SPECIAL OPS

G·K
Hall
&Cº.

*Also by W.E.B. Griffin
in Large Print:*

Behind the Lines
Blood and Honor
The Fighting Agents
The Investigators
The Secret Warriors

This Large Print Book carries the
Seal of Approval of N.A.V.H.

*A Brotherhood
of War Novel #9*

SPECIAL OPS

W.E.B. GRIFFIN

G.K. Hall & Co. • Thorndike, Maine

Published in 2001 by arrangement with G. P. Putnam's Sons, a member of Penguin Putnam Inc.

G.K. Hall Large Print Core Series.

The text of this Large Print edition is unabridged.
Other aspects of the book may vary from the original edition.

Set in 16 pt. Plantin.

Printed in the United States on permanent paper.

Library of Congress Cataloging-in-Publication Data

Griffin, W. E. B.
    Special ops : brotherhood of war novel / W.E.B. Griffin.
    p. cm.
    ISBN 0-7838-9468-6 (lg. print : hc : alk. paper)
    1. Guevara, Ernesto, 1928–1967 — Fiction. 2. Congo
(Democratic Republic) — Fiction. 3. Large type books. I. Title.
PS3557.R489137 S6 2001b
  813′.54—dc21
                                             2001024180

For Uncle Charley and The Bull

RIP October 1979

And For Donn
Who would have ever believed four *stars?*

And For Russ
Who would have ever believed Pee-Wee's Dog Robber
would grow up to be
a major general, a division commander,
and a university president?

And For Mac
RIP December 1987

And for All Those
Special Operations Types
Who Laid Their Lives on the Line
To Keep Africa and South America
Free of the Communists

[ONE]

TOP SECRET

THE JOINT CHIEFS OF STAFF
WASHINGTON, D.C.

Duplication Forbidden   Copy **4** of Seven.

For Distribution By Officer Courier Only

8 November 1964

Commanding General, United States Strike
   Command
Commanding General, European Command
Commanding General, United States Air
   Force, Europe
Commanding General, Seventh United States
   Army

1.   By Direction of the President; by Command of His Royal Highness, the King of the Belgians; and at the request of the government of the Republic of the Congo, a Joint Belgian-American Operation, "OPERATION DRAGON ROUGE," will take whatever military action is necessary to effect the rescue of

---

American, Belgian and other European nationals currently being held hostage in Stanleyville, Republic of the Congo, by forces in rebellion against the legal and duly constituted government of the Republic of the Congo.

2.   By Direction of the President, Counselor to the President Sanford T. Felter (Colonel, General Staff Corps, USA) is designated Action Officer, and will be presumed, in connection to military matters, to be speaking with the authority of the Joint Chiefs of Staff.

3.   OPERATION DRAGON ROUGE is assigned an AAAA-1 Priority with regard to the requisitioning of personnel, equipment, and other U.S. military assets.

4.   Addressees will on receipt of this directive immediately dispatch an officer in the grade of colonel or higher to the United States Embassy, Brussels, Belgium, where they will make themselves available to Colonel Felter or such officers as he may designate to represent him.

FOR THE CHAIRMAN, THE JOINT CHIEFS OF STAFF:

Forbes T. Willis
Forbes T. Willis
Brigadier General, USMC
Executive Officer, JCS

TOP SECRET

[TWO]
Brussels, Belgium
1320 Hours 11 November 1964

Brigadier General Harris McCord, USAF, thought he had yet another proof, if one were needed, that life was full of little ironies. Sixteen hours before, he had been at the USMC Birthday Ball at the Hotel Continental in Paris, tripping the light fantastic with his wife. He had been wearing his mess dress uniform, complete with real medals rather than ribbons, and with more silver embellishments than a Christmas tree.

Now that he was about to engage in what promised to be a really hairy exercise, he was wearing a somewhat baggy tweed jacket and well-worn flannel slacks. Just before he had left Paris, he had been told to wear civilian clothing. What he had on was all that had come back from the dry cleaners.

There were five peers, most of whom he knew, at least by sight, all in civilian clothing in a none-too-fancy conference room in the U.S. Embassy, waiting for Colonel Sanford T. Felter and his staff. The whole damned continent had been socked in, and Felter's plane had had to sit down in Scotland to wait for Brussels to clear to bare minimums.

He had heard of Felter, but he had never seen him in person and he was not very impressed with him when he walked into the room. Felter was small and slight, and wearing a baggy gray suit. He looked like a stereotype of a middle-level bureaucrat.

"Sorry to keep you waiting, gentlemen," Felter said. He threw a heavy briefcase on the table, then

9

took a key from his pocket and unlocked the padlock that had chained — more accurately, steelcabled — it to his wrist.

"My name is McCord, Colonel," General McCord said, and went to Felter and offered his hand.

"I'm glad you were available, General," Felter said.

As the others introduced themselves to Felter, McCord considered that. Felter knew who he was, and there was an implication that he had asked for him by name. That was flattering, unless you were rank-conscious, and thought that general officers should pick colonels, rather than the other way around.

"I think the best way to handle this, gentlemen," Felter began, "is to give you a quick recap of what's going on in the Congo, specifically in Stanleyville, and then to tell you what we intend to try to do to set it right.

"There are 1,600 people, Europeans, white people, held captive by Olenga's Simbas in Stanleyville. A four-column relief force — in other words, four different columns — under the overall command of Colonel Frederick Van de Waele of the Belgian Army has been charged with suppressing the rebellion, which includes, of course, the recapture of Stanleyville.

"There have been some successes, as you probably know from your own sources, but there is no way that Van de Waele can make it to Stanleyville before the end of the month. That poses two problems. The first is the rebels' announced intention to kill the hostages, a threat we consider bona fide, before Van de Waele can get to them.

"The second is that we have hard intelligence

10

that since 20 October, at least two, and probably as many as four, unmarked Ilyushin-18 turboprop aircraft have been flying arms and ammunition into the Arau airbase in northern Uganda, from Algeria. Should they decide to do so, it would be easy for them to move the arms and ammunition to Olenga's forces. The possibility of their doing so, it is believed, increases as Van de Waele's mercenaries and ANC troops approach Stanleyville.

"The President has decided, in consultation with the Belgian premier, Spaak, that the first priority is to keep those 1,600 people alive. The Belgians have made available the First Parachutist Battalion of their Paracommando Regiment. I'm familiar with it. The First Battalion was trained by the British Special Air Service people in World War II, and they pride themselves now on being just as good. The regiment is commanded by Colonel Charles Laurent, who is a fine officer, and who I suspect will lead the First Battalion himself.

"They will be carried to Stanleyville in USAF C-130 aircraft. After the airfield is softened up with some B-26s, they will make a parachute landing and seize the airport. Part of the force will remain at the airport to make the airport ready to receive the C-130s, and the balance will enter Stanleyville, find the Europeans, and bring them to the airport. They will be loaded aboard the C-130s and then everybody leaves. No attempt will be made to hold Stanleyville. I don't want any questions right now. I just wanted to give the rough idea."

"These gentlemen," Felter went on, turning to indicate the men he had brought with him, "are Lieutenant Colonel Lowell, Captain Stacey, Lieutenant Foster, and Sergeant Portet. They're

11

Green Berets. Colonel Lowell is on the Strike staff, and wrote Dragon Rouge. Captain Stacey and the others have been practicing a somewhat smaller operation intended for Stanleyville, now called off. But they know the town, and rebel dispositions and the probable location of the Europeans, and I brought them along to share their expertise."

The light colonel, Lowell, General McCord thought, *looks like a bright guy, if not much like a Green Beret. Stacey looks like a typical young Green Beret captain, a hard charger, tough, mean, and lean. The black lieutenant, Foster, looks as if he could chew railroad spikes and spit tacks. The sergeant . . . there's something wrong with him: His face is scratched and blotchy and swollen. He can hardly see out of his eyes. And whatever's wrong with his face is also wrong with his hands.*

"Colonel Lowell," Felter went on, "as soon as we wind it up here, will be available to explain any questions you might have about the OPPLAN for Dragon Rouge. Stacey and Foster are going to go liaise with the Belgians."

Felter looked at General McCord.

"I'm going to give Sergeant Portet, to you, General. He's a former airlines pilot, with extensive experience in the Congo — including, of course, Kamina and Stanleyville — and equally important, because he was involved in getting the B-26-Ks to the Congo, he knows most, if not all, the Cubans who will be flying them."

A former airlines pilot? McCord wondered. *What's he doing in the army as a sergeant? A Green Beret sergeant?*

"Glad to have all the help I can get," McCord said.

He had another thought: *I wonder if "the airlines pilot" caught whatever is wrong with his face and hands in the Congo? I wonder if it's contagious?*

Felter looked around the room. "I have rough OPPLANs here. Study them overnight, and be prepared to offer fixes for what is wrong with the OPPLAN tomorrow morning." He paused, then went on. "That will be all for now, gentlemen. Thank you. But keep yourselves available."

Felter and three of the three Green Berets started to leave the room. Lowell opened a well-stuffed briefcase. Felter caught the sergeant's attention and nodded toward General McCord. The sergeant went to General McCord.

"Colonel Felter said I am to make myself useful, sir," he said.

McCord resisted the temptation to offer his hand.

"You've been into Stanleyville, Sergeant? *Flown* into Stanleyville?"

"Yes, sir."

"Purely as a matter of idle curiosity, I've looked at the Jepp charts," General McCord said. "I know we can get 130s in there."

"Yes, sir, easily."

"But I should have looked closer," McCord said. "How many will it take at once?"

Portet's swollen face wrinkled in thought.

"No more than six at once, sir," he said. "To be safe, I would say no more than five. There's not much of paved tarmac, and the unpaved areas won't take the weight of a C-130."

"Colonel Felter said you were an airline pilot?"

The rest of the question went unspoken, but Sergeant Portet answered, smiling wryly.

13

"I got a postcard from my friends and neighbors at the draft board, General."

Then, as if he was no longer able to resist an awful temptation, he put his hand up and scratched at the open blotches his face — with a hand that was similarly disfigured with suppurating sores.

"What's wrong with your face, son?" General McCord asked. "And your hand?"

"It's nothing, sir. A little rash."

"A little rash, my ass," General McCord said. "How long has it been that way?"

"It started on the plane from the States, sir," Jack said. "It's some kind of an allergy, probably. Nothing to worry about."

"Where were you in the States? Bragg?"

"Yes, sir."

"Come with me, Sergeant," McCord said.

He had seen the military attaché's office on the way to the conference room, and he led Jack there.

There was a captain on duty, who glanced up and was not very impressed with what he saw. Two messy Americans in mussed clothing, one of them with what looked like a terminal case of scabies on his face.

"Yes?" he asked.

"I'm General McCord," McCord said, which caused the captain to come to his feet and to stand to attention.

"Yes, sir."

"Would you be good enough to get me the commanding officer of the nearest U.S. military medical facility on the telephone, please?"

"General," Jack said. "I'll be all right. I don't want to get put in a hospital now."

"I expected as much from a Green Beret,"

14

McCord said. "But I would be very surprised if they'll let you get on the airplanes, much less jump on Stanleyville. It looks to me as if the whole purpose of the Belgians is to keep Americans out of it."

"My stepmother and stepsister are in Stanleyville, General. I'm going in."

McCord looked at him. Before he could frame a reply, the captain handed him a telephone.

"Colonel Aspen, sir."

"Colonel, this is General McCord. This may sound a little odd, but I want you to dispatch, immediately, one of your best medical officers. I am in the U.S. Embassy, and I have a young sergeant with me who, if my diagnosis is correct, has been rolling around in poison oak." There was a pause. "No, Colonel, he cannot come there. I don't want to argue about this. I expect to see either you or one of your doctors here within twenty minutes."

He hung the phone up, and turned to smile at Jack.

"They give you a shot," he said. "It clears it up in a couple of hours. I had it in survival school in Utah a couple of years ago."

"Thank you very much, sir," Jack said.

"Don't get your hopes up about anything else, Sergeant," General McCord said. "I know they won't let you jump on Stanleyville."

"Yes, sir," Jack said.

"So tell me what else I should know about the airport in Stanleyville," General McCord said.

[THREE]
Stanleyville, Republic of the Congo
0600 25 November 1964

As a tradition, the men of the First Battalion, the Paracommando Regiment, Royal Belgian Army, continued to use the English-language jump commands the battalion had learned in England in World War II.

"Outboard sticks, stand UP!" the jumpmaster ordered.

The two outside files of men inside the USAF C-130, called "Chalk One" in the OPPLAN, stood up and folded up their nylon and aluminum pole seats back against the fuselage wall.

"Inboard sticks, stand UP!"

The two inside files rose to their feet and folded their seats.

"Hook UP!"

Everybody fastened the hook at the end of their static line to a steel cable.

"Check static lines! Check equipment!"

Everybody tugged at his own static line, to make sure it was securely hooked to the cable, and then they checked the harness and other equipment of the man standing in front of them — that is to say, in the lines that now faced rear, and led to the exit doors on either side of the aircraft.

Now the jumpmaster switched to French: *"Un minute!"* and then back to English: "Stand in the door!"

Chalk One was down to 700 feet or so, and all dirtied up, flaps down, throttles retarded, close (at 125 mph) to stall speed.

"Go!"

Sergeant Jack Portet, wearing the uniform of a

16

Belgian paratrooper, was the sixth man in the port-side stick. The Belgians had been sympathetic to someone who wanted to jump on Stanleyville because his mother and sister were there.

And if he got into trouble with the U.S. Army, *c'est la vie.*

Jack felt the slight tug of the static line almost immediately after exiting the aircraft, and a moment later, felt his main chute slithering out of the case. And then the canopy filled, and he had a sensation of being jerked upward.

There was not enough time to orient himself beyond seeing the airfield beneath and slightly to the left of him, and to pick out the twelve-story, white Immoquateur apartment building downtown before the ground seemed to suddenly rush up at him.

He knew where he was now. He landed on the tee of the third hole of the Stanleyville golf course. He landed on his feet, but when he started to pull on the lines, to dump a little air from the nearly emptied canopy, there was a sudden gust of air and the canopy filled and pulled him off his feet.

He hit the quick release and was out of the harness a moment later. He rolled over and saw that the sky was full of chutes from Chalk Two and Chalk Three.

And then there were peculiar whistling noises, and peculiar cracking noises, and after a moment Jack realized that he was under fire.

And there didn't seem to be anybody to shoot back at.

And then, all of a sudden, there was: There were Simbas firing from, of all places, the control tower.

17

He dropped to the ground, worked the action of the FN assault rifle, and took aim at the tower. As he lined his sights up, the tower disappeared in a cloud of dust. In a moment, he had the explanation. Two paratroopers had gotten their machine guns in action.

Jack got to his feet and ran toward a trio of Belgian officers. When there was transportation, either something captured here, or the jeeps or the odd-looking three-wheelers on the C-130s that were supposed to land, the officers would get first crack at it. And he wanted to be there when it arrived. He had to get to the Immoquateur, and he needed wheels to do that.

A sergeant drove up in a white pickup with a Mobil Oil Pegasus painted on its doors.

One of the Belgian officers looked around and then pointed to Jack.

"That one, *l'Americain,* knows the town. Put half a dozen men in the back, and make a reconnaissance by fire."

And then he made his little joke.

"You better hope you get killed," he said to Jack. "When Le Grand Noir, ["The Big Black," by which he meant, of course, Lieutenant Foster] was looking for you and couldn't find you, he said if you jumped with us, he was going to pull your legs and arms off, one by one."

Jack smiled and got on the running board of the Mobil Oil pickup, holding the FN in one hand.

But he was suddenly very frightened. Not of fighting, or even of dying, but of what he was liable to find when he got to the Immoquateur.

They first encountered resistance three hundred yards down the road, just past the Sabena Guest House. A Simba wrapped in an animal

18

skin, with a pistol in one hand, a sword in the other, charged at them down the middle of the road. Behind him came three others, armed with FN assault rifles, firing them on full automatic.

The pickup truck screeched to a halt. Jack went onto his belly, his rifle to his shoulder. As he found a target, baffled to see that the Simba's weapon was firing straight up into the air, there was a short burst of 7-mm fire over his head. The Simba with the sword stopped in midstride and then crumpled to his knees. Before he fell over, a torrent of blood gushed from his mouth.

The Simbas with him stopped and looked at the fallen man in absolute surprise. Then they stopped shooting and started to back up. There was another burst of the fire from the pickup, this time from several weapons. Two of the three Simbas fell down, one of them backward. The remaining Simba, the one in Jack's sights, dropped his rifle and ran away with great loping strides. There was another burst of fire from the truck, no more than four rounds from a paratrooper's assault rifle. The Simba took two more steps, then fell on his face to the left.

Jack scrambled to his knees and turned to look for the truck. It was already moving. He jumped onto the running board as it came past, almost losing his balance as the driver swerved, unsuccessfully, to avoid running over the Simba who had led the charge with a sword.

There was a furious horn bleating behind them, and the pickup pulled off the shoulder of the road. A jeep raced past them, the gunner of the pedestal-mounted .30-caliber Browning machine gun firing it, in short bursts, at targets Jack could not see.

The pickup swerved back onto the paved surface, almost throwing Jack off.

There was the sound of a great many weapons being fired, but none of the fire seemed directed at them. They reached the first houses. There were more Simbas in sight now, but none of them were attacking. They were in the alleys between the houses, and in the streets behind them.

The jeep that had raced past them was no longer in sight, but Jack could still hear the peculiar sound of the Browning firing in short bursts.

The Mobil Oil pickup truck came to an intersection and stopped. Jack looked at the driver.

"You're supposed to be the fucking expert," the driver said to him. "Where do we go?"

"Right," Jack ordered, without really thinking about it. The Immoquateur was to the right.

The pickup jerked into motion.

Fifty yards down the road, they came across the first Europeans. Three of them, mother, father, and a twelve- or thirteen-year-old boy, sprawled dead in pools of blood in the road, obviously shot as they had tried to run.

Jack felt nausea rise in his throat, but managed to hold it down.

Ahead, over the roofs of the pleasant, pastel-painted villas, he saw the white bulk of the Immoquateur.

Then there was fire directed at them.

The pickup screeched to a stop in the middle of the street. Jack felt himself going, tried valiantly to stop himself, and then, bouncing off the fender, fell onto the pavement, on his face.

He felt his eyes water, and then they lost focus.

Jesus Christ! I've been shot!

He shook his head, then put his hand to his face.

There was something warm on it.

Blood! I've been shot in the face!

He sat up. Someone rushed up to him. Indistinctly, he made out one of the paratroopers leaning over him, felt his fingers on his face.

And then the sonofabitch laughed.

"You're all right," he said. "All you've got is a bloody nose."

He slapped Jack on the back and ran ahead of him.

Jack's eyes came back into focus. He looked at his lap and saw blood dripping into it.

He looked around and saw his assault rifle on the street, six feet from where he was sitting. He scurried on his knees to it, picked it up, fired a burst in the air to make sure it was still functioning, and then looked around again, this time at the Immoquateur. There were bodies on the lawn between the street and the shops on the ground floor, Simba and European. He got to his feet and ran toward the Immoquateur.

Jack recognized one of the more than a dozen bodies on the lawn before the Immoquateur. It was the Stanleyville station manager of the Congo River Steamship Company. He had met him when they had shipped in a truck. He had been shot in the neck, probably, from the size of the wound, with a shotgun. The stout, gray-haired woman lying beside him, an inch-wide hole in her forehead, was almost certainly his wife.

Jack ran into the building itself. There were two dead Simbas in the narrow elevator corridor. One of them had most of his head blown away. The other, shot as he came out of the elevator, had taken a burst in the chest. It had literally blown a

21

hole through his body. Parts of his ribs, or his spine, some kind of bone, were sticking at awkward angles out his back.

He was lying in the open elevator door. The door of the elevator tried to close on his body, encountered it, reopened, and then tried to close again.

Jack laid his FN assault rifle against the wall, put his hands on the dead man's neck, and dragged him free. The elevator door closed, a melodious chime bonged, and the elevator started up.

"Shit!"

Jack went to the call button for the other elevator and pushed it. It did not illuminate. He ran farther down the corridor and pushed the service elevator call button. It lit up, but there was no sound of elevator machinery. He went back to wait for the first elevator.

One of the Belgian paratroopers from the pickup truck came into the corridor, in a crouch, his rifle ready.

"The sergeant said you are to come back to the truck," he said.

"Fuck him, my mother's upstairs," Jack said.

The Belgian paratrooper ran back out of the building. The elevator indicator showed that it was on the ninth floor. Then it started to come down.

The Belgian paratrooper came running back into the building. Jack wondered if he was going to give him any trouble.

"I got a radio," the Belgian said. "They are leaving us."

Jack felt something warm on his hand, looked down and saw blood.

The elevator mechanism chimed pleasantly, and the door opened. Jack stepped over the dead Simba. The Belgian paratrooper followed him inside and crossed himself as Jack pushed the floor button.

The door closed and the elevator started to rise.

It stopped at the fourth floor.

A Simba in parts of a Belgian officer's uniform did not have time to raise his pistol before a burst from Jack's assault rifle smashed into his midsection.

The noise in the closed confines of the elevator was painful and dazzling. Jack's ears rang to the point where he knew he would not be able to hear anything but the loudest of sounds for a long time. The paratrooper with Jack jumped, in a crouch, into the corridor and let loose a burst down the corridor. It was empty.

The Simba he had shot had backed into the corridor wall and then slid to the floor, leaving a foot-wide track of blood down the wall. Jack thought he saw life leave the Simba's eyes.

He took the Simba's pistol, a World War II–era German Luger, from his hand, stuffed it into the chest pocket of his tunic, and then backed into the elevator. The paratrooper backed into it after him. The chime sounded melodiously again, the doors closed, and the elevator started up again.

When the door opened, they were on the tenth floor. There was no one there.

Neither Jack nor the paratrooper moved.

The chime sounded again, and the door closed.

Jack reached out with the muzzle of his FN and rapped the rubber edge of the door. The door started to open again.

Jack, copying what the paratrooper had done on

23

the fourth floor, jumped, in a crouch, into the corridor. But the corridor was empty.

Jack ran to the door of the Air Simba apartment. It was battered, as if someone had tried to batter his way in, and there were bullet holes in it. He put his hand on the doorknob. The door was locked.

He banged on it with his fist.

"Hanni!" he shouted. "Hanni, *c'est moi! C'est Jacques!*"

There was no answer.

He raised the butt of the FN and smashed at the door in the area of the knob. The butt snapped off behind the trigger assembly.

He felt tears well up in his eyes. He pulled the trigger to see if it would still work, and there was another painful roar of sound, and a cloud of cement dust as the bullets struck the ceiling.

He raised his boot and kicked at the door beside the knob with all his might. There was a splintering sound, and the lock mechanism tore free.

Jack kicked it again, and it flew open. The Belgian paratrooper, in his now-familiar crouching stance, rushed into the apartment.

There was not the expected burst of fire.

Jack ran into the room.

Hanni was standing in front of the bedroom door, white-faced.

"Bonjour, madame," the Belgian paratrooper said.

Hanni saw Jack.

"Oh, my God! It is you! I thought I was losing my mind!"

"Hanni!" Jack croaked.

The bedroom door opened. Jeanine appeared.

"Jacques!" she screamed.

And there was somebody with her. Black.

24

Wearing an animal skin.

"Don't shoot!" Hanni screamed. "He's a friend!"

"Jacques, don't!" Jeanine said when Jack trained what was left of the FN at him.

"Who the hell is he?"

"Captain George Washington Lunsford," the man in the animal skin said, "United States Army, at your service, sir."

He walked into the room with his hands above his shoulders.

"Jacques, for God's sake," Hanni said, "he saved our lives. Put the gun down."

Jack saw Ursula Craig holding her baby in her arms in the bedroom. Beside her, a large knife in each hand, was an enormous, very black woman.

"Mon Dieu," the black woman said. *"C'est Jacques!"*

Jack went to the bedroom. Mary Magdalene dropped the knives and enveloped him in massive black arms. As her huge body heaved with sobs and tears ran down her cheeks, she repeated over and over, *"Mon petit Jacques, mon petit Jacques."*

"I hate to break that up," Lunsford said, "but there are savages all over the building, and I'd feel a lot more comfortable if I had my rifle."

Jack freed himself.

"You okay, Ursula?"

"I am now," she said.

Jack turned to Lunsford.

"Captain, I heard there were Green Beanies here, but I didn't expect to find one dressed like that."

"He knew what the Simbas would do once they saw the paratroopers," Hanni said. "He came to protect us."

"I was undercover. If I go get my rifle," Lunsford said, nodding at the Belgian paratrooper, "does he know what's going on, or . . ."

"*Je suis à votre service, mon capitain,*" the Belgian paratrooper said, coming to attention, and then added, almost as if he was embarrassed, "I speak good the English."

Lunsford went into the bedroom and came back with his rifle.

"That radio work?" he asked.

"*Oui, mon capitain,*" the Belgian said.

"Then you get on it, and tell somebody important where we are, and to come fetch us," Lunsford ordered.

"*Oui, mon capitain,*" the Belgian paratrooper said.

"You close the door," Lunsford ordered Jack. "We'll put the ladies back in the bedroom until the cavalry gets here."

"Yes, sir," Jack said.

[FOUR]
Quarters #1
Fort Myer, Virginia
0605 25 November 1964

The door to Quarters #1 was opened by one of the chief's orderlies, a pleasant-looking young man wearing a crisp white jacket.

"Good morning, General. The general is expecting you, sir. The general is in the kitchen, sir. Straight ahead to the rear of the house."

The chief of staff of the United States Army was wearing a white apron, in the act of slicing a steak from a baked ham with all the precision of a surgeon.

He looked up when he saw Bellmon, and smiled.

"Just a couple of us for breakfast, Bob," he said. "There's coffee. Help yourself."

He pointed to the coffeemaker on a countertop.

"Thank you, sir," Bellmon said.

Bellmon, a stocky, ruddy-faced forty-six-year-old, had been surprised, and just a little worried, when his aide-de-camp, Captain Richard Hornsby, the previous afternoon had told him that the aide-de-camp of the chief of staff of the United States Army had told him that it was the desire of the chief that General Bellmon present himself at Quarters #1 at 0600 for breakfast.

Bellmon knew the chief of staff — both were from Army families, both were West Pointers, and both of their fathers had also worn the stars of general officers — but this was Washington, the Pentagon, and there were a large number of major generals around, very few of whom were ever invited to take breakfast with the chief of staff at his quarters.

Bellmon, who commanded the Army Aviation Center at Fort Rucker, Alabama, had flown to Washington early the previous morning to confer with the deputy chief of staff for operations (known as Dee Cee Ess Ops.). DCSOPS was a three-star, and also a West Pointer, the son of a general officer, and an old acquaintance, but he had not invited Bellmon to his quarters.

"I wonder what the hell that's all about?" Bellmon had asked, not expecting an answer. "Okay, call Rucker, and tell them we'll be back as soon as we can tomorrow."

He had things to do at Rucker, but it had never entered his mind to decline the invitation.

"There's something about ham and eggs," the chief of staff said. "I don't know what the hell it is, but if you take a slice of baked ham, fry it a little in ham fat, and then fry eggs in the same fat and the same pan . . ."

"Yes, sir," General Bellmon said.

The chief carefully sliced another ham steak from the baked ham and laid it on a plate beside the first.

Bellmon poured a cup of coffee for himself, and was idly stirring it when another man entered the kitchen. Without thinking about it, Bellmon came almost to attention. The senior uniformed member of the Armed Forces of the United States had just walked into the kitchen.

"Good morning," the Chairman of the Joint Chiefs of Staff said.

Jesus, Bellmon thought, *did the Chairman forget to shave, or has he been up all night?*

"You two know each other, right?" the chief said.

"We've met," the Chairman said, putting out his hand. "Good to see you again, Bellmon."

"Good morning, Admiral," Bellmon said.

"I can use some of that," the Chairman said, indicating Bellmon's mug of coffee, "although God knows I've used up my month's allocation of caffeine in the last eight hours."

The Chairman took a sip and then raised the mug to Bellmon.

"Thank you," he said. He met Bellmon's eyes. "I spent the night with the President," he said. "Would you be surprised, Bellmon, to hear that at midnight, Washington time, a battalion of Belgian paratroops was dropped by USAF C-130s on Stanleyville?"

"How did it go?" the chief asked as he put ham fat in a large cast-iron frying pan.

"The Simbas made good on their promise to start executing the Europeans the moment they saw a parachute," the Chairman said. "But the Belgian paras lived up to their reputation: They took the city in less than two hours, and the Europeans that are left are already either in Léopoldville, or on their way."

He looked at Bellmon again.

"You don't seem overwhelmed by surprise, General," he said.

"I expected that some action would be taken, sir."

"You're telling me you never heard of Operation Dragon Rouge, is that it?"

"No, sir. I've heard of it."

"Your name is not on the list of those cleared for Top Secret–Dragon Rouge," the Chairman said. "Who brought you into the picture, your friend Colonel Sanford T. Felter?"

"No, sir."

"Do you think that Colonel Felter would be surprised if he heard that you heard about Dragon Rouge?"

"No, sir, I don't think he would be."

"May I infer that the Colonel arranged for you to be brought in on Dragon Rouge?"

"Hey, Charley," the chief said. "You promised this was supposed to be friendly."

"So I did. I apologize to both of you."

"How do you like your eggs, Charley?" the chief asked. "Your choices are up, over, or scrambled."

"Up, but no slime, please," the Chairman said.

The chief took two fried eggs from the cast-iron flying pan and laid them atop a ham steak and

29

handed the plate to the Chairman.

"Bob?" the chief asked.

Inasmuch as I suspect my ass is in a crack, I don't really want any eggs, thank you very much. But I can't say that, can I?

"Up is fine with me, General," he said.

The chief, a moment later, laid two more eggs on a ham slice and handed it to Bellmon, who, seeing no other possible action on his part, sat down at the kitchen table beside the Chairman.

"This isn't half bad, Bob," the Chairman said.

"Not bad, my ass," the chief said as he splashed ham fat on eggs in the pan. "This is one of God's Good Meals."

The Chairman looked at General Bellmon.

"So tell me, Bellmon, out of school, of course, who told you about Dragon Rouge?"

When Bellmon did not immediately reply, the chief called, "You can trust him, Bob. For a sailor, you can really trust him pretty far."

The Chairman of the Joint Chiefs of Staff gave the chief of staff of the U.S. Army the finger.

"I was always taught, Admiral," Bellmon said, "that a good officer protects juniors."

"A lieutenant colonel, in other words, with a big mouth?" the Chairman said, not seeming either surprised or angry. "It is hard to keep a secret, isn't it?"

The chief sat down beside them.

"Actually, sir, it was my daughter's boyfriend," Bellmon said.

"A lieutenant, then? Maybe a captain?" the chief said.

"Actually, sir, he's a sergeant," Bellmon said.

"A sergeant?" the chief parroted incredulously.

"A sergeant," Bellmon repeated. "I should have

30

shut him up, but I didn't. He simply presumed that as a general officer, I knew all about it. I didn't, but I was curious, and let him talk."

"Marjorie's boyfriend is a sergeant?" the chief asked. "And how does that go with Barbara?"

"He's a very fine young man," Bellmon said testily. "Barbara likes him, I like him. Before he was drafted, he was an airline pilot."

"A sergeant who knew about Dragon Rouge because he was involved in it, right? Does this sergeant work for Colonel Felter, by any chance?"

"Yes, sir, he does."

"Tell me about him," the Chairman said.

"His name is Jacques Portet, and —"

"I meant Colonel Felter," the Chairman interrupted. "I understand you're acquainted with him."

"Colonel Felter is a friend of mine, sir."

"Some people define 'friend' as anyone they call by his first name. I define a friend as someone you'd go to the mat for, and vice versa. Which is it with you and Colonel Felter?"

"Colonel Felter is a close personal friend, sir."

"Then you know what he does for a living?"

"I know he works for the President, sir. I think his job title is 'Counselor to the President.' "

"He's President Johnson's personal spook," the Chairman said. "As he was for Kennedy, and before that, for Eisenhower." He paused, and looked directly at Bellmon. "He has been described as 'one ruthless sonofabitch who runs over anybody who gets in his way.' "

"Sir," Bellmon said coldly, "I would not categorize Colonel Felter as either ruthless or a sonofabitch."

"Then you're out of synch with the Com-

31

mander-in-Chief, General. The President used — sometime around oh three hundred this morning, and admiringly, I thought — precisely those words."

The Chairman chuckled, then went on: "How'd you get involved with someone like Felter, General?"

"I'm not sure what the admiral means by 'involved,' sir," Bellmon said.

"Well, for example, where did you first meet him?"

Bellmon paused thoughtfully, then shrugged.

"At 1330, 8 April 1945," he said. "Outside a stable, in Zwenkau, Saxony, in what is now East Germany."

Both the Chairman and the chief looked at him curiously.

"You tend to remember precisely where and when you're liberated," Bellmon said. "Maybe especially if, sixty seconds before, you were convinced you were on your way to Siberia."

"I'm not tracking you, General," the Chairman said.

"I was captured in North Africa, Admiral," Bellmon said. "On 17 February 1943. I was a POW for two years, one month, and eighteen days, most of it in Stalag XVII-B, near Szczecin — Stettin — Poland. As the Russians advanced through Poland, the camp commandant was ordered to move us westward, toward Berlin. We didn't make it. We were overrun by the Russians —"

"Lucky for you," the Chairman interrupted.

"No, sir," Bellmon said. "Our Russian allies almost immediately made it clear they had no intention of turning us loose. Quite the contrary, we were informed that transportation was being arranged to take us to 'safety' in the Soviet Union."

"I've heard the stories, but —"

"I'm afraid they're all true, Admiral. In some cases, we have no idea why, they held on to our men. In this case, there's good reason to believe that they were trying to shove their murder of Polish officers in the Katyn Forest under the rug. Russian intelligence officers asked each of us if we had any knowledge of American officers being taken from Stalag XVII-B by German officers to visit the Katyn Forest."

"And had there been?"

"Yes, sir, there had. *I* had. I was taken to the Katyn Forest by a German officer who had been a friend of my father's. He wanted to make sure, when the war was over, that the Germans weren't held responsible for that particular atrocity."

"You were at Katyn?" the chief asked, surprised.

"Yes, sir. I was there. None of my officers, my fellow POWs, told the Russians I'd not only been taken from the Stalag but had in my possession photographs and other material which implicated the Russians in the murder of five thousand Polish officers, including two hundred and fifty cadets, none of them older than fifteen."

"Christ, you hear these stories, but . . ."

"Well, there I was," Bellmon went on, as if eager to relate the story, "at 1330, 8 April 1945, in a stone stable in Zwenkau — in the dark; the Russians had closed all the doors, and there were no windows — with two hundred thirty-eight other American officers, all prisoners of the Russians, with what I had seen at Katyn running through my mind, when I thought I was losing my mind. . . ."

"I can understand that," the Chairman said.

"First I heard a trumpet," Bellmon went on. "Playing 'When the Saints Come Marching In' — and then the enormous door of the stable came crashing down, and a half-track with a multiple .50-caliber machine-gun mount backed into the barn, and I thought the decision had been made to eliminate us all. Then I saw who the gunner was. He was about six feet three, weighed a good 250 pounds, and was as black as the ace of spades. And standing beside him was another enormous black trooper, blowing 'The Saints' on his trumpet."

"Elements of Colonel Philip Sheridan Parker's 393rd tank destroyer regiment," the chief said. "I'd heard that story, of course, Bob. But I had no idea until just now you were one of those he liberated."

Bellmon nodded.

"The half-track moved out of the barn," he went on, "and I staggered outside into the sunlight. My eyes grew accustomed to the light, and I saw another half-dozen tracks, and a sea of black faces, and in the middle of them, standing next to Colonel Parker, carrying a Thompson submachine gun, one skinny little white first lieutenant, who stood about five feet five."

He paused and looked at the Chairman.

"That was the first time I ever saw Sandy Felter, Admiral."

"What was he doing there?" the Chairman asked softly.

"He was a POW interrogator, and he'd found out about us. He'd taken the information to his division commander, General Waterford, together with a plan to send a flying column in to get us. General Waterford thought it would smack of favoritism —"

"What?" the Chairman asked.

"Charley," the chief said, "General Waterford was Bob's father-in-law."

The Chairman's eyebrows rose, but he said nothing.

"And — my father-in-law — nixed Felter's plan," Bellmon went on. "So Felter took it to Colonel Parker, who put it into execution, which almost certainly cost him the star — or stars — to which he was so certainly entitled."

He met the Chairman's eyes.

"Colonel Felter, Admiral, has been my friend since that time."

"Let me tell you, General, what this is all about," the Chairman said. "When Colonel Felter was named action officer for Dragon Rouge, I was curious about him. That's not the sort of responsibility normally given to a colonel. So I told my aide to get me his records. And then I forgot about it, since we were all up to our asses in alligators. But then, the day before yesterday, when Dragon Rouge was put in execution, I remembered about the records, and asked my aide about them."

"Yes, sir?"

"Ordinarily," the Chairman went on, "when an officer is detailed to the CIA, or another intelligence agency, his records are maintained there, and available to people on a need-to-know basis. Colonel Felter's records are maintained in the White House. When my aide asked for them, he was told he didn't have the need-to-know. When he explained that he was asking for me, he was told that my need-to-know would have to be approved by the President. Under the circumstances, I didn't pursue the issue."

"But you're the Chairman of the Joint Chiefs," Bellmon blurted.

"Yes," the Chairman said. "Anyway, I mentioned this to Bob, here, and he told me he thought you and Felter were friends. So I thought I could get a picture of him from you, out of school, without having to go to the President to ask for a look at his records."

"I understand, sir. But there's not much I can tell you."

"You said you've been friends for years," the Chairman countered. "How did he wind up as counsel to Presidents?"

"I have an idea, sir, but it's a rather long story."

"We have all the time we need. They know where to find me if they need me," the Chairman said. "Start at the beginning, please."

[FIVE]
Office of the Deputy Director
The Central Intelligence Agency
Langley, Virginia
26 November 1964

"Come on in, Howard," the deputy director said to Howard W. O'Connor, the assistant director for administration of the Central Intelligence Agency. "What have you got?"

The deputy director was a slight man in his early fifties who wore his still-blond hair very short. O'Connor was a stocky, ruddy-faced man with a full mane of white curly hair.

36

O'Connor waved a long sheet of teletypewriter paper.

"The manifest of the Americans rescued from Stanleyville, being flown via Frankfurt to the States," he said. "It just came in from Léopoldville."

"Something, someone, on it is interesting?"

"A woman named Hanni Portet and her daughter, Jeanine," O'Connor said. "Mrs. Portet is a German national, married to a chap named Jean-Phillipe Portet. He's an American — he was Belgian, but served in our Army Air Corps in World War II and got his citizenship that way. The little girl — she's eleven — got her citizenship via the father. There is also a son, Jacques, also an American citizen whom the long arm of the draft caught in Léopoldville, and when last heard of was at Camp Polk, Louisiana taking basic training."

"Why are the Portets of interest?"

"We've been looking around for someone to bankroll in setting up Air America II," O'Connor said.

"Don't call it that, Howard. Air America is a painful subject. No one was supposed to know of our interest in it. We need an airline that doesn't have parenthesis CIA close parenthesis painted on the tail of its airplanes."

"There have been several suggestions," O'Connor said. "The one I like best is 'Intercontinental Air Cargo.' We can set it up in Miami; there's half a hundred one- and two-airplane 'airlines' operating out of Miami."

"What about just 'Intercontinental Air'?"

"There is already an Intercontinental Air," O'Connor said. "That was one of the reasons I like 'Intercontinental Air Cargo.' We can even hide behind their logo and color scheme."

"Why don't we just buy into Intercontinental Air?"

"The people that own it aren't interested in partners," O'Connor said. "They're willing to sell, but we need somebody to buy it who can't be tied to us."

"This guy Portet?"

"Yeah. Right now he's chief pilot for Air Congo, but he also has his own two-bit airline, Air Simba, flying mostly World War II Boeing C-46s around Southern Africa."

"You think he'd be interested?"

"Things are not good in the Congo," O'Connor said. "And they're unlikely to get better, whether or not Che Guevara goes over there and starts causing trouble."

"That's not funny, Howard," the deputy director said. "We told the President that's not going to happen."

"I think Portet would be very interested," O'Connor said. "I wanted your permission to approach him."

"You want to go over there?"

"No. He's coming here with his family. I want J. Richard Leonard of the Gresham Investment Corporation to approach him."

"Do it. Do you know when and where he's going to be in the United States?"

"We're the CIA, Paul. We can find out."

"Do it, and let me know what happens," the deputy director said.

[SIX]
Office of the Commanding General
Pope Air Force Base, North Carolina
1520 1 December 1964

Brigadier General Matthew Hollostone, USAF, the forty-two-year-old general officer commanding Pope AF Base, was at his desk reading with fascination a rather detailed report by the Fort Bragg provost marshal.

On the one hand, it was encouraging to be reassured that the fighting spirit was as present in this generation of junior officers as it had been in his, when he had been a twenty-two-year-old captain. The detailed list the provost marshal furnished of the damage done to a Fayetteville night spot when a local beauty had aroused the mating instinct simultaneously in one of Pope's pilots and one of Bragg's parachutists was clear proof of that.

On the other hand, there was no question that the behavior chronicled by the provost marshal was conduct unbecoming officers and gentlemen, and he would have to come to some understanding with the commanding general of Fort Bragg vis-à-vis a suitable punishment for both miscreants.

Sitting on the credenza behind General Hollostone's desk was a small Air Force blue box containing a speaker. It brought to General Hollostone the radio traffic of the Pope control tower. It was on all the time, but very rarely did anything being said come to General Hollostone's conscious attention.

He was a command pilot with more than five thousand hours in the air, and over the years had learned to listen subconsciously to radio traffic. In

39

other words, he heard only those things that had an effect on him. It was not an uncommon characteristic, or ability, of pilots, but the only other people he had ever seen do something similar were experienced radio telegraph operators, who could carry on a conversation with one part of their brain while transcribing the dits and dashes of Morse code at forty words a minute.

What the speaker transmitted now —

"Pope, Air Force Three Eleven, a Learjet, at flight level two five thousand sixty miles north of your station. Estimate ten minutes. Approach and landing, please."

— caused him to stop thinking about suitable punishments for the battling junior officers and consciously await the reply of the Pope control tower operator.

There were very few Learjets in the U.S. Air Force, and as far as General Hollostone knew, all but two of the small, fast little airplanes were assigned to the special missions squadron in Washington. The other two were assigned to the four-star generals commanding the U.S. Air Force, Pacific, and the U.S. Air Force, Europe.

It was illogical to think that the commanding generals of the Air Force in the Pacific or Europe were about to drop in unannounced at Pope Air Force Base, but that left open the logical probability that the Learjet was carrying someone of the upper echelon of the military establishment, ranging downward from the Secretary of Defense to a lowly lieutenant general representing a four-star general.

No one with fewer than three stars would be aboard the Learjet. Riding in a Learjet was a symbol of power.

Hollostone waited until the Pope tower had told Air Force Three Eleven how to get on the ground at Pope, then stood up. He walked into his outer office, which was occupied by his secretary, his sergeant major, and his aide-de-camp.

"Steve," General Hollostone ordered, "get on the horn and tell Bragg there's a Learjet nine minutes out, and we don't know who is aboard."

"Yes, sir," the sergeant major said, and reached for the telephone. He understood that Bragg meant the Office of the Commanding General XVIII Airborne Corps and Fort Bragg, who would also be interested to hear that a Learjet was about to touch down at Pope.

"You and I will just be walking out of Base Ops when the mysterious stranger arrives," General Hollostone said to his aide-de-camp. "Make sure the car is available."

"Yes, sir," the aide-de-camp said.

Seven and a half minutes later, General Hollostone marched through the door of Base Operations onto the tarmac in front of it. He looked first skyward, and picked out a tiny shining object that had to be the Learjet.

Then he looked around him, to see if there was anything in front of Base Ops that shouldn't be there.

There was.

There was a soldier — a soldier, not an airman — in fatigue uniform, green beret, and parachutist's jump boots leaning against the concrete blocks of the Base Ops building.

And he didn't even come to attention when he saw a general officer. That's unusual. Usually the Army — especially the paratroops at Bragg — carries that sort of thing too far.

41

Then General Hollostone understood why the Green Beret in fatigues hadn't popped to attention when he saw a general officer. He was not required to do so, because he was senior by three months to Brigadier General Hollostone.

Salutes were exchanged.

"It's cold out here, Red," General Hollostone said. "Why didn't you go inside?"

Inside Base Ops was a VIP lounge for colonels and up.

"I didn't want to get your carpet muddy," Brigadier General Paul "Red" Hanrahan, the slight, wiry forty-three-year-old who was commandant of the Special Warfare School at Fort Bragg, said as they shook hands.

"What brings you here?" Hollostone asked.

Hanrahan pointed skyward.

The tiny shining object had grown into a recognizable Learjet making its approach to Pope AF Base.

"Anyone I know aboard?" Hollostone asked.

"I don't think so, Matt," Hanrahan said, chuckling. "Several of my people."

"Nobody important, in other words?"

"Probably not to you, Matt," Hanrahan replied. There was reproof, perhaps even contempt, in his voice.

"I didn't mean that the way it sounded, Red," Hollostone said.

"Good," Hanrahan replied.

"Anything you need, Red? Anything I can do for you?"

"No. But thanks anyway, Matt."

"Come see us," General Hollostone said.

"You, too," General Hanrahan said.

Salutes were exchanged, and then General

Hollostone marched back inside the Base Ops building trailed by his aide-de-camp.

He returned to his office and got there in time to see — through the mostly closed venetian blinds of his window — the Learjet taxi up to the tarmac in front of Base Ops and stop.

The fuselage door opened and two people got out. One of them was a skinny black man in a white linen suit that looked five sizes too big for him. The other man was white, and wearing a strange, none-too-clean parachutist's uniform. After a moment, General Hollostone recognized it to be that of the Belgian Paracommando Regiment. The Belgian paratrooper had a bandaged nose.

The door of the Learjet closed and the plane immediately began to taxi off. General Hanrahan made a signal with his hand, and a Chevrolet staff car appeared around the corner of the Base Ops building.

It was not flying the checked flag required of all vehicles driving on the flight line.

It's a clear violation of safety regulations. And that goddamned Hanrahan, who knows better, should have his ass burned.

But if I personally report him, he will think I'm chickenshit. And who do I report him to? He's not under the command of the commanding general of Fort Bragg. He gets his orders directly from the chief of staff of the Army.

I am not about to call the chief of staff of the U.S. Army and announce that I am an Air Force brigadier onto whose tarmac Red goddamn Hanrahan drove his staff car without flying a checkered flag.

And who was the black guy in the white suit? Probably the same Congolese, with something to do with

Operation Dragon Rouge.

It has to be something like that.

The black guy in the white suit meets the chief of staff of the Army at a cocktail party, says he'd like to see Green Beret training, and the chief says, "My pleasure, Mr. Prime Minister/Your Excellency/Mr. Secretary./Whatever the hell. I will call the Special Missions Squadron of the Air Force and see if they won't give you a Learjet to fly you down there."

It has to be something like that. You don't get to ride in a Learjet unless you are unquestionably a VIP. Or a four-star.

Brigadier General Hanrahan turned from the front passenger seat of the Chevrolet staff car to the black gentleman in the far-too-large-for-him white suit.

"Father," he said. "You look like death warmed over."

"Flattery will get you everywhere, *mon général*," Captain George Washington Lunsford said. Only close friends and commanding generals got to call him by his nickname, a shorthand for "Father of His Country," derived from the obvious source.

"Have you been drinking, Father?" Hanrahan asked.

"I cannot, *mon général*, in the noble tradition of my namesake, tell a lie. Yes, I have. And, if this could be arranged, I would be ever so grateful for a little belt right now."

"Not right now, I don't think, Captain Lunsford," Hanrahan said. "I think what you need right now is a cup of black coffee."

In the interests of good military order and discipline, General Hanrahan decided it would be far better if, when the word got around that Father Lunsford had returned alive from a really hairy

44

assignment, it was not gleefully bandied about that he had returned in a white suit that didn't fit, and as drunk as an owl.

He touched his driver, a nice-looking young Green Beret sergeant, on his sleeve.

"You better take us to the house, Tony."

"Yes, sir."

"First things first," General Hanrahan said as he walked into the sun porch of Quarters 107, a two-story brick home that had been built in 1938 as quarters suitable for a captain. "Your coffee, Captain Lunsford."

Lunsford, who was slumped in a wicker armchair, reached for it.

My God, he really looks awful.

"*Merci, mon général.*"

"Where'd you get the suit?"

"It belongs to Jack's father. It was in his apartment in the Immoquateur — that's the apartment building in Stanleyville?"

Hanrahan nodded his understanding.

"When the C130s started dropping the Belgians, I was wearing my Simba uniform, and I knew that the first Belgian to see me would take a shot at me, so I borrowed it from Jack's stepmother," Lunsford explained.

"Tony," Hanrahan said to his driver. "Go find the sergeant major. Tell him Captain Lunsford needs a clean uniform. There's a duplicate key to the captain's locker in my safe."

"Yes, sir."

"And, Sergeant, on your way back, stop by Class VI and pick up a bottle of scotch, will you?" Captain Lunsford said.

Hanrahan looked closely at Lunsford.

"You need a drink that bad, do you?"

"I really would like a little taste, General."

"I'll give you a drink," Hanrahan said. "Tony, get him his uniform."

"Yes, sir," the sergeant said.

Hanrahan poured scotch in three glasses, handed one to Lunsford and the other to Jack Portet, and then raised his own.

"Welcome home, the both of you," he said.

Portet took a sip of the straight scotch. Lunsford downed all of his at once.

When he sensed Hanrahan's eyes on him, Lunsford said: "It tranquilizes my worm, sir."

"What?"

"My tapeworm, sir. I have a world-class tapeworm."

I will deal with that later.

"What happened to your nose, Portet?" General Hanrahan asked. "And what's with the Belgian uniform?"

"Mon général," Captain Lunsford said. "Sergeant Portet has asked that I serve as his legal counsel. As such, Sergeant Portet, I advise you to claim your rights under the 31st Article of War and respectfully decline to answer the general's question — at least until you get your medals — on the grounds it may tend to incriminate you."

"What medals?"

"I have it on the best authority, *mon général,* that this splendid young noncommissioned officer is to be decorated by both the Belgian and Congolese governments for his heroic participation in Operation Dragon Rouge."

" 'Heroic'?" Hanrahan parroted. "What he was supposed to do was brief the Air Force about the airfield, and see if he knew anything about Stanleyville the Belgians didn't already know."

"Actually, sir, Sergeant Portet's contribution to Operation Dragon Rouge went a little beyond that."

"For example?"

"He jumped on Stanleyville with the Belgians, sir," Lunsford said. "That's where he got that uniform. And the busted nose. He fell out of a truck in Stanleyville."

"He was not supposed to jump anywhere," Hanrahan said. "And I specifically ordered Foster to make sure he didn't."

He looked at Portet, who looked very uncomfortable.

"Sir, Lieutenant Foster made it very clear that I was not to go with the Belgians."

"And you figured, fuck you, and jumped anyway?"

Hanrahan heard the angry tone in his voice and vowed to keep his temper.

"General, his family was in Stanleyville," Lunsford said.

"I know that," Hanrahan snapped, and then asked, more kindly, "Are they all right, Portet?"

"When I got to the Immoquateur, sir, Captain Lunsford was there. He protected them. They're fine. They're on their way to the States, via Germany."

"Geoff Craig's wife and baby, too?"

"Yes, sir. Thanks to Captain Lunsford."

"Well, thank God for that," Hanrahan said.

"How'd you come back?" Hanrahan asked.

"With Fath . . . Captain Lunsford, on the Special Missions jet."

If my family had been in Stanleyville, I would have

47

jumped on Stanleyville.

"The shit's going to hit the fan, you understand, when it gets out that you jumped with the Belgians," Hanrahan said.

"That's why I got him the medals, sir," Lunsford said. "I figured, what the hell, with the Belgians and the Congolese calling him a hero . . ."

"You got him the medals?"

"Colonel Van de Waele, the Belgian leading—"

"I know who he is," Hanrahan interrupted.

"Came to Kamina just before we left. I explained the situation —"

"The military situation, or Portet's?" Hanrahan interrupted again.

"Both, actually," Lunsford said.

"Sir, what Colonel Van de Waele really came to Kamina to do —"

"I don't recall having given you permission to speak, Sergeant," Lunsford said. "Shut your mouth."

"You were saying, Sergeant?" Hanrahan said.

"The King sent him," Portet said. "With orders to give Captain Lunsford the Grand Order of Leopold, First Class," Portet said.

Whatever medal the King of the Belgians gave him, he deserved.

"Did he?" Hanrahan said.

"Well, since the subject of medals had come up," Lunsford said, "I told Van de Waele about how Portet had come into the Immoquateur like John Wayne, his weapon blazing, dropping bad guys all over. . . ."

"And?"

"Van de Waele said he was pretty sure he could get Jack a medal, Second Class, and then some

48

Congo colonel got in the act and said he was sure General Mobutu, the Congolese chief of staff, would want to decorate the both of us —"

"Was this before or after you mentioned Jack wasn't supposed to be in Stanleyville in the first place?"

"Now that you mention it, that may have come up in the conversation." Lunsford paused, and met Hanrahan's eyes. "It wasn't all bullshit, what I told Van de Waele about Jack. He's one hell of a soldier, General."

"Who, by his own admission, disobeyed a direct order to jump on Stanleyville."

Lunsford shrugged, and then he began to cough. His body shook with the effort, and when he finally stopped, his face was sweat-soaked.

"Why aren't you in Walter Reed?" Hanrahan asked. "For that matter, why aren't you in the 97th General Hospital in Frankfurt?"

"Now that you mention it, *mon général,* it might be a good idea to call Walter Reed and tell them where I am. I think they might be wondering where I am about now."

"Goddamn it, Father! You're AWOL from Walter Reed, aren't you?"

"In a manner of speaking, sir."

"Why the hell did you come here?"

"When I looked out of the window of the Immoquateur and saw John Wayne here leading the cavalry to the rescue, I figured I really owed that guy, whoever he was. Then I found out who he was and what he had done, and I figured I owed it to him to do what I could to get him off the hook. So I came here."

"Did you see Colonel Felter over there, Father?"

"Yes, sir, he was at Kamina."

"So he knows about Portet?"

"Yes, sir."

"And?"

"There was an Air Force colonel flying the presidential Special Missions DC-9 at Kamina. Felter told him to get Portet to Fort Bragg by the most expeditious means. When we got to Washington, the Learjet was waiting for us, and we came here."

"Instead of you checking into Walter Reed, right?"

"Yes, sir."

Hanrahan shook his head in resignation.

"And did Colonel Felter have anything to say to you, Sergeant Portet?"

"Yes, sir. He told me to report to you and keep out of sight until I heard from him."

"That's all?"

Portet hesitated, then dug in his pocket and came up with a set of Belgian parachutist's wings.

"He gave me these, sir."

"Why aren't you wearing them?"

"I wasn't sure I was entitled to them, sir."

"You're entitled to them," Hanrahan said. "You earned them the hard way. The medals are something else. You need to get congressional approval to accept them."

"Colonel Felter told Colonel Van de Waele he didn't think there would be any problem about that, sir," Lunsford said.

Hanrahan shook his head again.

"Well, gentlemen, as I said before, welcome home," he said. "Now, before I throw your ass in the hospital, Father, and bury you at Camp Mackall, Sergeant, is there any little thing I can do for either of you?"

"I could use another little taste of the scotch, General," Captain Lunsford said.

"One more, Father, and that's it."

"Yes, sir."

"Jack?"

"I'd like to call Marjorie, sir."

"There's a phone in the kitchen."

II

[ONE]
Quarters #1
Fort Rucker, Alabama
1605 1 December 1964

As Major General Robert F. Bellmon, sitting in the rear seat of his 1963 Chevrolet staff car, rolled up the driveway to the quarters provided for the commanding general, U.S. Army Aviation Center and Fort Rucker, he had a thought he frequently had under the circumstances:

If I wasn't the CG, I damned sure wouldn't live here.

It did not mean that he felt honored and grateful that the U.S. Army was providing him, as a token of its respect for him personally, or the office he held, with such magnificent living accommodations, but quite the reverse.

He hated the place. He thought it was the sort of home in which a manager of the Farm Bureau Insurance Company would live; or the assistant vice president of a very small bank; or a moderately successful used car salesman.

He knew where the commanding general of Fort Benning, Georgia, a fellow major general, hung his hat. Quarters #1 at Benning was "Riverside," a charming old southern mansion. And he knew where the commanding general of Fort Knox, Kentucky, another fellow major general, hung his: in a very nice two-story brick colonial house with a very nice rose garden behind it.

Quarters #1 at Fort Rucker was a single-story frame building built just a few years before. You had to look close to see that it was larger — only slightly larger — than the sea of officers' quarters built nearby. Among the many other adjectives that frequently came to his mind when thinking about it was "pedestrian."

But he was the commanding general, and he had to live in the commanding general's quarters, although he would have much preferred to live elsewhere. There were a number of nice houses available on the civilian market in Ozark and Enterprise and Dothan, the nearest towns to Fort Rucker. And he could afford the rent. He was not a wealthy man, but he was comfortable; he didn't have to live on his Army pay.

There were two cars in the carport — the damned place didn't even have a garage — and three more on the concrete pavement in front of it. And the driveway was inadequate. If, for example, Barbara (Mrs. Robert F.) Bellmon wanted to go someplace in her Oldsmobile 98, now in the car-port, at least two of the other cars would have to be moved out of the way. The Oldsmobile had a blue sticker, an officer's sticker, on its bumpers, reading FORT RUCKER ALA 1.

Parked beside the Oldsmobile was a glistening, flaming-red Jaguar V12 convertible. It carried a red bumper sticker reading FORT RUCKER ALA 9447. Red stickers were issued to enlisted men; civilian employees of the post got green stickers.

The Jaguar was the POV of Sergeant Jacques Portet, whom Barbara Bellmon referred to as "Marjorie's Young Man." Jack had left the Jaguar in Marjorie's care while he was off on what was euphemistically called "temporary duty."

Jack had been assigned to Fort Rucker when he finished basic training. He was not the only young man with a commercial pilot's license to be drafted — although as far as Bellmon knew, he was the only one with an Air Transport Rating (ATR) in multi-engine jet and piston aircraft — or to decide that two years' service as an enlisted man was preferable to three years as a lieutenant, and some provision had been made to use their special talents.

Not nearly enough provision, in Bellmon's opinion. He regarded the army regulations that governed people like Jack as incredibly stupid, to the point where he'd written the assistant chief of staff for personnel about them.

It would be a sound Army policy, he had written, to send young men possessed of a college degree and a commercial pilot's license, with instrument ticket, before an officer selection board. If they got through that, they could be commissioned, sent to a short course in how to be behave as an officer, then another short flying course, to familiarize themselves with military flying, and then be sent to a unit.

That would, he had written, provide the Army with experienced junior officer pilots in far less time than it presently took to train young officers how to fly. Based on what he called "an informal survey of such enlisted men" (by which he meant that he had sought out and spoken with the dozen or so at Fort Rucker), an "overwhelming major-ity" (by which he meant all but one of the men he had talked to) had expressed willingness to serve as pilots, even if that meant service in Vietnam if the Army would permit them to do so.

What they were not willing to do was serve more time in the service than other draftees. The Army, so far as Bellmon was concerned, compounded the original stupidity of not directly commissioning such young men by adding what they regarded as a punishment for having gone to college and knowing how to fly.

If they accepted a commission, which meant they would have to serve three years in uniform instead of two, that three years would start the day they were commissioned, with no credit given for the time they had spent as enlisted men, which would be at least six months, and often longer. And then this stupidity was further compounded, should they volunteer to fly, by recomputing the three years' service required to start the day they were awarded their wings.

The reply to Bellmon's letter from the assistant chief of staff for personnel said, in effect, and more or less politely, We don't try to tell you how to run Army Aviation, please don't try to tell us how to run our officer procurement programs.

Bellmon was very sympathetic to Jack Portet's refusal to accept a commission, but he often thought that his mother and father — especially his mother — were spinning in their graves at the thought that Marjorie's Young Man was not a commissioned officer and gentleman.

What Jack would ordinarily have done at the Army Aviation Center was become a teacher of navigation, or radio procedures, or something similar in ground school, or find himself assigned to the Army Aviation Board, or the Instrument Examiner Board, where there were many places an experienced pilot forbidden to fly could make himself useful.

Private Portet, because of his ATR, had been assigned to the Instrument Board. That raised the number of ATRs at the Board to two. The other belonged to Major Pappy Hodges, the president of the Board.

When Private Portet opened a bank account at the Bank of Ozark, the teller on duty was Miss Marjorie Bellmon, on her first job out of college. Bellmon thought privately that his previously level-headed daughter had suddenly lost her senses. His wife called it "love at first sight." Bellmon thought of it as pure and unbridled lust at first sight, with Marjorie cooing like a dove, and Jack pawing at the ground like a stallion in heat.

At first, Romeo and Juliet had thought, with good reason, that they were lucky. Jack had immediately been declared an "essential to mission" enlisted man, which would keep him from being stolen by other aviation activities who would kill to have someone with an ATR. That meant he would spend the remainder of his draftee service at Fort Rucker, which meant he would not be sent to the growing war in Vietnam as an infantry private.

What Marjorie and Jack did not know was that Private Portet had come to the attention of Colonel Sanford T. Felter even before he had completed basic training.

Felter was convinced the United States was about to become involved in the ex–Congo Belge. There were very few people in the Army who spoke Swahili. At Felter's orders, records were scoured for anyone who spoke the language, and Portet's name had come up.

The situation in the Congo had grown much

worse much more quickly than anyone, including Colonel Sanford Felter, thought it would.

Thousands of square miles of the ex–Congo Belge, including Stanleyville, had fallen to the "Simba Army of Liberation," commanded by Joseph Olenga. There was no question that Olenga was a savage, and there was considerable reason to believe that he was insane, as well. Neither was there any question that he was being supported to some degree by the Soviet Union.

Sixteen hundred "Europeans" were being held hostage by Olenga, who regularly proved his willingness to execute them all if he didn't get his way by murdering two or more a day in the Center Square of Stanleyville.

The "Europeans" included the staff of the U.S. Consulate in Stanleyville, and sixty-odd other Americans, including Jack Portet's stepmother and sister who had been caught there returning to Léopoldville from Europe with Ursula Craig and her infant son. Ursula's husband was a Green Beret lieutenant undergoing flight training at Fort Rucker.

The President of the United States had signed "a finding," which meant that he had determined that a covert operation was necessary. Something had to be done about the Simbas, and not only because of the Americans the Simbas held captive.

Covert operations of this type are normally given to the CIA. The President gave Operation Dragon Rouge to the military, and specifically named Colonel Sanford T. Felter as "action officer." It was generally believed this was the President's method of expressing his dissatisfaction with the CIA and its formal conclusion that there would be no trouble in the Congo in the foreseeable future.

Felter had immediately taken several steps to accomplish his mission. The first had been to instruct the John F. Kennedy Center for Special Warfare to prepare to mount an operation that would be landed by parachute to seize the airfield at Stanleyville. Brigadier General "Red" Hanrahan was advised that he would be sent a young man who knew the Congo, and Stanleyville in particular, intimately, to help plan the operation.

The "essential to mission" classification of Private Portet at the Instrument Board fell to his being essential to the presidentially directed mission of Colonel Sanford T. Felter.

Bob Bellmon's reaction to the sudden transfer of Private Portet to Fort Bragg was relief. "Out of sight, out of mind" occurred to him, and he had never believed that "absence makes the heart grow fonder."

The next thing Bellmon had heard about Private Portet was from a very upset Marjorie, who returned from a brief weekend visit to Fort Bragg to announce that Jack was now a PFC, having qualified as a parachutist in a "special course" and was looking forward to becoming a sergeant, which would take place immediately on his graduation from a Special Forces "special course" at Camp Mackall.

"What the hell's going on, Daddy?" Marjorie, torn between fury and tearful concern, had demanded. "They can't do that, can they? Doesn't it take four weeks for jump school and a year to get through Special Forces training?"

The reply that came to his lips and nearly escaped was "Nothing those crazy bastards do surprises me anymore, honey."

What he said was "I'll see what I can find out, honey."

There was a grain of reason in the madness, he found out, by making an en-route-to-Washington fuel stop in North Carolina, and cornering his old friend Brigadier General Hanrahan in his quarters.

"You're not supposed to know anything about Dragon Rouge, Bob, and you know it, and I have never even heard the name. But hypothetically speaking, do you really think that if there were such an operation, I would send a kid — he's a really nice young man, by the way, and Marjorie's really gone on him, isn't she? — on it?"

"It would appear that way. You were saying, Red?"

"If there were such an operation, and we both know there isn't, but if there were, and your expert about the landing zone was a private soldier, would you pay as much attention to him as you would if he were a Green Beret and a sergeant?"

"Meaning what?"

"Three master parachutists gave him a thirty-six-hour course that taught him more than he would have learned in four weeks at Benning. And now he's getting the same sort of training by one of my A Teams at Mackall. He'll come out of Mackall trained, and qualified to wear a beret. When he talks to people, they'll listen to him. But he's not going anywhere near where this hypothetical operation we're talking about is going down. He probably won't even leave the States."

When Major General Robert F. Bellmon walked into his living room, Marjorie was sitting before the television, but not seeing anything.

"How goes it, honey?" he asked.

Until today, there had been very little about Dragon Rouge in the newspapers or on TV, except that an action to rescue the Europeans was under way. No journalists had been permitted to accompany the parachutists, and Joseph Kasavubu, the President of the Congo, had imposed an embargo on any news of the operation that had been lifted only twelve hours before.

"Did you find out anything for me?" Marjorie asked.

"No. I told you I have no need-to-know, and I know better than to ask. If something had happened to Jack, we would have heard. Sandy would have got word to us."

"No news is good news, right?" she said sarcastically. He chose to let it pass.

"If I had to make a guess," he said, "Jack is probably on Ascension Island. That's as far as they would let him go. And the C-130s probably didn't return that way; their mission was to get the people rescued back here as quickly as they could. So he's out there waiting for transportation."

He handed her *The New York Times* and the Atlanta *Constitution*.

"I asked somebody to get these for me," he said. "For you. They'll have more in them than that goddamned Dothan *Eagle*."

The same picture was on the front page of both newspapers, over the caption "Bloody-Bandaged, Battle-Weary, Belgian Paratrooper Tenderly Comforts Rescued Girl In Stanleyville."

Marjorie glanced at the picture and started reading the story.

"They killed that doctor," General Bellmon said.

"What?" Marjorie asked, and looked up at him.

"I said they killed that doctor, the missionary? Carlson? It's in there. Just shot him down in cold blood, as the parachutists were taking the town."

"Oh, my *God!*" Marjorie wailed.

General Bellmon looked at his daughter in surprise.

"What?"

"Look at that!" she said, thrusting the *Constitution* at him.

"What am I looking at?"

"That's no Belgian paratrooper," Marjorie said, tears running down her face. "That's my Jack! I can tell by his eyes! And that little girl is his sister. I've seen pictures of her. Oh, my God, he's been shot in the face!"

General Bellmon examined the photograph carefully.

"I'll be damned," he said. "I think that's Jack, all right." Then he raised his voice. "Barbara! Come take a look at this!"

Second Lieutenant Robert F. Bellmon looked at the photograph after his mother, then informed his sister that he had been shown a film at West Point demonstrating what miracles of reconstructive surgery were now possible.

Marjorie, her mother saw, was about to respond when the telephone rang.

"Bobby, answer that," Barbara Bellmon ordered, very quickly.

"Your brother gets his tact from his father," Barbara said to Marjorie. "But Bobby's right, honey, they can work miracles."

"Hey, Marj!" Second Lieutenant Bellmon called.

"Now what?" Marjorie snapped.

"We got a collect call from Sergeant Jack Portet at Fort Bragg. You want to pay for it?"

[TWO]
Quarters #9
Fort Bragg, North Carolina
0215 2 December 1964

In a failed attempt to get out of bed to answer the goddamned doorbell without waking his wife, Brigadier General Paul Hanrahan painfully stubbed his toe on the leg of the bed.

He swore.

"My God, what are you doing?" Patricia inquired, sitting up in bed and turning on a light.

"I was trying not to wake you. There's somebody at the door."

"Well, get your bathrobe on. Don't go down there in your underwear."

She turned the light off and dropped back into the bed.

General Hanrahan found his bathrobe in the dark, left the bedroom, turned on the hall lights, and made his way gingerly down the stairs.

This better be important, he vowed, *or I will burn whoever is at the goddamned door at this goddamned hour a new anal orifice.*

He snapped on the porch light and pushed the curtain away from the small triangular window in the center of the door.

"Shit," he said softly, and unlocked and opened the door.

"What can I do for you, Marjorie?" he asked, as

kindly as he could manage under the circumstances.

"Where is he, Uncle Red?" Miss Marjorie Bellmon asked. "I know he's here, he called me from here, but the duty officer wouldn't tell me anything."

He turned and wordlessly waved her into the house.

He picked up the telephone and dialed a number.

Miss Marjorie Bellmon and Patricia Hanrahan — who, her husband became aware, was now coming down the stairs — heard only the following:

(Politely): "Let me speak to the duty officer, please."

(Less politely): "Then wake him up, goddamn it!"

(Impatiently): "General Hanrahan."

(Apologetically): "I should have told you who I was, Sergeant. No problem."

(Politely): "Sorry to wake you up, Captain. I don't suppose Sergeant Portet is readily available?"

(Long silence during which the duty officer reports, somewhat uneasily, that there had been sort of a little "Welcome Home, Jack" party sponsored by the staff, which had ended when the beer ran out about oh-one-thirty, and that so far as he knew Sergeant Portet was asleep. *Soundly* asleep.)

(Politely): Hold one, please, Captain.

"Marjorie, Jack's in bed at Camp Mackall. He was all worn out from the flight. Do you want me to have them wake him up?"

"Can I see him in the morning?"

(Normal tone of voice): "Captain, first thing in the morning, put him in an ambulance and deliver him to my quarters. Tell him his girl is here."

(Somewhat impatiently): "Yes, an ambulance. You weren't told we're keeping him under a rock?"

(More politely): "Oh-six-thirty would be fine, Captain. Thank you. Good night."

" 'Under a rock'?" Patricia Hanrahan quoted, quizzically.

"Why does he need an ambulance?" Marjorie Bellmon inquired.

"Jack will be here at half past six," General Hanrahan said.

"I'll go to the guest house and be back then," Marjorie replied.

"Don't be silly, Marjorie, you'll do no such thing," Patricia Hanrahan said.

"What did you do, Marjorie? Drive all night to get here?" General Hanrahan inquired.

Stupid goddamn question. Unless she flew here on the wings of young love, how else would she get here?

"Are you hungry, honey?" Mrs. Hanrahan inquired.

"A little. I didn't stop except for gas."

"Red, why don't you make her an egg sandwich or something while I get her bed made?"

(Somewhat strained enthusiasm): "Sure."

[THREE]
Quarters #9
Fort Bragg, North Carolina
0530 3 December 1964

General Red Hanrahan came suddenly out of a deep sleep with the realization — *Christ, why didn't I think of this last night?* — that if he had Jack Portet delivered to his quarters in an ambulance at 0630, it would be all over Colonel's Row in ten minutes — and all over the Special Warfare Center ten minutes after that — that there had been some sort of before-reveille emergency at his quarters.

The Army, he thought, could give How To Gossip lessons to a dozen Italian widows gathered around the village water pump.

The concerned and the curious would descend on his quarters like flies onto a corpse, and he couldn't have that. For one thing, he had been told to keep Jack out of sight, and for another, tongues would really start to wag if it became known that he was playing Cupid's Helper to a fellow general officer's daughter and her sergeant boyfriend.

He very carefully got out of bed so as not to wake Patricia again, found his bathrobe without trouble, and made it almost to the bedroom door before stumbling into a footstool that was where it shouldn't have been.

"Shit!"

"For God's sake, Red, what are you trying to do, wake Marjorie?"

"Go back to sleep, baby. I've got to make a phone call."

"Hah!"

When he walked into his kitchen, he saw that

65

Miss Marjorie Bellmon was already wide awake, fully dressed, and had made a pot of coffee.

"I didn't mean to wake you, Uncle Red. Sorry."

"No problem, honey."

"I couldn't sleep."

"Well, let's see when Jack will be here," Hanrahan said, and picked up the handset of the wall telephone.

"U.S. Army Special Warfare Center, Staff Sergeant Abraham speaking, sir."

"This is General Hanrahan, Sergeant. Sometime in the next few minutes, someone from Mackall is going to bring a sergeant named Portet —"

"They're here, sir, waiting for 0615 to bring him by your quarters," Sergeant Abraham interrupted.

"The original idea was to bring him in an ambulance," Hanrahan said. "I don't want to give my neighbors something to talk about."

"I'll run him over there in the duty jeep when it's time, sir."

"Thank you," Hanrahan said. "You might as well bring him now. I'm up."

"Yes, sir."

"Thanks, Sergeant."

Marjorie kissed him.

"Thank you, Uncle Red."

He smiled at her and looked at his watch.

0537. He's already on the post. Which means he left Mackall at, say, 0445. Which means they woke him up at 0400. Good. I hope he was really hungover when they woke him up.

"I'm going to go back to bed for a while, honey. Make yourself at home."

Marjorie heard the jeep drive up, and peered around the drapes of the living-room window.

Her heart jumped when she saw him get out of the jeep.

Oh, my God, his nose is bandaged!

My God, I really love that man!

As she went quickly to the door to open it before he would have a chance to ring the bell and wake up the Hanrahans, she had a second thought:

My God, he looks like a soldier! He looks like one of them!

The last time she had seen him in uniform, he looked like what he was, a draftee fresh from Basic Training, a buck private in combat boots and a baseball cap and ill-fitting mussed fatigues bearing only the legend US ARMY over the left breast pocket and PORTET over the right.

She opened the door and he trotted quickly up to her.

He is one of them!

There was a green beret on his head, and sergeant's stripes and the insignia of Special Forces on the sleeves of his starched and form-fitting fatigues. There were U.S. Army parachutist's wings pinned above the US ARMY patch, and what she correctly guessed were Belgian paratrooper's wings over his name on the right. And he was wearing glistening paratrooper's jump boots.

"You're a long way from home, Marjorie," he said.

"How's your nose?" she asked.

And then she was in his arms, his face buried in her neck.

She felt him grow and stiffen against her abdomen.

"Oh, baby, I'm so glad to see you," he said.

She freed herself.

"So I noticed," she said.

He smiled.

"That's what they call an 'involuntary vascular reaction to a stimulus,' " he said.

She felt herself blush.

He leaned down to her and kissed her, very chastely, on the lips. The innocence of the kiss lasted perhaps three seconds, and then she was aware that she was pressing herself against him with a hunger that matched his.

She freed herself again.

"The Hanrahans," she said, nodding toward the stairs.

"Jesus," he said.

"You were supposed to teach them about the airport," she challenged. "Nothing else."

"It didn't work out that way," he said.

"You could have been killed, damn you!"

"I wasn't," he said simply.

"Good morning, Jack," Patricia Hanrahan said from the staircase.

Last night's carousing obviously hasn't hurt his appetite, General Hanrahan thought. *When I was a young buck and drank beer all night until there was no more, the last thing I wanted to see — even think about — the next morning was a fried egg.*

Sergeant Jack Portet was seated at the kitchen table, eating ham and eggs under the adoring gaze of Miss Marjorie Bellmon. Mrs. Patricia Hanrahan, wearing an apron over her negligee, was leaning against a kitchen counter wearing a look that Red Hanrahan thought was either maternal or *Ain't They Sweet!*

The telephone on the wall rang, and Hanrahan answered it on the second ring.

"General Hanrahan."

"Colonel Swenson, sir. I hope I didn't wake you."

"Good morning, Swede. No problem. I've been up for some time. What's up?"

"General, there's a lieutenant here asking for Sergeant Portet. I didn't know how to handle it."

"Very simple, Swede. We never heard of him."

"I tried that, General," Swenson said. "He says he knows Portet's here." He added: "He's one of ours, sir. I think he just came from where Portet came."

"Has 'one of ours' got a name, Swede?"

"Craig, sir. Lieutenant Geoffrey Craig."

"Damn!" Hanrahan said. He hesitated just perceptibly. "Okay, Swede. Send him over here."

He put the handset into its cradle and turned to look at Sergeant Jack Portet.

"Geoff Craig is here, Jack. Looking for you. Do you have any idea what that's all about?"

"No, sir."

"No idea at all?"

"Well, sir, it probably means that everybody's back. They came back via the Army Hospital in Frankfurt."

"Is there some kind of problem, honey?" Patricia asked.

"My orders are to keep Jack under a rock," Hanrahan said. "With a lot of people knowing he's here, that's getting to be difficult."

"Do you think he has Ursula and the baby with him?" Marjorie asked.

"That's why I think everybody's here," Jack

69

replied. "I can't imagine Geoff being here without them."

"He was with them in the Congo?" Hanrahan asked.

"They were flown to Léopoldville in the C-130s," Jack answered. "And then on Air Congo to Frankfurt. My stepmother and sister, too, and probably my father went along."

Hanrahan nodded, as if he agreed with Portet's thinking.

The telephone rang again, and Hanrahan snatched it almost angrily from its cradle, muttering, "Now what?"

"General Hanrahan," he snarled into the instrument.

His wife shook her head.

His caller chuckled.

"Should I call back later when you just haven't rolled out of the wrong side of the bed?"

He recognized the voice as that of Lieutenant Colonel Craig W. Lowell.

"I was actually in a very good mood until I heard your voice."

"Honest to God, Red, I waited until I thought you would be up before I called."

"I'm touched by your concern," Hanrahan said. "What's on your mind, Craig?"

"Where did you hide Portet? At Camp Mackall?"

"Uh-huh."

"How's his nose?"

"It's broken, but, aside from a bandage, there's nothing that can be done to it or for it."

"How long will it take to get him to Bragg from Mackall?"

"As a matter of fact, he's sitting here in my

kitchen. Marjorie's here."

That caught the attention of Mrs. Hanrahan, Miss Bellmon, and Sergeant Portet, who looked at him.

Hanrahan covered the mouthpiece with his hand.

"Craig Lowell," he explained.

"Why doesn't that surprise me?" Lowell said, chuckling. "Listen, Red, Geoff Craig's on his way there. He should be there within the hour."

"He's here," Hanrahan interrupted.

"Pappy Hodges is with him," Lowell said. "They're in my Cessna."

"And?"

"Geoff's going to drop Pappy at Rucker, and then bring Portet here."

"Where's here?"

"Florida."

"Where in Florida? McDill?"

Lowell was the army aviation officer on the staff of the commanding general, U.S. Army Strike Command at McDill Air Force Base, Florida. Strike was an in-place headquarters organization commanded by a four-star general. When needed, tactical forces of all the armed services were placed under its command for operations around the world. It had been the headquarters for Operation Dragon Rouge.

"No. Actually, Miami. And actually a little south of Miami, near Key Largo. For a little well-deserved R and R."

"Craig, my orders are to keep him under a rock."

"Obviously, this has the blessing of His Holiness, Moses I," Lowell said. "He's here. You want me to put him on the horn, even if that means

71

waking him from a sound sleep?"

Colonel Sanford T. Felter, Counselor to the President of the United States, had a staff of two. They were a bishop and nun, which he had to admit sounded a little funny, although he deeply regretted telling Lieutenant Colonel Craig W. Lowell where he had got them. Lowell thought it was hilarious, and had taken to calling Felter "His Holiness, Moses I, the First Jewish Pope."

The bishop was really a bishop, not of the Roman Catholic Church, but of the Church of Jesus Christ of Latter-Day Saints. James L. Finton was a career soldier who had risen to chief warrant officer, W-4, in twenty-three years. He was a cryptographer by training. Felter had found him in the Army Security Agency and arranged for his transfer to the White House Signal Detachment. He was a devout Mormon, and had told Felter that the church had saved his sanity after his wife had died of cancer. He spent his free time in one Mormon church function or another in the District. He had come to Felter with a Top Secret clearance, and a number of endorsements to that. He had a cryptographic endorsement, a nuclear endorsement, and several others.

The nun was really a nun, and of the Roman Catholic Church. Mary Margaret Dunne had been temporarily relieved of her vows to provide for her aged and senile father. When he died, she would return to the cloistered life as Sister Matthew. She spent her life in one of three places: with her father in a small apartment; on her knees in Saint Mary's church; or in Felter's small but ornate and high-ceilinged office in the old State, War and Navy Building.

Mary Margaret Dunne had been taken on by

the Kennedy White House following a quiet word from the bishop. She needed a job, and could type. She had gone to work for Felter the same morning President Kennedy had introduced Felter at a briefing as the only man in the White House who didn't answer his phone.

They were fiercely devoted to Felter, and, about as important, were both quietly convinced that the Communists were the Anti-Christ, and that what Felter was doing, what they were helping him do, was as much the Lord's Work as it was the government's.

"Sandy's in Miami, with you?"

"We're at McDill. The R and R will be in Miami. Portet's mother and father are there. My cousin Porter and his wife — Geoff's parents — are there. Geoff's wife and baby are there. Okay?"

"How long will he be gone?"

"Sandy hasn't made up his mind where to assign him."

"I thought he was here on TDY only until Dragon Rouge was over."

"Sandy hasn't made up his mind where to assign him," Lowell repeated, and Hanrahan understood there was something going on that Lowell was unwilling to talk about on the telephone.

"Okay."

"So he'll probably be coming back there," Lowell said. "In a week, ten days, something like that."

"Okay. I don't know how he's fixed for uniforms. Can he travel in fatigues?"

"No problem. We can get him something to wear here."

"Okay. He'll be ready when Craig gets here,

which should be any minute. Anything else?"

"Is Patricia handy?"

"Hang on," Hanrahan said, and handed the telephone to his wife, who beamed when he handed her the phone, and whose affection for Craig Lowell was evident in her voice and visible on her face.

He had no idea what Lowell said to his wife, although it produced peals of laughter, and when he had finished speaking with her, she handed the telephone to Marjorie.

He had no idea what Uncle Craig said to Marjorie, but at one point she blushed attractively and stole a look at Jack Portet, and when she was finished she handed the telephone to Jack.

He had no idea what Lieutenant Colonel Lowell said to Sergeant Portet, but it had Jack chuckling.

Finally, Jack put the telephone in its cradle.

"The condition of your nose permitting, Sergeant Portet, you are about to take an R and R in the vicinity of Key Largo, Florida," Hanrahan said.

"An R and R?" Jack questioned curiously.

"It stands for Rest and Recuperation Leave," Hanrahan said.

It is sometimes called I&I, which stands for Intercourse and Intoxication. I am looking at the only Special Forces sergeant in history who doesn't know that.

But on the other hand, there are a number of Special Forces sergeants who have never heard a shot fired in anger. This one, according to Father Lunsford, behaved damned well when he was being shot at.

General Hanrahan had more or less the same thought when, a few minutes later, he opened his door to a tanned young man in expensive civilian clothing:

This one behaved well, too, although to look at him, you would never suspect that he's a Green Beret officer, and a Vietnam veteran who's entitled to wear Combat Infantry Badge, the Silver Star, two Bronze Stars, and three Purple Hearts.

Geoffrey Craig had been a sergeant with an eight-man A Team on an isolated hilltop. They had fifty of the Mung tribesmen with them. The Vietcong had attacked with a battalion. Geoff and twenty-odd Mung had lived through the assault, and he had come off the hilltop with a Silver Star, his third Purple Heart, and a battlefield commission.

"Hey, Geoff," Hanrahan said, putting out his hand. "We've been expecting you."

"Good morning, sir," Geoff Craig said. "I hope going by the headquarters was the right thing to do?"

"Absolutely. Come on in. Have you had your breakfast?"

"Coffee and a fried egg sandwich, sir."

"Patricia will be happy to remedy that," Hanrahan said, then asked, "I thought Pappy Hodges was with you?"

"He has friends here, sir. We're to meet him at Pope at eleven hundred. Will that give us time to get Portet in from Mackall?"

"He's here. And so is Marjorie Bellmon."

"I saw the car," Craig said, inclining his head toward the driveway, where a red Jaguar convertible was parked.

Hanrahan hadn't noticed the car when Marjorie arrived.

"She drove up last night," Hanrahan said.

75

And won't that give my neighbors something to talk about over their morning coffee. "Did you see the Jaguar, with the enlisted man's sticker, in the Hanrahan driveway? I wonder what that's all about?"

"Jack told us that Ursula and the baby came through that nightmare all right," Patricia Hanrahan said as he walked into the kitchen. "I'm so happy for you, Geoff."

"Thank you. They're at Ocean Reef with my father and mother. And Jack's folks. That's where we're headed," he said, and went to Jack Portet, who stood up as he approached. They embraced each other briefly and wordlessly, but the affection between them was clear.

"And Miss Marjorie," Geoff said, turning to her. "You're a long way from the bank, aren't you?"

"If I wasn't so glad to see you, I'd tell you to go to hell," Marjorie said. "Ursula and the baby are really all right?"

"Absolutely. No small thanks to your boyfriend. You heard about his John Wayne act?"

"Why don't you shut up, Geoff?" Jack Portet said.

"No, I haven't," Marjorie said.

"Quickly changing the subject —" Jack said.

"Cutting to the chase," Geoff said, interrupting him, amused. "He's about to be invested in the Order of Leopold, in the grade of Chevalier, for conspicuous gallantry in action —"

"Jesus!" Jack said.

"But the gratitude of the King of the Belgians toward our modest hero is nothing like that of my parents. You are really going to have a good time

76

in Florida, Marj, basking in the reflected glory of our Jacques."

"He wasn't supposed to be anywhere near Stanleyville," Marjorie said.

"I heard whispers about that, come to think of it," Geoff said. "But it's no longer a problem. All is forgiven, so to speak."

"And I can't go to Florida," Marjorie said.

"Why not?" Jack asked, shocked. "I want you to meet my parents."

"Well, I have a job, for one thing."

"Screw the job. Let's get married."

Geoff Craig laughed.

"That will certainly rank high on the list of never-to-be-forgotten romantic proposals," he said. "Correct me if I'm wrong, Sergeant, but I think you are supposed to make propositions of that nature on your knees."

"Let's get married, Marjorie," Jack repeated. "As soon as we can."

She looked at him but didn't say anything.

"Oh, Jesus," he said. "Okay."

He got up from the table and dropped to his knees.

Marjorie, sobbing, fled the room. Patricia Hanrahan chased after her.

"Somehow, Jack, I get the feeling you didn't handle that very well," General Hanrahan said.

[FOUR]
Office of the Commanding General
The Army Aviation Center
Fort Rucker, Alabama
1545 3 December 1964

Captain Richard Hornsby, a rather good-looking,

very natty young man of twenty-five, who was wearing for the first time the insignia — a shield bearing two stars on his lapels, and an aiguillette hanging from his epaulette — identifying him as the aide-de-camp of a major general, looked up from his desk, first with idle curiosity and then with greater interest as a sergeant wearing fatigues entered his office.

For one thing, the sergeant had a large bandage covering his nose. For another, he was a Green Beret, and there were no Green Berets, as far as Hornsby knew, stationed on Fort Rucker.

"Can I help you, Sergeant?" Captain Hornsby asked.

"Sir, I'd hoped to see Captain Oliver," the sergeant said.

"Captain Oliver has been reassigned," Hornsby said. "How can I help you?"

"I'd like to see General Bellmon, please, sir."

Captain Hornsby's last instructions in that regard, that very morning, were *Dick, an important, very important part of your job will be to shield me from people who want to see me who really don't have to. You'll be astonished at the number of idiots who want to waste my time.*

The sergeant didn't look like an idiot, but the odds were, whatever he wanted, Hornsby could do it, and without disturbing General Bellmon.

"The general's tied up at the moment, Sergeant. Perhaps I can help. What's on your mind?"

"It's a personal matter, Captain," the sergeant said, a little uncomfortably. "I think if you tell him I'm out here — my name is Portet — he'll see me."

"Think of me as the guardian of the portals,

Sergeant," Captain Hornsby said, not unkindly. "I have the duty of deciding who can have some of the general's time, and as I'm sure you can understand, there's a hell of a demand for his time."

"Yes, sir."

"But whatever it is, Sergeant, I think it's even money that I could be of some help."

The sergeant didn't respond for a moment, and then he shrugged.

"Captain, would you believe me if I told you that if I told him I came to see him and you wouldn't let me in, he would be pissed?"

"No, Sergeant, I don't think I would," Captain Hornsby said, just a little testily.

Sergeant Portet opened his mouth as if to say something else.

The door to General Bellmon's office opened and General Bellmon came through, holding a sheaf of paper in his hands. Only after a moment did he raise his eyes and see the sergeant.

"Can I have a couple of minutes, General?" Sergeant Portet asked.

"Sir, I explained to the sergeant that you're tied up," Captain Hornsby said.

"Go on in," General Bellmon said, nodding with his head toward his office. He handed the sheaf of paper to Hornsby and added, "We'll get to this in a minute, Dick," then went into his office, closing the door behind him.

"Welcome home, Jack," General Bellmon said, offering his hand.

"Thank you, sir."

"We saw your picture in the paper," Bellmon said. "What happened to your nose? Is it serious?"

"Not serious. I took a dive off a truck in

Stanleyville," Jack said. "General, I want to marry Marjorie."

"Actually, Marjorie saw it first. She said, 'That's my Jack, and that's his sister.' It was on the front page of every newspaper in the country."

"Yes, sir. General, I want to marry Marjorie."

Bellmon took a moment to reply.

"I've been expecting this, Jack, but now that I'm faced with it, I find myself collecting my thoughts."

"Yes, sir."

"Presumably, you've asked her?"

"Yes, sir. This morning. In General Hanrahan's house."

"What did you do, drive straight back here?"

"No, sir. We're in Colonel Lowell's Cessna."

"Lowell loaned you his Cessna?"

"No, sir. He sent it after me. I'm headed for Florida. My parents are there. I want to take Marjorie with me, to meet them."

"I have no objection to that," Bellmon said. "Where in Florida?"

"Someplace called Ocean Reef," Jack said.

"I've been there. Lowell owns a house there. So does his cousin. Lieutenant Craig's father?"

"Yes, sir, but speaking of objections . . ."

"Is Lieutenant Craig there, with his parents?"

"No, sir. I mean he's here at Rucker. He and Pappy . . . Major Hodges . . . were flying the Cessna. I'm going to fly it to Florida. His wife and the baby are there. His parents, too, I think."

"I see," General Bellmon said. "Well, all's well — including this nightmare — that ends well, isn't it?"

"Yes, sir."

"No objections, Jack, to you and Marjorie getting married. I really don't have much choice, do I?"

"I'd like to have your approval, sir."

"Well, you have it, Jack," General Bellmon said. "And I know Mrs. Bellmon shares my high opinion of you."

"Thank you, sir."

"When were you thinking of getting married?"

"I thought right away, sir."

Bellmon's voice was cold when he asked: "Is there some reason you feel you should get married right away?"

"Yes, sir, now that you bring it up, there is."

"Well, those things happen. It certainly won't be the first time in recorded history, will it? Has she seen a doctor?"

"Sir?" Jack asked, confused, and then comprehension dawned.

"It's not what you're thinking, General," he said. "What I was thinking was that I realize this whole situation is a little awkward for you —"

"What situation is a little awkward?" Bellmon asked.

"I'm an enlisted man, and she's a general's daughter," Jack said.

"Why should that be awkward?" Bellmon challenged.

Jack looked at him helplessly.

"What I thought was that it would be easier for everyone all around if we got married right away, in a quiet ceremony, in Florida, just my family, and of course you and Mrs. Bellmon. . . ."

"Is this what Marjorie wants?"

"I don't know. I didn't ask her."

"You don't think she'll have an opinion?"

Jack didn't reply.

"Mrs. Bellmon and I were married in the Cadet Chapel at West Point," Bellmon said. "As were our parents. Both sides."

"I didn't go to West Point," Jack argued. "But if that's what she wants, why not?"

"Mrs. Bellmon will probably think of Chapel One here at Rucker," Bellmon said. "With a reception at the club."

"General, I'm a sergeant. I don't belong to the officers' club."

"Incidentally, I did notice the stripes. Congratulations. When did that happen?"

"Just before we went to Europe."

"And what are those, Belgian paratrooper's wings?"

"Yes, sir."

"Well, I guess you earned them the hard way, didn't you?"

Jack didn't reply.

"Jack, I am not the rambling idiot I sound like," Bellmon said. "I had no idea that facing the fact of Marjorie getting married would scramble my brains like this."

"General, I love her, and I'll take good care of her."

"Yes, I'm sure you will," Bellmon said.

He put out his hand.

They shook solemnly.

"Where is she?" Bellmon asked.

"At your house, asking permission to come to Florida with me."

"There would be room in the Cessna for Mrs. Bellmon, wouldn't there be?" Bellmon asked, distractedly, obviously thinking out loud. "I could get an L-23 over the weekend, take Bobby. . . ."

"Yes, sir," Jack said hesitantly.

Bellmon looked at him.

"You're implying Mrs. Bellmon wasn't invited?" Bellmon asked.

Jack didn't reply.

"Since you're about to join the family, Jack," Bellmon said, "let me tell you about my wife and Colonel Lowell. Anything she wants, she can have. I think he does it to piss me off. We have an open invitation to Ocean Reef — my wife does. If one of the houses isn't available, they put us up in a hotel."

"Yes, sir," Jack said.

"And the way it works, Jack, is that women do weddings. All the man has to do is show up sober at the church."

He smiled at his own wit, then touched Jack's arm and prodded him toward the door.

Captain Hornsby rose from his desk as they came into the outer office.

"If anybody wants me, I'll be at my quarters," General Bellmon said.

"Yes, sir."

"And Dick, call the post chaplain. Give him a heads-up. Mrs. Bellmon will probably call him tomorrow about a wedding."

"Yes, sir."

[FIVE]
Base Operations
Cairns Army Airfield
Fort Rucker, Alabama
1710 3 December 1964

When Major Daniel McCarthy, the AOD (Airfield Officer of the Day) returned to the Base Operations building from his first quick tour of the field — he

83

had come on duty at 1615 — there was a black Oldsmobile 98 with a blue sticker FORT RUCKER ALA 1 parked in the spot marked COMMANDING GENERAL.

McCarthy was made a little nervous, and was annoyed with the AOD he had relieved, who had said nothing about the general being on the program for the evening.

He got quickly out of the staff car — which had a large black-and-white checked flag flying from a mast on the rear bumper — and entered the building.

The sergeant on the desk pointed to the flight planning room, and Major McCarthy walked quickly to the door and pushed it open.

The general, a civilian, and a sergeant were bent over one of the worktables. Mrs. Bellmon and the general's daughter were standing before a huge map of the southern portion of the United States, which filled a wall.

There were other pilots in the room, obviously trying to stay out of the general's way.

Major McCarthy recognized the sergeant, despite the bandage over his nose. He had recently taken his annual instrument exam, and the sergeant had been in the office of the Instrument Board. McCarthy remembered someone telling him that he was a drafted airline pilot who had opted for two years' service as an enlisted man, rather than three or more years as an officer/pilot.

That explained what he was doing, making a flight plan, but it didn't mesh with McCarthy's memory that the drafted airline pilot had been a just-out-of-basic-training private, not a Green Beret sergeant with two sets of parachutist's wings.

84

"Good evening, General," McCarthy said. "Major McCarthy, the AOD. Can I be of some help?"

Bellmon turned and looked at him.

"Thanks, but no thanks, Major," he said, smiling. "But maybe the girls would like a Coke or a cup of coffee in the lounge."

"My pleasure, sir," Major McCarthy said. He turned to the women. "Would you like to come with me, ladies?"

"I'd like to see what's Jack's doing," Marjorie said. "Would I be in the way?"

"Help yourself," Jack said, and she walked to the table.

Barbara Bellmon smiled at Major McCarthy.

"I'll pass on the coffee, but thank you, Major."

Jack drew a straight line on a plastic-covered map of the area. It ran directly from Cairns Field to Hollywood, Florida, north of Miami. The route passed east of Crestview and Panama City, Florida, and then would take them over Appalachacola and the Gulf of Mexico, reaching land again northeast of Clearwater, Florida, and then across the Florida peninsula to Hollywood on the Atlantic coast.

"You're not going IFR?" — instrument flight rules — General Bellmon asked, surprised, and just a little disapproving.

Jack shook his head, no.

"They'd vector me into Georgia," he explained, drawing a course with his finger on the map. "And then down the peninsula. That'd add a couple of hundred miles, and this way I'll pick up a tailwind."

"That's what?" General Bellmon asked, and made a compass of his fingers to measure the dis-

85

tance on the map. "That's two hundred and something miles over the water."

General Bellmon obviously did not approve of the flight plan, and Major McCarthy was surprised that the sergeant, ex–airline pilot or not, did not immediately concur with the general's judgment.

"Daddy, Jack knows what he's doing," Marjorie said.

You said that because he's your knight in shining armor, but the fact is that he probably does, General Bellmon thought. *He's got more hours in the air than I do.*

"I'm sure he does," Bellmon said, smiling with a visible effort, "and he's the pilot."

Well, Major McCarthy thought, *if the sergeant is the pilot, that explains the Cessna 310H parked on the visitors' tarmac, doesn't it?*

And what's going on with him and the general's daughter?

[SIX]
Over Hollywood, Florida
2125 3 December 1964

"Miami, Cessna Six-oh-one," Jack said into the microphone.

"Six-oh-one, Miami."

"I'm on a VFR '— Visual Flight Rules —' Direct Cairns Field Alabama–Hollywood. You got it?"

"Hold one," the Miami controller said, and then, a moment later, "Got you, Six-oh-one."

"I'm at seven thousand over Hollywood. I want to extend to a private strip about twenty miles south of Miami. Okay?"

"Permission granted. I have you on radar. Close

86

out again when you're on the ground."

"Beginning descent at this time. And thank you, Miami," Jack said, and turned to Geoff Craig.

"Okay, now what?"

Geoff handed him the Jeppesen chart for the Miami area and pointed out a private landing strip on a narrow reef a few miles east of Key Largo.

"A private strip?" Jack asked dubiously. "Has it got lights?"

"Oh, ye of little faith!" Geoff replied. He dialed a frequency on the transceiver and picked up the microphone.

"Ocean Reef, Cessna Six-oh-one."

"Ocean Reef, go ahead."

"We're over Hollywood. Estimate fifteen minutes. Will you light it up in a couple of minutes and call Mr. Porter Craig and tell him we're on our way in?"

"Certainly. Give us a call, please, when you get close."

"Will do. Thank you, Ocean Reef," Geoff said, and turned to Jack. "You may start going down now, sir. In that direction, sir."

He pointed down with his index finger.

Jack smiled, shook his head, and put the Cessna into a gentle descent.

The hotels and condominiums along the beach, and Miami itself, were visible to their right, as were airliners making their descents toward Miami International.

"It's beautiful!" Marjorie said, leaning forward from the rear seat. Her fingers grazed Jack's neck. He shifted his neck backward to press against them.

Two minutes later, Geoff picked up the microphone again.

"Ocean Reef, Six-oh-one at 5,000. We have Miami in sight."

"Six-oh-one, Ocean Reef, we're lighting up now. The winds are five, gusting to fifteen, from the south. You will be met."

"Thank you kindly," Geoff said, and turned to Jack again. "The way I usually find it is to find A1A, and then Key Largo. We're about ten miles south."

He pointed vaguely to the southwest, and then to the southeast. Jack nodded.

"You better strap yourself in, Marjorie," Jack said, turning his head. She caressed his neck a moment more, then her fingers were gone.

A moment later, Geoff said, pointing to parallel rows of landing lights, "Either that's it or somebody's *really* got their boats in a row."

"Oh, Jesus," Jack said disgustedly, and turned slightly to the right to line up with the runway.

Three minutes later, the sleek twin-engine aircraft touched down smoothly just past the clearly marked threshold of what turned out to be a narrow but smoothly paved runway.

Jack saw that there was one small hangar; a neat-looking operations building with a small control tower on top of it; and maybe a dozen aircraft, mostly small, expensive light twins like the one he was flying, on the ramp.

It was, he decided, a very nice little airport.

A man in a sport shirt holding lighted wands appeared on the runway and directed him to a parking space.

He got on the horn and told Miami he was on the ground, then went through the shutdown procedures.

"That's Uncle Craig," Marjorie said happily,

and Jack looked out the side window of the airplane and saw that the man with the wands was indeed Lieutenant Colonel Craig W. Lowell.

He was the last person out of the airplane, and, deciding that caution was the better part of valor, Jack saluted him.

Lowell returned the salute.

"That's very nice, Sergeant, but we don't do very much of that around here." He paused and added, amused, "But I must say, Sergeant, that you really look awesomely military. Doesn't he, Geoff? A regular recruiting poster for Special Forces!"

"Well, he certainly would scare me to death," Geoff said.

"Leave him alone, Uncle Craig," Marjorie said. "And you, too, Geoff."

"Said the bride-to-be, protecting her man," Lowell went on, unabashed. "My, you two have had a busy, busy day, haven't you?"

"Craig, is that what I think it is?" Barbara Bellmon asked.

"Is what what you think it is?"

She pointed to an ancient, enormous, canary-yellow convertible sedan parked just off the runway.

"It is!" she said. "God, I thought it would be in a museum by now!"

"What is that?" Jack asked.

"It's a 1941 Packard 180 with a body by Rollson," Lowell said. "I will not explain further, because I am sure the mother of the bride-to-be will do so later in great detail. But I will say, Madame Bellmon, that the last offer I had for it — an excited little bald-headed man actually chased me down the highway in Key Largo waving his

89

checkbook — was ten times what I paid for it in Louisville."

"It's beautiful," Jack said. "I don't think I've ever seen one before."

"They made only thirty-two of them, the four-door," Lowell said. "Okay, here's the game plan. Jack's family are in House A. The Bellmon ladies will stay with them. Geoff — the whole Craig family — are in his parents' place, hereinafter referred to as House B. What we are going to do now is drop everybody off at House B, where festivities are already in progress. Except Jack and me, who will instead proceed to my house, House C, where Jack will be staying with me. There he will divest himself of his martial garb, slip into something more suitable, and then we will proceed to House B, where, unfortunately, Jack, you will receive a long, and probably tearful, speech of gratitude from Geoff's mother for saving her grandchild from the Simba."

"I didn't do anything like that —" Jack started to protest.

"Yeah, you did," Geoff said. "Ursula told me."

"Colonel, I don't have anything to change into," Jack said.

"Your ever-efficient stepmother took care of that," she said. "You have a full set of gear awaiting."

He gestured toward the car.

[SEVEN]

From what Jack had been able to see from the back seat of the Packard, Houses A, B, and C were — although their architecture was individual — alike in that they were large, substantial, and surrounded

90

by manicured greenery to assure the privacy of the inhabitants.

If he could judge by what he found in House C, they were luxuriously furnished and equipped. In addition to a glass-walled shower, plus a pool-sized tub, his bathroom had a black marble bidet. One rarely encountered bidets in the United States, much less black marble bidets.

The towels he found in the bathroom were too large and too thick to be wrapped around his waist, as was his custom, but that was not really a problem, because there was a terry-cloth robe hanging on a hook.

He put it on and walked into the bedroom, where he found Lieutenant Colonel Lowell sprawled comfortably in a chaise lounge. He had a whiskey glass in his hand, and there was another on the table beside the lounge.

Lowell got off the lounge.

"I knocked, but you were in the shower, I guess," Lowell said.

"No problem, sir."

"I've got two things you need," Lowell said. "Which would you rather have first, a nice, new king-sized Band-Aid for your nose? Or the drink?"

"The drink, please, sir. It's been a long day."

"And a long night before, according to General Hanrahan," Lowell said, a little smugly. He waited a moment, indicated the glass of whiskey, and waited until Jack had it in hand before going on: "These are your orders, so pay attention, Sergeant."

"Yes, sir?"

"You will not talk to the press, and will not permit your photograph to be taken by the press," Lowell said.

He's serious. What the hell is that all about?

"Sir?"

"Starting at about the time you left Kamina, the press was all over the place, and there is a rumor that an American Green Beret jumped with Belgians on Stanleyville. Everybody denies it, of course."

"I understand, sir."

"They are looking for an American hero right now, and if they could find you, get your name, it would be you. Felter thinks the frenzy will die down quickly. But then, when your permission to accept a foreign decoration goes through Congress, it's liable to come up again. Felter does not want your name or your photograph published. Got it?"

"Yes, sir. That's fine with me, Colonel."

"For the immediate future, you can count on ten, twelve days, two weeks here. Have a good time. I'm going to McDill in the morning, so the house will be yours alone."

"I'm awed by these houses, Colonel," Jack confessed. "Are they all yours?"

"This one's mine. And my cousin's is his. House A is owned by the company."

"You spend a lot of time here?"

"This is the first time this year. If you're looking for some place to take Marjorie on your honeymoon, this might be ideal."

"I don't know what to say, sir."

"Try thank you," Lowell said. "I'll set it up. All you have to do is call, and tell them when you're coming, and they'll send somebody over to turn up the air conditioner, make the beds, et cetera, et cetera. . . ."

He paused and changed the subject.

"We haven't finished with your orders," Lowell said. "Felter wanted to keep you at Mackall indefinitely, but I convinced him that sending you back to Rucker made more sense. So, in the absence of orders to the contrary in the meantime, you'll report to Rucker on 17 December. Back to the Instrument Board."

"Yes, sir."

"And get a regular cap. If you show up wearing a Green Beret, it'll cause talk. And we don't want talk."

"Yes, sir."

"That was Felter's idea. To hell with him. You earned it, you want to wear it, wear it. Just don't talk about Stanleyville."

"Yes, sir."

"That's it. Now let me look at your nose, and then we'll have to go face my sister-in-law."

"Yes, sir."

[ONE]
"Soft Breezes" (aka House B)
33 Ocean View Drive
The Ocean Reef Club
Key Largo, Florida
2345 3 December 1964

Hors d'oeuvres — plates of shrimp and oysters on beds of ice — and cocktails — served from behind a wet bar made of coral by a white-jacketed barman — and dinner — steaks and chicken to be broiled over charcoal by a chef in full white uniform on the patio by the pool — had been waiting for them in the enormous, L-shaped, open-to-the-rafters living room.

And so was the thank-you speech by Geoff's parents, which didn't go as badly as Colonel Lowell hinted it would.

When they walked into the house, Geoff's mother — a tall, elegant, silver-haired woman — and father — a somewhat portly, balding man — had walked quickly to him.

She put her hand up and touched his cheek and looked into his eyes.

"I'm Helene Craig," she said softly. "You're very welcome here, and I want you to know that I will pray for your health and happiness every night for the rest of my life."

Geoff's father had been worse. He looked as if

he was going to say something, then couldn't find his voice. He wrapped Jack in a bear hug, and his body shook with sobs.

"My God, Helene," Colonel Lowell said. "What will our guests think? They've only been here half an hour, and Porter's already as drunk as an owl."

"He is not!" Helene Craig said, somewhat indignantly, but by then the laughter had started, and what could have been far more awkward for everyone had passed.

Porter Craig shook his head, patted Jack on the back, and, still unable to find his voice, led him to the bar, where he gestured to the barman to give Jack a drink.

Marjorie came up to him and kissed him, on the cheek, and then Ursula, and then Hanni, his step-mother, and his father.

"Jeanine really wanted to wait up for you, Jacques," Hanni said. "But she was playing tennis all day and she just collapsed."

Jeanine was his eleven-year-old half sister.

"I'll see her in the morning," Jack said. "And Mary Magdalene?"

"Where do you think Mary Magdalene is?" his father said. "With her, of course."

"I really can't wait to meet both of them," Marjorie said, "Jack's told me so much about them."

"We're going fishing in the morning," Captain Jean-Philippe Portet said. "If you feel up to it?"

"Great."

"Am I invited?" Marjorie asked.

"Of course," Hanni said. "We're all going."

"It'll give us a chance to talk, Jacques," his father said. "About the business."

Jack looked at him curiously but said nothing.

"I think it's time to leave the Congo," his father said, then added, "we'll talk about it tomorrow."

"Fine," Jack said.

Helene Craig clapped her hands.

"Why don't we all go out by the pool and get something to eat?" she said.

They went out to the netting-protected grill by the pool and watched the chef cook. Marjorie's shoulder touched Jack's as they watched, and Marjorie's foot caressed his calf beneath the table by the pool as they ate. This caused him to have an involuntary vascular reaction to stimuli, and he was afraid his condition would be evident in his new white tennis shorts if he had to stand up.

He also reached the conclusion that there was not going to be an opportunity to be alone with Marjorie, at least tonight, with all these people around, and with her staying in a different house.

After dinner they went back into the living room. Jack took one of the stools — they were actually red-leather-upholstered captain's chairs on very long legs — at the wet bar and asked for a beer. Marjorie sat beside him and asked for a Tom Collins. Not at all accidentally, he decided, Marjorie's knee pressed against his.

That's her second Tom Collins. She is not used to drinking.

If we were not in this living room out of a Fred Astaire/Cary Grant movie, the chances are pretty good that I could get a little. Not only is she on her second Tom Collins — and one drink usually wipes out her maidenly inhibitions — but we are now engaged to be married, and that should eliminate whatever other objections she might raise.

But we're not even in the same house, and if I suggest we go for a walk, everyone will know what I have in mind, and I don't want to embarrass her. So I'm screwed. Correction, I am not screwed.

I suppose that's the way things go. The bitter with the sweet, et cetera.

Think of your goddamn nose, or something else unpleasant; the last thing you want is a hard-on poking out of your shorts.

Barbara Bellmon and Hanni Portet came in from the pool, arm in arm, laughing and smiling at each other.

"Oh, look at that!" Barbara cried happily, pointing upward.

His mother-in-law-to-be was, Jack decided, a little plastered. And so was Hanni. They were each on their third Tom Collins.

"Helene, I love your fish!" Barbara added.

Jack looked up. The living room was open to the rafters, and from them, suspended by nearly invisible wires, a huge sailfish moved slowly in the breeze from the air-conditioning. The ceiling was painted a soft blue, and it appeared the fish was swimming overhead.

"That's Geoff's first big fish," Porter Craig said. "He caught it when he was eleven."

"He insisted on having it mounted, of course," Helene Craig picked up the story, "and I didn't have the heart to tell him no. So we had it stuffed, and then we didn't know to where to put it, so it wound up there."

"I think it looks great there," Barbara Bellmon said, and giggled. "But I want to be here when someone tries to dust it!"

"It takes two people, on two ladders," Helene said. "One holds the fish, and the other vacuums it. Very delicately."

The mental picture was amusing, and Jack smiled.

Colonel Lowell joined them.

"Have you got a pocket in your shorts, sweetheart?" he asked.

"That's an odd question," Marjorie said. "But yes, I do."

He handed her a sheet of typewriter paper, folded twice.

"Stick this in it, and don't let anybody see it," he said.

"What is it?"

"Take a look at it later, when you go to bed," he said.

"What is it?" Jack asked.

"None of your business, Sergeant. Butt out. This is between the young lady and me."

She put the sheet of paper in her hip pocket.

Barbara and Hanni walked up to them.

"Is this the time to tell everyone about Second Lieutenant Lowell and his Packard?" Barbara said. "Or has liquor loosened my tongue?"

"I'd love to hear it," Jack said.

"I've heard it," Marjorie said. "So you can start, Mother, while I powder my nose."

She touched Jack's arm, smiled at him, and walked away.

"I think I'll have another one of these, please," Barbara said to the barman. "I really don't know where to begin. There are so many twists and turns. . . ."

"Well, I remember when he went in the Army," Helene said. "Porter and I had just come from our honeymoon, and their grandfather had us to dinner and told us — I'm sorry, Craig, but this is true — that Craig had been . . . asked to leave Harvard. . . ."

" 'Kicked out' is the term," Colonel Lowell said. "It seems to be a family tradition. Geoff got the ax, too, from Fair Harvard, didn't you, Geoff?"

"Guilty," Geoff said.

"Do they send you those once-a-month pleas to send them a check?"

"As regularly as clockwork," Geoff said.

"Anyway, Jack," Geoff's mother said. "Both Craig and Geoff started out as enlisted men, like you. They . . . left college . . . and as a consequence were drafted."

"I finished college, and I still got drafted," Jack said.

"And they earned their commissions on the battlefield," Helene Craig said proudly.

"I can't let that slip by, Helene," Lowell said. "Geoff got his commission that way, but I earned mine on the polo field."

"Excuse me?" Jack said.

Barbara Bellmon giggled. "That's absolutely true."

"There I was, Jack, the happiest draftee in the United States Constabulary," Lowell said. "In Bad Nauheim, Germany. I was the golf pro for the brass. I got paid to play at least eighteen holes a day. I had a private room at the golf club, no reveille, no formations, no chicken —"

"What's the Constabulary?" Jack asked.

"It was a military force consisting mainly of eighteen-year-olds," Lowell said seriously, "who raced around Germany in highly simonized tanks and armored cars, sirens screaming, while the Germans, who were supposed to be awed, had a

99

hard time to keep from laughing out loud."

"It was more than that, and you know it," Barbara said, adding, "My father was the commanding general."

"Her father played polo, and hated the French, which is certainly understandable," Lowell said. "And then it came to his attention that I also played a little polo. I soon found myself playing as number three on the U.S. Constabulary polo team. That was even better than being the golf pro."

"Daddy was determined to beat the French team —" Barbara said.

"Determined to really whip, *humiliate*, the French team," Lowell interrupted. "A wholly commendable ambition. But there was a little problem. Frog officers won't play with enlisted men, theirs or anybody else's. And the star — I say, with all modesty — of the U.S. Constabulary polo team was PFC Lowell."

"So Daddy got Craig a commission," Barbara said, chuckling.

"Just like that?" Jack asked.

"One day I was a PFC, and the next day a second lieutenant, Finance Corps — detailed Armor," Lowell said. "My understanding of the arrangement was that I would get out of the Army as scheduled, and that my new exalted status as a commissioned officer and gentleman was my reward for helping Ol' Porky kick the sh— soundly defeat the French."

"Porky?" Hanni asked.

"Major General Porterman K. Waterford," Lowell said. "His pals, of whom I was *not* one, called him 'Porky.' "

"And then my father passed on," Barbara said softly.

"At Baden-Baden," Craig Lowell said. "The score was nine–two for the good guys. In the last minutes of the last chukker, Porky got his mallet on the ball, and with me keeping the Frogs out of the way for him, galloped three quarters of the way down the field, took a magnificent swat at the ball, and drove it *squarely* between the posts. That made it ten–two. Porky raised his hand to acknowledge the applause and fell out of his saddle dead. God, what a good way to go!"

My God, Jack thought, *that's a true story.*

"Bob — he was a major — and I were at Fort Bragg when Dad died, so I didn't meet Craig until later, at Fort Knox. He went to Greece first."

"Leave Greece out," Craig said. "This is supposed to be the story of the Packard."

"I can't leave Greece out," Barbara said. "It's part of the Craig Lowell saga."

Marjorie returned. She went to Lowell, hugged him, and kissed his cheek.

"You're a wicked, wicked man, and I love you very much."

Obviously, she is a little plastered, not that it's going to do me any good, and just as obviously, she's read whatever's on that piece of paper he gave her, Jack thought. *I wonder what the hell it was?*

"Greece?" Jack's father asked. "What were you doing in Greece?"

"Eating a lot of lamb, mostly," Craig said. He looked at Jack. "Sandy Felter was there, and Red Hanrahan. He was our colonel. After which the Army sent me to Fort Knox. Pick up the saga there, Barbara."

"Okay," she said. "Craig arrived at Fort Knox, and shortly thereafter the Greek ambassador and entourage arrived. There was a retreat parade,

101

and the ambassador hung the largest medal I have ever seen on Craig."

"Cut to the chase, Barbara," Lowell said. "This is supposed to be about my prescience in buying the Packard at a distress sale price."

She ignored him.

"It's absolutely enormous," she went on. "It's called . . . the Order of St. George and St. Andrew, and it's about the size of a saucer, and it hangs around his neck on a purple thing — a sash, I guess."

"Well, there I was, Jack, in downtown Louisville," Lowell interrupted, "and there in a showroom was the Packard. And I realized — I come from a family of bankers, as you know — that it would certainly, and rapidly, appreciate in value, so I naturally took advantage of the investment opportunity and bought it."

He obviously doesn't want to talk about the medal, Jack decided. *I never heard of it, but if it was presented by the Greek ambassador, it's not the Greek good conduct medal.*

"You bought it because you were tiddly," Barbara said, laughing. "You and Phil Parker had been drinking all afternoon in the bar at the Brown Hotel." She paused and looked at Geoff. "You know Major Parker, don't you, Geoff?"

"The great big black guy? Flies Mohawks?"

"Right," she said.

"He and Craig were roommates in the student officer company," Barbara Bellmon explained. "So they took the car to Knox and started driving it around the post."

"*I* drove it around the post," Craig corrected her, "with the top down, and with Phil riding in the backseat, graciously returning the salutes of all who saw us." He smiled at the memory.

"They were blissfully unaware that the post commander also had a yellow Packard convertible of which he was very proud . . ."

"He had the cheap one, the 120, two doors, straight-eight engine, with the spare tire hidden in the trunk," Lowell said. "The one outside is a V-16, and proudly carries its spare tires in the front fenders."

". . . and the post commander," Barbara went on, "naturally came to the conclusion that there were two second lieutenants in the student officer company who were ridiculing him. It was awkward for Bob. The general knew that Phil's father had rescued Bob —"

"Which is another story, Mother," Marjorie said. "Which you can tell everyone tomorrow. Jack and I have had a busy day, and want to go to bed." She stopped, horrified at what she had just said.

"Presumably separately?" Lowell said, making it worse.

"Craig," Helene Craig said indignantly, "that was uncalled-for."

"So you just kept the car, Colonel?" Jack asked, quickly changing the subject.

Lowell looked at him with gratitude in his eyes.

"I gave it to my mother's husband, for services rendered," Lowell said. "He collected cars. He had it restored from the frame up. And when he died, he left it to me, and I didn't have the heart to sell it, so I shipped it down here."

He looked at Marjorie.

"Sweetheart, everyone knows that was a slip of the tongue. Now kiss Jack, chastely, and go to bed. I'll take Jack to *Jack's* bed, and he'll see you in the morning."

"I'll kiss him later," Marjorie said. "It's not a spectator sport. Good night, everyone."

She turned and marched out of the room.

Christ, I don't even get a good-night kiss, chaste or otherwise.

"Barbara Bellmon, especially with a couple of drinks in her, tends to take long trips down memory lane," Colonel Lowell said to Sergeant Portet just inside the door to House C. "But she's one of the world's good people. And you're damned lucky to be able to marry a girl just like the girl who married dear ol' Bob Bellmon."

"I think so, sir."

"I'm going to get out of here at first light," Lowell said. "The Packard will be at the airstrip, and the keys in the ashtray."

"Colonel, I don't know . . . I don't want to ding that magnificent car," Jack said.

"Then don't ding it," Lowell said. "The boat — House C is closest to the ocean — will be here at half past seven." He pointed to the rear of the house. "Breakfast aboard. Have a good time, Jack. And welcome to the family. The first time I saw you and Marjorie together, I thought that was going to happen."

"Thank you, sir."

"Good night, Jack," Lowell said. "Sleep well."

Fat fucking chance of that. And it's probably a good thing I didn't get a good-night kiss. Then I would really have a pair of blue-balls.

"Thank you, sir. Good night, Colonel."

Lowell touched his shoulder and walked toward his bedroom, and Jack walked to his, which was

104

on the opposite side of the house.

He turned on the television set and flipped through the channels. There was a Cuban channel, on which a splendidly bosomed Cuban beauty undulated as she crooned a love song.

Exactly what I don't need.

There was nothing else on he was interested in watching.

Fuck it!

He took off his clothing, decided they were all he would need to go fishing in the morning, tossed them on a chair, and got in bed naked and turned off the lights.

He had tossed and turned for perhaps ten minutes when he became aware of a banging on the sliding glass door of the room.

What the hell is that?

With my luck, it's an alligator.

More likely, the wind picked up and is knocking a chair or something against the glass.

Christ!

He got out of bed, stormed to the window, moved the curtain out of the way, and slid open the door.

Marjorie stood there, in a bathrobe.

"Holy Christ!" he said, and opened the door.

"Obviously, he told you to expect me? Or do you always sleep in the raw?"

"Jesus, wait a minute," he said, and covered his groin with his hands and went for the bathrobe.

He went back to her.

She handed him a sheet of paper.

It was obviously the same sheet of paper Colonel Lowell had given her.

On it was drawn both a map and a surprisingly good cartoon. The cartoon showed Jack sitting

105

glumly, forlornly alone in a room. Above his head was a picture of what he was thinking: Marjorie, in a bathing suit, with an angel's crest around her head, kneeling, her hands folded in prayer.

The map showed the route Marjorie should take from House B to House C if she felt the urge to join him.

There was a message:

"If Saint Marjorie would like to bring comfort to a lonely soldier, here's the route. Love, Uncle Craig."

"Oh, baby," Jack said.

"God, I love you," Marjorie said.

She turned and closed the door and the curtains, then walked to the bed and, with her back to him, took off her bathrobe and pajamas. Then she turned to him.

"I think you can take the bathrobe off now," she said.

[TWO]
Helene's Passion VI
15 Nautical Miles SSE of Key Largo, Florida
1225 4 December 1964

Captain Jean-Philippe Portet sat in one of the two, heavy, stainless-steel fishing chairs in the stern of the boat, and Sergeant Jacques Portet sat in the other. They both held bottles of Heineken beer.

Jeanine Portet, who was eleven, gangly, and freckled, was standing, her arms folded over her chest, waiting impatiently for one of the rods to get something on its line. *Helene's Passion VI* was trolling for whatever might be down there — Geoff suggested they might get lucky and run into Spanish, and maybe even king mackerel — with four lines, one port, one starboard, and two centerboard.

Jeanine didn't care what kind of fish took the bait, just as long as she could jump to the bent rod, take it from the holder, and wrestle the fish into the boat.

She was one of three females aboard. The other two, Marjorie Bellmon and Ursula Craig, were sunning themselves on the forward deck. Barbara Bellmon, Hanni Portet, and Helene Craig "thought they'd pass," and Porter Craig excused himself without giving any reason.

"He wants to play with the kid," Geoff said. "He's nuts about the kid, but playing Grandpa is beneath his dignity."

Geoff was running the boat. Her full-time captain, a deeply tanned, muscular man in his forties, found himself reduced to being more or less the steward. He didn't seem to mind either being the steward or having Geoff at the controls. He told them he had joined the Craigs with *Helene's Passion III*, and had absolute faith in Geoff's ability to handle the boat, because he had taught him, starting at age nine, the fine points of small-boat handling.

Jack was half dozing, thinking of, for perhaps the tenth time, what Marjorie had told him in the very early hours of the morning. It was astonishing, in this day and age, but he believed it.

"You may not believe this, or even want to hear it, but I will only be a partial hypocrite when I march down the aisle in bridal — virginal — white."

"What the hell are you talking about?"

"Our first time, on the beach at Panama City,

107

was my first time, period."

"Really?"

"Yes, really, and I thought you should know."

"Well, you may not believe this, or even want to hear it, but you certainly show a natural talent for the sport."

"You bastard!" she had said, and straddled him, and started to pound his chest with her fists. He had caught her hands and they'd looked at each other, and she had changed her mind about what she wanted to do to him.

"I've decided it's time to get out of the Congo," his father said suddenly, breaking Jack's reverie. "Out of Africa, period."

"Really?" Jack asked, surprised. "Why, all of a sudden?"

His father raised his hand and pointed to Jeanine.

"That's reason one," he said. "When I was sitting in Léopoldville, wondering what that lunatic Olenga might do to her — might already have done to her and Hanni — I was sick with shame that I hadn't gotten them out when I first began to think about it."

"Dad —"

"Let me finish," his father said.

Jack made a "have at it" gesture with his hand, and took a pull at his Heineken.

"The first time I thought about it was when Kasavubu made Mobutu chief of staff of the Army. That was more than four years ago."

Joseph Kasavubu became the first president of the Republic of the Congo when it became independent in 1960.

"Why?" Jack asked. "I thought you liked Mobutu. I do."

108

"I do," Jean-Phillipe Portet said. "I liked him when he was a corporal in the Force Publique and I liked him when he was working for *L'Avenir.* And I still like him — a little less, frankly — now. But he was — is — no more qualified to be a lieutenant general and chief of staff of the Army than I am. I knew that, but I didn't want to face facts."

Captain Portet took a pull at his beer, then went on:

"Our friend Joseph Désiré Mobutu is now calling himself Mobutu Sese Seko. And did you see the leopard-skin overseas hat?"

Jack chuckled.

"Yeah, I saw the hat. What the hell, he's an African. Why not?"

"I had dinner with him the night before the Belgians jumped on Stanleyville," Jack's father said.

" '*The* Belgians'?" Jack quoted. "Not, with chauvinist pride, '*We* Belgians'?"

His father chuckled, but not, Jack sensed, really happily.

"Let me put it this way," his father said. "I had dinner with Mobutu Sese Seko the night before my American son, making his American father's heart beat with pride, jumped on Stanleyville with some other parachutists, who I understand were Belgians."

"I'm missing something here, Dad."

"When we got off the airplane from Frankfurt," his father said, "The immigration guy looked at my passport, did a double take, and then said, 'Well, you've really been away a long time, haven't you? Welcome home, Mr. Portet.' "

"I forgot you had an American passport," Jack said. "You used that to get into this country?"

"More important, I have American citizenship," his father said. "Awarded for the faithful service during wartime of Captain Portet, J. P., U.S. Army Air Corps, 0-785499. I never thought much about it, really, until she was born." He inclined his head toward Jeanine. "We had three choices: Hanni's German, so we could have gone to the German consulate in what was then Léopoldville, and registered her as a German. Or, going to the U.S. Consulate, and getting her an American passport. Or going to the Belgian Registry office, making her a Belgian. It didn't take Hanni and me long to decide that Jeanine would be better off all-around as an American. So Jeanine 'came home,' too, after eleven years abroad."

"You never told me any of this, Dad," Jack said.

Captain Portet chuckled again.

"The immigration guy took a look at Jeanine's passport and said, 'This has expired. You'll have to get her another one before she leaves the country again.' "

"But this isn't her first trip here?"

"She always traveled, as we all did, from the time I went down there to start up Air Congo, on a Congolese passport," his father said.

"What are you going to do, move here?" Jack asked incredulously.

His father did not respond directly.

"I had dinner with Mobutu the night before the drop on Stanleyville," Captain Portet said. "Several significant things were said. He told me he had just come from seeing Kasavubu, who was drunk, and in a rage against the Belgians, who were, he is absolutely convinced, behind Olenga. Mobutu said nothing he could say would shake this conviction, and he quickly stopped trying."

"My God, where did he get that idea?"

"It fits neatly in with Kasavubu's belief that the Belgians will do whatever they have to take the Congo back," Captain Portet said. "He thinks the Belgians were behind the Katangese Rebellion —"

"The Belgians sent troops to put the Katangese Rebellion down," Jack argued.

"Kasavubu believes it gave them an excuse to send troops down to restore colonialism. And he believes the jump on Stanleyville was going to be more of the same thing."

"Jesus!"

"What Mobutu said was that Kasavubu's unwillingness to accept this — Kasavubu's willingness to accept the Belgian intervention at Stanleyville, in particular — proves that Kasavubu is unfit to lead the country, and will have to be replaced."

"Did Kasavubu really think the Belgians were going to stand idly by as the Simbas killed the Europeans one by one?" Jack asked angrily.

"Kasavubu believes the Congolese Army, under the leadership of Lieutenant General Mobutu, would have dealt with the problem in good time," Captain Portet said sarcastically. "Mike Hoare's mercenaries, much less the Belgian paras, were not necessary."

"Jesus," Jack said. "Was it the booze talking?"

"Sure. But *in vino veritas,* Jacques."

"You said Mobutu thinks Kasavubu has to be replaced. Who does he have in mind?"

"Who do you think? He almost came out and said it, and believe me, Jacques, there is no question in my mind that sooner or later, probably sooner, Mobutu is going to stage a coup against

111

Kasavubu, and probably succeed. I want to get out before that happens — or the other inevitable thing happens. The result in either case being chaos."

"What other inevitable thing?"

"The Communists have another shot at taking over that part of the world. They're not through, and I don't like to think what would have happened in Stanleyville if they had managed to get arms to Olenga."

"What will happen to Air Simba?"

"I'm going to sell it to one of Joseph Désiré Mobutu's cousins," Captain Portet said. "That was another interesting thing he said at dinner. He said that he has a cousin who would like to 'take a position' in Air Simba. I wondered who taught him to say 'take a position.'"

" 'A cousin'?"

Again his father didn't respond directly.

"And I realized that once the camel's nose came under the tent, we could kiss Air Simba goodbye, anyway. In two months, there would be fifty more cousins on the payroll, fighting over which one got to put his hand in the cash register today."

"Where would he get the money?"

"He told me his cousin 'found himself in a strong cash position' and was 'looking for a suitable investment opportunity.' I told him that while I was here, I would come up with a price. I know what it's worth, so the price will be that, plus the price of the house, the cars, the furniture, everything else. For that his 'cousin' can have a fifty-percent 'position' in Air Simba."

"And you won't go back for the rest?"

His father shook his head, no.

"I'll come out of the Congo considerably richer

112

than when I went in," he said. "Which is more than a lot of other people can say."

"And what are you going to do?"

"There's a lot of old Boeing 707s on the market," Captain Portet said. "I'm going to buy a couple of them, maybe three or four, and start up an air cargo, or maybe air cargo/passenger charter operation here. Operating into South America, and maybe, even probably, into Vietnam. That war seems to get bigger by the day."

"Yeah," Jack agreed.

"Are you going to have to go over there?"

"I don't know. Christ, I hope not. Before the Stanleyville thing came up, I didn't think so. They assigned me to the Instrument Examiner Board at Fort Rucker —"

"You were flying?"

"They don't let enlisted swine fly. What they had me doing was writing the written parts."

"Any regrets about not being an officer?"

"Not until Marjorie. Or until that got serious. I don't think Marjorie cares, but her family, both sides, have been officers for generations."

"I think you made a good choice there, but with her background, is she going to be happy married to an airplane driver?"

"I guess we'll have to find that out," Jack said. "But to keep the record straight, I did a little flying. When they were getting the B-26s ready for the Congo, they didn't have anybody who knew how to fly them, so they looked the other way and turned me into an IP."

"Where'd you get B-26 time?"

"I got about twenty hours just before I became an IP," Jack said. "They were really desperate. I even flew one to Kamina, because there was no

113

one else around who could. But to answer your question, what I'm hoping to do is finish my time giving written instrument exams at Fort Rucker."

"I wouldn't count on it," his father said.

"You know something I don't?"

At that moment, what turned out to be a fifteen-pound grouper struck the port line, the rod bent nearly double, the reel screamed, and they jumped out of their chairs to help Jeanine. Jack's question never got an answer.

[THREE]
Walter Reed U.S. Army Medical Center
Washington, D.C.
0930 Hours 12 December 1964

Brigadier General James R. McClintock, Medical Corps, U.S. Army, a tall, silver-haired, hawk-faced man of forty-six, arrived in the ward unannounced. He was wearing a white smock over a uniform shirt and trousers. The smock bore an embroidered caduceus, the insignia of the U.S. Army Medical Corps, but it did not have pinned to it, as regulations required, the small oblong black piece of plastic he had been issued, and on which was engraved his rank and name and branch of service.

He did not, General McClintock often informed his aide-de-camp when the question of the missing name tag came up, have to look down at his chest to remind himself who he was, and if there was a question as to his identity in the minds of the staff, the aide should tell them.

General McClintock was alone when he got off the elevator. Usually he was trailed by at least his aide, and most often by a small herd of medical personnel, and these people were most often

114

smiling nervously. In addition to being an internist of international repute, General McClintock had a soldier's eye. When he visited a ward, in other words, he was just as likely to spot a military physician whose hair was too long, or whose shoes needed a shine, as he was to find a misdiagnosis or something wrong with a patient's chart.

He walked across the highly polished linoleum floor to the nurses' station. There were three nurses and two enlisted medical technicians inside. The nurses looked busy, so General McClintock addressed one of the medical technicians:

"Hand me Captain Lunsford's chart, will you, son?"

"Yes, sir," the technician, a specialist six (an enlisted grade corresponding to sergeant first class), responded. He knew who General McClintock was, and, consequently, his response was far more enthusiastic and militarily crisp than usually was the case. So much so that it caught the attention of the senior nurse, Major Alice J. Martin, ANC, who had been standing with her back to the counter, talking on the telephone. She glanced over her shoulder, hung the phone up in midsentence, and walked quickly to the counter.

"May I be of help, General?" she asked.

"I thought I'd have a last look at Captain Lunsford before he's discharged," McClintock said.

He took the chart, which was actually an aluminum folding clipboard, and which with all the forms clipped in various places inside was nearly three inches thick, from the medical technician, nodded and smiled, and said, "Thank you."

115

Major Martin headed for the opening in the nurses' station.

"That won't be necessary, Major," he said. "I won't need you. Thank you."

"Sir, he has visitors," Major Martin said, more than a little annoyed and disappointed not to be able to exercise her prerogative of accompanying the chief of internal medical services while he saw a patient on her ward.

"Well," General McClintock said, "he's about to have at least one more."

"He's in 421, General," Major Martin said.

"Yes, I know," General McClintock said. "Thank you."

He walked down the corridor, his rubber-heeled and soled shoes making faint squeaking noises on the waxed linoleum.

When he pushed open the door to 421, there were three men inside, including the patient, who was sitting, dressed in civilian clothing, smoking a very large light green cigar, on the bed. The patient started to get off the bed when he saw General McClintock, but McClintock, smiling, quickly put up his hand to stop him.

"Stay where you are, Captain," McClintock said.

General McClintock saw that the room was decorated for the holiday season as seen through the eyes of an officer like this one. The patient had obviously visited the Post Exchange Branch, where he had purchased not only a plastic model of the HU-1B "Huey" but four adorable little dolls. One of them was Santa Claus; two were dressed as nurses and one as a doctor.

The Huey was hanging from the central light fixture. The adorable nurse and doctor dolls were hanging, their necks realistically broken, from pipe-cleaner nooses attached to the Huey's skids. Santa Claus straddled the tail boom of the helicopter, cradling a machine gun in his arms.

The chart described the patient as a Negro male, twenty-six years old, five feet eleven and one half inches tall, weight 144 pounds. There was a note stating that this was twenty-one pounds less than he had weighed at his last annual physical examination.

Dr. McClintock noted quickly, professionally, that the patient's eyeballs were clear. When they had brought him in, he looked as if he had been liable to bleed to death through the eyeballs. And he had been ten pounds lighter then than he was now.

Dr. McClintock guessed the patient's visitors to be his father and brother, not because they looked alike, but because he had been ordered to restrict his visitors to his immediate family. The younger of them, the brother, a tall, light-skinned, hawk-faced man, was well, even elegantly, dressed in a superbly tailored glen plaid suit and a white-collared faintly striped blue shirt. The father was short, squat, flat-faced, very dark, and what Dr. McClintock thought of as "comfortably crumpled." He wore a tweed jacket, rumpled flannels, rubber soled 'health' shoes and a button-down collar tattersall shirt without a necktie.

"How do you feel, Captain?" Dr. McClintock asked.

"Frankly, sir," Captain Lunsford said politely, "not quite as happy as I was an hour ago, when I thought I was being turned loose."

Dr. McClintock raised his eyes from Lunsford's chart and smiled. "All things come to he who waits, Captain," he said. "We're still going to turn you loose. But not just now. Soon."

"Today?" Lunsford asked.

"Today," McClintock said. "Shortly."

"May I see the chart, Doctor?" Lunsford's father asked. When McClintock looked at him in surprise, he added, "I'm a physician."

"Excuse my manners, General," George Washington Lunsford said. "Doctor, may I present my father, Dr. Lunsford? And my brother, Dr. Lunsford?"

"How do you do, Doctor?" McClintock said, handing the elder Dr. Lunsford the chart.

"Dad is a surgeon, Doctor. My brother is a shrink," Lunsford said. Then, when McClintock smiled, he added, "Before Charley became a shrink, Dad used to say that shrinks were failed surgeons."

"George, for Christ's sake!" the younger Dr. Lunsford snapped.

"I've heard that," Dr. McClintock said, smiling, "but rarely when one of them was in the same room."

"My God!" the elder Dr. Lunsford said. "I have never seen a case of that before." He extended the chart to Dr. McClintock, pointing at a line with his finger.

"It's pretty rare," Dr. McClintock said. "Your son has been regarded as a gift from heaven by our parasitologists. I understand he has his own refrigerator in their lab."

"I'll bet he does," the elder Dr. Lunsford said, and showed the chart to his other son, who shook his head in disbelief.

"And they are going to give him his own glass cabinet in the Armed Forces Museum of

118

Pathology," Dr. McClintock said, smiling. "Several of our intense young researchers suggested, more or less seriously, that we just keep him here as a living specimen bank."

"Do you *realize* how sick you were?" Dr. Lunsford demanded of his son. "For that matter, still are?"

"I didn't really feel *chipper,* now that you mention it, Dad," Captain Lunsford said, "but there is a silver lining in the cloud. I have been given so many different antibiotics that it is not only absolutely impossible for me to have any known social disease, but I may spread pollen, so to speak, for the next six months or so without any worry about catching anything."

Dr. McClintock and the elder Dr. Lunsford chuckled. The younger Dr. Lunsford shook his head in disgust.

"We think, Doctor," Dr. McClintock said, "that everything is under control. We were a little worried, frankly, about the liver, but that seems to have responded remarkably —"

He stopped in midsentence as the door to the room opened suddenly and two men in gray suits walked briskly in. One of them quickly scrutinized the people in the room, then walked quickly to the bathroom, pulled the door open, and looked around inside. Then he stepped inside and pushed the white shower curtain aside.

The other went to the window and closed the vertical blinds, then turned to Dr. McClintock.

"Who are these people, General?" he demanded.

"Who the hell are *you?*" Captain Lunsford demanded icily.

The wide, glossily varnished wooden door to

the corridor opened again.

The President of the United States walked in. On his heels was Colonel Sanford T. Felter, who was wearing a rumpled and ill-fitting suit.

"You can leave, thank you," the President said.

"Mr. President —" one of the Secret Service men began to protest.

"Goddamn it, you heard me!"

The two Secret Service men, visibly annoyed, left the room.

"How do you feel, son?" the President asked Captain Lunsford with what sounded like genuine concern in his voice.

"I'm all right, sir, thank you," Lunsford replied, a tone of surprise in his voice.

"This your dad?" the President asked.

"Yes, sir, and my brother."

"Well, you can be proud of this boy, Mr. Lunsford," the President said. "He's something special."

"It's 'Dr.' Lunsford, Mr. President," Captain Lunsford said.

"No offense, Doctor," the President said. "I didn't know. Usually Colonel Felter tells me things I should know, like that."

"None taken, Mr. President," Dr. Lunsford said.

The President turned to Captain Lunsford.

"I'm having a little trouble with Congress about your Belgian and Congolese medals," he said. "You'll get the authorization — you and the sergeant — but it may take a while. So, in the meantime, I thought maybe this might make up for it."

He held out his right arm behind him. Felter put an oblong blue box in it. The President opened the lid and took out a medal.

"That's the Silver Star, Captain," the President said. "I understand it will be your third. I can't believe the others are more well-deserved than this one."

He stepped to Lunsford and pinned the medal to the lapel of his coat. He did not do so properly; it promptly fell off. Lunsford, in a reflex action, grabbed for it, and the open pin buried itself in the heel of his hand.

"Shit!" he said involuntarily, and then, immediately, "Excuse me, sir."

"I understand," the President said, chuckling, "that 'it's the thought that counts.'" And then there was concern in his voice, as Lunsford pulled the pin free from his hand. "You all right, son?"

"Yes, sir," Lunsford said.

"I told the chief of staff to find out if there is some reason your name can't be on the next promotion list to major. I have the feeling he's not going to find any."

Lunsford looked at him but didn't say anything.

"You're one hell of a man, Captain," the President said. "I'm grateful to you. Your country is grateful."

He shook Lunsford's hand, then punched him affectionately on the shoulder, and then shook the hands of Lunsford's father and brother.

The President nodded at Dr. McClintock, murmured, "General," and, adding, "Let's go, Felter," walked out of the room.

"See you soon, Father," Felter said, and followed the President out of the room.

"It was very good of you, Mr. President, to make the time for Captain Lunsford. I appreciate it," Colonel Felter said as the presidential limousine headed back to the White House.

"If I had the time, I'd go to Fort Bragg and pin a medal on that sergeant who parachuted with the Belgians, too," the President said. "Goddamn, men like that make you proud to be an American."

"Yes, sir, I agree," Felter said.

"What's going to happen to him now? When he's fit for service?"

"He'll be an instructor at the Special Warfare Center at Bragg."

"Teaching what?" The President chuckled. "How to run around in a leopard skin in the jungles of Africa and stay alive?"

"Yes, sir. That sort of thing."

"I thought I was making a joke. You're implying we're going to continue to be involved in the Congo."

"In sub-Saharan Africa, yes, sir, I'm afraid we will be."

"But the Simbas are finished," the President argued, and then asked, almost menacingly, "Aren't they?"

"I think it's safe to say that Olenga is finished, Mr. President. But I think there will be others like him, and the next time, the Soviets will be prepared to help them."

"Why didn't they do more for Olenga?"

"I think they were as surprised by Olenga as we were, Mr. President. He really came out of nowhere —"

"That's not the answer I was looking for, Felter," the President interrupted.

"Sir?"

"The Russians knew I wouldn't stand for anything like that," the President said. "That's why they didn't supply him with arms."

Felter said nothing.

"Goddamn you, Felter," the President said after a long moment, "you can say more with your mouth closed and that dumb look on your face than most members of Congress can say in a two-hour speech."

Felter said nothing.

"Felter, you're paid to tell me what you think, not what you think I want to hear."

Felter looked at him.

"Mr. President, before Dragon Rouge, there were four Soviet transports flying weapons from Algeria into Uganda —"

"According to the CIA, there were *reports* of *one or two* airplanes, which may or *may not* be Soviet aircraft which *may have* carried weapons. . . ."

Felter almost visibly chose his words carefully before replying:

"Mr. President, the CIA is constrained by their obligation to give you facts. I believe you wish me to tell you what I think."

"What do you think, Colonel?" the President snapped sarcastically.

"I believe that at the time Dragon Rouge occurred, at least two — and most probably four — Ilyushin-18s, which is a turboprop transport much like our C-130s, were engaged in transporting arms from Algeria to the Arau air base in northern Uganda. The aircraft were black —"

"A figure of speech?" the President interrupted. "Or really black?"

"They were painted black, Mr. President," Felter said. "To make them black, if you follow my meaning."

"In other words, you've seen them? You *know*

they were painted black?"

"I didn't see them personally, but I trust my source."

"Which is?"

"With all respect, Mr. President, I'd rather not say."

"You are aware that the President is the ultimate authority on need-to-know? *I* decide who needs to know, not you."

"I would prefer that the CIA didn't learn of my source, Mr. President."

"You and the CIA are supposed to be on the same side, something you don't always remember," the President said. "Let me spell it out for you, Colonel. You will tell me, and I will decide whether or not I'll tell the CIA. Got it?"

"Yes, sir. The West Germans have an agent in the East German Embassy in Algeria. His intelligence was passed on to me."

"Why shouldn't I tell the CIA that?"

"Because the CIA would pressure the Germans to use him, sir."

"And what's wrong with that?"

"If that happened, in this case, sir, I think it would shut off my flow of information from Bonn."

"Okay. That will go no further."

"Thank you, sir."

"In the sure and certain knowledge that what you will tell me will not be what I would hear if I asked the CIA, Felter, what — or who — is going to cause me the most trouble in the immediate future in Africa?"

"Che Guevara, Mr. President."

"*Guevara?*" the President parroted incredulously. "Castro's guy? The one who can't grow a decent beard?"

"Yesterday, Mr. President, he was in New York. He addressed the General Assembly of the United Nations."

"Nobody paid any attention to him," the President said disparagingly. "They call that 'tweaking the tail of the lion.' It goes back to the days when there really was a British Empire. He got a lot of applause, not because of what he said, but because the people clapping — the ambassadors from 'countries' the size of Rhode Island — knew it would piss us off."

"Yes, sir, I'm sure that's true. Tomorrow, he's going to be on CBS's *Face the Nation*."

"So what? More of the same."

"He has a certain stature, sir. His coming here — to the United States, and the UN — will increase it. If he can cause trouble for us in Africa, it will increase his stature in South America, and make it easier for him to cause us trouble there. He makes an excellent Soviet surrogate, sir. And a cheap one."

"The CIA thinks he's going to try to cause trouble for us in the banana republics. And now."

"He will try that, too. And if he's successful in Africa, that will make it so much easier."

"Africa?" the President said dubiously.

"He leaves the U.S. for Algeria on 17 December, Mr. President."

The President looked at him but said nothing.

The presidential motorcade — smaller than usual, but still consisting of two District of Columbia police motorcycles, a District police car; a Secret Service Suburban, the presidential Lincoln limousine, a second Secret Service Suburban, and a trailing D.C. police car — turned off Pennsylvania Avenue onto the White House grounds.

The limousine turned off the interior drive and stopped at the private entrance.

As a Secret Service agent trotted up to open the door, the President leaned forward and locked it.

"Felter," he said. "Right now I think you're as full of shit as a Christmas turkey, but I'm going to think about this, ask some questions."

"Yes, sir."

"Don't get too far away," the President said, then unlocked the door and got out of the limousine and walked into the White House.

Felter got out of the limousine, then walked toward his office in what was now called the Executive Office Building, but had been built, in simpler days, as the State, War and Navy Departments Building.

[FOUR]
226 Providence Drive
Swarthmore, Pennsylvania
1735 Hours 12 December 1964

"Charlene," Major (Designate) George Washington Lunsford said to Charlene Lunsford Miller, Ph.D., Stanley Grottstein Professor of Sociology at Swarthmore College, "you don't know what the fuck you're talking about."

Major Lunsford offered this opinion of Professor Miller's assessment of the political situation in the Congo at an unfortunate time, two seconds after their mother had pushed open the door to his room, bearing a tray of Camembert on crackers and bacon-wrapped oysters.

126

"George!" their mother, a slight, trim, light-skinned, gray-haired woman wearing a simple black dress with a single strand of pearls, said, truly shocked.

"Sorry, Mother," Father Lunsford said, truly embarrassed.

"You apologize to your sister!"

"Sorry, Charlene," Father Lunsford said, not very sincerely.

"It's all right, Mother," Professor Miller said, pushing herself out of an upholstered armchair. "I know what he's been through."

Just in time, Father Lunsford stopped the reply that came to his lips: "Screw you, don't you dare humor me."

"I thought you might want something to nibble on," Mrs. Lunsford said, setting the tray on Father Lunsford's desk. There was an old blanket covering part of the desk, on which were the disassembled parts of a Colt Combat Commander .45 ACP automatic pistol. Lunsford had been cleaning the pistol when his sister came up to welcome him home.

"Not for me, Mother, thank you," Professor Miller said. "I'd better go keep my husband away from the gin."

She walked out of the room.

Lunsford popped a bacon-wrapped oyster into his mouth and chewed appreciatively. He sort of mumbled his approval.

Mrs. Lunsford waited until she heard Charlene's heels on the wide wooden steps leading from the second floor to the foyer, then asked: "What was that all about?"

Lunsford shrugged. "It's not important, Mother. My mouth ran away with me. I'm sorry."

"What was it about, George?" Mrs. Lunsford insisted.

"The professor delivered a lecture," Lunsford said, "apparently the collective wisdom of the faculty of Joseph Stalin U, equating what we did in the Congo with some of the more imaginative excesses of Adolf Hitler."

His mother looked at him with troubled eyes, then smiled.

"As a special favor to me, George, could you refrain from referring to Swarthmore as 'Joseph Stalin University' tonight?"

He stepped quickly to her, put his arms around her, and lifted her off her feet.

"You're my girl," he said. "Your wish is my command."

She kissed his cheek as he set her down.

"If you mean that, no politics tonight, agreed?"

"I don't start it," he said. "They start it. They get so excited to have a real live fascist in their midst that they slobber all over themselves waiting for their chance to tell me off."

"I don't think you're a fascist," she said. "Neither does your father. And I don't think the President would have personally given you that medal if he thought you were."

"On that subject," Lunsford said, taking a Camembert cracker, "I don't think we should bring up that medal tonight. Not with half the faculty of *Swarthmore College* at the table."

She laughed, not entirely happily.

"Too late," she said. "Your father's put it on the phone table in the foyer. He's greeting people, 'Good evening, and incidentally, let me show you what President Johnson gave George today.'"

Lunsford laughed.

128

"I wondered where the hell it was," he said.

Her eyebrows rose.

"I wondered where, delete expletive, it was," he said.

"Better," she said. "George, these people just don't understand."

"That's what's known as a massive understatement," he said.

"I'm not sure I do," his mother said. "All I know is that I'm proud of you, and I thank God you're home."

"Then nothing else matters, Mom," Lunsford said. "And I give you my word as a field-grade, designate, officer and gentleman, that I will behave myself tonight."

"Then finish whatever you're doing with that gun, and get dressed, and come down. Just about everybody's here, and they're all anxious to see you."

"For one reason or another," Lunsford said dryly. Then: "Sorry. Yes, ma'am. I will be right down. Thank you for the oysters."

She raised her hand and gently touched his cheek. Then she walked out of the room.

Lunsford sat down at his desk again. He opened a drawer, took from it a bottle of Johnny Walker Black Label scotch, and took a pull at its neck.

Then he started putting the Colt Commander back together.

He had been downstairs thirty minutes when he was called to the telephone.

"Captain Lunsford."

"I understand they cured the clap okay, but that they're having trouble with the scabies, crabs, and blue balls," his caller said.

Captain Lunsford didn't reply for a moment.

He was surprised at the emotion he felt.

Then he said, "Oliver, you asshole, where are you?"

"In Philly," Oliver said. "Just passing through."

"In a pig's ass," Lunsford said. "You will come out here. Got a car?"

"Hey, I don't want to intrude. You just got home."

"Don't argue with me, I'm a goddamned major designate. All I want to hear from you is 'Yes, sir.' "

"Yes, sir."

"Where are you?"

"Out by some athletic stadium. I just got off I-95."

"South Philly," Lunsford said. "Got a pencil?"

[FIVE]
The Presidential Apartments
The White House
Washington, D.C.
1110 13 December 1964

"Colonel Felter, Mr. President," the Secret Service agent announced.

"Let him in," the President ordered. "And nobody else, until I tell you. Got it?"

"I understand Mr. President."

"Good morning, Mr. President," Felter said, entering the room.

The President was wearing a shirt, trousers held up by suspenders, and bedroom slippers. He was sitting in an armchair. On the floor around it were the Sunday editions of the *Washington Post*, *The New York Times*, and the *Dallas Morning News*.

"Lady Bird went to church," the President said.

"Which means I can have one of these. Help yourself."

The President pointed to a stainless-steel thermos sitting on a tray with a bowl of ice and two glasses.

Felter realized that what he had originally thought was a glass of tomato juice was a Bloody Mary.

"Go on, Felter," the President said when he sensed reluctance. "You've worked for me long enough to know I don't like to drink alone."

"Thank you, Mr. President," Felter said, and went to the table and made himself a Bloody Mary.

"Too hot for you?"

"No, sir, I like them this way."

"I like lots of Tabasco," the President said. "I can't handle some of those Mexican chili peppers, but I like Tabasco."

"Yes, sir."

"Did you know that the guy who owns that company, the Tabasco Company, is a colonel in the Marine reserves?"

"No, sir, I didn't."

"The commandant told me," the President said. "He said the guy fought on Guadalcanal as a lieutenant, and wants to come back on duty now and go to Vietnam."

"Yes, sir."

"The commandant says he's tempted to take him; this guy is apparently a crack shot. He knew him on Guadalcanal. But there's really no place for him. He wouldn't want to come back in to push paper, and he's really not qualified to command a regiment."

Felter didn't reply.

131

"I thought of you when the commandant told me about this guy," the President said. "You'd really rather be commanding a regiment, wouldn't you, than what you're doing?"

"Yes, Mr. President, I would."

"There are probably five hundred colonels in the Army qualified to command a regiment," the President said. "But you're the only one I know qualified to do what you do for me. I know that, and I want you to know I appreciate what you do."

"Thank you, Mr. President."

"Would you be surprised to hear that the director and you agree about something?"

"We often agree, Mr. President," Felter said. "You only hear of our disagreements."

The President laughed.

"Okay. The director agrees with you that unless he's stopped, Che Guevara is going to cause us a lot of serious trouble in South America and Africa."

"That's my assessment, sir. It's nice to know I'm not the only one who sees the problem."

"You can get rid of him, can't you, Felter? Soon, quietly, and of course, outside the country?"

"I don't believe I understand the question, Mr. President."

"The euphemism the director used was 'terminate.' He thinks Guevara should be terminated, and he thinks you're the guy to do it. You have a problem with that?"

"I have very serious problems with that, Mr. President," Felter said.

"Really?" the President replied, as if surprised. "You've 'terminated' people before, Colonel, haven't you?"

"Yes, sir, I have."

"Then what's the problem here?"

"In my judgment, Mr. President, the assassination of Che Guevara is not only unnecessary, but would be counterproductive."

"You're the one who came to me and said he was going to cause trouble, Felter."

"That can be dealt with, Mr. President."

"Do you believe in capital punishment, Felter?"

"Yes, sir, I do."

"You sit a murderer in the electric chair and fry him, there's one thing you can be sure of, he won't murder anybody else, right?"

"Yes, sir."

"Is there some kind of difference in your mind between a murderer who shoots his girlfriend, or a bank guard, and a guy who orders the killing of other people, but doesn't pull the trigger himself?"

"Not much of a difference, sir."

"That was one of the arguments the director made when he was trying to get me to authorize the elimination of Guevara. He says there's pretty good proof that when Castro shot all those people on the baseball field in Havana, Guevara was really the man in charge. You think that's so?"

"There doesn't seem to be any question about it, Mr. President."

"Then you would agree the sonofabitch *is* a murderer? Just like the guy who shoots the guard when he's robbing a bank?"

"I can only repeat, Mr. President, that in my judgment the assassination of Che Guevara is both unnecessary and would be counterproductive."

"What you're saying is that *you* could . . . what

133

did you say? . . . *deal with* the trouble you say he's going to cause?"

"I believe he can be kept from causing any serious problems, yes, sir."

"The question was, you think *you* could control him?"

"With a relatively small unit, and a large amount of money, yes, sir."

"Why would eliminating him be counterproductive?"

"He would then be a martyr, Mr. President."

"And if I ordered you to terminate the sonofabitch, then what?"

"I would be forced to resign my commission, Mr. President."

"Do you mean that, Felter? Or do you think you can get away with bluffing me?"

"I would be forced to resign my commission, Mr. President," Felter repeated.

"You arrogant little sonofabitch!" the President said angrily. "You're about to learn you cannot bluff the President of the United States."

Felter came to attention.

"Permission to withdraw, sir? You will have my resignation within the hour."

The President glowered at him for a long moment.

Then he walked to a telephone on a table, picked it up and said, "Get me the Chairman of the Joint Chiefs," and hung up.

He glowered at Felter for the perhaps ninety seconds it took the White House operator to get the Chairman on the line and to ring the presidential phone.

He snatched the telephone almost angrily from its cradle.

"This is the President, Admiral," he said, and then he winked at Felter. "I've just given Colonel Felter a special mission. I want you to make sure that whatever he asks for, he gets. Clear? *Whatever* he asks for."

He put the telephone back in its cradle.

"Relax, Sandy," the President said. "We just called each other's bluff. You won."

Felter remained at attention.

"Sit down, Sandy, and finish your drink," the President went on.

Felter looked at him, bent down and picked up his Bloody Mary, and drained it. He held the glass up and looked at the President. "With your permission, sir?"

"And give me another little taste, too," the President said, extending his empty glass.

As Felter was refilling their glasses, the President called his name, and Felter turned and looked at him.

"To keep the air clear between us, Sandy," the President said, "I had already decided that shooting the sonofabitch would be about the dumbest thing we could do. And just between you and me, I knew what the Director was trying to do: He thought he had himself a win-win. You got rid of Guevara for him, and the trouble that would cause would make me get rid of you."

Felter nodded, finished pouring the drinks, and walked to the President and handed him his. The President raised his glass and knocked it against Felter's.

"Pick yourself a good deputy for this," the President said. "I don't want you spending all your time 'controlling' Señor Guevara."

"Yes, sir."

135

IV

H. Wilson Lunsford, M.D., answered the door of his home.

"Good afternoon, Doctor," Colonel Sanford T. Felter said. "It's good to see you again, sir, and I apologize for the intrusion."

"I'm sure you consider it necessary, Colonel," Dr. Lunsford said. "Won't you please come in?"

"How is he?"

"He and his buddy have been at the scotch since lunch," Dr. Lunsford said, and then, when he saw the look on Felter's face, added: "Dr. McClintock at Walter Reed gave me tranquilizers for George to dispense as I saw fit. He said he thought there might be some depression. He and his buddy are having a good time, and the only price they're going to have to pay is a hangover. I'm a lot happier giving him scotch than some exotic chemical."

He motioned for Felter to precede him into the house, then down a corridor, and then stepped quickly ahead of him to open a door. Through it, Felter saw that it was a game room. There was an antique billiards table in the center of the room, and there were leather armchairs and a couch

136

against one paneled wall, and there was an octagonal card table with a green felt playing surface in a corner.

"Your guest, George," Dr. Lunsford said.

When Father Lunsford saw him in the doorway, he — a Pavlovian response — came quickly out of his chair.

"Good afternoon, sir," he said, just a little thickly.

Felter waved him back into his chair and walked up and gave him his hand.

"Sorry to intrude, Father," Felter said. "It couldn't be helped, and I won't be long."

Then he turned to make his manners to Father's buddy, who had also stood up when he entered the room, and was standing now.

Felter had been mildly curious about whom Father Lunsford would have for a buddy, and mildly concerned that, in the company of some high school or college chum, the scotch might loosen Father's tongue a little too much.

"Good afternoon, sir," Father's buddy said, also a little thickly.

The last time Felter had seen Captain John S. Oliver was in the office of Major General Robert Bellmon. Oliver — whom Bellmon has described as "as good an officer as they come" — was Bellmon's aide-de-camp.

"Hello, Oliver," Felter said. "Good to see you." Then he blurted what was in his mind. "I didn't know you two knew each other."

He was genuinely surprised. Oliver was an Army aviator, a Regular Army officer out of Norwich, who had already been accepted into what Felter thought of as the establishment. He knew that Bob Bellmon would have been happy if

John Oliver and Marjorie had hit it off. This was, he realized, the first time he had ever seen Oliver — and he had been with him often — looking as if he had as much as sniffed at the neck of a beer bottle.

"Captain Oliver and myself, Colonel, have been anal orifice comrades since he saved my bacon in Vietnam," Father said.

"Sit down, Johnny," Felter said.

"With the colonel's kind permission, I will adjourn to the gentlemen's facility," Oliver said, carefully pronouncing each word, and walked a little unsteadily out of the room.

Father looked at Felter.

"His lady love told him it was either her or the Army," Father said. "He chose the Army, and she wasn't bluffing."

"I had no idea," Felter said.

"And now he is sadly contemplating all those nights in the future, alone in a soldier's bed."

"What did she have against the Army?"

"She lost one husband, and decided she wasn't equipped to lose another. No problem with him, Colonel. I'll take care of him. He's one of the good guys."

"General Bellmon thinks very highly of him," Felter said, thinking out loud.

"He's Johnny's general?" Father asked, and when Felter nodded, went on: "Yeah, he got Johnny a deal —"

" 'Deal'?"

"You know he's no longer a dog-robber?"

"No, I didn't."

"Well, he's not. He was good at it, but he hated it, and he was up for reassignment, and his general got him some kind of special job — executive assistant or something — to a General Rand,

138

who's going to have some new kind of division at Benning . . ."

"George Rand," Felter supplied. "They're calling it the 11th Air Assault Division."

"Right," Father said. "Anyway, Johnny told me that his general — Bellmon, you said his name is?"

"Bellmon," Felter said. "He's an old friend of mine."

". . . *Bellmon* told him that if he did a good job for this General Rand, he could expect to make major on the five percent list within a year."

Up to five percent of the promotions on any promotion list may be awarded without regard to their seniority (time in grade) to officers who have demonstrated outstanding capabilities.

That makes sense, Felter thought. *He's an unusually bright officer; he worked hard for Bob Bellmon, and because he worked for Bellmon he knows a lot more than most captains do about aviation, and he'll work hard for George Rand, who'll write him another outstanding efficiency report, and he'll earn a place on the five percent list.*

"I'm sure he could," Felter said. "Father, quickly, before he comes back: I don't need an answer right now, although I'd like one, but would you be willing to continue working on Africa?"

"Jesus Christ, I haven't been home seventy-two fucking hours, and you're asking me to go back to the fucking African jungle?" Lunsford flared, then got control of himself. "Sorry, sir. I know you wouldn't ask if it wasn't necessary. What went wrong over there now?"

"I don't think you'll have to go back in the jungle, Father," Felter said. "The deal is this. I've managed to convince the President that Che

139

Guevara has to be watched —"

"In *Africa?*" Lunsford asked dubiously.

"Yeah, in Africa. Later, Central and South America. But right now in Africa."

"Why don't we just shoot the sonofabitch? I heard he shot, or had shot, a thousand people in cold blood in Havana. . . ."

"The figure was higher," Felter said. "And that's what the CIA wants to do — terminate him."

"It sounds like a good idea to me. But why me?"

"I'm not asking you anything like that, Father. And actually, we don't — the President and I don't — want him terminated. We don't want to turn him into a martyr."

"You don't want to turn who into a martyr?" Captain John S. Oliver asked, cheerfully, as he came back into the game room.

And then he saw the looks he got from Felter and Lunsford, and it cut through the alcohol.

"Sorry, sir," he said. "I'll wait outside."

"Come in, close the door behind you, and sit down, Captain," Felter ordered.

The tone of Felter's voice, too, cut through the alcohol.

"Colonel, no excuse, sir, but I've had a couple of drinks," Oliver said. "Maybe it would be better if I . . ."

Felter pointed to a chair, and Oliver sat down.

"You are advised, Captain, that what we are discussing is classified Top Secret," Felter said.

"Yes, sir."

"When there is time, there will be another classification, Top Secret Slash Something. You understand?"

"Yes, sir."

140

"There's no reason not to label this right now," Felter said. "Okay. The material we will discuss is classified Top Secret Slash Ernesto . . . make that Top Secret Slash Earnest. Got that, the both of you?"

"Yes, sir," they said, nearly in unison.

"I understand you will be going to work for General Rand at the 11th Air Assault at Benning," Felter said.

"Yes, sir."

"General Rand will not be cleared for Top Secret/Earnest, and neither will anyone else at Benning," Felter said. "Which means that he cannot be made privy to Slash Earnest information. Clear?"

"Yes, sir."

"When are you going to Bragg, Father?"

"Actually, we were talking about driving down there tomorrow," Lunsford said. "Not for duty. We know some people down there we haven't seen since Vietnam."

"The only person at Benning who will be, for the foreseeable future, cleared for Earnest will be General Hanrahan."

"I understand, sir," Lunsford said.

"I don't, sir," Oliver said.

"We're going to keep an eye on Che Guevara," Felter said. "Maybe cause him some trouble, but we are not, repeat not, going to terminate him, and we're going to do our damndest to make sure Langley doesn't terminate him, either."

"It's probably the alcohol, sir, but I still don't understand," Oliver said. "Che Guevara in Cuba?"

"He's leaving for Africa in a couple of days," Felter said. "To get to the point here, I want to make Father the project officer."

"He just got of there, barely," Oliver said.

"I don't want him to get involved with anything like that again," Felter said. "I want him to run this."

"Explain 'run this,' please, Colonel," Lunsford said. "And 'project officer.' "

"Set up a team, as small as possible, but as large as you need. You'll run it. The first priority will be to keep me up to date on what he's doing, and where."

"Won't the CIA be doing that?"

"Yeah, they will, and I will have — which means you will have — access to what they develop. But I want independent reports. And, where and when possible, I want to destroy his image."

"His image?"

"Right now, he's sort of like a movie star, David the guerrilla taking on the nasty North American Goliath, and so far, winning. If Goliath terminated him, that would make Guevara a martyr, and that would cause us a lot of trouble. Goliath would look like a real sonofabitch, for one thing, and Castro and/or the Soviets would quickly replace him, and we would be no better off. What I think Guevara has in mind is taking a small force, no more than two hundred men — which is how many people Castro took into the Sierra Maestra mountains — to Africa, to the Congo, and repeating what Castro did in Cuba. I'd like him to fail."

"The Russians are going to help him, of course," Lunsford said. "And Mobutu and Kasavubu aren't going to stand by and let Guevara take over the Congo. And 'termination' is about the first thing that's going to occur to Mobutu."

"If we had absolutely nothing, and I mean absolutely nothing, to do with it — and I don't mean credible deniability, Father, I mean we have absolutely nothing to do with it — that wouldn't be too big a problem. But what I'd like to see is Señor Guevara leaving Africa with his tail between his legs."

"Humiliated, is what you're saying?" Lunsford asked thoughtfully.

"Right."

"Money talks," Lunsford said. "I learned that over there. Keeping track of him wouldn't be much trouble."

"Money will not be a problem," Felter said.

"Do I get to pick my people?"

"Yes."

Lunsford looked at Johnny Oliver.

"Doubting Thomas," he said. "There's a certain exquisite irony, wouldn't you say?"

Oliver chuckled.

"Who's he?" Felter asked.

"Master Sergeant William Thomas," Lunsford said. "He was with us when we walked out of Laos."

"Actually, sir," Oliver said. "He carried Major-Designate Lunsford out of Laos, bitterly complaining every step of the way."

"And when he returned to Bragg, when offered his choice of language training at the Presidio, chose Swahili in the smug, if naive, belief that it would see him sent not only as far from Vietnam as possible, but would see him sent to the land of his ancestors, teaching the savages close-order drill, and where his position would offer him a never-ending procession of willing, nubile, sixteen-year-old maidens."

"Where is he?" Felter asked.

"At Bragg," Oliver said. "Teaching escape and evasion. I called him to tell him Father had made it out of the Congo."

"And will he volunteer?"

"Sure," Lunsford said, as if the question surprised him. He looked at Felter. "And I want Jack Portet, too."

"That may pose a problem," Felter said.

"Colonel, he knows the country, he speaks Swahili and French, he knows people, white, black, colored, and savage all over —"

"Define 'savage' for me, Father," Felter said.

"There are four kinds of people in Africa," Lunsford said. "The whites, the blacks, the colored — the mixed-bloods and, for some reason I haven't entirely figured out, the Portuguese — and the savages, who are the Africans who came out of the trees last week."

He looked between them.

"Okay. So it's not a very nice word. Do you know a better word for somebody who beheads somebody else with a machete, then broils his or her liver for lunch? I saw them do that in Stanleyville."

Neither Felter nor Oliver responded.

"And just for the record, my liberal friends, that great humanitarian, Albert Schweitzer, who spent his life trying to help them, called them 'les sauvages'," Lunsford said.

"Sergeant Portet is about to get married to Marjorie Bellmon," Felter said. "And is therefore unlikely to be willing to volunteer for anything."

"They're going to get married?" Oliver asked. "I thought I saw that coming."

"I'll need him, Colonel," Lunsford said.

"I gather you're going to take the job?" Oliver asked.

"What the hell, Johnny, I've already seen Vietnam, and I don't want to spend the next three years of my life at Bragg teaching clowns to make fire by rubbing two sticks together."

[TWO]

S E C R E T

Central Intelligence Agency
Langley, Virginia

FROM: Assistant Director For Administration

DATE: 18 December 1964 0405 GMT

SUBJECT: Guevara, Ernesto (Memorandum # 1.)

TO: Mr. Sanford T. Felter
Counselor To The President
Room 637, The Executive Office Building
Washington, D.C.

By Courier

In compliance with Presidential Memorandum to The Director, Subject: "Ernesto 'Che' Guevara," dated 14 December 1964, the following information, provided by the FBI, is furnished: (Reliability Scale Five).

SUBJECT departed John F. Kennedy airfield, New York City, aboard Air France Flight

---

305 at 2105 GMT 17 December 1964. He was accompanied by Héctor GARCÍA and José R. MANRESA. All are traveling on Cuban Diplomatic passports, and are ticketed to Paris, France, with an intermediate stop scheduled at Gander, Newfoundland.

CIA surveillance of SUBJECTS will begin at Gander, and dossiers of SUBJECTS GARCÍA and MANRESA will be furnished for your possible interest within 24 hours.

Howard W. O'Connor
HOWARD W. O'CONNOR

SECRET

[THREE]
Office of the Commanding General
The Army Aviation Center and Fort Rucker,
** Alabama**
18 December 1964

Major General Robert F. Bellmon was, as he privately thought of it, up to his ass in paper, and it took some time before he noticed Captain Richard J. Hornsby was standing in the office door.

"Have you got something for me, Dick?"

"Yes, sir," Captain Hornsby said. "This TWX just came in, and I thought you would like to see it."

Bellmon took it and glanced at very quickly. It

was a Routine message, signed by some colonel for the adjutant general. It was probably, he decided, one more admonition to him to limit drinking by the troops over the holidays, or failing that, to keep them from killing themselves on the highway full of holiday cheer. Whatever it was, it probably could have waited until he wasn't quite so up to his ass in paper. Hornsby, who was new, didn't have the experience to make judgments about what messages were worthy of his immediate attention.

"Thank you, Dick," Bellmon said, and picked up the TWX, which was printed on a roll of yellowish teletype paper, and read it. His lips tightened. He clenched his teeth and was aware that his temples were throbbing.

"Sonofabitch!" he said, and reached for his telephone.

Then he reminded himself of his solemn vow to count to twenty slowly twice before picking up a telephone when he was angry. He slumped back in his chair and read the TWX again.

ROUTINE
HQ DEPT OF THE ARMY WASH DC 1005
18DEC64
COMMANDING GENERAL
FORT RUCKER AND THE ARMY AVIATION
CENTER ALA
ATTN: AVNC-AG
INFO: PERSONAL ATTN MAJ GEN BELLMON

    1. SO MUCH OF PARAGRAPH 23,
GENERAL ORDER 297, HQ DEPARTMENT OF
THE ARMY 29 NOVEMBER 1964 PERTAINING

TO CAPT JOHN S. OLIVER ARMOR AS READS
"IS RELIEVED OF PRESENT ASSIGNMENT
AND TRANSFERRED TO HEADQUARTERS
COMPANY 11TH AIR ASSAULT DIVISION
FORT BENNING GA EFFECTIVE 1 JAN 1965"
IS AMENDED TO READ "IS RELIEVED OF
PRESENT ASSIGNMENT AND TRANSFERRED
TO HEADQUARTERS JOHN F. KENNEDY
CENTER FOR SPECIAL WARFARE FORT
BRAGG NC EFFECTIVE 1 JAN 1965."

2. IT IS SUGGESTED THAT SUBJECT
OFFICER BE NOTIFIED OF THIS CHANGE AS
SOON AS POSSIBLE.

FOR THE ADJUTANT GENERAL
J. C. LESTER LTCOL AGC
ACTING ASSISTANT ADJUTANT GENERAL

Johnny Oliver had been a good aide, a very good aide, a *goddamned* good aide for a year. And not only that, he'd gone above and beyond the call of duty, and stuck his neck out as a friend for the Bellmons.

He wasn't supposed to know, and Barbara and Bobby certainly didn't know he knew, but he had his sources and he had found out that Bobby was about to be given an elimination check ride, and was almost certain to flunk it. And then, all of a sudden, Bobby had miraculously polished his skills literally overnight. He had passed the check ride and gone on and gotten rated.

Bellmon didn't believe in miracles, so he checked that out, first with the instructor pilot, who told him he wouldn't pass Jesus Christ himself if he didn't think he was safe to fly and up to snuff. Bellmon believed him, and looked elsewhere for the answer.

It had been Johnny Oliver. Fully aware that if he got caught at it he would be permanently taken off flight status himself (not to mention getting the lousy efficiency report Bellmon would have been obliged to give him), he had taken Bobby out in a helicopter and taught him enough to get him past the check ride.

And he had not waived his general's aide's insignia in anybody's face, either, hiding behind the throne. He had taken the risk knowing that if Bellmon had caught him at it, he could kiss his career goodbye. He had done it because he liked Bobby, and because he knew Bobby's father would be heartbroken if Bobby busted out.

Bellmon, in the end, had — not without a certain uneasiness — decided that more harm than good would come from his becoming officially aware of what had taken place. The Army would lose two pilots, and in Johnny Oliver's case, anyway, a bright young officer with great potential.

And that potential was going to be enhanced working for George Rand in the 11th Air Assault. He would come out of that assignment knowing how a division, not any division, but the Army's first airmobile division, functioned in combat. And probably with a gold leaf on his collar point, too. He would have unusual knowledge and experience for an officer of his age and length of service. It was a damned good assignment for him, and for the Army. And now the orders were changed. Johnny was assigned to the John F. Ken-

149

nedy Center for Special Warfare.

Those sonsofbitches in Green Berets again!

He was not going to stand still and have those bastards take a perfectly decent, upstanding, *out*standing young officer and ruin him!

He lit a cigarette, and when he saw that his hand was hardly shaking at all, he punched his intercom button and, proud of the control he was now exercising over his voice, very calmly and politely asked his secretary to see if she could get Brigadier General Hanrahan at the JFK Center at Bragg for him.

"If he's not in his office, Mrs. Delally, try his quarters, please."

General Hanrahan was not in his headquarters. He was not in his quarters, either. General Bellmon spoke with Mrs. Hanrahan, and wished her a merry Christmas, and she told him Red was off somewhere with Craig Lowell, and that she didn't really expect him back until Christmas Eve.

If he was off with Lieutenant Colonel Craig Lowell, God only knew where they would be. And God, if he had any sense, would probably not want to know.

When Mrs. Delally called the Office of the Adjutant General in the Pentagon, the only officer he could get on the phone, a light colonel, obviously didn't have the brains to blow his nose without illustrated instructions.

"No problem, thank you, Colonel, I'll call again in the morning."

He had less trouble getting Brigadier General George R. Rand on the telephone.

"I have a TWX here, George," he said. "Assigning Johnny Oliver to Red Hanrahan and the snake eaters. You know anything about it?"

"You don't?" Rand asked.

"First I'd heard of it. What do you know?"

"He called me a couple of days ago and very politely said that he'd been offered another job —"

"By Red Hanrahan?" Bellmon interrupted.

"He said 'at the Special Warfare Center,' but I'm sure he meant Red, because . . . after I told him I wouldn't stand in his way . . . Red called me and asked if I minded. He said he had a job for him, with a little less pressure than he's been under. But that if I really needed him . . . et cetera et cetera."

"Hanrahan wanted him when he first became my aide," Bellmon said.

"But you didn't know about this, huh?"

"Oliver is on leave. It must have come up all of a sudden. George, if I can talk some sense to you, will you still take him?"

"Sure. Love to have him."

"I'm going to look into this. I'll probably get back to you. Thank you, George."

General Bellmon hung up, and then broke, one by one, six #2 lead, rubber-tipped pencils into inch-long pieces. Then he walked out of his office, smiled at Mrs. Delally, and said that he would be going to his quarters now, and if it was important, he could be reached there.

[FOUR]
Annex #1, Officers' Open Mess
Fort Rucker, Alabama
1505 18 December 1964

Second Lieutenant Robert F. Bellmon, Jr., sat at the bar of Annex #1 drinking Miller's High Life beer from a can and feeling more than a little sorry

151

for himself. He was about to lose the companion-ship of the officer sitting beside him at the bar, Captain John S. Oliver. Johnny Oliver was to report to the 11th Air Assault Division at Fort Benning, on 1 January 1965.

Bobby was staying on at Rucker to get transitioned into fixed wing. After that, he didn't know what was going to happen to him. But an era, clearly, was over. He was being separated from the best friend he had ever made in his life, and nothing would ever be the same again. Bobby didn't think much of his father's new aide. God-damned stuffed shirt.

It was difficult for a second lieutenant to be stationed on a post where the commanding general had the same name. His peers were generally divided into two categories, those who thought getting close to the general's son was dangerous, and those who thought they might somehow be able to turn it to their advantage. Bobby was naive but not a fool.

The test of a friend, Bobby believed, was when someone did something for you that either cost him, and/or not because something was in it for him. The proof that Johnny Oliver was a friend had been several instances where he had done things for Bobby *despite* the fact that he was General Bellmon's aide rather than because of it. If it hadn't been for Johnny, Bobby knew, he wouldn't be wearing wings, period.

Bobby realized that what he really admired in Oliver was his self-confidence. He decided what was right, and then did it. Bobby privately thought that he was still thinking like a plebe: *If a thing is not specifically permitted, it is prohibited.* Johnny reversed that: *If something isn't specifically pro-*

scribed, screw it, let's do it!

Captain Johnny Oliver had signaled the bartender for another round of beers, and the bartender had just stooped over the cooler to get them when the phone rang. Bobby picked it up.

"Annex Number One, Lieutenant Bellmon, sir," he said in the prescribed manner.

"Is Captain Oliver in there?" a male voice asked. "This is Major Ting. I'm the AOD." The aerodrome officer of the day.

"Hold one, please, sir," Bobby said, and covered the microphone with his hand. "It's for you. Major Ting. The AOD."

When Bobby handed him the telephone, Captain John S. Oliver had also been thinking of 1 January 1965. On that date, he believed, it would be possible for him to put Liza Wood — and the kid — out of his mind once and for all.

Obviously, it wasn't meant to happen. Love couldn't overwhelm the obstacles to their getting married and living happily ever afterward.

He understood Liza's position, and was aware that a lot of people — including himself, from time to time — would think she was absolutely right.

She had lost one soldier husband — Allan's father — and had been devastated by the loss, and determined not to let it happen again, to her or to Allan.

"He's already lost one daddy, Johnny, and I'm not going to put him through that again."

The implication there, of course, was that he had become Allan's daddy, and that was true. He liked the kid, and the kid liked him, and he would have been perfectly happy to raise him as his own.

And it was not as if he would have to take off his officer's uniform and get a job selling used cars or life insurance. He was a millionaire, which — although it was hard to really comprehend — was absolutely true.

His sister and her husband had tried to cheat him, screw him, out of his half of their father's estate, which consisted primarily of Jack's Truck Stop, in Burlington, Vermont. It was painful to think that your own sister, your only living relative, would consciously plan to screw you of what was rightfully yours, but that's what she had done.

His father's will had said that either his sister or he could offer to buy the other one out. His sister had sent him a letter saying she and her husband wanted to buy him out, and his share was worth so much.

At that point, he had the option of sending her that much money, and he would own all the truck stop. Or taking her offer, which meant that she would send him a check and she and her husband would own it. Actually, she didn't offer to send him a check, she said that she and her husband would pay him off "over time."

His first reaction when he got the letter was that — even knowing nothing about it — the truck stop was probably worth a little more than twice what she was offering. But that was a moot point, because he had about two thousand dollars in the bank, which wasn't even in the same ballpark as the two hundred sixty-eight thousand he would have had to send her to buy her out.

At that point, Lieutenant Colonel Craig W. Lowell had entered the picture. Lowell said that he didn't want to intrude in Johnny's personal business, but business was business, and a quarter

154

of a million dollars was a lot of money, and it couldn't hurt to get a professional opinion of the offer.

Lowell said that Geoff Craig's father was chairman of the board of Craig, Powell, Kenyon & Dawes, Investment Bankers, of New York. They had experts on the staff who knew about such things, and Lowell felt sure they would be happy to help.

"Thanks, Colonel, but I don't want to lean on Geoff to lean on his father."

"I'm vice chairman of the board," Lowell had said. "Let me give them a call, Johnny."

A funny little man showed up at Johnny's BOQ and handed him a card identifying him as Foxworth T. Mattingly, Esq., Attorney-At-Law. Mattingly said that he was from Craig, Powell, Kenyon & Dawes, and had been instructed by Colonel Lowell to take care of the details of the truck stop purchase. Johnny had signed a power of attorney authorizing him to handle the deal.

And had promptly forgotten about the deal until his sister had telephoned, hysterical, furious, and, he suspected, drunk. After she delivered a ten-minute lecture about what an ungrateful sonofabitch he was, he finally understood that she had received a letter from Craig, Powell, Kenyon & Dawes, Investment Bankers, informing her that John S. Oliver, Jr., was exercising his right to purchase her share in Jack's Truck Stop, for the amount she proposed, and enclosed please find a cashier's check in the amount of $268,000.00.

Johnny had called Colonel Lowell.

"Mattingly found out the property's worth a little more than four million, Johnny," Lowell said. "So I told him to buy it for you, for — what

155

did she offer? — a quarter of a million."

"I don't have $268,000," Johnny said.

"The firm loaned it to you," Lowell said. "That's what we do, Johnny, we're investment bankers. This was a very good deal for an investment banker. We knew our money was safe."

In the end, his sister got to keep Jack's Truck Stop, and Johnny deposited a certified check in the First National Bank of Ozark for $2,327,000.00.

With that kind of money, Liza argued, they could really build a life for themselves, if he would only get out of the goddamned army.

He found he couldn't do that. He did not want to go into the real estate business, or buy a Ford dealership, or even a charter boat in the Florida keys. He was a soldier. He was a good soldier. He liked being a soldier, and he knew that he would be miserable doing anything else.

Liza told him the decision was his, and it was either her and Allan, or the goddamn army.

Now she wouldn't even talk to him on the telephone. It really hurt to know she was only seven miles away and wouldn't talk to him.

On 1 January 1965, he would report to the Special Warfare Center at Bragg — new surroundings, new duties, and maybe the pain wouldn't be as bad.

"Captain Oliver, sir," Johnny Oliver said to the battered telephone at the end of the green linoleum bar in Annex #1.

"Major Ting, Oliver. I'm the AOD."

"Yes, sir?" Oliver said.

"The tower just got a call from a civilian Cessna 310-H," Major Ting said. "They're thirty min-

156

utes out. They have a Code Seven aboard. No honors, but they request ground transportation."

Major Ting obviously doesn't know that I have been replaced as aide-de-camp to the commanding general.

A Code Seven, based on the pay grade, was a brigadier general. "No honors" meant the general didn't want a band playing, or an officer of suitable — that is, equal or superior rank — to officially welcome him to Fort Rucker. All this Code Seven wanted was a staff car to take him to Ozark.

There was little question in Oliver's mind who it was. It was Brigadier General "Red" Hanrahan, Commandant of the U.S. Army John F. Kennedy School for Special Warfare at Fort Bragg. Oliver was sure that it was Red Hanrahan for a couple of reasons. When he'd seen him at Bragg the week before, when he'd gone there with Father Lunsford, Hanrahan had told him he would be coming to Rucker on Monday anyway, to deliver a briefing on Army participation in Operation Dragon Rouge to Rucker officers.

More important, he was arriving in a 310-H. That almost certainly meant Lieutenant Colonel Craig W. Lowell's 310-H.

But it never hurt to check.

"Sir, have you got a name for the O-7?"

"General Hanrahan," Major Ting said.

"Thank you very much for calling me, sir," Oliver said. "I appreciate it."

It was not the time to mention that he was no longer aide-de-camp to General Bellmon, and that calls like this should be directed to his replacement.

"My pleasure," Major Ting said, and hung up.

Captain Johnny Oliver, with visible reluctance,

pushed his beer can away from him, then made several calls, dialing each number from memory.

He called the general's driver and told him to get a one-star plate, and the staff car, and to pick him up at Annex #1.

He called the billeting office and told them to make sure the Magnolia House, the VIP quarters, were set up and prepared to receive Brigadier General Hanrahan and a party of God-only-knew.

He called the main club, and told them to be prepared to reset the head table for General Bellmon's dinner party on short notice; there would probably be Brigadier General Hanrahan and who else God-only-knew.

Finally, he called Quarters #1. Mrs. Bellmon answered.

"Johnny, Mrs. B.," Oliver said. "General Hanrahan will land at Cairns in about twenty minutes, in a Cessna 310-H."

"That probably means Colonel Lowell," Mrs. Bellmon responded.

"Yes, ma'am, I think so. I've called the club and Magnolia House and laid on the general's car. They requested ground transportation to Ozark, but I figured I'd better cover all the bases."

"You're supposed to be retired, Johnny," Barbara Bellmon said.

"My last hurrah," Johnny said. "I thought it would be better to spring General Hanrahan and Colonel Lowell on Captain Hornsby slowly. Or at least one at a time."

She laughed.

"Where are you?"

"At Annex One, with Bobby," Oliver said, then winced. Bobby, who did not like to be called

158

"Bobby," was shamelessly eavesdropping on the conversation.

"We'll see you at the club, then," she said. "Thank you, Johnny. Again."

"One last time," he said, and hung up and turned to Bobby. "Finish your beer, Roberto, duty calls."

Until now, Oliver hadn't paid much attention to the weather; it was important only when he was going to fly, but when they heard the horn of the Chevrolet staff car bleating and went outside, he grew concerned. It was drizzling and cold, which meant the real possibility of wing ice, and the visibility and ceiling were probably down to next to nothing.

It was a ten-minute ride before the general's driver pulled the nose of the Chevrolet into the parking space reserved for the commanding general at Base Operations.

"Come on, Bob," Oliver said. "The only way they're going to get into here is ILS. You ought to see that."

They entered the Base Operations building through the rear door, walked through the lobby past the oil portrait of Major General Bogardus S. Cairns, a former tank commander who crashed to his death in his white H-13 two weeks after he'd pinned on his second star, and climbed an interior stairway to the ILS Room.

ILS (Instrument Landing System), which permits an aircraft to land through fog without any visual reference to the ground until moments before touchdown, requires three things, in about equal priority: a high-quality, precision radar, so that the precise location of the aircraft is known second by second; a highly skilled ILS controller, who interprets the position (speed, altitude, attitude, and rate of descent) of the landing aircraft in relation to the runway; and a pilot of high skill who can instantly respond to the controller's directions with precision.

The controller, a plump, thirty-five-year-old sergeant first class, looked over and glared at them when they entered his preserve. They had no business there, but the aide-to-the-general is a more equal pig.

"Is that General Hanrahan's aircraft?" Oliver asked.

"Yes, sir," the sergeant said impatiently. "He's about five miles out."

Oliver then remained silent as Cessna Six-oh-three was talked down. It was not very exciting. The controller told the pilot what to do, and the pilot did it. Johnny was a little disappointed. He was pleased, of course, that everything went smoothly, but it would have been more of an education for Bobby had there been terse, quick commands to change altitude, or direction, or even an excited order to break it off.

But there were no such commands. The first Cessna Six-oh-three was heard from was when Lieutenant Colonel Craig Lowell's voice came over the speaker.

"We have the runway in sight, thank you very much, ILS."

"My pleasure, sir," the sergeant said.

"We probably would have done much better if we were sober," Colonel Lowell's voice said.

The sergeant laughed, and turned to them.

"You know the colonel, Captain?"

"Yes, sir."

"Quite a guy," the sergeant said. "Hell, that

landing was textbook. Couldn't have been any better."

"We better go down and meet them," Oliver said. "Thank you, Sergeant."

They went down the stairwell, and then through the plate-glass doors leading to the transient ramp. As they pushed them open, the Cessna's engines could be heard, and then it could be seen, taxiing from the active runway.

"With a little bit of luck, Bobby," Oliver teased, "Sergeant Portet will have been given a ride over here by the general. Wouldn't that be a nice surprise?"

"Shit!" Bobby said.

General Robert F. Bellmon was finally reconciled to having his daughter marry a common enlisted man. Second Lieutenant Bobby Bellmon was not similarly adjusted, or even resigned, to having Jack Portet, the EM who had been fucking his sister outside the bonds of holy matrimony, accepted into the Bellmon platoon of The Long Gray Line.

The Cessna taxied past them. Sergeant Jack Portet, smiling broadly, waved at them from the pilot's seat.

"Well," Oliver said, chuckling. "That explains that textbook ILS, doesn't it, Bobby?"

"Goddamn it, will you stop calling me 'Bobby'?"

Lieutenant Colonel Craig W. Lowell came out of the sleek Cessna first. He was wearing civilian clothing: a Harris tweed jacket; gray flannel slacks; loafers; and an open-collared, yellow, button-down shirt. There was a paisley foulard around his neck.

He stood on the wing root and stretched his

161

arms over his head. Then he looked down at Captain Oliver and Second Lieutenant Bellmon and smiled.

"Hello, Bobby," Colonel Lowell called down cordially. "How nice of you to come out here in the rain to meet us."

"Hello, Uncle Craig," Bobby said. He had known Lowell since he was a little boy; that, Oliver had noticed, gave Lowell the right to call him "Bobby" without his taking offense.

Lowell came down off the wing and offered his hand to Johnny Oliver.

"I thought you'd been retired," he said. "But thanks anyway, Johnny."

"My pleasure, Colonel," Johnny said. "How was the flight?"

"Humbling," Lowell said. "Safe, but humbling. You know we had to come in ILS?"

"Yes, sir. We watched your approach. The ILS operator said it was textbook."

"What made it humbling was that he carried on a conversation with us while he was doing it," Lowell said. "When I make an ILS approach in weather like this, I resent the intrusion on my concentration of a watch ticking."

Brigadier General Paul R. Hanrahan came out of the Cessna's cabin next. He was in uniform, wearing only his combat-jump-starred parachutist's wings and his Combat Infantry Badge with the star above the flintlock that indicated a second award.

"Oh, hell," he said. "I didn't expect you to come out to meet me," he said. "All we asked for was a ride."

"Our pleasure, General," Oliver said, saluting.

"And you, too, Bobby. Well, I appreciate it,"

162

Hanrahan said as he came off the wing root.

Lowell went to the baggage compartment and took out their luggage.

Sergeant Jack Portet came out last. He stood on the wing root and pulled up his tie, rolled down and buttoned his shirt cuffs, and then reached back into the airplane for his uniform blouse. He put that on and buttoned it, then reached inside a last time and came out with a green beret. He put that on, then stooped to adjust the "blouse" of his trousers around the top of his highly polished parachutist's "jump" boots.

He came off the wing root and saluted Johnny Oliver.

"Hello, Jack," Oliver said, returning the salute and then offering his hand. "That was a nice ILS."

"That wasn't quite what I hoped to hear," Portet said.

"So far as I know, she's at Quarters One."

"And doesn't know I'm coming?"

"She probably does by now," Oliver said. "I called Quarters One."

Jack mockingly saluted Second Lieutenant Bellmon.

"Good afternoon, Lieutenant," he said. "How are you, today?"

Not knowing what else to do, Bobby returned the salute. Hanrahan and Lowell smiled at Oliver. Lowell winked.

Portet went to a compartment in the side of the airplane and took out wheel chocks and a cover for the pitot tube, then walked around the plane, putting them in place. While he was doing that, Oliver took tie-down ropes from the compartment and tied the wings down. Then they walked together toward Base Operations.

163

"Now, let's get this show on the road," General Hanrahan said. "The first priority, Johnny, when it can be arranged with his schedule, I'd like a few minutes with General Bellmon, the sooner the better."

"I don't think that will be a problem, sir," Oliver said. "You're in the Magnolia House. Why don't you call him when you get there?"

"Okay," Hanrahan said. "How did he react to the news that you're coming to work for me?"

"I haven't told him, sir," Oliver said.

"You haven't?" Hanrahan asked sharply. "Why not?"

"I . . . sir, I was about to say there hasn't been the opportunity. But the truth is, I haven't made the opportunity. I plan to tell him tonight at his party."

"He already knows," Hanrahan said. "The orders were changed by DA TWX. I have a copy."

"Oh, God!" Oliver said.

"You should have told him, Oliver," Hanrahan said.

"Yes, sir, I should have."

Hanrahan started to say something else, but stopped when Marjorie Bellmon came out the door of the Base Operations building.

"The USO has arrived," Lowell said sotto voce. He shifted into a thick, but credible, southern accent. "Why, Miss Marjorie, *whatever* brings you heah?"

"Oh, shut up, Uncle Craig," Marjorie Bellmon said. She went to General Hanrahan and kissed his cheek. "Thank you," she said.

"Thank me, it's my airplane," Lowell said. He extended his cheek.

"Okay," she said, and kissed him. "Thank you, too."

Then she went to Jack Portet and kissed him, lightly, on the cheek. And looked out of her intelligent gray eyes into his for a moment, and kissed him again.

She put her hand under Jack Portet's arm and leaned her head against his shoulder.

"May I presume," Lowell said, "from that awful display of affection, that I will not have to concern myself with Sergeant Portet's well-being while we're here?"

"I'll take care of him," Marjorie said. "You won't have to worry about him at all."

"In that case, let's get out of here," Hanrahan said.

[FIVE]
Daleville, Alabama
1615 18 December 1964

Jack Portet, as they rode in Marjorie's MG-B through Daleville, the small town that sits between Cairns Army Airfield and Fort Rucker — known as "The Post" — decided that discretion was the better part of lust, and did not, as he was sorely tempted to do, put his hand on Miss Bellmon's knee.

"I've got to stop by the officers' sales store, baby," he said.

"Will it wait? It's quarter after four."

"Mine not to reason why, mine but to gallop into the valley of the officers' sales store," Jack said.

"He's got you running errands, doesn't he?" she said, annoyed, but then added, "But I will forgive him, for he has brought my baby to me."

She reached over and caught his hand, and squeezed it, and when she let go to downshift, it was over her knee, and he gave in to the temptation and let it drop onto her knee. After a moment, her hand covered his.

"I wonder what you and I can do to pass the time when everybody else is at Johnny's farewell party?" she asked innocently.

The MP at the gate spotted the blue officer's sticker on the MG-B's bumper, popped to attention, and saluted.

Jack returned it.

"I don't know if sergeants are supposed to do that or not," Jack said. "But if I were on the gate, and saluted another EM, I would be annoyed."

"It's supposed to be 'a greeting between warriors,'" Marjorie said.

The staff sergeant in charge of the officers' sales store saw Marjorie's car pull up outside and had time to go in the back and tell the lieutenant in charge that the general's daughter was coming into the store.

"Good afternoon, Miss Bellmon," the lieutenant said when Jack and Marjorie walked in. "How can I be of service?"

"I'm with the sergeant," Marjorie said. "Thanks anyway."

I wonder what the hell that's all about? the lieutenant thought, but he smiled at Jack and asked, "How can I help you, Sergeant?"

"I'll probably need one of everything," Jack said. "But I think I'll leave precisely what up to Miss Bellmon."

He handed Marjorie a thick sheaf of mimeographed paper. She looked at him curiously and then read it.

HEADQUARTERS

DEPARTMENT OF THE ARMY
WASHINGTON, D.C.

16 December 1964

SPECIAL ORDERS

NUMBER 307

E * X * T * R * A * C * T

101. SERGEANT Jacques Emile PORTET, US52397606, Hq & Hq Company USAAVN Center Fort Rucker, Ala is HONORABLY DISCHARGED from the military service for the convenience of the government under the provisions of AR 615-365. EM auth travel pay and appropriate per diem to his Home of Record, 404 Avenue Leopold, Léopoldville, Republic of the Congo.

102. FIRST LIEUTENANT Jacques Emile PORTET, Inf, 0-391123, US Army Reserve, having reported for extended active duty for a period of no less than three (3) years is assigned to Hq & Hq Company, John F. Kennedy Center for Special Warfare, Fort Bragg, N.C. Travel pay and appropriate per diem

---

from officer's Home of Record, 404 Avenue Leopold, Léopoldville, Republic of the Congo, is authorized.

103. FIRST LIEUTENANT Jacques Emile PORTET, Inf, 0-391123, Hq & Hq Company, JFK Center for Spec War, Ft Bragg, NC, is placed on TDY for a period not to exceed forty-five (45) days and will proceed USAAVN Center, Fort Rucker, Ala for the purpose of undergoing special flight training by the Ft Rucker Instrument Flight Examiner Board leading to his designation as an Army Aviator, fixed and rotary wing, single and multi-engine with Special Instrument Rating. Off is auth per diem and travel by Privately Owned Vehicle. AUTH: Verbal Orders of the Chief of Staff, US Army to Comm Gen JFK Center for Special Warfare Ft Bragg, NC 0830 Hours 15 Dec 1964.

E * X * T * R * A * C * T

OFFICIAL:

John B. Stevenson
Major General, The Adjutant General

Distribution:

Special
201-Portet, Jacques E., 0-391123

"Oh, my God!" Marjorie said.

She looked at Jack, and he shrugged and smiled.

"You did this for me!" she accused. "Oh, Jack, you damned fool!"

"I did it because Colonel Felter said he needs me," Jack said. "And I think he does. I thought you'd be pleased."

"Pleased that you're going to be around Sandy and Craig and Geoff and the rest of those snake-eating lunatics?" she asked incredulously. "I wanted you safe and sound at that goddamned Instrument Examiner Board!"

She thrust his orders at him as if they burned her.

Jack turned to the quartermaster lieutenant and handed him the orders.

"I'm going to need uniforms," he said. "And one Class A right now. I'm a 42-long. Is that going to be a problem?"

"We can take care of everything but cuffing the pants, Lieutenant," the QM officer said. "The seamstress has already taken off for the day."

"I'll cuff your goddamned pants for you, *Lieutenant*," Marjorie said. "Oh, Jack, why?"

[SIX]
The Magnolia House
Fort Rucker, Alabama
1715 18 December 1964

Major General Robert F. Bellmon pulled his Oldsmobile into the driveway of Magnolia House — the transient quarters for visiting general officers and VIPs — got out, and walked quickly to the door. He knocked at the door, but entered without waiting for a reply.

He found Lieutenant Colonel Craig W. Lowell in the sitting room, in civilian clothing. He was watching the news on the television, holding a drink in his hand. His dress mess uniform was hanging on a hanger over the door to what was probably his bedroom.

"Hello, Craig," he said, signaling for him to remain seated. "Where's Red?"

"On the horn, checking in with his wife," Lowell said. "Would you like a little taste?"

"Please," Bellmon said. "What are you having?"

"Scotch," Lowell said. He got up and walked to a sideboard on which sat a row of bottles and shining silver accoutrements. Before he got there, the steward, a moonlighting GI in the employ of the officers' club, came into the room from the dining room. He wore a white jacket and shirt and a bow tie.

"That's all right, Sergeant," Lowell said. "I'll pour the drinks. As a matter of fact, why don't you just pack it in?"

The steward, surprised, looked at General Bellmon for guidance.

"I've known these gentlemen long enough, Sergeant," Bellmon said, "to know they need absolutely no help in getting at the whiskey. Why don't you go over to the club, and see if you can't help out with the bar for my party?"

"Yes, sir," the steward said with a smile.

Lowell mixed a scotch and soda and handed it to Bellmon.

"Mud in your eye, Robert," he said.

"Nastrovya," Bellmon said, and took a sip. "That's good. What is it?"

"McNeil's," Lowell said.

170

"Never heard of it," Bellmon said.

"I have it sent over," Lowell said.

"From Scotland, you mean?" Bellmon asked. Lowell nodded. Bellmon shook his head from side to side.

"It must be nice to be rich," Bellmon said.

"It is, as you well know," Lowell said, smiling. "Don't poor-mouth me, Bob. I know better."

"Not that I'm not delighted to see you, Craig," Bellmon said, just a little sarcastically. "Especially since you brought your mess dress . . . I presume you brought the golden saucer, too?"

"I never leave home without it," Lowell said, gesturing toward one of the armchairs. On it, suspended from a purple sash, was the four-inches-across golden symbol of membership in the Greek Order of Saint Michael and Saint George.

"That always gives people something to talk about when the conversation pales," Bellmon said.

"A regular conversation piece," Lowell said.

"As I was saying, while I'm thrilled you're here, I can't help but wonder *why* you're here."

"Well, I was invited, for one thing," Lowell said.

"You know what I mean," Bellmon said.

"Okay. I suspected you were going to be annoyed with Red about now, and I came here to protect him from your righteous wrath."

"Then you know? Maybe you're involved?"

"Tangentially," Lowell said. "Peripherally."

"Well, Red better have a damned good explanation, or I'm going to fight it, right up to the chief of staff, if necessary. I like Johnny Oliver, and I'm not going to see him throw his career down the toilet . . . have it thrown down the

171

toilet by you cowboys."

Brigadier General Paul R. Hanrahan appeared at the living room. He was in his shirtsleeves.

"Howdy, Tex," Lowell said. "Go for your gun. It's high noon. I told you he was going to be pissed."

Bellmon flashed Lowell a coldly furious look, then faced Hanrahan.

"Goddamn it, Red, I wasn't even consulted!"

"I think I better have a drink," Hanrahan said.

"I think you better tell me what the hell you're trying to do to Johnny Oliver," Bellmon said.

"All right," Hanrahan said as he mixed himself a drink. "Captain Oliver came to me, asked if he thought there was someplace around the Center where he could be useful, and I said there was."

"He came to you?" Bellmon asked, genuinely surprised. "He had his assignment. George Rand, who is writing his own TO and E, came up with an 'executive assistant' slot for him. It's a damned good assignment."

"He came to me," Hanrahan repeated.

"I just don't understand that," Bellmon said.

"Well, he got together with his pal Lunsford —" Hanrahan said.

"He's mentioned him. Who is he?" Bellmon interrupted.

"They knew each other in 'Nam. He was the A Team commander Johnny was trying to extract when he got shot down. Felter had him in the Congo, walking around in the woods with the Simbas. He got a Silver Star for it . . . from the President, incidentally. Who put him on the major's list. Good officer."

"And this is his idea, then?" Bellmon asked.

172

"No, it was Oliver's idea. They showed up drunk."

"Drunk?"

"Drunk. That didn't surprise me about Lunsford, but I was surprised about Oliver. And then it occurred to me, Bob, that he was damned near as emotionally exhausted as Lunsford."

"You're suggesting I burned him out?" Bellmon asked coldly.

"I'm suggesting he broke his hump working for you," Hanrahan said. "He thinks the only reason you don't walk on water is that you don't like wet shoes. And then he had some personal problems."

"You mean the reluctant widow?" Bellmon asked.

"Yeah," Hanrahan said. "She told him fish or cut bait. Her and the kid, or him and the Army. He chose the Army."

"And then there was the beloved sister," Lowell said.

"I don't know about that," Bellmon said.

"When he wouldn't let her cheat him out of a million point three, she told him what an ungrateful sonofabitch he was."

"I didn't hear about that," Bellmon said. "There was something about a sister, but —"

"From what I hear, she is a real bitch," Lowell said. "But she did raise Johnny from a kid. . . . I know why it bothers him."

"He told you all this?" Bellmon asked.

"No. He told Father Lunsford, and when I asked Father why Oliver wanted to join the Foreign Legion, he told me."

"Tell me?"

"Right now, it's those two against the world," Hanrahan said. "Lunsford's on the outs with his

173

family — or some of them, anyway. And Oliver has been kicked in the balls by both his sister and the widow."

"And he thinks running around in the woods with you guys, eating snakes, is going to make things better?"

"They both need a rest," Hanrahan said. "After which, I can find something for them to do. I don't intend to have them running around eating snakes. They've had all the on-the-job training they need in that area."

"If he goes to work for George Rand," Bellmon said firmly, "there is absolutely no question in my mind that he would make the major's five-percent list in a year. I just wrote him one hell of an efficiency report."

"What he does *not* need at this point in his career is another year or so of sixteen-hour days working for a general officer," Hanrahan said just as firmly. "Can't you see that? As soon as he gets home from 'Nam, you put him to work. He would work just as hard for George Rand. And with his lady love giving him the boot . . . That's a prescription for a breakdown if I ever heard one."

"I vote with the redhead," Lowell said.

Bellmon looked at him coldly, shrugged, and then turned back to Hanrahan.

"So what would you do with him? Notice the tense. *If* you had him. I am still ten seconds away from calling the chief of staff."

"I think you better tell him, Red," Lowell said.

Hanrahan looked at Lowell for a long moment, obviously making up his mind.

"I suppose Bob will get involved sooner or later, won't he?" he said finally, and looked at Bellmon.

"Involved with what?" Bellmon asked.

174

"Operation Earnest," Hanrahan said. "It's a Felter operation. And it's classified Top Secret/Earnest."

"What the hell is it?" Bellmon asked.

"Lunsford's the action officer, and Oliver will be handling the aviation for him."

"I asked what the hell it is," Bellmon said impatiently. "What is 'Operation Earnest'?"

Hanrahan looked at Lowell before replying. Lowell shrugged.

"Felter has information that Che Guevara's going to Africa to cause trouble. They're going to keep an eye on him," Hanrahan said.

"His Christian name," Lowell said dryly, "is Ernesto."

"I'm not quite sure I understand," Bellmon said. He obviously did not like what he had heard. "You're going to try to locate him, is that what you're saying? Isn't that the CIA's business?"

Hanrahan shrugged.

"What are you going to do if you find him?"

"Reason with him," Lowell said dryly. "Try to point out the error of his ways. He wasn't always a murderous sonofabitch who beats prisoners to death with baseball bats; and as Father Whatsisname of Boys' Town said, 'there is no such thing as a bad boy.' "

"You mean assassinate him," Bellmon said.

"No, that's absolutely not an option," Lowell said. "I told you what the orders are. Keep an eye on him. Maybe cause him a little trouble, but that's all."

"That's the CIA's business," Bellmon argued.

"The President gave the job to Felter," Hanrahan said.

Clearly, Bellmon thought, *after the Felter-run*

175

operation to rescue hostages from Stanleyville had gone off so well, he enjoyed, for the moment at least, the admiration of the President. The President admired results.

"If the CIA had to run around in the Africa jungle," Lowell offered, "keeping an eye on Guevara, they'd get mud on their shiny loafers. Couldn't have that, could we?"

"I don't see why Felter would put Johnny Oliver in something like that," Bellmon said. "He has neither the training nor the experience for something like that."

When neither Hanrahan nor Lowell replied, Bellmon added, "I still think he'd be better off working for George Rand."

"It's done, Bob," Hanrahan said. "If you raised a lot of hell about it, you might get it undone. But I'm not sure. Why don't you just let it be? If nothing else, for his sake, give him a little time to get over the woman. I'm probably betraying a confidence when I say this, but Major Lunsford told me he broke down and cried like a baby."

Bellmon looked at him. It was a moment before he spoke.

"Just within these walls, I am about out of patience with that goddamned widow." Then he shrugged. "Okay. If the best thing for Johnny to do is go eat snakes, *bon appétit!*"

"There's one more thing, Bob," Lowell said. "He had planned to tell you about this tonight. Apparently, he was afraid of your reaction. Red told him you already knew — that he'd gotten a copy of the TWX changing his orders."

"I'm not about to add to the poor guy's problems. A crazy widow and you two, plus Felter, is more than enough of a burden for a young captain to bear."

Lowell smiled and chuckled.

"Well, now that we're all old pals again," Lowell said, "would anybody like another drink?"

"Please," Generals Bellmon and Hanrahan said, almost in unison.

V

[ONE]
Quarters One
Fort Rucker, Alabama
1825 18 December 1964

Second Lieutenant Robert F. Bellmon entered his parents' home via the kitchen door and found Jacques Portet standing on the kitchen table, and his sister fussing with Jack's trousers' cuffs.

"What the hell is going on?" Bobby demanded.

"Ask the lieutenant," Marjorie said.

"Jack, what the hell is going on?"

"That's 'what the hell is going on, sir?' " Jack said. "See if you can remember that in the future."

"Oh, Jesus!" Marjorie said disgustedly. But there was a hint of a smile on her lips.

"Those are officer's trousers," Bobby observed in surprise, having seen the black stripe down the trousers' seam that differentiates officer's trousers from those of enlisted men.

"Splendid!" Jack said. "Perception is a characteristic to be encouraged in junior officers."

"Marjorie?" Bobby asked, sounding young and confused.

"The damned fool took a commission," Marjorie said.

"*Took* a commission?"

"As a first lieutenant," Jack said. "You don't have to stand at attention in my presence, Bobby, but a little respect would be in order."

"You can get off the table," Marjorie said. "And put your other pants back on."

Jack jumped nimbly off the table.

"Stick around, Bobby," Jack said. "I need a favor."

He walked out of the kitchen, and Marjorie followed him.

Two minutes later, he walked back in. He laid a uniform tunic and a handful of plastic-boxed insignia on the table.

"I don't know where that stuff goes, Bobby," Jack said. "Would you show me?"

"You're really an officer?" Bobby asked.

Jack nodded.

Bobby regained his composure.

"Then let me offer my congratulations, Jack."

He put out his hand, and Jack took it.

"Thank you," Jack said. "Your sister is less than thrilled, as you may have noticed."

"What's that all about?" Bobby asked.

"She wanted me safe and sound at the Instrument Examiner Board," Jack said.

Major General Robert F. Bellmon entered the kitchen a few minutes later. Bobby was bent over the kitchen table, pinning the crossed rifles of Infantry to the lapels of Jack's tunic.

"Hello, Jack," he said, offering his hand.

"Good evening, sir," Jack said. "I'd hoped to have this finished before you got home."

"What's going on?" Bellmon said.

"Bobby's pinning my new insignia on for me," Jack said. "I don't know where it all goes."

Bellmon looked at the tunic and then at Jack.

Jack handed him a copy of his orders.

"Felter?" he asked when he had read them.

179

"Yes, sir," Jack said. "Colonel Felter thought it would solve a lot of problems if I was commissioned."

"And he arranged it?"

"Yes, sir."

"Does Marjorie know?"

"Marjorie's pissed," Bobby said. "She called him a 'damned fool.' "

Bellmon shook his head, then looked at Jack.

"May I show these to Bobby?" he asked.

"Yes, sir, of course."

Bellmon handed the orders to Bobby, then turned to Jack.

"There's no question in my mind that, with your professional qualifications and character, you'll make a fine officer, Jack," he said, and put out his hand. "Congratulations."

"Thank you, sir," Jack said.

"And it will solve a lot of problems about your marriage, won't it?" Bellmon said.

"That may be on hold, sir," Jack said.

Bellmon looked at him for a moment.

"Marjorie'll come around," Bellmon said. "I think what she had in mind was you being out at the Instrument Examiner Board, and not in Vietnam, and is honest enough to admit it."

"Yes, sir. I think that's it."

"You start working for Felter, you may both wish you were in Vietnam," Bellmon said, then added: "Sorry, I shouldn't have said that. I just found out that Johnny Oliver is also going to work for Colonel Felter, and I'm a little less than thrilled about that."

"Yes, sir, I'd heard."

"Well, first things first," Bellmon said, and went to a cupboard and took out a bottle of Martel

180

cognac and three snifter glasses. He poured drinks and handed glasses to Jack and Bobby.

"A successful career, Jack," he said.

"Hear, hear," Bobby said, then touched glasses.

"When you have Lieutenant Portet's insignia where it should be, Bobby, call Captain Hornsby, and tell him to provide places at the head table tonight for Lieutenant Portet and his lady," General Bellmon said.

"Yes, sir," Bobby said.

[TWO]
Dining Room A
The Officers' Open Mess
Fort Rucker, Alabama
2115 Hours 18 December 1964

Dining Room A of the officers' open mess was usually the cafeteria. It was on the main floor of the club, separated from it by folding doors. When it was in use for a more formal purpose, such as the Commanding General's Christmas Dinner-Dance, the glass-covered steam trays of the cafeteria serving line were hidden by folding screens, and the plastic-topped tables rearranged and covered with linen.

The tables tonight had been arranged in a long-sided U, with a shorter line of tables in the middle of the U. Seating was determined by protocol, modified slightly by the unanticipated presence of Brigadier General Paul Hanrahan and First Lieutenant Portet and his lady.

The commanding general and his lady sat, naturally, at the head of the table, in the center of the U. To their left sat the chief of staff and his lady, and to the right, Brigadier General Hanrahan. No

181

one sat across from the general officers and their ladies.

People were seated on both sides of the legs of the U, their proximity to the head of the table determined, for the most part, by their rank, and sometimes by their seniority within that rank.

A corkboard the size of a sheet of plywood mounted on the wall of the small office of General Bellmon's aide-de-camp had been used. Every invitee was represented by a small piece of cardboard on which had been typed his name, grade, and date of rank. These were thumbtacked to the corkboard onto a representation of the arrangement of the tables in Dining Room A, and re-arranged as necessary.

One of the things that would be useful to him in his later career that Johnny Oliver had learned during his tour as aide-de-camp was that General Robert F. Bellmon looked forward to the official parties (there were half a dozen a year) with slightly less enthusiasm than he would look forward to a session with the post dental surgeon where the agenda was the removal, without anesthesia, of all of his teeth.

This was not evident to the guests, or to their wives. Bellmon had decided that the parties, which were more or less an Army tradition, were part of his duties, and his duty was very important to him. He and Mrs. Bellmon, and the chief of staff and his wife (and both aides-de-camp, who took turns discreetly whispering the invitees last name, read from invitations), stood in the foyer for forty-five minutes, shaking hands with, and smiling at, and more often than not coming up with a personal word of greeting for everybody who showed up.

Once, sometime during Johnny Oliver's year's tour as aide-de-camp, General Bellmon had come to his office late at night and found Oliver standing before the corkboard rearranging the guests for an official affair.

"It began, these official damned dinners, with the Brits," Bellmon told him. "Regimental 'dining in' once a month. Good idea. Once a month they got together, shop talk was forbidden, and they got a little tight. And it worked here, before the war, when there was rarely more than a regiment on a post. Thirty, forty officers on a post, including all the second lieutenants. This is out of hand, of course. But how the hell can you stop it? If it wasn't for these damned things, a field-grade officer could do a three-year tour on the post and never get to see the commanding general except maybe at an inspection, or a briefing. And the wife never would. The most important element in command, Johnny, is making the subordinate believe he's doing something important. If he doesn't feel he *knows* the commanding officer . . ."

Johnny Oliver had also learned that sometimes getting to *personally* know the commanding general could get out of hand. Officers' wives were the worst offenders, but not by much. One of the aides' functions at official dinners was to rescue the general from people who had backed him into a corner, either to dazzle him with their charm and wit, or to make a pitch for some pet project of theirs, ranging from getting use of the post theatre for amateur theatrics, to revamping the entire pilot training program.

"General, excuse me, sir," Captain Oliver had often said, to separate General Bellmon from pressing admirers, "General Facility is calling."

General Facility was a white china plumbing apparatus hung on the gentlemen's rest room tiled wall.

Nobody in the men's room would bend his ear while the general was taking a leak. But from what Oliver had seen of the women, especially with a couple of drinks in them, the general would not be equally safe in the ladies' room.

When Johnny Oliver entered the club, Captain Richard Hornsby, the new aide-de-camp — wearing, Oliver knew, his dress mess uniform for the first time — was standing, where Oliver had stood so often, behind General Bellmon, with a clipboard and a stack of invitations in his hand. He smiled, and softly said, "Captain Oliver and Lieutenant Bellmon."

General Bellmon put out his hand.

"Good evening, sir," Johnny Oliver said.

"Good evening, Captain," Bellmon said. "An officer is judged by the company he keeps. Try to remember that."

Then he withdrew his hand and offered it to his son.

"Good evening, sir," Bobby said.

"Good evening, Lieutenant," Bellmon said. "I'm glad you could make it."

Barbara Bellmon violated protocol. After she took Captain Oliver's hand, she pulled him to her and kissed his cheek.

"We're going to miss you, Johnny," she said.

"Me, too," John Oliver said.

"So will I, Oliver," the chief of staff said.

"Thank you, General," Oliver said, touched by the comment.

"Well," Mrs. Chief of Staff said, "you're only going to Benning. We'll see you."

Next in the reception line was Brigadier General Paul R. Hanrahan. Oliver knew that he was in the reception line only because Bellmon had insisted that he be there. If it was true that it was a good thing for officers remote from the command post to shake the hand, and look in the eye, of the commanding general, it therefore followed that it was a good thing for officers to do the same thing with visiting (and in Hanrahan's case, near-legendary) general officers.

"Hello, Johnny," Hanrahan said.

"Good evening, General."

"Do me a favor?"

"Yes, sir. My privilege."

"Keep an eye on Colonel Lowell, amuse him, see if you can keep him out of trouble."

"I'll do what I can, sir," Oliver chuckled.

The two bachelors entered Dining Room A. Captain Oliver spotted Lieutenant Colonel Craig W. Lowell at almost the instant Lowell spotted him. Lowell was standing near the bar, holding a drink in his hand. He looked, Oliver thought, *splendiferous* in his uniform. He was in the center of a group of people, predominantly female. Oliver remembered what Mrs. Bellmon had said about Lowell attracting the ladies as a candle draws moths.

Lowell beckoned to Oliver with his index finger. The three of them walked over.

"Good evening, sir," Oliver said.

"Lieutenant Bellmon," Lowell said by way of greeting. "Now that you're here, go around and locate our place cards — mine, Oliver's, Lieutenant Portet's, Marjorie's and yours — and relocate them to one of the tables at the rear of the room."

185

"Sir?" Bobby said.

"See if you can explain what I thought was a simple command to him, will you, Captain?"

Oliver chuckled.

"Do it, Bobby," he said.

Lowell turned to the others he was standing with.

"I have a standing rule at official dinners," he explained, "to sit as close to the back of the room, and the exit, as possible."

There was laughter, some genuine, some a little nervous. Bobby, visibly uncomfortable, started to comply with his orders.

Major General Bellmon stood up and looked around the room. Some conversation stopped, but by no means all of it. Bellmon tapped on an empty wine bottle with the handle of a knife until the room fell silent.

"You all have met General Hanrahan," he said. "And I know that many of you are wondering what he's doing here."

He gave that a moment to sink in, and for a scattering of applause to die down.

"One rumor I heard going around is that they ran out of rattlesnakes for General Hanrahan's Green Berets to eat in North Carolina, and that he's here to talk me out of some of ours," Bellmon went on.

There came the expected laughter.

"That's not true, of course," Bellmon said. "The truth is that this party has very strong personal meaning for Mrs. Bellmon and myself. It's become, for us, a family affair, and as General Hanrahan is a longtime friend of the family, he belongs here with us."

There was some applause.

186

"During the past year, as you all know," Bellmon went on, "Captain John S. Oliver has had the toughest job on the post — he's been my aide-de-camp. When General Hanrahan unfailingly mentioned Captain Oliver's all-around competence and high intelligence, I simply chalked that up as Captain Oliver's due. For he has indeed been a fine aide, and I like to think a friend, too. We will all miss him. The command group, my family, everybody on the post."

There was a round of applause and heads turned, looking for him.

"As those of you who have been around a couple of years know, there's sort of a new custom: At this Christmas Dinner, with everybody gathered together, I announce my departing aide's new assignment. There are many places in the Army where an officer of Captain Oliver's experience, devotion to duty, and extraordinary competence could be assigned. I made several recommendations along that line. Captain Oliver, will you please stand up?"

Oliver stood up.

"Attention to orders," Bellmon said, and read from a sheet of paper: " 'Headquarters, Department of the Army, 29 November 1964. General Order 297, Paragraph 23. Captain John S. Oliver, Armor, is relieved of present assignment and transferred to Headquarters, John F. Kennedy Center for Special Warfare, Fort Bragg, N.C., effective 1 January 1965.' "

There was a scattering of applause, several audible snorts.

"General Hanrahan tells me that you will be assigned as the aviation officer on his special staff," Bellmon went on. "And I'm sure you will

187

serve him as well and faithfully as you have served me, and that he will in time become as fond of you as is the Bellmon family."

There was more applause.

"Now if you'll come up here, Johnny, we have a few little things to prepare you for your new assignment. There's a snakebite kit, and a Bowie knife, and an earring, and a book entitled *101 Tasty Rattlesnake Recipes*."

Captain Johnny Oliver looked at Lieutenant Colonel Craig W. Lowell.

"He really is still pissed, isn't he?" Lowell said softly.

Oliver looked at him a moment, then started walking toward the head table.

General Hanrahan got to his feet as Oliver approached the head table. He smiled and handed Oliver a green beret.

"Put it on, Johnny," Mrs. Barbara Bellmon said. Oliver did so, and turned to face the room.

There was applause, in which General Bellmon joined. But when Oliver looked at him, there was no laughter in his eyes.

"I think I should point out that Captain Oliver is entitled to the Green Beret," Bellmon said. "He earned it the hard way, by on-the-job training. He was shot down in Vietnam, flying a D-Model Huey, while trying to extract a Special Forces A Team behind the enemy's lines. Because the A Team commander was rather badly wounded, Oliver assumed command and led the team, on foot, through enemy-held territory to safety. His valor earned him the Silver Star and the Combat Infantry Badge.

"General Hanrahan and Special Forces think of him as one of their own, but, whether General

Hanrahan likes it or not, I will — Army Aviators will — continue to regard him as one of our own."

There was a good deal of applause at that, and people got to their feet.

"And finally, there is another Special Forces officer here tonight, in the rear of the room, for whom Mrs. Bellmon and I have a great deal of affection, and our daughter Marjorie has even more affection. Lieutenant Portet, will you stand up, please?"

Jack got uncomfortably to his feet.

"Lieutenant Portet was supposed to be sitting at the head table tonight, because he will shortly be our son-in-law, and it was my intention to introduce him to everybody."

More applause.

"But he's a Green Beret, and we all know about Green Berets. They do what they want to do, not what someone else wants them to do, so he's sitting in the back of the room where he wants to be."

There was nervous laughter at this.

"With him is another old and dear friend of the family — our children call him 'Uncle Craig' — who is more or less one of us, an old-time Army Aviator who now wears a Green Beret, Lieutenant Colonel Craig W. Lowell. And our son, Bobby, who very recently won his wings and became one of us."

There was polite applause at this.

"And I would like, in the friendliest possible way, to suggest to General Hanrahan, and Colonel Lowell, and Captain Oliver, and Lieutenant Portet, that if I hear even the hint of a rumor that they are trying to get my son to go to Fort Bragg with them and become a snake-eater like they are,

189

when I am through with them, they will be the first male soprano quartet in the history of the U.S. Army."

There was laughter, some hearty and some a little nervous, that the commanding general would, even as a joke, threaten to castrate anybody.

And only Colonel Lowell and Lieutenant Bellmon knew, of course, that Bobby had three minutes before asked Uncle Craig what he thought about his applying for Special Forces, and would he help get him in?

[THREE]

S E C R E T

Central Intelligence Agency
Langley, Virginia

FROM: Assistant Director For Administration

DATE: 19 December 1964 1505 GMT

SUBJECT: Guevara, Ernesto (Memorandum # 2.)

TO: Mr. Sanford T. Felter
Counselor To The President
Room 637, The Executive Office Building
Washington, D.C.

By Courier

In compliance with Presidential Memorandum to The Director, Subject: "Ernesto 'Che' Guevara," dated 14 December 1964, the following information is furnished:

(1) (Reliability Scale Five) (From CIA, Paris, France) SUBJECT and party landed at Orly Field, Paris, France, 2305 GMT 18 December 1964. They were met by Cuban Ambassador to France and French Foreign Ministry officials. They were taken to VIP waiting room, and at 0315 19 December 1964, they boarded Air France Flight 1727 for Algiers, Algeria.

(2) CIA surveillance was terminated at this time. CIA Algiers, Algeria has been advised, and will attempt to pick up surveillance in Algiers.

Howard W. O'Connor
HOWARD W. O'CONNOR

SECRET

[FOUR]
Room 2012
The Daleville Inn
Daleville, Alabama
0555 20 December 1964

There had been verbal orders from Lieutenant Colonel Craig W. Lowell to augment the Department of the Army Special Orders vis-à-vis 1st Lt. PORTET, Jacques E., which explained his presence in the Daleville Inn.

"From now on, Jack," Lowell said as they had flown to Cairns Field in Lowell's Cessna 310-H, "the name of the game is not attracting attention to yourself. The reason you're on per diem, for example, is not to provide you with a place to fool around with Marjorie at government expense, but to keep you out of the BOQ."

Jack knew he could not indignantly proclaim his and Marjorie's innocence. Marjorie had, after all, followed Lowell's map at Ocean Reef, and Lowell knew it.

Lowell had smiled at him and then gone on:

"The BOQs are full of lieutenants undergoing flight training, and the sudden appearance in their midst of a Special Forces lieutenant taking a special flight training program would make them naturally curious, and they would ask questions which you could not answer. Get the picture?"

"Yes, sir."

"This way, in the Daleville Inn, it will look like you're staying there waiting for the glorious day of your being joined in holy matrimony to the beautiful Miss Marjorie."

"I get the picture, sir."

"There will be a telephone in your room, a private number, not going through the switchboard. It won't be a secure line, but it will be a lot more private than the phone on the wall of the corridor in a BOQ."

That telephone had rung at 2135 the previous evening, shortly after Miss Marjorie and Jack had entered the room "to watch a little TV."

Jack had picked it up on the second ring. "Hello!?"

"The way that's done, Lieutenant," Major Pappy Hodges's gruff voice had announced, "is 'Lieutenant Portet,' or even better, 'Lieutenant Portet speaking, sir.' "

He wondered how Pappy had known (a) that he had been commissioned; (b) was in the Daleville Inn; and (c) the number of the private telephone line. He hadn't seen Pappy since Kamina, in the Congo. That made him wonder why Pappy hadn't been at General Bellmon's party; they were friends.

"Yes, sir."

The door to the bathroom opened, and Miss Marjorie stood there wearing a look of curiosity on her face, and a pair of black panties (and nothing else) on her body.

Goddamn, she's beautiful!

"Have you got a flight suit and a helmet?" Pappy asked.

"Yes, sir."

"I'll meet you at the Board at 0630," Pappy said.

"What's up?"

"Oh-six-thirty at the Board," Pappy had said. "If you eat breakfast, have it eaten by then."

The phone had clicked in Jack's ear. Pappy had hung up.

"Who was that?" Marjorie asked.

"Pappy Hodges," Jack said. "Apparently we're going flying in the morning. Oh-six-thirty, as we officers and gentlemen say."

Marjorie nodded, then went back into the bathroom.

"Either turn the light off, or put your eyes back

in your head," she called to him.

She didn't stay in the bathroom long, but she was no longer in the bed when the desk called to tell him it was his five-minutes-to-six wake-up call. But the smell of her was, and Jack shamelessly buried his nose in the pillow where her head had lain before getting up.

There was also a Kleenex with her lipstick on it in the bathroom, and, when he picked up his hairbrush, several of her hairs.

As he showered, he thought, *All things considered, living with Marjorie is going to be great, and it's really going to be nice to wake up and find her beside me.*

When Jack pulled the Jaguar into a RESERVED FOR STAFF parking slot at the Instrument Examiner Board building, Pappy was already there, leaning against the fender of his car.

Jack got out and walked up to him and saluted.

"Good morning, sir," Jack said.

Pappy snorted as he returned the salute almost contemptuously.

"You have egg yolk on your chin," Pappy said, and walked away, around the corner of the building to the Board's aircraft parking area.

Jack wiped the yolk off his chin and hurried after him.

The Board had been assigned what amounted to a private fleet of Army Aircraft to discharge its responsibilities of making sure pilots who would fly in instrument conditions were qualified to do so.

Lined up before the Board building were three twin-engine airplanes: a Grumman Mohawk, an ominous-looking twin turbojet electronic surveillance aircraft; a sleek high-wing L-26 Aero Commander; and a Beechcraft L23D "Twin Bonanza." There were three helicopters: a Bell UH-1D "Huey," the mainstay of the Army's rotary wing fleet; a Boeing Vertol Model 114/CH-47 Chinook, a large, dual-rotor helicopter capable of carrying a 105-mm howitzer, its crew, and a basic load of ammunition; and a Hughes OH-6, called the "Loach," a fast, high-performance single-rotor aircraft. There were three single-engine fixed-wing aircraft: There was the de Havilland U-1A "Otter," the largest single-engine aircraft in the world, capable of short-field performance carrying up to ten passengers. Beside the "Otter" sat its older little brother, the de Havilland L-20 "Beaver," a six-place short-field-capable aircraft originally developed for use in the Canadian and Alaskan bush, and used extensively by the Army in the Korean war.

And at the far end of the line sat a Cessna L-19, a small two-place, high-wing observation and liaison aircraft, also used for basic fixed-wing flight training. The Instrument Board's L-19 had been equipped with the radios and other instruments necessary for instrument flight.

"Preflight the L-19," Pappy Hodges ordered.

"Yes, sir."

"And prepare an instrument flight plan from here to Pope Air Force Base, with a fuel stop at Fort Gordon, Georgia."

"We're going on instruments in this weather?" Jack asked incredulously. He had called for the FAA weather prediction from the Daleville Inn. It couldn't be any nicer, and was almost certainly going to stay that way for 48 hours.

Pappy nodded. Jack shrugged, then remem-

195

bered where Pope Air Force Base was, how far away it was.

"In the Cessna?" Jack asked incredulously. "At eighty-five miles an hour?"

"The way it works, Lieutenant," Pappy said, "is the major tells the lieutenant what to do, and the lieutenant says, 'Yes, sir.' Got it?"

"Yes, sir."

I wonder what I've done to piss him off? There's more to this than his getting out of the wrong side of the bed.

Pappy was waiting for him in the flight planning room, and stood over his shoulder as he made out his instrument flight plan. Pappy said nothing when he was finished, simply walked out of the room and the building carrying his parachute and a small bag. Jack grabbed a parachute and walked quickly after him.

Pappy climbed in the rear seat of the small airplane and strapped himself in.

Jack decided the best thing to do under the circumstances was to cross every *t* and dot every *i* in the procedure to fly an aircraft under instrument flight conditions, and did so.

There was not a peep from the backseat.

At 5,000 feet over Eufala, Alabama, on a course for Fort Gordon, Georgia, Jack turned in his seat to see what Pappy was doing. Pappy's little bag had apparently contained a rubber pillow, for Pappy, his head resting against a rubber pillow, was sound asleep.

Jack almost gave in to the temptation to wake Pappy by make a hard landing at Gordon, considered this briefly, and then did the opposite. He greased it in, and the proof that it was a greaser came when he turned and looked, at the end of the landing roll, and Pappy was still asleep.

They were directed to a parking space at the Fort Gordon airstrip — and it wasn't much of an airstrip, Jack noted — by a soldier, and Jack started to shut the aircraft down.

Pappy's voice came metallically in his earphones. "How much fuel do you have remaining, Lieutenant?"

"About forty minutes, sir."

"That should be sufficient, Lieutenant," Pappy ordered. "It is my professional opinion, as an instructor pilot in L-19 Series aircraft, that I have given you sufficient instruction and that you have demonstrated sufficient basic piloting skills to be allowed to attempt solo flight."

"What?" Jack blurted.

"As soon as I exit the aircraft, Lieutenant, you will attempt solo flight as follows: You will request permission to taxi to the end of the runway, where you will request to take off under visual flight rules for a local flight. When permission is granted, you will take off, climb to three thousand feet on a due north course, and then request permission to shoot a touch-and-go landing. When permission is granted, you will make such a touch-and-go landing, and again climb to three thousand feet, at which point you will request permission to land. You will then land. Got that all? Won't it be necessary for you to write your orders down?"

"No, sir."

"On landing, you will tie the aircraft down in the prescribed manner, arrange for it to be refueled, supervise such refueling, and then you may join me in the coffee shop."

"Yes, sir," Jack said.

Pappy opened the door and got out and walked

to the small Base Operations building.

Shaking his head, Jack reached for the microphone.

"Gordon, Army Sixteen Twenty-Six, an L-19 aircraft, by Base Ops, request taxi and takeoff permission for a local flight under visual rules."

"Sir, the aircraft has been serviced and is tied down," Jack said to Pappy at the coffee shop in Base Ops.

Pappy put out his hand.

"Congratulations on your first solo flight," he said.

Jack ignored the hand.

"Actually, I soloed when I was twelve," Jack said.

"I have had several telephone calls concerning you lately," Pappy said. "The first came from Craig Lowell. He said you were getting a commission and wanted to know if there would be any problem in getting you checked out in an L23. I told him I didn't think so."

Then what's all this nonsense about soloing in that damned L-19?

"Call two was from Bob Bellmon. He had two concerns. The first one was for your well-being, and the second that he didn't want it bandied about that the general's son-in-law was getting special treatment. He asked me if I would personally check you out, as opposed to doing it with a ballpoint, and I said sure. Bob Bellmon is one of the good guys."

"I understand," Jack said.

"Not yet, you don't. Call three was from Miss Marjorie, who I literally bounced on my knee when she wore diapers. *'Uncle Pappy,'* she said, *'he* doesn't even know how to pin his bars on. When he's out there with you, will you teach him how to act like an officer? He'll take it from you, and he doesn't like it when I say something.' So I told her sure, too."

"I didn't know that," Jack said.

"You still don't know that," Pappy said. "But still no problem. Then came call number four. Sandy Felter. Another of the good guys, and I owe him. He called last night, at half past nine. He wanted two things. He wants you to be checked out yesterday in everything with a special instrument ticket to go along. And he wants us both to meet with Father Lunsford — you heard the President got him promoted to major?"

Jack nodded.

". . . at twelve today at Bragg. I figured no problem. We'd hop in the Mohawk about nine o'clock, which would give us plenty of time to be there by noon. I also figured I could check you out in the Mohawk on the way. But then I realized I couldn't do that."

"Why not?"

"As of yesterday, you have an Army record of your Army flying. I can fudge a little on that. You need a minimum of four hours dual instruction before you can solo. By the time we get to Bragg, you'll have that four hours, so I will say you soloed en route. That's more or less honest, and we'll have the L-19 tail number in the records . . . understand?"

Jack nodded.

"I could not get away with saying you soloed in a Mohawk," Pappy said. "Nor do I want your records to say that on the day you soloed, you also got checked out in the Mohawk, and satisfied the cross-country IFR requirements for an instru-

199

ment ticket, much less a special instrument ticket. I realized we're going to have to do this one step at a time. From here to the Beaver, from the Beaver to the Otter, then the L-23. Somewhere along the way, you'll get an instrument rating, and then the special instrument ticket. I have no idea how the hell we're going to teach you how to fly rotary wing."

"I see the problem."

"If I was a little gruff on the phone last night, it was because I realized I was going to have to get up at oh-dark-hundred and fly all the way to Bragg in a goddamned L-19. And then back."

"No problem, Pappy," Jack said, enormously relieved that Pappy was pissed not at him, but over things over which he had no control.

"Of course there's no problem," Pappy said. "One of the things I think Miss Marjorie would like me to teach you is that what a lieutenant has to understand is that majors don't have to explain to lieutenants why they have a hair up their ass."

He smiled at Jack and put out his hand again.

"So congratulations again on your solo flight."

"Thank you, sir."

"Now go untie the goddamned L-19 and we'll be on our way."

"Yes, sir."

[FIVE]

SECRET

Central Intelligence Agency
Langley, Virginia

FROM: Assistant Director For Administration

DATE: 20 December 1964 1505 GMT

SUBJECT: Guevara, Ernesto (Memorandum # 3.)

TO: Mr. Sanford T. Felter
Counselor To The President
Room 637, The Executive Office Building
Washington, D.C.

By Courier

In compliance with Presidential Memorandum to The Director, Subject: "Ernesto 'Che' Guevara," dated 14 December 1964, the following information is furnished:

(1) (Reliability Scale Five) (From CIA, Algiers, Algeria) CIA Surveillance of SUBJECT resumed on SUBJECT and party's landing at Algiers 0915 GMT 19 December 1964.

(2) (Reliability Scale Four). They were met by members of the Algerian Council of Ministers and the Cuban Ambassador and transported to residence of Cuban Ambassador.

Howard W. O'Connor
HOWARD W. O'CONNOR

SECRET

[SIX]
Base Operations
Pope Air Force Base, North Carolina
1135 20 December 1964

George Washington Lunsford was standing just outside the plate-glass doors to the Base Operations building when Major Pappy Hodges and Lieutenant Jack Portet walked across the tarmac from the transient parking area. He was in fatigues, and there were major's leaves on his collar points and pinned to his green beret.

Jack, as he saluted, was not surprised at the rank insignia. Pappy was.

"Patton did that in North Africa, you know," he said. "Considered himself promoted — pinned on a third star — before his promotion orders came down."

"That wasn't very nice of him, was it?" Father said. "I myself modestly waited until I had my promotion orders in my hot little hand before I pinned my major's things on."

"No kidding. They came down already?"

"Yesterday," Lunsford said. "I haven't even had time to wash them down."

"Congratulations, Major," Jack said.

Lunsford looked at him.

"And this newly commissioned young officer, to judge by his bare-of-any-insignia flight rompers, is carrying modesty to the extreme."

He raised his eyebrows, then wrapped an arm affectionately around Jack.

"How the hell are you, sport? What happened to the bandaged nose?"

"It kept coming off in the shower. I never figured out what it was supposed to do, anyway."

202

"Well, come to think of it, you are properly dressed for what I have in mind for you."

"Sir?"

"Among friends, you may address me as 'Father,' but when we get to Mackall, hit the 'sir' and 'major' a little heavily."

"Yes, sir, Major," Jack said.

"Is that where we're going, to Mackall?" Pappy asked.

"You're going to see our noble leader, General Hanrahan. Jack and I are going to Mackall. Is there any reason Jack can't fly me there in the L-19?" He paused. "And frankly, Pappy, I am surprised to see the L-19. Are you on somebody's shitlist at Rucker? I expected at least an L-23, maybe even a Mohawk."

"It's a long story," Pappy said. "What's Hanrahan want?"

"He's going to bring you up to speed on Operation Earnest, give you some heads-up. And Felter wants to talk to you on the secure line."

"Which means I am going to be involved up to my ass in this, right?"

"A succinct and correct, if somewhat obscene, assumption. Yes, you are. We need you, Pappy. The rear echelon is an important facet of any military operation."

"Damn," Pappy said. He looked thoughtfully at Jack.

"Do you think you can put the L-19 down at Mackall without killing yourself and the major?"

Jack nodded.

"If you don't bend the bird, I could sign you off on Unprepared Fields," Pappy said. "If you bend it, I'll swear under oath you stole it. Okay, Father. He can fly you out there. It would save time, and

I'd like to go home today."

Lunsford didn't reply.

"Why do I suspect you know something I don't know?" Pappy asked.

"Hanrahan wants to pick your brains," Lunsford said. "I hope you brought a change of undies, as that may take some time."

"I didn't," Jack said. "I thought we were going to fly around the pattern at Rucker."

"Well, when we come back from Mackall, you can buy some at the PX when you're buying your bars," Lunsford said.

"How do I get from here to Hanrahan?" Pappy asked.

"Hanrahan's car and driver are outside," Lunsford said. "I think he's even going to buy you lunch."

Pappy looked at both of them, and then, without a word, walked into the Base Operations building.

"Anytime you're ready, Father," Jack said.

"I know you were an airlines pilot," Lunsford said. "But why was Pappy worried about you bending the L19? How much experience do you have flying puddle-jumpers?"

"Not much," Jack said. "As a matter of fact, the first time I flew one of these all by myself was on the way down here."

"Oh, what the hell," Lunsford said. "Live on the edge, I always say."

"I think I can get us back and forth to Mackall in one piece," Jack said.

"When we get to Mackall," Lunsford ordered as they overflew Fort Bragg en route to the "dormant, former base" twenty miles from Fort

Bragg that was used for Special Forces training, "go along with whatever I say. Don't ask questions, and don't volunteer any information."

"Yes, sir," Jack said.

There was a stocky black master sergeant sitting in a jeep at the dirt airstrip when Jack landed the L-19.

Jack had been here before during his "special course" in becoming a Green Beret. He had never been inside one of the buildings then, and only when he had been put on ice at Mackall had he learned that they contained showers, cots, stoves, and refrigerators for the use of the training cadre. Trainees washed in creeks, slept on the ground, and ate as well as they could from field rations, and/or from what they could catch, kill, and cook over open fires.

The master sergeant waited until Jack had parked the airplane and was starting to tie it down before driving the jeep up and getting out.

He saluted Father.

"Those leaves look good on you, sir," he said. "Congratulations."

"Thank you," Father replied in Swahili. "I told you I wanted you guys to speak nothing but Swahili between us."

"Sorry," the sergeant said in Swahili.

"And on the subject of Swahili, the AG turned up this officer, who studied it in college, and may join us." He turned to Jack. "You get that, Lieutenant?" The adjutant general's department handled Army personnel matters.

"Yes, sir," Jack said.

"Can you say that in Swahili?"

"Yes, sir," Jack said in Swahili.

205

"Lieutenant Portet, Master Sergeant Thomas," Father said.

"How are you, Lieutenant?" Thomas said. "I didn't know they taught Swahili in college."

"They do at the Florida Baptist College," Father answered for him. "The lieutenant was studying to be a missionary in Africa when he got drafted, and decided he'd rather fly airplanes. Isn't that so, Lieutenant?"

"Yes, sir," Jack said.

"He had just finished flight school when the AG found him. I asked for black guys, but they sent him anyway. No offense, Lieutenant."

"None taken, sir."

"And since he had flown all the way here from Rucker, I figured nothing would be lost if I showed him around. If nothing else, he'll see if anybody understands him when he tries to speak Swahili."

"I get the idea, sir," Thomas said.

"I'll remind you again, Lieutenant," Lunsford said, "that anything you see here is classified, you're not to discuss it with anyone — are you married?"

"No, sir."

"You seemed to hesitate, Lieutenant."

"I'm about to married, sir — 23 December, sir."

"That will probably keep you from being assigned to us," Lunsford said thoughtfully. "Maybe we shouldn't show you around. Oh, to hell with it. We're here. To get back to what I was saying: You will not discuss anything you see here in any way with anyone, and that includes your fiancée, or, when she becomes your wife, with your wife. Clear?"

"Yes, sir."

"Does the young lady speak Swahili?"

"No, sir."

"I thought perhaps she was also studying to be a missionary," Lunsford said. "Okay, Sergeant, if you'll give the lieutenant a thirty-minute tour of the establishment, I'll have time to snoop around here and see how you've been screwing things up."

"Yes, sir," Sergeant Thomas said.

"Make sure he speaks to every man," Lunsford said. "Have everybody on the team explain his function. In Swahili."

"Yes, sir. If you'll get in the jeep with me, Lieutenant?"

When Master Sergeant Thomas was sure they had driven far enough to be out of Major Lunsford's sight, he turned to Jack.

"Lieutenant, is your Swahili good enough for you to understand what I'll be saying? No offense, sir."

"I'm having a little trouble understanding you, Sergeant," Jack said. "But maybe if you spoke slowly . . ."

"I'll try, sir," Sergeant Thomas said. "Now, what we are trying to do here, Lieutenant, is simulate, as well as we can, what life would be like for a Special Forces team operating clandestinely in a sub-Saharan African country."

"Very interesting," Jack said.

When they returned to the landing strip, and the small collection of tarpaper-roofed crude frame buildings around it, thirty minutes later, they found Lunsford sitting on the steps to one of the buildings.

He did not get up as they approached, and

returned their salutes with a casual wave of the hand.

"See anything interesting, Lieutenant Portet?" he asked in Swahili.

"Yes, sir. It was very interesting."

"And did the lieutenant have any trouble conversing with you, or any of the men, in Swahili?"

"Not much, sir," Master Sergeant Thomas answered graciously.

Lunsford raised his hand in the manner of a clergyman blessing his flock.

"By the power vested in me by God, the President of the United States, and General Hanrahan, I declare a training schedule amnesty for all hands," Lunsford said. "You will go get them, Sergeant Thomas, and bring them back here. And when you do, Lieutenant Portet will critique our little operation."

"Sir?" Thomas asked incredulously.

"It's truth time, Sergeant Thomas," Lunsford said. "And the first truthful answer I would like from you is whether you have had your run today."

"No, sir," Thomas said.

"Then why don't you kill two birds with one stone, so to speak, and jog out to the men, and lead them as they jog back here for the lieutenant's critique?" He turned to Jack. "We in Special Forces have found, Lieutenant," he went on, "that a daily jog of no more than five miles keeps the body in tip-top shape for our strenuous duties. Isn't that so, Sergeant Thomas?"

"Yes, sir," Sergeant Thomas said.

"Put your heart in it, Sergeant," Lunsford said. "We don't want to keep Lieutenant Portet waiting around, do we?"

"No, sir," Sergeant Thomas said, visibly fuming.

He turned and started to trot off down the road. Jack looked at Lunsford.

"Are you going to tell me what's going on?"

"This is what is known as setting the stage, Lieutenant," Lunsford said. "Unless I am truly mistaken, what Sergeant Thomas is going to do, when he arrives, huffing and puffing, at the campsite, is say, 'You're not going to believe this, but what we're going to do is jog back to the airstrip where that honky-motherfucker of a candy-ass airplane driver is going to tell us what we're doing wrong,' or words to that effect."

Jack chuckled.

"Why are you trying to piss him — everybody — off?"

Lunsford said, "If you're trying to teach somebody something — anything —" Lunsford said, very seriously, "the first thing you have to do is get their attention. That's particularly true with a group like this. The junior man out there is a staff sergeant. They're all fully qualified Green Berets, and with more than a little justification, they think — they know — they're pretty hot stuff. And unless I can get their attention, that's likely to get them killed."

He pushed himself off the stairs.

"Come on," he said. "I'll need some help, and I think Thomas — who is about as good a noncom as I've ever known — is going to set a speed record out there and back."

He led Jack into one of the tarpaper-roofed buildings. There was a huge refrigerator in one room, and a huge freezer sat beside it. The doors to both were locked shut with heavy chains through their handles, and secured with massive padlocks.

Lunsford opened both.

He pointed to two galvanized iron washtubs.

"I load," he said. "You chop the ice."

The freezer held huge blocks of ice, and the refrigerators cases of beer, as well as food.

There were ice tongs in the freezer, and Jack picked them up.

"Shit!" he proclaimed. They had frozen to his hand.

"You don't look that stupid," Lunsford said, and hurried him to a water spigot and got him unfrozen after a moment.

"I don't think you'll have to write this down, Lieutenant, having had a painful lesson, which caught your attention, but metal at forty degrees below zero sticks to the hand."

"I feel like a fucking fool," Jack said, examining his angry red fingers. "I knew better than that."

"Feeling like a fucking fool is the first step to acquiring — more important, remembering — knowledge," Lunsford said unctuously. "Can I trust you with the ice pick, or will you stab yourself in the hand with it?"

Jack picked up one of the blocks of ice, put it into the galvanized tub, and began hacking at it.

"After you ram knowledge down the throats of the unwilling to learn, it is necessary to pat them on the head," Lunsford said. "It's something like giving a dog a bone. Unfortunately, the Army doesn't recognize this universal truth, and officers have to pay for the beer themselves."

When there were three cases of beer covered with ice in the tubs, Lunsford carefully chained the refrigerator and freezer doors again.

"Now we go outside, and act as if we haven't moved, until our reluctant students show up, huffing and puffing and feeling sorry for themselves," he said.

With Thomas leading the column, the men trotted up to them five minutes later.

Master Sergeant Thomas saluted.

"Sir, the detail is formed," he said.

Lunsford returned the salute casually. He did not get up.

"Put the men at at ease, please, Sergeant," Lunsford said.

Thomas executed an about-face movement and bellowed, "At ease!"

The men relaxed, and put their hands behind their backs.

"As Sergeant Thomas may have told you," Lunsford said. "Lieutenant Portet will now critique our little operation. Lieutenant, will you please stand up and face the men?"

Jack, feeling very awkward, got to his feet and looked at fifteen black, scornful, unfriendly faces.

"We are now going to play truth or consequences," Lunsford said. "And we will start with Lieutenant Portet. Lieutenant, what is the first thing you think of when you hear Sergeant Thomas attempt to speak Swahili?"

Jack looked at Thomas and was horrified to hear himself blurt, "He sounds like a white man."

That was too much for Master Sergeant Thomas.

"With all respect, Lieutenant, I think I learned my Swahili the same way you learned yours, from a missionary."

"At the Presidio, you mean, Sergeant Thomas?" Lunsford asked sympathetically.

The Army Language School was at the Presidio, in San Francisco, California.

"Yes, sir," Thomas said righteously. "The instructor told us he learned Swahili as a missionary in the Congo."

"All those who remember what I said to you the first time we met about 'never trust anyone,' and 'always remember that things are very seldom what they first appear to be,' raise your hands," Lunsford said.

One by one, fourteen soldiers, feeling like schoolchildren, raised their hands.

"You don't remember me saying that, Sergeant Thomas?" Lunsford asked.

Sergeant Thomas raised his hand.

"You may now lower your hands," Lunsford said.

There were some smiles as they did so.

"Since you all obviously need it, I will now prove that you should never trust anyone," Lunsford said. "I told Sergeant Thomas that Lieutenant Portet was studying to be a missionary, and that he learned how to speak Swahili in the Florida Baptist College. I lied."

He let that sink in a moment.

"He is not, in other words, what he appears to be. I happen to know his teacher, and she assures me that Lieutenant Portet speaks Swahili, and several other Congolese dialects, as well as anyone born and raised there. Lieutenant Portet wasn't born there, but he was raised there. He learned how to speak Swahili at the knee of the toughest black lady I have ever met. Her name is Mary Magdalene Lotetse. She's got three inches and fifty pounds on Sergeant Thomas, and if she says Lieutenant Portet's Swahili is perfect, I am not about to argue with her. But just for the record, I know his Swahili is better than mine."

He let that sink in for a moment.

"Is there among this band of would-be warriors, Lieutenant Portet, in your judgment, any one who would not be spotted as a tool of the Imperialist Devils — the prize for which, gentlemen, is having your head sliced open, or off, on the spot, with a dull machete — the minute he opened his mouth in the woods around Stanleyville?"

Two of the men had spoken surprisingly good Congolese, and Jack found their faces. He could not recall their names, but that didn't matter, he realized with relief, because Lunsford had said they were all at least sergeants.

"The sergeant there, sir," Jack said, pointing. "And the sergeant there, sir. They could, with a little luck, pass themselves off as Congolese."

"Let the record show the witness identified Sergeant First Class DeGrew," Lunsford said. "And Staff Sergeant Williams. Try to remember their names, Lieutenant. I know all we Negroes look alike to you honkies, but if you're going to be with us, I would appreciate it if you would try to learn people's names."

Now there were a number of smiles. *The major's giving it to the lieutenant, too.*

"Sergeant DeGrew and Sergeant Williams, you have an additional duty from this moment forward," Lunsford said. "Every time, and I mean every time, you hear anyone — including our beloved Master Sergeant Thomas — saying anything wrong in Swahili, you will not only correct him on the spot, but make him repeat it and repeat it for however long it takes until he's got it right. Clear?"

213

"Yes, sir," Williams and DeGrew said in unison.

"The U.S. government has invested a lot of my tax dollars in you people," Lunsford said. "And I don't want it flushed down the toilet, as it would be if you're running around the bush, open your mouth to some bona fide African, and he says, 'Hey, that brother speaks Congolese like a honky' or words to that effect, and cuts your stupid head off. Clear?"

There were shrugs of acknowledgment, admitting the logic behind Lunsford's orders.

"And now another show of hands, please. If I announced that this honky airplane driver wants to join our little private army, but that I was leaving it up to you, how many of you would vote to take him?"

After a long pause, one hand went up, and it was evident from the look on his face that he had done it to get a laugh. He got it.

"And I was just starting to hope that maybe at least of couple of you weren't as stupid as you look," Lunsford said.

He waited until that had time to settle in, then went on.

"Let me set the scene for you. You are a Belgian paratrooper. You have just landed in Stanleyville, where some really nasty people have been practicing cannibalism on white people, possibly including your relatives. You go to the apartment house where you hope your relatives are. There are dead white people all over the lawn, and in the elevators. You break into your apartment, and there is this barefoot black guy in a Belgian officer's tunic, a leopard skin, and shorts. And, of course, holding a gun. You'd blow the motherfucker away, right?"

There were no smiles now.

"Teeter?" Lunsford said, pointing to one of them.

"Yes, sir, that's what I'd do."

"Anybody who wouldn't blow the motherfucker away, raise your hand."

No hand raised.

"Well, lucky for me — I was the black guy in the Simba suit — that paratrooper thought before he pulled the trigger. Lucky for me, that Belgian paratrooper had control of himself under pressure. I don't think I would have had that control myself. That Belgian paratrooper did."

"You're talking about the lieutenant, aren't you, sir?" Master Sergeant Thomas said. "We heard that an American jumped with the Belgians. . . ."

Lunsford didn't reply.

"Anybody who wants to change his mind about the lieutenant," Sergeant Thomas said, "raise your hand."

His hand rose.

"Jesus, Major, how were we supposed to know?" one of them asked as his hand went up.

"You were supposed to think," Lunsford said. "The only way you're going to stay alive is if you think."

Lunsford waited until they all had raised their hands.

"Enough with the hands bullshit," he said. "You all look ridiculous. And this is the Army — we don't take votes."

Now there was laughter.

"From this moment, Lieutenant Portet is our resident expert," Lunsford said. "If he says some-

215

thing, you treat it like it came from me. I just hope you're smart enough to understand how lucky we are to have him." He paused. "One more thing. If one of you runs off at the mouth and repeats what I said about Lieutenant Portet being the American who jumped on Stanleyville, I'll feed him his balls."

He paused.

"You have anything else, Lieutenant?"

"There's just one problem, sir. There's a lot of beer in that building that's going to get warm unless someone starts to drink it."

"So there is," Lunsford said. "Okay, what happens now is that you will form a line, walk past Lieutenant Portet, state your name, and say that you are happy to meet him, or words to that effect. With a little bit of luck, he'll remember them the next time you see him."

One by one, they filed past Jack and shook his hand, and said they were happy to meet him, or words to that effect. Jack had the feeling they meant it.

"If you've got something on your mind, Jack, say it," Lunsford said as they were riding from Pope Air Force Base to the Main PX at Fort Bragg.

"Although there was a lot of bullshit in that session," Jack said, "it was masterful."

"But?"

"I'm not the heroic, calm-under-pressure officer you made me out to be, and you know it."

"Neither am I heroic, or calm under pressure. The trick is not letting the troops find out."

"I don't know if I can pull that off."

"You can if you try. I've been doing it for years.

216

You owe it to the troops, Jack, to make them think you're something special. They need to think their officers are something special. And you're an officer now."

Jack shrugged uncomfortably.

"And speaking of the troops, you owe me . . . three times two ninety-eight is eight ninety-six, divided by two is four forty-eight. You owe me four dollars and forty-eight cents, and I would like it now, please."

"What for?"

"Your share of the beer."

VI

[ONE]
123 Brookwood Lane
Ozark, Alabama
1550 20 December 1964

"Good, she's home," Marjorie Bellmon said aloud when she saw Liza Wood's Buick station wagon in the carport.

She turned the Jaguar off the street and drove up the drive.

Liza, a tall, lithe, strikingly beautiful twenty-four-year-old who wore her flamboyantly red hair in a pageboy, was in the carport, stuffing bags into a garbage can.

When she saw Marjorie, she smiled and walked up to the car.

"Hi," Marjorie said.

"It must be love. He's letting you drive his Jaguar," Liza said.

"I had to take it to the provost marshal's to get him a temporary sticker for it," Marjorie said, and added, "a blue sticker."

"A blue sticker? What's that all about?" She didn't give Marjorie time to reply before adding, "It'll wait until we get in the house. It's cold out here."

She opened the kitchen door for Marjorie, who walked in.

A small boy ran to her and wrapped his

arms around her leg.

"M'Jeri," he cried happily in his best, if failing, attempt to say her name.

Marjorie scooped him up.

"Hello, handsome," she said. "Where in the world have you and Mommy been? Aunt *Mar-jor-ee* has been looking *all over* for you."

She looked at Liza as she spoke.

"I'm about to have a drink," Liza said. "You want one?"

Marjorie thought it over for a moment.

"Yeah, why not? What are you offering?"

"Whatever you'd like. I'm going to have a Bloody Mary."

"Sounds fine," Marjorie said. "Where the *hell* have you been?"

"Skiing in Colorado."

"For three weeks? Your mother-in-law wouldn't tell me where you were."

"I told her not to tell anyone," Liza said. "Tell me about the blue sticker."

"I heard about you and Johnny," Marjorie said. "I'm sorry."

"I wanted to get away from here, and I suppose in the back of my mind, there was the hope that I would find some handsome stud by the fireplace in the ski lodge, who would take my mind off the goddamned army."

"The goddamned army, or Johnny?"

"Both."

"And?"

"I wouldn't want this spread around, it would ruin my reputation, but when it came to the nitty-gritty, I decided there had to be a better way to get my act together than letting some moronic sun-tanned ski bum into my pants."

"And is your act together?"

"God, I hope so. Tell me about the blue sticker."

"Bmari," Allan said. "Bmari, bmari!"

Liza handed him a glass with red liquid in it.

"No booze, of course," Liza said. "But he likes it, Tabasco and all. I live in fear I'm going to give him the wrong glass sometime."

She handed Marjorie a Bloody Mary.

"There is gin in there, so make sure he doesn't pick it up. Now, what about the blue sticker? The *temporary* blue sticker, I think you said."

"Did they have newspapers where you were?"

"No, they communicate with tom-toms and smoke signals out there. Blue sticker?"

"Then you read about what happened at Stanleyville?"

"Sure. God, that was terrible. They were actually . . . cannibals."

"Specifically, did you see the picture of the Belgian paratrooper carrying the little girl in his arms?"

Liza searched her memory.

"Yeah, I did. It looked like he'd been shot in the nose."

"He wasn't shot in the nose. He fell off a truck. That was Jack."

"I have the strangest feeling that you're not pulling my leg," Liza said after a long moment.

"Girl Scout's Honor," Marjorie said. "Cross my heart and hope to die, et cetera."

"What the hell was he doing in Africa?" Liza asked.

"He wasn't supposed to jump with the Belgians, but he did anyway. The Belgians are going to give him a medal."

Liza shook her head.

"And we're going to get married," Marjorie said.

"That's even worse news," Liza said. "Sorry, I shouldn't have said that."

"No, you shouldn't have," Marjorie agreed. "And he came back, and I drove to Bragg to see him, and he proposed in words I will remember to my dying day. *'Screw your job,'* my knight in shining armor said, *'let's get married.'* "

Liza smiled at her.

"And you apparently were overwhelmed by the eloquence and said 'yes.' "

"Yeah," Marjorie said.

"Well, you're obviously happy about it, so I'm happy for you. And he's an officer now, with his own blue sticker?"

"Yeah," Marjorie said, and chuckled. "First lieutenant. Bobby had to pin his insignia on for him. He didn't know how."

"First lieutenant? That ought to make things easier for you at home."

"And I want you to be my maid of honor."

"I don't think so, honey."

"Why not?"

"He whose name I have sworn never again to say out loud, your daddy's dog-robber, will be there, right?"

"What's that got to do with anything?"

"Let me pass, Marjorie, please," Liza said.

"That's an admission you *don't* have your act together," Marjorie accused. "You still love him."

"I didn't say I don't love the sonofabitch," Liza said. "I said I wasn't going to go through the pain of losing a husband again, or, worse, put Allan through something like that. I gave him the choice, the Army, or Allan and me, and it wasn't Allan and me."

Marjorie didn't reply.

"I don't want to be a camp follower, Marjorie. And there's no reason we have to be. You heard about the money he got from his father's estate?"

"Not in much detail," Marjorie said. "I overheard Craig Lowell tell my father that his sister and brother-in-law had tried to cheat him."

"They did. And didn't get away with it. Jack came out of that with two million three hundred twenty thousand dollars. And change."

"I had no idea it was that much," Marjorie said.

"It would have been more, if he had been willing to stick her the way she tried to stick him. But he's an officer and a gentleman, and he wanted 'to be fair.' "

"That's hardly a character flaw," Marjorie said.

"With that kind of money, and with what I've got, we could have really built a life for ourselves. I'd have done anything he wanted, the whole 'whither thou goest' routine, as long as it wasn't someplace the Army could find him and send him off somewhere to get killed."

"My father spent his entire life in the Army, and he's alive," Marjorie said.

"And all her life, your mother worried herself sick that he would be," Liza said. "I've been down that road. You're about to start down it yourself. I don't have that kind of strength. Not an opinion. A fact. I waited for Allan to come back, I prayed — my God, how I prayed — that he would come back. And he did. In a casket. And I damned near died. I'm not going to go through that again, because I know I couldn't handle it again."

They looked at each other a moment.

"We're on opposite sides on this one, Marjorie," Liza said. "I hope the same thing doesn't happen to you. I'll pray that it doesn't happen to you, but thank you just the same, I'll pass on being your matron of honor."

"You don't have to talk to him," Marjorie said. "All you have to do is be there for me. You're the best friend I've ever had."

Liza looked at her and raised her empty glass.

"You want another one of these?"

"I'm not half through with this one," Marjorie said.

"But you don't mind if I do, right?" Liza said, and went to the counter to fix herself another drink.

"Not so long as you don't get plastered and give Allan one with gin in it," Marjorie said, and then, very softly, "Please, Liza?"

Liza didn't reply until she had made herself a fresh drink and walked up to Marjorie.

"It would be understood that I wouldn't try to talk to the sonofabitch, right? And that nobody tries 'to fix things'?"

"Deal," Marjorie said.

"Okay, then. Tell me all the giddy details."

[TWO]
Flight Planning
Base Operations
Pope Air Force Base, North Carolina
0730 21 December 1964

"You check the weather, Lieutenant?" Major Pappy Hodges said when he walked up to Jack, who

223

was laying out an IFR course to return to Fort Rucker.

"Yes, sir."

"And?"

"Couldn't be any better, sir," Jack said.

"What is that you're doing, Lieutenant?"

"Preparing an IFR flight plan for your approval, sir."

"Usually, when I'm going from here to Rucker, I head catty-cornered across South Carolina until I find Aiken or North Augusta, or maybe Bamberg for a piss and fuel stop, then cut across Georgia to Fort Benning, and then fly down the river until I start recognizing the local area around Rucker. Do you think you could do that without flying us into the ground?"

"Yes, sir, I think I can handle that."

"Doing it that way will be quicker than going IFR, so file a VFR to Bamberg," Hodges ordered. "You can change it en route, if we're closer to North Augusta."

"Yes, sir."

"If I didn't mention this before, Lieutenant Portet, you have successfully completed your check ride in cross-country flight using instrument flight rules."

"Thank you, sir."

"And since you came back from the boonies, you have also successfully completed your check ride in landing on unimproved strips."

"Thank you, sir."

"You see anything interesting out there?"

Jack hesitated.

"You can tell me, Lieutenant," Hodges said. "As I am now, goddamn it, possessed of a Top Secret/Earnest security clearance."

"Father's training a dozen or so guys, black guys, out there to go to the Congo. A couple of them speak pretty good Swahili."

"Felter's fucking him, too, after what he went through, to get him involved over there again so soon."

"I don't think he minds," Jack said. "He seemed happy doing what he was doing. And Jesus, did I get a lesson in leadership."

"Meaning what?"

"All these guys are Green Berets, tough and smart, and here comes a honky airplane driver."

"That must have been interesting," Pappy said, smiling.

"By the time Father was through with them, he had them believing I was John Wayne, and the best thing that happened to them this year. Christ, it was masterful!"

"Just so long as you don't start believing it," Pappy said. Then he added, thoughtfully, "There's a very few guys — a very few — around who are natural leaders. Father's one of them."

"Yeah," Jack said, and took a chance. "You learn anything interesting?"

"You're not supposed to ask questions, Lieutenant, you know that."

"Sorry, sir."

"Felter's going to Germany, but he'll be back in time for your wedding," Pappy said. "And as soon as I can do it, I'm to get you checked out in the L-23. Then you and I are going to go out to Wichita, Kansas, and pick one up from the factory. We'll ferry it back to Rucker, where it will be equipped with the navigation equipment — and maybe auxiliary fuel tanks — necessary for a flight to Buenos Aires, Argentina, and subsequent service in what Felter calls 'the Southern Cone of South America.' "

"Buenos Aires? What the hell is that all about?"

"You're not supposed to ask questions, Pappy, you know that," Pappy said, in a perfect mimicry of Felter's New York accent.

Jack smiled at him.

"Craig Lowell's probably involved in this somehow," Pappy said. "He's going to Germany with Felter." He paused, then, making it clear the subject of the their conversation had changed, asked, "I don't suppose you have any Beaver time, do you, Jack?"

"I've got about eight hours in one," Jack replied. "DeHavilland really tried to sell them in Africa; they loaned us one for two weeks, even paid for the fuel. They're great little airplanes, but the distances in the Congo didn't make them practical for us."

"That's next on your agenda," Pappy said. "When we get to Rucker, I'll give you an hour or so in ours, then arrange for someone to give you a check ride in the morning. Then from the Beaver to the Otter, and then the L-23."

"Yes, sir."

"Let's get this show on the road, Lieutenant," Pappy said.

"Yes, sir."

As he climbed out of Pope, Jack turned and looked in the backseat and saw that Pappy was already asleep with his head resting on the pillow he had brought with him.

THREE

SECRET

Central Intelligence Agency
Langley, Virginia

FROM: Assistant Director For Administration

DATE: 20 December 1964 2305 GMT

SUBJECT: Guevara, Ernesto (Memorandum # 4.)

TO: Mr. Sanford T. Felter
Counselor To The President
Room 637, The Executive Office Building
Washington, D.C.

By Courier

In compliance with Presidential Memorandum to The Director, Subject: "Ernesto 'Che' Guevara," dated 14 December 1964, the following information is furnished:

(1) (Reliability Scale Five) (From CIA, Algiers, Algeria) SUBJECT met 1600-1825 GMT 19 December 1964 with Ben Bella, Chief of State of the Algerian Government at the Presidential Palace. No official announcement of the meeting was made.

(2) (Reliability Scale Five). SUBJECT at 1905 GMT 19 December 1964 returned to

residence of Cuban Ambassador. There have been many visitors to the residence, identities are being developed.

Howard W. O'Connor
HOWARD W. O'CONNOR

SECRET

[FOUR]

The Southern Star, Ozark, Alabama, 23 December 1964:

MISS MARJORIE BELLMON MARRIES

By Joe Adams

Fort Rucker Dec 23 — Miss Marjorie W. Bellmon, of Fort Rucker, was united in marriage this afternoon to First Lieutenant Jacques E. Portet, in an Episcopal Ceremony at Chapel Number One at Fort Rucker.

The bride, a graduate of Southern Methodist University, is the daughter of Major General and Mrs. Robert F. Bellmon. General Bellmon is the Commanding General of Fort Rucker and the Army Aviation Center. Prior to her marriage, she was employed by the First National Bank of Ozark.

Lieutenant Portet, a graduate of the Free University of Brussels (Belgium), is the son of Mr. and Mrs. J. P. Portet of Ocean Reef, Florida. He is stationed at Fort Bragg, N.C.

The bride was attended by Mrs. Allan Wood, of Ozark, as her matron of honor, and the groom's sister, Jeanine Portet, served as flower girl. Miss Bellmon was given in marriage by her father. Mr. Portet served as his son's best man. Mrs. John D. Roberts, of Ozark, sang "I Love You Truly" during the ceremony. The organist was Mrs. Nancy Higham, of Ozark.

The newly united couple left the chapel beneath an arc of sabers, following military tradition. The saber bearers were commanded by Captain John S. Oliver of Fort Rucker.

A reception followed at the Fort Rucker Officers' Open Mess. Following a wedding trip to Florida, the couple will reside in Fort Bragg, N.C.

The Army Flier, Fort Rucker, Ala., 23 December 1964:

COMMANDING GENERAL'S DAUGHTER MARRIES

By PFC Charles E. Whaley

Fort Rucker 23 Dec — Miss Marjorie Waterford Bellmon, daughter of Fort Rucker Commanding General and Mrs. Robert F. Bellmon was married this afternoon at Chapel #1 in a ceremony conducted by Chaplain (Col.) H. Dennis Smythe to First Lieutenant J.E. Portet, Inf.

Major General Bellmon gave the bride in marriage, and her brother, Second Lieutenant Robert F. Bellmon, Armor (USMA '64), served as an usher. Miss Bellmon was attended by Mrs. Allan Wood as her matron of honor.

Captain Jean-Philippe Portet, who "flew the Hump" in the China-Burma-India Theater as a Captain, US Army Air Corps, during World War II, and is now Chief Pilot of Air Simba, the state airline of the former Belgian Congo, served as Lieutenant Portet's best man.

Major General Bellmon (USMA '39) is the son of the late Major General and Mrs. Herbert Bellmon, USA, and Mrs. Bellmon is the daughter of the late Major General and Mrs. Porterman K. Waterford, USA. Her brother, Brig Gen Porterman K. Waterford IV (USMA '42), is Commandant of Cadets at the US Military Academy, West Point, N.Y.

First Lieutenant Portet, who is an Army Aviator and Parachutist, is qualified in multi-engine aircraft, and holds a Special Instrument Rating. He has also completed Special Forces ("Green Beret") training. He is assigned as an Aviation Officer on the staff of the Commanding General, at the John F. Kennedy Center for Special Warfare, Fort Bragg, N.C.

Following the nuptial ceremony, 1st Lt and Mrs. Portet exited the chapel beneath an arc of swords. The honor platoon of officers was commanded by Captain John S. Oliver, Armor, until recently aide-de-camp to Major General Bellmon.

A reception was held at the Fort Rucker Officers' Open Mess, following which First Lieutenant and Mrs. Portet departed for a wedding trip to Florida. They will reside at Fort Bragg, N.C.

Mrs. Liza Wood did not speak to Captain John S. Oliver during the wedding rehearsal, nor the wedding dinner, nor during the wedding itself, and she did not attend the reception.

[FIVE]
Room 1105
Ocean Breeze Motel
Panama City, Florida
0845 24 December 1964

Mrs. Jacques Emile Portet leaned over her husband, who was asleep on his back, took his nipple between her fingers, and pinched it.

"*Mon Dieu!*" he yelped, and sat up. "What the hell was that all about?"

"Oh, I *like* it when you talk French!" she said. "Good morning, husband. Sleep well?"

"Oh, yeah. And you obviously have something against that?"

"No, not at all," Marjorie said. "But now that we are married, and that marriage has been duly — and I must say well — consummated . . ."

"Thank you very much. Be sure to tell your friends."

"We have to talk, and the way you looked, you were going to sleep until noon."

"Talk about what?"

"What happens now."

231

"I think the plan was to get up, have breakfast, and take off for Ocean Reef."

"I mean, after Ocean Reef."

"We go back to Rucker. I have to be there January second — but, as we discussed, wife, we could go back in time for New Year's Eve at the club, if that is your desire."

"Then?"

"Then Pappy and I go out to Wichita and pick up an L-23 at the Beechcraft plant, which I will then fly back to Rucker. I will then stand around the SCATSA hangar and watch them do whatever they're going to do with the L-23. And when they've finished doing whatever they're going to do with the L-23, I will take it to Bragg, while my bride drives the family Jaguar up there."

" 'Family Jaguar'? Didn't I hear you say, before God and a chapel full of people, that you were about to endow me with all your worldly goods?"

"I wasn't thinking about my Jaguar when I made that promise," he said. He paused. "But if you want the jag, baby, it's yours. Wedding present. And if driving it up there bothers you, honey, I could deliver the L-23 up there, catch a commercial flight back to Rucker, and we could drive up there together, in your Jaguar."

"You do understand I was pulling your leg?"

"I don't know. I don't have much experience dealing with a wife."

"So far, you're doing very well," she said. "And now that I've had a chance to think about it, I sort of like the sound of 'family Jaguar.' "

"Whatever I have is yours, baby," Jack said.

She lowered her face to his and kissed him, at first very tenderly.

Five minutes later, lying with her face against his chest, she asked:

"What's that all about?"

"What's what all about?"

"The L-23."

"I don't really know," he said.

"You don't really know, or it's classified, and you don't think you can tell me?"

"I'm sure it's classified," he said. "Everything around Colonel Felter seems to be classified Top Secret."

"First reminding you that your wife is not some airhead you picked up in a honky-tonk outside the gate, but a fifth-generation Army brat who knows all about security classifications, and is not going to say anything about anything to anybody, are you going to tell me or not?"

"I wondered about that," he said seriously. "Every time they tell you a secret, the usual line is 'This goes no further, and that includes your wife.' And I wondered how I would handle that with you."

"And?"

"And, I figured, fuck it, I'll tell her everything."

"I don't like the language, but I approve of the decision," she said.

"Sorry."

"So what's with the L-23?"

"I really don't know. It's a Felter operation. He told Pappy to pick up the airplane at Beech, take it to SCATSA — what the hell is SCATSA, anyway?"

"It stands for Signal Corps Aviation Test and Support Activity," Marjorie said. "It's not under Fort Rucker. It's what they call a Class II activity;

233

it takes its orders from the chief signal officer. Among other things, it provides avionic support to the Aviation Test Board and Combat Developments. And this won't be the first nobody-talks-about-it job they've done for Uncle Sandy. You don't know what they're going to do to it?"

"Equip it with navigation equipment, and maybe auxiliary fuel tanks so that it can be ferried to Argentina and used there."

"What's that got to do with you? Which raises the question: What are you going to be doing at Fort Bragg?"

"I can't imagine how it will have anything to do with me. I think all I'm going to do is fly it up there. Felter probably has some other iron in the fire. And what I'm going to be doing at Bragg has its own security clearance. Top Secret Slash Earnest. Felter found out somewhere that Che Guevara — Ernesto Guevara, hence Earnest — is going to try to cause trouble in the Congo. And we're going to stop him."

"I don't think I like the sound of that," Marjorie said. "You're going back over there? When?"

"Now you're going to be told stuff I was expressly ordered not to tell anyone," Jack said. "Father Lunsford — the guy who went to the Immoquateur in Stanleyville to try to help my stepmother —"

"I know who he is," Marjorie interrupted.

"— is putting together a team of black Green Berets to go to the Congo to screw up Guevara. I'm going to help him do that, teach them about the Congo, try to teach them how to pass themselves off as Congolese, that sort of thing."

"You're not going to the Congo?"

"I'll probably go over there with them when

234

they're ready, to introduce them to people who can help them, but if the question is 'Are you going to be involved in their operation,' no, I don't think so. Too many questions would be asked. Felter is determined that our operation there be invisible."

"So we'll be at Bragg together for a while?"

"Yeah, I think so. Did I tell you that Father found us an apartment?"

"No. But why should you tell me? What could be less important than where we're going to live?"

"Father said the lieutenant's family quarters at Bragg are pretty crummy, so, if I can afford it, he can get me permission to live off post, in an apartment complex, where he lives — and where Johnny Oliver is going to live with him. So I told him, 'Yes, please, I can afford it.' "

"Write this down, husband," Marjorie said. "What you should have said was 'Thank you very much, Major. I'll ask Marjorie and get back to you.' "

"Honey, I didn't think. You don't like the idea?"

"I don't like the idea that you didn't ask me," she said.

"Hey, baby. This is all new to me."

"I'm trying to remember that."

"Look, unless you've got your heart set on Ocean Reef, we could go from here to Bragg, you could look the apartment over. . . ."

"No, that would hurt Craig's feelings," she said. "We have to go to Ocean Reef."

"Up to you," he said.

"Now you're learning," she said.

She got out of bed and walked naked to the bathroom.

"I'm for a shower," she said. "And then we'll get on the road."

"Leave the water running," he said.

"Better yet, how about you wash mine, and I'll wash yours?"

[SIX]
Office of the Army Attaché
United States Embassy
Sarmiento 663
Palermo, Buenos Aires, Argentina
1445 24 December 1964

Colonel Richard J. Harris, Jr., Infantry, the tall, slim, forty-two-year old army attaché of the United States Embassy, looked up from his desk and inquired of Master Sergeant Douglas Wilson, his thirty-six-year-old rather chubby chief clerk (who as a courtesy was referred to as the "sergeant major"):

"What have you got, Doug?"

Both were in civilian clothing, Harris in a well-cut poplin suit, and Wilson in a seersucker jacket and khaki — civilian khaki — trousers. Perón was gone, but there was still a good deal of leftover anti-American feeling in the Argentine capital, and uniforms were worn only when they were necessary. And poplin and seersucker because December in Argentina is the beginning of summer.

"This just came in," Wilson said, "and if I'm reading this right, boss, Santa Claus is being very good to us this year."

He handed a sheet of teletype paper to Colonel Harris.

HQ DEPT OF THE ARMY WASH DC 1305 22
DEC 1964

ROUTINE
CONFIDENTIAL

TO: ASSISTANT CHIEF OF STAFF FOR
PERSONNEL, HQ DEPT OF THE ARMY
ASSISTANT CHIEF OF STAFF FOR LOGISTICS,
HQ DEPT OF THE ARMY
INFO: US ARMY ATTACHÉ US EMBASSY
BUENOS AIRES ARGENTINA

REFERENCE IS MADE TO "SPECIAL TABLE OF
ORGANIZATION AND EQUIPMENT, OFFICE
OF ARMY ATTACHÉ US EMBASSY, BUENOS
AIRES ARGENTINA" AS APPROVED 15
SEPTEMBER 1964.

(1) REFERENCED TO&E IS AMENDED AS
FOLLOWS:

SECTION 13A COMMISSIONED AND
WARRANT OFFICERS IS AMENDED TO ADD 1
(ONE) CAPT OR LT BRANCH IMMATERIAL
MULTI-ENGINE FIXED-WING INSTRUMENT
QUALIFIED ARMY AVIATOR AND 1 (ONE)
WARRANT OFFICER GRADE IMMATERIAL
MULTI-ENGINE FIXED WING INSTRUMENT
QUALIFIED ARMY AVIATOR.

SECTION 13B ENLISTED PERSONNEL IS
AMENDED TO ADD ONE MASTER SERGEANT
OR SERGEANT FIRST CLASS QUALIFIED AS

CREW CHIEF L-23 SERIES AIRCRAFT; ONE SERGEANT FIRST CLASS OR STAFF SERGEANT QUALIFIED AS AIRCRAFT AND ENGINE MECHANIC L-23 SERIES AIRCRAFT AND ONE SERGEANT FIRST CLASS OR STAFF SERGEANT QUALIFIED AS DEPOT LEVEL AVIONICS TECHNICIAN.

SECTION 19 SPECIAL EQUIPMENT IS AMENDED TO ADD 1 (ONE) L-23 SERIES AIRCRAFT.

(2) DCSLOG AND DCSPERS WILL EXPEDITE THE IMPLEMENTATION OF THE AMENDED TO&E. PRIORITY AAAA-1 IS ASSIGNED. DIRECT COMMUNICATION WITH US ARMY ATTACHÉ BUENOS AIRES IS AUTHORIZED TO DETERMINE AND PROVIDE NECESSARY SUPPORT. DCSLOG WILL MAKE EVERY EFFORT TO ENSURE THAT OFFICER AND ENLISTED PERSONNEL ASSIGNED WILL POSSESS KNOWLEDGE OF THE SPANISH LANGUAGE. A WEEKLY REPORT OF PROGRESS WILL BE FURNISHED TO THE OFFICE OF THE CHIEF OF STAFF.

FOR THE CHIEF OF STAFF, US ARMY

CHARLES M. SCOTT, JR.
LT GEN US ARMY
DEPUTY CHIEF OF STAFF

"I will be damned," Colonel Harris said. "When I asked for a Beaver, they as much as laughed at me."

"I remember," Master Sergeant Wilson said.

"If something is too good to be true, it usually is," Harris said.

"You want me to get on the horn and see if I can find out anything?"

"No. It's Christmas Eve, and nobody who knows anything will be working in the Pentagon anyhow. We'll wait a couple of days, at least until 2 January, and then if we don't hear anything more, we can give them a call."

"Yes, sir."

"At the risk of repeating myself, it's Christmas Eve. Why don't you take off?"

"Yes, sir. Thank you, Colonel. Merry Christmas, sir."

"Same to you," Colonel Harris said, getting out of his chair to shake Wilson's hand.

When the sergeant had gone, Harris started to sit down again, but changed his mind, picked up the teletype message, and walked down the third-floor corridor to the office of Colonel H. Robert McGrory, USAF, the defense attaché of the U.S. Embassy.

He already had a difficult relationship with Colonel McGrory, and he suspected the L-23 was going to make it worse.

Buenos Aires was an "air force post." That is to say, the defense attaché was always an air force officer, and the army and navy officers, called the "army attaché" and the "naval attaché," were subordinate to him. Other embassies were "army posts," or "naval posts," and the defense attaché was an army officer or a navy officer.

Harris had no idea where the stupid idea had started, but he knew there was nothing he could do about it, so he tried to live with it as best he could. Which was difficult for a number of reasons, starting with the fact that Colonel Bob McGrory, who had spent most of his career driving airplanes, knew very little about anything else.

He spent most of his lunches, and the afternoons following, in the Argentine air force officers' club, where he regaled his Argentine peers with flying stories, which he could afford to do because he delegated just about all of his duties to Colonel Richard J. Harris, Jr., the army attaché, and Captain Sam Duckworth, USN, the naval attaché.

The problem was further compounded by seniority. Harris outranked McGrory by more than a year. Harris had been asked, when offered the Argentine assignment, if he could deal with that, and almost without thinking about it, had said it would pose no problem.

Certainly, there would be little problem between two officers with nearly thirty years of service simply because one of them outranked the other. And Harris had wanted to come to Buenos Aires because he thought he could do some good in the assignment, build a relationship between the Argentine officer corps and the American, among other things.

But McGrory, who was led around by the nose by his wife, had made it very clear from the beginning that he regarded Dick Harris and Sam Duckworth as not only subordinate officers on his staff, but junior officers. And Mrs. Constance McGrory held the belief that she was in command of the military and naval ladies.

Joanne Harris had put up with that for a while, but had finally told Constance McGrory where to head in, about which Constance had complained to Bob. Bob McGrory had called Harris in for a little chat, during which — to his lasting chagrin — Harris had lost his temper.

McGrory had referred to Constance as the "senior military lady, deserving of more respect than your wife is apparently paying her," and that had pushed Harris over the edge.

"I don't think wives wear their husbands' rank, Bob, but if we're going to play that game, Joanne is the 'senior military lady,' as I'm the senior military officer attached to the embassy. I outrank you by a year, which means I can order you around, and I'm ordering you to keep your wife away from my wife."

From that moment on, it had been "Colonel Harris" and "Colonel McGrory" when they spoke, and Harris spoke to McGrory as little as possible.

But the assignment of an airplane to the embassy was clearly of legitimate interest to the defense attaché, and Dick Harris knew he had to tell the stupid sonofabitch about it.

The door to McGrory's office was open, and the defense attaché, who was in uniform, complete with attaché aiguillette, and of course wearing his wreath-starred command pilot's wings, was at his desk, reading the *Buenos Aires Herald*.

Harris debated, and decided against, knocking at his door.

I'm not a goddamn PFC.

"Have you got a minute for me, Colonel?" he called.

McGrory raised his eyes from the *Herald*.

"Come in, Colonel. What's on your mind?"

Harris walked in and laid the teletype on his desk.

241

McGrory read it.

"Why wasn't I advised of this previously?" McGrory asked when he had finished reading it.

"It was delivered to me ten minutes ago, Colonel."

"If there is to be an aircraft at this embassy, it should be an air force aircraft," McGrory said.

When Harris didn't reply, McGrory added: "Wouldn't you agree, Colonel? An air force aircraft for an air force post?"

"Colonel, I get my orders from the chief of staff of the U.S. Army. And I have never questioned one of his orders before, and I am not going to start now."

"I would hate to think, Colonel, that you have gone over my head with this," McGrory said.

"I don't know how it is in the air force, Colonel, but in the army we can't go over another officer's head unless he's senior."

"Be advised, Colonel," McGrory said, his face flushed, "that I intend to get to the bottom of this."

"I stand so advised," Harris said.

"Is there anything else, Colonel?" McGrory asked.

"I don't think so, Colonel," Harris said, and leaned over and took the teletype from McGrory's desk.

"I'd like a copy of that, Colonel," McGrory said. "If you don't mind."

"I'll get you one, Colonel," Harris said.

He walked to the door and turned around.

"There is one more thing, Colonel, now that I think of it."

"Which is?"

"Merry Christmas, Colonel McGrory," Colonel Harris said, and walked out of the office before McGrory could reply.

He was almost back at his own office when he had the thought *That dumb sonofabitch is right. This is an air force post. So how come I'm getting an army airplane, and army pilots and mechanics?*

What the hell *is this all about?*

[SEVEN]

SECRET

Central Intelligence Agency
Langley, Virginia

FROM: Assistant Director For Administration

DATE: 27 December 1964 1805 GMT

SUBJECT: Guevara, Ernesto (Memorandum # 5.)

TO: Mr. Sanford T. Felter
Counselor To The President
Room 637, The Executive Office Building
Washington, D.C.

By Courier

In compliance with Presidential Memorandum to The Director, Subject: "Ernesto 'Che' Guevara," dated 14 December 1964, the following information is furnished:

(1) (Reliability Scale Two) (From CIA sources in Bamako, Mali) SUBJECT met with

243

President Modibo KEITA of Mali at 1105 GMT 26 December 1964 for one hour and fifteen minutes. No details of their conversation or identities of other (if any) personnel attending are available.

(2) (Reliability Scale Four) SUBJECT held a press conference at 1605 GMT 26 December, during which he expressed his belief that Africans and Cubans have a common goal in defeating U.S. Imperialism.

Howard W. O'Connor
HOWARD W. O'CONNOR

[EIGHT]
Office of the Commander-in-Chief
The Army of Argentina
Edificio Libertador
Buenos Aires, Argentina
1015 Hours 28 December 1964

Lieutenant General Pascual Angel Pistarini, the commander-in-chief of the Argentine Army, was sitting behind his huge, ornately carved desk, his back turned to it, his glistening riding boots resting on the sill of the window of his ninth-floor office, sipping a coffee as he looked out over the River Plate.

Pistarini was a tall, slim, rather sharp-featured

man of forty-six. He had intelligent blue eyes (his maternal grandmother was German), and when he smiled — rarely — he displayed a set of teeth so perfect some people suspected they were not his. They were. He attributed this to his mother, who had listened to her mother, and fed all of her five children as much milk as possible, well into their teenage years. This was not common in Argentina, where most children went from their mother's breast to coffee, but Pistarini's children were fed cow's milk and they all had fine teeth.

What General Pistarini was thinking, when his aide-de-camp came into his office, was that he had made a serious error in agreeing to take the parade of the First Regiment of Cavalry — the Húsares de Pueyrredón; named after the Pampas *estanciero* who had turned two-hundred-odd gauchos into cavalrymen and run the English out of Buenos Aires — at Campo de Mayo that afternoon.

It was hot as hell, and humid, and after sitting for an hour or so on a horse in the afternoon sun, he was going to be sunburned, dehydrated, and his fresh-from-the-dry-cleaner's-uniform sweat-soaked.

There was nothing that could be done about it now, it was too late, and he consoled himself with thinking that it was his duty, as a cavalry officer, as former colonel commanding, and commander-in-chief.

"Mi general?" Teniente Coronel Ricardo Fosterwood, his aide-de-camp, called from the office door.

Pistarini waved him into the office without turning around or taking his boots off the windowsill.

"Mi general, el Coronel Stumpff is in the office, and asks to see you."

Colonel Hans-Friedrich Stumpff was the military attaché of the German embassy.

"Do I have an appointment with him?" Pistarini asked.

"No, sir."

"Can't you deal with him?"

"Sir, he apologizes for the intrusion, but says that it is important that he see you personally at your earliest convenience."

"Give me a minute, then send him in. *Bring* him in. And after three minutes, if he is still here, remind me of a meeting."

"Yes, sir."

Pistarini reluctantly took his boots off the windowsill, turned around, opened a drawer in his desk, put the coffee cup and saucer into it, and then opened one of the folders on his desk and pretended to read it.

"Mi general," Fosterwood announced, *"El Coronel* Stumpff."

Colonel Stumpff marched into the office, came to attention, and saluted.

He was in uniform. Pistarini privately thought the two-tone blue uniform of German officers made them look like pilots of some third-rate airline.

Pistarini returned the salute.

"Thank you for seeing me, *mi general,*" Stumpff said in Spanish.

"Always a pleasure to see you, Colonel," Pistarini replied, then, extending his hand, switched to German. *"Wie geht's, Hans?"*

The German was another inheritance from his maternal grandmother, who to her dying day proclaimed that German was the only language of precision, and that someone who did not speak German could not consider himself educated.

"Gut, und Sie?" Stumpff said, smiling, as he shook Pistarini's hand.

Then he reached into his briefcase and took from it a large manila envelope. He opened this and took from it a smaller, letter-size envelope and handed it to Pistarini.

"What have we here?" Pistarini asked.

"It was in this morning's diplomatic pouch, General," Stumpff said.

Pistarini tore open the crisp, expensive embossed envelope.

Schlöss Greiffenberg
Marburg an der Lahn

22 December 1964

Teniente General Don Pascual Angel
  Pistarini
Commander-in-Chief
Argentine Army
Edificio Libertador
Buenos Aires

By Hand of Officer Courier

My dear friend Pascual:

   I had the privilege of receiving here over the weekend my dear American friend Sanford T. Felter, and Lieutenant Colonel Craig W. Lowell, U.S. Army.

It came out that Colonel Lowell will shortly be visiting the military attaché of the U.S. Embassy in Buenos Aires, and I would regard it as a personal service if you would receive him while he was there, and perhaps even see that he has the opportunity to sample some of your magnificent Argentine beef.

Colonel Lowell, as you and me, is a Cavalry/Armor officer and very nearly as good a polo player as you are. I'm sure you will find that you have many interests in common.

With the warmest possible fraternal greetings, and my most sincere best wishes for a joyous Christmas and a happy and prosperous New Year,

Von Greiffenberg
Von Greiffenberg

Pistarini's eyebrows rose, and his lips pursed thoughtfully as he read the letter.

"It was very kind of you to bring me this, Hans," he said.

"Not at all, General."

"May I offer you cup of coffee?"

"I won't take any more of your valuable time, *mi General.*"

"Well, if I can't get you to change your mind, then *auf Wedersehn,* Hans," Pistarini said, putting out his hand.

Fosterwood showed Stumpff out of office and then returned. Pistarini held out the letter to him. Fosterwood read it.

"I don't believe I know this gentleman, Sir," he said.

"It would perhaps be a good idea, Ricardo, if you remembered that my good friend Lieutenant General Count Peter-Paul von Greiffenberg is the chief of West German intelligence. Sometimes knowing odd little facts like that can be useful."

Fosterwood flushed.

"Yes, sir."

"Call the American attaché — what's his name?"

"Colonel McGrory, sir."

"No. Not him. McGrory's that Irish Air Force idiot. The other one."

"Colonel Harris, sir. The American *army* attaché."

"Right. See when he expects this Colonel Lowell."

"Yes, sir."

"From today, any invitations to the American military will include Colonel Lowell."

"Yes, sir."

"Call the Círculo Militar and have them prepared to put Colonel Lowell in the best available of the general officer's suites."

"Yes, sir."

"And call SIDE and see what they have on Colonel Lowell, in addition to what you're going to find out for me by checking the U.S. Army Register." SIDE was the acronym of the Argentine Secret Intelligence Service.

"Yes, sir."

"And have the sergeant bring me another

249

coffee, would you, please?"

"Yes, sir. Sir, may I ask a question?"

"Certainly."

"Would it be helpful for me to know something about the other gentleman in the letter, Señor Felter?"

"It certainly would," Pistarini said. "I'll tell you all I know about him. He's an American, with obvious ties to the intelligence community, and with many high-placed friends around the world. That's it. That's all anyone seems to know about him."

"Central Intelligence Agency, sir?"

"I don't think so," Pistarini said. "I once had a conversation with a senior CIA official. The name Felter came up, and I was left with the distinct impression that he is cordially detested by the CIA."

"Perhaps that was disinformation, sir."

"I don't think so. My CIA official had too much to drink to try to be clever in that way. He really hates Señor Felter, whoever he is."

[NINE]
123 Brookwood Lane
Ozark, Alabama
1250 31 December 1964

"Boy," Liza Wood said as she opened the door to find Lieutenant and Mrs. Jacques Portet standing there, "that was a quick honeymoon."

"Jack has to report back on the second —"

"The second is Saturday," Liza interrupted.

"Yeah, I know," Marjorie said. "So we figured since we had to be here anyway, we'd go to the New Year's party at the officers' club —"

"On your *honeymoon?*" Liza interrupted incredulously.

"— so we drove up here, and are stopping here first, even before we get a motel and pick up Jack's dress blues at the uniform store, because we want you to go with us."

Liza motioned them into the kitchen without replying.

"You look like you could use a drink, Jack," she said.

"Thank you ever so kindly," Jack said.

Allan came running into the kitchen, looked up at Jack, and, visibly disappointed, asked, "Johnny?"

"Shit," Liza muttered, then squatted beside her son.

"Mommy's told you, darling, that Johnny had to go away, and that it will be a long time before we see him again."

"Shit," Allan said, kicked at her, and ran out of the room.

Liza looked at Marjorie and Jack but said nothing. She went to one of the cupboards and opened it.

"Scotch for you, Jack, right?"

"Please."

"Marjorie?"

"Why not? Thank you."

Liza made the drinks and handed them to them.

"Now, where were we? Oh, yeah. As I remember, there were three parts to your statement requiring a reply. First, there's absolutely no reason to get a motel. There's plenty of room here."

"We couldn't do that," Marjorie protested.

"Why not? The honeymoon's over, isn't it?"

"No, as a matter of fact, it's not. But I told my mother Jack and I would take a motel, and if she found out we were here with you, her feelings would be hurt."

"The invitation remains open," Liza said. "Statement two. Based on my own painful experience as an army wife, if the uniform place promised the uniform today, it won't be ready."

"I don't know," Marjorie said. "My mother said she would check on it. That may inspire them to keep their promise to have it ready."

"RHIP, right?" Liza asked, shaking her head.

"Excuse me?" Jack said.

"Rank Hath Its Privileges," Liza said.

"Really, is that what they say?" Jack said, amused.

"Boy, has he got a lot to learn," Liza said.

"He'll have a very good teacher," Marjorie said.

"And as to the third part of your statement, me going out to the club for New Year's, thank you very much, but I have made other plans."

"I don't believe that," Marjorie said flatly.

"Cross my heart, et cetera, et cetera," Liza said. "Not that I would go out there anyway, if I had nothing whatever planned for tonight."

"What are your *other* plans?" Marjorie pursued. "Sitting here by yourself?"

"Allan and I are going to walk through the back-yard to Ursula and Geoff's —"

"They're here?" Jack asked, surprised. "I thought they were going to Ocean Reef."

"I left a note under their door at Ocean Reef, saying we were coming here," Marjorie said.

"Geoff wanted to go down there," Liza said, "but gave in to Ursula when she said you two would probably want to be alone. Proving once again, I suppose, that no good deed ever goes unpunished." She paused and added, bitterly, "Jesus Christ!"

"I think I'm missing something here," Marjorie said.

"He whose name I am desperately trying to forget was always saying that," Liza said. She looked at Jack. "Geoff was looking for you, come to think of it. At least, he called me and asked if I had heard from you two."

He looked at her curiously. She pointed to the telephone and said, "six-four-eight-four."

"Just four digits?"

"Everything in Ozark is seven-seven-four," Liza said.

Jack took the handset from the wall-mounted cradle and dialed the number.

Geoff answered it on the third ring.

"Lieutenant Craig."

"Lieutenant Craig, sir, this is Lieutenant Portet, sir. I understand the lieutenant has been looking for me, sir."

Geoff was not amused.

"Jesus, Jack, you're going to have to get in the habit of letting people know where you are," he said.

"I'm on leave, on my honeymoon, for Christ's sake."

"Felter doesn't know the word," Geoff said. "Where are you?"

"In Liza's kitchen."

"Don't go anywhere," Geoff said, and hung up.

Two minutes later, he appeared at the kitchen door.

"Funny, you don't look exhausted," he said. "I

expected skin and bones, dark rings under your eyes, trembling limbs, the whole panoply of symptoms of sexual excess."

"Very funny, Geoff," Marjorie said, blushing.

"What the hell are you doing here?" Geoff asked.

"Marjorie wants to go to the New Year's Eve party at the O Club," said Jack. "I have to report back on Saturday."

"You really want to go out there? Why?"

Jack pointed at Marjorie.

Geoff shrugged.

"There's a term for unquestioned obedience to a wife like that that an officer and gentleman such as myself would not repeat in mixed company," he said, and handed Jack a sheet of pocket notebook paper.

Marjorie gave him the finger.

"Finton," Geoff said. "You better call him right now. He's been looking all over for you."

"Who's Finton?"

"The Bishop," Marjorie said. "The warrant officer who works for Sandy in Washington. I'm really starting not to like *Uncle Sandy*."

"You don't even know what he wants," Jack said. "Can I use the phone, Liza?"

"Get the charges, Jack," Marjorie said.

"Go in one of the bedrooms," Liza said. "If I'm liable to overhear anything I shouldn't."

Jack shook his head and reached for the telephone and dialed the number. It was answered on the second ring.

"Liberty 7-5686," a gentle female voice announced.

"Mr. Finton, please."

"May I ask who's calling?"

254

"My name is Portet."

"Oh, Lieutenant Portet, Mr. Finton will be so pleased. He's been looking all over for you. Just one moment, please."

Jack covered the microphone with his hand.

"A woman answered," he said.

"That's the nun," Marjorie said.

"The *nun?*" Liza asked in disbelief.

"She's really a nun," Marjorie said.

"This is Warrant Officer Finton," a male voice announced. "Lieutenant Portet?"

"Right."

"You're a hard man to find, Lieutenant," Finton said. "You really ought to let people know where you are."

"I was on my honeymoon," Jack said. "On leave."

"I know," Finton said. "I tried all the numbers in Ocean Reef, and the golf club, and the marina, and wherever else I could think of. Where are you now?"

Jack looked at Geoff.

"With Lieutenant Craig in Ozark."

"He told me he didn't know where you were."

"When he told you that, he didn't know. What's on your mind, Mr. Finton?"

"I have a message from the colonel for you. You got a pencil and paper?"

Jack saw there was a blackboard and chalk on the wall. He reached for the chalk.

"Yeah."

"Start. Enrico de la Santiago is in Room 24, BOQ 107, Hurlburt. Telephone Hurlburt Military 6674. I thought you would like to know. Happy New Year. Signature is S.T.F. End. Got that?"

255

"Six-six-seven-four?"

"Right."

"Got it," Jack said.

"What the colonel likes, Lieutenant, is for you to have at least three people on the list know where you are at all times. He didn't tell you that?"

"No, as a matter of fact, he didn't. What list?"

"The list of people on whatever project you're working on," Finton said. "Most people find it easier to let me or Mary Margaret know."

"Okay. Now I know."

"If you leave Craig's place, Lieutenant, let someone know where you'll be," Chief Warrant Officer Finton said, and hung up.

"Well?" Marjorie asked.

"A friend of mine, Enrico de la Santiago, is at Hurlburt," Jack said.

"Who's he?"

"He's a Cuban, used to be in the Cuban Air Force, used to work for us in Air Simba. He was in the Congo flying B-26s for the CIA."

"Oh, yeah," Geoff said. "I wonder what he's doing at Hurlburt?"

"I have no idea, but Hurlburt's no place to be spending New Year's Eve alone. His wife and kids are still in Cuba."

He looked thoughtful for a moment, then picked up the telephone again and dialed the Fort Rucker number.

"Major Hodges's quarters, please," he said when the operator came on the line. Pappy answered on the fifth ring, just as Jack was concluding he wasn't home.

"Hodges."

"Portet, sir."

"Are you aware that Finton's looking for you?"

"Yes, sir. I just talked to him."

"Why do I suspect I'm not going to like this call?"

"Major, could I get an airplane for a couple of hours this afternoon?"

"You're here?" Pappy asked, and then went on before Jack could reply. "Where do you want to go in an airplane?"

"Hurlburt," Jack said. "Finton gave me a message —"

"Who is Santiago, anyway?" Pappy interrupted. "I mean to you. Finton told me what he's been doing."

"He's an old friend. He used to fly with me at Air Simba."

"You want to go there and bring him here?"

"Yes, sir."

"Why not?" Pappy said. "Here's on the way."

"On the way to where, sir?"

"Bragg, where Felter wants you to fly Santiago on Saturday morning, just as soon as you report off leave. Okay. I'll call out there and have them get the L-23 ready. And I'll see you at 0700 Saturday."

"Yes, sir."

Hodges hung up, and Jack put the phone back in its cradle.

"Jack," Marjorie said. "My parents expect us at the club tonight."

"It's only an hour or so to Hurlburt," Jack said. "I'll be back in plenty of time."

"You don't even know if your friend is there, or will want to come here," Marjorie protested.

"He'll come," Jack said. "When you get us a

motel room, get another one for him."

"You're going to stay with me," Liza protested.

"And the Cuban can stay with us, and have some fun while you and the bride are out at the post playing Officers and Ladies. And sucking up to the brass."

"Go to hell, Geoff," Marjorie said.

"You want some company?" Geoff asked, ignoring her.

"Love some. Pappy gave me an L-23." He paused. "I better call and tell him we're coming," Jack said, and reached for the telephone again.

Three minutes later they were gone, in the Jaguar, Geoff having told Marjorie to tell Ursula he'd be back in a couple of hours, and to put clean sheets on a bed in one of the guest rooms.

"From the look on your face, Marjorie, my love, it is apparent that you have just realized the honeymoon is over," Liza said.

Marjorie didn't reply.

"Some women thrive on exciting little incidents like this," Liza said. "Where all well-laid plans are tossed out the window by a telephone call. They are called Good Army Wives. It's a little late to ask you if you're sure you want a life like that, but I will anyway."

"Jack did what he thought he had to do."

"That's always their excuse — it has to be done."

"Maybe you're right," Marjorie said.

"Of course I'm right."

"I was talking about you breaking it off with Johnny Oliver," Marjorie said. "Maybe that was the right thing for you to do."

"I'm not going to be a goddamned camp follower," Liza said. "That's it. Period."

"Can I borrow a car to go get Jack's uniform?" Marjorie asked.

"Oh, hell, I'll drive you out there."

VII

[ONE]
Hurlburt U.S. Air Force Field
Mary Esther, Florida
1505 31 December 1964

"Hurlburt," First Lieutenant Geoff Craig said into his microphone, "this is Army Six-one-niner."

"Go ahead, Six-one-niner," the Hurlburt tower replied.

"Six-one-niner, an L-23 aircraft, is at two thousand feet, oh, maybe three miles from your station, above the beautiful blue Gulf of Mexico. Request a straight-in approach to your Runway Zero Five."

"Army Six-one-niner, this is a closed field."

"Thank you, Hurlburt. We have the runway in sight."

"Army Six-one-niner, you are denied permission to land, I say again, you are denied permission to land."

"Thank you, Hurlburt. We will not require any services."

"Six-one-nine, go around, I say again, go around, permission to land is denied."

"Hurlburt, Army Six-one-niner on the ground at five past the hour."

"Army Six-one-nine, turn left on Taxiway One-five-A and hold your position. I say again, hold on Taxiway One-five-A. You will be met."

"Roger, Hurlburt, Six-one-niner holding on Taxiway One-five-A."

Geoff reached in the knee pocket of his flight suit, pulled out his green beret, and put it on.

"I hope you brought yours," he said to Jack Portet, in the left seat.

Jack nodded, took off his headset, pulled his beret out, and put it on.

"Never leave home without it," Geoff said solemnly. "Sometimes it's more useful than a credit card."

Two jeeps, both painted in checkerboard black and white, one of them with a pedestal-mounted .30-caliber Browning machine gun, came racing up the taxiway.

"Make nice," Geoff said. "We probably woke them up, and they're liable to be pissed."

He started to wave cheerfully at the approaching jeeps.

There were four Air Force men in the jeeps, all in fatigues, all wearing the flap-pinned-up-on-one-side, wide-brimmed hat that is the mark of the Air Force's air commandos.

The jeeps stopped. The two air commandos in the lead jeep trained the machine gun on the L-23. An air commando first lieutenant, whose jacket bore both pilot's and parachutist's wings, and who had a .45 pistol slung low — cowboy style — across his hips got out of the second jeep and walked in front of the first. He had an AOD brassard on his right arm.

"Smile and wave, goddamnit," Geoff ordered. Jack complied.

The air commando lieutenant looked at the airplane, shook his head in disgust, turned to the air commandos manning the machine gun, and signaled for them to point the machine gun in another direction.

Then he pointed at Jack and indicated that he wished for him to get out of the aircraft.

"I think he wants to talk to us," Geoff said. "You better shut it down."

"What the fuck are you guys up to?" the air commando lieutenant asked. "Didn't you hear the tower deny you permission to land?"

It was not normally the way he would have questioned the crew of an aircraft that had violated a direct order not to land at the air commando base.

But this crew was something special. They were Green Berets in addition to being pilots, which made them almost as good as air commandos, and thus entitled to a little professional courtesy.

"No," Geoff said, "what I heard him say was 'you are number one to land, there are no other aircraft in the area.' Isn't that what you heard him say, Jack?"

"That's what I heard him say," Jack said.

"You know you need prior permission to land here," the air commando said.

"We didn't remember that until we were halfway down here," Geoff said, "and the guy that sent us here apparently didn't remember at all."

"This is official? You're not just fucking around?"

"It's official," Geoff said. "We're going to pick up a guy and be out of here in five minutes."

"What guy?"

"His name is Santiago," Jack said. "De la Santiago."

"That's on the schedule for Saturday morning," the air commando lieutenant said.

"The early bird gets the worm," Geoff said. "You never heard that before?"

"Jesus!" the air commando said. He looked more closely at Jack. "Don't I know you? You've been here before, right?" His memory filled in the blank. "With the B-26's for the Congo, right?"

"Right," Jack said.

Intending them for service in the rapidly expanding war in Vietnam, the Air Force had taken a number of World War II B-26 bombers from the Air Force "graveyard" at Davis-Monthan Air Force Base and had them rebuilt. One of the first things Colonel Felter had done when given responsibility for the Congo was to order a dozen of them diverted to the air commando base at Hurlburt Field. There their American insignia was removed, and replaced with that of the air force of the Republic of the Congo.

Since there were no B-26 pilots in the Congolese Air Force, which existed mostly on paper, and the President didn't want the trouble he would get from the American people, and the Russians, if an American pilot was shot down, or crashed, non-American pilots, most of them formerly officers in the pre–Cuban Air Force, were hurriedly recruited to fly them to the Congo, and then into action against the Simbas.

"I figured your guy Santiago — he's Cuban, right? — was involved in that."

"You know him?"

"He walked into Base Ops about twenty minutes ago and said somebody was going to pick him up. I told him nothing was scheduled, and he should come back on Saturday. He just smiled at me, and went outside and sat down against the building."

"He's been flying B-26s in the Congo —" Jack said.

"While I sit on my ass here," the air commando pilot interrupted, more than a little bitterly.

"— and now he's back, and we were sent down to get him."

"With a little luck, maybe you can get yourself sent to Vietnam," Geoff said.

"You realize the crack you guys put my ass in?" the air commando asked.

"Just let us pick up Santiago, and then forget we were here," Geoff said.

"All that 'you are denied permission to land' conversation is on tape, how the hell can I forget it?" the air commando said. "Oh, hell, I'll think of something."

"Thank you," Geoff said.

"If I went to Base Ops and brought your guy out here," the air commando asked thoughtfully. "Could you get someone to cancel the pickup scheduled for Saturday morning?"

"Consider it done," Geoff said.

"Don't go anywhere," the air commando said.

He turned, walked to his jeep, got in, and motioned first for the driver to turn around and then for the other jeep to follow them.

"I think we ruined the day of the guys with the machine gun," Geoff said. "They thought they were finally going to get a chance to shoot somebody."

"Jacques, *mon ami,*" Enrico de la Santiago said when he got out of the air commando lieutenant's jeep. "They are finally letting you fly airplanes?"

264

But then Latin emotion took over and he ran to him, grabbed his arms, kissed both of Jack's cheeks, then wrapped him in a bear hug.

He was a slight man, with a swarthy skin, a full head of thick black hair, and a neatly manicured pencil-line mustache. He was wearing powder-blue trousers, a flamboyantly colored shirt of many colors, and an ex-USAF leather flight jacket, to which had been sewn a cloth patch reading CUBA, a painted-on-leather squadron insignia, and a leather patch with embossed Cuban pilot's wings over "E. de la Santiago, Capitaine, Forces Aero de Cuba."

Jack finally freed himself, and he and Geoff shook hands.

"The face I remember, but the name . . ." Enrico said.

"We used to see each other at Kamina," Geoff said. "In the Congo."

"Oh, yes. You were flying one of these," Enrico said, indicating the L-23. "It is very good to see you again."

"I like your jacket," Geoff said.

"A painful souvenir of times past," Enrico said, and shrugged.

"I hope we didn't get you in real trouble," Geoff said to the air commando.

"No problem," he replied. "I'll figure some way to really fuck you up sometime."

"Thank you," Enrico said to him.

"I'm sorry I ran you off before," the air commando said. "I really didn't know your friends were coming."

"Don't be silly."

"Okay, put the captain's bag in your little airplane, wind it up, and get it out of here," the air commando said.

He saluted, and held it, until Enrico realized the salute was intended for him. Then he came to attention and returned the salute.

Jack pulled the throttles back from TAKEOFF power, skillfully synchronized the engines, set a course for Rucker, set the trim for a slow climb, and turned to Enrico.

"So what's up?"

Enrico just perceptibly nodded in Geoff's direction, wordlessly asking, *Can I talk in front of him?*

"You ever hear the phrase 'Operation Earnest'?" Jack asked.

Enrico shook his head, no.

"Okay. But you can say anything in front of Geoff," Jack said. "What's going on?"

"I don't know what's going on," Enrico said. "Let me tell what happened. I took a C-46 from Kamina to Léopoldville. Your air force flies supplies into Léopoldville; I think they're worried about sending them into Kamina. Anyway, when I got to Léopoldville, there was a man waiting who took me to the American Embassy, to the military attaché, an Army colonel. He gave me a note from Colonel Felter. It said that he needed me to go after Che Guevara, and was I willing to do so? And if I was, would I accept appointment as a U.S. army warrant officer? The colonel, the one in the embassy, said I had to make up mind right away."

"And obviously, you decided to answer 'yes' to both questions," Geoff said.

"There wasn't much of a choice for me between bombing and strafing ignorant black savages wearing soldier's uniforms, and having a chance to kill Señor Guevara slowly and painfully."

Both Jack and Geoff were surprised, and made a little uncomfortable, by the icy intensity of de la Santiago's answer.

"You don't like him, huh?" Geoff said, jokingly, after a moment.

"The perverted obscenity personally murdered my grandfather, with my grandmother and my mother watching," de la Santiago said.

"Jesus!" Geoff said.

"Why perverted?" Jack asked.

"He is a doctor of medicine," Enrico said. "He took an oath to God never to take life. Is the murder of an innocent man, in front of his wife and his daughter by a doctor of medicine, not perverted behavior?"

"Well, I can't argue with that reasoning," Geoff said.

"So you agreed," Jack said. "Then what?"

"When the USAF C-130 left Léopoldville that same afternoon, I was on it," Enrico went on. "We came here. I was met by a warrant officer named Finton, who told me that I would be taken to Fort Bragg on Saturday, by you." He paused, smiled at Jack, and went on. "When you came back from your wedding trip."

"Yeah," Jack said. "December thirty-first."

"I knew when I first saw you two that it would happen. You have my prayers for a long and happy marriage."

"Thank you," Jack said. "Have you heard anything about your wife and children?"

De la Santiago held up both hands helplessly.

"They are in the hands of God," he said.

"Sonofabitch," Geoff muttered.

"What will happen to me at Fort Bragg?" Enrico asked.

"I haven't a clue," Jack said. "I guess you'll find out on Saturday."

"I'll give you this advice, de la Santiago . . ."

"I would be honored if you would call me by my Christian name."

"Okay. Thank you. I'm Geoff. The advice is, don't go around telling anybody you want to kill Guevara —"

"But I do."

"— painfully or otherwise. That's not on Felter's agenda for the bastard."

Enrico looked at Jack, who nodded.

Enrico shrugged.

"Perhaps if I am sent into Cuba, I would be able to learn something of my family."

"Guevara's not in Cuba," Geoff said. "He's in Africa."

"What's he doing in Africa?"

"My guess is that he wants to train the savages to do it right, the next time they try to take over the country," Geoff said.

"I was in Stanleyville, Jacques, right after the Belgians jumped — before they left. I saw what happened there. Only God's infinite mercy saved your mother and your sister."

"And my wife and baby," Geoff said. "It gave me a whole new perception of the efficacy of prayer."

"Your wife and baby were in Stanleyville?"

"Yeah. And so was John Wayne here," Geoff said. "He jumped with the Belgians."

"I didn't know that."

"He's a regular fucking hero."

"Fuck you, Geoff," Jack said conversationally.

"Does Colonel Felter understand what happened there?" Enrico asked.

"Oh, yeah," Geoff said. "He knows all about it."

"And that Guevara wants to start it all over again?"

"Yeah," Geoff said.

"And Colonel Felter is still unwilling to have him killed?"

"The Lord and Colonel Felter move in mysterious ways, Enrico," Geoff said. "You better keep your thoughts about killing Guevara to yourself, or you're going to find yourself out of his operation."

Enrico nodded.

What that means, Jack thought, *is that he will no longer announce his intention to kill Guevara, but not that he has given up his ambition to kill him, preferably slowly and painfully, but any way he can, just as soon as he has the opportunity.*

The question is, do I tell Father Lunsford or Colonel Felter?

[TWO]
Office of the Army Attaché
United States Embassy
Sarmiento 663
Buenos Aires, Argentina
0800 2 January 1965

"Anything interesting?" Colonel Richard J. Harris, Jr., inquired of Master Sergeant Douglas Wilson when the sergeant major walked into his office carrying the thick stack of messages that had come in over New Year's Day.

"The Pentagon has been heard from, Colonel," Wilson said, and handed him a sheet of teletypewriter paper.

HQ DEPT OF THE ARMY WASH DC 1100 31
DEC 1964

ROUTINE
CONFIDENTIAL

FROM: DSCOPS (AVIATION)
TO: US ARMY ATTACHÉ US EMBASSY
BUENOS AIRES ARGENTINA

1. REFERENCE IS MADE TO "SPECIAL TABLE
OF ORGANIZATION AND EQUIPMENT,
OFFICE OF ARMY ATTACHÉ US EMBASSY,
BUENOS AIRES ARGENTINA" AS AMENDED
22 DECEMBER 1964.

2. LT COL CRAIG W. LOWELL AND MAJOR
GEORGE W. LUNSFORD WILL ARRIVE IN
BUENOS AIRES 3 JAN 1965 TO DISCUSS
IMPLEMENTATION OF REFERENCED
AMENDED TO&E. SUBJECT OFFICERS ARE
TICKETED ABOARD AEROLINEAS ARGENTINE
FLIGHT 9790 WITH SCHEDULED TIME OF
ARRIVAL 1130 HOURS BUENOS AIRES TIME.

FOR THE ASSISTANT DCSOPS FOR
AVIATION:

RALPH J. LEMES, CAPT, SIGNAL CORPS

"I wonder if Colonel McGrory is going to come in today," Colonel Harris wondered out loud.

Master Sergeant Wilson read his boss's mind. Today was Saturday. It was very unlikely that

Colonel McGrory would come to work on Saturday; he rarely did. And tomorrow, when these two paper pushers from the Pentagon would arrive at Ezeiza, Buenos Aires' International Airport, was Sunday. There was almost no chance at all that Colonel McGrory would come to work on Sunday. If he did, it would be the first time either of them could remember.

"Colonel, why don't I go out there and pick these officers up?" Sergeant Wilson asked. "Where are we going to put them?"

"Does a lieutenant colonel rate the VIP transient apartment?" Colonel Harris asked rhetorically. "In the absence of any opinion to the contrary, and knowing there's no one in there right now, I have decided that this one does. He is, after all, about to give us not only an airplane but a twin-engined airplane. And pilots to fly it, and mechanics to fix it. Doesn't that make him a VIP?"

"I would certainly think so, Sir," Sergeant Wilson said. "What about the major?"

"I think that simple courtesy requires we give the major the benefit of the doubt, and put him in with the lieutenant colonel. You go out there at 11:30 and meet them, and when they're through customs and immigration, which should take no more than an hour or two, you call me and I will be at the VIP apartment when you deliver them there."

"Yes, sir."

"And perhaps the lieutenant colonel and I can have a little chat before he gets to meet Colonel McGrory the next morning. Give him the lay of the terrain, so to speak."

"Excellent thinking, Colonel," Master Sergeant Wilson said.

"Great minds run in similar paths, Sergeant Wilson," Harris said.

"What are you going to do about the Argentines, Colonel?"

Teniente Coronel Ricardo Fosterwood, aide-de-camp to the commander-in-chief, Argentine Army, had called and politely inquired if there was a Lieutenant Colonel Lowell visiting the U.S. Embassy. When told there was not ("Never heard the name, Colonel, Sorry," Master Sergeant Wilson had said.) Teniente Colonel Fosterwood had told Wilson that he would consider it a personal service if he were notified if such an officer did visit in the future.

"God, I forgot about that," Harris said. "I still can't figure out how he knew this Lowell character was coming before they told us." He paused. "I'll call him. I don't think he'll be working today, but I can leave a message."

Colonel Harris guessed right. Teniente Coronel Fosterwood had not come into the Edificio Libertador, and was not expected to do so until Monday. But he had left word, his subofficial mayor (sergeant major) told Colonel Harris, that if either Colonel Harris or Subofficial Mayor Wilson telephoned, the call was to be transferred to wherever he was.

That turned out to be his home. Fosterwood told Harris he very much appreciated being informed of the arrival of Teniente Coronel Lowell and — what was the other officer's name? And as soon as they could find the time, they were going to have to have lunch, or better, dinner.

When he hung up from speaking with Fosterwood, and after some thought, Harris thought he had the answer to deal with Colonel

272

Bob McGrory. He would Xerox the TWX from DCSOPS, put it in an envelope, stamp the envelope CONFIDENTIAL, and hand it to whatever Air Force NCO had been stuck with the over-the-weekend duty. On the envelope, he would write:

McGrory:
0835 Sat 2 Jan
Sorry I missed you. This just reached me.
Harris

Colonel Harris did all of this, and feeling just a little smug, walked down the corridor to Colonel McGrory's office to find his NCO on duty and found instead Colonel Robert McGrory sitting behind his desk, drinking a cup of coffee and reading the *Buenos Aires Herald.*

"I didn't think you'd be coming in today, Colonel," Harris said. "So I put this in an envelope so that you would have it first thing when you did."

"What have you got, Colonel?" McGrory asked.

Harris handed the xeroxed copy of the TWX to him, and McGrory read it.

"Who are these people, Colonel?" McGrory asked.

"I never saw their names before, Colonel."

"I want to see this man the minute he arrives, Colonel," McGrory said.

"So you'll go to Ezeiza to meet him, Colonel?"

The airport was an hour's ride through usually maddening traffic from either downtown Buenos Aires, or from the suburb of Olivos, where both Harris and McGrory — and senior State Department officers — lived.

"I didn't say that, Colonel," McGrory said. "I

meant the minute he walks in the Embassy on Monday morning."

"I see. I'll tell him that, Colonel."

"You're going to meet him?"

"Sergeant Major Wilson will meet them, Colonel."

"And take them where?"

"I'm going to put them in the transient VIP apartment."

"You're going to do what?"

"I think you heard me, Colonel."

"The transient VIP apartment is for VIPs, Colonel. I don't want to find myself trying to explain to the Ambassador why someone on my staff put a lieutenant colonel — who is not a VIP — and a major in there."

"If the ambassador asks me, Colonel, why I did it, I will tell him that since I knew the apartment was empty, I thought it was the courteous thing to do."

"These Army officers, Colonel, are not going to stay in the transient VIP apartment. Are we clear on that?"

"We're clear on that, Colonel," Harris said, and mentally added, *you chickenshit sonofabitch.*

"And as far as having your sergeant meet these officers, Colonel — they are, after all, field-grade officers, and entitled to the appropriate courtesies — I don't like that at all."

"And how would you prefer that be handled, Colonel?"

"I was about to say that someone on your staff, a field-grade officer, should be given that duty, but on reflection, Colonel, I'll have one of my field grades handle it. This is, after all, an Air Force post, and I want to make sure these people get the message that I want to see them first thing Monday morning."

"Whatever you say, Colonel," Harris said, and walked out of the office very aware that he was teetering over the brink of telling the Dumb Mick Fly-Boy chickenshit sonofabitch to go fuck himself.

[THREE]
Pope Air Force Base
Fort Bragg, North Carolina
1125 2 January 1965

"Office of the Commanding General, Special Warfare Center, Captain Zabrewski speaking, sir."

"Captain, my name is Portet, and —"

"The general has been expecting your call, Lieutenant. You're at Pope? Base Operations?"

"Yes, sir."

"I'll have a car there in ten minutes. Be waiting outside."

"Yes, sir."

Jack put the phone back in its cradle and shook his head. He had called Hanrahan's office in desperation, after fifteen minutes on the telephone trying, with absolutely no success, to find Major Father Lunsford. First the SWC operator had firmly denied knowing anything about a Major Lunsford, then when Jack had said he was at Mackall, that she knew anything about a place called Camp Mackall, and when he'd finally worked his way past the operator's supervisor and gotten the signal sergeant to patch him through to the Mackall switchboard, that operator, a man, had firmly denied knowledge of a Major Lunsford or a Master Sergeant Thomas. He had finally gotten Thomas on the line.

"Hell, he doesn't tell me where he's going, Lieutenant," Thomas had told him in Swahili. "I don't have a clue where he is. You try his apartment?"

To try the apartment, it had been necessary to find a pay phone, because the Pope/Bragg telephone system did not allow off-post calls from Class B telephones, and then find change to feed the pay phone, and when he finally got the number to ring, it rang and rang and rang, making it clear that Father wasn't at home, either.

As he had dialed the SWC number again, he wondered if Mr. Finton ate Father's ass for not letting people know where he was the way he had eaten his.

"The general will see you now, Lieutenant," said Captain Zabrewski, who stood six feet four inches tall, weighed 230 pounds, and had a voice like a bass tuba.

Jack marched into Hanrahan's office and saluted.

"Hey, Jack," Hanrahan said, returning the salute with a wave in the general direction of his forehead, and smiling. "Where's your friend?"

"Outside, sir. Sir, I was looking for Major Lunsford —"

Hanrahan silenced him with a raised hand and punched the lever on his intercom.

"Ski, run down Mr. Zammoro. When he shows up, send him and Mr. de la Santiago in, please."

"Father's not here," Hanrahan said to Jack.

"Pappy Hodges told me to take Santiago to him, sir. Can I ask where he is?"

Hanrahan thought that over perceptibly.

"He's on his way to Buenos Aires with Colonel Lowell."

"Buenos Aires?" Jack asked incredulously.

"It may have something to do with this," Hanrahan said. "Which Colonel Felter, for reasons I can't imagine, felt he should share with me. It just came over the secure photo line."

He handed Jack what was a wire photograph of a CIA memorandum.

SECRET

Central Intelligence Agency
Langley, Virginia

FROM: Assistant Director For Administration

DATE: 1 January 1965 1310 GMT

SUBJECT: Guevara, Ernesto (Memorandum # 8.)

TO: Mr. Sanford T. Felter
Counselor To The President
Room 637, The Executive Office Building
Washington, D.C.

By Courier

In compliance with Presidential Memorandum to The Director, Subject: "Ernesto 'Che' Guevara," dated 14 December 1964, and in consideration of the fact that SUBJECT holds Argentinian citizenship by birth, the following information is furnished:

---

(1) (Reliability Scale Three) (From CIA Buenos Aires) The Argentine Foreign Ministry has been informed by Argentine Ambassador in Madrid that former President Juan D. PERÓN has chartered an aircraft and intends to travel today from Lisbon, Portugal via Asuncion, Paraguay to an undisclosed location in Argentina, presumably to make good on his promise to return to Argentina by 1 Jan 65. ARG FORMIN previously believed promise was meaningless.

(2) CIA sources in Madrid and Lisbon know of no overt or covert charter.

Howard W. O'Connor
HOWARD W. O'CONNOR

Jack finished reading it, and looked at General Hanrahan.

"And then again, it may not," Hanrahan said.

"General Perón? Argentina?"

"Like it says in there, Señor Guevara was born there," Hanrahan said. "How's married life?"

"So far just fine, sir."

"Johnny Oliver reported in this morning. He's getting settled in. If Father and Oliver living together can ever be called settled. In a garden apartment in Fayetteville."

"Father — excuse me, Major Lunsford — offered to find an apartment for Marjorie and me there, sir."

"Jack, very quickly: A senior can call a junior by his first name; the reverse is not true unless they are really friends, and among friends. Example: So far as I'm concerned, you can call Father Father and Oliver Johnny when you and I are alone, but don't let my aide hear you do it. It would deeply offend his sense of proprieties. You'll learn, Jack. It's not hard, but it's important."

"Thank you, sir," Jack said, meaning it, realizing that Hanrahan, like Pappy, like Marjorie, like even Geoff, was trying to help him learn how to act like an officer.

"Father told me about the apartment. When are you coming up here?"

"General, you know about the L-23 we're to pick up in Wichita?"

Hanrahan nodded.

"Well, as soon as it gets modified at SCATSA, sir, I'll bring it here. There was some talk about teaching me how to fly choppers, but that seems to have died."

"Not died. Put on hold. When you get up here, Oliver will transition you into choppers. In addition to your other duties."

"Yes, sir."

"How close is Geoff Craig to finishing up down there? Do you know?"

"He rode down to Hurlburt with me when I picked up de la Santiago —"

"Today?"

"No, sir. On New Year's Eve. We spent New Year's Eve together at Geoff's."

"I thought Marjorie would want to display her new husband to the brass at the O Club."

"First we went there, and then to Geoff's," Jack

said, and then answered the question. "Geoff's just about finished with the course, sir."

"Nobody knows, of course, when this Guevara business is about to start. The possibility exists Felter may be wrong. If I wanted to take over South America, I think I'd start in Central America, or maybe Chile or Bolivia, not in the Congo."

"I wondered about that, sir."

"On the other hand, from the moment I met him, a long time ago, in Greece, Felter's track record has been perfect. In the end, he's usually turned out to be right, and everybody else wrong. So it behooves us to get this operation in place as soon as possible."

"Yes, sir."

"I wonder where the hell Zammoro is?" Hanrahan asked, and looked impatiently at his closed officer door.

"Sir," Mr. Zabrewski's voice boomed over the intercom, as if he had been waiting for the question, "Mr. Zammoro is here."

Hanrahan smiled at Jack and chuckled. He depressed the SPEAK lever on his intercom.

"Bring them in, please, Ski," he ordered.

The door opened and a large, swarthy man in fatigues came in first, clutching his green beret in a massive hand, followed by Enrico de la Santiago and Captain Zabrewski. Zabrewski stood by the side of the door; de la Santiago looked as if he didn't know what to do.

The large man walked to Hanrahan, came to attention, and barked, in the approved military manner, "Sir, Warrant Officer Zammoro reporting as ordered, sir." He had a slight Spanish accent.

280

Hanrahan returned the salute. Zammoro remained at attention. Hanrahan gestured for him to relax, and turned to de la Santiago.

"I'm General Hanrahan, Mr. de la Santiago."

"How do you do, sir?" de la Santiago replied, coming almost to attention.

"Ski, close the door, please, and stick around."

"Yes, sir."

"Zam, this is Lieutenant Portet," Hanrahan said.

"How do you do, sir?" Zammoro asked.

"Lieutenant Portet, Zam, and Mr. de la Santiago are old friends. You two don't happen to know each other, do you?"

"Yes, sir. We knew one another, in Cuba," Zammoro said.

"Mr. Zammoro was a major in the Cuban Army, Lieutenant Portet, and you were, as I understand it, Mr. de la Santiago, a captain in the Cuban Air Force?"

"Yes, sir," de la Santiago said.

"There is a special program, not very well-known, begun during the Hungarian Uprising of 1956, which authorizes certain foreign nationals to be taken into the U.S. Army if they possess certain skills and characteristics that convince a board of U.S. Army officers, one of whom has to be a general officer, they will be of unusual value to the Army," Hanrahan said.

De la Santiago nodded but didn't say anything.

"Mr. Zammoro is such an individual," Hanrahan said. "The board of officers before whom he appeared were convinced that he was a bona fide refugee from Señor Castro's government, rather than an intelligence officer sent to penetrate our

281

Army. And the board of officers was convinced further that the skills acquired while he was a major in the pre-Castro Cuban Army would be of value to the Army, and specifically to Special Forces."

"Yes, sir," de la Santiago said.

"He was therefore permitted to enlist as a private in the U.S. Army, which required that he take an oath of allegiance to the United States, disavowing any previous allegiances, and that he swore to obey the orders of the officers appointed over him, and to defend the Constitution of the United States against all enemies, foreign and domestic."

"I understand, sir," de la Santiago said.

"Shortly after Private Zammoro was sworn in as a private soldier — I believe it was the same day, was it not, Zam?"

"Yes, sir," Zammoro said, smiling.

"It was brought to his attention that he was eligible to apply for direct appointment as a warrant officer, junior grade, U.S. Army, because of his linguistic skills. He is fluent in Spanish as well as English, as I believe you are, Mr. de la Santiago?"

"Yes, sir," de la Santiago said.

"And he applied, and went before another board of officers, which also included one general officer, which not only decided that he possessed the requirements to be a warrant officer, junior grade, but that if he were an American citizen, he would be eligible for direct appointment as a captain, and that when and if he became an American citizen, which is possible, under another special provision of the law, for a foreign national who has served faithfully for eighteen months as an

282

enlisted man or warrant officer, in the U.S. Army, that he be so commissioned."

He paused and looked at de la Santiago.

"You're following all this, Señor de la Santiago?"

"Yes, sir."

"And questions, Señor de la Santiago?"

"At the risk of sounding flippant, sir, how soon could I expect to go before the board of officers you mentioned?"

"You're in front of it now, Mr. de la Santiago," Hanrahan said. "And let the record show that the president of the board has been advised by Mr. Sanford T. Felter, Counselor to the President, Executive Office Building, Washington, D.C., that he is personally familiar with Mr. de la Santiago's counterintelligence dossier and states that he is not an intelligence officer of Cuba or any other foreign power."

Captain Zabrewski, who had been leaning against the wall, came to attention.

"Yes, sir," he said.

"For your information, Mr. de la Santiago," Hanrahan said, "it is the custom of the U.S. Army, when polling a board such as this one, that the junior member thereof be polled first, so his opinions will in no way be influenced by the opinions of his superiors."

Hanrahan paused.

"Mr. Zammoro, is there any question in your mind that Mr. de la Santiago, should he be allowed to enlist as a private in the U.S. Army, would be of special value to Special Forces?"

Zammoro popped to attention.

"No, sir."

"Or, should he be enlisted as a private soldier,

283

that his application for appointment as warrant officer, junior grade, be approved?"

"No, sir."

"Thank you, Mr. Zammoro. I believe you are next senior, Lieutenant Portet?"

"Yes, sir," Jack said. "I agree with Mr. Zammoro, sir."

"Captain Zabrewski?"

"I agree with Mr. Zammoro and Lieutenant Portet, sir."

Hanrahan turned and rapped his knuckles on his desk.

"The board approves. Let the record show the decision was unanimous."

"Yes, sir," Captain Zabrewski said.

"If you'll take one step forward, Mr. de la Santiago, I will now enlist you into the United States Army," General Hanrahan said.

[FOUR]

SECRET

Central Intelligence Agency
Langley, Virginia

FROM: Assistant Director For Administration

DATE: 2 January 1965 1805 GMT

SUBJECT: Guevara, Ernesto (Memorandum # 10.)

TO: Mr. Sanford T. Felter

Counselor To The President
Room 637, The Executive Office Building
Washington, D.C.

By Courier

In compliance with Presidential Memorandum to The Director, Subject: "Ernesto
'Che' Guevara", dated 14 December 1964,
the following information is furnished:

(1) (Reliability Scale Three) (From CIA
Sources in Bamako, Mali). SUBJECT spent
New Year's Eve in the Cuban Embassy in
Bamako. No other information is available.

Howard W. O'Connor
HOWARD W. O'CONNOR

SECRET

[FIVE]
Ezeiza International Airport
Buenos Aires, Argentina
1130 3 January 1965

When the Aerolineas Argentina Flight 9790, a
Boeing 707, landed, completing its nonstop flight
from Miami, it taxied close to the terminal and shut
down. Two stairways mounted on Chevrolet trucks
drove up to the aircraft as the doors were opened. A
black Ford Falcon drove up, and a tall, rather
sturdy-looking man in a well-cut suit got out. As

soon as the forward stairway was in place, he went up it and entered the airplane. Sixty seconds later, he came down the stairway and got back in the Falcon, which immediately drove to the terminal building.

A train of baggage carts rolled up to the aircraft, as did two passenger buses. The passengers began to deplane as the luggage was unloaded.

The first-class passengers were disembarked first, the idea being this would give them first shot at the limited seats available on the buses for the five-hundred-meter trip to the terminal. The fifth and sixth first-class passengers to come down the stairway were a tall white man and a stocky black man, both wearing tweed sport coats, open-necked polo shirts, gray flannel slacks, and loafers.

As they had gotten on the bus first, they had to wait, at the terminal, for the standees to get off first; they were the last two passengers to get off their bus.

As they entered the terminal, the sturdy-looking man who had been aboard the 707 stepped in front of the tall white man and smiled.

"Colonel Lowell?" he asked.

"That's right."

"*A sus órdenes, mi coronel,*" the man said. "General Pistarini has asked me to assist you in passing through Customs and Immigration."

"How very kind of him," Lowell said. "This is Major Lunsford."

"I am very pleased to meet you, Major," the sturdy-looking man said, and gave Lunsford his hand. He did not volunteer his own name.

"If you'll be kind enough to give me your baggage checks, we can be on our way. Your luggage will follow whenever this inefficient system of ours

286

finally gets it off the aircraft."

Lowell and Lunsford handed him their baggage checks.

The sturdy man snapped his fingers, and another well-dressed man appeared, neither as sturdy nor as tall. The sturdy man handed him the baggage checks and then, smiling, motioned for Lowell and Lunsford to precede him toward a row of booths, behind which sat officers of the Immigration Service of the Republic of Argentina.

"May I have your passports, please?" the sturdy man asked, and Lowell and Lunsford handed them over. The sturdy man handed them to an Immigration officer. It took him only long enough to find blank pages to stamp before he said, "Welcome to Argentina," and waved them through.

The sturdy man led them into the reception area of the airport, where people gathered to meet incoming passengers. Among these was a U.S. Air Force major, holding a sign reading, "Lt. Col. Lowell."

"Just a second, please," Lowell said to the sturdy man, and walked up to the major holding the sign.

"My name is Lowell, Major," he said.

"Major Daley, Colonel. Colonel McGrory sent me to meet you and Major Lunsford."

"Colonel who?"

"Colonel McGrory, sir. The defense attaché."

"What happened to Colonel Harris?"

"Colonel Harris is the *army* attaché, Colonel. This is an Air Force post. Colonel McGrory is the *defense* attaché."

"Please tell Colonel McGrory I very much appreciate his courtesy in sending you out here,

Major, and tell him that I hope he can find time to see me while I'm in Argentina."

"Sir, Colonel McGrory asked me to take you to your quarters, and then bring you to report to him."

"To *report* to him, you said, Major?"

"Yes, sir."

"Please tell Colonel McGrory I hope he can find time for me to pay him a courtesy call while I'm in Argentina," Lowell said. "And I'm sorry you wasted your time coming out here, Major."

He walked back to the sturdy man, who led him outside the terminal where three cars, two Ford Falcons and a black Buick, were parked in an area clearly marked FOR TAXIS ONLY.

The sturdy man opened the rear door of the Buick and smilingly motioned for Lowell and Lunsford to get in, and when they had, got in the front seat. The Buick pulled away from the terminal. One of the Falcons followed.

Neither car even slowed when they came to the tollbooths for the airfield parking lot.

The sturdy man in the front turned.

"General Pistarini regrets, *mi coronel*," he said, "that he was unable to meet you himself. The press of duty . . ."

"I understand, of course," Lowell said. "We have reservations at a hotel called the Plaza."

For the first time, the sturdy man frowned.

"The general has arranged accommodation for you and the major, *mi coronel*, in the Círculo Militar. Will that be a problem?"

"The general's hospitality is overwhelming," Lowell said.

"And our baggage will be going there, right?" Father Lunsford asked.

"It should be there within the hour," the sturdy man said. "And there is no problem about your staying at the Círculo Militar?"

"I'm looking forward to it," Lowell said.

It was a forty-five-minute trip through traffic to downtown Buenos Aires.

"This is Plaza San Martín, *mi coronel*," the sturdy man said. "We will pass the Foreign Ministry, on our left, and then come to the Círculo Militar. The building directly ahead is the Círculo Militar."

He pointed to an enormous, French-style building, with a fifty-foot-tall, heavily gilded cast-iron double gate. Two soldiers, in field gear, armed with automatic rifles, stood guard.

Actual guard, both Lunsford and Lowell decided at about the same moment. *Those rifles are not ceremonial.*

"Beautiful building," Lowell said.

"It was given to the Army in the early years of the century by the family who owns *La Nacion*, our major daily newspaper."

"How interesting," Lowell said.

"The Plaza Hotel, *mi coronel*, is on the far side of the Plaza," the sturdy man said, and pointed.

They came close to the Círculo Militar. The huge gates swung inward, and in a moment Lowell saw that they had been pulled open by two men in white jackets. The soldiers with the automatic rifles unslung them, came to attention, and held the rifles stiffly in front of them, in a maneuver not unlike Present Arms in the *U.S. Army Manual of Arms*, as the Buick rolled through the gates.

One of the white-jacketed men walked quickly to the car and opened the rear door.

Lowell and Lunsford got out.

A tall officer, in a splendidly tailored uniform — brown tunic, Sam Browne belt, pink riding breeches, and glistening riding boots — came out of the building, walked up, came to attention, and saluted.

"Colonel Lowell, Teniente Coronel Ricardo Fosterwood, *a sus órdenes*. I have the honor to be aide-de-camp to Teniente General Pistarini."

"How do you do, Colonel? This is Major Lunsford."

They all shook hands.

"Why don't we go inside and get out of this beastly summer heat?" Fosterwood said, and waved them into the building.

Beside a curving marble staircase there was an elevator. There was hardly enough room for the three officers.

Fosterwood apologized for the size of the cramped elevator.

"I have always wondered if the Frenchman who designed this building did so in the belief that Argentines were all dwarfs, or whether he thought we liked to stand really close to ladies in the lift," he said.

The three smiled at each other.

The elevator stopped, and Fosterwood slid the folding door open, then motioned them outside. He led them down a wide corridor, opened the left half of a huge, massive, heavily carved door, and waved them through it.

"I took the liberty of placing the major in one of the bedrooms in this suite," Fosterwood said as he came into the elegantly furnished living room of the suite. "It would be no trouble at all to arrange —"

290

"I'm sure that Major Lunsford will be completely comfortable here," Lowell said.

"General Pistarini has ordered me, as our first order of business, to go through a custom he said he learned at your Fort Knox while on a visit there. 'Cutting the dust of the trail'?"

"One of our most sacred customs," Lowell said.

Fosterwood bowed them through another door. It turned out to be a bar, with a white-jacketed bartender in attendance.

"And I believe bourbon whiskey is the dust-cutter of choice?"

"Actually," Lowell began, stopped, and then went on. "Actually, two things. I'm a scotch drinker, and actually it's a little early in the day for me to start on anything."

"In that case, let me introduce you to an Argentine custom," Fosterwood said. "We say it's never too early, or too late, to have a glass of champagne."

"We of the infantry say the same thing," Lunsford said.

"I think we'll find French champagne and Argentine," Fosterwood said.

"Argentine, if you will," Lowell said.

The bartender produced a bottle of champagne and glasses.

"To your very pleasant stay in Argentina, *mi coronel*," Fosterwood said, raising his glass.

"Thank you," Lowell said. "And when would you say it would be convenient for General Pistarini to receive me, so I can offer my thanks for his magnificent hospitality?"

"Odd that you should ask," Fosterwood said. "There is a small problem at the moment, nothing that can't be managed, but bothersome enough that General Pistarini feels he should be at Campo de Mayo until it is resolved. . . ."

"And Campo de Mayo is what?" Lowell asked.

"It's one of our major bases, on the outskirts of Buenos Aires. Our military academy is there, and one of our cavalry regiments."

"I see."

"The General asked me to ask you, if you felt up to it, after your long trip, if you might not like to play a little polo with him this afternoon at Campo de Mayo."

"I'm not really an Argentine-class polo player," Lowell said.

"Oh, this would just be a friendly game between friends," Fosterwood said. "To help pass the time, so to speak."

"I'd be happy to play with the general," Lowell said. "There is the problem of breeches and boots. . . ."

"Not a problem at all. I'm sure we can outfit you with no difficulty. May I tell the general you will join him?"

"How do we get from here to there?" Lowell asked.

"The car, of course, is at your disposal," Fosterwood said.

"The Buick?"

"And the drivers will all speak English. So, *mi coronel?*"

"Please tell General Pistarini that, even with the knowledge that I will be a rank amateur playing with the world's best, I am delighted to accept his kind offer."

"And you, Major?"

"I am not a polo player, Colonel. Thank you just the same," Lunsford said.

"But you will come anyway? There will be a — you call it barbecue — I'm sure."

"Yes, I will. Thank you very much."

"If you left here at three, or a little after," Pistarini said. "The driver will know where to take you."

"And the car will be downstairs?"

Pistarini nodded. "The car is at your disposal during your visit."

"Thank you."

"And, now, with your permission, I will leave you to get settled. I suspect my general needs me. He usually does."

"Did you expect this, *mi coronel?*" Lunsford asked. "The Red Carpet?"

"Not quite this way."

"Those guys at the airport were spooks," Lunsford said.

"They're called the SIDE. Felter told me that."

"And who was the Air Force guy at the airport?"

"He said that this was an Air Force post, whatever the hell that means, and that he had been sent by the Air Force, correction, defense attaché, to take us to our quarters, and then to report to him."

"I wonder how he knew we were coming," Lunsford said. "*Report* to him?"

Lowell nodded. "I told him to go fuck himself."

Lunsford laughed. "No, you didn't."

"I told him to tell his boss that I hoped he could find time in his schedule for me to pay a courtesy call on him."

"And this invitation to play polo?"

Lowell shrugged helplessly.

[SIX]
Office of the Defense Attaché
United States Embassy
Sarmiento 663
Buenos Aires, Argentina
1325 3 January 1965

"You wanted to see me, Colonel?" Colonel Richard J. Harris, Jr., USA, inquired of Colonel Robert McGrory, USAF, from the latter's doorway.

"Come in, Colonel," McGrory said.

"Hello, Charley," Harris said to Major Charles A. Daley, USAF, who was standing at a position pretty close to attention in front of McGrory's desk.

"Sir," Major Daley replied.

"Major, would you please repeat for Colonel Harris's edification what transpired when you were at Ezeiza this morning?"

"Yes, sir," Major Daley said.

"Those officers weren't on the plane?" Harris asked.

"Colonel, please be good enough to allow the major to give his after-action report," Colonel McGrory said.

"Sorry," Harris said.

"Sir, I went to the Reception Area of Ezeiza with a sign with 'Lieutenant Colonel Lowell' written on it. About the very first people to come off the airplane — through the doors from Immigration — were a tall white man and a Negro. They were with a man I believe was from SIDE. The white man —"

"Why do you think they were from SIDE, Charley?" Harris interrupted.

"Sir, I believe I have seen the man before, and later, when they left the airport, there were two of the cars, those little Falcons SIDE uses?"

"Yeah," Harris said.

"I suggest, Colonel, that the major's report could be more expeditiously completed if you could refrain from interrupting him."

"Sorry," Harris repeated.

"As I was saying, sir, one of the gentlemen with the man I believe was from SIDE came up to me and said he was Colonel Lowell. I told him who I was, and what I wanted."

"He delivered the message, Colonel," McGrory said, "that as soon as they were in their quarters he was to report to me."

"And?"

"Sir, Colonel Lowell said that I was to tell Colonel McGrory that he hoped Colonel McGrory could find time for him to pay a courtesy call while he was in Argentina, and that he was sorry I wasted my time going to the airport."

"To make things crystal clear to the colonel, Major," McGrory said, "did you make it absolutely clear to Lieutenant Colonel Lowell that it was an order to report to me, not a request?"

"Yes, sir. I made that perfectly clear, sir."

"Is that clear to you, Colonel?"

"Crystal clear, Colonel. Instead of reporting to you, Colonel Lowell replied that he hoped you would find time for him to pay you a courtesy call."

In other words, he told Charley to tell you to go fuck yourself. I like this guy already.

"I intend to make a full report of this," Colonel McGrory said. "It's disobedience to an order, clear and simple."

"And then these two people left the airport? With the man from SIDE?" Harris asked.

"Yes, sir. As I said before, there were three cars parked illegally in the taxi area, two Falcons and a Buick. Colonel Lowell, and the Negro man. . . ."

"I think we can safely presume, don't you, Charley, that the Negro man is Major Lunsford?" Harris asked.

"Yes, sir, I think we could do that."

"Go on, Charley," Harris said.

"Yes, sir. Colonel Lowell and Major Lunsford got in the Buick, and it drove off, with one of the Falcons following it."

"You have any idea where they went?" Harris asked.

"Are you telling me, Colonel, that you don't know where they are?" Colonel McGrory asked.

"I haven't the faintest idea where they are, Colonel."

"That better be the truth, Colonel. If I find out later —"

"The truth is, Colonel, that I deferred to your announcement that it was the business of the defense attaché to meet these officers, and left the matter entirely in your capable hands. Have you got something else for me, Colonel?"

"That will be all, thank you, Colonel."

Colonel Harris returned to his office, repeated the essentials of the conversation to Master Sergeant Wilson, and suggested that Wilson ask his buddy, the Assistant Administrative Officer (Housing & Medical Services) of the United States Information Agency, which was also housed in the Embassy Chancellery, if he had any ideas where the two Army officers might be found.

An hour later, Master Sergeant Wilson told him

that Lowell and Lunsford were in the Círculo Militar.

[SEVEN]

SECRET

Central Intelligence Agency
Langley, Virginia

FROM: Assistant Director For Administration

DATE: 2 January 1965 1110 GMT

SUBJECT: Guevara, Ernesto (Memorandum # 9.)

TO: Mr. Sanford T. Felter
Counselor To The President
Room 637, The Executive Office Building
Washington, D.C.

By Courier

In compliance with Presidential Memorandum to The Director, Subject: "Ernesto 'Che' Guevara," dated 14 December 1964, and in consideration of the fact that SUBJECT holds Argentinian citizenship by birth, the following information is furnished:

(1) (Reliability Scale Five) (From CIA Rio de Janeiro, Brazil) Former Argentine President Juan D. PERÓN arrived in Rio de Janeiro at 1307 GMT aboard scheduled Iberia

Airlines Flight 909. PERÓN and party of eight (8) Argentine nationals were detained by Brazilian Air Force at direction of Brazilian government.

　　(2) (Reliability Scale Three) (From CIA Rio) PERÓN and party intend to travel by air to Montevideo, Uruguay. PERÓN does not have visa required for such travel.

　　(3) (Reliability Scale Two) (From CIA Rio) It is intention of Brazilian government to deny PERÓN permission to enter Brazil. PERÓN does not possess the required visa.

　　(4) (Reliability Scale Five) (From CIA Buenos Aires) Argentine government has re-inforced border crossing points with Army officers under orders to deny PERÓN en-trance to Argentina. Surreptitious entry, how-ever, is believed possible.

Howard W. O'Connor
HOWARD W. O'CONNOR

SECRET

298

VIII

[ONE]
Círculo Militar
Plaza San Martín
Buenos Aires, Argentina
1440 3 January 1965

Lieutenant Colonel Lowell and Major Lunsford, both now dressed in seersucker suits — Lowell had considered proper dress, decided against uniforms, and against too much informality, as open-collar polo shirts might have been — walked through a smaller gate in the huge gates of the Círculo Militar toward the Buick.

The driver saw them coming and got quickly out of the car and opened the door for them. He tried to take a small leather bag from Lowell's hand, but Lowell declined, saying, "I'll just put it in the back with me. And before we go to Campo de Mayo, I have to stop at the Plaza Hotel for a minute."

"Of course, sir."

The bag contained a change of linen and toilet articles.

"What's that for?" Lunsford had asked when he saw him packing the bag.

"Polo, for your general edification, my dear major, is a sport in which the riders sweat as much as their mounts. The ponies are replaced at least once each chukker; the players are not. I am desperately going to need a shower and a change of undies when the Argentines are through with me. If not hospitalization."

"You're not any good at polo?"

"When I was a young man, I thought I was a very good polo player," Lowell said, "and so did Barbara Bellmon's father. My skill kept me from simonizing a lot of tanks and armored cars, which is how the other enlisted men of the United States Constabulary spent their time. I had a four-goal handicap."

"What does that mean?"

"You're rated, one to ten, on your skill. Ten is top. Four guys on a team. You add up the handicaps and get, say, a five- or six-, or maybe even a ten- or twelve-goal handicap team. I thought I was pretty hot stuff with my four-goal handicap. And then, at Ramapo Valley, in New York, I played my first game against an Argentine team. They trotted happily onto the field with forty goals between them. *Everybody* had a ten-goal handicap."

"You played any lately, *mi coronel?*" Lunsford asked, chuckling.

"Indeed I have. And I have been rated again, and now I am a *one*-goal-handicap player, which I think reflects their opinion of me as a very nice fellow, rather than my skill on the field."

He paused and then added, "Before we go out there, I want to go to the hotel to see if someone canceled my reservations."

"Can't you call?"

"I would like to know, if they're canceled, who did it," Lowell said.

When the Buick pulled out of the parking area

reserved for guests of the Círculo Militar, a black Ford Falcon followed it. They moved about halfway around the wide avenue that circles Plaza San Martín, then turned off it and into a drive under one corner of the Plaza Hotel.

A doorman in a silk top hat opened the door of the car for them.

"This won't take long," Lowell said to the driver. "How will I find you?"

The passage under the hotel was obviously a drop-off/pick-up-and-get-moving-quickly area.

The driver acted as if the question surprised him.

"I will wait for you here, *mi coronel*."

Lowell smiled and walked into the hotel with Lunsford trailing him.

"What is that, some pigs is more equal than other pigs?" Lunsford asked quietly. "And you noticed the old Ford?"

"Actually, it's probably a new one," Lowell said. "They still make them down here."

He walked to the reception desk.

"My name is Lowell," he said. "I think I have a reservation."

"Oh, Mr. Lowell," the desk clerk said immediately. "I am so sorry you didn't connect with the car at Ezeiza."

"I didn't know you were sending a car," Lowell said. "But no problem, a friend met me."

"And your luggage, sir?"

"That will be along after a while," Lowell said.

"Will you excuse me just a moment, Mr. Lowell?" the desk clerk said.

A moment later a man in formal clothing appeared in front of the desk.

"Mr. Lowell, I am Dominic Frizzelli, the assistant manager. I would like to apologize for our driver not being able to find you."

"A friend met us; it was no problem. And I very much appreciate your courtesy in sending it."

"You are very gracious. If you'll come with me, please?"

He led them to an elevator, which took them directly to the foyer of a suite on the top floor.

The suite was large and elegantly furnished, and its windows provided a view of the ancient trees in Plaza San Martín, and, beyond, of the River Plate. There was a large basket of fruit and a bottle of champagne in a silver cooler. The suite was not as large nor as elegantly furnished as their accommodations in the Círculo Militar.

"This is very nice," Lowell said.

"Mr. Delaplaine of the Bank of Boston personally inspected it, sir, and thought you would find it satisfactory. This is where they often accommodate their distinguished visitors."

"How kind of Mr. Delaplaine," Lowell said. "If you see him before I do, will you express my gratitude?"

"Of course, sir."

"We may not be back tonight," Lowell said. "I suspect we'll be asked to spend the night."

"I understand perfectly, sir."

The Buick was parked exactly where they had left it in the passageway.

"Okay," Lowell said to the driver. "I am now ready to be humiliated by Argentine polo players."

"Oh, I'm sure," the driver said, missing the intended humor completely, "that nothing like that will happen, *mi coronel*."

"It doesn't look much like Fort Bragg, does it?" Lunsford asked after they had entered the parklike Campo de Mayo. "I'm beginning to think I'm in the wrong army."

Lowell chuckled.

"And I'm really beginning to think you're in the wrong business," Lunsford went on. "You could really live like that all the time, couldn't you?"

"And be bored out of my mind, sure," Lowell said. "And I'm going to get a large piece of Lieutenant Craig's ass for that suite at the Plaza."

"What's he got to do with it?"

"He's been down here a couple of times with his father, so I told him to get us a nice hotel."

"Well, he did that."

"We didn't need a suite arranged for by the Bank of Boston," Lowell said. "The last thing I need is bankers — worse, journalists — chasing me around asking for my opinion of world economic affairs, or the trends in sow belly futures."

"I get the point," Lunsford said. "Hell, he was probably just trying to be nice."

"I'd feel a lot better if I wasn't beginning to question his smarts," Lowell said.

Lunsford raised his eyebrows but said nothing.

The Buick pulled up before a long, red-tile-roofed building, surrounded by a verandah, and as the driver opened the door, Teniente Coronel Ricardo Fosterwood came off the verandah and down the shrubbery-lined walk toward them.

Fosterwood was dressed for polo, in a white polo shirt, white breeches, and boots. And these,

Lowell saw, were the battered boots of a polo player, rather than the glistening boots of a cavalry officer.

"Pray for me," Lowell said softly. "I suspect I am about to get my ass kicked."

"Colonel," Fosterwood said. "I'm glad to see you again, and you, Major."

"It's good to be here."

He waved them toward the building. As they approached the verandah, another man dressed for polo got out of a wicker armchair and waited for them.

"Colonel Lowell," he said, holding out his hand. "How good of you to come. I am Pascual Pistarini."

"It was very good of you to ask us, General," Lowell said. "May I introduce my assistant, Major George W. Lunsford?"

"And it is a pleasure to meet you, Major," Pistarini said. "I understand you are not a polo player?"

"No, sir, I am not," Father said.

"Then may I suggest that you join me here, and I will attempt to explain the game to you, while Ricardo takes your colonel and does his best to get him suited up?"

"You're very kind, sir," Lunsford said.

"And if you will be good enough to come with me, *mi coronel?*" Fosterwood said, motioning toward the door to the building.

"Inasmuch, *mi coronel,*" Lowell said, "as we are both of the same rank, and you are about to learn what a terrible polo player I am, could you find it in your heart to call me by my Christian name? Craig?"

General Pistarini laughed.

"Of course, Craig," Fosterwood said. "My friends — and if I may say so, I consider you one already — call me Ricky."

They shook hands, smiled, and Ricky waved Craig into the building.

Just inside the door were two soldiers in fatigues and web gear carrying automatic rifles, and there were others, officers, in fatigue uniform and armed with pistols and submachine guns in the large foyer of the building.

"Polo fans, no doubt?" Craig said to Ricky.

"There is, as I mentioned, a small internal problem at the moment," Fosterwood said uneasily. "What is the cliché? 'Better safe than sorry'?"

"Are you a betting man, Ricky?"

"Every once in a while I make a small wager, yes. Why do you ask?"

"I'll give you five to one the Brazilians don't let him the leave the country for anywhere but Spain."

Fosterwood, although he tried hard, could not keep his surprise off his face.

"Excuse me?" he said after a moment.

Lowell smiled at him.

"How good a polo player is General Pistarini?" he asked.

"He has a six-goal handicap," Fosterwood said, almost visibly relieved the subject had been changed.

"The locker room is right this way, Craig," he went on. "Unless you would like a little something to drink first?"

"I think, under the circumstances, that alcohol would not be wise," Craig said. "After the game . . ."

When Craig rode onto the field — which he saw was manicured, but bore the marks of frequent use — he saw that the tile-roofed building also had a verandah on the polo field side. Officers and their wives were sitting, waiting for the game to begin, at tables on it.

There was also a balcony cut into the attic of the building, providing a better view of the field, obviously for senior officers and their wives. There were four tables under umbrellas. No one was sitting at any of the tables.

And he saw, standing at maybe thirty-yard intervals against the ten-foot-high shrubbery that lined both sides of the field, more soldiers in field gear and carrying automatic rifles.

Perón really has these people worried. What if he manages to get back in, and takes over the country again? Where's that going to leave me?

Your immediate problem, Craig, my boy, is not to fall off your horse while playing far out of your league. Worry about that.

Not only is this a first-class shower room, Lowell thought an hour and a half later, standing in a large, tile-walled shower stall under a powerful stream of hot water, *but there is obviously an even better one reserved for the commander-in-chief of the Argentina Army. I don't see him here, and he needed a shower just about as bad as I do.*

Fosterwood, now wearing a polo shirt and slacks, was waiting for him in the locker room.

"You are too modest, Craig," he said. "Of our five goals, two were yours."

"God takes care of fools and drunks, Ricky, and

I qualify on both counts."

Fosterwood laughed delightedly.

That's a funny line, but not that funny.

"I will have to remember that," Fosterwood said. "When you're finished dressing, the general asks that you join him."

Fosterwood led him up a stairway to the upper-level balcony. Pistarini, dressed in slacks and a polo shirt like Fosterwood, was sitting in a wicker chair at one of the tables with Father Lunsford and a ruddy-faced man of forty-odd in a suit. There were glass mugs of beer sitting in front of Lunsford and the ruddy-faced man.

And there were two soldiers in field gear with automatic rifles, standing in the inside corners of the area, simultaneously scanning the area and trying to make themselves inconspicuous.

Pistarini rose to his feet, smiled, and offered Lowell his hand.

"We have a rule that anyone who scores two or more goals can cut the dust of the trail with absolutely anything he desires," he said.

"In that case, I will have a large glass of water, followed by a glass, perhaps two, of your excellent Argentine champagne," Lowell said.

Fosterwood went to fill the order.

"Oh, excuse me, Hans," Pistarini said, in German, to the ruddy-faced man and then switched to English. "Lieutenant Colonel Lowell, may I present my friend Colonel Hans Friedrich Stumpff, the German military attaché?"

Lowell rose from his wicker chair.

"I'm very pleased to meet you, Herr Oberst," Lowell said in German.

"And I you, Herr Oberstleutnant. Are you with the U.S. Embassy?"

"No, Herr Oberst, Major Lunsford and I are just visiting the army attaché," Lowell said, shook Stumpff's hand, and sat down again.

"You must be a cavalryman," Stumpff said. "You're a very good polo player."

"I'm an armor officer, Herr Oberst. As I'm sure you know, our cavalry now rides helicopters."

"I have been watching that development with great interest," Stumpff said.

"As have I," Pistarini said, now in German. "It is one of the things I look forward talking to Colonel Lowell about."

Fosterwood reappeared, trailed by a young soldier in a white jacket carrying a tray with glasses, and a second carrying a champagne cooler.

The glasses were filled, and touched together.

"To old friends and new," Pistarini said.

"Hear, hear," Fosterwood said.

Pistarini took a sip of his champagne and looked at his watch.

"I really had no idea it was so late," he said. "Hans, I need a word with Colonel Lowell, and we are both pressed for time. Would you be offended if I asked Teniente Coronel Fosterwood to take you and Major Lunsford to the bar?"

"Absolutely not," Stumpff said, immediately getting to his feet.

Lunsford looked at Lowell for guidance. Lowell just perceptibly nodded his head.

"Ricky, I think we'll need another bottle of the champagne," Pistarini said. "And then will you see we're not disturbed?"

"Yes, sir," Fosterwood said.

When they had gone, and another champagne cooler had been delivered, Pistarini looked directly at Lowell.

"You had never met my friend Stumpff before, had you, Colonel?"

"I never had the privilege of meeting the colonel before, sir."

"Interesting man," Pistarini said. "As is Major Lunsford. Stumpff and I both tried to draw him out, and got hardly anywhere. What is it he does in the Army, Colonel?"

"He's a Special Forces officer, sir."

"I thought perhaps an intelligence officer."

"A Special Forces officer, General."

"And what, exactly, does a Special Forces officer do in the U.S. Army?"

"They do all sorts of things, sir. Major Lunsford, until recently, was in the Congo."

"I was under the impression the U.S. government flatly denied the presence of U.S. forces in the Congo."

"I believe that to be the case, sir."

"But you say your major was there?"

"He infiltrated the Simba army that captured Stanleyville, sir. He speaks Swahili, and was wearing a uniform consisting of a Belgian officer's tunic, topped off with a leopard skin."

Pistarini thought a moment before going on.

"You're just about fluent in German, aren't you?"

"It's not as good as yours, General."

"You spent some time in Germany, I gather?"

"Yes, sir."

"And that's where you met our mutual friend Lieutenant General von Greiffenberg?"

"Yes, sir."

"May I ask how that came to be?"

"My wife introduced us, sir."

"Your wife?" Pistarini asked, surprised.

"Generalleutnant Graf von Greiffenberg is my father-in-law, General."

"How interesting," Pistarini said. "I wonder why he didn't mention that in his letter. You know about the letter?"

"He was good enough to show it to me, and to Mr. Felter, before he sent it, General."

"You should have brought your wife to Argentina, Colonel. It would have given my wife great pleasure to show General von Greiffenberg's daughter our country."

"My wife passed on, General."

"I'm so sorry," Pistarini said.

"An auto accident, in Germany, while I was in Korea," Lowell said.

"How very tragic," Pistarini said. "You served with great distinction in Korea, didn't you? Earning your country's second-highest award for valor."

Lowell didn't reply.

"And before that, you were awarded the Greek order of Saint George and Saint Andrew."

Lowell said nothing.

"What were you doing in Greece?"

"We were trying to — and succeeded — in keeping the Communists from taking over the country."

"And you seem to know that Colonel Perón is at this very moment trying to reenter Argentina via Brazil," Pistarini said. "Let a simple soldier, Colonel, try to put this all together. You have apparently spent a good part of your career fighting the communist menace."

"That's a fair statement, sir."

"Would it be also be fair of me to conclude that you have a professional as well as a personal relationship with General von Greiffenberg?"

"Yes, sir, it would."

"And a professional relationship with the mysterious Mr. Felter, as well?"

"Professional and personal, General. He is my closest friend."

"To a simple soldier, this suggests that you are an intelligence officer, probably attached to the Central Intelligence Agency."

"No, sir. I have no connection of any sort with the Central Intelligence Agency."

"But you realize, of course, that I would expect you to deny such a relationship?"

"Would the general accept my word of honor as an officer about that?"

Pistarini leaned forward in his chair and looked into Lowell's eyes. Then he slumped back in his chair.

"Yes, I will," he said. "You come here bringing with you an officer, a Special Forces officer, who you tell me has been in the Congo, despite the flat statement by your government that the U.S. Army was not involved in the Congo."

"Yes, sir."

"In your judgment, Colonel, was the situation in the Congo Communist-inspired?"

"My best information, sir, is that the Simba movement was spontaneous. As soon as Moscow heard of it, they attempted to get arms and ammunition, and other support, to the Simbas. The parachute envelopment of Stanleyville by the Belgians —"

"Dropped from U.S. Air Force aircraft," Pistarini interrupted.

"— came just in time to make that impossible for them," Lowell concluded.

311

"And now this simple soldier wants to know what, if anything, this has to do with Argentina?"

"We believe — and I have been authorized by General von Greiffenberg to tell you he shares this belief — that the Communists have by no means abandoned their intentions for Africa."

"I'm sure that's true, but what is it you want from Argentina?"

"We also believe that an Argentine national will shortly become very actively involved in fresh efforts to have the Congo fall under communist control."

"That's difficult for me to accept," Pistarini said. "What Argentine national? You're not talking about Che Guevara?"

"The most recent information I have on Dr. Guevara is that he spent New Year's Eve in the Cuban Embassy in Bamako, Mali," Lowell said. "Prior to that, he was in Algiers. We have reason to believe that he will next go to Brazzaville, in the former French Congo."

"You're sure of this information?" He was visibly surprised.

"We believe it to be absolutely reliable, General."

Pistarini slumped back in his chair and sat there for a full ninety seconds.

"Even if it comes slowly to a simple soldier, there is usually a reason for everything," he said finally. "Colonel, you may tell both the mysterious Mister Felter and General von Greiffenberg that should Dr. Guevara suffer an unfortunate accident, it would of course be fully investigated by our SIDE — the assistant director of which met you at the airport — who would conclude they found nothing, *absolutely nothing,* suspicious in the events surrounding his death."

He looked at Lowell and smiled.

"And between you and me, between Pascual and Craig, the sooner that despicable anti-Christ communist sonofabitch met a painful death, the better I would like it."

"General," Lowell said. "Believe me, I understand your feelings. But the fact is I was sent here to solicit your cooperation in keeping the despicable anti-Christ communist sonofabitch alive."

Pistarini looked at him intently. He shrugged, then picked up the champagne bottle and refilled their glasses.

"You are a man of many surprises, Colonel," he said. "When you say you were sent here, you mean by Mr. Felter?"

"Yes, sir. But General von Greiffenberg is aware of my mission, and has authorized me to tell you that he and Mr. Felter are in complete agreement about this."

"Did they share their reasoning with you? And if so, are you able to share it with me?"

"They believe, sir — and I have come to believe they're right — that Guevara alive will pose fewer problems than Guevara dead, especially if the Communists can allege — not necessarily prove, simply credibly allege — that he was murdered by fascist forces who wanted to keep him from liberating the poor and oppressed."

"I'm going to have a hard time selling that argument to Rangio," Pistarini said.

"Sir?"

"I was thinking out loud," Pistarini said. "Coronel Francisco Bolla is the Chief of SIDE, which is directly under President Illia. Bolla works for Illia, in other words. Teniente Coronel

313

Guillermo Rangio, who met you at the airfield, is the deputy director. He works for me. My orders to him are that Dr. Guevara is not to return to Argentina alive, despite what orders he may have from anyone else to the contrary."

Lowell said nothing.

Pistarini drained his champagne glass.

"What I really would like to have right now is a large scotch," he said. "But as you know, I have another problem on my hands at the moment. . . ." He paused. "Did you mean what you said to Fosterwood? The odds are five to one the Brazilians will not allow him to come here?"

"I was gambling from a position of ignorance, General," Lowell said. "If I were the Brazilians, that's what I'd do."

"Do they teach 'never underestimate your enemy' in the U.S. Army, Colonel?"

"Yes, sir."

"If you and Major Lunsford are free for dinner tonight, Colonel, I would be pleased if you would dine with Coronel Rangio and me."

"We would be honored, sir," Lowell said. "Where and when?"

"Probably about ten," Pistarini said. "I think I should have some word as to how things are going in Brazil by then. Is ten too late for you?"

"No, sir. Dress?"

"This will be very informal," Pistarini said.

"Yes, sir."

"And as to where, the driver will know. If you wouldn't mind, if you would either be in the Círculo Militar from nine-thirty — or in the car, there's a radio in the car — it would make things easier for me."

"Yes, sir."

Pistarini got quickly to his feet.

"And if you will excuse me before I give in to the temptation to have the rest of the champagne?"

Lowell jumped to his feet.

"Thank you very much, General," he said.

"I will send another of my aides up here with the Major and Colonel Stumpff, and you can finish it," Pistarini said, and walked off the balcony.

Both of the soldiers with the automatic rifles followed him.

[TWO]
Círculo Militar
Plaza San Martín
Buenos Aires, Argentina
2105 3 January 1965

"Would you please see who that is, Major Lunsford?" Lieutenant Colonel Craig Lowell asked. "Your beloved colonel's ass is really dragging."

Lunsford pushed himself out of his armchair and walked to the door of the suite. An elderly steward in a white jacket extended a silver tray to him. It held a calling card. Lunsford picked it up.

"Beloved Colonel, sir," he called. "Mr. J. F. Stephens is downstairs and seeks audience with you."

"Who?"

"According to his card, Mr. Stephens is the administrative officer for housing and medical services of the United States Information Service."

"Jesus!" Lowell said.

"He probably wants to ask you about hog belly futures."

315

"Let him come up," Lowell said.

When he stepped into the suite, it was impossible to tell if Mr. Stephens was an old-looking twenty-five-year-old or a young-looking thirty-five-year-old. He stood about five feet seven in his mussed seersucker suit, was pale-skinned and starting to bald, and his shoes needed both heels and a shine.

"My name is Lowell, Mr. Stephens," Lowell called from what he thought of as his overstuffed red leather chair of pain. "You wanted to see me?"

Stephens walked to Lowell and handed him a curling sheet of paper from a photo transmission machine.

"I was asked to get this to you, Colonel," he said. His voice sounded as he looked: soft, inoffensive, and more than a little tired.

Obviously, Lowell thought as he started to read it, *a secure photo transmission machine.*

SECRET

Central Intelligence Agency
Langley, Virginia

FROM: Assistant Director For Administration

DATE: 3 January 1965 1005 GMT

SUBJECT: Guevara, Ernesto (Memorandum # <u>11</u>.)

TO: Mr. Sanford T. Felter
Counselor To The President

Room 637, The Executive Office Building
Washington, D.C.

By Courier

In compliance with Presidential Memorandum to The Director, Subject: "Ernesto
'Che' Guevara," dated 14 December 1964,
and in consideration of the fact that
SUBJECT holds Argentinian citizenship by
birth, the following information is furnished:

(1) (Reliability Scale Five) (From CIA Rio
de Janeiro, Brazil) Under threat of loss of
Brazilian landing rights for non-compliance,
the pilot of the Iberian Airlines aircraft which
carried Former Argentine President Juan D.
PERÓN to Rio was ordered by the Brazilian
Air Force authorities to fly non-stop to Madrid with PERÓN and party aboard.

(2) (Reliability Scale Five) (From CIA Rio)
PERÓN and party were placed aboard Iberian aircraft by Brazilian Air Force authorities,
and denied access to the more than 100
members of the press who had gathered at
the airfield, apparently informed of PERÓN's
presence by party or parties unknown. The
aircraft took off immediately, with PERÓN
and party, three of whom were armed, the
only passengers.

(3) (Reliability Scale Two) (From CIA
Rio) Brazilian military aircraft (possibly a
DC-8) will accompany Iberian aircraft over

317

Atlantic Ocean until the Point Of No Return.

(4) (Reliability Scale Five) (From CIA Buenos Aires, Argentina) Borders remain closely watched by Army augmented authorities. ARG Foreign Minister Miguel A. Z. ORTIZ stated PERÓN travel was "a maneuver in a campaign of provocation and subversion."

Howard W. O'Connor
HOWARD W. O'CONNOR

SECRET

"Thank you, Mr. Stephens," Lowell said, handing the document to Father Lunsford. "Can we repay your courtesy by offering you a small libation of your choice?"

"Right about now, I'd kill for a martini," Stephens said, surprising both Lowell and Lunsford. "It's been a lousy day for me."

"Among his many other talents, Major Lunsford is known for making wicked martinis," Lowell said. "If you please, Major Lunsford?"

"Sit down, please," Lowell said.

"Thank you."

Stephens sat on the edge of a couch.

He looks, Lowell thought, somewhat unkindly, *like a none-too-hopeful applicant for a job selling life insurance.*

"Clever, if battered, bruised, and exhausted, fellow that I am, I deduce you have access to a secure photo transmission line."

"I believe there is one somewhere around the embassy, Colonel."

"I was afraid you were going to say that, Mr. Stephens," Lowell said.

He pushed himself out of his armchair, grunting with the pain, walked into his bedroom and came back a moment later with an envelope, and handed it to Stephens.

HEADQUARTERS

United States Strike Command
McDill Air Force Base, Tampa, Florida

28 December 1964

Special Orders:
Number 360:

EXTRACT

    6. Lt Col LOWELL, C.W., this hq, and Maj LUNSFORD, G.W. Hq USASWC Ft Bragg NC are placed on TDY and WP to Buenos Aires, Argentina, and such other places as their mission requires for a period not to exceed thirty days. Travel by US Govt and Commercial Air, Land, and Sea T and POV is auth. Off possess TOP SECRET security clearances, and are authorized to transmit material up to TOP SECRET over US Govt facilities. Off will remain under command

---

of their respective units during this TDY.

EXTRACT

OFFICIAL:

Rupert K. McNeil
Brigadier General

"Do you have any trouble understanding the last two sentences of our orders?" Lowell asked.

Stephens shook his head, no.

"I went by the embassy about an hour ago," Lowell said. "Asked to see the military duty officer. I got an Air Force captain. I showed him the orders, and told him that I had a very short message, classified Secret, to send, and would he do that for me? And he wouldn't. Said he couldn't. Said the defense attaché had to sign off on any classified messages, and he wouldn't be available until the morning. My most persuasive arguments fell on deaf ears."

"I think I can find someone to send your message, Colonel," Mr. Stephens said.

Father came back in the sitting room with a squat glass.

"Mr. Stephens is going to send our message," Lowell said.

"What's with this defense attaché, anyway?" Lunsford asked. "Catch-22. We can't send a message without his approval, and he's not available to give his approval."

"His name is McGrory," Stephens said. "He likes to know everything that's going on."

Lowell handed him a sheet of paper.

"This is the message," he said.

"May I read it?"

"How nice of you to ask! I can tell just by looking at you that someone like yourself would never dream of reading other people's mail under any circumstances."

What could have been the hint of a smile appeared on Stephens thin, pale lips.

SECRET

To White House Signal Agency

Buenos Aires 1900 3 Jan

Mr. Sanford T. Felter
Room 637, Executive Office Building

I played polo with Peter's friend this afternoon, and he's buying Father and me dinner later. He is reluctant to talk about life insurance, but we will work on him.

Craig

SECRET

"I'm pretty sure I can get this off for you, Colonel," Stephens said.

"Tonight?"

"I wouldn't be surprised if it was in the Executive Office Building within the hour."

"You're an amazing man," Lowell said. "Whatever would the country do without the U.S. Information Agency?"

Stephens stood up and drained his martini.

"So are you," he said. "Most of the people watching you play polo this afternoon couldn't believe you were an American."

Then he nodded at Lunsford, turned, and walked out of the room.

[THREE]
Círculo Militar
Plaza San Martín
Buenos Aires, Argentina
2305 3 January 1965

Lieutenant Colonel Craig W. Lowell and Major George Washington Lunsford were both asleep in armchairs in the sitting room of their suite when the driver of the Buick appeared at the door and in British-accented English announced that if it was convenient for them, General Pistarini wished them to join him for dinner.

The Buick, again trailed by a black Ford Falcon, drove between the tall buildings of downtown Buenos Aires, crossed the Avenida de 9 Julio, supposed to be the widest avenue in the world, passed the Colón Opera House on the far side, and then moved again between tall office buildings.

"For your general fund of cultural knowledge, Major Lunsford," Lowell said. "That building is the Colón Opera House, built 1896–99, and it is larger than both the Paris and Vienna opera houses."

"You're a cornucopia of information, aren't you, *mi coronel?*"

"There was a book in English in my bathroom providing all sorts of information about Buenos Aires. Are you an opera fan, by any chance, Major Lunsford? This Wednesday they're doing *The Flying Dutchman.*"

"Would you be surprised if I told you, *mi coronel,* that I am very fond of *Die Fleigende Hollander?*"

"Nothing about you would surprise me, Major," Lowell said.

Lowell glanced out the window and saw they had doubled back and were headed back toward the bright lights of the Avenida de 9 Julio.

Then the Buick braked suddenly and turned off the street into what looked like the service entrance to one of the office buildings. The headlights picked out two soldiers in uniform, with 9-mm Uzi submachine guns slung around their necks.

There was a whining of electric motors, and then the large metal door to the street began to close. When it was just about closed, lights came on, and Lowell saw that the black Falcon that had been trailing them had pulled in beside them.

And then he saw Teniente Coronel Fosterwood, in uniform, coming down a flight of steps set into the concrete loading dock toward the car. The driver of Buick barely beat him to the door and opened it.

"Ah, Craig, so sorry we're so late," he said. "I understand that Americans like to eat in what we call the afternoon."

"Frankly, Ricky, we have just about emptied

that magnificent basket of fruit," Lowell said. They shook hands.

He waved them up the concrete steps to the landing dock and down a corridor to an elevator and into it.

The elevator operator had an Uzi slung under his arm.

The elevator stopped, and Fosterwood led them down a paneled corridor, in which there was another man with an Uzi, and waved them through a double door.

It was an office. The large sturdy man who had met them at Ezeiza was seated behind a large, ornately carved desk. There were two Argentine flags against the wall behind the desk, on either side of an antique sword — a cavalry saber, Lowell corrected himself — in a glass case.

There was a bottle of Johnny Walker Black Label scotch on the desk, and a water pitcher.

"Good evening, gentlemen," General Pascual Angel Pistarini said, rising from a leather armchair. "Thank you for joining us."

He put out his right hand. His left held a large square glass dark with something Lowell suspected had come from the bottle on the SIDE guy's desk.

"We're honored to be here, General," Lowell said, shaking his hand.

"Let me first formally present Teniente Coronel Guillermo Rangio, the deputy director of SIDE," Pistarini said. "You have met both of these gentlemen, Guillermo."

Rangio rose from behind the large desk and shook hands, wordlessly, with both of them.

"That out of the way," Pistarini said, "I think under the circumstances we should address one another by our Christian names, or better still, what is your phrase, our 'nicknames'?"

Craig Lowell had an immediate flashback to Bad Nauheim, Germany, in 1946. Major General Porterman K. Waterford, commanding general of the U.S. Constabulary, had assembled his newly formed polo team in a stable.

"Gentlemen, on the polo field, we will relax somewhat military courtesy," he said. "I will address you by your Christian names, or your nicknames, whichever you prefer, and you, in turn, may address me either as 'Sir' or 'General.' "

Lowell had laughed then, and he barely managed to suppress a laugh now. No one in this room was about to call Pistarini "Pascual."

"Craig knows that Ricky is Ricky, Willi," Pistarini said to Rangio. "But I don't know what Major Lunsford is called by his friends."

"Father, sir," Lunsford.

Pistarini's face tightened. "Isn't that how one refers to priests in English?"

"Yes, sir," Lunsford said. "But in my case, it makes reference to my Christian names George Washington, as in 'Father of his Country.' "

"I see," Pistarini said, visibly relieved. "Well, then, Father, that's what we'll call you, with your permission, of course."

"I would be honored, sir," Father said.

Fosterwood nudged Lowell's arm, and when Lowell looked, handed him one of the square glasses. Then he handed Lunsford one.

"I thought we should drink to the successful transoceanic flight of a man who once sat behind that desk," Pistarini said. "Have you heard about that, Craig?"

"Yes, sir. Did you hear, General, that the Brazilian Air Force is accompanying the plane to the Point of No Return?"

"No, I didn't," Pistarini admitted.

And that got your attention, didn't it, Willi? Lowell thought. *There was a visible crack in your studiously stern countenance.*

"Would you say, Craig," Pistarini asked, "that your government had something to do with the departure of the man we're talking about?"

"I don't know that, sir. But I would certainly think so. We don't want him back here any more than you do."

"Let's drink to his successful, nonstop transoceanic flight," Pistarini said, and raised his glass.

There was nothing in the filled glass but Johnny Walker Black and ice, and not much of that.

"We are going to be completely open with you, Craig, in the belief you will be the same to us."

"Yes, sir."

"This is the office of the deputy director of SIDE," Pistarini said. "Willi's office. SIDE's director, who has rarely been a career intelligence officer, serves at the pleasure of the President, and maintains his office in the Casa Rosado, our White House, near the office of the President. The deputy directors of SIDE — including Willi — are customarily career intelligence officers who serve at the pleasure of the commander-in-chief of the Army."

He let that sink in, then went on.

"The director of SIDE very rarely comes to this building. Very few people do. Willi and I were talking before, and we really think that

326

you and Father are the first Americans, and very probably the only foreign officers, ever to be where you are now."

"Then we are very honored, sir."

"There are in this office two symbols of what has been great about Argentina, and what has been very, very disgraceful and bad for the country," Pistarini said. "The sword is that of General Simón Bolívar. He was, I'm sure you will agree, a great man, who at the risk of his life, his fortune, and his honor did great things not only for Argentina but for the entire Western Hemisphere."

"He is one of our heroes, too, sir. One of General MacArthur's most trusted lieutenants was General Simón Bolívar Buckner."

"So I have heard," Pistarini said. "The other symbol is the desk behind which Willi sits. It was formerly used by Juan Domingo Perón."

"I don't know what to say, sir, except that it's a beautiful desk."

"There are many objects of beauty in Argentina, Craig," Pistarini said. "Unfortunately, Perón thought — probably still thinks — they all belonged to him, and/or to the woman he married."

He walked across the office and pulled open a door.

"I think you should see this," he said, "although I hope you won't tell anyone you did."

Lowell and Lunsford walked across the room and into the small room beyond.

"I don't think there are one hundred Argentines who know this," Pistarini said. "But this is where, after God took pity on Argentina and removed Evita from our midst, SIDE held her body for six weeks. Perón had it specially embalmed — he had a Spaniard come here to do it — in the manner of Lenin, and it was the intention of the Peronists to build a enormous monument to Señora de Perón, in which her body would be on permanent display."

"I'd never heard that before," Lowell said.

"We knew that once the parasites around Perón got their hands on her body, very little could be done to stop the Leninization of her, so we took control of the body to prevent that from happening. A young SIDE major was given the duty, with orders to guard the remains with his life."

Lowell felt suddenly sure that he was talking about Willi Rangio.

"Curiosity is about to overwhelm me, General."

"Where is the body now? I hope you can control your curiosity, Craig. I don't think you need to know, but I will tell you if you ask."

"I will not ask, sir. Forgive me."

"I have told you our secrets, and over dinner, I hope you will tell us yours," Pistarini said.

He took Lowell's arm and led him back through Rangio's office to another room where a table had been set for dinner.

A stocky man wearing a white jacket over uniform trousers served as the waiter. He reminded Lowell very much of Master Sergeant Doubting Thomas. An old soldier, tough as nails, and absolutely to be trusted to do whatever he was told to do.

"There's wine, of course," Pistarini said as he waved them into chairs. "A very nice Merlot from Mendoza, but if you would like another whiskey?"

"The wine will be fine, sir."

"And you haven't finished the first, have you? Either of you."

It was a challenge, however tactfully phrased.

"Waste not, want not, my general," Lowell said, raised his glass, and drained it. Father did the same thing.

The old soldier filled their wineglasses. It took nearly two bottles before he was finished.

Then, with a grace surprising for his bulk, he served the first course, prosciutto ham wrapped around chunks of melon.

"Delicious," Lowell said. "Argentine?"

"Oh, yes," Willi Rangio said. "Tell me, Craig, would Sanford T. Felter eat that?"

It was the first time he had said anything. His English was perfect, but without an identifiable accent, neither British, nor American, nor any variation of those dialects.

"Would he eat the ham, Willi? Oh, yes, and with relish. Is he Jewish? Which, if it's what you're asking, yes he is."

"Is he CIA?" Rangio asked.

"No, he's not. Actually, Willi, I suspect that his service is much like yours. Are you a graduate of the military academy here?"

"All Argentine officers are."

"Most Americans are not. I'm not, Father's not. Felter is a West Pointer."

"He's not listed in your Army Register," Fosterwood said.

"I didn't know that," Lowell said. "But it doesn't surprise me. Anyway, Felter is a serving officer. A full colonel."

"You told General Pistarini that he is your closest friend," Rangio said, making it a question.

"Yes, he is," Lowell said, and put a chunk of

melon and prosciutto in his mouth.

"Really delicious," he said.

"Tell us how you met him," Rangio said.

"I was a very young officer in Greece, a second lieutenant. Felter was there, as a first lieutenant. He had served in the war against Germany. He saved my life."

"How did he do that?" Fosterwood asked.

"This is one of my secrets," Lowell said, looked at Pistarini, and then went on: "I was serving with a Greek company on the Albanian border. We were attacked by Communists, Greek and Albanian, and nearly overrun. I was pretty badly shot up, and there were other wounded. A Greek relief column was sent, under an American captain — a West Pointer, by the way — to reinforce us. This 'officer' concluded that under the circumstances fifty dead Greeks, thirty wounded Greeks, fifteen unwounded men, and a second lieutenant did not justify moving the column in such a manner that would bring it under fire and he himself might be hit."

"And what happened?" Pistarini asked.

"Felter did what he concluded was necessary for an honorable officer to do under the circumstances," Lowell said matter-of-factly. "He shot him, took over the column, and, as the expression goes, saved my bacon."

"I never heard that story before," Father blurted.

"And you probably won't again. It's not for repeating. This is a special situation," Lowell said.

"So he was an intelligence officer as early as your involvement in Greece?" Rangio asked.

"No," Lowell said. "He got involved with intelligence — actually counterintelligence — after

Greece. In Germany. Probably because he spoke German."

"I understand that you had many German Jews in Germany running down Nazis," Rangio said.

"We did, but from the beginning, Felter has been involved with the Communists."

"And do you think he had a connection with the Gehlen organization?" Pistarini asked, almost innocently.

"He did, and does, General," Lowell said.

"Am I allowed to ask what that is?" Fosterwood asked.

"You don't really know, Ricky?" Pistarini asked.

"Sir, I'm just a simple soldier," Fosterwood said.

"General Gehlen was the Abwehr officer, under Admiral Canaris, in charge of Eastern intelligence, Russian intelligence," Pistarini said. "When the war was over, he offered to turn his entire operation over to the Americans, providing that they didn't go after any of his men in the de-Nazification program."

"And we agreed?" Father asked incredulously. "To let some Nazis walk?"

Lowell nodded.

"Either Eisenhower or President Truman — probably Truman, no one else would have had the authority — decided we couldn't have done without what Gehlen was offering."

The waiter who reminded Lowell of Doubting Thomas took the prosciutto and melon plates away, replaced them with plates of enormous grilled chunks of filet mignon, and then refilled the wineglasses.

When he had finished, General Pistarini asked,

"And is that how Mr. — Colonel — Felter became close to General von Greiffenberg?"

"In a way, General," Lowell said. "Felter learned that my father-in-law was in Siberia, with several thousand other German POWs the Russians never intended to send home. He arranged for the Gehlen organization to get him out."

"Because he was your father-in-law?" Rangio asked.

"That was a happy by-product of getting him out," Lowell said. "I think — and Felter's told me this — that he could justify the effort because von Greiffenberg, whose anti-Nazi credentials are impeccable, was fully aware of what happened in the Katyn Forest."

"The Katyn Forest?" Fosterwood asked.

"When the Red Army moved against Poland," Lowell said, "they took a large portion of the Polish army officer corps, thousands of them, including several hundred teenage officer cadets, into the Katyn Forest, shot them in the back of the head, and buried them in unmarked mass graves. And then, when it came out, tried to blame it on the Germans."

"How did Felter know what happened in the Katyn Forest?" Rangio asked. "That General von Greiffenberg knew about it?"

"While General von Greiffenberg — he was then a colonel — was recuperating from wounds during the war, he ran a prisoner-of-war camp for American officers. He took several of them to the forest and let them judge for themselves, from the evidence, who had been responsible."

"In the face of all the evidence," Rangio said, "I am absolutely unable to understand why so many people refuse to believe the truth about the Russians."

"Willi," Pistarini said resignedly, "how many Argentines absolutely refuse to believe the truth, despite the evidence, about Perón and his wife?"

Rangio shrugged.

"I also think Felter, and probably Gehlen," Lowell went on, "agreed that with von Greiffenberg's anti-Nazi credentials, plus his Russian experiences, he would almost certainly attain high rank in the German Army, might even become chief of intelligence. Getting him out was costly; they had to think carefully about doing it. But to answer your basic question, Willi, they did not get him out because he was my father-in-law."

"I didn't mean to imply —"

Lowell waved his hand in a dismissal of that, then went on:

"Anyway, the Korean War came along, and Felter went over there, by then an intelligence officer."

"It must be hard to be an intelligence officer if you don't speak the language," Rangio mused out loud.

"Felter speaks Korean," Lowell said. "And Russian. And Greek. And Vietnamese, and . . ."

"And Spanish?" Pistarini asked.

"Probably. I never asked him, but it wouldn't surprise me. In fact, I'd bet on it."

"He's like your General Vernon Walters,[*] then?"

[*] Lieutenant General Vernon Walters, USA, who spent much of his military career as an interpreter for senior military and government officials at high-level international conferences, was later Ambassador to the United Nations.

Pistarini asked.

Lowell looked at him in surprise.

"I met the general in Washington," Pistarini said. "An amazing man. I heard he only has to hear a language for a couple of hours, and he can speak it."

"I don't know if Felter is as good as General Walters, but he's close," Lowell said.

"And that is how he reached his — what shall I say? Current position. As a linguist?"

"Something like that," Lowell said. "When Eisenhower was elected, before he was inaugurated, he went to Korea. Felter was assigned as his interpreter, and when Ike left Korea, Felter was on the plane with him. And he's been a counselor to the President ever since. Kennedy after Eisenhower, Johnson after Kennedy."

"But you would agree, would you not, that he is more than a presidential interpreter?" Pistarini said.

"I think that would be a fair statement," Lowell said.

"And is President Johnson aware of the decision that he and General von Greiffenberg have reached about Dr. Guevara?" Pistarini asked.

"It was Colonel Felter's recommendation, sir. President Johnson went along with the logic. Felter was sent to tell von Greiffenberg of the President's decision, and he took me along to help convince him of the wisdom of the decision. There was no argument — von Greiffenberg and Felter are in complete agreement that everybody's best interests are served by keeping Guevara alive."

"And you're here on the same sort of mission?"

"Yes, sir, as I told you."

"If it were up to you personally, Father," Pistarini asked, "how would you handle the problem of Dr. Guevara?"

"I'm a soldier, General," Father said, just a little thickly. "I do what I'm told, but if it were up to me, I'd blow the murdering sonofabitch away the first chance I got."

And so, Lowell thought, *would you, Willi, to judge from your no longer expressionless face.*

And then Pistarini read Lowell's mind.

"It would seem that Willi and Father are having trouble understanding the reasoning of your president and von Greiffenberg, Craig," he said.

"And you, sir?"

"I agree with the decision," Pistarini said. "Argentina already has one modern-day martyr in Evita. The country doesn't need another one."

Willi's face showed disappointment.

"What are you proposing, Colonel Lowell?" Pistarini asked.

"We will share our intelligence on his activities with you," Lowell said. "We would like that to be reciprocal."

"Willi?"

"That raises questions," Rangio said, looking at Lowell, "how do we know what we're getting is all you have, and that it can be trusted?"

"It's in our interest to see that you have everything, and I hope you will see that it is in yours to give us what you have."

"Anything else?" Pistarini asked.

"The army attaché at our embassy here is about to get an airplane, a twin Beech, what we call the L-23."

"Very nice. I know the aircraft," Pistarini said.

"How much does Colonel Harris know of all this?"

"Very little. I'm going to see him tomorrow, and I will tell him as little as possible."

"What about the airplane?" Fosterwood asked.

"It will be used to transport our military attaché personnel around Argentina, Uruguay, Paraguay, and Chile, visiting as many bases and places as we can get the army attaché and his staff invited to."

"And you don't want me to pay much attention to it, right?" Rangio asked.

"I hope you do more than that," Lowell said. "The copilot will be a U.S. Army warrant officer named Enrico de la Santiago. I think you might become friends."

"Why is that?"

"He really hates Señor Guevara. Guevara personally murdered his grandfather in Havana, with Enrico's mother and grandmother watching."

"What did they do?" Pistarini asked.

"His grandfather was a lawyer," Lowell said, "who was known for saying unkind things about Communists. And then Guevara knew that Enrico had flown a Cuban Air Force fighter to Florida, saying that as a Catholic he was obliged to fight Castro."

"And what does he think of the decision to keep Guevara alive?"

"He's every bit as enthusiastic about it as you and Father," Lowell said.

Rangio laughed. "I look forward to meeting him," he said.

"When the airplane is delivered, and that should be shortly, there will be other people concerned with this aboard. A master sergeant named Thomas, who will be going to the Congo with

Father; an officer who was raised in the Congo, and is helping train Father's people; and another officer who will be coordinating things at Fort Bragg. I'd like them to learn as much as they can about Guevara — what you have on him, where he was raised, that sort of thing."

" 'Know your enemy,' eh?" Pistarini said. "Work out the details between you, Willi."

"Yes, sir."

"And now, gentlemen," Pistarini said, "I think we should have a brandy and call it a night. It's been a very busy day."

IX

[ONE]
Círculo Militar
Plaza San Martín
Buenos Aires, Argentina
0915 4 January 1965

Lieutenant Colonel Craig W. Lowell came into the sitting room of the suite in a tropical worsted uniform. It bore the silver-leaf oak leaves of his rank on its epaulets: four rows of four-wide colored ribbons, plus one on top of these. The single ribbon was that of the Distinguished Service Cross, the nation's second-highest award for gallantry in action. The other ribbons represented other decorations, United States and foreign, including the Purple Heart medal with two oak-leaf clusters, indicating he had three times been wounded in combat, and what he thought of as his "I was there" ribbons, attesting that he had served in the European Theatre of Operations, the Army of Occupation in Germany, Korea, and the Republic of Vietnam.

Immediately below the ribbons were the wings of the parachutist, and immediately above them the silver wings with a wreathed star indicating he was a Master Army Aviator. Above these was the only device he thought meant a damn, a wreathed blue oblong box with a musket inside, the Combat Infantry Badge. His had a star within the wreath, indicating the second award.

338

Over the other breast pocket were devices indicating and representing the Distinguished Unit Citations of the United States and the Republic of Korea, and pinned to the blouse pocket beneath was the badge attesting that he had served on the General Staff of the U.S. Army. His lapels carried the insignia of the General Staff Corps.

Major George Washington Lunsford was similarly uniformed. He had fewer ribbons, the one on top of the others the Silver Star, with clusters indicating he had won the third-highest decoration three times. He, too, had won the Combat Infantry Badge, but only once. His parachutist's wings, however, had a wreath and a star, indicating he was a Master Parachutist. His lapels carried the crossed rifles of infantry, and there was no GSC badge, but that pocket of his uniform carried the parachutists wings of the Vietnamese, the Australians, and the Germans.

He held a leather-brimmed uniform cap in one hand, and a green beret in the other.

"If I may be permitted to say so, *mi coronel*, you look like death warmed over in a splendidly tailored uniform," Lunsford said.

"I was doing all right until Pistarini said 'Let's have a brandy and call it a day,' or words to that effect," Lowell said. "What he obviously meant was let's have a bottle of brandy, each."

"What was that all about?" Lunsford asked.

"I think by then he understood that Perón was really on his way back to Spain, and he could really relax."

"If Perón had come back, Pistarini would have been in trouble?"

"And so would we," Lowell said. "Perón hates all things American, or North American, as I

339

learned to say last night. We would have gotten zero help with him running things."

"My memory is a little fuzzy, but we did come out of the place smelling like a rose, didn't we?"

"Yeah, I think we did," Lowell said. "I don't think that was the booze talking. And Rangio has contacts in Chile, Bolivia, the other places, that we can't come close to."

"And you think he's on board?"

"I think (a) he's on board, and (b) will do what Pistarini tells him to do."

"Which hat, boss?" Father asked, holding up the green beret and the service cap.

"The brimmed one," Lowell said.

"Did you forget yours?"

"No. It's in my briefcase, and when we accept Pistarini's kind offer — let's hope he remembers it — to join him for the cocktail hour at the Edificio Libertador, I'm going to wear it. But brimmed caps for the embassy, I think."

Lunsford opened his briefcase and stuffed the green beret in it.

"You don't wear yours much, do you?" he asked.

"It makes me a little uncomfortable," Lowell said. "I got fathered into Special Forces. I've made only seven parachute jumps, I never went through Mackall, and I really don't know how to bite the head off a chicken."

Father smiled. "One of them was a HALO,[*] I understand?"

"My *first* was a HALO," Lowell said. "Red Hanrahan did that to me. I thought I was going to

[*] A High Altitude, Low Opening parachute descent is made by exiting an aircraft at a very high altitude, and falling close to the ground before deploying the canopy.

watch a HALO, and the next thing I know, two of his thugs grabbed my arms and dragged me off the open ramp of a C-130 at 30,000 feet."

Father laughed.

"That was Hanrahan's way of announcing that the army had decided that since Special Forces had really gotten started in Greece, and people who had served there — you knew Hanrahan was our colonel there, Felter's and mine? —"

Lunsford nodded.

"— so anybody who was there could consider himself a Green Beret."

"I thought it got started in Korea?"

"Not by that name," Lowell said. "Bull Simon came back from Korea and started it at Bragg."

"Just for the record, *mi coronel,* I think you're as entitled to the beret as anybody I ever met," Lunsford said.

Lowell looked at him for a moment.

"Thank you," he said simply.

"My name is Lowell, Corporal," Lowell said to the Marine guard in the lobby of the American Embassy. "This is Major Lunsford. We'd like to see Colonel Harris, the army attaché, please."

"Sir, Colonel McGrory left word that if you showed up here, I was to send you to his office."

"You've relayed Colonel McGrory's message, Corporal. Now please call Colonel Harris and tell him that I'd like to see him," Lowell snapped, and was immediately sorry. "Corporal, the truth is I'm just a little hungover. I didn't mean to snap at you."

The Marine corporal didn't reply, but he picked up his telephone, dialed a number, and told whoever answered, "U.S. Army Lieutenant Colonel

Lowell and one other officer to see Colonel Harris."

Master Sergeant Douglas Wilson came into the foyer less than two minutes later. He saluted.

"Good morning, sir. We've been expecting you. Sir, the defense attaché, Colonel McGrory, wants to see you right away."

"Sergeant, I'll see Colonel McGrory when I've completed my business with Colonel Harris."

"Yes, sir. Right this way, please, gentlemen?"

The moment they were out of sight, the Marine Corporal called the office of the defense attaché.

"Office of the defense attaché, Master Sergeant Ulrich speaking, sir."

"Corporal Young at Post One, Sergeant. That Army colonel your colonel was looking for just came in the building. With a major."

"I'll come get him."

"Sergeant, he told me to call Colonel Harris's office, and Colonel Harris sent his sergeant to fetch him."

"Okay. Colonel McGrory's on the can. The minute he comes out, I'll tell him. Thank you."

The Marine corporal broke the connection and dialed another number.

"Mr. Stephens, this is Corporal Young at Post One. That Army officer you were asking about just came into the building. He's on his way to Colonel Harris's office."

Lowell, with Lunsford on his heels, marched into Colonel Harris's office, came to attention, and saluted.

"Sir, Lieutenant Colonel Lowell and Major Lunsford. Thank you for seeing us."

Harris returned the salute.

"Colonel, did my sergeant major tell you that Colonel McGrory has expressed a strong desire that you report to him immediately, whenever you came into the embassy?"

"Yes, sir, he did," Lowell replied, still at attention. "I have no business with Colonel McGrory, but I'll see him when I'm finished here."

"Colonel, Colonel McGrory's request is really in the nature of an order."

"Sir, may I show you my orders?" Lowell said. "They specifically state that both Major Lunsford and myself remain —"

Colonel H. Robert McGrory, USAF, visibly agitated, stormed into the room.

"Colonel Lowell," Colonel Harris said, "Colonel H. Robert McGrory, the defense attaché."

"Do you know how to obey orders, Colonel?" McGrory inquired.

"Yes, sir, I think I do."

"Then, it might be fairly said, you have willfully disobeyed my orders?"

"Sir, with respect, you are not in a position to issue orders to me or Major Lunsford."

"Goddamn your impertinence!" McGrory flared. "I am the senior military officer attached to the U.S. Embassy and —" he stopped in midsentence, having seen Mr. J. F. Stephens, the administrative officer for housing and medical services of the United States Information Service standing in Harris's open door.

"Mr. Stephens," McGrory said. "If you're here to see Colonel Harris, give me just a minute, and these officers and I will be out of here."

"Actually, Colonel," Stephens said softly. "I'm here to see Colonel Lowell. Could you give me a minute, please?"

"Yes, of course," McGrory said. "Colonel Lowell, you understand that you are to report to me immediately after Mr. Stephens concludes his business with you?"

"Yes, sir," Lowell said.

McGrory left. Stephens closed the door.

"I called the Círculo Militar, and they told me you were coming here," Stephens said. He took a folded sheet of paper from his pocket and handed it to Lowell.

SECRET

Central Intelligence Agency
Langley, Virginia

FROM: Assistant Director For Administration

DATE: 3 January 1965 2115 GMT

SUBJECT: Guevara, Ernesto (Memorandum # 17.)

TO: Mr. Sanford T. Felter
Counselor To The President
Room 637, The Executive Office Building
Washington, D.C.

By Courier

In compliance with Presidential Memorandum to The Director, Subject: "Ernesto 'Che' Guevara," dated 14 December 1964,

---

the following information is furnished:

(1) (Reliability Scale Five) (From CIA, Brazzaville, Congo (Brazzaville) SUBJECT arrived Brazzaville 0835 GMT 2 January 1965 aboard UTA Flight 4505. He was met at airfield by Prime Minister Pascal LISSOUBA and taken to Cuban Embassy.

(2) (Reliability Scale Five) (From CIA, Brazzaville) SUBJECT met with President Alphonse MASSEMBA-DEBAT and LISSOUBA at Presidential Residence at 1245 GMT 2 January 1965 for lunch.

(3) (Reliability Scale Three) (From CIA source) At luncheon MASSEMBA-DEBAT and LISSOUBA asked for Cuban military aid and expressed willingness to cooperate with liberation movement. SUBJECT promised to furnish instructors for guerrilla operations, weapons, and money.

Howard W. O'Connor
HOWARD W. O'CONNOR

SECRET

Lowell read it and handed it to Lunsford.

"Colonel, I'm sorry," he said to Harris, "but I happen to know you don't have the right clearance for that."

"I understand," Harris said.

"Will there be a reply, Colonel?" Stephens asked.

"Not a reply, but I sure would like access to your hot line, Mr. Stephens."

"None of my business, of course, but could your message have something to do with Colonel McGrory?"

"Indeed it does," Lowell said.

"Same address as before?" Mr. Stephens asked.

"Right," Lowell said. "Colonel, could I have a sheet of paper?"

Stephens gestured with his hand that that would not be necessary. He walked to Harris's desk and held his hand over one of the telephones on it.

"Okay, Dick?"

"Help yourself," Colonel Harris said. "Would you like me to step outside for a moment?"

"Up to Colonel Lowell," Stephens said as he picked up the telephone.

"Is that what I think it is?" Lowell asked.

"This is Stephens," the mousy little man said. "Put me through to the farm, please."

There was a slight pause.

"Put me through to the White House switchboard," Stephens said. He handed the phone to Lowell. "I presume you know the extension?"

"White House Secure," a male voice said.

"Two-two-seven, please."

"Mr. Finton speaking, sir."

"Finton, Lowell."

"Yes, sir?"

"Is he there?"

"I can reach him in ninety seconds, sir."

"Get a message to him. Ready?"

"Yes, sir."

"Life insurance sold, but the defense attaché here, an Air Force absolute asshole colonel named McGrory, is going to screw things up, and he has to be told firmly and immediately to butt out."

"I'll take care of it, Colonel."

"The operative word, Finton, is immediately."

"I'll take care of it, Colonel," Mr. Finton said. "Anything else, sir?"

"No. That's it."

"Yes, sir," Mr. Finton said.

There was a click on the line.

"White House Secure. Have you finished?" the male operator asked.

"Yes, I have, thank you," Lowell said, and hung the telephone up.

He looked at Colonel Harris.

"Sir, I regret my intemperate language."

"Colonel, I think that's what's known as calling a spade a spade," Colonel Harris said. "Do you think it's going to work?"

"I devoutly hope so," Lowell said.

"Why don't you take a few minutes to collect your thoughts before reporting to Colonel McGrory?" Colonel Harris suggested. "Can I offer you and the major a cup of coffee?"

"That would be very kind, sir. And if you happen to have an Alka-Seltzer, something like that?"

"The Colonel and the Major were out until the wee hours last night," Stephens said.

"Coming right up," Harris said.

"For two, please, sir," Father chimed in.

"So you sold our friend the life insurance, huh?" Stephens asked. "I didn't have a clue whether you were going to get away with that."

"You're curious about that, are you, Mr. Stephens?" Lowell asked.

"What I'm curious about is what's inside that building," Stephens said. "It sure doesn't look a place for an all-night party."

"Just some old soldiers sitting around swapping war stories," Lowell said. "You know how that goes."

Stephens chuckled.

I'm probably not thinking too clearly, Lowell thought, *but obviously Stephens has put together (a) Felter has got the CIA doing a "where-is-he" on Guevara with (b) that I'm in that loop and with (c) that I'm talking about it with Pistarini and SIDE and with (d) that I reported to Felter that I sold the life insurance. And he's come up with Felter's surrogate has sold the Argentines on not blowing Guevara away. Langley will hear about that, and probably within the next fifteen minutes.*

You don't get to be the CIA station chief anywhere unless you're bright as hell, and this guy's brighter than most; and that selling life insurance line didn't need a rocket scientist to figure out.

Question: Why didn't Felter arrange for me to have access to that secure radiotelephone? Why did he send that CIA report to Stephens to give to me?

Answer: (Probably severely influenced by most of a bottle of Argentine cognac, which went down as smoothly as Martel's best) Sandy Felter does not share my high opinion of the CIA or its station chiefs. He wanted the CIA to know I'm down here, hoped they would send the station chief a heads-up. And since that might not happen, and in any case the presumption was this guy couldn't find his ass with both hands, he set it up for him to find out himself. It would come to the CIA's attention that a visiting officer was sending classified material, and he would want to know what that's all about.

The CIA will now know that Pistarini — the C-in-C of the Argentina Army — is going along with him, and they can't bitch that he's interfering with their mission of making deals like this, because they don't officially know about it.

Felter, you Machiavellian sonofabitch!

"We do that in the U.S. Information Agency, too," Stephens said. "Sit around over a couple of drinks and tell propaganda stories, come up with the best way to win hearts and minds. You know how it is."

"Yeah." Lowell chuckled.

Colonel Harris handed him a glass with an Alka-Seltzer fizzing in its bottom.

"Sir," Lowell said. "You may just have saved my life."

"For example, apropos of nothing whatever, one of the times we were sitting around," Stephens said, "one of the guys said that Che Guevara . . . you know who I mean? The guy with the beard and the beret?"

"I've heard the name," Lowell said.

"Anyway, one of the guys said Guevara was going to give us hearts-and-minds problems, but maybe we would get lucky and he would have a fatal accident or something."

"And what did you say to that?"

"I said if the sonofabitch had an accident, he would become an international saint, and that would really give us hearts-and-minds problems."

"I have no idea what you're talking about, of course, Mr. Stephens, but as a shot in the dark, I'd say you're right on the money," Lowell said.

From the smile that just flickered across your lips, Colonel Harris, I don't have to be a rocket scientist either to figure out that despite our cutesy-poo talking around the subject, you know exactly what Stephens and I are talking about. And if there are any questions unanswered, Stephens will answer them. And just as soon as Lunsford and I are out the door, you will tell Stephens what the L-23 is really for, and who the players are.

But we didn't tell Stephens, and he probably won't tell Langley, because if it came out they knew, Harris would have his ass in a crack. And if I can get Felter to keep that Air Force asshole out all of this, that's going to be very useful.

And you had that all figured out, Sandy, didn't you?

"How long are you going to be down here visiting Colonel Harris, Colonel?" Stephens asked. "I mean, if that's not classified and you can tell me?"

"Another couple of days, but not long."

"If there's anything I can do for you — like set up a tour of the sights of Buenos Aires for you — or anything else, let me know."

"I don't think there's going to be time for that," Lowell said. "But I'm sure the officers and noncoms who are going to be coming down here to join Colonel Harris would really like something like that."

"Consider it done," Stephens said. "Well, I'll leave you fellows alone. I know you've probably got military secrets and stuff like that to talk about."

He held out his hand.

"It's been a pleasure, Colonel," he said, and then we walked to Lunsford and tapped

Lunsford's Silver Star.

"I heard where the last one came from, Major," he said. "If you ever want to change employers, give me a call."

He shook Lunsford's hand and walked out the door.

Major Charles Daley, USAF, knocked at the door of the defense attaché, waited until permission to enter was granted, and then opened the door and stood in the center, almost at attention.

"Lieutenant Colonel Lowell to see you, sir."

"Permission granted," Colonel H. Robert McGrory said.

Lowell marched into the office, stopped thirty inches from Colonel McGrory's desk, came to attention, saluted, and said, "Sir, Lieutenant Colonel Lowell reporting to the defense attaché as ordered."

McGrory crisply returned the salute.

"Major, I do not wish to be disturbed," he said.

"Yes, sir," Major Daley said, and left the office.

"You took your time getting here, Colonel," McGrory said. "I will want, of course, to get into the nature of your business with Mr. Stephens, but we will get to that in a moment."

Lowell, who was still standing at attention, his eyes focused six inches over McGrory's head, did not reply.

McGrory had a yellow lined pad on his desk. Lowell dropped his eyes very quickly, long enough to see that it was a list of his sins, which Colonel McGrory was arranging sequentially.

The door opened. Major Daley was standing in it.

"You may stand at ease, Colonel," McGrory said.

351

You sonofabitch, you didn't "forget" to put me at ease. If that major hadn't shown up, I'd still be at attention.

"Major Daley, I thought I made it clear that I did not wish to be disturbed."

"Sir, it's the vice chief of staff," Major Daley said.

"What?"

"It's the vice chief of staff of the Air Force, sir."

"Would you like me to step outside, Colonel?" Lowell asked.

"You stand right where you are!" McGrory flared, and added, "At attention."

Lowell popped to attention.

Colonel McGrory picked up his telephone.

"Colonel McGrory speaking, General," he said.

"Yes, sir. He's in my office at this moment, General."

"Yes, sir," Colonel McGrory said.

He repeated this at least ten times in the next ninety seconds, and then put the telephone back in its cradle.

He looked at Lowell. His face was white.

"My orders, Colonel, are to ask of you how I may be of service to your mission here. Is there anything I can do for you?"

"No, sir."

"In that case, we have nothing to discuss, do we?"

"I don't believe we do, sir."

"You may take your post, Colonel."

"Yes, sir," Lowell said. He saluted. The salute was returned. Lowell executed an About-Face movement and walked out of Colonel McGrory's office.

As he passed Major Daley, he winked.

352

[TWO]
Dependent Services Branch
Office of the Assistant Chief of Staff for
Personnel
Headquarters, XVIII Airborne Corps and
Fort Bragg, North Carolina
0830 5 January 1965

It was not the first time she had registered a car on a post, and when Mrs. Marjorie Portet walked into the rambling, one-story frame building (built in 1940 and intended to last no more than ten years), she was reasonably convinced that she had everything that she would need with her.

First, a copy of Jack's orders assigning him (*them*, as she now thought of it) to Fort Bragg. The car's title. The certificate of insurance. A Xerox of his driver's license, and a just-issued-by-the-provost-marshal certificate that the Jaguar's headlights and stoplights worked and were properly adjusted; that the tires had an adequate amount of tread depth; that the brakes had an adequate amount of lining; that the horn made a proper amount of noise and the exhaust system did not make an excessive amount of noise and did not emit a cloud of noxious fumes.

There were people in line ahead of her, women "getting stickers" for the family car, and a half-dozen lower-ranking enlisted men, younger men who did not have a wife, a helpmeet, a life's partner to get a sticker for them. It took her about fifteen minutes to reach the sergeant behind the desk.

She laid all the documentation out for him, including the neatly-filled-out-in-block-letters-with-ballpoint-pen Request for Privately Owned

353

Vehicle Registration, in triplicate.

The sergeant examined the provost marshal's Report of Safety Inspection of Privately Owned Vehicle carefully. It identified the POV as a 1964 Jaguar Convertible, Guards Red in Color, Two Doors, twelve cylinders.

"Nice wheels, ma'am," the sergeant said.

"It's a nice car," Marjorie agreed.

He examined everything else.

"It run all right? I read in *Car & Driver* they have electrical problems a lot."

"Not so far," Marjorie said.

The sergeant examined all the documents.

"It all looks fine," he said. "All I'll need is a dollar and a quarter for the sticker, and your AGO card."

The Adjutant General's Office issues identification cards to military personnel and their dependents. It is sealed in plastic, and bears the owner's photograph, date of birth, and rank, or in the case of dependents, the rank of the soldier, who is known as the sponsor. It is necessary to make use of Army facilities, such as the hospital, the dental clinic, and the post exchange.

"I don't have an AGO card," Marjorie said.

That was not the truth. She had an AGO card in her purse. It listed her name as Marjorie W. Bellmon and stated that her sponsor was Major General Robert F. Bellmon.

The sergeant looked at her strangely.

"I just got married," Marjorie said.

That was the truth. She was still having trouble believing it.

"You got to have it, ma'am," the sergeant said, not unkindly. "Not only for the sticker, but to get in the PX, the hospital, places like that."

354

"Where do I get one?"

"For that, you're going to have to go to the AG," he said. "On the main post. A big sign out in front says, 'Headquarters XVIII Airborne Corps and Fort Bragg.' "

She knew where it was. Her father had once been G-3 of XVIII Airborne Corps.

"You're going to have to have your wedding certificate," the sergeant said. "It won't take long. All they have to do is take your picture with a Polaroid camera, and your thumbprint, and type up the card and put it in plastic. Then you can come back here, and you can get your sticker."

Marjorie left the building and got in the Jaguar and drove to the headquarters of XVIII Airborne Corps & Fort Bragg. It was a three-story brick building. She knew it had been built as a hospital before the war.

She found a parking space with some trouble, and as she was getting out of the car, a military police car pulled in beside her. She was searching in the sturdy plastic-reinforced envelope marked "Personal Papers" when an MP knocked on the window.

She rolled it down.

"Excuse me, ma'am," the MP said. "You visiting the post?"

"No. We've just been assigned here."

"You don't have a visitor's sign," he said. "You're supposed to stop at the MP shack at the main gate and get one."

"I didn't know that," she said.

That was the truth.

Then she remembered that whenever she had been at Bragg before, on the times she'd come to see Jack, the Jaguar had had his red Fort Rucker sticker on it. It didn't now. When she'd "cleared the post" for him at Rucker and taken off the temporary blue sticker, she'd spent fifteen minutes with steel wool and lighter fluid taking off his red sticker.

The Jaguar had no sticker at all, and the MP was just doing his job.

"Yes, ma'am," the MP said. "Can I see your driver's license and AGO card, please?"

There was a terrible temptation to give him the AGO card in her wallet. MPs are often sympathetic and understanding to the dependents of major generals.

She resisted it. She was no longer Miss Marjorie Bellmon, dependent daughter of Major General Robert F. Bellmon; she was now Mrs. Jacques Portet, dependent wife of First Lieutenant Portet.

"The driver's license I have," she said. "I'm here to get my AGO card. When I have that, I'm going to get the sticker for the car."

"Lost card?"

"I just got married," Marjorie said.

"You got orders or something, ma'am?"

She handed over Jack's orders and her driver's license.

He took a pad and started writing on it.

"Nothing to worry about, if you're telling me the truth," the MP said matter-of-factly. "This'll come down through channels to the Special Warfare Center, and they'll check to see if you applied for a sticker within seventy-two hours —"

"I got here last night," Marjorie said.

"Yes, ma'am," the MP said. "— of reporting on post, and if you did, they'll endorse it back, and there won't be no problem. And I don't think they'll give you any trouble for not getting a visitor's pass."

He extended the pad to her.

"Sign there on the bottom by the X," he said. "All you're doing is acknowledging getting the citation."

Marjorie signed "Marjorie Bellmon" and added "Portet" when she saw what she had written.

She handed the pad to him. He tore a copy of the citation off and handed it to her.

"Thank you, ma'am," the MP said. "This is a really nice set of wheels."

"Thank you," Marjorie said. She put the citation in the envelope and got out of the car and walked into the redbrick building housing Headquarters XVIII Airborne Corps & Fort Bragg.

There was a sign on the wall in the corridor of the second floor:

Hours of AGO Card Issuance
1030–1200 and 1500–1630

She looked at her watch. It was quarter past nine.

She sat down to wait.

At 1125 Mrs. Marjorie B. Portet, dependent wife of First Lieutenant Jacques Portet, now possessed of an AGO card attesting to that status, got back in the Jaguar, drove back to the Dependent Services building, presented the AGO card and $1.25, and was issued two stickers, with blue printing, reading "Fort Bragg NC 56787."

She applied them to the front and rear bumpers of the Jaguar before driving away.

And I'll bet, she thought, *that he'll be pacing up*

357

and down in front of the SWC headquarters building, wondering where the hell I have been, how it could take all that time to get a couple of lousy stickers for the car.

Jack had said he would try to "break ground" at Rucker with the L-23 at half past seven. That would put him into Pope at about 9:30, give or take ten minutes. Figure ten minutes to tie it down, and another ten or fifteen minutes to get from Pope to the SWC, he had arrived at 10:00, certainly no later than 10:15, which meant he would have been waiting for her more than an hour. And no one knew where she was.

Johnny Oliver would have the keys to their new apartment. They would take a quick look at it to see how big it was, and then go to a furniture store and buy at least enough — a refrigerator, a kitchen table and chairs, a small television set, and, of course, a bed — to spend their first night together in their very own home/apartment/love nest.

The apartment would be furnished slowly. As soon as she could get to The Farm, she could have her pick of the furniture in The Barn, or, for that matter, within reason, in The House.

The Farm, in Virginia, outside Washington, had been in the Bellmon family for four generations, and The House was furnished with the best of a century's accumulation of furniture. The Barn held the less desirable pieces, including, she thought she remembered, some really beautiful pieces of Philippine Mahogany acquired when then Lieutenant Colonel Porterman K. Waterford had been assigned to the 26th Cavalry outside Manila before the Second War.

And then, of course, there would be wedding presents. They had been married so suddenly there had been no time for that, but she knew they would start coming almost immediately.

And Hanni, Jack's stepmother, had said she was going to ship all the furniture in their house in the Congo to the United States, and it was far more than enough to furnish the house they were going to build or buy in Ocean Reef.

But it would be a nice memory for later, to remember their first night together, when she'd driven up from Rucker, and Jack had flown up, and they'd bought their first furniture together.

Jack was not pacing up and down in front of the SWC headquarters building, nor anywhere in sight.

There was a sergeant on duty in the lobby of the building, charged with keeping unauthorized visitors out.

"Sergeant, I'm Mrs. Portet," Marjorie said. "I wonder if there are any messages for me?"

"You want to spell that for me, please?"

"Pee Oh Are Tee Eee Tee."

"Oh, you mean, Por*tet*."

"Why not?"

The sergeant stiffened.

Brigadier General Paul R. Hanrahan, the commanding general of the John F. Kennedy Center for Special Warfare, was marching purposefully across the lobby, trailed by his aide-de-camp, Captain Stefan Zabrewski.

He changed course when he saw Marjorie.

"We were getting a little worried, Margie," he said. "We expected you early this morning. What are you doing here? Why didn't you go to the house?"

"I was supposed to meet Jack here, Uncle Red," she said.

"What was the message, Ski?" Hanrahan asked.

"There was a delay at Rucker, sir," Zabrewski boomed. "He'll let us know when he has an ETA."

"Sorry, honey," Hanrahan said. "Why don't you go over to the house? I'll have messages forwarded there, and Patricia's worried about you."

"Uncle Red, I'm sort of anxious to see the apartment. Johnny was supposed to have the keys."

"Sergeant," Zabrewski boomed. "You got an envelope there for Mrs. Portet? From Captain Oliver?"

"Yes, sir," the sergeant said. He handed over an envelope. "Sir, that's not what the lady said. She said 'Por-tay' or something."

Zabrewski handed her the envelope. It contained two door keys, and two maps, one of the route from Fort Bragg into Fayetteville and the Foster Garden Apartments, and the other of the Foster Garden Apartment complex itself, showing her the location of Apartment B-14, and where to park the car.

"Great," Marjorie said. "I'll go see Aunt Patricia and then have a look."

"Patricia said she'd go with you and get the car registered," Hanrahan said. "For some reason, Eighteenth Airborne Corps is on a death-to-unregistered-POV kick."

"I've already done that, Uncle Red," Marjorie said.

It did not seem to be the time to tell him about the MP citation.

"Good girl," he said. "Honey, I've got to run. See you later."

Aunt Patricia was almost visibly hurt that Marjorie and Jack weren't going to stay with them until they had a chance to settle in, and Marjorie didn't have the heart to decline her invitation to lunch.

It was a little after two before she found Apartment B-14 in the Foster Garden Apartments complex and managed to get the door open.

It was a nice apartment, she decided. It had two bedrooms, one of which, she thought, Jack could use as a home office, an area that was obviously intended to be used both as a dining room and living room — she *knew* there was an elaborately carved Philippine wooden screen, courtesy of Grandfather Waterford, in The Barn. There were animals and naked women carved on it, which Jack, she was sure, would like, that would fit there. The bathroom was all right, and the kitchen, while small, had room for a table and chairs. There was even a small balcony overlooking a grassy interior courtyard.

The only "furniture" in the apartment were a stove and a telephone. The stove lighted right up when she tried, which pleased her. When she bent over and picked the telephone from the floor, intending to call Patricia Hanrahan to see if there was an ETA on Jack, it was as dead as a doornail.

She took a small notebook from her purse and wrote "TELEPHONE!!!!!!" in it, and then set out in search of Fayetteville Furniture and Interiors.

She explained to a salesman what she was after right now, just a bed and a kitchen table and chairs, and that she would be back later for other things, and then asked him if she could first use the telephone before looking at what he had to offer.

The telephone company said they would be happy to reactivate the telephone already installed in B-14 of the Foster Garden Apartments. They would call her previous telephone company to check her credit, and that out of the way, turn it right on. When they learned she had never had her own telephone before, the telephone company said in that case she would have to come by the office and leave a deposit of $125.

She decided on a natural-wood–looking kitchen table with matching captain's chairs; a small-screen TV; a large, two-door refrigerator with an ice maker; a Simmons Best Quality King Size mattress and spring, and a bed to hold it.

She paid for it with check number 0001 drawn on the account of Lieutenant and Mrs. J. E. Portet, in the First National Bank of Ozark, Alabama.

"Would delivery, let's see," the salesman said, consulting a sheet of paper, "the day after tomorrow, in the afternoon, be all right with you?"

"I need this stuff today," Marjorie said. "Right now. I told you that."

"Oh, I'm afraid that just wouldn't be possible, Mrs. Portet," he said, pronouncing it "Poor Tet."

"Then forget the whole thing," she said, hoping he couldn't see how close to tears she was. "Give me my check back."

"Just a minute, I'll see what I can do."

The furniture, promised for delivery at four, arrived at half past five, and by then it was too late to go to the telephone company and leave a deposit.

With the mattress and bed — that came in

362

pieces, and she had no idea how she was going to manage to assemble it — in the larger of the two bedrooms, the bedroom seemed a lot smaller than it had originally.

When the refrigerator was installed in the kitchen, the door opened the wrong way.

She went in search of a pay telephone, found one outside the apartment complex manager's office, and then found that she didn't have any change to feed it.

She went in search of a shopping center, found one, with pay phones outside, and then had to wait in the checkout line to get five dollars' worth of silver for the pay phones.

There was still no ETA on Jack, and Marjorie knew she had hurt Patricia Hanrahan's feelings again when she declined the invitation to come out to the post and wait for him there.

"God, you ought to know, baby, you never know when they're going to show up."

"I'm getting the apartment set up," Marjorie said. "But I really appreciate it."

She went back into the supermarket to buy just enough food to get by until she could really go shopping, and at the commissary at Bragg, of course, to save money. By the time she was finished, the shopping cart was overloaded.

She had a little trouble getting the supermarket to accept check 0002, but finally beat the supermarket's manager down.

Whatever the other virtues of the Jaguar XKS, there is not much trunk space, and what there was was occupied by Marjorie's suitcases. She finally managed to get everything she had bought in the passenger compartment, but not before she had ruptured a milk carton, which gushed milk which would be sour in the morning and all over Jack's precious carpets unless she took them out tonight and washed them.

She telephoned the Hanrahans and General Hanrahan said there was still no ETA on Jack, but if his flight was aborted he would have heard. And why don't you come out and wait here?

She was halfway back to the Foster Garden Apartments complex when she realized that she had a bed and mattress and spring, but no pillows or sheets. And, for that matter, no towels.

Back to the shopping center, where Bed & Bath had some very nice sheets and pillows and nice big thick terry towels, but absolutely refused to take check number 0003.

That left her with $19.40, until she noticed she was almost out of gas. She purchased $9.40 cents of gasoline and drove home.

She put the groceries in her new refrigerator. She slid the pieces of her bed out of their long cardboard box, managed to get them more or less together, and then reached the inevitable conclusion that there was no way she could get her new Simmons Best Quality King Size mattress and spring on it by herself, so she took it apart.

When she cut the cardboard box the mattress came in, the mattress fell out as she predicted it would. When she cut the cardboard box the spring came in, the falling spring gouged a hole in the freshly painted wall of the bedroom.

By then, she decided she needed a shower. That reminded her of the suitcases in the car, and she went to get them, which reminded her of the milk-soaked carpet. It took her two trips to get her suitcases from the car up the stairs to B-14, and another trip to get the carpet, which was already starting to smell.

She went down a final time to use the pay phone to call the Hanrahans.

This would be the last call, she decided. *I am making a real pain in the ass of myself.*

There was no ETA on Jack.

When she started to unpack her clothing and hang things up behind the sliding doors of her new bedroom closet, there were no hangers.

She laid her clothing out as neatly as she could on the floor of Jack's office, then took a shower with Jack's carpet. That was made somewhat more difficult because the only soap in her new apartment came in a plastic bottle and was intended for use on dishes.

When she hung Jack's freshly washed carpet on the shower door, it was sufficiently heavy to cause the screws of its hinges to pull out.

I am not going to scream, and I am not going to cry. I am going to go out there, put my nightie on, get in my bed, and watch television until I hear from Jack.

And there is no reason to modestly wrap a towel around myself. I'm all alone. Oh, God, am I all alone!

She went into her bedroom and then started for Jack's office to get the goddamned nightgown. Halfway through her new living room, she heard a strange thumping noise and looked at the sliding glass door to the balcony.

Jack was standing there, in his flight suit, holding a bottle of champagne, his appreciation of her stark nudity written all over his face.

How did he know how to find the apartment? How the hell did he get up to the balcony? Answer: He's a Green Beret. They can do anything.

She finally managed to operate the door's lock, and slid it open.

"Boy, talk about timing!" Jack said. "Shall we do it right here on the balcony, or do we have a bed?"

She threw herself into his arms.

After a moment, he asked, "Hey, baby. What's with the tears?"

"I'm happy," Marjorie said. "That's all. Welcome home, baby."

[THREE]

SECRET

Central Intelligence Agency Langley, Virginia

FROM: Assistant Director For Administration

DATE: 7 January 1965 1415 GMT

SUBJECT: Guevara, Ernesto (Memorandum # 32.)

TO: Mr. Sanford T. Felter
Counselor To The President
Room 637, The Executive Office Building
Washington, D.C.

By Courier

In compliance with Presidential Memorandum to The Director, Subject: "Ernesto 'Che' Guevara," dated 14 December 1964, the following information is furnished:

(1) (Reliability Scale Five) (From CIA Conraky, Guinea) SUBJECT met at 1945 GMT 6 January 1965 with Guinean President Sékou TOURÉ at the presidential palace. Also present was Senghor a LABE, President of Senegal.

(2) (Reliability Scale Three) (From CIA sources) Both TOURÉ and a LABE expressed sympathy for African liberation movements, but neither requested any kind of assistance from SUBJECT to achieve liberation, nor offered any Guinean or Senegalese help, even though SUBJECT repeatedly suggested Cubans could safely offer aid covertly.

Howard W. O'Connor
HOWARD W. O'CONNOR

SECRET

[FOUR]
Room 637, The Executive Office Building
Washington, D.C.
1505 10 January 1965

Room 637 actually was a small suite. There was an outer office, with room for two desks, facing each other, with room to pass between them; two filing cabinets against one wall, and a battered leather couch against the other. Next to the couch there was a clothes tree and a door leading to a small washroom. Directly across from the door to the corridor was a door leading to the inner office. It was smaller than the outer office, and held a desk pushed up against the wall, two straight-backed chairs, and a clothes tree.

Chief Warrant Officer James L. Finton sat at one of the desks in the outer office, and Miss Mary Margaret Dunne at the other.

Five minutes before one of the telephones — the one connected to the White House Secure telephone switchboard — had rung, and when she answered it, a male voice had demanded, without any other preliminaries, "Is Felter there?"

"Yes, Mr. President," Mary Margaret had replied.

The line had gone dead.

Mary Margaret had immediately informed the colonel of the call and she had been keeping one eye on the telephone ever since, expecting a second call, ordering the colonel to immediately report to the Oval Office, or the Presidential Apartments, or the private entrance to the White House, or the lawn, where the helicopters landed.

The door to 637 opened, and the President of the United States walked in.

"Afternoon," he said to Mary Margaret.

"Wait here," he said to the two Secret Service agents who followed him into the office.

"Stand at ease, son," he said to CWO Finton, who had popped to rigid attention behind his desk.

"There?" he asked of Mary Margaret, pointing to the washroom door.

"There, Mr. President," Mary Margaret said, pointing to the door to the colonel's office.

The President walked to the door and opened it without knocking.

The three men in the room, two of them in uniform, stood up.

"Good afternoon, Mr. President," Felter said. "I didn't know you were coming here, sir."

"I needed a breath of fresh air," Johnson said, "and I realized I had never seen your office. So here I am."

"Yes, sir."

"This is a pretty shitty office," Johnson said. "You want me to get you a better one?"

"This serves my needs very well, sir. But thank you."

Johnson turned to look at the two men in uniform.

"Well," the President said, offering his hand to one of them. "Look who's here! And looking a hell of a lot better than the last time I saw you. How are you, Major?"

"Very well, thank you, sir," Father Lunsford said.

"Who are you?" the President inquired of the other man in uniform.

"My name is Lowell, Mr. President," Craig Lowell said.

"I've been hearing about you," he said. "You don't look like an investment banker."

"I try not to, Mr. President," Lowell replied.

"They told me about that," the President said, and then stabbed at Lowell's chest with his finger. "But not about that. I guess the Distinguished Service Cross doesn't fit in with the picture somebody was — just a couple of minutes ago — trying to paint of you as a Wall Street investment banker playing at being a soldier."

Lowell didn't respond directly.

"Permission to withdraw, Mr. President?" he asked.

"I'll tell you when you can, Colonel," Lyndon Johnson said sharply.

"Yes, sir."

"Your uniform looks like you slept in it, Colonel," Johnson said.

"Yes, sir, I did," Lowell said.

"You just flew up here from Buenos Aires?"

"Yes, sir."

Johnson turned to Lunsford.

"You were with him, right?"

"Yes, sir."

"I heard that Lowell was down there with another guy; they didn't have your name. What the hell were you doing down there?"

Lunsford looked uncomfortable, as if he was phrasing his reply.

"You can tell me," Johnson said sarcastically. "I'm the President."

"Sir, we were seeking the cooperation of the Argentine government with regard to Che Guevara," Lunsford said.

"The last I heard, Colonel Felter," Johnson said, looking at him, "we have an ambassador down there who's paid to deal with the Argentine government."

"I'm afraid Major Lunsford misspoke, Mr. President," Felter said. "Colonel Lowell and Major Lunsford met, unofficially, with General Pistarini."

"Who's he?"

"Commander-in-chief of the Argentine Army, sir."

"Doesn't the chief of the Army down there take

his orders from the President?"

"In a manner of speaking, Mr. President, President Illia of Argentina serves at the pleasure of General Pistarini," Felter said.

"He's another Perón, in other words?"

"No, sir," Felter said. "From what I know of him, and from what Colonel Lowell and Major Lunsford have been telling me about him, he is not at all like Juan Perón."

"In what way different?" Johnson asked.

"For one thing, if he considers a coup to remove President Illia necessary in the best interests of Argentina, he will order the coup with great personal reluctance, and appoint someone else — probably General Ongania — to the presidency. Perón, on the other hand, would like to be president for the sake of Juan Perón."

Johnson turned to Lowell.

"You talked to this guy — Pistarini, you said? — and he told you this?"

"Yes, sir."

"And you believed him?"

"Yes, sir."

"Why?"

"It was in the wee hours of the morning, Mr. President, and we'd all had a good deal to drink."

"You were drinking with this Pistarini at three, four o'clock in the morning?" Johnson parroted wonderingly. He chuckled. "You got along with him pretty good, huh?"

"Yes, sir," Lowell said, and then blurted, "It was all I could do to keep him from giving me a medal."

"Why would he want to do that?" Johnson asked.

"That was never made clear, sir," Lowell said.

"But at three o'clock in the morning, General Pistarini seemed to think that decorating both Major Lunsford and myself was a splendid idea."

Johnson shook his head and smiled.

"You know, every time I go south of Brownsville, I see all these Latin American generals marching around, covered from eyeball to belly button with medals, and I know most — maybe none — of them never heard a shot fired in anger."

"I've noticed, sir," Lowell said.

"Why didn't you take it?" Johnson asked.

"I was under orders to maintain as low a profile as possible, sir."

"Your low profile didn't escape the attention of the secretary of state, Colonel. He thinks you two were pissing on his grass."

"I'm sorry to hear that, sir."

"Before you and he hit the bottle, how was this Pistarini planning on dealing with Señor Guevara?"

"He was not to be allowed to enter Argentina alive, Mr. President," Lowell said. "And General Pistarini told me that should Dr. Guevara meet an accident anywhere, not only would he not be unhappy, but also that the accident would be investigated by the Argentine intelligence service — it's called SIDE — who would find, and announce, that they had found absolutely nothing suspicious about it."

"And after you'd had a couple of belts?"

"He and the man who runs SIDE became convinced that your feeling that Guevara should be kept alive and allowed to fall on his face was in everybody's best interests."

"Can we do that, Lunsford?" the President

asked. "Make the sonofabitch fall on his face in the Congo?"

"Yes, sir. I think we can. I'm building a pretty capable team at Fort Bragg."

"Did Colonel Felter make it clear to you that nobody can find out we're involved?"

"Yes, sir."

"You think — all three of you — that this Pistarini character can be trusted?"

"Yes, sir, I do," Lunsford said, and then Felter and Lowell chimed in simultaneously with the same reply.

"Okay. That's it," Johnson said. "If the secretary of state is still waiting outside the Oval Office, and I know goddamned well he will be, I'll tell him what I told the Joint Chiefs Chairman yesterday."

He looked at Felter.

"Which is, Mr. President?" Felter asked.

"That I know all about what you're doing for me, that they're to give you anything you ask for, and that I don't want to talk about it."

"Thank you, sir," Felter said.

"One more thing," Johnson said, turning to Lowell and Lunsford. "I don't want to have to pin another medal on either of you. Or send one to your next of kin. Clear?"

"Yes, sir."

He shook their hands, then marched out of the small office.

X

[ONE]
Room 1322
The Fountainbleau Hotel
Miami Beach, Florida
1605 9 January 1965

J. Richard Leonard of the Gresham Investment Corporation, a somewhat portly forty-five-year-old, came out of the shower with a towel around his middle.

He sat down on the double bed and reached for the telephone.

There was a knock at the door.

"Room service."

Leonard went to the door, admitted a bellman carrying a champagne cooler holding four bottles of Bass Ale, signed the tab, and handed it to the bellman.

"That was quick, thank you," he said.

He had ordered the ale before going into the shower, thinking it would take at least half an hour for it to be delivered.

"Anything else I can get for you, sir?" the bellman asked suggestively.

A lone forty-five-year-old businessman in a nice suite often wanted more in Miami Beach than sand and sun.

"No, thank you," Leonard said. "I like to catch my females on the hoof."

"Well, if you change your mind, ask for Richard," the bellman said, and left.

Leonard found a bottle opener in the bathroom, opened a bottle of the ale, and went back to the bed and picked up the telephone again. He gave the operator a number in northern Virginia.

"Twenty," a female voice answered.

"Dick Leonard, sweetheart, is the boss available?"

"I'll see."

Howard W. O'Connor came on the line a moment later.

"What's up, Dick?"

"I spoke with Captain Portet this afternoon," Leonard said. "Which was more difficult than I thought it would be. There's a place down here called Ocean Reef —"

"I know it. When Nixon was Vice President, he used to go there with his buddy Bebe Rebozo. Very nice."

"Also hard to get into," Leonard said. "Anyway, Portet's got a house there. I think he's renting it to give his family a vacation."

"Well, that blows your 'he's probably broke' theory, doesn't it?"

"Yeah, I guess it does. Anyway, after heavily bribing the security guard to let me in, I went to his house this morning, just as he was leaving. So I followed him. He went to the airport in Miami and was nosing around, asking about used airplanes. I struck up a conversation with him in a coffee shop, and made a preliminary pitch, told him Gresham was thinking of buying into a small airline, or starting one up, and that I'd gotten his name because of what he's been doing in the Congo."

"And he was interested?"

"A little," Leonard said. "I didn't get the enthusiasm I sort of expected. He told me to make him a proposition, and he'd think it over."

"Well, make him one, and let me know what happens. We have to get this thing moving, Dick."

"I'm going to hang around here a couple of days more, snoop around a little more. I don't want to seem too eager."

"Just don't sit on the dime, Dick," Howard W. O'Connor said, and hung up.

[TWO]
"Bonne Visage" (aka House A)
24 Golf Club Lane
The Ocean Reef Club
Key Largo, Florida
1820 10 January 1965

Captain Jean-Philippe Portet had just gone to the poolside wet bar and made himself a drink when the door chimes went off.

"There's the door," he called, in case Madam Portet hadn't heard it.

"Get it," Hanni called back from their bedroom. "I'm not dressed."

"Give whoever it is a thrill."

"Mein Gott!"

Captain Portet walked through the house to the front door and opened it.

Lieutenant Colonel Craig W. Lowell was standing there, in uniform. His enormous ancient Packard was in the drive.

God, he's got more medals than Patton.

"Excuse me for just showing up like this, JP," Lowell said, smiling. "I am about my master's

376

work, and there is no rest for the weary."

"Oddly enough, I was just thinking about you," Portet said. "We need to talk."

"That's my line," Lowell said. "Look JP, I put this uniform on in Buenos Aires. I need a shower badly. What I'd like to do is buy you dinner, if that would be possible. But before that, could you come with me to my place while I change clothes? What I have to say won't take long, but it's the sort of thing I'd rather Hanni and the girl didn't hear."

Why the hell not? What I have to say won't take long, either.

He pushed the TALK and MASTER SUITE buttons on the intercom panel mounted to the exterior wall by the door.

"Hanni, baby," he announced. "I'm going over to Colonel Lowell's place for a couple of minutes. We'll be back in a little while. And then we're going to dinner."

As he was closing the door, Hanni pushed the TALK and FRONT DOOR buttons on the intercom panel mounted on the wall and inquired, incredulously, "What did you say?"

Captain Portet did not respond, but instead walked to the Packard and got in.

I am almost certainly going to piss Lowell — probably his whole family — off, and/or cut off my own nose to spite my face — Hanni really loves that house — but I know myself well enough to know that if I don't get this straight between us, it will get much worse. It's better to settle it right here and now.

"I came down in a Learjet," Lowell said. "A little less than two hours from wheels up."

"I thought you said you just came from Argentina," Portet replied.

"Buenos Aires, Miami; Miami, Washington;

Washington, here. I am worn out and need a drink and shower badly," Lowell said. "And in that order, I have just decided."

"What were you doing in Argentina?" Portet asked, his curiosity overwhelming his intention to be polite but distant.

"I hope I succeeded in talking the Argentines out of blowing Che Guevara away," Lowell said.

"I don't think I understand that."

"I shouldn't have told you that much," Lowell said. "Can you forget I said that?"

"Certainly," Portet said.

"There's an operation going on," Lowell said. "If you're willing to come to Washington, Colonel Felter will explain it all to you."

"Why would he do that?"

"We need your help," Lowell said. "That's why I'm here. To ask for it."

Lowell pulled up in front of 12 Surf Point Drive (aka House C). The lights were on, and as they got out of the car, the door was opened by a white-jacketed young man.

"Welcome home, Colonel," he said. "How long will you be with us?"

"If I don't leave tonight, I'll be out of here before daylight," Lowell said.

"I put things for breakfast in the refrigerator, Colonel."

"You better come back tomorrow and freeze what you can, and get rid of the rest," Lowell said. "And put the car back in the garage, too. I'll leave it at the strip."

"I saw that Air Force Lear come in. Was that you?"

"Yeah. And honest to God, this is business," Lowell said.

"Yes, sir. Will there be anything else, Colonel?"

"That'll do it. Thank you very much."

"Good night, gentlemen," the young man said, and walked to a golf cart and drove off.

"You didn't tip him," Portet said.

"No, we don't tip here," Lowell said. "Oh, God! JP, have you been trying to grease palms? I should have said something."

"No problem," Portet said. "But I didn't know."

And I thought that everybody's refusal of a tip was another indication of Lowell's family's gratitude run amok.

"It's a complicated system," Lowell said as he walked to the bar. "I don't really understand how it works; Helene Craig calls me once a year and tells me how much of a Christmas present I just made. Ask her to do the same for you until you learn the system."

He pulled a bottle of a scotch Portet could not remember ever having seen before from an array behind the bar.

"I highly recommend this," he said.

"Colonel, I don't think we'll be staying here, living here, at Ocean Reef," Portet said.

" 'Colonel'?" Lowell parroted. "There's a certain icy *I am pissed at you* formality in that, *Captain*," Lowell said. "You want to tell me what's got your back up?"

He handed him a glass half full of scotch.

"If we ain't buddies no more," Lowell said, "fuck you, get your own ice."

It was hard for Portet not to smile, but he managed not to.

"I thought I made it quite clear to Mr. Craig that his gratitude to Jacques for what happened at Stanleyville —"

"You're stuck with that, JP, I'm afraid," Lowell said. "My cousin's only grandson, the apple of his eye, was in your Stanleyville apartment with a good chance of having really terrible things happen to him when Jack showed up and did his John Wayne routine. That happened. He has a reason to be grateful to Jack. We all do."

"We don't need a financial expression of that gratitude, Craig," Portet said. "I made that point, I thought, to Porter Craig, but I apparently didn't get through to him."

"For example?"

"At first I thought I was being paranoid," Portet said. "When I applied for a mortgage on the house, the banker told me I was stealing it. So I had it appraised. The price Porter quoted me was ninety thousand under the appraisal I paid for."

"Okay. I'm beginning to see what's going on in your mind. We have our own appraisers. Everything we own is appraised on a regular basis so we don't get raped by the tax collector. When you told Porter you wanted to buy that house, he called me and said this should be the one exception to The Rule. And I agreed."

" 'The Rule'? What rule?"

"The family buys property, but never sells it. We lease it, sometimes by the year, sometimes by the century, but we never sell it. I agreed we should break The Rule for you and Hanni. You're more than friends — you're family."

"Ninety thousand under its appraisal value?"

"You're going to have to trust me on this, JP," Lowell said. "When I told him, sell it to JP, Porter called our appraiser and asked him what was on the books. Whatever figure Porter quoted you was the figure he got from our appraiser. We're a bank, not a benevolent society."

Portet looked at him for a long moment.

He took his wallet from his pocket and handed Lowell a business card.

Gresham Investment Corporation

J. Richard Leonard
Vice President

Suite 1107
27 Wall Street
New York City 10022
212 555-9767

"What's this?" Lowell asked.

"You don't know?" Portet asked.

"No. I never heard of them."

"I really want to believe you, Craig," Portet said.

"I never heard of these people, okay?" Lowell said coldly. "Where'd you get it?"

"At the airport in Miami," Portet said. "I've been going over there to see what's available on the used-airplane market, maintenance facilities . . . you understand."

"And?"

"This fellow came up to me while I was having a coffee — not in the terminal, across from it, in the cargo area. He knew who I was, called me Captain

381

Portet, and said he heard I was at the airport, and that it was a fortunate coincidence, because he had been thinking of contacting me in the Congo."

"He say why?"

"He said that he 'and his associates' were on the edge of setting a charter company, half a dozen convertible 707s; that they were not happy with the people they'd been looking at to manage it; and that a search had come up with my name as someone with just the experience they were looking for. My long-haul jet operations, between Europe and southern Africa, and my short-haul piston operations in the Congo area, he said, were just about what they wanted to start up between the States and the Far East — I think he meant French Indochina, Vietnam. If I was interested, they were prepared to really talk seriously about it, and were prepared to offer me participation, which I took to mean a substantial piece of the company, plus a salary 'commensurate with my background.' "

"It sounded too good to be true, right?"

"I had talked to Porter Craig about buying into a small airline," Portet said. "Yeah, Craig, it sounded too good to be true."

"My first reaction is to tell you that Craig, Powell, Kenyon and Dawes does not employ people to wander around airports looking for people to loan money to," Lowell said. "People come to us, usually on their knees. But sometimes Porter does go overboard. And we own Twenty-seven Wall Street, and that piques my curiosity."

He pulled a telephone out from under the bar and dialed a number from memory.

Portet could barely hear someone answer the telephone.

"The Craig residence."

"Hello, Stephen, is my portly cousin there?"

Lowell held the telephone away from his ear so that Portet could hear the conversation.

"What can I do for you, Craig?"

"Give me a straight answer. Have you been trying to help Captain Portet with his plans to buy an airline? Straight answer, please, Porter."

"I would be happy to, but when I offered to help in any way I could, he politely but firmly told me no, thank you. I have respected his wishes. Does he want help now? Has he come to you?"

"What do you know about the Gresham Investment Corporation?"

"I never heard of it."

"How about a guy named J. Richard Leonard?"

"I don't know the name."

"They have offices in Twenty-seven Wall."

"So do a hundred other firms. That's a large building. I never heard of them, sorry."

"Who can you call to find out?"

"If it's important to you, I'll make inquiries in the morning."

"I mean right now."

"Good God, Craig! For one thing, it's after business hours."

"This is important, Porter."

"What would you like me to do?"

"See how much space they have, who they gave as credit references. That should be on the lease."

"I don't even know who manages that building."

"Porter, if I let you off the hook tonight, will you make it your first business in the morning? I'll be in the apartment in the Hotel Washington."

"I heard you were going to be using it," Porter Craig said. "Geoff called me and told me you would be there."

"And I can't tell you why, Porter, except that there will be the usual complement of loose women. And seeing that tomorrow will be during business hours, check them out with Dun and Bradstreet — the confidential reports. I want to know who they're loaning money to."

"I'm beginning to think this is really important to you. You want to tell me why?"

"It is, and no."

"All right. I'll get on it first thing in the morning. Let me write all that down."

Lowell put the telephone back under bar, picked up his drink, and looked at Captain Portet.

"Porter has not been playing Santa Claus," he said. "And by ten o'clock tomorrow morning, I think we're going to have a pretty good idea of just what the Gresham Investment Corporation is."

"I guess you think I'm an ass," Portet said. "I feel like one."

"Yeah, JP, I do," Lowell said. "But I will forgive you if you come to Washington with me, either tonight, after dinner, or in the very wee hours tomorrow morning."

"What's that all about?"

"Felter wants to pick your brains about Joseph Désiré Mobutu," Lowell said. "Following which, he will return you here in the Lear."

Lowell drained his drink.

"I'm for the shower," he said, and walked toward his bedroom. "You think of some plausible reason you can give Hanni for rushing away with me in the middle of the night."

"You seem pretty confident that I'll go."

"I think you're almost as curious about the Gresham Investment Corporation as I am," Lowell called over his shoulder.

[THREE]
Apartment B-14
Foster Garden Apartments
Fayetteville, North Carolina
2105 10 January 1965

Dinner had been a little late, and if Mrs. Marjorie Portet had been asked, she would have admitted that she would have preferred to dine alone with her husband, rather than with two of his fellow officers.

But just before five, when he had been expected home, Jack had called from Camp Mackall and said he would be a little late, he had to go to the PX at Bragg. He arrived at half past seven, both arms loaded with groceries, and trailed by Captain John S. Oliver and Warrant Officer Enrico de la Santiago, who were each carrying a case of beer.

They were all in fatigue uniforms.

Jack had kissed her, and she had returned the kiss with considerably less enthusiasm than she planned.

The groceries and the beer had been deposited in the kitchen, and the three had left the apartment, to return a few minutes later, staggering under the weight of an enormous cardboard carton.

"What the hell is that?" Marjorie had asked after they had pushed her new coffee table out if the way so they could set the carton down on her new carpet in the middle of the living room.

"I have a speech to make, Miss Marjorie, but

385

first I need a beer," Johnny Oliver said.

Beer bottles were opened and passed around. The officers, having declined the use of her new Pilsner beer glasses, partook of them directly from their necks.

"That, Miss Marjorie, is a wedding present," Johnny Oliver said. "From Mr. de la Santiago and myself. More precisely, two-thirds of it is a wedding present from Enrico and me. The other third is a small token of my appreciation to you personally for two things. First, for being the only general's daughter in the history of the Army who did not make a royal pain in the ass of herself to her daddy's dog-robber."

"Oh, Johnny!"

"And the second for your deeply appreciated, if doomed to failure, efforts on my behalf with the Ice Princess."

"Oh, Johnny," Marjorie had repeated, genuinely surprised that tears had formed in her eyes.

"Unveil the present, Mr. Santiago," Oliver ordered.

"Yes, sir," Enrico said.

De la Santiago pulled a wicked-looking knife, which Marjorie hadn't noticed before, from his boot and slit the carton open.

It held a not-assembled bottled-gas-powered grill, the largest one Marjorie had ever seen.

"I think we have two little problems," Johnny said. "First, the assembly of that device will require tools, and second, it may not fit on the balcony."

"There's a tool set in the Jag," Jack said.

"You go get it," Oliver said. "And if Miss Marjorie can come up with a piece of string, for use as a measuring device, we will determine whether or not it will fit on the balcony."

Jack went to fetch the tool kit. Marjorie found a ball of twine and gave it to Johnny, who gave it to Enrico.

When they were alone in the living room, Marjorie asked softly, "You haven't heard from Liza at all?"

"When she hears my voice, she hangs up," he said.

"Keep trying," Marjorie said.

"Yeah," he said. He met her eyes. "I really miss Allan; that makes it worse."

Jack appeared with the tool roll from the Jaguar and handed it to Oliver.

"It's my wedding present —"

"*Our* wedding present," Marjorie corrected him.

"— you put it together."

"Can the bride handle putting aluminum foil around the spuds?" Johnny asked.

"I'll supervise," Jack said.

Marjorie guessed correctly that it would take Enrico and Johnny at least as long to assemble the grill as it would take to bake the potatoes; they were done five minutes before the gas under the artificial charcoal lit.

This was followed by the smell of the preservative being burned off the interior parts of the stove, which lasted about five minutes. Cooking the thick steaks from the commissary took another fifteen minutes, but finally they were all sitting at her new dining-room table, and Jack was pouring wine into her new wineglasses.

The new telephone rang.

An hour after the dead telephone she had found

on her first day in the apartment had been brought to life by a man from the phone company, another man from the phone company arrived at her door.

"It's already working, thank you very much," Marjorie had told him.

"Is this B-14, Lieutenant Portet?"

"Yes, it is."

He handed her his Installation Order:

One unlisted private line telephone to be installed Apt B-14, Foster Garden Apartments (Lieutenant Portet) Bill to Finance Officer, JFK SWC Fort Bragg. No deposit required. (US Govt).

Jack reached over his shoulder and picked up the new telephone from her new dining-room sideboard.

"Hello?"

The acoustics were such that the caller's voice could be clearly, if faintly, heard.

"Jack, is Johnny Oliver there with you?" General Hanrahan asked without any preliminaries.

"Yes, sir."

"De la Santiago?"

"Yes, sir."

"Would it be reasonable of me to presume that all of you have had a couple of beers?"

"Yes, sir."

"Put Oliver on."

"Yes, sir."

Jack held out the phone to Oliver, who got up, went to the sideboard, and took the telephone from him.

"Captain Oliver, sir."

"I just had a call from Felter. He wanted you up there tonight," Hanrahan said.

"Up where, sir?"

"I will now call him back, and tell them that none of you are in any condition to fly tonight. Tomorrow's Special Orders will contain a paragraph confirming and making a matter of record the following verbal order of the commanding general. You, Portet, and de la Santiago are placed on five days' temporary duty to Headquarters, Department of the Army, Washington, D.C. Travel by U.S. government aircraft is directed."

"Yes, sir."

"Supplemental orders: Take Felter's L-23. You serve as instructor pilot for de la Santiago, as the flight will also serve as his cross-country check ride in L-23 aircraft."

"Yes, sir."

"Schedule your flight so that you can present yourself, in suitable civilian clothing, to Lieutenant Colonel Lowell, at the National Aviation Club — You know where that is, Johnny?"

"Yes, sir. In the Hotel Washington. General Bellmon goes there a lot."

"— not later than noon. Reservations have been made for the three of you in the hotel."

"Yes, sir. For five days, sir?"

"That's not set in concrete," Hanrahan said. "When was de la Santiago supposed to finish his parachute qualification?"

"Two more jumps tomorrow afternoon, sir, and the night jump tomorrow night."

"I'll have Ski reschedule that. Any questions, Johnny?"

"No, sir."

"Good night, Johnny."

Hanrahan hung up.

Oliver hung up the telephone.

"Everybody get that, or do I have to repeat it?" he asked.

"Five days?" Marjorie asked.

What the hell am I going to do here by myself for five days?

"He said he wasn't sure about that," Oliver said, and then went on, thinking out loud: "It's about two-twenty up there. Call it two-thirty. Another hour to get them to give us a car and get into Washington, three-thirty. Thirty minutes to change clothes. Four hours. Plus an hour for the You Damned Well Better Not Be Late factor, five hours. So we want to break ground at 0700."

He looked down at the table.

"The twelve-hour rule be damned," he said. "I'm going to have wine with my steak."

He sat down and reached for his knife and fork.

"As part of your flight training, Mr. de la Santiago," he said. "You can get on the horn and check the weather for us."

"Did he say what Uncle Cr— what Colonel Lowell wanted?" Marjorie asked.

Johnny shook his head.

"Now that you're married to a junior officer, Miss Marjorie, you better understand that they don't tell us peasants nothing."

"I'll call when I know something, baby," Jack said.

De la Santiago went to the telephone and dialed a number from memory.

"We may not get out in the morning," he said when he had finished listening to the weather forecast. "Or at least into Washington. There's a front coming in from the West."

"We're going to have to try," Oliver said. "You

can ride out there with us, Jack. We'll be at my car at six."

"I'll take him out to the field," Marjorie said.

"You don't have to do that, baby."

"I want to," she said. "I'll even throw in breakfast for your friends."

And then I'll come back here and wash the breakfast dishes, and see if I can get the dirt from the stove out of my new carpet, and then I will twiddle my thumbs for five days.

"I accept," Johnny said.

"Thanks, baby," Jack said.

[FOUR]
Room 914
The Hotel Washington
Washington, D.C.
0830 11 January 1965

When the doorbell chimed, Lieutenant Colonel Craig W. Lowell, wrapped in a terry-cloth bathrobe, got up from the room-service breakfast table, walked to the door, and opened it.

Two men were in the corridor. One was a bellman, carrying a uniform in a plastic bag. The other was Colonel Sanford T. Felter.

"Good morning, Colonel," Lowell said cheerfully. "Let me have a couple of bucks, will you, please?"

Felter shook his head, but took out his wallet and handed Lowell two one-dollar bills. Lowell gave them to the bellman.

"Thank you," he said, and took the uniform from him.

Felter walked to Captain Portet, who was sitting in his shirtsleeves at the table.

391

"Thank you for coming, Captain Portet," he said. "I realize it's an imposition."

"I got to ride in a Learjet," Portet said. "Good to see you, Colonel."

"Did Craig explain what this is all about?" Felter asked.

Lowell ripped the plastic cover from the uniform, balled it up, threw it at a wastebasket, missed, shrugged, and then laid the uniform against the back of a couch and began to pin insignia and ribbons on it.

"He led me to me to believe you wanted to ask me about General Mobutu," Portet said.

The telephone rang.

Lowell picked it up.

"Craig, Powell, Kenyon and Dawes," he said, then: "Good morning, Porter. Hold it a minute, will you?"

He waved at Portet and Felter.

"It's my cousin," he said. "I want you to hear this. Both of you."

Felter looked annoyed, but he followed Portet to where Lowell was standing, and both stood behind him so as to be able to listen to the conversation.

"Okay, Porter, what have you got?" Lowell said.

"Who's with you?"

"Colonel Felter and Captain Portet," Lowell said.

"The Gresham Investment Corporation has a two-room suite, 1107, in 27 Wall," Porter Craig announced. "They have been in there four months, on a two-year lease."

"What does Dun and Bradstreet have to say about them?"

"Not much. They've got a little over two million in Chase Manhattan. No other assets that D and

B knows about. The officers were listed, of course, but I never heard of any of them, including J. Richard Leonard."

"What about their credit references?"

"They gave us the Riggs Bank in Washington as a credit reference. I called a fellow I know there, and he assures me their credit is impeccable. I asked him how he knew, and he said I should trust him, they were as solid as the U.S. Treasury."

"Interesting," Lowell said.

"I thought so. I called their office a minute ago. A woman answered the telephone. I asked for Mr. Leonard. She wanted to know who was calling, and I lied to her; I said I was my friend in the Riggs bank. She told me Mr. Leonard was in Washington, and she knew I had that number. I didn't ask for it."

"Porter, you're wonderful," Lowell said.

"You want me to inquire further?"

"No, thanks," Lowell said. "I just hope this Leonard guy doesn't call your friend at Riggs, and he remembers you called him."

"I don't think that's likely," Porter Craig said. "I told him that it was a random check of credit references by the 27 Wall Street Corporation, and that I thought we could probably save us both time and money by me calling him."

"Thanks again, Porter. I owe you one," Lowell said, and hung up.

"What was that all about?" Felter asked.

"You tell him, JP," Lowell said. "While I finish with my uniform."

"Hurry up with that, will you?" Felter said, a tone of annoyance in his voice.

Lowell looked at him a moment.

"Pardon me all to hell, Mouse," he said. "The

393

Commander-in-Chief, himself, as you will recall, gave me two demerits for a mussed uniform. I am trying to straighten up and fly right."

Felter was not amused.

"I want to get out of here before the others arrive," he said. "I had Finton send the ASA over to sweep one of the private rooms in the club." The Army Security Agency was charged with signal counterintelligence, which often entailed "sweeping" rooms to detect electronic eavesdropping devices.

"Why do I suspect there is more to this meeting than you've told me?" Lowell asked.

Felter flashed him an angry look, then announced: "I just learned that Kasavubu has told our Ambassador (a) if Guevara shows up in the Congo, he will put him in front of a firing squad; and (b) that he has the entire situation under control; and (c) he absolutely refuses to have any American military personnel in the Congo."

"Guevara?" Captain Portet asked. "Che Guevara? In the Congo?"

Lowell looked as if was going to say something, but at the last minute did not.

"When you're finished," Felter said. "Please bring Captain Portet to the club. I want to make sure the ASA has been there."

[FIVE]
The National Aviation Club
The Hotel Washington
Washington, D.C.
0955 11 January 1965

Lowell led Captain Portet into a small, private meeting room in the Aviation Club. The roof of the

U.S. Mint could be seen through the windows. Felter was sitting at a round table surrounded by red-leather-upholstered captain's chairs. There was a coffee thermos and the associated paraphernalia on the table.

"They were still here when I got here," Felter said. "For a minute, I didn't think they were going to let me in until Finton cleared me."

"Yes, thank you," Lowell said, "I will have some coffee. Thank you so much."

"I'm really in no mood for your sophomoric humor, Craig," Felter said. "I think the first thing we should do is clarify the telephone call. Porter was suggesting the long hand of Langley was involved in something, wasn't he?"

"Yes, he was," Lowell said.

"What?"

"You tell him what happened, JP," Lowell said. "I have to take a leak."

"Well, Sandy?" Lowell asked when he came back into the room.

"They already own Air America," Felter said. "Why not another airline?"

" 'They'?" Captain Portet parroted. "You're talking about the CIA?"

"The CIA," Felter said. "The question is where did they get your name? Off the top of my head, I don't think they have made any connection with Earnest."

" 'Earnest'?" Portet parroted again. "I have no idea what you're talking about."

"Sandy, I think you better start with Earnest," Lowell said. "Hold off on Kasavubu until Jack gets here."

"What have you told him about Earnest?"

"Just that I was in Argentina trying to convince the Argentines not to blow him away," Lowell said.

"You shouldn't have told him that much," Felter snapped, then turned to Portet. "Captain Portet, some time ago I asked Colonel Lowell to look into the CIA's financial practices. Would you please tell Captain Portet what you learned, Colonel?"

"Yes, sir," Lowell said, and Felter did not miss the sarcasm.

"We're pressed for time, Craig," Felter said.

Lowell looked at him for a long moment.

"Okay," he said finally. "JP, from what I understand — actually, from what Porter found out for me — the Agency, the Company, is into all sorts of businesses. They look for a business that seems to be a suitable cover for their covert operations. Preferably one in financial difficulty. They send somebody to see the guy, let him know — they don't say they're the agency, of course, they probably have a half-dozen variations of the Gresham Investment Corporation scattered around — that they're interested in making an investment in a business like his."

"And people aren't suspicious?" Portet asked.

"People in financial difficulties tend to believe they need just a little help to weather the storm," Lowell said. "Okay, so since they're not trying to buy him out at distress prices, just invest in his business, the guy sells them a piece — say, thirty, forty percent. Business starts to pick up; he thinks he made the right decision, and then it goes bad again, and he needs just a little more help to weather the storm, and the agency winds up with fifty-one percent."

"And eventually they own the whole thing?" Portet asked.

"No. They don't want to own it. They want, should something come up, to be in a position to control it. Day to day, they want Mr. Clean to continue to operate a legitimate business in which they can hide their covert operations, and they see to it that it doesn't go under. And Mr. Clean is happy because he's still running the business and making money."

"It doesn't seem very ethical."

"This is the intelligence business, JP," Felter said. "Ethics in intelligence is about as common as honesty in politics."

Both Lowell and Portet chuckled.

"There are two possibilities," Felter went on. "The most logical, I think, is that the CIA's right hand doesn't know what the left hand is doing. The right hand — in this case, the Asian desk — already has one airline, and they want another. Redundancy is the term. If the right hand has talked to the left — the African desk — the chances are it was only to get confirmation of what they had already learned about Air Simba."

"How can you be so sure that Gresham Investments is the CIA?" Portet asked.

"The Riggs bank is the CIA bank, for one thing," Lowell said. "And for another, it sounds like one of their projects."

"What shape is Air Simba in, Captain Portet?" Felter asked.

"We *were* in the black. . . ."

" '*We*'? Who are your investors?"

"Me. Jacques and Hanni are the officers."

"They'd find that interesting," Lowell said.

"You were saying, Captain?" Felter said.

"Could I get you to call me JP?"

"Thank you," Felter said. "My friends call me 'Sandy.' "

"We were in the black before the Simba uprising," Portet said. "I was actually talking to Credit Lyonaisse about borrowing enough to buy a 707 or a DC-8. The Simba uprising changed all that, of course."

"I don't understand that," Lowell said. "Wasn't there an increase in demand for air freight? Military and civilian?"

"Air Simba is chartered in the Congo, and is required by law to serve the government first," Portet said. "And the government has been paying with vouchers that will be redeemed 'when the emergency is over.' They give the same vouchers to Mobil Oil for our fuel, and they cash enough of the vouchers to give us money to pay the crews and maintenance personnel, but we get a little deeper in the hole every day."

"And the CIA in the Congo would know that, wouldn't they?" Felter said thoughtfully. "My scenario — scenarios, there are several — is that maybe their report on what Kasavubu was doing to his civilian airlines was sent to Langley and passed to the Asian desk, and somebody there said, 'Hey, this guy is just what we're looking for. He's an American citizen, about to go broke, and he knows how to run the kind of operation we want.' "

"Yeah," Lowell agreed softly. "Or they did a database search for American pilots flying for foreign airlines, came up with JP's name. Same result. They checked him out with CIA in the Congo, and got the same report."

"Well, it doesn't really matter, does it?" Portet

said. "I certainly don't want to get involved with the CIA."

"Don't be too hasty about that," Lowell said. "Let's think that over."

"Think what over?"

"You could turn the agency's interest in you to your advantage, JP."

"I'm not sure I'd want to," Portet said. "But how could I do that?"

"By letting them finance your airline, which would in effect make it an interest-free loan, and then not letting them get fifty-one percent."

"How would I do that?"

"Every time they up the ante, you match it," Lowell said.

"Where would I get the money to do that?"

"Craig, Powell, Kenyon and Dawes is always ready to put money into a business guaranteed not to fail by the U.S. government," Lowell said. "And that's business, not personal."

"You want to go over that again?" Portet asked.

"That's a very interesting thought, Craig," Felter said. "But let's put it on the back burner for the present. I think it's time we brought JP up to speed on Operation Earnest."

He turned to Portet.

"What I am about to tell you, for reasons that will be self-evident, is highly classified. Ordinarily, when it is necessary to give highly classified information to someone outside the system, there is a stock speech threatening all sorts of dire consequences if he reveals that information to someone else. That's absolute nonsense. You can't take someone to court for revealing a secret unless you're willing to reveal in open court *what* secret, and that's the last thing you want to do. All I can do is rely on your good sense and patriotism."

"Thank you," Captain Portet said.

"We have reliable intelligence indicating that Che Guevara intends to go to the Congo — he's in Africa now —" Felter began, "to pick up the chaos where the Simba movement left off, and take the country over."

"You *are* talking about the Cuban?" Captain Portet asked, surprised.

"Actually, he's an Argentine. Ernesto Guevara de la Serna, M.D., born June 14, 1928, in Rosario. His father is of Irish descent, his mother of Spanish."

"Why the Congo?" Captain Portet asked.

"His ultimate ambition is to take over all of South America," Felter said. "The Congo is the first step. I don't think he gives a damn about the Congo, except that if he can take it over, he will appear unstoppable, prove that Cuba was not an aberration. And, of course, I suspect that he believes it'll be relatively easy for him."

"That's bad news for the Congo," Captain Portet said, and then asked, "Did I understand you to say he's a doctor?"

"Class of '53, the University of Buenos Aires," Lowell said.

"There are two ways to deal with the problem," Felter said. "One is to terminate him. . . ."

"You mean kill him? Or have him killed?"

Felter nodded. "That would, of course, turn him into a martyr. Recognizing this, President Johnson has approved a plan in which he will be kept alive while his operations in the Congo are thwarted. We intend to make him fail in the

Congo. Covertly, of course."

"Interesting," Captain Portet said thoughtfully.

"There are a number of people, and governments, who think that terminating him is the best solution for the problem. Colonel Lowell and Major Lunsford have just returned from Argentina, where they succeeded in convincing the Argentines that keeping Guevara alive makes more sense than killing him."

"Hell, I'm almost on the side of those who would like him dead," Captain Portet said. "Emotionally, I certainly am. I finally got Hanni to tell me what she saw the Simbas do in Stanleyville."

"Lunsford and Jack are forming a team of Green Berets, Swahili-speaking American Negroes, at Fort Bragg. They will go to the Congo with the dual mission of making sure that Guevara fails and isn't killed while failing."

"You're sending Jacques to the Congo?" Captain Portet asked. His tone made it clear that he didn't like that at all.

"Not into the bush," Felter said. "His skin is the wrong color. We can't take the chance that someone would see him, or, worse, that he would be captured. But it was my intention to send him there, for short trips, to help Major Lunsford make contacts — and, of course, to take advantage of his knowledge of the Congo."

" '*Was* your intention'? Does that mean you're *not* going to send him?"

"What I have in mind for Jack to do now is to go there and see what he can do to get General Mobutu to get around the 'no-American-military-under-any-conditions' disaster our ambassador has created with Kasavubu. The Ambassador tried this, and Mobutu literally pushed him out of

401

his office. I'm hoping Jack can do better."

"Joseph can be difficult," Captain Portet said wryly. "Particularly if he's been drinking, which, rumor has it, is whenever the doctor's not around, and sometimes when he is."

"I got the impression that he and Jack are pretty close," Felter said.

"Mobutu's known Jacques since he wore short pants," Captain Portet said. "He was still Sergeant Major Mobutu of the Force Publique."

"And *Lieutenant General* Mobutu made good on his promise to decorate Jack for what Jack did at Stanleyville," Felter said. "A private bill will be introduced in Congress tomorrow, so that Jack can accept it."

"I asked Mobutu one time why he was only a lieutenant general when every other chief of staff in Africa was at least a full general or a field marshal," Captain Portet said thoughtfully. "And he told me the doctor had given him a life of George Washington to read — that if being a lieutenant general was good enough for the Father of the United States, it was good enough for Joseph Désiré Mobutu."

"Interesting," Lowell said. "Who is this doctor you keep mentioning?"

"Actually, he's a physician," Portet said. "He's a Mormon. A missionary, I guess."

"And what's his relationship to Mobutu?"

"One of the few white men he trusts," Portet said.

"Like you and Jacques?" Felter asked.

Lowell noticed that Jack had become Jacques.

"More than that," Captain Portet said. "He's sort of a . . . Mormon Jesuit, I guess. Mobutu turns to him for advice."

"What's his name?"

"Howard Dannelly," Captain Portet said.

"How do you get along with Dr. Dannelly?" Felter asked.

"We know each other," Captain Portet said. "He's a good man. He's good for Mobutu."

"How does Dr. Dannelly feel about Jacques?" Felter asked.

"He's . . . uh . . . not in Jacques's legion of admirers," Portet said.

"Why not?" Felter asked.

"Well," Portet said, smiling. "You know the Mormons. They don't drink, they don't smoke, they don't believe in sex outside of marriage. You might not believe it, looking at clean-cut young Lieutenant Portet, but, pre-Marjorie, he drank like a fish, smoked big black cigars, and was working his way through the white female population of the Congo, without regard to anyone's marriage vows."

Lowell laughed.

"Was there something specific?" Felter asked, a tone of annoyance in his voice.

"He was in Kolwezi one time, in the Hotel Leopold, with a friend, and Dr. Dannelly accosted him in the lobby and told him he and the friend should be ashamed of themselves, their conduct was inexcusable, and Jacques . . . told him to go fuck himself."

"The friend was female?" Lowell asked.

Portet nodded.

"So Dr. Dannelly is not about to give Jack a character reference?" Lowell asked.

"That would be highly unlikely," Portet said, and then added: "I'll talk to Mobutu if you want."

"That's a thought," Lowell said. "Particularly if

403

you play the Mormon card, Sandy."

"Excuse me?" Captain Portet said.

"Sandy, those Mormons are tight with each other. If we can get Finton to go with JP and Jack to see Mobutu . . ."

"You'd be willing to go to Mobutu?" Felter asked.

"I spent a large part of my life in the Congo," Portet said. "I like it. I like the people. They don't need a Cuban revolutionary making things worse than they already are."

"I told Finton to come here for lunch," Felter said. "Let's see what he thinks. Not during lunch. Afterward."

He paused and looked at Captain Portet.

"A man who works for me is a devout Mormon," he said. "When you meet him at lunch, try to guess how well he'd get along with Dr. Dannelly."

Captain Portet nodded.

[SIX]
The Hotel Washington
Washington, D.C.
1105 11 January 1965

"Good morning," Johnny Oliver said politely to the reception clerk at the Hotel Washington. "I'm Captain Oliver, and I believe you have reservations for myself and these officers?"

"Yes, sir. We do. You're in 914."

He passed out keys to each of them.

"All of us?" Oliver said.

"All of you," the reception clerk said, and tapped the bell for a bellman to handle the luggage.

"Why do I suspect the SWC has just run out of TDY money?" Oliver asked softly in the elevator. "Rank will have its privileges, gentlemen. *I'm* not going to share a bed with either of you."

"We should have told the guy to get us another room — rooms," Jack Portet said.

"Let's take a look at this, and see what we're going to need, and then call him on the phone?" Oliver suggested, but they both understood it to be an order.

The bellman stopped his cart outside 914, then knocked at the door.

"Come!" a male voice called.

The bellman pushed the door open and waved them through.

914 was a large, well — even luxuriously — furnished living room.

"Oh, thank God, the lost birdmen have been found!" Lieutenant Geoffrey Craig called out.

He was sitting in one corner of the room, in civilian clothing, about to finish a club sandwich. There was a coffee service on the coffee table. Major Pappy Hodges, sipping at a cup, was slumped into an armchair across from him.

"What do you mean, lost?" Johnny Oliver asked. "What is this, old home week?"

He walked to Pappy and shook his hand.

"Good to see you, Johnny," Pappy said, then raised his voice: "You, Portet, change clothes right now and go see Felter in the Aviation Club."

"Yes, sir," Jack said. "Where do I do that?"

"Top floor."

"I meant change out of uniform?"

"There's four bedrooms in here," Geoff said. "Wherever you find that ugly luggage of yours is yours."

"What is this place, anyway?" Jack asked.

"It belongs to the firm," Geoff said.

Jack found his luggage in a large L-shaped bedroom furnished with two king-size beds, a desk, a wet bar, and an upholstered chair and table set that made the room in effect a small suite.

He wondered if he had time for a quick shower, and decided he didn't; Pappy had said "right away." He shaved quickly with an electric razor, sprayed himself with cologne, changed into a sports jacket and tie, and went back into the living room.

Pappy was on the telephone. He waved impatiently for Jack to get moving.

As he left the room, he heard Pappy say, "Colonel, he should be there any second. . . ."

He wondered what Colonel Lowell wanted with him; he was, except for Enrico de la Santiago, the least experienced of all of them. And this, he sensed, was business, not social. He got in the elevator and rode up to the National Aviation Club.

The receptionist expected him.

"You're Captain Portet, right?"

"No. I used to be. Now I'm Lieutenant Portet," Jack said.

"If you'll come with me, please?" she said, smiling strangely at him.

She led him through the bar to a corridor, then knocked at a door.

"Yes?"

"Lieutenant Portet is here, Colonel," she said, and then, to Jack, "Go on in."

Lieutenant Colonel Craig W. Lowell was sitting at a table with Colonel Sanford T. Felter, which surprised him a little, and so was Captain Jean-Philippe Portet, which surprised him a great deal.

Completely ignoring what he thought was probably the proper military protocol, he went directly to his father, and they hugged and kissed in the European manner.

"And how is married life?" his father said.

"I think I better salute, or do whatever else I'm supposed to do in a situation like this, before I get into that," Jack said.

"Now that everybody's here, why don't we order drinks?" Lowell suggested.

"It's not even noon," Felter protested. "Do you need the alcohol?"

Lowell ignored him.

"Scotch for you, right, Jean-Philippe?" Lowell asked.

"Please."

"Jack?" Lowell asked, and then when he saw the look on his face, added, "Go ahead, you're not going to be flying anytime soon."

"Then please," Jack said.

"Mouse?"

"Get me a cup of tea, please," Felter said.

Lowell picked up a telephone.

"Bring in a bottle of scotch, please. Is any of mine left? And the necessary ancillary equipment." He hung up the phone and looked at Felter. "You don't need tea, Mouse. You need a drink."

"I'll be a sonofabitch," Felter said.

"You *are* a sonofabitch, Mouse. *Everybody* knows that," Lowell said unctuously.

Felter glared at him.

" 'Mouse'?" Captain Portet asked.

"He's the only sonofabitch in the world who can call me that to my face."

"I see," Captain Portet said.

"And you, Lieutenant," Lowell said, "may call Colonel Felter, and myself, either 'Colonel' or 'sir.' "

"Yes, sir."

Captain Portet chuckled.

"That line's not original," Lowell said. "I heard it first years ago — from your mother-in-law's father, Jack — and I thought of it a couple of days ago in Buenos Aires, when Pistarini, the commander-in-chief of their army, wanted us all to be buddies."

"You didn't call him Pascual?" Felter asked, smiling.

"I can't vouch for the hours between two and four A.M., but the rest of the time I made a real effort to call him *mi general*," Lowell said.

There was a knock at the door, and a waiter appeared carrying a tray on which sat a bottle of the same obscure Scottish distillery whiskey Lowell had given Portet in Florida, a bowl of ice, and both a water pitcher and a soda siphon.

"We'll do it, thanks," Lowell said to the waiter, and poured generous drinks in each of the glasses.

When the waiter was out of the room, he turned to Jack.

"Your father has been regaling us with tales of your romantic escapades in the Congo," Lowell said.

Jack looked at his father in surprise.

"Which, he suggests, have put you on Dr. Dannelly's shitlist."

"Which is important, Jack," Lowell went on, "because Colonel Felter has just learned that Mobutu threw our ambassador out of his office when he asked for his help with Operation Earnest."

"Shit!" Jack said. "That sounds like Dannelly. And he's got Mobutu's ear."

"My original thought was to send you there, with Father, to talk to Mobutu," Felter said.

"Colonel, I'm sorry, but if Dannelly is involved, me showing up would only make matters worse. I . . . uh . . . once told him, in a hotel lobby —"

"To go fuck himself," Felter interrupted. "We know." He paused. "Your father has volunteered to go to Léopoldville and speak with Mobutu."

"You told him what's going on?" Jack asked.

Felter nodded.

"What do you think?" Lowell asked.

"If anybody can get Joseph to change his mind, he can."

"Would you recommend that he go alone? Or that you go with him?"

"If Dannelly's going to be there, alone," Jack said without hesitation.

Felter nodded.

"We may have one more hole card," Felter said. "I don't know if we'll get to play it."

"Sir?"

"Mr. Finton is a highly respected member of the Church of Latter-Day Saints," Felter said. "A bishop."

"He's coming to lunch, Jack," Lowell said. "We want you and your dad to try to guess how well he would get along with Dr. Dannelly. Separate opinions, please. Don't compare notes."

"Yes, sir."

One of the rooms opening off the sitting room was a conference room with a huge mahogany table and a dozen red leather-upholstered captain's tables. Its windows, too, overlooked the roof of the U.S. Mint, with the White House visible farther down Pennsylvania Avenue.

The table was now set for lunch, and there were two rolling steam carts standing against one wall. Pappy Hodges, Father Lunsford, Geoff Craig, Enrico de la Santiago, and Johnny Oliver were sitting at the table.

"You didn't have to wait for us," Felter said as he led Lowell and the Portets into the room. "Help yourselves, and let's get this started. We have a lot to talk about."

He led by example by raising the chrome domes of the steam tables and picking up a plate. There was a tureen of clam chowder, bowls of vegetables, and platters of baked ham and roast beef.

Everybody but de la Santiago had, so to speak, gone through the chow line when Chief Warrant Officer W-4 James L. Finton came into the room. He was a lithe, sharp-featured man in his early forties, wearing a gray suit, a crisp white shirt, and a dark blue necktie.

Without a word, he went to the windows, closed the drapes, and then went to the steam tables. He bent over, raised the linen drapes on one table, peered under the table intently, and then repeated the process on the second table. Finally, he took a

410

plate and helped himself to food.

"ASA swept this room at ten, Colonel," he announced as he sat down. "Anyone been in here alone since?"

Felter shook his head, no.

"Then I would say we're secure," Finton said.

"Thank you," Felter said.

Finton bowed his head, put his fingertips together, and closed his eyes. He was obviously saying grace.

Then he opened his eyes and reached for his knife and fork.

Felter laid down his soup spoon and dabbed at his mouth with a napkin.

"I'm going to go over where we are and where we're going," he said. "I suppose Argentina's as good a place as any to start. Lowell and Lunsford did a good job down there; the Argentines are on board. The next step is to get the L-23 down there. Finton is working on finding us a Spanish-speaking Army aviator who will be the pilot down there, diverting, it is to be hoped, attention from de la Santiago. We also need one with a Top Secret security clearance — not for Top Secret/ Earnest; this guy will be told as little as possible about that, but because it's a requirement for anyone assigned to an embassy. So the pilot may not be immediately available. Oliver, Portet, and de la Santiago will fly it down there, taking with them Warrant Officer Zammoro from Bragg, Master Sergeant Thomas, and one of Father's guys . . ."

He paused and looked at Lunsford.

"Sergeant First Class Otmanio," Lunsford furnished.

". . . who, it turns out, speaks Spanish Harlem

Spanish," Felter finished. "Zammoro was a major in the Cuban army, making it possible he's friendly with some Argentine army officers. As a young officer, he went to a couple of schools down there. Which is why he's going. He may stay, but right now, the only ones we know that are going to stay down there are de la Santiago and Otmanio."

He paused again.

"Questions?"

There were no questions.

"So what we need from you, Pappy, is to make sure the L-23 is all right to make the trip. And lay out the flight plan. And we have to get de la Santiago rated as an L-23 pilot, the sooner the better."

"Can we talk about that?" Pappy asked.

Felter made a come-on-with-it gesture with his hand and returned to his clam chowder.

"These hurry-up, rate-them-yesterday, screw-the-regulations, Mickey Mouse pilot-qualification courses of yours are about to blow up in your face," Pappy said.

"How's that, Pappy?" Lowell asked. "What we've been trying to do is comply with the regulations. And none of these people learned to fly last week. So what's the problem?"

"Geoff learned to fly last week," Pappy said.

"You're saying he's not qualified?" Felter asked.

"Can he fly twin-engine airplanes? Yeah, he can. But he was sent to Rucker to learn to fly helicopters. Students are expressly forbidden to take private instruction. Geoff started taking private fixed-wing lessons about the day after he got to Rucker, and people know about that. They also know that half the time, Lowell's Cessna is at the

Ozark airport, and that Geoff is flying it, which is also against the rules. Students are forbidden to fly private aircraft while they're students. And those rules were always enforced. Until now."

"Well, that's water under the dam, isn't it?" Lowell asked. "I thought you were about to give him his L-23 check ride?"

"I am," Pappy said.

"When you pass him, he's gone from Rucker, right? So what's the problem?"

"They also know that Jack, who last week was a PFC, and is now Bellmon's son-in-law, suddenly shows up as an officer and gets himself rated in just about everything in a Mickey Mouse course."

"Okay," Felter said. "And?"

"And now Enrico shows up, to go through another Mickey Mouse course to get himself rated."

"Go on," Felter said.

"I happen to know there have been bitches to Bellmon," Pappy said.

"General Bellmon (a) has orders to give us whatever we need and (b) knows why all of this was necessary," Felter replied.

"And, being the good guy Bob Bellmon is, he's prepared to swallow the gossip that he's giving special treatment to his son-in-law. That hurts him."

"Yeah, I know," Lowell said.

"And Bellmon, of course, can't tell the people who asked him what the hell is going on what's behind it, and since they don't know, they can't explain it to the guys who have been bitching to them, who are understandably pissed. And sooner or later, probably sooner, one of them — maybe three or four of them — are going to go to the IG about it. Then what?"

"Oh, goddamn it!" Lowell said. "I never thought of that."

The inspector generals of the Army, almost invariably experienced senior officers, are in a sense ombudsmen. They investigate complaints of unfairness, illegality, and so on. They are on the staff of the local commander, but have the authority — and the duty — should the local commander not rectify a situation to their satisfaction, or be at fault himself, to take the issue to higher headquarters, and ultimately to the inspector general of the Army, who takes his orders only from the chief of staff of the Army.

The problem was not that anything Felter had done, including what Pappy called the "Mickey Mouse special courses," was illegal — he was acting with the authority of the President, the Commander-in-Chief; that was all the authority he needed.

But the inspector general at Rucker would certainly investigate allegations that officers were being rated as aviators without following the regulations prescribing precisely how this should be done, and further, perhaps reluctantly, but with no less dedication, that the commanding general's son-in-law had been given special treatment.

That meant that at least the IG at Rucker would have to be told of Operation Earnest. It was possible, perhaps even likely, because of the allegations of special treatment of Bellmon's son-in-law, that he would feel he had to make a report to the IG of the Third U.S. Army, in whose area Fort Rucker was located, and/or to Continental Army Command (CONARC), which supervised all training within the Continental United States.

414

And the IGs at Third Army and CONARC might feel they were obliged to bring the IG of the Army into the loop.

The rule of thumb — too often proven true — for classified matters is that the more people who knew a secret, the greater the chance it would be compromised. It was not that any of the IGs would have loose mouths, but there were other people involved: The junior officers, noncoms, and civilian clerks who would handle the paperwork would also learn what was going on, and experience proved this would be tantamount to unlocking the door on a secret.

"I'm not finished," Pappy said. "The L-23 Jack and I picked up at Wichita was supposed to go to the commanding general of III Corps at Fort Hood," Pappy said. "He's found out he's not going to get it, and he's highly pissed."

"How do you know that?" Lowell asked.

"His aviation officer is an old pal of mine," Pappy said. "He called me up and said, 'Pappy, my boss found out you stole his airplane from Wichita, and he wants it back.' "

"What did you say?"

"I told him I didn't know what he was talking about, and he said, 'Bullshit' and hung up."

"Great," Lowell said.

Felter stopped his spoon halfway between his bowl of clam chowder and his mouth.

"This will have to be nipped in the bud," Felter said calmly. "At both ends. Finton, call Mary Margaret and have her call the chief's office and ask for an appointment for me at his earliest convenience, and have her prepare a letter, on White House stationery, with the 'Counselor to the President' signature block on it, addressed to the com-

415

manding generals of Rucker and III Corps stating that Colonel Lowell is dealing with a classified operation at my direction."

"I'll go back to the office and do it myself, sir," Finton said.

"No, I need you for something else here. Call Mary Margaret."

"Yes, sir," Finton said, and got up from the table.

"What did you fly up here, Pappy?"

"A Mohawk. I wanted to be able to get home for supper."

"I want you to take Lowell to Hood, and stick around there until he sees the III Corps Commander, and then take him to Rucker."

Pappy nodded his acceptance of the order.

Felter finished putting the spoonful of clam chowder in his mouth.

Waiters were just about finished clearing the table.

"You and Pappy might as well head for Hood, Craig," Felter said. "There's really no reason for you to sit in on this."

"Was that an order, or is it open for discussion?" Lowell asked.

Felter visibly thought that over.

"You can stay, which means you won't be able to see the III Corps CG today."

"I don't know," Lowell said. "If I was the III Corps CG, and my aide told me there was a light colonel from the White House who wanted to see me at my earliest convenience, I don't think I'd make him wait until tomorrow morning."

"Let's hope you're right," Felter said. He raised his voice slightly. "Okay, everybody but Captain Portet, Lowell, Finton . . ."

He looked at Jack Portet for a moment, and then went on: ". . . and Lieutenant Portet, take your coffee into the living room."

When they had filed out, Felter waited patiently until the waiters had finished clearing the table and had pushed the steam tables out of the room. Then he went to the door and closed it.

"Talking to Captain Portet about Mobutu was worth the effort getting him up here, Jim," Felter began.

Finton nodded but said nothing.

"What do you know about Dr. Dannelly?" Felter asked.

"One of the CIA backgrounds said that he is close to Mobutu," Finton said, "that's all."

"Captain Portet tells me that he is very close to Mobutu," Felter said. "And that he is a devout member of the Church of Latter-Day Saints."

"That wasn't in any of the CIA backgrounds," Finton said.

"Captain Portet also tells me that without the approval of Dr. Dannelly, it is unlikely that Mobutu will change his mind about helping us to get around Kasavubu's refusal to let us operate over there."

"The backgrounds said that Captain Portet was very close to Mobutu," Finton said, but it was a question.

"Jacques Portet needs to be involved with our operations, and Mobutu needs to approve of that, too."

"The backgrounds also said that Lieutenant Portet is on a first-name basis with Mobutu," Finton said, another question phrased as a statement.

"Dr. Dannelly is not one of Jacques's

417

admirers," Felter said.

"Why is that?" Finton asked.

Felter cocked his head, then smiled.

"I was tempted to sugarcoat the situation by saying he disapproved of Jacques's sowing of wild oats," Felter said. "But it's worse than that."

"Specifically?"

"You tell him, Jacques," Felter said.

"I was in the Hotel Leopold in Kolwezi with a lady who was not my wife. Dannelly told me I was a disgrace, and I told him to go fuck himself," Jack said.

"I don't like to pry into your personal affairs, Lieutenant. . . ." Finton said.

"Ask him anything you want," Felter said.

"Was alcohol involved?" Finton asked.

Jack nodded.

"And was the lady someone else's wife?"

Jack nodded again.

"I thought it had to be something like that," Finton said. "The Bible teaches us, 'Judge not, lest ye be judged,' and we try to follow that teaching. Our church teaches us that a man's sins are between him and God. In this case, I would say that Dr. Dannelly believed not saying something to you, to try to turn you from your wicked ways, would be a sin of omission — 'we have not done those things we ought to have done' — and tried to counsel you."

"Jacques has turned from his wicked ways," Felter said. "How do we convince Dr. Dannelly of that?"

Jack thought: *That's the first time I have ever heard anyone say "wicked ways" in absolute sincerity, in a conversation. And they both did it. And I'll be damned if Felter didn't mean it just as sincerely as this Mormon bishop.*

"Have you, Lieutenant?" Finton asked. "Have you turned from your wicked ways?"

Jack saw from his father's raised left eyebrow that he was amused by the exchange.

Jack thought: *That's three times. And if I blow this answer, I'm really going to fuck things up.*

"I hope so," Jack said. "I think so. The day before I got married, I took Holy Communion with my fiancée. We're Anglican. There is a prayer of confession, with the same line you quoted before — 'we have done those things which we ought not to have done, and we have not done those things we ought to have done' — and the next day, before a priest, I swore to God that I would be faithful to my wife. The line is 'keep myself only unto her.' I'm really going to try to keep that promise."

Jack thought: *The strange thing is, I meant that; I didn't say it to get on the right side of this guy.*

"I am happy for you, then," Finton said. "If you keep that vow, it will give you joy in this world and the next."

"I hope so," Jack said.

"You might consider giving up alcohol," Finton said.

"How about 'take a little wine for your stomach's sake and thine other infirmities'? Didn't Christ say that?" Jack quipped.

Oh, shit, my mouth ran away with me again.

"Probably, if you'd limited yourself to a little wine, you wouldn't have found yourself locking horns with Dr. Dannelly," Finton said, smiling.

"Okay," Felter said. "How do we convince Dr. Dannelly that Jacques has turned from his wicked ways?"

419

"Correct me if I'm wrong, Colonel," Finton said, "but what you're really asking is if I will help you do that, as a bishop of the Church of Latter-Day Saints."

"Yes, I am," Felter said seriously.

"I will have to ask God's guidance about that," Finton said.

"Our cause here is noble, Jim," Felter reasoned. "We've talked about that."

"I will have to ask God's guidance," Finton repeated. "I will let you have my decision in the morning."

"Thank you."

"And now I'd better go back to the office," Finton said, "and see how Mary Margaret is coming with your appointment to see the chief. Would you like me to send her here with the letter for Colonel Lowell?"

"Please," Felter said.

Finton came to a position close to attention.

"With your permission, sir?"

"Granted. Thank you, Mr. Finton," Felter said.

Finton left the room.

"Interesting man," Captain Portet said. "And just for the record, Jacques, I'm glad you have turned from your wicked ways."

"What are you going to do if he says no?" Lowell asked.

"Try to do it without him, obviously," Felter said. "The next question is Father Lunsford. How do you think Mobutu would react to him?"

"Tough one," Captain Portet said. "I don't know how it would go, whether he would look at Lunsford as a fellow black soldier — he's in love with his own parachutists — or whether he would look at him as a mercenary. And he's death, literally, on them."

"Jacques?" Felter asked.

"Father speaks pretty good Swahili; that would go well with Mobutu. And we know he's impressed with what Father did before we jumped on Stanleyville."

"I go with the fellow parachutist notion," Lowell said. "All you parachute nuts recognize each other. It's you against the rest of the sane world."

"Okay," Felter said. "Father goes. I think it's important that Mobutu know him. Anybody else? Should we start infiltrating the team now?"

"I think you'd better wait to see how Mobutu reacts to this," Jack said. "If he goes along, it will make things a lot easier."

"You're going to go ahead with this in any event?" Captain Portet asked.

"We have to," Felter said.

XI

[ONE]
Room 914
The Hotel Washington
Washington, D.C.
0805 12 January 1965

"Good morning," Colonel Sanford T. Felter said as he came through the door to the living room.

Major G. W. Lunsford, Captain John S. Oliver, and WOJG Enrico de la Santiago quickly stood up, and a moment later, so did Lieutenant Jacques Portet.

Felter impatiently waved them back into the seats. He was wearing the same mussed suit he had worn the day before. The others were in their shirtsleeves.

Lieutenant Geoffrey Craig was on the telephone.

"We're ordering breakfast, Colonel," he said. "What would you like?"

"Toast and tea, please," Felter said. "My wife made breakfast at home."

Felter turned to Captain Portet and smiled.

"I think you may have been a good — or should I say 'sobering'? — influence on these hoodlums, JP," he said. "I see few of the usual signs of debauchery on their smiling faces."

"We went to the movies," JP said. "*Topkapi*. With Peter Ustinov. Pretty good."

"About a jewel robbery," Lunsford furnished.

422

"And then we came back here and, with enormous patience, Captain Portet let me grill him about the Congo."

"I asked you to call me JP, Father," Captain Portet said.

"You're like the colonel, Captain, one of those people people like me have trouble calling by anything but their rank."

"You mean I'm stuffy?"

"No, I mean you're one of those people — like the colonel — people like me have trouble calling by anything but their rank. It was intended as a compliment."

"I will buy a bigger hat," Captain Portet said. "Call me JP, Father."

"Yes, sir," Washington said.

"Learn anything interesting?" Felter asked.

"He understands their thinking, sir," Lunsford said. "I wish my guys had been here."

The door opened and CWO Finton came in.

"Good morning, sir," he said to Felter, then nodded at the others and added, "Gentlemen."

"Breakfast is on the way, Jim," Felter said. "And I heard Lieutenant Craig tell them to send an extra order of steak and eggs."

"Yes, sir. Thank you, Lieutenant, I haven't had any breakfast." He paused and looked at Felter. "Sir, if you think I would be useful in the Congo, I am prepared to go."

"Thank God," Felter said, and then heard what he had said. "I know you know I didn't mean that the way it sounded."

"I like to think I know you very well, Colonel," Finton said. "I took no offense."

"Lieutenant Portet just made the point that if we can get Mobutu's cooperation, things will be a lot easier for us. To infiltrate the team, for one thing."

"There's already a problem there," Finton said. "An immediate problem. Mary Margaret tells me the Congolese Embassy is being difficult about issuing visas."

"Did she say why?" Felter asked.

"She suspects it is an expression of unhappiness with our ambassador, sir."

"Slip the Congolese Consular officer a hundred bucks," Jack said. "That usually speeds things up miraculously."

"How many visas do you need?" Captain Portet asked.

Felter looked around the room and counted with his finger.

"Five," he said. "You and Jacques, Father, Jim, and me. I don't want to enter the Congo on an accredited to U.S. Embassy basis unless I have to."

"Jack and I have Congolese passports," Captain Portet said. "I think I can get visas for you and Father and Mr. Finton. When do you have to have them?"

"As soon as possible," Felter said.

"Well, can I suggest that as soon as we finish breakfast, we go over there? To the Congolese Embassy?"

[TWO]
Chancellery of the Embassy of the Republic
of the Congo
Washington, D.C.
0945 12 January 1965

The receptionist of the embassy was a tall, stunning Negro woman in her late twenties.

"Good morning, my darling," Captain Jean-Phillipe Portet greeted her in Swahili, smiling broadly. "Would you be so kind as to inform the ambassador that Captain Portet of Air Congo would like a moment of his time?"

It was evident even before she opened her mouth that the receptionist didn't understand a word he had said, but she made it official:

"Excuse me?"

"My father, my beauty," Jack said in French, "wishes to see the ambassador. Be a good girl and tell him we're here, won't you?"

It was equally evident that the receptionist had only a distant acquaintance with the French language.

Captain Portet laid a business card on her counter. It identified him as the Chief Pilot of Air Congo, 473 Boulevard de Antwerp, Léopoldville.

The receptionist studied it.

"I'll be right back," she said, and got up from her desk. She turned and added, a bit triumphantly, *"S'il vous plâit."*

"Merci, mademoiselle," Captain Portet said.

A young black man in a suit came into the reception area a minute later.

"How may I help you?" he asked in English.

"You're not the ambassador," Captain Portet said, not very pleasantly, in Swahili. "I wish to see the ambassador, and I am getting tired of waiting."

Father Lunsford, having figured out what was going on, chimed in.

"You are dealing with the chief pilot of Air Congo here, my good friend," he said.

"Chief," the young man said in Swahili, "I will inform his excellency that you are here."

425

The ambassador, a squat, very black man in his fifties, appeared two minutes later. He smiled broadly at Captain Portet, then came around the counter with his arms spread wide.

"My dear friend!" he said in Swahili. "How good it is to see you!"

He kissed both of Captain Portet's cheeks. He turned to Jack. "And the fruit of the lion's loins!"

He kissed Jack.

"Chief, you are looking well," Father said in Swahili.

The ambassador kissed Father.

He looked at Colonel Felter and CWO Finton and smiled, but did not kiss either one of them.

"What may I do for you?"

"I need a small favor," Captain Portet said. "I need to send a message to a mutual friend of ours, and, to be discreet, I do not wish to send it through commercial channels. I thought you might be able to help me."

He handed him a sheet of paper:

> *His Excellency,*
>
> *Lt. Gen Joseph Désiré Mobutu*
> *Chief of Staff, the Congolese Army*
>
> *Léopoldville*
>
> *My Dear Joseph:*
>
> *I have the price for that investment you are considering. Jacques and I are on our*

way home. Can you fit dinner with us into your schedule as soon as possible?

With the warmest regards,

Jean-Philippe Portet.

The ambassador read it.

"I was hoping you could send this using your diplomatic code," Captain Portet said in Swahili.

"It will be gone within the hour," the ambassador said.

"I very much appreciate your kindness."

"It is my pleasure. Is there anything else I can do for you?"

"No, I don't think so," Captain Portet said. "Except — I hate to trouble you with something unimportant, Chief."

"Nonsense. What are friends for? What can I help you with?"

"These gentlemen need visas," Captain Portet said.

It took the ambassador about twenty seconds to decide that his orders from Léopoldville to subject all applications from Americans for visas to enter the Congo to very careful — and thus very lengthy — evaluation obviously did not apply to friends of a man who addressed General Mobutu by his Christian name.

"Of course," the ambassador said. "It will take just a minute, if you'd be good enough to wait."

[THREE]
Apartment B-14
Foster Garden Apartments
Fayetteville, North Carolina
1620 12 January 1965

Mrs. Marjorie Portet was torn between joy at seeing her husband come through the door of their home and fury that he hadn't, as he had promised, telephoned her as soon as he knew what was going on.

Joy triumphed. She threw herself into his arms, and one thing led to another, and it was thirty minutes later before she raised the question about his unexpected appearance.

They were at the time on their new bed, and there had been proof that, due to an application of soap on various parts thereof, it no longer squealed in protest when subjected to vertical movements on the mattress.

"I thought you were going to be gone for five days," she said. "I was thinking of going to see my folks."

"You can go tomorrow," Jack said helpfully. "Actually, it's a pretty good idea. There's not much for you to do around here, is there?"

"Where are you going to be tomorrow?" she asked.

"On my way to the Congo," he said.

She didn't trust herself to speak. He interpreted this as a silent request for additional information.

"We're on the 8:20 Southern Airways flight to Atlanta; then the 12:10 Eastern Flight to La Guardia — we're going to meet my father there; he's coming up from Miami. Then we take the 5:17 Pan American flight out of Kennedy to

428

Amsterdam; and the 10:05 Air Congo flight to Léopoldville the next morning."

"Why do I suspect 'we're,' as in 'we're on the 8:20 Southern flight,' doesn't mean you and me?" Marjorie asked softly.

"Father and me, baby," Jack said. He saw the look on her face. "Hey, I'm a soldier. I go where they send me."

My God, Liza was right. I feel like screaming or weeping, or both.

"What are you going to do in the Congo?"

"Steal furniture, for one thing," he said, chuckling. "Or keep it from being stolen."

"What?" she asked incredulously.

"My father says we'll get a truck and get what we can — the best stuff — out of the house, call it personal stuff, and take it to KLM Air Freight at the airport and at least try to get it out of the Congo. Some of it's pretty nice, but I don't know where the hell it would fit in here."

"You're not going over there to steal furniture," Marjorie thought out loud.

"We're going to see Mobutu, and see if we can get him to help," Jack said.

"Your father, too?"

"Yeah. He was in Washington. He and Mobutu are pretty close."

"How long will you be gone?"

"Not long," he said. "A couple of days in Léopoldville, and a couple of days in Stanleyville."

"Stanleyville? You're not going back to Stanleyville? In God's name, why?"

"I want to introduce Father to people who can do us some good," Jack said. "And if there's anything left in the apartment, I'll bring it back with me to Léopoldville and ship it out of the Congo."

"For example?"

"Well, there's a Browning shotgun there," Jack replied. "I saw it when . . ." He paused, and then, obviously delighted with his wit, went on, ". . . I unexpectedly dropped in the last time. And my tennis racquets."

"My God!" Marjorie said.

"Hey, it's safe, baby, at least for the time being. Mike Hoare's mercenaries ran the Simbas out. And, come to think of it, probably stole everything that wasn't nailed down in the apartment."

"You'll be gone how long?"

"Two days to get there, five days there, two days to get back. I should be back on the twenty-second. We *have* to be back on the twenty-sixth."

"You *have* to be back on the twenty-sixth?"

"Yeah, we're going to Argentina on the twenty-eighth," Jack said.

"*Argentina?* Isn't that strange? I can't remember ever hearing a word from you about Argentina."

"A lot of this just happened in Washington, baby."

He saw the look on her face.

"What?" he asked.

"What what?"

"What are you thinking?"

"How long are you going to be in Argentina?"

"About the same time, ten, twelve days," Jack said. "But why do I suspect that's not what you were thinking?"

"I was thinking I was going to miss you," Marjorie said.

What I was thinking was that I'm going to go out of my mind in the apartment, wondering where the hell you are, and whether I'm ever going to see you again, or whether Red Hanrahan and the chaplain will show

430

up at the door here with uncomfortable looks on their faces.

"Hey, it's not as if I want to go," he said. "They're sending me."

You're not consciously lying, my darling, but that's not true. You want to go. Maybe you can't control it, but you want to go.

"I know, baby," she said. "Sorry."

She kissed him, and one thing led to another, and it was another thirty minutes before she got around to asking whether he was hungry, and did he want to eat in the apartment or go out.

[FOUR]

SECRET

FROM: CIA LANGLEY 12 JANUARY 1965 1805 GMT

TO: STATION CHIEF LÉOPOLDVILLE

SUBJECT: TRANSMISSION OF CIA MATERIAL

MR. SANFORD T. FELTER, COUNSELOR TO THE PRESIDENT, WILL BE IN THE REPUBLIC OF CONGO ON A PRESIDENTIAL MISSION, ETA 15 JAN 65.

CIA WILL TRANSMIT CERTAIN CIA CLASSI- FIED MATERIAL TO HIM VIA CIA COMMUNICATIONS. ON RECEIPT YOU WILL DECRYPT SAID MATERIAL AND FURNISH ONE COPY ONLY TO US MIL ATTACHÉ WHO WILL PASS TO MR. FELTER.

SHOULD MR. FELTER INITIATE CONTACT WITH YOU, YOU ARE DIRECTED TO PROVIDE WHATEVER ASSISTANCE HE ASKS FOR, TO INCLUDE ACCESS TO CIA CLASSIFIED MATERIAL. UNDER NO REPEAT NO CIRCUM- STANCES WILL YOU INITIATE CONTACT WITH MR. FELTER. CIA WILL BE ADVISED IMMEDIATELY OF ANY CONTACT INITIATED BY MR. FELTER AND OF ASSISTANCE REQUESTED AND FURNISHED.

FOR THE DIRECTOR:

HOWARD W. O'CONNOR
ASSISTANT DIRECTOR FOR
ADMINISTRATION

SECRET

SECRET

FROM SEC STATE WASH DC 12 JANUARY 1965 2110 GMT

TO AMBASSADOR LÉOPOLDVILLE (EYES ONLY)

COUNSELOR TO THE PRESIDENT SANFORD T. FELTER WILL SHORTLY TRAVEL TO LÉOPOLDVILLE AND POSSIBLY OTHER POINTS WITHIN THE REPUBLIC OF THE CONGO ON A MISSION ORDERED BY THE

PRESIDENT. HE WILL BE ACCOMPANIED BY A PARTY OF THREE US ARMY OFFICERS. FELTER HAS PRESIDENTIALLY AUTHORIZED ACCESS TO DEPARTMENT OF STATE CLASSIFIED MATERIAL OF WHATEVER NATURE.

CONTACT BETWEEN MR. FELTER AND US EMBASSY WILL BE THROUGH US ARMY ATTACHÉ UNLESS INITIATED BY MR. FELTER. FYI FELTER IS COLONEL, GSC, USARMY. FELTER IS AUTHORIZED ACCESS TO USEMBASSY COMMUNICATIONS FACILITIES AND MILATTACHÉ WILL BE DIRECTED TO PROVIDE WHATEVER ASSISTANCE HE REQUIRES, WHICH SPECIFICALLY INCLUDES USE OF AIRCRAFT UNDER CONTROL OF MILATTACHÉ. MILATTACHÉ WILL ALSO SERVE AS CONTACT BETWEEN FELTER AND CIA STATION CHIEF. MILATTACHÉ WILL BE ADVISED OF FELTER'S ETA AND WILL MEET HIM AT LÉOPOLDVILLE AIRPORT.

SECSTATE WILL BE IMMEDIATELY INFORMED OF ANY CONTACT INITIATED BY FELTER, AND REASONS THEREFORE, AND ANY ACTIONS TAKEN BY US EMBASSY IN REGARD THERETO.

FOR THE SECRETARY OF STATE

RONALD I. SPIERS, ADMIN ASST TO SEC STATE

[FIVE]
Schipol International Airport
Amsterdam, The Netherlands
1000 14 January 1965

Captain Jean-Phillipe Portet, chief pilot of Air Congo, boarded the Boeing 707 that was Air Congo's Flight 2117, nonstop service to Léopoldville as a passenger, but after stowing his briefcase in the overhead compartment, walked toward the cockpit and motioned Jack to follow him.

The pilot, a Belgian, Captain Henri Ratisse, and the first officer, Marcel Defarre, a Frenchman, turned in their seats.

"Bonjour, mon chef," he said, smiling. "Jacques."

"Bonjour, capitain," Jacques replied. "Marcel."

"I think I'll take it, Henri," Captain Portet announced. "I want to see how well Jacques can get us out of here."

He motioned for Jack to get in the right seat.

Captain Ratisse didn't like that much, but Jean-Phillipe Portet was the chief pilot and there wasn't much he could do about it. And Ratisse knew that the chief pilot's son was on the Air Congo Reserve Pilot's roster, rated as a first officer in the 707, and frequently flew in the right seat of one of Air Congo's 707 cargo planes when a first officer called in sick, or everyone on the roster had flown his hours for that month.

Jack had not been especially surprised when his father had come into the hotel dining room for breakfast wearing his Air Congo captain's uniform. He usually wore it when he traveled aboard Air Congo aircraft. He was, after all, the chief pilot, and as such almost invariably sat in the jump

434

seat during takeoff and landing. He had more than once told Jack that "it makes the passengers nervous if they see some guy in a sports coat coming out of the cockpit."

But Jack had been surprised when they got to Schipol and his father had taken him into the briefing room for the weather and the weight and balance procedures, and had motioned for him to follow when they had walked around the huge aircraft while Ratisse and Defarre and the flight engineer, Paul Dupose, another Belgian, had done the preflight examination.

But Captain Portet rarely took over from the pilot, and this was the first time he had ever ordered Jack into the right seat of a passenger-carrying 707, although he had often flown as his father's copilot in cargo versions of the aircraft.

But Jack knew his father didn't like questions, and he strapped himself in, looked at the flight documents for a moment, and then reached for the checklist.

Jack got the 707 off the ground without any trouble, although it took a little longer than he expected it would, and to cruising altitude and across the Netherlands, Belgium, and half of France before his father indicated to the captain, who was riding the jump seat, that he should resume command of the airplane and unstrapped himself. The captain had just about finished adjusting his seat when Jack became aware that the first officer was standing behind him, waiting for him to get out of the copilot's seat.

"Thank you, Captain," Jack said.

"My pleasure, Jack. Anytime," the captain replied.

He did not sound very sincere.

The first-class compartment had six rows of seats, four to a row, twenty-four in all. They were all full. Except for Felter — who was asleep — and Finton — who was reading a book — all the faces were black.

Captain Portet led Jack past their empty seats, to the galley that separated the first-class section from the tourist section, and helped himself to two cans of Coca-Cola from the refrigerator. He handed one to Jack, then tapped his can against Jack's.

"I hope you enjoyed that, Jacques," he said.

"What was that all about?" Jack asked.

"I'm going to land it," his father said. "Which, with a little bit of luck, will bring to a suitable conclusion my career as chief pilot of Air Congo, and yours as one of Air Congo's loyal legion of reserve pilots."

"You're quitting?" Jack asked.

Captain Portet nodded.

" 'With a little bit of luck'?" Jack quoted.

"Kasavubu's not going to like it," Captain Portet said.

He motioned for Jack to follow him, stepped into the aisle, and pushed aside the curtain to the tourist section.

There were seats for 130 passengers. Only a quarter of them were occupied. Half were white, and half black.

"Those are the paying passengers," Captain Portet said. "You can't fly a 707 from Schipol to Léopoldville on what you get paid for thirty-five, forty tourist-class tickets."

"The cargo bay is full," Jack said. "It took me a long time to get off; it felt like we were pretty close

436

to max gross weight."

"You didn't *know* we were pretty close to max gross weight?" Captain Portet challenged. "Why did you think I took you with me to flight planning?"

"I didn't think I would be taking it off," Jack said, a little lamely. "And you and Henri didn't seem concerned."

"Jesus Christ, Jacques," his father said. "I've taught you better than that. If you're flying, you get the necessary information yourself."

The trouble with this ass-chewing, Jack thought, *is that the old man is absolutely right.*

There followed a long pause.

"We were close to max gross weight, and the cargo bay is full," Captain Portet said finally. "The problem is that the cargo is being paid for with government vouchers. And so are the tickets of the passengers in first class, with the exception of Felter and Finton. The other first-class passengers are all Congolese bureaucrats of one kind or another who go to Brussels or Paris or London for consultation every other month, sometimes more often. One day of consultation, and three days to recuperate from that exhausting labor."

"I don't think I follow you," Jack said.

"Right after you got drafted, we got a notice from the Secretary of State for Finance: 'Temporarily, until the end of the current emergency, payment of government passenger and cargo vouchers will be delayed.' "

"Air Simba, too?" Jack asked.

"Air Simba first," his father said. "When that happened, I thought either Kasavubu or Mobutu was putting pressure on me to sell part of it. Now I'm convinced it's Mobutu."

"So what are you going to do?"

"Sell him all of it," Captain Portet said.

"Will we get paid?"

"I would be very surprised if we got half what it's worth, but if I can get that in cash . . ."

"Start a one-airplane airline all over again in the States?" Jack asked. "Will there be enough for that?"

"There might be," Captain Portet said. "Let me tell you what's happened. . . ."

"And if the CIA deal falls through?" Jack asked when he had finished.

"Then I guess I start looking for a couple of old DC-4s in which I can fly freight around the Caribbean," Captain Portet said. "I'm putting all my chips on what Felter said."

"What?"

"That they're looking for someone just like me," Captain Portet said.

"Did you tell Hanni?"

"This just happened. I haven't had the opportunity. So don't say anything to her before I do."

Jack nodded.

"And with me in the goddamned army, I won't be of much help, will I?"

"I think I'm just as annoyed with your friends and neighbors as you are," Captain Portet said.

The letter Jack had received from the U.S. government just over a year before had told him "your friends and neighbors have selected you for induction into the Armed Forces of the United States."

He had said then what he said now:

"Friends, my ass!"

Captain Portet laughed.

"On the other hand, no draft notice, no Fort

438

Rucker, no Marjorie," he said.

"Is that that goddamned silver lining people are always talking about?"

"That's what it looks like, doesn't it?" his father said.

"You could always go back to Sabena," Jack said. "Couldn't you?"

Jean-Phillipe Portet had been a captain in Sabena, the Belgian national airline, before he had been offered the position of chief pilot of Air Congo, in which Sabena was a major investor. At the time, he had been offered the opportunity to return to Sabena if things didn't work out.

"I don't think that would work out," Captain Portet said flatly, and Jack understood that his father had decided that option either was no longer valid, or that he didn't want to do it.

He smiled at his son.

"If I hadn't decided to land this thing in Léopoldville," he said, "I would now have a very stiff drink."

And once my poppa has made up his mind to do something, he does it. And he's apparently made up his mind to shoot his roll on this CIA deal.

"Well, since I'm not flying," Jack said, and then saw something on his father's face. "Do you want me in the right seat when we get to Léopoldville?" he asked.

"That's up to you, Jacques."

They looked at each other.

"Hand me another Coke, Pop, will you, please?" Jack asked.

[SIX]
Léopoldville, Republic of the Congo
2305 14 January 1965

Captain Portet greased the 707 in, with a long, low, right-by-the-book approach, with the wheels hitting just past the stripes at the end of the runway, followed by a gentle deceleration in the landing roll.

He almost always greases it in, Jack thought as they turned off the runway and began to taxi to the terminal. *He's that kind of a pilot.*

His finesse reminded Jack — painfully — of his carelessness in not checking for himself the weight and balance.

When he'd finished shutting it down, Captain Portet signed the logbook and then handed it to Jack for his signature.

They left the aircraft through the passenger compartment rather than down the ladder that had been wheeled up to the cockpit door. Jack wondered about that, but decided it was because they had boarded the airplane as passengers, not crew.

It was hot on the tarmac; it always was. Captain Portet stopped to light a cigar inside the terminal, but Jack suspected the purpose was more in seeing what happened when Colonel Felter and Father Lunsford and Mr. Finton passed through Immigration and Customs than in satisfying a craving for nicotine.

The three passed through Immigration and Customs without making a ripple, probably because, Jack thought, his father had told them to make a little present — really a little present; about two dollars' worth of Dutch guilders — to each of the Customs officers.

440

But when Jack and his father had gone through the AIR CREW line and had their passports stamped, however, they were nowhere in sight in the terminal.

"Look around outside," Captain Portet ordered. "I'll check in here."

Outside the terminal, Noki, the "head boy" of the Portet household, who somehow always knew when either one of them was aboard an Air Simba or Air Congo aircraft, was waiting for them with the air-conditioning running in their Ford station wagon.

And then Jack saw Felter and Finton talking to someone in a darkened doorway just outside the terminal doors.

He started to go to them, but changed his mind and went looking for his father. If there was some sort of problem, Captain Portet could deal with it better than he could.

He found his father in the men's room. The smell of that was familiar, too.

When the two of them walked up to Felter, Lunsford, Finton, and the other man, Jack recognized him. He was the military attaché of the U.S. Embassy.

"You know Colonel Jacobs, right?" Felter asked.

Captain Portet and Jack shook Colonel Jacobs's hand.

"Colonel Jacobs tells me that he saw Dr. Dannelly riding through town in Mobutu's motorcade, and that as far as he knows, he's staying with him in the chief of staff's villa," Felter said. "So that's good news."

Jack noticed that Felter was now carrying a leather briefcase he had not had with him on the airplane. After a moment, he decided that it probably contained messages for him from Washington, sent through the embassy.

Confirmation came, he thought, when Felter thanked Jacobs for coming to the field and told him he would be in touch, then indicated he was ready to go.

They got in the Ford and drove out to the house. It took them a little over half an hour. There was an Army roadblock at every major intersection, where Congolese soldiers armed with Fabrique National 7-mm automatic rifles examined their documents intently until Noki gave them a little present.

The house, too, looked like it always did.

In what Jack thought of as better times, his father had bought three hectares (about 5.5 acres) of land overlooking the Stanley Basin of the Congo River, built his house on the most desirable hectare, and then tried to sell off the rest to other Europeans as home sites.

That hadn't worked out. Europeans, after Independence, had wanted to get out of the Congo, not move in. The entire property was now surrounded by a barbed-wire-topped Cyclone fence three meters tall. There was a floodlight mounted on every other pole.

Dense shrubbery now hid the fence, which had been designed to keep people from looking in, but worked equally well to keep people from looking out.

Noki sounded the horn, and one of the barefooted security guards who endlessly circled the fence after dark, armed with shotguns and machetes, trotted up and unlocked the gate and opened it.

There was a large stack of messages for Captain Portet, but none was an acknowledgment — more important, an invitation to dinner — from Joseph Désiré Mobutu.

And neither was there an answer when Mr. Finton tried to call the number he had for Dr. Dannelly, which seemed to confirm that he was staying with Mobutu in the Chief of Staff's official villa.

"Why don't we get a good night's sleep and see what happens in the morning?" Captain Portet suggested.

Felter, Lunsford, and Finton were put into the guest room — actually, a three-room suite — and Jack went to his room — also a three-room suite — and was surprised that everything seemed to be as he had left it.

He wondered about that, since had been gone almost exactly a year, and his parents and sister since November 27 — the day after the jump on Stanleyville — but then realized that Noki and the others who ran the house found nothing unusual about their absence.

He had, after all, left the house to go to the Free University in Belgium every year for months at a time for four years, and before he had been drafted his mother and sister had often been gone for months on long trips to Europe.

But before he went to sleep, he wondered what Nimbi, the houseboy responsible for his room, had thought when he'd unpacked his luggage and found his U.S. Army tropical worsted officer's uniform and parachutist's jump boots.

[SEVEN]
404 Avenue Leopold
Léopoldville, Republic of the Congo
1235 16 January 1965

When, at breakfast — at half past ten — there had been no response to the message his father had sent General Mobutu from Washington, Captain Portet said that could mean any number of things, or nothing, but the best thing for him to do was go to his office at Air Congo and see what he could find out. Jack offered to go with him, but his father said it would be best if he stayed at the house, in case Mobutu called.

When Mr. Finton tried the telephone number he had for Dr. Dannelly, there was again no answer. Captain Portet told Noki to drive him into town in Hanni's Ford to see if he could make contact.

Colonel Felter had announced that he had some messages to write — confirming again, as far as Jack was concerned, that the briefcase he had seen at the airport had contained "traffic" for him from Washington — and went to his room.

With nothing else to do, Jack and Father had played — before it got too brutally hot — not quite a full set of tennis, and then, stripping down on the run to their tennis shorts, had dived into the pool. When they climbed out, Nimbi had placed a beer-and-ice-filled cooler, and a copy of *L'Avenir*, the major newspaper, by one of the poolside tables.

There wasn't much in *L'Avenir* but rather effusive reports of the many accomplishments of President Joseph Kasavubu.

"There's not one fucking word in here about

444

what's going on in the boonies," Father said, in mingled wonderment and disgust, as he tossed his part of the newspaper on the tiles.

"This is the Congo, Father. If you ignore a problem, maybe it will go away."

"Well, somebody should tell your pal Mobutu that what's going on in Stanleyville is going to get worse, not better. Ignoring it is not a viable option."

"Mobutu knows," Jack said. "Kasavubu is the problem. And we may not get a chance to tell Mobutu anything. My father really expected that there would be an invitation to dinner waiting for us."

"You think he's stiffing us?"

"This is the Congo," Jack said. "You never know."

Father reached into the cooler and tossed Jack a beer, then took one for himself.

A few minutes later, just as he realized his beer bottle was empty, Jack heard the sirens, but paid little attention to them. For one thing, sirens in Léopoldville didn't mean what they had before Independence. Then the use of sirens had been limited to the Force Publique, the local police, the fire department, and ambulances.

Father Lunsford did.

"What the hell is that?" he asked.

"Probably some Congolese general, or a second deputy assistant secretary of state for something or other, going home for lunch, or to his mistress's house," Jack said. "The larger your motorcade, the more sirens and flashing lights you have, the more important you are."

And the other standard symbol of power is the ele-

445

gance of the mistress, most often a Belgian, some-times a Frenchwoman, but almost always a pale-skinned blonde. I wanted to add that, but didn't. Because it would make me sound like a racist?

Fuck it. Father knows better than that.

"The other status symbol is a white mistress," he said.

"Really?"

"Usually Belgian, but sometimes French. The blonder, the better."

"Uh," Father said. Jack waited for him to go on, but that was all Father said.

From where they were sitting, the roads that cir-cled the property couldn't be seen, so there was no telling in which direction the motorcade was going.

He idly noticed that the sound of the sirens had died and decided that whoever was sounding them had arrived at his house — or his mistress's house — for lunch. That made him wonder what Mrs. Marjorie Portet was doing at this hour — it was almost half past six in Fayetteville; she was probably making supper; or else she had gone to Fort Rucker, where it was half past five and she was helping her mother prepare supper.

That thought led to another, of Mrs. Marjorie Portet making breakfast for him in Fayetteville, attired in one of his shirts — only — which cos-tume he found incredibly erotic. After a minute or so of this, he decided that what he was doing was torturing himself, and reached for another beer.

"Heads up!" Father said, softly but with great intensity.

Jack looked up from the ice-and-beer-filled cooler.

Four large Congolese paratroopers, in immaculate, heavily starched camouflage pattern fatigues, holding Fabrique National 7-mm automatic rifles, were trotting down the lawn from the house. They took up defensive positions — looking outward, toward the fence.

Jack twisted in his chair. There were two more paratroopers on the patio by the house, and another one walking across the lawn, smiling broadly. This one was armed with a Browning pistol in a web holster, and his collar tabs bore the insignia of a lieutenant general of the Congolese Army. A lanky white man in a linen suit walked beside him.

Jack got out of the chair, holding a beer bottle in his hand.

"Jesus Christ, Joseph," he blurted in Swahili. "You scared hell out of me."

"Jacques, my old friend!" Mobutu said, holding his arms wide.

They embraced, and kissed, in the European manner. Mobutu was liberally doused with cologne.

"You know my friend, Dr. Dannelly, of course?" Mobutu asked, and then switched to French. "Whose Swahili, while good, is not as easy for him as French."

"Yes, of course," Jack said in French.

And I have just fucked up again with Dannelly. I blasphemed, with a bottle of beer in my hand.

"It's good to see you, Doctor."

"How are you, Portet?" Dannelly said, giving Jack his hand. His grip was firm, but anything but cordial.

Fuck it.

"This is my friend, Major George Washington Lunsford," Jack said.

Mobutu and Dannelly looked at Father, but neither offered his hand, smiled, or said anything.

"Would you like a beer, Joseph, or something stronger?"

"I would like something stronger, but it's early in the day," Mobutu said, and walked to the cooler and helped himself to a beer.

Jack glanced at the house. Nimbi was standing there, looking terrified.

"Can I offer you a Coke, Doctor? Or perhaps orange juice?"

Jack got a dirty look from Father.

What the hell is that for? Oh, shit! Finton told you, you damned fool, that Mormons don't drink anything with caffeine in it. Like Coke.

Where the hell is my father?

"Orange juice would be nice," Dannelly said.

Jack ordered a pitcher of orange juice in Swahili.

"And you will stay for lunch, of course," Jack said, switching back to French. "My father will be here any minute."

"That's very kind," Mobutu said.

Jack waved them into the chairs by the table.

"Dr. Dannelly hoped to see a friend of yours, a Mr. Finton?"

"He went into town, Doctor, to see if he could find you," Jack said. "He should be here any minute, too."

Mobutu took a healthy swig from the neck of the beer bottle.

"So how do you like being a soldier?" Mobutu asked.

"Except when people are shooting at me, I like it," Jack said.

Mobutu laughed delightedly.

"But the most important thing that's happened to me since we last saw one another, Joseph, is that I have married."

"You're not old enough to be married," Mobutu said.

"That's what our parents thought," Jack said.

Mobutu laughed again, but then his smile suddenly vanished.

Jack followed his gaze.

Mr. Finton, who was wearing a suit, was on the patio by the house. One of Mobutu's paratroopers had his FN rifle leveled at his chest to make the point that he was to go no further.

"And that is?" Mobutu asked rather coldly.

"That's Mr. Finton, Joseph," Jack said.

Mobutu called out, in Swahili, orders to let Finton pass.

"I would like to speak to him privately, Joseph," Dr. Dannelly said.

Dannelly got up from the table and walked across the lawn toward the patio.

"Tell Nimbi to take you to my father's study, Dr. Dannelly," Jack called after him.

Dannelly nodded.

Mobutu watched until Dannelly and Finton had shaken hands and gone inside the house. Then he took another pull at his beer and turned to Lunsford.

"Did I understand Jacques to say that you are an American officer?" Mobutu asked in French.

"Yes, sir," Father said.

"You speak pretty good French for an American," Mobutu said.

"I like to think so, General," Father said.

"How is that?" Mobutu asked.

"Well, the Army sent me to our language school

at the Presidio in California," Father said. "And then to postgraduate study in Vietnam."

Mobutu thought that over for a moment, then smiled.

"Major — Jacques did say you were a major, didn't he?"

"Yes, sir. I'm a very junior major."

"*Major,* why do I suspect that you did more in the former French Indochina than study the French language?"

"Because you are a parachutist, sir, and airborne officers are known to be highly intelligent and very astute."

Mobutu laughed.

"You wouldn't, by chance, be a parachutist yourself?" Mobutu asked.

"I have that distinct honor, sir," Father said.

Mobutu laughed again.

They're really getting along, Jack thought. *Bringing Father along was a very good idea.*

"Languages are very important," Mobutu said. "It's a pity your ambassador does not speak it well enough to understand our president when he speaks it," Mobutu said.

Oh, shit, here it comes!

"Sir?" Father asked.

"President Kasavubu hoped to make it quite plain to him that he did not want any American soldiers — even a distinguished officer, a fellow parachutist officer, such as yourself — in the Congo," Mobutu said. "I can only presume you are here unofficially, as guests of my old friends the Portets, in which case, of course, you are more than welcome."

He turned to Jacques.

"I'm afraid the major and your friend Finton

450

have made a long trip in vain, Jacques," he said. "Dr. Dannelly is speaking to him only because there was a telephone call from someone in his church, in the United States, asking him to. Dr. Dannelly suspects that your friend is going to ask him to ask me to ask the President to change his mind. I have no intention of doing so, because I know he has no intention of doing so. And I think his decision was the correct one."

"Then you're making a mistake," Jack said.

"Don't strain our friendship, my young friend," Mobutu said coldly.

"I would not be a friend if I let you make a big mistake," Jack said.

"If Kasavubu is to lead this country, he cannot afford to be perceived as a man who has to have white assistance to handle every minor disturbance that occurs."

"General, you're not suggesting that Stanleyville was a 'minor disturbance'?" Father said.

"Perhaps, Major, 'minor' was a poor choice of words."

"Stanleyville was a disaster," Father said flatly. "And if the Belgians hadn't jumped on it when they did, the Simbas would now be marching on Léopoldville. And when Che Guevara starts operating in that area, training soldiers, arming them with Soviet weaponry, what happened before will look like a Boy Scout rally in comparison."

For a moment Jack thought Mobutu was either going to lash out at Father, remind him that he was speaking to the chief of staff of the Congolese Army, or simply get up and storm off.

But he surprised Jack. He took a moment to almost visibly restrain his temper, then smiled at Father.

"Jacques, you know, jumped with the Belgians," he said.

"Yes, sir, I know," Father said.

"And is Jacques, then, the source of your information about what happened in Stanleyville?" Mobutu asked. "With all respect to my young friend, he was only there for a few hours."

"I was there for five months, General," Father said in Swahili. "I know what went on in Stanleyville."

Both the statement and the Swahili surprised Mobutu.

"You're the man Colonel Supo told me about," Mobutu said after a moment, in Swahili.

Lunsford looked confused.

"He was the Congolese officer with Colonel Van de Waele at Kamina," Jack furnished.

"At his recommendation," Mobutu said, as if to himself, "I have decorated you for your extraordinary valor. What you did was incredible."

Father didn't reply.

"With that in mind, Joseph," Jack said. "Don't you think you could at least hear what Major Lunsford has to say?"

Mobutu took a long moment to consider that, but finally nodded his assent.

"Before I get into what we know about Che Guevara, and his plans to screw up your country, General," Father began, "let me try to put your mind at ease about one thing. Nobody will be able to accuse you of having to ask white men to help you out here. Everybody we want to send over here is black."

"Interesting," Mobutu said. "But let me perhaps save us both some time. What you have to do, Major, is convince me of two things. First that

452

this Cuban is actually going to come here —"

"Colonel Felter — he's in the house — has brought you proof of that, General, believe me," Father interrupted.

"— and if this is actually so, why the United States government does not believe my government is perfectly capable, if this man should come here and start an armed rebellion against the Congo . . . why the army I have the honor to command cannot arrest him, try him, and stand him before a firing squad."

"That's the last thing we want to happen, Joseph," Jack said. "We want to keep the sonofabitch alive."

"What?"

"What we want to do, General," Father said, "is very quietly — 'invisibly' may be a better word — help you frustrate everything Guevara tries to do. We want him humiliated, not turned into a martyr."

"Whose idea is that?" Mobutu asked incredulously.

"President Johnson's," Father said.

Mobutu looked at Jack, who nodded.

"Why should I believe that?" Mobutu asked, and looked toward the house, obviously seeking Dr. Dannelly.

Jack followed Mobutu's glance. Dannelly was not visible, but Colonel Sanford T. Felter was. He had apparently just that moment come out of the house and was standing on the patio where Finton had stood, with the same Congolese paratrooper who had pointed his rifle at Finton now pointing it at Felter.

Felter was in uniform, complete to jump boots and green beret.

453

He looked up with contempt at the paratrooper's face, and pushed the muzzle of the rifle away with his hand.

Mobutu called out to the paratrooper to let him pass, and when the paratrooper stepped aside, Felter marched off the patio and across the lawn toward them.

Jack thought very much the same thing his father had thought when Lieutenant Colonel Craig Lowell had appeared at his door in Ocean Reef.

Christ, he has more medals than Patton!

Felter walked up to the table.

"Joseph, may I present my chief, Colonel Felter?" Jack said. "Sir, this is Lieutenant General Mobutu."

Felter saluted.

"An honor, sir," he said.

Mobutu returned the salute.

"Please join us, Colonel," Mobutu said in French. "And let us know what you think of our Congolese beer."

"Thank you, sir," Felter said, and helped himself to a beer before sitting down.

"Major Lunsford was just telling me that despite the terrible things this Cuban plans for my country — that is, if he actually does plan terrible things for my country, of which I am yet to be convinced — that the President of the United States wants him kept alive. And I had just asked him why I should believe either thing."

"General," Felter said. "Insofar as Guevara's intentions are concerned, I've got material in my briefcase that should remove any doubts you may have. And I hope this will remove any doubts you might have about President Johnson."

Felter handed Mobutu a small, nearly square envelope.

Mobutu opened it, read it, and then laid it on the table where Jack could see it.

The White House
WASHINGTON, D.C.

January 12, 1965

**Lieutenant General Joseph D. Mobutu
Chief of Staff, the Army of the Republic of
    the Congo**

By Hand

Dear General Mobutu:

   This will introduce Counselor-to-the-President of the United States Colonel Sanford T. Felter, USA, who has my absolute confidence and speaks for me.

Lyndon B. Johnson
LYNDON BAINES JOHNSON

Mobutu looked at Felter for a long moment before finally speaking.

"So you are a little more than a parachute officer, Colonel?" Mobutu said.

"Like yourself, General, I am a parachute

455

officer whom fate has chosen to give additional duties."

Mobutu chuckled.

"I will have to give this matter some thought," Mobutu said.

By that he means he wants to ask Dannelly what he thinks he should do, Jack thought. *Which means we're right back at square one. His decision will be based on whether or not Finton can convince Dannelly that we're doing the righteous thing in the eyes of God.*

"Of course," Felter said.

[EIGHT]

Captain Jean-Philippe Portet showed up fifteen minutes later, interrupting Major Lunsford's lecture on the training of Special Forces soldiers, and the composition of Green Beret A and B Teams, which Mobutu had obviously found fascinating.

He and Mobutu embraced warmly, and when Captain Portet helped himself to a beer, Mobutu asked for another.

"It's good to have you back, my friend," Mobutu said. "I have missed you."

"And I have missed you," Portet said, tapping the neck of his beer bottle against Mobutu's, then slumping into one of the chairs. "And I'm going to miss the house — the Congo — very much. I can only hope it won't take long."

"What are you talking about?" Mobutu asked, confused.

"You don't know, obviously," Captain Portet said. "I thought Jacques or Colonel Felter would have told you."

Mobutu flashed a look of annoyance at both Jack and Felter.

456

"Told me what?"

"Jacques is not the only one who's been conscripted," Portet said.

"Conscripted?" Mobutu asked. "You mean into the Army?"

"Not exactly," Captain Portet said. "But into government service."

"Can they do that?" Mobutu asked incredulously.

"Well, it's about the same thing that happened to you, Joseph," Captain Portet said. "I know you didn't want to remain chief of staff. . . ."

In a pig's ass, he didn't, Jack thought.

"You had done your military service, as I had, and as Jacques is now doing," Portet said. "You had earned the right to take off your uniform and put soldiering behind you. But duty called. There was no one better qualified than you to command the army, and you knew it."

"I saw it as my duty," Mobutu said. "You and I talked about it."

"And when we talked about it, we talked about it meaning that keeping the position would mean a great loss of income for you."

"I saw it as my duty," Mobutu repeated modestly.

Christ, he's playing this for Father's benefit, maybe for Colonel Felter's too, but he really wants Lunsford to see what a noble man, what a patriot, he is. He's glad my father gave him the opportunity.

"How long did that last?" Portet asked.

"Eight days," Mobutu said. "Kasavubu and Lumumba should have known that after Independence the Force Publique would not serve under Belgian officers. I told them both the Force Publique would mutiny, and it did."

"And you knew then that only you could stop the mutiny. . . ."

"They saw me as a fellow soldier, one who understood their concerns," Mobutu said. "I did what had to be done."

You made colonels — including yourself — out of Force Publique sergeant majors, majors out of sergeants, lieutenants out of corporals, and every private who could read and write got to be a sergeant, Jack thought. *But, I have to admit, you did stop the mutiny. Those were hairy times.*

"And I know, Joseph, for we talked about it then, that it was only with the greatest reluctance that you became involved in the trouble between Kasavubu and Lumumba; you would have preferred to hold yourself and the Army distant from dirty politics."

"Lumumba proved incapable of governing," Mobutu said. "I was forced to chose between them, for the good of the Congo."

"Seizing control of the government for Kasavubu was something you had to do," Captain Portet said. "And history will record that as soon as you could, you gave the government back to the people."

"I did not want to be secretary of state for national defense," Mobutu said, "that was thrust upon me. I tried to tell Lumumba that Moise Tshombe was a Communist, but he wouldn't listen," Mobutu added righteously.

"The damage he has done to the Congo is by no means over," Captain Portet said. "He let the noses of the Russian and Chinese camels under the flap of the tent."

"I will meet fire with fire if they try something like that again," Mobutu said. "The Congolese

Army is now prepared to defend the Congo against any enemy."

Does he believe that? Christ, I hope not.

He's liable to decide the way to prove to Lunsford that he's in charge and that every day, in every way, everything's getting better and better is to refuse to let us send the teams in.

"Joseph," Captain Portet said, "I didn't mean to get into all this again."

Mobutu waved a hand to show he understood.

"What I wanted to do was tell you that, in my own way, I am going to do what you did. My country has asked for my help, and I see it as my duty to do what I can."

"What will you be doing?" Mobutu asked, almost impatiently.

Dad could have spent all afternoon here letting Lunsford know what a great man Joseph Désiré Mobutu is, and Mobutu would have loved every second of it.

"The war in Vietnam is growing larger by the day," Portet said. "They need my help in setting up an air operation, passenger and freight, to augment the Air Force, which isn't large enough to handle the job itself."

"It was large enough to send a fleet of transports to Stanleyville," Mobutu said.

"And doing so is what taught them they need a supplemental air fleet, and now."

"When will you be going? And for how long?"

"Almost immediately," Portet said, "and for at least a year."

Mobutu didn't reply.

"Which is going to pose problems for Air Simba," Portet went on. "I'm going to have to find someone to manage it, and I have even been thinking of putting it up for sale."

Mobutu looked at him.

"I can think of someone to manage it," he said. "And if you're not asking too much, perhaps I can even come up with a group to take it off your hands."

"I would be grateful if you could, Joseph," Captain Portet said.

"Nonsense, Jean-Philippe," Mobutu said. "We have been friends for a long time. Friends help one another, no?"

Particularly, Jack thought, *unkindly, when the helper, in helping the helpee, gets to buy something like Air Simba at a distress price, less fifty percent.*

And then he remembered what had happened in the casino in Baden-Baden just before he'd gotten his draft notice. His parents had been on vacation there, and he'd had a forty-eight-hour layover in Brussels and he'd driven down to join them.

After an initial run of luck playing vingt-et-un, he'd drawn a king to a ten and a two, and gone bust. He had gone through not only the money he had had in his pocket but two monthly paychecks from Air Simba.

When he stood up and turned from the table, his father had been standing behind him. He had been so concentrated on the cards that he hadn't been aware of it.

"Been there long?" he'd asked.

"Long enough," his father had said, and handed him a drink of scotch. "I thought you probably would need this."

"To precede a lecture on the price of gambling?"

"Hey, not only wasn't I dealing the cards, or

holding you down in your chair, but you're a big boy now. If you want to go bust trying to break the bank at Baden-Baden, that's your business."

"Sorry, Dad," he'd said, genuinely contrite. "I don't like making an ass of myself with people — especially you — watching."

"You want to know what you did wrong?" his father had asked.

"Gamble?"

"There's nothing wrong with gambling — life is a gamble. But what you haven't learned is when to quit. When the cards are running against you, you have to take what you've got left, and get up from the table. That leaves you with a stake for the next time you sit down to play."

That's what the old man is doing here, knowing when to quit, and walking away from this game with a stake — maybe a little one, but a stake — to play again, this time with the CIA.

Dr. Dannelly and Mr. Finton came out of the house a few minutes later.

"About ready for lunch, Joseph?" Captain Portet asked. "And where would you like to eat? Here, or in the house?"

Mobutu didn't reply.

Finton came off the patio and walked toward them; Dr. Dannelly stayed on the patio.

Mobutu, without a word, got up and walked across the lawn to the house, then followed Dannelly inside.

"Noki," Captain Portet called out in Swahili. "Lunch, here, whenever you're ready."

Noki and Nimbi had just finished setting a table when Dannelly and Mobutu came out of the house.

With Dannelly following him, Mobutu walked directly across the lawn to the luncheon table and sat down at the head of it. Dannelly sat down beside him. Mobutu signaled for Noki to get him a beer, then smiled and waved at Father Lunsford, Felter, Finton, and the Portets to join him.

Jean-Philippe Portet thought: *The first time Joseph Désiré Mobutu sat at my table, he was genuinely surprised at the invitation, and was made uneasy by the choices he was going to have to make between three forks, three spoons, and two knives. And I told him what my father had told me — if you don't know which fork to use, watch your host — and he was grateful.*

But of course, he was then Sergeant Major Mobutu of the Force Publique, and he's now Lieutenant General Mobutu, chief of staff of the Congolese Army. Now he sits at the head of my table — any table in the Congo — and doesn't have to worry about his manners.

"Sit by me, Major," Mobutu said to Lunsford, pointing to the chair across from Dannelly.

"And where would you have me sit, Joseph?" Captain Portet asked.

Mobutu looked at him coldly, but then smiled.

"Am I in your chair, Jean-Philippe?" he asked.

"If you are at my table as my old friend, you are," Captain Portet said. "If you are sitting there as chief of staff of the Congolese Army, you're not. The chief of staff, like a 250-kilo gorilla, can sit wherever he wants to."

A look of alarm — *My God, is Portet going to make Mobutu angry now?* — flickered across Felter's usually unreadable face.

Mobutu smiled, but there was no telling what the smile meant.

"In that case, let me say something to Colonel Felter as one soldier to another," Mobutu said. "And then we can have our lunch."

He looked at Dannelly, then at Felter.

"Your ambassador — I mentioned his French leaves something to be desired — apparently did not make it clear to President Kasavubu what he was proposing," Mobutu said. "He gave him the impression the U.S. government wanted to send troops here. That's obviously out of the question, and Kasavubu told him so. The Congolese Army is perfectly capable of dealing with the present emergency, and any emergency in the future, including the Cuban Guevara. That is not to say the Congolese Army might not find it useful to have the assistance, in a purely training capacity, of someone with the expertise of Major Lunsford, and with several caveats, I have no problem with that."

"What are the caveats, General?" Felter asked.

"First, that it not appear that President Kasavubu has changed his mind. He is a strong-willed man, who — as you well know, Jean-Philippe — has great difficulty admitting he has ever made a mistake."

"That's certainly true, Joseph," Captain Portet said.

"So, unfortunately, we are going to have to keep this purely military decision from him, you understand?"

"Yes, of course," Felter said.

"That may be putting the cart in front of the horse. I would decide that your *trainers*, Colonel Felter, would be of use to the Congolese Army only if Colonel Supo agrees that they would be of use to *him* —"

"Colonel Supo?" Felter interrupted.

"He's in charge of cleaning out the remaining insurgents in Oriental, Equatorial, and Kivu Provinces," Mobutu said. "He's already met Major Lunsford and Jacques. And second, it has to be clearly understood that your people would serve at Colonel Supo's orders, and only at his pleasure."

"Agreed," Felter said immediately.

"Then I suggest that Major Lunsford and Jacques meet with Colonel Supo as soon as possible," Mobutu said. "He's in Stanleyville, or perhaps Costersmanville."

"The army attaché has an airplane, an L-23, at his disposal," Felter said. "Would you have any objection, General, if Jacques and Major Lunsford were to fly there using it?"

Mobutu thought that over before replying.

"Would there be room for Dr. Dannelly and one of my aides?"

"Sure," Jack said.

Why is he sending Dannelly? So that he can report back what Supo said? His aide could do that. Maybe, even probably, to tell Supo that he really has the power to say no.

"Tomorrow morning?" Mobutu asked. "Say, eight o'clock at the airport."

Felter nodded.

"Then it is done," Mobutu said. "And we can have our lunch."

He started to get up from the table.

"Sit there, Joseph," Jean-Philippe Portet said. "I'll sit here."

He sat at the other end of the table.

Jack started to reach for his beer, when he saw that Dr. Dannelly's head was bowed in prayer.

464

With a quick look at Mr. Finton, he saw that he was also praying a silent grace, which didn't surprise him. But then he glanced at Mobutu, wondering if Mobutu would honor the praying of the others.

One hand on his beer bottle, the chief of staff of the Congolese Army had his head bowed in prayer, too.

XII

[ONE]
The Residence of the Ambassador of
  the United States
Léopoldville, Republic of the Congo
1845 16 January 1965

"Thank you for seeing me on such short notice, Mr. Ambassador," Colonel Aaron Jacobs said as he walked into the ambassador's study. Another man, also in civilian clothing, followed him into the room.

Jacobs was a tall, muscular man who wore his hair in a crew cut. The ambassador was tall and thin and wore rimless spectacles. A pleasant-looking man in his thirties, who looked as if he had played baseball, not football, in college sat in a leather armchair, a drink in his hand.

"Anytime, Aaron," the ambassador said, smiling. "You know that. Should I run the CIA away, or is he cleared for whatever you want to say?"

"I thought those fellows were cleared for everything," Jacobs said. "How are you, Charley?"

"Aaron. Hey, John," the CIA Léopoldville station chief replied.

The CIA station chief knew Major John D. Anderson, one of the assistant military attachés, well. Anderson, a tanned, lithe man in his early thirties, was an assistant military attaché. He was

466

the senior of the two army aviators assigned to the embassy, and thought of as "the embassy pilot."

"Charley," Anderson said.

"What's on your mind, Aaron?" the ambassador asked.

"I just had a call from Mr. . . . Colonel . . . Felter," Jacobs said.

"We were just talking about him," the CIA station chief said.

"He wants to go to Stanleyville and/or Costersmanville tomorrow morning," Jacobs said. "In our airplane."

"Did he say why?" Charley, the CIA station chief, asked.

"Uh-uh. What he said was that he wanted to go to Stanleyville and/or Costersmanville tomorrow morning, and would I make sure the airplane was ready at half past seven."

"And you said?" the ambassador asked.

"That you, Mr. Ambassador — I didn't mention you, Charley — were planning to go to Bujumbura, and that I didn't think you would have any problem with dropping him off at Bujumbura, that it's not at all far from Costersmanville."

"And he said?"

"He said that he was sorry but he was going to need the airplane for two or three days, and that there wouldn't be room to take you along, Mr. Ambassador."

"The sonofabitch!" Charley said.

"He's blessed by Lyndon himself," the ambassador said. "You saw the message — 'milattache is directed to provide whatever he requires, which specifically includes use of aircraft' — or words to that effect. So fly him to wherever he wants to go,

467

Aaron. And try to smile."

"Sir, I'm not sure about this — it was only after he hung up that the hairs on my neck started to rise — but I'm not sure he wants me to fly the aircraft."

"Who would fly it?"

"Well, he's staying with Captain Portet, I saw him at the airport. With his son and two other people," Jacobs said.

"The son's in the Army, right?" Charley asked, but it was a statement. "The long arm of the draft board caught up with him way over here in Darkest Africa."

"He's a pilot," the ambassador said. "He's a nice kid, who suffers from erectis permanitis." He waited for the expected chuckle, then went on. "Do you think he's going to fly it?"

"He couldn't be an Army aviator, Mr. Ambassador," Major Anderson said.

"Why not?"

"He was drafted a year ago," Colonel Jacobs answered for him. "That means he was an enlisted man. Three months in basic training, then six in Officer Candidate School. Flight training — and they usually don't send kids straight from OCS to flight school. Or if he went into the warrant officer program, to learn to fly choppers, that's eight months or so. He's not an Army aviator, I'll bet on that."

"So what you're asking me is what do you do if you go to the field and find that either Captain Portet or his son wants to fly our airplane?"

"Yes, sir."

"First of all, I don't think you should go to the field," the ambassador said. "John is the senior pilot — responsible for the airplane. Have him at the field at half past seven."

"Yes, sir," Colonel Jacobs and Major Anderson said, almost in unison.

"You will introduce yourself as the embassy pilot, John, and inform Colonel Felter that you are prepared to fly him anywhere he wants to go."

"Yes, sir."

"If it develops that he wishes either Captain Portet or his son to fly the aircraft, after (a) inquiring into their qualifications to fly an airplane of that type, which may be, probably are, nonexistent; and (b) making them aware of the extraordinarily hazardous flight conditions in the Congo, you will offer no further objections or comments. They will take the airplane —" the ambassador said.

"Which, with a little bit of luck, will never be heard from again," Charley said.

The ambassador gave him a dirty look.

"— and as soon as they are off the ground," he went on, "I will, in compliance with my instructions — 'SecState will be immediately informed of any contact initiated by Felter, and reasons therefore, and any actions taken by U.S. Embassy in regard thereto,' or words to that effect — I will inform the secretary that the counselor to the President commandeered the embassy aircraft for purposes unknown, and that said aircraft was flown by persons not believed to be qualified to fly such an aircraft here in the Congo."

"Yes, sir," Colonel Jacobs said.

[TWO]
404 Avenue Leopold
Léopoldville, Republic of the Congo
0615 17 January 1965

Since Mobutu had made it plain that he didn't want Kasavubu to suspect that he was going to defy the President's frequent, and apparently firmly meant, announcements that he didn't want American soldiers in the Congo, Jack would have guessed that Colonel Felter would have made the uniform of the day civilian clothing. Maybe, because he was going to fly the embassy's Army L-23, a flight suit over civvies, but civvies. But Felter had said uniforms, so that was that.

It was a strange feeling to be sitting on the bed that had been his since he was a kid and lacing up Corcoran jump boots.

When he had finished dressing and was examining himself in the mirror, he had a quick mental image of Marjorie pinning the insignia on the jacket in their apartment in Fayetteville. It was a twice-pleasing thought, first because it seemed to be a wifely take-care-of-your-husband thing for her to have done, and he liked that, and also because she had bent over their bed for the pinning, and he had had occasion to consider once again that she had the greatest tail in the whole wide world.

Father Lunsford was already in the breakfast room when he got there, his uniform sagging under an array of ribbons and qualification badges that reminded Jack what a rookie he really was in the world of soldiers.

And Felter was there, too, in civilian clothing, causing Jack to wonder again if he wore ill-fitting

470

suits because he *wanted* to look like a government clerk, or whether he just didn't give a damn how he looked.

"Good morning," Jack said.

"I thought I'd see that you got off all right," Felter said.

Jack nodded, and wondered if he should have said, "Yes, sir."

"Apparently, the ambassador had planned to use the aircraft today," Felter went on. "He seemed a little annoyed when I told him we were going to need it."

"Did you want to go with us, Colonel?" Father asked.

"No," Felter said. "Mobutu made it pretty plain he didn't want me up there, and when I thought about it, I decided the two of you can deal with this guy better if you're alone."

"If things go well," Father said, "I'd like to get Doubting Thomas over here as soon as possible."

"It's your show, Father," Felter replied. "You want me to get him on the next plane, or do you want to talk to him in the States first?"

"Can we message him to tell him that if he wants a leave, to take it now?"

"I'll send it just as soon as you get off," Felter said. "If this thing with Supo doesn't work out, then he'll just have to go back."

Noki came in a moment later and served breakfast. Since the Portet houseguests were Americans, he had naturally prepared what he thought was the — somewhat barbaric — American breakfast: orange juice, toast, hash brown potatoes, and ham and eggs.

Felter attacked everything, including the ham, with relish.

He's Jewish. Lowell tells me he takes it seriously. Ham?

Felter looked up and met Jack's eyes. A chunk of ham dripping with egg yolk was on his fork.

"Nothing like steak and eggs for breakfast, is there, Jack?" he asked with a straight face.

Christ, Jack thought. *He* can *read minds!*

Noki drove them in Hanni's Ford to the Air Simba hangar, where the embassy's L-23 was parked and maintained. Air Simba was the Beech Aircraft Corporation's recommended maintenance facility for both the former French and Belgian Congos and for the northwestern third of South Africa. Air Simba billed Beechcraft for whatever they did to the Army's airplane, and for hangar rent, and eventually the bill worked its way through the corporate and military bureaucracies, and there was a check.

He felt a moment's flicker of regret that Air Simba was shortly going to belong to one of Mobutu's cronies, but he knew his father was right about cutting his losses and getting out.

Dr. Dannelly and a short, squat, very black Congolese were already in the office, waiting for them.

"This is Mr. Hakino of the Defense Ministry," Dr. Dannelly introduced him in French. "The President thought it would be a good idea for him to go with us. Is that going to be a problem?"

"We are honored to have the chief with us," Father replied in Swahili.

"Let me get the weather and the keys to the airplane and we'll get going," Jack said in Swahili.

The weather report was of near-perfect flying weather en route and in Stanleyville. Jack knew from experience that the weather report could be trusted not quite as far as he could see, but every once in a while, when there was an enormous storm, Léopoldville sometimes heard about it, and might pass on the information. It was worth the call.

The keys to the L-23 were not in the office key locker where he expected to find them, but when he looked out the window down to the hangar floor, he saw the door of the airplane was open, and decided that Noki had called ahead and said M'sieu Jacques would be flying it, and that someone was making sure it was ready.

When they went down to the hangar floor, Jack quickly learned that Noki had not been involved. There was an Army aviator standing by the nose of the airplane, in a flight suit bearing wings, the golden oak leafs of a major, a name patch — ANDERSON — and the patch of the Army Aviation Center at Fort Rucker.

The major walked toward them, smiling. After a moment, Jack remembered to salute. Major Anderson returned it.

"You're the people I'm going to take to Stanleyville today?" he asked.

"Not quite," Father Lunsford said, smiling and offering his hand. "My name is Lunsford."

"Anderson," the major said. "Not quite?"

"We're going to Stanleyville," Lunsford said. "But we already have a pilot." He pointed at Jack. "He'll fly it."

"I don't even know who he is," Major Anderson said.

"His name is Portet," Lunsford said.

Major Anderson looked at First Lieutenant

Portet, who was a Green Beret, wearing aviator's wings, parachutist's wings, and what Anderson thought were Belgian parachutist's wings, and decided that Captain Portet must have two sons, the other one being the one who was drafted a year before.

Jack looked around for Felter. He was nowhere in sight. Dr. Dannelly and Mr. Hakino of the Congolese Defense Ministry were watching the exchange with interest.

"Let me start from square one," Major Anderson said. "My name is Major John D. Anderson. I am an assistant military attaché at the embassy. I am also the senior Army aviator assigned to the embassy. My orders were to be here at 0730 prepared to fly Colonel Felter and another American officer to Stanleyville. How am I doing so far?"

"Well, are you sure you got your orders straight?" Lunsford asked. "Is it possible that you were told to prepare the *airplane* for a flight to Stanleyville?"

"Is Colonel Felter here?" Major Anderson asked.

Lunsford looked around and found Felter, who was at a stand-up desk against the hangar wall with a telephone in his hand. He pointed at him.

"That's Colonel Felter?" Major Anderson asked in disbelief. He had not expected an Army colonel, or a man who was counselor to the President of the United States, to look like a clerk of the Internal Revenue Service.

"Sir, is there anything I should know about the airplane?" Jack asked.

"You really don't have to worry about the airplane, Lieutenant," Anderson said. "Believe it or not, Air Simba runs a first-class maintenance operation."

"That's nice to know," Jack said.

I wonder how long that reputation will last when one of Mobutu's friends takes over?

"What you have to worry about is flying in the Congo," Major Anderson said, and asked: "Have you got much L-23 time?"

"No, sir," Jack replied truthfully.

"How many hours is not much?"

"I'm rated as an instructor pilot in L-23 series aircraft, Major, okay?"

"I'm just trying to keep you — and your passengers — alive," Anderson said.

"Yes, sir."

"It's a long way from here to Stanleyville," Anderson said. "You sure you don't want me to come along?"

"Thank you, sir, but no thanks," Jack said.

"You want some help with your flight plan?"

"No, sir," Jack said without thinking. "But thanks."

Then he saw the look on Anderson's face — *You arrogant little inexperienced sonofabitch* — and quickly added: "With full tanks, and four people aboard, I figure that will give me about 1,200 nautical miles. . . ."

"I think the manual says about 1,500, Lieutenant," Anderson corrected him. There was a hint of sarcasm in his voice.

Jack ignored him.

"Stanleyville's about 785 nautical miles from here," he went on. "According to the manual, I'd have enough fuel aboard to make it nonstop. But I don't trust manuals."

"Is that so?" Anderson asked, and now the sarcasm was clear.

Father looked as if he was about to shut him up, but Jack signaled him with a small movement of his hand not to.

"What I'm going to do, Major, is fly up the Congo River to Colquilhatville; their ADF usually works. That's 350-odd miles. I'll top off the tanks there. Then it's a little under 500 nautical miles from Colquilhatville to Stanleyville. Their ADF is supposedly working again, but I don't want to count on that. If there's weather and I can't find it IFR, or if I get there and see that I can't land, I'll have enough fuel, with a reserve, to go back to Colquilhatville, or maybe, probably, even enough to make it to Costersmanville. If there's anything wrong with that, I'd be grateful if you would tell me what it is."

Anderson now examined him carefully.

"You've flown in the Congo before, Lieutenant?"

"Yes, sir, I have."

"Have we got some sort of a problem here, Major?" Father Lunsford asked, not very pleasantly.

"No problem, Major," Anderson said. "But if I wasn't under orders not to ask questions, I would have a couple."

"But you *are* under orders not to ask questions, Major, aren't you?" Felter said, softly.

Jack hadn't seen him walk up to them.

"My orders, sir," Anderson said, "if it turned out I wasn't to fly the aircraft, were to ask about the qualifications of whoever was to fly it."

Felter turned to Jack. "I'll deal with this, Jack. You get going."

"Yes, sir," Jack said.

He called out in Swahili to some Air Simba mechanics to open the hangar doors and push the L-23 outside.

Anderson was visibly surprised to hear Jack speak Swahili.

[THREE]
Stanleyville Air Field
Stanleyville, Oriental Province
Republic of the Congo
1340 17 January 1965

The weather en route to Colquilhatville had been perfect, and Jack picked up the Colquilhatville beacon long before he expected to. There had even been an English speaker in the Colquilhatville tower, which didn't always happen in the Congo. They touched down almost exactly three hours after they'd broken ground in Léopoldville.

A Mobil Oil truck had rolled up to them as they stopped, and Jack didn't even have to remind them to run the avgas through a *clean* chamois. There was even pastry and coffee in the terminal building.

From there, however, things had gone downhill. The station manager told Jack that he'd had in-flight reports of bad weather between Colquilhatville and Stanleyville and that he *knew* the Stanleyville ADF was down. Further, what before the Simba Uprising had been alternate airfields at Lisala, Bumba, and Basoko were no longer available. Wrecked trucks and cars and earthmoving equipment had been placed by the Simbas on the runways to deny their use to the Congolese Army.

Jack had decided the thing to do was try to make Stanleyville; if the weather was really bad, he could turn around.

An hour out of Colquilhatville there had been proof that the popular understanding of "Darkest Africa" — as in "The Heart of Darkest Africa," understood as a reference to the skin pigmentation of the native population — was wrong. Actually, it made reference to the weather conditions. Very frequently — sometimes daily, for weeks at a time — storm clouds began gathering around noon. The sky would continue to darken, actually growing black, until the clouds opened, releasing torrential rain, and then it would clear.

Today that phenomenon had begun early.

Father, who had been riding in the copilot's seat, had seen the black skies ahead of them, and looked wonderingly at Jack.

"Jesus, are you going to try to go through that?"

"Welcome back to Darkest Africa, Major," Jack said. "I have three choices. I can either try to get above it, which would be a reasonable solution, if there was a working beacon at Stanleyville, which there is not, making a descent through the soup rather difficult since I would have only a vague idea where I was. Or I can go down and fly the Congo River, which will produce a rather bumpy ride. Or we can go back to Colquilhatville, and have a shot at it first thing tomorrow morning. Your call, Major."

Father didn't hesitate.

"Your call, Jack. You know the sooner we see Colonel Supo the better, and I don't think you want to die any more than I do."

Jack banked to the left, dropped to 3,000 feet, and looked for and found the Congo River. He had just started to fly over it when he entered the soup.

"Rather bumpy" turned out to be a massive understatement.

Several times, Jack had almost turned back, deciding each time at the last moment that it couldn't possibly be this bad all the way to Stanleyville and continuing on "for a little more." And then, finally, that choice was not available; it was a greater distance to return than it was to continue to Stanleyville.

Mr. Hakino of the Defense Ministry got airsick first, and then Dr. Dannelly, which Jack more or less expected. But when, a half hour later, Father Lunsford got sick, Jack was afraid that it would be contagious, and he didn't like the notion of trying to fly through the storm while airsick, but he managed to fight it back.

Finally, the white bulk of the Immoquateur apartment building could be made out through the rain, and he knew the airfield was only a few miles farther. He was not surprised when the Stanleyville tower did not respond to his calls.

He dropped lower and made two low-level passes across the field, to make sure that no one had blocked the runway here with a burned-out truck or Caterpillar tractor. The runways were clear, but there were four crashed airplanes: two B-26s, a Douglas DC-3, and the blackened hulk of something with twin engines burned beyond recognition on the field. Parked near the terminal building was a Boeing C-46 with "Air Simba" painted on the fuselage and the leaping lion logotype on the tail. It appeared undamaged. Jack wondered who had flown it in, and when; no one in Léopoldville had said anything about an Air

Simba aircraft going to be in Stanleyville.

He made his approach and landed.

The downpour beating on the fuselage and wings also restricted visibility, and he taxied very slowly to the terminal building, trying to remember where there would be tie-down ropes for the airplane, and then finding them. The wind was gusting, and he was going to have to tie it down carefully.

He told Father, and when he turned to him to do so, Father was nauseated a last time. This time it was very nearly contagious.

When he shut the engines down, he turned to Dr. Dannelly.

In the old days, when a plane landed in rain like this, a dozen or more terminal employees would come out to the plane carrying enormous umbrellas, either to escort people directly into the terminal or to load them aboard the tarmac busses.

The tarmac buses were still there, all riddled with bullet holes, two of them with flat tires and smashed windows, and the third a fire-gutted hulk. Jack remembered seeing it on fire the last time he'd been at the airport.

No one came out of the terminal building now.

"Obviously, nobody's going to come out here with an umbrella," he said, turning in his seat to speak to Dannelly. "When Major Lunsford gets out, you and Mr. Hakino take a run for the terminal. See about getting us some wheels. Lunsford and I are going to have to tie the airplane down well."

Dr. Dannelly nodded but said nothing.

"You're going to have to run to the terminal, I'm afraid, Chief Hakino," Jack added in Swahili.

Hakino nodded.

Jack got out of his seat, walked through the fuse-lage, opened the door, and lowered the step. Dr. Dannelly and Mr. Hakino got out and ran across the tarmac to the terminal building.

Jack was soaked by the rain before he found the tie-down ropes on the ground under an inch of water, and by the time they were finished, there was no point in running to the terminal building. They were as rain-soaked as it was possible to get.

Jack pushed open the door to the passenger ter-minal, and had just enough time to see that the neon sign urging passengers to "Fumez Lucky Strike" was working when he was jabbed painfully in the stomach with the barrel of a Fabrique National 7-mm automatic rifle in the hands of a tall, dirty-looking Congolese soldier.

Jack looked over his shoulder worrying what Lunsford would do when similarly threatened.

A moment later, Lunsford came through the door and another Congolese soldier advanced on him with the barrel of his rifle.

"You touch me with that," Father snapped in Swahili, "and I'll take it away from you and stick it so far up your ass it'll come out your nose."

The soldier stopped.

"Identify yourself," a voice said in French, to Jack.

Jack saw that the speaker was a Congolese lieu-tenant, in a surprisingly immaculate uniform.

"My name is Major George Washington Lunsford," Lunsford replied in French, "and you will address any questions to me, preceded by a salute and the term 'sir.' "

The lieutenant hesitated just a moment.

"Sir, this field is closed by order of the military

481

commander —"

"Colonel Supo? Where is he?" Father interrupted. He turned to Mr. Hakino, switching to Swahili. "Chief, please tell this officer who you are."

Thirty seconds later, everything was sweetness and light. The lieutenant expressed profound regret that he had no word of the coming of the distinguished assistant secretary and his party, in which case he would have made preparations for their arrival.

Colonel Supo was en route by road from Costersmanville, he said, and expected within the hour, although, of course, with the rain there was no way of telling how long he might be delayed.

"We will require quarters, of course, and food," Lunsford said, not very pleasantly. "What is available?"

"The officers are billeted in the Immoquateur — it is an apartment building —"

"I know what it is," Lunsford snapped. "Is it habitable?"

"Yes, of course," the lieutenant said, as if the question surprised him.

Jack thought: *That probably means the roof is still in place.*

"Take us there," Lunsford ordered.

"Yes, sir," the Lieutenant said.

There was a Buick station wagon outside the terminal. Jack wondered if had been taken from the stocks of the Buick dealer who had once done business in Stanleyville, or whether it was one of the cars that had been left at the airfield with the keys in the ignition as the Belgians had fled — or tried to flee and failed — as the Simbas approached. Or whether it had been taken from

482

some Belgian's garage.

The lieutenant got behind the wheel, with the two soldiers crowded beside him. The others got in the back.

Three hundred yards from the terminal building, Jack saw that the Sabena Airlines guest house now housed Congolese soldiers; there were a dozen of them sprawled in lawn chairs on the verandah.

There wasn't any visible activity the rest of the way to the Immoquateur. There were still neat cottages lining the streets; here and there were cottages that had been set on fire and allowed to burn. There were abandoned automobiles all over, some of them looking as if they had just been parked, others with their windows and everything else breakable shattered with bullet holes or simply heavy objects, and some burned-out hulks.

He was surprised when they approached the Immoquateur that there were lights on all over the twelve-story building. The lieutenant pulled under the portico where there had once been a white-jacketed porter to open the doors. Now there were half a dozen Congolese soldiers, all armed with automatic rifles, two standing, the others sitting on the sidewalk.

He remembered then that the Immoquateur had emergency diesel generators in the basement. Obviously, someone had gotten them running.

The soldiers stood up when they saw the lieutenant get out of the Buick, but it was not as if someone had called "Attention" at the sight of an officer. And only one of them saluted the lieutenant.

They entered the lobby. Some of the leather furniture was still there, fewer pillows on the seats, and only the chrome frame remained of what had been a large glass-topped table.

But there were electric lights burning in the ceiling, and the elevators were apparently running, for the lieutenant led them to the narrow corridor leading to the elevators.

One of the elevators was waiting. There were only a few shreds of its mirrored walls left, and there were bullet holes in the side and rear walls.

The last time he'd been on this elevator, he'd had to drag the body of a Simba out of it, and the moment he had, the elevator door had closed, leaving him on the ground floor.

The lieutenant bowed them into the elevator. The door closed, and the elevator began to rise. At the fourth floor, it stopped.

On the corridor wall, there was a bullet-chipped area, and a dark splotch running from the chipped area almost to the floor.

The last time Jack had been on the fourth floor of the Immoquateur, when the door opened, there had been a Simba in parts of a Belgian officer's uniform standing in the corridor. He had not had time to raise his pistol — a 9-mm Luger parabellum — before a burst from Jack's assault rifle had smashed into his midsection.

Jack had taken the pistol and gotten back on the elevator and ridden to the tenth floor, absolutely terrified of what he would find there.

"No," Jack said in Swahili. "Take us to the tenth floor first."

The lieutenant gave him a strange look but pushed the tenth-floor button, and the door closed and they rode to the tenth floor.

Jack got out first and went to the door of the Portet apartment.

The door was closed but could not be locked. Jack had smashed the doorknob and lock first with the butt of his FN — which had caused the stock to break — and then with the heel of his boot.

He pushed the door open and entered the apartment, expecting almost anything but what he got; there was no question in his mind that the apartment would be stripped of anything that could be picked up or torn loose.

It was not. Everything was there. Furniture, lamps, rugs on the floor, and even Hanni's Grundig radio, tuned to the BBC's "Light Programme" from London.

"Mon Dieu, c'est Monsieur Jacques!" Tomo, the houseboy, exclaimed in surprise as he came into the living room from the kitchen.

He wasn't wearing his usual crisply starched white jacket, but he was alive, well, and apparently on duty.

The last Jack had heard of him, from Mary Magdalene, was that she had ordered him to go to his village and stay there until the trouble was over.

Jack, his eyes tearing and his throat painfully restricted, walked to Tomo and embraced him.

When he could find his voice, Jack said: "We'll be staying here, Lieutenant."

"When Colonel Supo gets to Stanleyville, tell him where we are," Lunsford said.

"Yes, sir," the lieutenant said.

"That will be all. You may go," Lunsford said.

"Yes, sir," the lieutenant said, and saluted.

"Tomo, when did you come back?" Jack asked.

"I did not go home," Tomo said. "I stayed in the bush across the river until the whites from

South Africa came. Then I came here and protected things."

"Tomo, you're wonderful."

"I am the number-one boy," Tomo said. "It was my duty."

Tomo took a good look at Lunsford.

"I know you," he challenged. "You are a Simba!"

"No," Jack said. "You saw him here?"

"I saw him enter the building when the Belgians came," Tomo said. "And then I saw him leave the building with Mary Magdalene and your mother and sister and the young white woman with the baby. He was a Simba."

"He is an American officer who was dressed like a Simba," Jack said, and then he felt overcome by an urge to giggle. He switched to English, and through his giggles said, "It's a good thing he recognized you as a Simba now, Major, sir, rather than later, or you would have woken up in the morning with your throat neatly sliced open."

"I am a friend, Tomo," Lunsford said in Swahili.

"If M'sieu Jacques says so," Tomo replied dubiously.

"First things first, Tomo. We have to get out of these wet clothes. Is there anything we can wear? And what about these clothes?"

"There are underthings," Tomo said. "I found them above the ceiling. Under things and your Browning gun, and some other things . . . Madame Portet's radio . . . but all the men's clothing is gone. I can dry those clothes, and iron them."

By "above the ceiling" Tomo meant between the concrete floor of the floor above and the false

486

ceiling of acoustic tiles in the apartment.

"And food?"

"Fish from the river, M'sieu Jacques. And manioc. And tomatoes. And eggs. No wine, but there is, of course, beer."

"He just said the magic word," Father Lunsford said. "Give him a hundred dollars."

"I think first the underwear, and then the beer. Then, if you will get us the fish, we'll cook while you see what you can do about our clothing."

At that point, Jack remembered Dr. Dannelly and Mr. Hakino.

"Tomo, these gentlemen are Mr. Hakino, who is a very important official of the government, and Dr. Dannelly, who is a very good friend of General Mobutu."

Tomo did not seem very impressed with either of them.

"They will be staying, M'sieu Jacques?"

"For not more than two days, or three."

"I think there is enough underthings for everybody," Tomo said.

[FOUR]
Apartment 10-C, The Immoquateur
Stanleyville, Oriental Province
Republic of the Congo
1645 17 January 1965

Colonel Jean-Baptiste Supo, military commandant of Oriental and Equatorial provinces, was a tall, muscular, 210-pound thirty-six-year-old with very black skin and sharp features. When, at eighteen, he had left his home in the Katanga Province to enlist in the Force Publique, his basic training instructors — black and white — had cruelly teased

487

him by saying his mother had obviously been very friendly with an Arab. They had called him "Camel Boy."

He had not understood the teasing. His mother was a fine Christian woman who had been educated by the Catholics and became a teacher. She had been very disappointed when he had finished secondary school at the head of his class and chosen the Force Publique over a career with Union Miniere, who were always looking for young men from good families and good academic records.

He had to take the teasing in training, but when he was assigned to his first unit, he knew he didn't want to and didn't have to. Five days after he had reported to his first unit, he found himself standing before the company commander, a Belgian captain named Dommer, charged with breaking three teeth from the mouth of his corporal by striking him with his fist.

Captain Dommer asked him, in Swahili, if he had anything to say before he announced his sentence; he expected at least ninety days, possibly longer, of punishment.

"If he insults my mother again, my captain," Private Supo had replied in French, "I will knock the rest of the teeth from his mouth."

"Exactly how did the corporal insult your mother?"

"He called me a motherfucker, my captain. My mother is a good Christian woman."

Captain Dommer had then asked him about his mother, and where he had gone to school, and what his father did, and he told him about his mother being assistant principal of St. Matthew's School in Kiowa; that he had graduated from

St. Matthew's with honors in mathematics and French; and that his father was maintenance supervisor for the Union Miniere mine at Kamundo.

At the evening parade that day, it was announced that Private Supo had been sentenced to four months' imprisonment for striking his corporal, and he was handcuffed and put into the back of a truck with everybody watching as the truck drove out of the compound.

He had a hard time keeping from crying. His mother and father would learn that he was in prison, and would be ashamed of him.

Five miles out of the compound, the sergeant driving stopped the truck and came in the back and took the handcuffs off and told him that Captain Dommer was giving him a second chance. He was not going to prison, but to the 23rd Company, which had need for someone who read and wrote French fluently and had a knowledge of mathematics.

The sergeant chef of the 23rd Company was a tall, large man in an immaculate, crisply starched khaki uniform.

If Private Supo ever even thought about hitting another noncommissioned officer, the sergeant chef of the 23rd Company said, or did anything that in any way made Captain Van de Waele, the commanding officer of the 23rd Company, sorry that he had given Private Supo a second chance when Captain Dommer asked him to, he would know about it and he would slice off Private Supo's balls and cock and feed them to the pigs.

The sergeant chef of the 23rd Company when Private Supo joined it was named Joseph Désiré Mobutu. When Sergeant Chef Mobutu left the

23rd Company three years later, it was to become the youngest sergeant major ever in the Force Publique. By then Private Supo had become Corporal Supo.

Five years later, Senior Sergeant Supo became sergeant chef of the 23rd Company and the youngest sergeant chef ever of the Force Publique. He received his sergeant major's chevrons at the same parade that honored Sergeant Major Mobutu on his retirement from the Army, and they saw one another frequently after that, when Mobutu was working as a journalist on the *L'Avenir* in Léopoldville.

When, after Independence, the Force Publique had mutinied against its Belgian officers, and Secretary of State for National Defense Mobutu had to find officers for the Force from the black ranks of the Force, the first colonel named was Sergeant Major Jean-Baptiste Supo.

Mobutu had placed him in charge of dealing with the Belgians who had returned to the Congo to stop the Simbas from massacring the people (white and black) at Stanleyville, mainly because the senior Belgian officer was Colonel Van de Waele, the same man who had given him his second chance after he'd beaten up the corporal for insulting his mother. He had been their captain in the 23rd Company, and was one of the very few Belgians they knew they could trust.

When he had been at the Kamina Air Base with Colonel Van de Waele, before and after the Belgians had dropped parachutists on Stanleyville — which was now officially Kisangani, although few people used the new name — his mother had come to see him, and he had introduced her to Colonel Van de Waele and she told him that she now knew she was wrong about not wanting him to go off and be a soldier and that she was very proud of him. And Colonel Van de Waele had kissed his mother and said he was very proud of him too, and this time he could not keep the tears from running down his cheeks.

Colonel Supo had traveled from Costersmanville in a six-vehicle convoy, because there were still some Simbas in the bush, and sometimes they ambushed single cars and trucks on Route National Number Three. The convoy consisted of an ex–Royal British Army "Ferret" reconnaissance car, armed with one .30-caliber Browning machine gun; two Swedish Scania-Vabis armored cars, each armed with three Browning .30-caliber machine guns — a dual mount in front and a single machine gun firing toward the rear; two Ford ton-and-a-half trucks, holding between them a platoon of paratroopers; and a GMC carryall. The Fords and the GMC still bore the logotype of Mobil Oil Congo. He knew he would have to give them back, but right now he needed them.

The Ferret and one Scania-Vabis led the convoy, followed by the GMC and the two Ford trucks. The second Scania-Vabis was at the tail. Colonel Supo had ridden in the carryall, most of the way driving it himself, as his driver, Sergeant Paul Wotto, while enthusiastic and a good man to have around, was not a very good driver. And neither were the four officers of his personal staff in the back of the carryall.

Route National Number Three took them along the north bank of the Congo past the airport, and Colonel Supo was very surprised to see a small twin-engine airplane with US ARMY lettered on its fuselage parked in front of the terminal building. He decided it was worth a look, and turned out of the convoy onto the airport access road.

The two Ford trucks and the Scania-Vabis bringing up the rear followed him. The Ferret and the leading Scania-Vabis were almost a mile down the road before someone realized they had lost the tail of the convoy and hastily turned around to look for it.

By the time they reached the airport, Colonel Supo had spoken with the officer guarding the airfield and learned that there had been four people on the airplane: the two American pilots, both of them Swahili speaking, one of them a *noir;* Assistant Secretary of State for Defense for Provincial Affairs, M'sieu Hakino; and a second *blanc,* who the lieutenant believed had been referred to as "Doctor." The lieutenant said they had requested quarters, and he had taken them to the Immoquateur, where one of the Americans had insisted on being taken to the tenth floor, where they entered the apartment formerly occupied by Air Simba and insisted on staying there.

As an afterthought, the lieutenant reported that the Assistant Secretary of State for Defense for Provincial Affairs had said he was in Stanleyville to see Colonel Supo, and that the black American had told him to tell Colonel Supo where they were.

Colonel Supo was back behind the wheel of his carryall when the lead elements of his convoy finally caught up with him.

Colonel Supo put his head out the window and ordered the driver of the Ferret to go to the Immoquateur, and after some hasty backing and turning around, the newly reassembled convoy set out for the Immoquateur.

When they rolled up to the portico of the Immoquateur, Sergeant Paul Wotto did not think the corporal of the guard reacted quickly enough to the appearance of Colonel Supo; did not think his belatedly rendered salute was crisp enough; and further, noted that his uniform was soiled. He expressed his displeasure by punching the corporal in the mouth, hard enough to knock him off his feet, and then trotted after his colonel.

Colonel Supo pretended not to see what had happened. Sometimes it was possible to inspire men. Sometimes you could speak with them. And sometimes it was necessary to do what Sergeant Wotto had done. He had learned that in the 23rd Company.

At the elevator, Colonel Supo motioned for Major Alain George Totse, his intelligence officer, and Sergeant Wotto to get on the elevator, and ordered the rest of his party and guards to wait for him.

On the tenth floor, when there was no response to Colonel Supo's knock at the door, he motioned for Sergeant Wotto to enter the apartment.

Wotto drew his 9-mm Fabrique National pistol from its web holster and entered the apartment cautiously, obviously expecting trouble. He made his way carefully through the living room, peered into each of the three bedrooms, worked his way through the dining room to the kitchen, and ultimately to the open balcony at the rear of the apartment. The balcony overlooked the wharves and warehouses lining the Tshopo River, which flowed into the Congo four miles downstream.

There he found three black men and two white men. One of the black men was standing at an ironing board, pressing a pair of trousers. He was obviously not the Assistant Secretary of State of Defense for Provincial Affairs, but it was quite impossible to tell which of the other two black men was that dignitary, for all four men were wearing nothing but white boxer shorts and undershirts. One of the white men was drinking a glass of water. The other three all held bottles of Simba beer in their hands.

"Put that goddamned gun away before I make you eat it," Father Lunsford snarled in Swahili.

Obviously, Sergeant Wotto decided, the short muscular man was the Assistant Secretary of State for Defense for Provincial Affairs.

"Chief," he announced as he hastily holstered his pistol, "Colonel Supo is here."

"Where?" Lunsford asked.

"I will fetch him," Sergeant Wotto announced, and fled from the balcony.

"They are in their underwear, my colonel," Sergeant Wotto reported. "Drinking beer on the servants' balcony."

"Are they indeed?" Colonel Supo replied, and gestured for Wotto to lead the way.

Father Lunsford rose to his feet when Supo came onto the balcony, and a moment later Jack did. Major Totse and Sergeant Wotto stayed just inside the door to the kitchen.

Supo knew both Assistant Secretary of State for Defense Hakino and Dr. Dannelly, who was Joseph Désiré Mobutu's good friend. He was relieved to see Dannelly. He knew the Air Simba apartment was really that of Captain Jean-Philippe Portet, who was another of Mobutu's very few close white friends. It was possible, even likely, that Dannelly and Portet were friends, and Dannelly was in Portet's apartment as his guest. Otherwise, the situation might be difficult.

Supo saluted Hakino.

"Chief," he said in Swahili, and then turned to Dannelly. "It is good to see you again, Doctor."

Supo turned to Lunsford and Jack and switched to French.

"I don't believe I know these gentlemen," he said, smiling.

"We have had the privilege of meeting the colonel before," Lunsford replied in French. "Major George Washington Lunsford and Lieutenant Jacques Portet, U.S. Army, at your orders, sir."

Supo's smile vanished. He knew for a fact that President Kasavubu had been offered, and had bluntly refused, the offer of American troops.

"At Kamina, sir," Lunsford went on, switching to Swahili. "Both yourself and Colonel Van de Waele at first thought I was a Simba prisoner, and Lieutenant Portet a Belgian para who had taken a bullet in the nose."

Supo's eyes widened as he looked between them and recognition came.

"*Mon Dieu*," he said. "I would not have recognized either of you!"

"*Mon Dieu*," Major Totse parroted in French, "it is him!"

"It is very good to see you again, sir," Lunsford said.

"And you're not Belgian?" Supo asked Jack.

"He's Jean-Philippe Portet's son," Dr. Dannelly said.

"Captain Portet is Belgian," Supo protested.

"My father and I are American citizens, Colonel," Jack said in French.

"You were wearing a Belgian para's uniform. You jumped with the Belgians at Stanleyville. You were wounded at Stanleyville."

"Actually, I fell off a truck," Jack said.

"He's a U.S. Army Special Forces officer, Colonel," Lunsford said. "Sometimes we find it necessary to wear other people's uniforms."

Supo, visibly considering that, looked intently at Lunsford but didn't reply directly.

"What are you two doing back in the Congo?" he asked.

"They have a proposition for you, Colonel," Hakino said. "The President wants you to listen to it."

"He told me to tell you, Jean-Baptiste," Dannelly said, "that the decision is entirely yours."

Supo looked at Lunsford.

"Before we get into this, Colonel, would you like a beer?"

"Yes, I would, thank you. Have you enough for Major Totse and Sergeant Wotto?"

"Of course," Jack said.

"Totse, do you remember these two officers? At Kamina?"

"Yes, my colonel, very well."

"I'm sorry," Lunsford said, making it clear he did not remember Major Totse at Kamina.

"I'm surprised you remember Kamina," Colonel Supo said. "You had just gone through —"

"Colonel, we have information that the Cuban Communist Che Guevara plans to come to the Congo and pick up where the Simbas left off —"

"Why should a Cuban Communist come here?" Supo challenged.

"Jean-Baptiste," Dannelly said, "to save time,

496

let me say that General Mobutu is convinced the threat is real. And so am I."

Supo nodded.

"With respect, Doctor, I would prefer to hear it all myself," he said.

"Certainly," Lunsford said. "As I was saying, sir, we have reliable intelligence that . . ."

"If I understand you correctly, Major," Supo said ten minutes later, "what you are offering is a small force of Special Services —"

"Special *Forces,* sir," Lunsford corrected him.

"— *Forces,* then," Supo went on, making it clear he did not like being interrupted, "specially trained for this sort of operation. The purpose of which, presumably, is to either kill or capture this man, and then what, if he is captured?"

"No, sir," Lunsford said. "We don't want to either capture him or eliminate him. We want to frustrate him; we want him to leave the Congo, Africa, with his tail between his legs."

"I'd like an explanation of that, if you please, Major," Supo said.

"I think I understand your reasoning," Supo said when Lunsford had finished. "But I must tell you I'm not sure I agree with it. As I'm sure you know, the rules of land warfare permit the trial and execution of anyone who enters a sovereign nation and undertakes an armed revolution against the legitimate government."

"I know what he did in Cuba, Colonel," Lunsford said, "and I saw what the Simbas did here. In my personal opinion, anyone who would arm and train more Simbas deserves to die painfully. But I'm a soldier, and my president has decided we want him humiliated, not killed, and that makes it orders I am sworn to obey."

"I am having trouble convincing my soldiers they cannot shoot on sight anyone they suspect might be a Simba," Supo said. "How would you suggest I keep them from shooting, or worse, a white man they suspect of arming the Simbas?"

Lunsford shrugged.

"We'll have to deal with that as it comes up," Lunsford said. "I had the same immediate reaction to this that you did. But I've come around to seeing the wisdom that the sonofabitch alive and humiliated will cause less trouble in the end than dead and a martyr."

"Joseph Désiré is in agreement with this?" Supo asked Dr. Dannelly.

"He is in agreement with the idea that killing this Cuban would be less wise than his becoming a martyr," Dannelly replied. "But as I said before, the decision whether you want the assistance Major Lunsford offers is entirely yours."

Supo looked at Lunsford.

"What I really would like to have as assistance is an airplane — airplanes," he said.

"What sort of airplane — airplanes?" Father asked.

Supo smiled.

"One like the one you came in would be nice," he said. "But I'd be happy with anything with wings."

"What would you do with an airplane if you had one, Colonel?" Lunsford asked.

"Reconnaissance," Supo replied immediately. "You can't fight an enemy if you can't find him."

"That's true," Lunsford agreed. "They're also handy for moving officers quickly around."

Lunsford, Jack thought, *is practically inviting*

Supo to ask for, even demand, an airplane. What the hell is he up to?

"That, too," Supo said. "I'm out of touch — we don't have good radios — far too much of the time."

"So if I understand you, sir," Lunsford said, "what you're telling me is that, in the absence of a minimum number of light aircraft — say a DeHavilland Beaver to move you and your staff around, a couple of Cessna L-19s for reconnaissance and a Bell H-13 helicopter — you don't think the assistance I'm offering would be of much use to you?"

Supo, with the hint of a smile on his face, looked at Lunsford for a long moment.

"What I'm saying, Major, is that if there were available to me the aircraft you mention — and some decent tactical radios — the assistance you offer would be of far greater value."

"And without the aircraft, and some decent tactical radios, to make sure I have this right, you don't think my team would be of any real value to you, and you wouldn't want it, right, sir?"

"You could put it that way, if you chose," Colonel Supo said.

"You heard the colonel, Lieutenant Portet. What do you think Colonel Felter would say if I reported to him that Colonel Supo doesn't think the team would be any good to him without the airplanes and radios he mentioned?"

"Sir, I think the colonel would immediately take steps to get the aircraft and the radios."

"There are problems with that," Hakino said. "Internal and external."

"Sir?" Lunsford asked.

"It is one thing for a U.S. Army aircraft assigned to the U.S. Embassy to move around the Congo

499

carrying passengers on embassy business, and quite another for U.S. Army aircraft to be actively engaged in supporting military operations," Hakino said. "The President has made it clear he does not want the U.S. Army operating in the Congo."

"Speaking hypothetically, Mr. Secretary," Lunsford said. "What if a U.S. Army Beaver, or an L-19, showed up here, mysteriously, as if someone had flown it across the border from South Africa when no one was looking. And then, somehow, the aircraft was painted black so that it didn't say 'U.S. Army' on the wings and fuse-lage . . ."

"And the pilot's face would be painted black, too?" Hakino asked, smiling.

"Still speaking hypothetically, of course," Lunsford said, "what if the hypothetical pilot of this hypothetical aircraft, and its hypothetical maintenance crew, all happened to be black?"

"I suppose this hypothetical aircraft could be given Congolese Army identification," Hakino said, smiling conspiratorially.

"With respect, sir," Lunsford said. "If it had no identification at all, then no one would know who it belonged to, would they? Everybody could say, 'What airplane?' "

Hakino and Supo chuckled.

"The decision is yours, Jean-Baptiste," Dannelly said, shaking his head.

"I think Major Lunsford and I understand each other," Supo said. "And that he understands the problems — tactical and political — here. I think he and his men could be very useful."

"We'll try, Colonel," Lunsford said. "We'll try hard."

Supo nodded and offered Lunsford his hand.

"I have an apartment here in the Immoquateur," Supo said. "I'd be pleased if you all joined me for dinner. At eight?"

"We would be honored, sir," Lunsford said.

Supo gave his hand to Jack, turned, and walked off the balcony.

With Hakino and Dannelly in the apartment, it wasn't until Lunsford and Jack were alone in what had been Jack's bedroom that Jack could ask, "Where are you going to get these airplanes you promised him?"

Lunsford looked at Jack for a long moment before replying, "I figured that if Felter can steal an L-23 from some general to send to Argentina, he can steal a Beaver, a couple of L-19s, and an H-13 to send here —"

"Felter doesn't know about your offer?"

Lunsford shook his head, no.

"Since we're dreaming, why not a Huey?" Jack asked sarcastically. "For that matter, a Mohawk?"

The sarcasm went right over Lunsford's head.

"It would be hard to credibly deny a Huey or a Mohawk," he said. "The South Africans and the Israelis have Beavers, L-19s, and H-13s. The problem we're going to have is talking enough black guys, with visions of flying a Mohawk or a Chinook gloriously in Vietnam in their heads, to come here and fly L-19s and H-13s in a war that doesn't exist, and never will, but from which, nevertheless, they stand a good chance of returning in a body bag."

"Can you do it?"

"Of course I can do it," Lunsford said. "I'm a Green Beret. I can do anything."

501

XIII

[ONE]
Camp David
The Catoctin Mountains, Maryland
1530 22 January 1965

The President of the United States and the chief of staff of the United States Army were shooting skeet when the peculiar *fluckata-fluckata* sound a Bell HU-1 helicopter makes caught the President's attention.

He looked skyward, in the direction of Washington. A U.S. Army Huey could be seen approaching.

"That's probably Colonel Felter, Mr. President," the chief said.

The chief of staff was at Camp David because of Colonel Sanford T. Felter. The red White House switchboard telephone on his desk had gone off — it was rigged so that it didn't ring until a red light had flashed five times; the chief had caught it, he hoped, on the second flash — at half past ten that morning.

"Have you got heavy plans for this afternoon?" the President of the United States had inquired without other preliminaries.

"No, sir."

No plan has priority over any plan of the Commander-in-Chief.

"Come over here so that we can take off for

502

Camp David — say, quarter to twelve," the President ordered. "Don't come by chopper; the goddamn press will interpret that to mean we're about to go to war."

"Yes, sir."

The phone had clicked off.

The chief and two aides-de-camp had arrived by Army sedan at the White House at a few minutes after eleven. The presidential helicopter had fluttered down on the South Lawn of the White House at twenty past eleven. At twenty to twelve, a Secret Service agent had come to the waiting room outside the Oval Office and told the chief of staff that it was time for the chief to board the presidential helicopter.

"Just you, General," the Secret Service agent said.

"I'll call when I know something," the chief told his aides, who would now have to wait for God Only Knew How Long.

Lyndon Johnson boarded the helicopter last, just after the Secretary of State. He delayed takeoff long enough to walk, stooped, to where the chief was sitting.

"Felter will land in New York in about twenty minutes. By the time they can get him to Andrews, and on a chopper, it'll be half past three before the sonofabitch can get to Camp David."

"Yes, sir," the chief had said.

The President had walked forward and taken his seat, impatiently waving away the crewman who wanted to help him strap himself to the seat.

The chopper took off and headed north-northwest toward the Catoctin Mountain presidential retreat that still bore the name of President Eisenhower's grandson.

503

The Secretary of State got off the helicopter at Camp David only to immediately get aboard a Huey that was waiting, rotor turning, and before they reached the main guest house was already airborne and presumably headed back to Washington.

The President took lunch privately with Mrs. Johnson.

At two o'clock, a Secret Service agent led the chief of staff to the skeet range, where the President, in a windbreaker and blue jeans, was practicing mounting his shotgun to his shoulder.

"Regular skeet, a dollar a bird?" the President asked.

"Fine, Mr. President," the chief said, wondering if the stock of the shotgun he was handed was going to soil the shoulder of his tunic, which was new.

"I've got Felter trouble again, as you may have guessed," the President said. He had volunteered no further details, but the chief noted that the President had said, "It will be half past three before the sonofabitch can get to Camp David."

When Lyndon Johnson heard the inbound Huey, he was on Station Three, about to fire on the low house. He turned to one of the Secret Service agents standing behind the firing line.

"If Colonel Felter is on that chopper, bring him here," he ordered. "Only him."

"Yes, sir," one of the Secret Service agents said, and started to walk toward the helicopter pad.

"Pull!" the President called, and then, in one smooth movement, turned around and raised his shotgun — a Winchester Model 12 pump 12-gauge — to his shoulder.

After a moment, a clay pigeon emerged from the low house. The President fired and missed, and then quickly worked the action and fired again. This time the clay disc disappeared in a small cloud of black dust.

The President worked the action again, ejecting the fired shell, peered at the shotgun to make sure that there was no round in the chamber, and then turned and stepped off the station.

"I'm not taking that as a miss," he announced. "The way it's supposed to work is that when I call 'Pull,' you're supposed to pull, right goddamn then, not when you come back to paying attention to what you're supposed to be doing."

"Sorry, Mr. President," the Secret Service agent who was "pulling" targets said.

"That all right with you, General?"

"It was a bad pull, Mr. President," the chief said.

"Goddamn right it was," the President said, and waved the chief of staff on to Station Three.

Colonel Sanford T. Felter, who was wearing a gray suit in need of pressing and who had a leather briefcase chained to his wrist, was led onto the skeet range as the President fired at the high house from the center station. He broke the bird.

"I'm out of shells," the President announced. "I had that bad pull on the low house three, and had to shoot at it twice. But that's twenty-four, and you can't win anyway, General, can you?"

"I have an extra shell, Mr. President," the chief said, and offered it to Johnson, who dropped it into his shotgun, called for the low house bird, and broke it.

"That's straight, right?"

"Yes, Mr. President," the Secret Service agent keeping score agreed.

"Your shot, General," the President said.

The chief, who was firing a Remington Model 1100 semiautomatic, broke the high house and "dropped" the low.

"The President is straight, and the general is twenty-two," the Secret Service scorekeeper said.

The President held out his hand, and the chief of staff counted out three one-dollar bills into it.

"No good deed goes unpunished, General," the President said. "If you hadn't given me that shell, it would have cost you only two dollars."

The chief chuckled.

"How are you, Felter?" the President called.

"Good afternoon, Mr. President," Felter said. "Very well, thank you, sir."

The President walked toward Felter, with the chief of staff following. A Secret Service agent came forward and took the President's, and then the chief's, shotguns.

"You know each other, right?" the President said.

"Actually, sir, no," the chief said. "I know who Colonel Felter is, of course, and we have mutual friends, but —"

"How do you do, sir?" Felter said.

"I'm really glad to finally meet you, Colonel," the chief said, putting out his hand.

"He's really a legend in his own time, right?" the President said, chuckling. "Everybody knows who he is, but hardly anybody actually knows him."

"I suppose that's true, Mr. President," the chief said.

"You ever shoot any skeet, Felter?" the President asked.

"Yes, sir."

"You a gambling man, Felter?"

"Every once in a while, sir."

"You want to shoot a round of Humiliation for a buck a bird, winner take all?"

"I don't know what Humiliation is, Mr. President," Felter said.

"All doubles," the President explained. "You don't get off the station until you break both birds. A buck in the kitty for each missed bird. If you get left behind when everybody moves to the next station, you're humiliated. Get the picture? Okay with you?"

"Yes, sir," Felter said.

"You better take the briefcase off," the President said. "What have you got in there, anyhow?"

"I had my assistant bring my accumulated overnights to meet my plane in New York, Mr. President. I hoped to have time to read them on the plane to Washington."

The President beckoned to a Secret Service agent with his finger, and when he quickly walked over to him said, "Sit on Colonel Felter's briefcase while we're shooting."

"Yes, sir," the Secret Service agent said, and waited for Felter to unlock the padlock.

"And he'll need a shotgun. An 1100 all right with you, Felter?"

"Is there another Model 12, Mr. President?"

"Imitation is the sincerest form of flattery, right?" the President said. "Get him a Model 12."

"Yes, sir."

Felter, now in his shirtsleeves, suspenders

showing, with a shell pouch hanging low on his leg, stood at Station One.

"When was the last time you shot skeet, Felter?" the President asked.

"I don't remember, sir. Some time ago."

"You want a couple of don't-count shots to bring you up to speed?"

"Yes, sir. I think that would be a good idea."

"Two, four, how many?"

"I'd like four, if I can have them, sir. I'd like two singles and then a double."

"Have at it."

Felter broke the first — high house — single, and dropped the low house single. Then he called for doubles, which caused clay pigeons to be thrown simultaneously from the high and low houses. He broke both of them.

"Ready now?" the President asked.

"Yes, sir."

"Have at it," the President ordered.

Felter loaded a round in the magazine and pumped it into the chamber and then loaded a second round in the magazine.

"Pull," he called.

Both birds disintegrated.

The President took his turn and broke both birds.

The chief of staff took his turn; he broke the high house and missed the low.

"He has to stay there while we move on to Station Two," the President said. "That's why it's called Humiliation."

"Yes, sir," Felter said.

Felter and the President both fired two shots from Station Two, and both broke both birds. The chief fired again from Station One, and this time broke both birds.

Felter broke both of his birds on Station Three; the President dropped the low house. The chief dropped the high house when he fired from Station Two.

When the round was over, Felter had gone straight, which left him standing alone at Station Eight. The President had failed three times to break both of his targets, which left him at Station Five. The chief had failed six times to break both targets, which left him on Station Three.

They walked back to the rear of the range.

The President gave Felter three dollars, and the chief of staff counted out six.

"You ever think that's why you're not a general, Felter?" the President said.

"Sir?"

"The President outranks the chief of staff, so he lets me win," Johnson said. "The chief of staff — any general — outranks you, so you were supposed to let him win. Instead you humiliated the both of us."

"I thought that was the name of the game, sir," Felter said.

"I think they call that tunnel vision," the President said. "Set your eyes on what you want to do, and pay attention to nothing else. Like a horse with blinders."

"You may be right, sir," Felter said.

"The Secretary of State says that our ambassador to the Congo is going to be very humiliated if President Kasavubu finds out that you — which means the U.S. government — have gone to this General Mobutu behind his back," the President said. "And that if you could only have found the time in your busy schedule to speak with him, he

509

could have told you your efforts were doomed to failure."

"I'm sorry he feels that way, Mr. President," Felter said.

"The Secretary of State tells me he has every confidence that after a cooling-down period, and after he sees the situation develop, Kasavubu will agree to accepting some help, and that all you did, more than likely, was make the sonofabitch dig in his heels more than he already had."

"General Mobutu has agreed to accept a Special Forces team to operate covertly to deal with Guevara, Mr. President."

"No shit?" the President asked, genuinely surprised. "What's that going to cost us?"

"A Beaver, two L-19s, and an H-13, Mr. President."

"What's a Beaver?"

"A large, single-engine, six-place airplane designed for use in Canada and Alaska —"

"Oh, yeah," the President said. "That's all?"

"Some tactical radios, Mr. President. And a handful of additional personnel — pilots, maintenance people."

"Goddamn, Felter, you really pulled that off?"

"Actually, sir, Major Lunsford did."

"What's with you commandeering the embassy's airplane?"

"General Mobutu said the final decision would be up to Colonel Supo, the military governor in that area of the Congo. Lieutenant Portet — the young officer who jumped on Stanleyville with the Belgians — flew Major Lunsford, the assistant secretary of defense for provincial affairs, and General Mobutu's friend, Dr. Dannelly, to Stanleyville to talk to him."

"You couldn't have told the ambassador what you were going to do with his airplane?"

"I couldn't take the risk, Mr. President, that the ambassador might think it was a bad idea, or insist that he be part of the negotiations. In my judgment, any delay might have been fatal."

"In other words, you're telling me that not only didn't you care to hear the ambassador's opinion, but that you thought you could negotiate a deal better than he could?"

"With respect, sir, the ambassador's negotiations had failed."

"So the end justifies the means?"

Felter didn't reply.

"After the Secretary of State complained about you, again, this morning, Colonel, I decided to hell with it. I asked the chief to join us here for two reasons. First, to inform him Operation Earnest was to be transferred to the CIA as soon as possible, and second, to tell him that despite the mess you had made of things, you had acted in good faith, and when you went back to the Army, I didn't want them giving you command of a supply depot somewhere, that you had earned the command of a regiment you'd always wanted."

"Yes, sir," Felter said. "Thank you."

"Mr. President," the chief said uncomfortably. "I'm not personally involved in the selection of regimental commanders. There is a process —"

"Well, I am," Lyndon Johnson said coldly. "I'm the Commander-in-Chief. If I say he gets a regiment, he gets a regiment."

"Yes, sir," the chief said.

"Now that we understand each other on that," Johnson went on, "it's actually moot. I should have known Felter was going to pull his chestnuts out of the fire before they got burned."

"Sir?" the chief asked.

"See that Colonel Felter gets whatever he thinks he needs," the President said.

"Yes, sir," the chief said.

"Give my best regards to Major Lunsford when you see him, Felter."

"Yes, sir."

"And don't worry about the State Department. I'll deal with Foggy Bottom."

"Thank you, sir," Felter said.

The President looked like he was going to say something else, but didn't.

He beckoned to his Secret Service detail to follow him, and walked toward his private quarters.

[TWO]
Apartment B-14
Foster Garden Apartments
Fayetteville, North Carolina
0645 23 January 1965

Mrs. Jacques Portet, although she and her husband had retired early — actually, very early — the previous evening, had not actually gotten much sleep during the night, and she was therefore annoyed when the door chimes sounded, and even more annoyed when she glanced at the bedside clock and saw that it was only quarter to seven.

She nudged her husband, who, like her, was sleeping au naturel, because he could, she reasoned, more quickly slip on a pair of pajama bottoms and answer the door than she could modestly cover her nakedness and do the same thing.

His groan of protest, which was almost a groan

of agony, made her regret her selfishness. He was exhausted. He had every right to be exhausted. Not only had he flown all over the Congo when he was there, but he had spent twenty-eight hours returning from the Congo and then, on arrival the previous late afternoon and evening, expended considerable energy on the nuptial couch.

She pushed herself upright and then out of bed, finally found her bathrobe, which had somehow wound up under the bed, and walked through the living room to the door.

There was a small lens through which she could examine callers. She peered through it, deciding as she did that it would have to be Jesus Christ himself out there before she opened the door this time of morning, thereby depriving herself of rest — and very possibly, some physical manifestation of husbandly affection — in her bed.

It was not Jesus Christ. It was instead Major George Washington Lunsford, in a class A uniform.

She opened the door anyway.

"Whatever it is, no," Marjorie Bellmon Portet said.

"We have a small problem," Major Lunsford said.

"*You* have a small problem," Marjorie said. "Jack's exhausted. I won't wake him up."

"Johnny is supposed to fly me to Rucker this morning," Father said. "Last night, he drank about a quart of scotch. He's still drunk."

Johnny was obviously Major Lunsford's room-mate, Captain John S. Oliver, Norwich '59, and former aide-de-camp to Major General Robert Bellmon. Mrs. Portet had never seen him drunk, or heard of him being drunk.

"What happened?" Marjorie asked.

"When he called the Goddamn Widow to tell her he was going to be at Rucker, she hung up on him."

"Goddamn her," Marjorie said as she opened the door wide enough for him to enter.

"Was Jack drinking last night?" Father asked, quietly.

"I had a bottle of champagne on ice when he got here," Marjorie said. "We drank that early. That's all."

"I'm sorry, Marjorie," Lunsford said.

"Where's Johnny?" Marjorie asked.

"In the apartment. I called Doubting Thomas. He's on his way from Mackall to baby-sit him."

"You weren't with him?"

"I thought he was over that woman," Lunsford said. "If I'd known he'd called her, I would have stayed home."

"Put some coffee on, you can take a thermos with you," Marjorie said. "I'll wake Jack up and get him showered."

"I'd like to say we'll be back tonight," Father said. "But it will probably be tomorrow or the day after."

"No problem," Marjorie said. "This will give me a chance to go back to Sears Roebuck and count the tools in the hardware department again."

"Is it that bad for you?" he asked.

"Yeah, it is," Marjorie said. "You say you think you're going to at least RON?" — Remain Over Night.

"I think we'll have to."

"Stay in the Daleville Inn," she said. "Separate rooms."

514

"You're going to fly down?"

"If I can get on an airplane, I will. If I can't, I'll drive the Jag. Don't tell Jack."

"Okay."

[THREE]
Base Operations
Cairns Army Airfield
Fort Rucker, Alabama
1115 23 January 1965

The parking space immediately before the Base Operations building is reserved for transient aircraft. Fort Rucker's aircraft park elsewhere on the field. There are exceptions to every rule.

For example, when Captain Darrell J. Smythe, at the controls of a Grumman Mohawk, got on the horn and requested of the Cairns tower landing and taxi instructions: "Cairns, Army Six-oh-six, five miles out, landing and taxi, please," he added another phrase: "I have a Code Seven aboard."

The Cairns tower operator understood that there was a general officer in the Mohawk. In the Army rank structure, a second lieutenant is identified as an O-1, a first lieutenant as an O-2, and so on up to through the grades to O-10, which is the code for a full, four-star general. A Code Seven is a brigadier general.

"Army Six-oh-five, Cairns," the Cairns tower replied, "you are number two to land on twenty-seven, behind the L-23 on final. The winds are negligible, the altimeter is two-niner-niner. Take the first taxiway to the Base Operations tarmac."

Fort Rucker airplanes with a brigadier general aboard get to park in front of Base Operations.

"Six-oh-six," Captain Smythe said into his

515

microphone. "I have the L-23 in sight."

As Captain Smythe lined up with Runway 27, he saw the L-23 touch down. On his landing roll, Captain Smythe saw the L-23 taxiing toward the Base Operations building, and decided it was a transient aircraft, or possibly a Rucker airplane with a colonel aboard. Exceptions were often made for full-bull colonels, too.

As ground crewmen directed him to park immediately adjacent to the just-landed L-23, its crew and passenger debarked. There were three people aboard. All were wearing flight suits. They were all wearing green berets. One of them was slight, and very fair-skinned, and looked like a boy, and Captain Smythe at first decided he was the enlisted crew chief, being taken along for a ride.

As Captain Smythe helped Brigadier General Edward J. Devlin, Assistant Chief of Staff for Plans and Training of the III Corps at Fort Hood, disconnect himself from his seat and shoulder harness and the connections to his helmet, Smythe noticed, idly, that the two officers in the L-23 were tying the aircraft down, while the young-soldier-who-was-probably-the-crew-chief stood by watching, and wondered what that was all about.

It could be, he decided, that the kid was not the crew chief, but rather an enlisted man at Fort Bragg who had caught a ride to Rucker.

"Goddamn Green Berets," General Devlin said.

"Sir?"

"My general is long overdue for an L-23, and when he was finally advised it was on the way, the next day they told him the goddamn Green Berets were going to get it instead. That one looks brand new; that's probably it. What the hell do they need an aircraft like that for?"

"Yes, sir," Captain Smythe said.

"There is no place in the Army for a quote elite force unquote," General Devlin said. "The Marines understand that. I have never been able to understand the mystique surrounding the goddamn Green Berets."

"Yes, sir," Captain Smythe said.

By the time a ladder had been produced so that General Devlin and Captain Smythe could climb down from the cockpit of the Mohawk, the three people from the L-23 had entered the Base Operations building.

When General Devlin and Captain Smythe entered the Base Operations building, the two Special Forces officers were leaning on the wall under the oil portrait of Major General Bogardus S. Cairns, for whom the field had been named. Neither showed any interest when they saw General Devlin.

General Devlin had served — as a major — with General — then colonel — Cairns in the 1st Armored Division, and had admired him greatly. The entire armor community had been saddened when Cairns, shortly after receiving a well-deserved second star as commanding general of Fort Rucker and the Army Aviation Center, had crashed to his death in an H-13. There was a story that it was his own fault, that as a nearly brand-new pilot, he had forgotten to turn on his carburetor heat, whatever the hell that meant, but Devlin didn't believe it.

What he did believe was that junior officers should come to attention in the presence of a general officer, maybe especially when they were standing under a portrait of a distinguished general officer, and these two Green Beret clowns had not done so.

He marched purposefully toward them to deliver a small lecture on the military courtesy expected of majors and lieutenants and had almost reached them when a female voice called his name.

"Hello, Eddie," Mrs. Barbara Bellmon called. "Bob didn't say anything about you coming here."

General Devlin had the highest possible regard for Major General Robert F. "Bob" Bellmon, with whom he had served at three different occasions during his career. Mrs. Mary-Catherine O'Hare Devlin and Barbara Bellmon were friends from the start, at least to the extent that the wife of a captain can be friends with the wife of a senior colonel.

The two Green Beret clowns would have to wait.

He went to Barbara Bellmon and kissed her cheek.

"I'll only be here for lunch," he said. "Bob called me and said it was high time I had a good orientation ride in the Mohawk, and sent Captain Smythe to Hood to pick me up in one." He turned. "Captain?"

Captain Darrell Smythe walked to General Devlin and Mrs. Bellmon.

"Do you know Mrs. Bellmon, Captain?"

"Sir, I haven't had that privilege," Smythe said.

"How do you do, Captain?" Barbara Bellmon said, smiling at Smythe and offering him her hand.

"A pleasure, ma'am," Smythe said.

A very attractive young woman in a sweater and skirt walked up to them.

That's Marjorie, General Devlin thought. *God, I remember her when she had braces on her teeth. What did Mary-Catherine tell me? That she was involved with an enlisted man? Yes, but she also told me that she had married an officer.*

"Hello, Marjorie," General Devlin said. "How nice to see you again."

"General Devlin," Marjorie Bellmon Portet said.

"I understand you've been married," he said.

"You and Mary-Catherine were invited, Eddie," Barbara Bellmon said. "You sent regrets."

"And a 220-volt toaster, which you said you were sure we would get to use, sooner or later. Thank you again," Marjorie said.

"Our pleasure, honey," General Devlin said.

"Jack," Barbara Bellmon called, and when she had his attention, beckoned him over. And then beckoned again, to Major Lunsford.

"Jack, this is an old, old friend of the family, General Edward Devlin," Barbara said. "Eddie, this is my new son-in-law, Jack Portet."

A Green Beret! That's worse than an enlisted man.

"How do you do, sir?" Jack said politely.

"Congratulations, Lieutenant, I'm really sorry we missed the wedding," General Devlin said, and then his mouth ran away with him. "That was you in the L-23, wasn't it?"

"Yes, sir."

"Brand-new, I think?"

"Yes, sir."

"General Hanrahan's aircraft?"

"Actually, sir, I guess you could say it's Major

519

Lunsford's airplane," Jack said, nodding at Lunsford.

"Sir," Lunsford said.

Devlin offered him his hand.

"Special Forces gives L-23s to majors?" Devlin asked, trying hard to smile, to seem interested in a friendly way.

"Well, sir, it's mine only in the sense that it's been given to a project they gave me," Lunsford said.

"What project is that?"

"I'm sorry, sir, I'm not at liberty to discuss that," Lunsford said.

"Of course," General Devlin said, somewhat coldly, but still trying hard to smile.

Goddamn Green Berets. They classify everything they do.

"Well, Barbara, it was nice to see you and Marjorie again, and to meet these officers," General Devlin said.

"Give my love to Mary-Catherine," Barbara Bellmon said.

General Devlin shook hands with Jack and Father, and walked to the door to the parking area, where Captain Smythe and a staff car waited for him.

When the door had closed behind him, Barbara Bellmon turned to her daughter, her son-in-law, and Major Lunsford.

"Are you out of your minds?" she asked.

"Jack got back yesterday," Marjorie said. "I wanted to be with him."

"You're not authorized to fly in Army aircraft," Barbara Bellmon said.

"She wore a flight suit and put her hair up," Jack said.

"I authorized it," Father said.

"And if General Hanrahan hears that you 'authorized' it?" Barbara snapped. "Or my husband?"

"That's one of those bridges we'll cross if we get to it," Lunsford said.

"*Why?*" Barbara Bellmon asked in exasperation.

"Johnny was supposed to fly Father here," Marjorie said. "He called Liza Wood to tell her he was coming, and would she see him, and she hung up on him. And then he got drunk."

"And we didn't want General Hanrahan to hear about that . . . ," Jack said.

"Johnny got drunk?" Barbara asked, genuinely shocked.

Marjorie nodded.

"How sad!" Barbara said. "My God!"

"So Jack flew me down here, and Marjorie said she was going to drive down so she could be with him, and I figured, what the hell . . ." Lunsford said.

"We owe Johnny, Mother," Marjorie said. "Among other things, the only reason Bobby has his wings is because Johnny broke the rules and coached him."

"We owe Johnny, agreed. But what you did?"

"She's going back commercial," Jack said. "It's done."

"You mean, you got away with it," Barbara said.

"It looks that way, wouldn't you say?" Lunsford said.

Barbara looked at Marjorie.

"I don't know what these two are going to do here, but you and I, my irresponsible daughter, are going to have a long talk about the responsibilities of being an officer's wife."

"Mother, a half-dozen — more — times, I've heard you described as the perfect officer's wife. I think that's true, and I also think in the same circumstances, you would have done the same thing I did. I wanted to be with my husband. I needed to be with my husband."

Barbara Bellmon looked at her daughter, opened her mouth to reply, closed her mouth, shrugged, and then said, "The car's outside."

Captain Darrell J. Smythe escorted Brigadier General Devlin to the office of the commanding general, and after General Bellmon had personally come to the door of his office to beckon General Devlin to enter, had telephoned the office of the director of fixed-wing training to report that he had picked up General Devlin on schedule at Fort Hood, flown him to Fort Rucker, demonstrating en route the capabilities of the Mohawk, had just now turned him over to General Bellmon, and planned, while General Devlin was having lunch with General Bellmon, to prepare the aircraft for the return flight to Fort Hood.

"Major Calhoun will take him back to Hood, Darrell. At 1300 you will present yourself to the office of the chief of staff."

"Sir?"

"The chief of staff telephoned me and said, 'Have Captain Smythe report to me at 1300.' I told him you were doing a dog-and-pony show for General Devlin, and he replied, 'Have Captain Smythe report to me at 1300.' What's this all about, Darrell?"

"Sir, I have no idea. You don't?"

"Thirteen hundred. Chief of staff's office."

"Yes, sir."

"I'm sending Major Calhoun over there now, in case you want to take a shower and put on a nice uniform or anything before 1300."

"Yes, sir."

As Captain Smythe looked down the narrow flight of stairs that led from the commanding general's office to the main floor of the headquarters building, the two Green Berets were coming up them, and, deferring to the Green Beret major's seniority, Captain Smythe waited for him to come up before starting down himself.

"Hey, bro," the Green Beret major said, "people are going to talk if we keep meeting like this."

Captain Smythe smiled with an effort. He hated the term "bro." He did not consider himself to be a brother of every other Negro/colored/black man/whatever in the world.

"So, Eddie," Major General Bellmon said to Brigadier General Devlin, "what do you think of the Mohawk?"

"It's an amazing aircraft," Devlin said honestly, as he nodded his head in reply to Bellmon's gesture of offering a cup of coffee. "That side-looking radar capability has enormous potential."

"You have to see it work before you really believe it," Bellmon said. "And the Signal Corps is working on an infrared version. The prototype I saw shows little images, tanks, trucks, people . . ."

"We're really a long way from directing artillery fire from the side window of a Piper Cub, aren't we?" General Devlin mused. "And what I thought on the way up here was that the pilot of that sophisticated airplane was really a professional pilot, not an artilleryman, or whatever, who also knew how to fly."

"That's one of our problems," Bellmon said. "It's asking a hell of a lot of a pilot like Smythe to be a pilot, and, in his case, armor, keeping up with all he has to know to command a tank company."

Devlin grunted.

"What did you think of him?" Bellmon asked.

"Truth to tell?" Devlin asked. "He impressed me from the moment I saw him, and I wondered what the hell he was doing driving an airplane, when I really need bright young officers to command tank companies."

"That was before your first Mohawk ride?" Bellmon asked, smiling.

"Yeah," Devlin said.

"Well, Captain Smythe is about to get command of a platoon," Bellmon said.

"A *platoon?*"

"We're forming a Mohawk platoon, for Vietnam. We chose from among ten of the best and the brightest captains we could find; Smythe was the final choice."

"Captains commanding platoons . . ."

"We're accused, of course, of inflating, or diluting, the rank structure, of course," Bellmon said. "But it's just not that way. When III Corps gets a Mohawk platoon —"

"Will that be before or after Bob Grisham gets his Corps Commander's L-23?"

Bellmon ignored the dig.

"— it will consist of six Mohawks. Each aircraft requires two aviators, and of course you need spares. The draft TO and E calls for ten aviators, all commissioned officers, because we are not yet at the point where we can train warrant officer pilots to fly them. There's also a maintenance officer, commissioned, and a deputy, warrant, and an avionics officer, commissioned, and a warrant deputy. And a supply officer, commissioned. From that perspective, you wonder if a captain isn't a little junior to command."

"And all of the officers have to stay current in their branch?"

"The brightest of us," Bellmon said jokingly, "can do both. Command a tank unit and fly. Me, for example," he paused. "Craig Lowell."

Devlin shook his head.

"Where is he now?"

"McDill," Bellmon replied. "Aviation officer for STRIKE command."

"I heard he's a Green Beret," Devlin said.

"Unfortunately," Bellmon said.

"I was in Task Force Lowell, you know," Devlin said. "I thought Lowell was what you find when you look up 'combat commander' in the dictionary."

"He's a fine combat commander," Bellmon agreed. "And I have to keep telling myself that what he's doing as a Green Beret is important. But I find myself wondering if he shouldn't be commanding an aviation company in Vietnam."

Devlin grunted.

"Or a tank battalion at Hood," he said.

"And they're attracting the bright young officers, or stealing them —"

"Stealing them?" Devlin interrupted.

Bellmon didn't reply directly.

"You remember my aide, Johnny Oliver?" he asked. "He's up at Bragg, eating snakes with Red Hanrahan. Even my son, who should know better, put in an application for Special Forces. And my daughter married one of them."

"I just met him," Devlin said, and when Bellmon looked surprised, went on: "He was at the airfield when we got here. With Barbara and Marjorie."

"You ever hear 'the general is the last to know'?" Bellmon said. "I had no idea either of them were here."

"They came in just ahead of us in an L-23," Devlin said, "which I strongly suspect is the one Bob Grisham expected and didn't get."

"For God's sake, don't tell him you got this from me, but it is. The reason I know is that my son-in-law went out to Wichita to pick it up."

"Seems like a very nice young man," Devlin said.

"Unfortunately, he is. Otherwise, I could hate him. Marjorie took one look at him, and that was it."

"Academy?"

"No. He got drafted and then took a direct commission. He was an airline pilot."

"And now he's a Green Beret?"

"Don't ask, Eddie. For those of us who like to go by the book, it's painful."

The General's intercom went off:

"General, Major Lunsford and Lieutenant Portet are here. Major Lunsford says you expect him."

"Give them a cup of coffee and tell them I'll be available shortly," Bellmon replied. He looked at Devlin. "Last night, the chief called me at my quarters. He said two officers would be coming here from Bragg, from the Special Warfare Center, on a recruiting mission. Read 'steal my brightest officers.' "

"Those two?" Devlin asked, pointing to the door.

Bellmon nodded.

"The chief didn't say who was coming, but two and two are four, right? And the chief said they can have whoever they want — the priority came from the President himself."

"Jesus Christ!"

"The chief told me I was to prepare a list of ten officers meeting certain criteria —"

"Such as?" Devlin interrupted.

Bellmon ignored the question.

"And have them available for interview at 1300 today. And like the good soldier I like to think I am, I said, 'Yes, sir' and called the personnel officer at his quarters and told him to make up the list."

"What the hell is going on? Do you know?"

"I can make a couple of good guesses," Bellmon said. "But what it boils down to is that it has the President's approval. He's the Commander-in-Chief. I'm not going to second-guess him about priorities."

He leaned forward and pressed the lever on his intercom.

"Ask Major Lunsford and Lieutenant Portet to come in, please."

Their arrival, at least, was by the book.

There was a knock at the door, Bellmon called, "Enter"; they marched in, came to attention before his desk, and saluted; Bellmon returned it; Lunsford said, "Major Lunsford, sir," and Bellmon said, "At ease, gentlemen."

He stood up and offered his hand, first to Lunsford and then to Jack.

"Sir, General Hanrahan's compliments," Lunsford said. "He said you would be expecting us."

"My chief of staff's office at 1300," Bellmon said. "I came up with only eight officers meeting the criteria."

"Thank you, sir."

"You've met General Devlin, I understand?"

"Yes, sir," Lunsford said, "at the airfield."

"Lieutenant, if you don't mind my asking," General Devlin said, "what are those wings? I don't think I've ever seen —"

"Not to go further than this office, Eddie?" General Bellmon said.

"Of course."

"Those are Belgian paratrooper's wings," Bellmon said. "Jack earned them jumping into Stanleyville with the Belgians."

"Jesus!"

"And when he got there, he found Major Lunsford waiting for him. He'd been there, covertly, through the entire episode. The President gave him the Silver Star — his third — personally."

"I'm very impressed," General Devlin said.

"Whenever I become really annoyed with Special Forces, I think of people like these two, and it calms me down," General Bellmon said.

Devlin looked at him but said nothing.

"I will buy all the officers in this room lunch," General Bellmon said, "with the following ground rules: We will not discuss Special Forces, or who has General Grisham's L-23. Perhaps General Devlin will regale us with tales of Captain Craig Lowell and Task Force Lowell."

"I can talk about that all day," General Devlin said.

[FOUR]
Conference Room
Office of the Chief of Staff
U.S. Army Aviation Center and Fort Rucker, Alabama
1545 23 January 1965

Before the first of the eight officers who had been ordered to report to the office of the chief of staff actually entered the conference room itself, they had a chance to examine each other and wonder what the hell was going on.

The only things they had in common were that they were all black/Negro/colored/whatever and rated Army aviators. There were two majors, both of whom had the star of a senior aviator mounted above the shield of their wings. There were two captains and four first lieutenants.

"What the hell is this?" one of the majors inquired, "the Rucker Black Caucus?"

The other major gave him a dirty look but said nothing.

"If one more goddamned white liberal asks me if I have experienced racial prejudice, I'll throw up in his lap," the other captain asked. He, too, was a senior aviator.

There was laughter, in which Captain Smythe did not join.

"Is that what this is?" one of the lieutenants asked.

"Christ, I hope not," the major who made the Black Caucus crack said. "I'm supposed to be giving Caribou right-seat check rides, and this is really going to fuck up a lot of scheduling."

The chief of staff entered at that point. He was a tall, slim, crew-cutted full-bird colonel who everyone knew had been selected for promotion to brigadier general. He was one of the very few people whose wings were topped by a star within a wreath, identifying him as a master Army aviator.

The only other master Army aviator with whom Captain Smythe was familiar was Major Hodges, the president of the instrument examiner board, who had given him his final check ride on finishing Mohawk Transition; his annual instrument rating check ride; and, most recently, his check ride leading to his certification as a Mohawk instructor pilot.

All eight had risen to their feet when he entered his outer office.

"As you were, gentlemen, good afternoon," the chief of staff said. "I will not entertain questions, primarily because I don't have any answers. But I will tell you this, and with whatever emphasis is required to make you understand, it's not bovine excreta. You will not discuss what transpires here this afternoon between yourselves, or with your superiors — if they have questions, refer them to me — your subordinates, your girlfriends, and especially not your wives. Are we all clear on that?"

There was a chorus of "Yes, sir."

"Okay, Les," the chief of staff said. "You first."

"Yes, sir," the major of the Black Caucus crack said. He stood up.

"When Major Levitt leaves, he will inform you who is next," the chief said.

The chief of staff walked into his office, and Major Levitt walked into the conference room, closing the door behind him.

Captain Smythe decided entry into the conference room would be by rank, which would make him either third or fourth to enter. This logical presumption proved to be in error. He was the last man to enter the conference room.

He entered the conference room and found the two Green Berets he had seen at Cairns at one end of the conference table. There was a stack of what certainly were service records on the table. They were in shirtsleeves. There was a coffee thermos on the table. The lieutenant was puffing on a cigar.

Captain Smythe saluted.

"Sir, Captain Smythe, Darrell J., reporting as ordered, sir."

The major returned the salute with a casual wave in the general direction of his forehead.

"Sit," he ordered, indicating a chair at the other end of the table.

Captain Smythe sat down.

"If I didn't know better, bro," Father said. "I'd suspect you were following us around."

Captain Smythe neither smiled or replied.

"The *J* is for Jeremiah, right?" Father asked.

"Yes, sir."

"Was your mother carried away with seventh-century Hebrew prophets, or did she pick that out of a phone book?"

The lieutenant chuckled.

"Sir," Captain Smythe said, "may I ask what this is all about?"

"What this is all about, Darrell, is that I ask the questions, and you answer them."

"Yes, sir."

"What I'm really curious to know about you, Jeremiah, is how come a nice black fellow like you from Swarthmore passed up the chance to go, not to Joseph Stalin U, right there in Swarthmore, or the U of P, or even Drexel, but all the way to Norwich in frozen Vermont?"

"I'm not sure I understand the question, sir."

"Think about it. Have a shot at it. Isn't the Norwich motto 'I will try'?" He turned to Jack. "For your general fund of knowledge, Lieutenant, Swarthmore College was founded in 1833 by an abolitionist named James Mott."

"Thank you, sir," Jack replied in English. Then he switched to Swahili. "Why are you trying to piss this guy off?"

In Swahili, Father replied: "It's very useful, sometimes, Jack, to know how well an officer can control his temper." He switched back to English: "You've got something against abolitionists, Jeremiah?"

Captain Smythe, obviously, had never previously heard Swahili spoken.

"Sir," Captain Smythe said icily. "I went to Norwich in anticipation of a military career."

"You ever run into a guy named Gordon Sullivan up there?"

"He was '59, sir. I'm '60."

"Is there anything to the story that he and another Norwich lunatic named Bob Johnson took a mule into the commandant's office and left it there overnight? Causing, the story goes, certain equine excreta damage to the commandant's carpet?"

"I've heard that story, sir."

"How about John Oliver? You ever run into that Norwich maniac?"

"No shit?" Jack asked in Swahili.

"You ain't seen nothing yet," Father replied in Swahili.

"Sir, Captain Oliver and I are classmates,"

Captain Smythe said.

"And you admit it?"

"Sir," Captain Smythe said, on the edge of losing his temper, "Captain Oliver is a fine, highly decorated officer I am proud to claim as a friend."

"Is that so?" Father asked. "Well, they say appearances are deceiving, don't they?" He turned to Jack. "Get Doubting Thomas on the phone, please, Lieutenant."

"Yes, sir," Jack said, and went to a credenza against the wall and got on the telephone.

"Tell me, Jeremiah," Father said, "what kind of an L-19 pilot are you?"

"Sir, I'm rated in the L-19, of course, but I'm also rated as an IP in the Mohawk."

"You're too good to fly L-19s, is that what you're suggesting, Jeremiah?"

"Sir, an L-19 is really a rather basic aircraft. The Mohawk is really at the other end of the scale, in terms of sophistication and required pilot skill."

"And as a Mohawk pilot you feel you have risen above the L-19, is that what you're saying, Jeremiah?"

"Sir, I didn't say that at all," Smythe protested.

"Then what did you say?" Father asked.

"Sir, you asked me what kind of an L-19 pilot I am —"

"And I never got an answer, did I? Let me rephrase. Are you a competent L-19 pilot? Confine your response to 'Yes, sir' or 'No, sir.'"

"Yes, sir."

"That wasn't really that hard, was it, Jeremiah?"

On the telephone, in Swahili, Jack said, "Jack Portet, Doubting. Hold one."

533

In Swahili, Father said, "Get the village drunk on the phone, Jack."

In Swahili, Jack said, "Put Captain Oliver on the phone, please."

Captain Smythe picked up on the "Captain Oliver," and his eyes widened.

"Jack?" Johnny Oliver said a moment later. "I owe you a big one."

"Forget it," Jack said, then changed his mind. "Yeah, come to think of it, Captain, you do. Hold one."

He held up the phone to Father Lunsford, who held up his hand, indicating he didn't want it right then.

"Jeremiah, if I were to ask Captain Oliver what kind of an officer you are, what kind of an L-19 pilot you are, what do you think he would say?"

"Sir, I have no idea," Captain Smythe said.

"I do. I already asked him," Lunsford said.

He took the phone from Jack.

"Say hello to Jeremiah, Johnny. Welcome him to the team."

He signaled for Smythe to go to the telephone.

The conversation took no more than twenty seconds. Father signaled that he wanted the telephone.

"Just for the record, Johnny, you're on my shitlist, and you really owe Jack," Father said. "We'll be back tomorrow or the day after, depending on how we do recruiting mechanics and radio people. Spend the time thinking about how you can square yourself with us."

He hung up and turned to Smythe.

"Might one inquire into the nature of your conversation with Captain Oliver, Jeremiah?"

"Sir, Captain Oliver said, 'Welcome to the team, and the first rule is don't ask questions.'"

"I thought it might be something like that," Father said.

"Sir, I have no idea what's going on."

"Did that sound like a question to you, Jack?" Father said.

"That was more of a statement than a question," Jack said.

"In that case, I think I should try to satisfy Jeremiah's natural curiosity, don't you?"

"Yes, sir."

"From here on, this is Top Secret/Earnest," Lunsford said.

"Sir, I have a Top Secret clearance, but . . . what did you say?"

"As of this moment, Captain Smythe," Lunsford said, "you are authorized access to material classified as Top Secret/Earnest."

"Yes, sir."

"In the very near future, Smythe," Lunsford said, "you will find yourself flying over the lands of our ancestors in an L-19, and a little later, in a Beaver and an H-13 — Johnny said you went to chopper school together — assisting our merry little band of covert warriors in fucking up Che Guevara's intentions of taking over the Congo, with the important caveat that we are absolutely forbidden to waste the sonofabitch. Any other questions?"

Father was now smiling.

"I hardly know where to begin, sir," Smythe said. "But there is something I think I should tell you."

"Which is?"

"Sir, I am on Department of the Army general

535

orders to assume command of a Mohawk platoon."

"You were. What happened was that as soon as Johnny remembered you were here, we started the process of having your orders changed. It may already be done."

"As a statement," Smythe said. "The word 'volunteer' doesn't enter any of this."

Father shook his head, no.

"That bother you?"

Smythe thought that over for ten seconds.

"No, sir. I'm a soldier. I go where I'm sent and do my best to do what I'm told."

"That's what Johnny said you'd say," Lunsford said. "The reason we kept you 'til last — since you didn't ask — is because we knew we wanted you. And because I think you and I should now go someplace for a quiet beer, while I fill you in. Jack and his bride have other plans for the evening, right?"

"Did you hear what she said on the plane?" Jack asked.

"About going to see the Goddamned Widow?"

Jack nodded.

"Good luck," Father said.

[FIVE]
Quarters #1
U.S. Army Aviation Center and Fort Rucker, Alabama
1905 23 January 1965

Surprising Jack not at all, his mother- and father-in-law, acting separately and in concert, insisted that he and Marjorie stay with them, rather than taking a room at the Daleville Inn.

"Don't be silly," Barbara Bellmon said. "Marjorie's old bed is big enough for the two of you."

"And you're really going to have to start thinking about money," General Bellmon said. "I don't even like to think how much it cost you to fly Marjorie down here for just two days."

Supper was broiled chicken halves and baked potatoes, both prepared on a charcoal grill by General Bellmon, who put on a white apron with a red cartoon of a man in a chef's hat printed on it.

Marjorie and her mother worked in the kitchen, sipping on white wine; General Bellmon and Jack worked on a bottle of Merlot on the patio while they watched the chicken cook.

Bellmon asked what had happened in the Congo, and Jack decided to tell him. Bellmon not only had a Top Secret/Earnest clearance, but was also a major general and his father-in-law.

He got as far in the story as flying to Stanleyville when Second Lieutenant Robert F. Bellmon, Jr., appeared, uninvited. The story was necessarily interrupted there, as Bobby was not possessed of a Top Secret/Earnest clearance.

"I called Johnny Oliver to ask if he's heard anything about my application," Bobby announced. "He told me you were here."

"And?" General Bellmon asked.

"So I came over," Bobby said. "You should have called me, Jack."

"I meant about your application," General Bellmon said.

"He said he hadn't heard anything," Bobby said. "Jack, could you ask?"

"Bobby, I am a very unimportant lieutenant in Bragg," Jack said.

"Like hell," Bobby said. "God, it's all over the

post that you and Major Lunsford are here recruiting people for some hush-hush operation."

"Where did you hear that?" General Bellmon asked, rather sharply.

"From a guy in my Mohawk class," Bobby said. "Tony Stevens. Black guy. Lieutenant. He said he and Captain Smythe, one of the IPs, and every other black aviator he knew were ordered to report to the chief of staff's office at 1300."

"And how did Major Lunsford's name come up?" General Bellmon asked. "And Jack's?"

Bobby looked uncomfortable.

"Well?" Bellmon asked impatiently.

"Mother said I was to get out of the habit of coming here whenever I wanted and drinking up all your beer," Bobby said. "So on the way over here, I stopped by Annex One to pick up a six-pack. And there was another black guy at the bar talking, and he said he'd been interviewed this afternoon for a hush-hush assignment by two Special Forces officers, one of them a black major named Lunsford and the other one . . . 'the guy who married the general's daughter.' "

"Good God!" Bellmon said, adding, "Do you know this officer's name, Bobby?"

Bobby shook his head, no.

"Presumably your friend Lieutenant Stevens does," Bellmon said coldly. "You go to him, Bobby, right away, tonight, and you tell him I said that if I ever hear another report of his irresponsibly loose mouth he will find himself counting snowballs on ground duty in Alaska. And tell him to pass the word."

"Yes, sir," Bobby said.

"Is this going to cause any damage, Jack?" Bellmon asked.

"I don't think so, sir," Jack said after a moment's reflection. "With one exception — Captain Smythe — Lunsford didn't go beyond 'classified mission' to explain what we were looking for."

"What about Smythe?" Bellmon asked. "We just gave him command of the Mohawk platoon we're sending to Vietnam."

"He was at Norwich — and in Vietnam — with Johnny Oliver, sir," Jack said. "Major Lunsford had already decided we were going to take him before we got here."

"Six senior officers spend God knows how many hours picking the right man for an important assignment, and one Major comes along and steals him," Bellmon said, bitterly. "Goddamn it!"

Jack didn't reply.

"I know it's not you, Jack," Bellmon said. "Please excuse the temper flare." He turned to Bobby. "If memory serves, Bobby, my words were 'right away, tonight.' "

"Yes, sir," Bobby said. "Dad, I — I'm sorry."

"I know," Bellmon said. "But you've just got to learn that 'sorry' doesn't put things back the way they were."

"You going to be here later, Jack?" Bobby asked.

"Marjorie wants to go into Ozark to see Liza Wood," Jack said. "After that —"

"Right away, goddamn it, Bobby," General Bellmon flared.

Bobby fled.

He had almost made it to the corner of the house when Bellmon called after him.

"Your schedule permitting, come for breakfast, Bobby. You can talk to Jack and Marjorie then."

[SIX]

"What did you tell Liza on the phone?" Jack asked.

Lieutenant and Mrs. Portet were in Barbara Bellmon's Oldsmobile, approaching Ozark on the Fort Rucker/Ozark Highway. Marjorie was driving.

"Nothing. Just they we were here and wanted to see her."

"At the risk of destroying this marriage-made-in-heaven, my darling, in my studied judgment, this is a dumb fucking idea," Jack said.

"Why?"

"For one thing, it's none of our business, and for another, you can talk yourself blue in the face all night and not change her mind."

"I was thinking maybe I could make her ashamed of herself for what she's doing to Johnny."

"Right now, your sainted Captain Oliver is not one of my favorite people," Jack said.

"Really?"

"If he wasn't behaving like a lovesick calf, I would at this moment be chasing you around our apartment, while you pretended to want to get away."

"Oh, really?"

"Instead, because he got sauced last night, I get jerked out of my nuptial couch in the early hours of morning, have to fly down here, and now face the prospect of having to chase you around your girlhood bedroom with Mommy and Daddy listening."

"You are, in other words, in what could be described as a self-pitying, lustful, frame of mind?"

540

"In words of multiple syllables, Madame, you bet your sweet fucking ass I am."

"Is that how you think of it?" Marjorie asked.

"Do what you want to do, baby," Jack said. "On the way just now, I realized I'm already henpecked."

"I thought you tough Green Beret masculine types called that 'pussy-whipped'."

Jack didn't reply.

"How about this for an alternate plan?" Marjorie said. "We go to see Liza. We have one drink, no more than two. We play with Allan. We don't mention the name of Captain John S. Oliver, Jr., and if she does, we say 'Who?'. Then we leave, we drive to Highway 231, we take a motel room. I will let you catch me before you get too tired, and later, much later, we will go to sleep in my girlhood bed."

"God, if you could cook, I think I'd marry you," Jack said.

XIV

[ONE]
Foster Garden Apartments
Fayetteville, North Carolina
1400 25 January 1965

When Major George Washington Lunsford let himself into the apartment he shared with Captain John S. Oliver, Jr., he found Oliver sprawled on the couch in fatigues. The television was on, but unless Oliver had suddenly developed an interest in *As the World Turns*, he wasn't paying a hell of a lot of attention to it.

"Hey," Father said.

"Hey," Oliver replied.

"I need a beer. You want one?"

"No, thanks," Oliver said.

Lunsford walked into the kitchen and returned a minute later holding two bottles of Heineken beer. He handed one to Oliver, then slumped into an armchair facing the couch.

Oliver held the beer bottle up.

"I really think I've had enough of this for a while," he said.

"Moderation in all things, as it says in the Good Book," Lunsford said. "And I happen to agree with the patron saint of the Green Beanies, John Wayne, who said he never trusted a man who turned down a drink."

"I don't think John Wayne said that," Oliver said.

"If he didn't, he should have."

"Is Jack in his apartment? I want to apologize face-to-face."

"Jack's still at Rucker," Lunsford said. "Jeremiah flew me up. I had things to do here. Jack's stripping the markings from an L-19, and getting SCATSA to check the radios. Jeremiah went back. Jack will bring the plane up here, and Jeremiah will bring Marjorie with him when he drives up here."

" 'Things to do up here,' " Oliver parroted. "Presumably including dealing with the drunk-on-duty Captain John S. Oliver, Jr.?"

"Among other things, yeah," Lunsford said.

"I'm sorry, Father, for what that's worth."

"You should be, buddy, and no, it's not worth much."

"Shit," Oliver said, and took a pull at his beer.

"On the way down there, Marjorie said she was going to see the Goddamned Widow and give her a piece of her mind for abusing Poor, Dear Johnny, driving him to the bottle."

"Oh, God, no!" Oliver said. "Did she?"

"At the last moment, according to Jack, wisdom prevailed. They went to see the Goddamned Widow, but neither side invoked the name of John Oliver."

"You stuck your neck out pretty far flying Marjorie down there," Oliver said.

"We got away with it," Lunsford said. "By the skin of our teeth, as it turned out. When we parked at Cairns, Jeremiah — he was giving a Mohawk dog-and-pony show to some brigadier from Hood — parked right next to us. If he had known Marjorie —"

"Jesus!" Oliver said. "He hates being called Jeremiah — as you obviously know."

"How long do you think it will take the team to start calling him 'Aunt Jemima'?" Lunsford asked. "He's got a tough skin. I did my best to piss him off, and couldn't."

"He's a good man," Oliver said.

"Anyway, I figured I owed Jack for saving your ass. And he's going to Buenos Aires on Friday. He's entitled to a little time with his bride."

"Yeah," Oliver agreed.

"What are you going to do about the Goddamn Widow, Johnny?" Lunsford asked.

Oliver met his eyes but didn't respond.

"The bottom line is that I'm wondering if I can trust you to handle things in Buenos Aires," Lunsford said.

"If I were you, I wouldn't," Oliver said. "If I were you, Father, I would have turned me in to Hanrahan."

"No, you wouldn't have," Father said. "And I need you, Johnny. But you've got to settle this Goddamn Widow business once and for all."

"You ever been in love?" Oliver asked.

"A hundred times, which probably means never."

"This is my first time," Oliver said. "It sneaks up on you, then whacks you in the back of the head. I can't believe the effect it's had on me."

"The other option, of course, is to take off the suit, settle down in a vine-covered cottage by the side of the road, and start spending your money."

"I'm a soldier, Father."

"Soldiers — good soldiers — don't get shitfaced when they're supposed to go on duty."

"Yeah. That thought has occurred to me more than once in the last couple of days."

"I can't let this hang in the breeze, Johnny," Lunsford said. "You have to get off the dime."

"All suggestions gratefully accepted."

"Jack will be back here tomorrow or the day after," Lunsford said. "I'll send you to Rucker in the L-23 to 'check on the L-19.' While you're there, go see her and get this settled, once and for all."

Oliver looked at him but did not reply.

"Option Two," Lunsford said. "I can probably arrange for you to take that assignment with the Air Mobile Division at Benning."

"Pass the problem of the lovesick drunk to some one else?"

"I can't deal with it, Johnny. If I can't have you bright-eyed, bushy-tailed, and sober, I don't want you," Lunsford said.

They exchanged looks again.

"How does the Goddamned Widow feel about Benning?" Father asked. "Is she pissed because you came here, or with you being in the Army, period?"

"Me being in it, period. She says she can't go through having another husband blown away — put Allan through that again."

"It's up to you, pal," Lunsford said. "When Jack brings the L-23 back, you can go to Rucker with the understanding that if you can't get your act together, you're out of here."

Oliver nodded.

"What have I got to lose?" Oliver said. "Thank you, Father."

"There is yet another option," Father said. "Which I don't think will interest you."

"Which is?"

"I have been satisfying my carnal hungers with

the Puerto Rican nurse in C-27."

"Good for you."

"She has a roommate," Lunsford said. "Who has expressed an interest in you."

"Bullshit."

"Cross my heart and hope to die," Lunsford said. "I'm headed there now. Maybe a little piece — *i-e* piece — would relieve the pressure on your gonads and clear your brain."

"You're serious, aren't you?"

"I'm desperate, pal. I don't want to lose you."

Oliver looked at him for a long moment.

"For the absolutely last time," Oliver said finally. "I'll try to get her on the phone. And if what I think will happen happens, I'll join you in C-27."

"And go to Rucker later? Overwhelmed with shame and remorse?"

"If what I think will happen happens, I won't be going to Rucker."

Lunsford nodded.

"One last word. If what you and I both think will happen happens, and I come back here and find you shitfaced, that'll be it."

"Understood."

"Give me a couple of minutes for a quick shower and some cologne behind my ears, and I'll be out of here," Father said.

Five minutes later, Lunsford, now in a sport coat and slacks, stood at the apartment door.

"I hope it works out, pal," he said, and then left.

Oliver stared at the door for a moment, then looked at the television, saw what was playing, uttered a disgusted "Shit," and turned the television off.

He walked to the telephone, looked down at it

for a long moment, then picked up the receiver and dialed.

"This is it," he said aloud when it started to ring. "Whatever happens, this is it."

After the fifth ring, Liza's voice informed him that she was sorry she was not at home, but if he left his name and number, she would get back to him just as soon as she could.

He put the receiver back in its cradle.

"Fuck it," he said aloud. "I don't know what the hell I would say if you did answer the goddamned phone."

Well, I can still fly down there tomorrow, or whenever Jack brings the L-23 back, and face her face-to-face.

Fuck that! I've made enough of an ass of myself. I said that would be it, that was it.

The Heineken bottle was on the chair side table.

I will finish that beer, and I will have another one, or two, with the girls in C-27. If I can't handle that, and get shitfaced, I will admit I can't handle the booze, and will join Alcoholics Anonymous.

And who knows, maybe Father is right, a piece of ass might be just what I need to come to my senses. And I suspect that the other Puerto Rican nurse will be a very interesting roll in the hay.

He drained the Heineken and went into his bedroom, stripped, showered, and was almost dressed when the doorbell rang.

What the hell is that?

Did Father, knowing that what we both knew would happen, happened, come back to hold my hand? To make sure I stayed off the sauce?!

He went to the door, opened it, and said after a moment, "What's this?"

Liza Wood was standing there, holding Allan's

hand. There were four suitcases on the floor beside them.

"What does it look like?" Liza asked. "It's a goddamned camp follower and her fatherless child."

He didn't know what to do, or trust his voice to speak, so he scooped Allan up, and growled in his neck.

"*Horsey*, Johnny," Allan said.

He swung the child so that he was on his shoulders, and then he put his arms around Liza and held her tight against him, and the three of them bounced up and down together.

[TWO]

SECRET

Central Intelligence Agency
Langley, Virginia

FROM: Assistant Director For Administration

DATE: 25 January 1965 1510 GMT

SUBJECT: Guevara, Ernesto (Memorandum # 37.)

TO: Mr. Sanford T. Felter
Counselor To The President
Room 637, The Executive Office Building
Washington, D.C.

By Courier

In compliance with Presidential Memorandum to The Director, Subject: "Ernesto 'Che' Guevara," dated 14 December 1964, the following information is furnished:

(Reliability Scale Five) (From CIA Conraky, Guinea) SUBJECT departed Conraky 1525 GMT 24 January 1965 aboard chartered aircraft, announced destination, Cotonou, Dahomey.

Howard W. O'Connor
HOWARD W. O'CONNOR

SECRET

[THREE]
Apartment B-14
Foster Garden Apartments
Fayetteville, North Carolina
1735 Hours 27 January 1965

As Mrs. Jacques Portet put her key in the lock of B-14, she had a sudden chill. Jack expected her. They had telephoned an hour before to report themselves an hour out of Fayetteville. Jack was a lunatic. That translated to the very real possibility of him answering the door in his birthday suit, with a lustful leer on his face.

Ordinarily, she would have been privately pleased, but Captain Darrell J. Smythe was standing behind her. Despite her assurances that she could make it from his Buick to her door without assistance, he had insisted on walking up with her.

Captain Smythe, she had learned, was something of a prig.

When Marjorie pushed the door open she found her husband fully clothed, sitting on the living room floor. Also sitting on the floor was Major George Washington Lunsford. Major Lunsford was assisting Master Allan Wood in the driving of a toy, wire-controlled M-48 tank. Lieutenant Portet was in command of a toy, wire-controlled Russian T-34 tank. There were three bottles of Heineken beer sitting upright on the carpet.

Terrain had been improvised using pillows from the couch, a silver champagne cooler, three empty Heineken bottles lying on their sides, and an empty Heineken six-pack.

"Hey there, Jeremiah," Major Lunsford called. "You're armor. Come on in and give Jack a hand; Allan and I are whipping his . . . armor tactics."

"Hi, Aunty Marjie," Allan called.

"Hi, sweetheart," Marjorie replied tenderly. And then, less tenderly: "What's going on here?" and then, as Allan reached for one of the upright Heineken bottles, "My God, you're not giving that child beer?"

Allan picked up a Heineken bottle, cried, "Beer, beer, beer," and took a healthy swig.

Marjorie ran to take it away from him.

"As in root beer, light of my life," Jack said. "What did you think?"

"What's he doing here?" Marjorie asked.

"Allan's mommy and uncle Johnny are discussing world ecological problems in my apartment," Father said. "We are taking care of Allan."

"If she sees him drinking out of that beer bottle, she'll be furious," Marjorie said.

"God, I hope so," Father said. "Johnny may have forgiven her, but Jack and I damned sure haven't."

"When did she get here?" Marjorie asked. "What's going on?"

"She confessed, in the few minutes we've seen either of them, that she was inspired by our married bliss when we called," Jack said. "Actually, what she said was that when we didn't talk about Johnny, she thought there was something wrong. She was too proud to ask, of course, but after we left, especially when Allan wanted to know where Johnny was, and threw a fit when she told him he was going to have to forget about Johnny —"

"Oh, God," Marjorie said.

"— she realized (a) that had been selfish of her and (b) that she really cared about him, leading her to conclude (c) that she would really rather be a camp follower after all, and immediately loaded Allan in the car and came here."

"I'll be damned," Marjorie said.

"Come on in, Jeremiah," Lunsford said. "We'll take you out to the post in the morning. After you have a beer, you and I will go to my apartment and throw buckets of water on Romeo and Juliet to cool them down long enough to discuss sleeping arrangements."

"Father," Marjorie said, "that's disgusting."

"You haven't seen them," Father said.

"I should be mad at you," Marjorie said, "and happy for them. Instead, I want to cry."

[FOUR]
Office of the Commanding General
The John F. Kennedy Center for Special
Warfare
Fort Bragg, North Carolina
1015 28 January 1965

"Sir, Colonel Martin asks for a minute," Captain Ski Zabrewski boomed from the open door.

Brigadier General Paul R. Hanrahan nodded, then raised his voice.

"Come on in, Padre!"

Chaplain (Lt. Col.) T. Wilson Martin marched into Hanrahan's office, stopped twelve inches from Hanrahan's desk, came to attention, and saluted.

"Good morning, General. Thank you for seeing me."

Chaplain Martin was almost — not quite — as large as Captain Zabrewski, and if anything, his voice was even deeper. His crisply starched uniform bore the wings of a master parachutist, and he had earned the hard way the green beret he clasped in his left hand.

"At ease," Hanrahan said, and rose from behind his desk to offer Martin his hand. He waved him into the chair in front of the desk.

"Coffee?"

"No, thank you, sir, I'm trying to cut down."

"What's on your mind, Padre?" Hanrahan asked.

Padre is the Spanish word for father. Roman Catholic priests are called "Father," and thus Padre. Chaplain (Lt. Col.) Martin was of the Protestant persuasion — a Presbyterian, or an Episcopal, or maybe a Lutheran, Hanrahan

552

thought; not a Baptist. Chaplain Martin had a cultivated taste for French cognac — and preferred to be addressed as "Chaplain" or "Colonel."

Hanrahan, who privately thought that chaplains should not wear the insignia of rank, because it made their relationships with enlisted men that of officer to enlisted man, rather than shepherd to a member of the flock, called all chaplains "Padre," even if they were Jewish rabbis.

"May I speak frankly, General?"

"You know you can."

"General, I have serious concerns about Captain Oliver and Mrs. Wood."

"How so?"

"I feel they are entering this marriage impetuously."

"What gives you that idea?"

"Sir, when I spoke with them . . . I said I was going to speak frankly . . . it was obvious, forgive the bluntness, that they are very strongly attracted to one another in a physical sense."

"In heat, you mean?" Hanrahan asked, smiling.

"I wouldn't have used those words, but yes, sir."

"Doesn't it say somewhere in the Good Book that we're supposed to be fruitful, to go forth and multiply?"

"Sir, it has been my painful experience that young people often mistake that physical attraction for one another we're speaking of for love. With disastrous results later, when . . . that sort of attraction . . . disappears in the realities of marriage."

"I'm sure that's true," Hanrahan agreed.

"General, as you know, with your approval, it has been my policy that when young people come to me for prenuptial counseling, I invariably ask them to think it over, prayerfully, for two weeks, and then come back."

"I think that's a very good idea," Hanrahan said.

"When I suggested this to Captain Oliver and Mrs. Wood, Captain Oliver said that he was getting married tomorrow — which is today — whether by me in the chapel, or by the nearest justice of the peace."

"That's what he said, huh?"

"And Mrs. Wood seems equally determined."

"Well, he's going on TDY tomorrow for a couple of weeks," Hanrahan said. "Obviously, he wants to tie the knot before he goes."

"Several weeks of separation might be just what the situation calls for," Chaplain Martin said. "It would give the both of them time to cool off . . . that was an unfortunate choice of words, forgive me . . . think things over seriously."

"So what you're thinking of is declining to perform the ceremony?"

"What I'm thinking of, General — and I realize this is an imposition — is that you speak with Captain Oliver."

"Padre, at sixteen hundred hours this afternoon, you are going to marry them in the chapel," Hanrahan said. "That's what they call an order."

"Yes, sir."

"Believe me, Padre, those two have really given this a whole hell of a lot of thought. And with a little bit of luck — he is an officer and a gentleman, after all — he will refrain from sprinkling any more pollen on her until after the wedding and the reception. Which Mrs. Hanrahan and I are giving at the O Club, and to which you

554

are, of course, invited."

"Yes, sir."

"Anything else, Padre?"

Captain Martin got out of the chair, came to attention, and saluted.

"No, sir," he said. "By your leave, sir?"

"Granted," Hanrahan said, and returned the salute.

Chaplain (Lt. Col.) Martin executed a perfect about-face movement and marched out of the office.

[FIVE]
Room 637, The Executive Office Building
Washington, D.C.
1045 28 January 1965

"Major Lunsford on two-two, Colonel," Mary Margaret Dunne said.

Felter grabbed the red secure phone on his desk before he remembered Mary Margaret had said "two-two." He dropped the red phone, picked up the black, multiline phone and punched the illuminated button.

"Felter."

"Lunsford, sir. The line is not secure."

"Go."

"Sir, how would you feel about me sending Doubting Thomas to Supo instead of south?"

"Reasoning?"

"I don't want Colonel Supo to have second thoughts," Lunsford said. "The sooner we get him the airplane, the better, and once he's got it, he's sort of committed."

"And Doubting Thomas and Supo are going to get along?"

"Master Sergeants understand master sergeants, sir."

"And Supo and what's the captain's name?"

"Smythe, sir. I don't think that's going to be a problem. Oliver likes him."

"Do it," Felter ordered, then asked, "What's the status of the L-19?"

"It's painted, sir," Lunsford said. "And the radios are in. Smythe wonders why we can't fly it here at night, instead of waiting for the Air Force."

"Do it."

"Yes, sir."

"Any problems with the trip down south?"

"No, sir. Departure is scheduled for 1400 29 January; ETA they don't know, but probably no later than 2 February. It's about thirty-six hours in the air."

"Keep me advised."

"Yes, sir."

"Anything else?"

"I'd like to go on the 130 with the L-19, sir. Put Supo together with Smythe and Thomas."

"Let me think about that. Oliver will be south with Portet. Who'd be minding the store?"

"Yes, sir."

"Anything else?"

"Oliver's getting married at sixteen hundred, sir."

"To the lady who lost her husband?"

"Yes, sir."

"Does General Bellmon know?"

"I don't know, sir. Perhaps Marjorie told him. Or Mrs. Bellmon. I'll find out for sure, sir."

"I'll handle it. Anything else?"

"No, sir."

Felter hung up without another word.

"Mary Margaret?" he called.

"She's in the ladies' room, Colonel," Warrant Officer Finton called, then appeared in the door.

"Call the Air Force, lay on a Lear for right now. Destination, Fort Bragg and possibly Fort Rucker first. They can drop me and pick me up later."

"Yes, sir."

Felter reached for the red secure telephone.

"Get me General Bellmon at Fort Rucker," he ordered when the White House operator came on the line.

[SIX]
Office of the Deputy Director
The Central Intelligence Agency
Langley, Virginia
1115 28 January 1965

"Thanks for fitting me in, Paul," Howard W. O'Connor, the assistant director for administration of the Central Intelligence Agency said to the deputy director.

"Happy to," the deputy director said. "But I have to be in the District not later than half past twelve. What's on your mind?"

"Egg on my face," O'Connor said.

"How did it get there?" the deputy director asked with a smile.

"Multiple choice," O'Connor said. "Carelessness, stupidity, incompetence, or all of the above."

The deputy director smiled again, and wiggled his fingers in a sign for O'Connor to go on.

"What are we talking about?"

"Intercontinental Air Cargo."

"The last I heard about that is that you'd found the guy you wanted to run it, and Gresham Investments was about to make him an offer."

"That's right."

"But there has been a bump on the road, I gather?"

"The guy they — which means me, Paul, I'm the deputy director for administration, I'm responsible — the guy *I* came up with is Captain Jean-Phillipe Portet."

"So you told me. And cutting to the chase?"

"Che Guevara and Colonel Sanford T. Felter," O'Connor said. "I am, as you know, reporting on Guevara's whereabouts to Felter. . . ."

"I took that call from President Johnson myself," the deputy director said. "What's it got to do with this?"

"Felter has an operation going called Operation Earnest, the purpose of which is to stop Guevara in the Congo."

"We're off on a tangent, aren't we?"

"I'm beginning to think that Felter may be onto something. Guevara's been all over Africa. You know that."

"I still don't think he's going to try anything in the Congo; all he's doing is public relations."

"I suppose you've read the unconfirmeds from Havana that they're recruiting black troops for an international peace force?"

"I have, always keeping in mind the operative word is 'unconfirmed.' "

"Felter has just come back from the Congo. He went there to change Mobutu's mind about no American troops in the Congo. . . ."

"Don't tell me he was successful?"

"He got General Mobutu to agree to take a small

team of Special Forces types. He's already got people training at Bragg to go over there. You know what — more precisely, who — changed his mind?"

"Go on."

"Captain Jean-Philippe Portet."

"How did he get involved?"

"It gets worse. Portet's son, I have just found out, is a Green Beret lieutenant assigned to Operation Earnest."

"Felter's operation, right?"

O'Connor nodded. "Father and son went to the Congo with Felter, and now Mobutu's letting a Special Forces team in to deal with Guevara."

"How 'deal'?"

"Felter thinks he should be frustrated, humiliated, not terminated."

"I don't think I agree."

"The President does. Felter also sent a light colonel named Lowell to Argentina to talk the Argentines out of eliminating Guevara."

"They'll have a hard time doing that, fortunately. When the Argentines, in their own good time, take out one of their own named Guevara, it will solve a lot of our problems."

"This Colonel Lowell is an interesting chap. . . ."

"I've heard the name."

"His father-in-law is General von Greiffenberg."

"That is interesting."

"Felter is about to send a small Army airplane down there and a couple of ex–Cuban Army officers now in Special Forces to work with the Argentines. That wouldn't be happening if the Argentines weren't going along."

"Damn!"

"And guess who's flying the airplane down there? Young Lieutenant Portet."

"How good is your information, Howard?"

"Five all the way. State routinely gets copies of orders sending Army officers out of the country not in connection with a troop movement. And of augmentation to defense attaché staffs. I have a friend over there. They're as unhappy with Felter as we are."

"Unfortunately, President Johnson is happy with him."

"We have to consider that Felter is entirely capable of dropping into one of their private conversations that we're setting up young Portet's daddy in a covert airline."

"What's young Portet got to do with the President?"

"When the Belgians parachuted into Stanleyville, one of them was young Portet in a Belgian uniform. The King of the Belgians, and Mobutu, are giving him medals. The President thinks young Portet is the all-American boy of fame and legend."

"That goddamn Felter has his nose in everything," the deputy director said.

"The conversation I don't want to take place is as follows," O'Connor said. "Felter: The Agency is bankrolling another Air America–type airline. Maybe this one they can keep secret. Johnson: How do you know that? Felter: The front man is young Portet's father. Chuckle, chuckle. They don't know I know, or who Captain Portet is."

"Shit," the deputy director said bitterly. "You're right, Howard, you should have known about the Portets, *pere et fils*."

"The last word I had was that the son was a

560

draftee private taking basic training, and his step-mother and half sister had just been rescued from Stanleyville."

"I thought you just said he was an officer?"

"When he came back from the Congo, they commissioned him," O'Connor said.

"I'll have to bring the director in on this," the deputy director said. "And he will ask me what I think should be done. What are the choices?"

"I tell the Gresham Investment Corporation to terminate their negotiations with Portet as of the day before yesterday —"

"Which would give us this conversation: Mr. President, chuckle, chuckle, I guess the Agency just found out the man they were setting up to run a really covert airline, since Air America has become sort of an open secret, is all-American boy Portet's father. They broke off negotiations just as they were about to write the check. For some reason, chuckle, chuckle, they don't seem to want to have anything to do with me. Pity, he really could have done a good job for him."

"Yeah," O'Connor agreed.

"Or," the deputy director said, "you get on the telephone in the next few minutes, and you tell Dick Leonard that you're sick and tired of their feet-dragging with Portet, and to get off the dime."

O'Connor considered that for a long moment.

"That's another possibility," he said. "Which would give us this conversation: You, or the director himself: Mr. President, I thought you might be interested in knowing that we've set up another covert airline, now that Air America isn't the secret we hoped it would be. And we've found a fine man to run it for us, as a partner. All sorts of

561

the right kind of experience, and, as a matter of interest, the father of that fine young all-American boy who jumped with the Belgians on Stanleyville. Oh, sure, Mr. President, we knew all about that."

The deputy director picked up on the imaginary conversation: "Me, or the director: As we knew all about Felter being in the Congo, and his man Lowell in Argentina, we still feel that it's highly unlikely that Guevara's going to cause any serious trouble in the Congo, but we can't be too careful, can we?"

Howard W. O'Connor grunted approvingly and smiled.

"I like that conversation a lot better," the deputy director said. "If Portet's holding out for something — money, whatever — give it him. Get it done."

"It's done."

"Just to be sure, keep me advised. Off paper."

"Certainly."

The deputy director looked at his watch.

"I've got to get going," he said. He looked at O'Connor. "Try not to get any more egg on your face, Howard."

[SEVEN]
Pope Air Force Base
Fort Bragg, North Carolina
1325 29 January 1965

Mrs. Marjorie Bellmon Portet, Mrs. Elizabeth Wood Oliver, Mrs. Carmen Sanchez Otmanio, Captain Stefan Zabrewski, and Warrant Officer Junior Grade Julio Zammoro drank coffee in the VIP lounge in the Base Operations building while waiting for the pilots — and other interested parties — to finalize the flight plan of the first leg — Fort Bragg–Fort Lauderdale, Florida — of their flight to Buenos Aires.

The room was furnished with chrome, plastic-upholstered chairs and couches, a coffee machine, a television set, and two coffee tables, on which sat an array of out-of-date magazines. A speaker mounted high on the wall relayed the radio traffic of the Pope tower.

Captains, warrant officers junior grade, and the wives of captains, lieutenants, and sergeants first class are not normally given access to the VIP lounge, but the AOD, a major, on duty had heard Brigadier General Paul R. Hanrahan order Captain Zabrewski to "take the ladies and Zam in there while we're in flight planning" and was highly unlikely to challenge the general's desires.

Through the window they could see three soldiers — two of them Green Berets — in camouflage fatigues stuffing luggage into an L-23 parked on the transient ramp. They were Major George Washington "Father" Lunsford; SFC Jorge Otmanio, and Captain Darrell J. Smythe, who had already become known to the team as "Aunt Jemima."

There wasn't much luggage. Weight was a real consideration. There was a uniform and a set of civilian clothing for each of the five who would be aboard, plus linen for three days and toilet gear.

Six footlockers labeled PRIORITY and addressed to the U.S. Army attaché, Buenos Aires, had been entrusted on Thursday to the Air Force, which flew a weekly round-robin around South America delivering cargo and sometimes passengers to the various embassies.

563

They contained the uniforms, civilian clothing, and personal gear Zammoro, de la Santiago, and Otmanio would need to stay in Buenos Aires, and additional clothing and uniforms for Oliver and Portet to use while they were there. There was no promise when the footlockers would actually arrive in Buenos Aires.

Planning the flight had mostly taken place in the kitchen of the Portet apartment, with time-outs for various distractions, including the wedding and reception of Captain and Mrs. John S. Oliver, Jr.

The first leg, Fort Bragg–Fort Lauderdale, was, in comparison to the rest of the trip, about as complicated as driving to a gas station and filling up. From there on, it got complicated.

It was impossible of course, to overfly Cuba. The first fueling stop from Lauderdale would be South Cariocas Island, which was 635 miles from Fort Lauderdale and about 250 miles northeast of the U.S. Naval Base at Guantánamo, on the eastern tip of Cuba. This would be about a four-hour flight in the L-23, which cruised at about 150 knots. If they left Fort Lauderdale as planned at 0800, they would make South Cariocas about noon.

Landing there posed no problems, because South Cariocas was a British possession, and there was a long-standing bilateral agreement that military aircraft of one nation could land at airfields of the other.

If they took off, as planned, from Cariocas at 1400, it would be a four-hour flight to cover the 600 miles to St. Maarten in the Leeward Islands. The Netherlands and France have shared administration of the island since 1648. To get permission to land there and at Paramaribo, Suriname, in Dutch Guinea, Mary Margaret Dunne had had to go the Netherlands Embassy in Washington. Colonel Felter had brought the documentation with him when he arrived at Bragg in a presidential Lear jet, with General and Mrs. Bellmon aboard, "coincidentally" just in time to witness the Oliver/Wood nuptials.

They would spend the night in St. Maarten, Jack had decided, both because they could probably get a much better dinner in St. Maarten than they could have in Port of Spain, their next stop, and because by then, they would have spent eight hours–plus in the L-23 and be tired.

If they left St. Maarten at 0730, as planned, they could make the 520 miles to Port of Spain, Trinidad, by noon. Trinidad, off the northeast tip of Venezuela, was a British possession and there was no problem landing there.

From Port of Spain to Paramaribo, Suriname, was 560 miles, or another four hours. If they left Port of Spain at 1330, as planned, it would take them four hours — until 1730, or thereabouts — to Belém, on the northern coast of Brazil.

The military attaché of the Brazilian Embassy in Washington, who handled military flight permissions over Brazil, smilingly told Mary Margaret that his friend, the U.S. military attaché at the U.S. Embassy in Brasília, would be green with envy and probably red in the face as well, when he heard that he was going to be asked to provide overnight accommodations for the crew of an L-23 ferrying the aircraft to the U.S. attaché in Buenos Aires. The American attaché in Brasília, he reported, had been trying for years, without success, to get an L-23 to fly between Brasília, in the center of the nation, to Río de Janeiro and Sâo Paulo, the two largest cities in Brazil, both many hundreds of miles from Brasília.

They would spent the night in Belém, before taking off at 0800 on the longest leg — right at 1,000 miles — to Brasília. That meant about seven hours in the air — approaching what Jack called the Bladder Limit Factor of the flight — but there was nothing that could be done about that except to remember to take the two empty quart plastic milk bottles from the baggage department before takeoff, and hope than no one had bowel problems.

They would spend the night in Brasília, and take off at 0800 for Sâo Paulo, on the Brazilian coast south of Río de Janeiro. That was a 550-mile leg — another four hours or so. After a quick fuel stop there, they would take off at 1230 for Pôrte Alegre, on Brazil's Atlantic Coast, not far from the Uruguayan border, another 500-odd mile, four hour, plus or minus, leg.

It was another 520 miles from Pôrto Alegre to Buenos Aires, or a final four hours in the air, most of it over Uruguay. If they could take off from Pôrto Alegre at 1800, that would put them into Ezeiza, Buenos Aires's international airfield, at 2200 or thereabouts.

"All of this," Jack had announced, "presumes that nothing will go wrong. Does anyone wish to offer me odds that nothing will go wrong?"

"You sure you want to spend twelve hours in the air the last day? And the final four hours at night?" Lt. Col. Craig W. Lowell asked. Lowell had flown up from Strike Command at McDill Air Force Base to "check final arrangements," his trip "coincidentally" permitting him to witness the

Wood/Oliver nuptials.

"Why not?" Major Pappy Hodges asked. He had flown up from Rucker in a Mohawk to review the flight plan, and had been genuinely surprised to learn this his visit coincided with the Wood/Oliver nuptials.

"There's three pilots aboard," Pappy went on. "If Oliver flies the first leg, one of the other two can sleep in the back. And the other one can on the second leg. That would put Jack and de la Santiago at the controls for the final leg. De la Santiago speaks Spanish, if that comes up. That your thinking, Jack?"

"Yes, sir," Jack said.

"You're the experts," Lowell said.

That's true, Marjorie had thought in wifely pride. Of all the pilots who had "helped" Jack with the flight planning, only Major Pappy Hodges was more experienced, and he hadn't offered a suggestion to improve — much less a criticism of — what Jack had laid out.

Captain Oliver, Lieutenant Portet, and WOJG de la Santiago came out of the flight planning room twenty minutes later. Behind them trailed General Hanrahan, Lieutenant Colonel Lowell, and Major Pappy Hodges. Everyone but General Hanrahan was wearing a flight suit and carrying a large, squarish case — much like a salesman's sample bag.

They were Jeppesen "Jepp" cases, and they contained the approach charts for every major — and just about every other — airport in the world, plus the tools of aerial navigation, and sometimes a change of linen.

Lieutenant Portet walked up to his bride, who

was trying very hard to be cheerful and pleasant, and handed his Jepp case to her.

"Hang on to it for me, will you, baby?"

"Won't you need it?" Marjorie asked, surprised.

"We only need one. We can get by with de la Santiago's," he said. "There's no sense hauling Johnny's and mine all the way to Argentina, just to haul them back."

"Sure," Marjorie said, taking the case. She immediately put it on the floor. It was heavier than it looked.

Captain Oliver handed his Jepp case to Liza without saying anything. She smiled and set it on the floor beside the other one.

"I hope, Mrs. Oliver," Lieutenant Colonel Lowell said, "that you realize how lucky you are?"

Liza eyed him suspiciously.

"How is that, Colonel?" she asked.

"Well, when the wives start swapping stories about how the Army has interfered with their marriages, you can top them all. 'I was married at four in the afternoon, and at noon the next day the Army sent my husband to Argentina.' "

"I'm not exactly the virgin bride, Colonel," Liza replied. "And knowing the Army as I do, I wasn't even surprised."

Lowell was visibly surprised at the tone of her reply, and there was an awkward silence for a moment, until General Hanrahan patted Liza's shoulder approvingly.

"Good for you," he said. "Score one for the captain's lady."

Lunsford, Smythe, and Otmanio came into the lounge, shivering and rubbing their hands.

"I have just had a cheerful thought," Lunsford announced. "It's summer in Argentina. Out there" — he nodded toward the parking ramp — "it's as cold as a witch's . . . broom handle."

Neither Mrs. Oliver, Mrs. Portet, nor Mrs. Otmanio seemed amused.

"Smythe, you about ready to go?" Pappy Hodges said.

"Yes, sir."

"Where are you going, Smythe?" General Hanrahan asked.

"Rucker, sir."

"What I meant to ask is why are you going?" Hanrahan asked.

"I'm going to bring the L-19 up here tonight, sir."

"What's that all about?" Lowell asked. "The Air Force is — somewhat reluctantly — going to pick it up at Rucker."

"Colonel, Aunt Jemima wanted to test the radios they put in at Rucker with the team's radios here," Lunsford answered.

Lowell's eyebrow rose at "Aunt Jemima," but he didn't say anything.

"You're talking about the black L-19, right?" General Hanrahan asked.

"Yes, sir."

Hanrahan stopped, and looked uneasily at the three wives, who didn't have Top Secret/Earnest security clearances.

"Captain Smythe's going to bring it up tonight, sir," Lunsford said. "Take it to Camp Mackall."

"How's he going to land it there at night?" Lowell asked.

"The team is going to improvise runway lights, sir," Smythe said.

"I don't know . . ." Lowell said.

"Sir, I have Colonel Felter's permission," Lunsford said.

"What about the Air Force picking it up at Rucker?" Lowell asked.

"Mr. Finton changed that, sir. I talked to him this morning."

Major Hodges ended the conversation.

"Let's get our circus on the road, Smythe," he ordered. "Try not to bend the bird, you guys. We can't afford to piss off another Corps Commander by stealing another one."

He tossed General Hanrahan a casual salute. Smythe saluted more crisply, and the two of them walked out of the room.

"I'll preflight it," de la Santiago said, and followed them out of the lounge.

In a moment, they could be seen walking toward a Mohawk and an L-23 on the transient tarmac.

"Have a good flight," General Hanrahan said. "The priority is to get there — don't worry about how long it takes."

He shook their hands, called "Let's go, Ski," to Captain Zabrewski, and walked toward the door.

"That was not permission to take a week in Fort Lauderdale," Father Lunsford said. "Have a good flight."

He walked out of the lounge.

Lowell took an envelope from his pocket and handed it to Johnny Oliver.

"You have the letter Felter wrote to General Pistarini?"

"Yes, sir."

"This is for Teniente Coronel Guillermo Rangio. . . ."

"The intelligence guy?" Oliver asked, to be sure.

"Deputy director of SIDE," Lowell confirmed. "I wouldn't be surprised if he was there when you land — probably not in uniform."

"May I ask what's in here, sir?"

"Another of the CIA's memos to Felter. The purpose is really to show Rangio you're in the loop."

"I understand, sir."

"If you need any help, yell," Lowell said. He turned to the women.

"For what it's worth, I really hated to send your guys off like this."

"But we're Army wives, right?" Liza said.

"That was your choice, you will recall," Lowell said. He kissed Marjorie on the cheek, shook hands with Mrs. Otmanio, nodded somewhat coldly toward Liza, and walked out of the VIP lounge.

The husbands and wives were alone.

In a moment, Lowell could be seen walking toward a U.S. Air Force T28, a single-engine tandem-seat advanced trainer.

"Hey," Oliver said. "Why the gloom? We're going to Argentina, not Vietnam, and we'll be back in a week or ten days?"

"And we have to go now," Jack said. "I hate long farewells."

Marjorie gave him a hurt look, then hugged him.

"Be careful," she said, and whispered "I love you" in his ear.

"Me, too," he said, and walked quickly out of the lounge.

"We'll have some when I get back, baby," Johnny Oliver said to his bride, and then followed.

She smiled at him but didn't reply, then hugged him.

SFC Otmanio kissed his wife, who looked to be on the edge of tears, and then followed Oliver.

Out the window, the women could see that the propellers of the Mohawk were turning. As they watched, the engine of Lowell's T-28 started in a cloud of blue smoke.

"Pope, Army Nine-three-three at Base Ops tarmac, IFR Fort Rucker, taxi and takeoff, please," Pappy Hodges voice came metallically over the speaker on the wall.

"Pope, Air Force Double-zero-four, same place, IFR McDill. Put me after the Mohawk, please," Craig Lowell's voice came over the speaker.

"Pope Army Eight-seven-seven, next to the T-28," Jack Portet's voice came over the speaker. "Let me follow the old folks out of here, please. IFR Fort Lauderdale."

It was a moment before the tower responded.

"Pope to the Mohawk. Take taxiway one to the active, Two-seven. Hold on the threshold. T-28, follow the Mohawk. Seven follow the T-28. You are cleared as one, two, and three for takeoff, one-minute intervals, after a C-130 on final. Await my clearance."

"Pope, Nine-three-three will wait for clearance at the threshold of Two-seven," Pappy responded.

Liza Wood walked to where she was standing under the speaker. Then she stood on the couch, reached up, and turned the speaker off.

She went to the window and watched as the three airplanes moved off the tarmac. Marjorie walked up and stood beside her, and so, finally, did Mrs. Otmanio.

A C-130 came out of the sky a moment later and touched down. A minute later, Pappy's Mohawk turned onto the runway and, without slowing down, began to move down it, finally lifting into the air. A minute later, the T-28 took off, and a minute after that, the L-23.

Liza looked at Marjorie, shrugged, and then walked to where she had put Johnny's Jepp case down and picked it up. Marjorie exhaled audibly and walked to Jack's Jepp case and picked it up.

Mrs. Otmanio stood with her forehead pressed against the window.

Liza and Marjorie looked at each other, set the Jepp cases on the floor again, walked to Mrs. Otmanio, and put their arms around her until she stopped crying.

[EIGHT]

Jack Portet was in the left seat and de la Santiago in the right, but Johnny Oliver, who was in the back with Otmanio and Zammoro, like most other pilots, never fully trusted any other pilot, and waited until the L-23 was at 10,500 feet, trimmed up, on course, and on autopilot before satisfying his curiosity about what the CIA report he was to pass to the intelligence guy in Argentina said.

He opened the envelope and took it out and read it.

S E C R E T

Central Intelligence Agency
Langley, Virginia

573

FROM: Assistant Director For Administration

DATE: 28 January 1965 1345 GMT

SUBJECT: Guevara, Ernesto (Memorandum # <u>39</u>.)

TO: Mr. Sanford T. Felter
Counselor To The President
Room 637, The Executive Office Building
Washington, D.C.

By Courier

In compliance with Presidential Memorandum to The Director, Subject: "Ernesto 'Che' Guevara," dated 14 December 1964, the following information is furnished:

(Reliability Scale Five) (From CIA Algiers, Algeria) SUBJECT arrived Algiers on Air Mali flight 1121 from Cotonou, Dahomey at 2005 GMT 27 January 1965, and went directly to Cuban Embassy.

Howard W. O'Connor
HOWARD W. O'CONNOR

S E C R E T

He handed the document to Zammoro and then unstrapped himself and went forward to kneel behind Portet.

"At the risk of revealing my monumental ignorance, where the hell is Cotonou, Dahomey?"

"On the Gulf of Guinea, between Nigeria and Togo," de la Santiago answered. "Why?"

"Where the hell is the Gulf of Guinea?" Oliver asked. "And, for that matter, where is, or what is, Togo?"

"West Coast, Atlantic. Togo is a country," de la Santiago answered, chuckling.

"Why do you think Che Guevara went to Cotonou, Dahomey?" Oliver asked.

"Beats the shit out of me," Jack Portet replied. "I didn't know anybody went there on purpose."

De la Santiago chuckled.

"If he's there —" Jack added, his tone now serious.

"*Was* there. Now he's in Algeria," Oliver interrupted.

"If he *was* in Dahomey," Jack went on, "and is now in Algeria, I guess that proves Felter was right. He damned sure wasn't in Cotonou to take a swim. There's a lot of sharks in the ocean there. The sonofabitch is obviously trying to get support for what he wants to do in the Congo."

"And we're supposed to stop him? How?" Oliver asked.

"Hell, I thought you Green Beanies can do anything," Jack said.

"That's *we* Green Beanies, Lieutenant," Oliver said. "Write that down."

"I know how to stop him," de la Santiago said. "I'd love to stop him. But blowing the bastard's brains out is a no-no, isn't it?"

"I'm sure you will think of something else,

Mr. de la Santiago," Oliver said, and went back to his seat.

[NINE]
Apartment B-14
Foster Garden Apartments
Fayetteville, North Carolina
1545 29 January 1965

"Tank! Tank! Tank!" Master Allan Wood cried the moment Marjorie had unlocked the door to the apartment.

He had been under the grandmotherly care of Patricia Hanrahan while they had seen their husbands off from Pope.

Marjorie smiled.

"A true son of armor," she said, and led the child to the couch, behind which the toy tanks had been parked.

"A male," Liza said. "They like to destroy things, preferably with as much noise as possible."

Marjorie's smile tightened, but she didn't say anything.

She knelt on the floor and found the switch that turned the battery on. Allan gleefully drove the tank into the leg of the coffee table, where the treads churned uselessly.

She went into the kitchen to get him a couple of plastic cups, which he could batter around with the tank.

Liza Wood was squatting before the open refrigerator door.

"There's enough food left over to feed an army," Liza said. "Unfortunately, our Army is on its way to sunny Florida and points farther south."

576

"Well, at least we won't have to cook," Marjorie said.

"I knew there would be beer in here," Liza said. "You want one, or would you prefer something stronger?"

"Beer's fine," Marjorie said.

She found the plastic cups she was looking for, and took them to Allan. When she returned, she saw that Liza had taken two bottles of Heineken from the refrigerator and opened them. Liza handed one to Marjorie and then took a healthy pull from the bottle's neck.

"Don't you want a glass?" Marjorie asked.

"Why?" Liza asked taking another swig. "When it's only us camp followers, what's the point in being dainty and ladylike?"

"Liza," Marjorie said. "I'm in no mood for bitter."

Liza looked at her and shrugged.

"Sorry," she said. "You know what I thought on the way here?"

"I'm not sure I do," Marjorie said.

"I asked myself, did I do the right thing?" Liza said. "And I decided, yeah, Liza, you did the right thing. You love him and he needs you, and Allan needs him, and he loves Allan, and if the price I have to pay for that is putting on a smile while I wave bye-bye, then it's a hell of a bargain."

"Yeah, it is," Marjorie agreed.

"One last bitter," Liza said, "and then I'll quit."

"Okay."

"You know one thing the Army has got down pat? The better an officer is, the more they expect of him, the more they drain him."

Marjorie didn't reply.

"Think about it," Liza said. "Johnny — who

577

was pretty well drained himself by his year working your father — told me what terrible shape Father Lunsford was in when he came back from the Congo. Did Father get a plush, sit-on-his-ass-and-play-golf assignment? Hell, no. Neither of them did. Your Jack did a John Wayne in Stanleyville, and what happened? 'Pin a bar on that one, we can squeeze him a lot more.' "

"What's your point?"

"No point, I just felt like saying that."

"Okay. And for what it's worth, I agree. But that was the last bitter, agreed?"

"Agreed," Liza said, and walked to Marjorie and tapped her beer bottle against hers. "From now on, all will be sweetness and light."

There was the sound of door chimes.

"Who the hell can that be?" Marjorie asked.

She walked to the door and opened it, carefully concealing her beer bottle behind the door.

Two women in their late twenties were standing in the corridor, in heels, good dresses, hats, and white gloves.

"Hello," Marjorie said.

"Mrs. Portet?"

"That's pronounced 'Por-tay,' but yes."

"I'm Helen Davidson, and this is Paula McCarthy," the other woman said. "Welcome to the ranks of Army wives."

"I beg your pardon?"

"We're the co-chairladies of the Welcome New Wives Committee," Mrs. Davidson said. "Our honorary chairlady is Doris Lowze."

When that obviously rang no bell with Marjorie, Mrs. McCarthy quickly said, "Doris Lowze. General Lowze is assistant division commander of the

Eighty-Second Airborne."

"What can I do for you, ladies?" Marjorie asked.

"May we come in?" Mrs. Davidson said. "We were here earlier, and you weren't in." This statement came out as an accusation.

"Certainly," Marjorie said, and immediately regretted it.

"Oh, what a nice apartment," Mrs. McCarthy said. "When Jack and I were married — we were married right after he graduated from the Military Academy — we didn't have anything nearly as nice as this."

Liza came out of the kitchen holding her beer bottle.

"These ladies are the co-chairladies of the Welcome Wives Committee —"

"That's Welcome *New* Wives Committee," Mrs. Davidson corrected her.

"Well, you certainly came to the right place," Liza said. "Can we offer you a beer?"

"This is my friend, Liza Wood," Marjorie said.

"Thank you, but no thank you," Mrs. McCarthy said. "Actually, I've found it best to avoid alcohol until the cocktail hour."

"Have you really?" Liza asked.

"Especially when there is going to be a social event later on, during which alcohol will be served," Mrs. McCarthy said.

"Which is why we're here, actually," Mrs. Davidson said. "Mrs. Lowze feels that it's very important to get new wives involved as soon as possible. I really hope you don't have plans for tonight."

"Actually," Liza said. "Not a goddamn one. How about you, Marjie, baby?"

"The monthly Welcome New Wives Get To Know One Another cocktail party is tonight, Mrs. Portet — Por-tay," Mrs. McCarthy said, "and Mrs. Lowze would really be very disappointed. . . ."

"She really would," Mrs. Davidson chimed in. "She asked us to make a special effort to find you and make sure you came."

"How did you find me?" Marjorie asked.

"The sergeant at POV registration gave us your address," Mrs. McCarthy said.

"Is he supposed to do that?" Marjorie asked.

"Well, of course, dear," Mrs. Davidson said. "Otherwise, he wouldn't have, right?"

"And whose adorable little boy is that?" Mrs. McCarthy asked.

"Mine," Liza said. "Marjorie hasn't been married long enough to have a rug rat of her own."

"Your husband's not in the Army, I take it?" Mrs. Davidson asked. "Mrs. Wood, is it?"

"Actually, it's Mrs. Oliver," Liza said. "And actually, yes, he's in the Army."

"But not stationed at Fort Bragg?"

"Actually, yes, he is stationed at Fort Bragg."

"I can't imagine why we don't have your name on our list," Mrs. McCarthy said.

"Actually, neither can I," Liza said. "Does that mean I don't get to come to the party?"

"Really, ladies," Marjorie said. "While we both appreciate the invitation, and please thank . . . Mrs. Lowze, you said? . . . for thinking about us —"

"What time is this affair, actually?" Liza asked.

"Seventeen thirty," Mrs. McCarthy said. "At the Main Officers' Club, on the main post. Do

580

you know where that is?"

"And there's child care, of course," Mrs. Davidson said. "Right next to the Club."

"Oh, the kid can't come to the party?" Liza asked.

"Mrs. . . . Oliver, you said?"

"That's right."

"This is a cocktail party for the ladies. No children."

"Perhaps the next time, ladies," Marjorie said.

"Nonsense," Liza said. "We'll be there with bells on."

"The suggested dress is a dressy dress, hat, and gloves," Mrs. Davidson said.

"Well, if it's inconvenient, perhaps it might be best if you did wait until next month's Get To Know One Another," Mrs. McCarthy said.

"I think I can scrounge up a dressy dress, hat, and gloves," Liza said. "How about you, Marjie, baby?"

"I don't know, Liza," Marjorie said.

"Nonsense, we'll find something," Liza said. "What time did you say the bar opened?"

"Actually, the procedure is that you first go through the reception line," Mrs. Davidson said, "and then, if you like, you can have a cocktail."

"Or two, or three?" Liza asked.

"However many as you would like, of course," Mrs. Davidson said, rather coldly.

"If you would wait for us in the foyer, we'll take you through the reception line," Mrs. McCarthy said.

"That's before I can go to the bar, right?"

"That would be better, Mrs. Oliver," Mrs. McCarthy said. "And now, if you'll excuse us?"

"You sure you don't want a little nip for the road?" Liza asked.

Mrs. McCarthy and Mrs. Davidson declined and left the apartment.

"How many of those have you had?" Marjorie demanded. "My God, Liza!"

"This is the first and only," Liza said. "I haven't been so happy since the Chaplain said, 'I pronounce you man and wife.' "

"What?"

"I hate women like that," Liza said. "How long did it take her to tell you her husband went to Hudson High and that she was here at the orders of Mrs. General Whatsisname? Twenty seconds?"

"Closer to ten," Marjorie said, smiling.

"And from now until we show up out there, they'll be worried sick that we're going to show up smashed and cause a scene that'll get them on Mrs. General Whatsisname's shitlist."

"I'm not going out there with you if you're going to pretend to be smashed," Marjorie said. "Much less really smashed."

"You don't get it, do you? We're going to go out there and show those two quote ladies unquote how two officers' ladies, no quotes, behave."

From Liza Wood Oliver's point of view, at least, the monthly Welcome New Wives Get To Know One Another cocktail party could not have gone better.

Mrs. Davidson and Mrs. McCarthy were waiting for them in the foyer of the club. There were about thirty young women gathered in a herd to be led through the line. Both ladies were visibly surprised to find Marjorie and Liza in nearly identical simple black dresses, each with a

582

single strand of pearls.

Liza quickly managed to erase the smile of approval on Mrs. McCarthy's face by asking her if she couldn't get a quick one in the bar, then come back to go through the reception line.

"Please just take your place with the others, dear," Mrs. McCarthy said, and placed Marjorie and Liza at the end of what would be the line passing the senior officers' wives.

As the line started to move, Liza grabbed Marjorie's arm and went to the head of the line.

Short of wrestling Liza to the floor, there was nothing Mrs. McCarthy could do.

There were seven senior officers' wives in the line, lined up according to their husbands' rank, with the most junior closest to the door.

This turned out to be Mrs. General Lowze. Mrs. General Hanrahan was third in line.

Following Mrs. McCarthy's rather precise directions, Mrs. Oliver and Mrs. Portet gave their names to Mrs. General Lowze and the general's wife (Mrs. 82nd Division artillery commander) standing beside her.

Both ladies said they were very happy to make their acquaintance.

The third general's lady leaned forward and kissed Mrs. Oliver, and then Mrs. Portet.

"I didn't expect to see you two here," Patricia Hanrahan said. "Good for you."

She then turned to the ladies to her right, who were Mrs. 82nd Division Commander, Mrs. Assistant XVIII Airborne Corps Commander, and Mrs. XVIII Airborne Corps Commander herself.

"I think you all know Marjorie Portet, Bob Bellmon's daughter," she called out, "and I know you all knew his aide, Captain Johnny Oliver. This is the brand-new Mrs. Johnny Oliver, Liza."

The orderly flow of the reception line was interrupted for a good three minutes, while the two brides received the best wishes of the senior officers' ladies.

Neither Mrs. Davidson nor Mrs. McCarthy found occasion to speak with Mrs. Oliver or Mrs. Portet for the remainder of the Get To Know festivities.

XV

[ONE]
Office of the Chairman of the Board
Craig, Powell, Kenyon & Dawes
101 Wall Street
New York City, New York
1525 29 January 1965

Porter Craig, when he saw the light flashing on one of his telephones, pushed the lever of his intercom.

"Gladys, that had better be important. I am savoring my very last cup of coffee. I won't get any on the plane, or in Florida."

"Mrs. Porter is just trying to keep you alive, I can't imagine why. It's the Colonel. What do I tell him?"

"You're a lady, Gladys. I can't use the language I'd like to."

He leaned forward and reached for the telephone.

"Good morning Craig," he said. "And how are you going to ruin what so far has been a nearly perfect half-day?"

"Aside from getting fall-down drunk, what are your plans for the weekend?"

"Florida. Geoff is flying Ursula and the baby down to Ocean Reef in your airplane. If you could tear yourself away from whatever war you're fighting this weekend, you're of course welcome."

"Wonderful!" Craig Lowell said.

"Why am I suspicious about 'wonderful'?"

"And you're going down when?"

"I was just about to leave for the airport."

"I accept your kind invitation," Lowell said. "I'll fly down either tonight or first thing in the morning."

"And why does that also make me suspicious?"

"Because you are insecure," Lowell said. "I've told you that many times before."

"What the hell do you want, Craig?"

"I just had a call from Jean-Philippe Portet," Lowell said. "Mr. J. Richard Leonard of the Gresham Investment Corporation just called him, and wants to present their proposal to him tomorrow."

"What's that got to do with me?"

"I think he could use some advice in dealing with them."

"He's at Ocean Reef?"

"Yeah."

"Why me?"

"Hey, Porter, you're the one who's been whining about not being able to properly express your gratitude. . . ."

"I meant, why don't I bring someone — Hoover Daniel, for example, he's our legal VP — down with me?"

"Christ, if you can't negotiate a contract, Porter, what are you doing sitting at Grandpa's desk?"

"I want the very best for Jean-Philippe, Craig, is what I mean."

"Jean-Philippe will take your help as a friend," Lowell said. "I think he might say 'thanks but no thanks' about Daniel."

"Yeah," Porter Craig agreed grudgingly. "What

do I do? Walk over to his house and say I understand you need some contract advice and here I am, you lucky fellow?"

"I'm going to call him right back," Lowell said, "and tell him you and I are going to be down there, and suggest he ask you to sit in on the negotiations. I think he'll be grateful. If he isn't, I'll tell him what a dumb shit he's being."

[TWO]
33 Ocean View Drive
The Ocean Reef Club
Key Largo, Florida
1530 30 January 1965

"Where's Jean-Philippe?" Lieutenant Colonel Craig Lowell asked when Porter Craig, in tennis whites, came into his home and found his son and cousin floating in truck tire inner tubes in the pool.

"Having a shower," Porter said. "He will be here directly."

"So what happened?"

"That will have to wait until I have my shower, and Jean-Philippe shows up," Porter said. "Suffice it to say, for the moment, that I am going to stop by the kitchen and make sure there is champagne on ice."

"It must have gone well," Craig Lowell said to Lieutenant Geoff Craig. "Your old man is never that happy unless he has evicted a widow, or otherwise destroyed somebody financially."

"We didn't do too bad," Porter Craig said. "I'll tell you that."

He walked off in the direction of the kitchen.

"I would now like to propose a toast," Porter Craig said, raising his champagne glass fifteen minutes later. He was now wearing a short-sleeved shirt of many colors and pink slacks. Captain Jean-Philippe Portet was wearing a polo shirt and seersucker slacks. Colonel Lowell and Lieutenant Portet were still in their bathing suits.

"To our very good friend, Jean-Philippe, the new president of Intercontinental Air Holding, Ltd.," Porter Craig said, "a Bahamas corporation which is going to make everybody a little money."

"The translation of that is that your old man just screwed the CIA," Lowell said.

"You remember Granddad always saying that it's very hard to cheat an honest man?" Porter said.

"And God knows, he tried often enough," Lowell said.

Geoff and Jean-Philippe chuckled.

"That's not true, and you know it," Porter said.

"Are you just going to stand there and smirk in self-satisfaction, Porter?" Lowell asked. "Or tell us what happened?"

"He's entitled to smirk, Craig," Jean-Philippe said. "He was magnificent!"

"What the hell happened, for Christ's sake?" Geoff asked.

"I want you to hear this, son," Porter said.

"Hear what?" Lowell egged him.

"The greatest advantages one can have in negotiations are for the other party to think (a) that your position is weaker than it actually is and (b) that your knowledge of the situation is less than his and (c) that you are not nearly as smart as he is. We had all three going for us."

"Leonard showed up with a lawyer," Jean-Philippe said. "A fellow named Eichold. He said he was there to help me explain the details of what they were going to propose."

"How did you explain Chubby here?" Lowell asked.

"I told them I was his tennis buddy and down-the-road neighbor," Porter said, visibly pleased with himself. "I told them I was in real estate, and had handled a contract or two, and that he asked me to sit in."

"Craig," Helene Craig said, "I've asked you again and again not to call him that."

"Put him on a diet, Helene," Lowell replied, then asked: "What did they propose?"

"What they've done is set up a Bahamas corporation," Porter explained, "Intercontinental Air Holding, Ltd., capitalized at three million, already paid in. They used not quite two million to purchase all the assets of Intercontinental Air, a Delaware Corporation, based at Miami. The assets consist primarily of a Boeing 707 and two Douglas DC-7s, all configured for cargo, and a lease on a hangar with office space. Getting to the bottom line, the people who owned Intercontinental Air walked away with about half a million, since the debt on the aircraft was about 1.5 million."

"This is going over my head," Mrs. Helene Craig said.

"All you have to do, my darling," Porter said, "is sit there and be beautiful and make sure the champagne flows."

"Go to hell, Porter," she said.

"They have also set up a Delaware corporation," Porter went on, "Intercontinental Air Cargo, Inc., which is a wholly owned subsidiary of Intercontinental Air Ltd., and at the moment has zero assets."

"What shape is the 707 in?" Lowell asked.

"So-so. The engines are half gone," Jean-Philippe said. "And it's getting pretty close to its annual. It was one of the airplanes I looked at when I went out there . . . before Leonard found me. The DC-7s are pretty well down the road to rebuild."

"Leonard didn't know that," Porter said. "I mean he didn't know there was as much useful life left in the 707 as Jean-Philippe did."

"What did they propose?" Lowell asked.

"What they proposed was thirty-three percent to Jean-Philippe for his services as president," Porter said. "What we agreed on was thirty-five percent to Jean-Philippe, who will be in any case the chief operating officer, subject to the orders of the president, who will be elected by the stockholders."

"You're losing me here," Lowell said. "They'll have sixty-five percent of the votes."

"Jean-Philippe has the option of purchasing additional stock, when and if the sale of Air Simba goes through, before a sixty-day period has elapsed. They were happy to grant that, inasmuch as they think Mobutu has Jean-Philippe over a barrel, and there won't be any sale within sixty days, even at distress prices," Porter said.

"And?"

"Just as soon as the contracts are signed — and they can't back out; we have a memorandum of agreement; they wouldn't want us to take that to federal court for noncompliance — Jean-Philippe hands them a check for a million . . . maybe, just to be sure, a million point five. That gives him enough votes to elect himself president."

"Where does he get the million point five? From

us?" Lowell asked.

"Yes, of course. We loan him a million point five against Air Simba. And then we wait Mobutu out. As long as Mobutu eventually comes through with a million five, and Air Simba's worth, bottom figure, at least twice that, we can wash our hands. For an investment of a million five, plus his services, Jean-Philippe gets control of Intercontinental Air Ltd., with assets of over two million."

"They're going to want to buy aircraft for the new company," Lowell said. "What about that?"

"That can be handled in several ways," Porter said. "As president, Jean-Philippe will have the authority to either borrow money to purchase aircraft, to lease aircraft, or to offer additional stock to raise the necessary capital. What I think will happen is that if President Portet is unwilling to offer additional stock, and the stockholders go along with him —"

"And he will have the votes to say 'no way', won't he?" Lowell said, smiling. "Porter, I take back most of the unkind things I've been saying about you over the years."

"— Mr. Leonard's associates will have the choice between leasing aircraft, which I don't think they'll want to do, because people who lease aircraft want to know where they'll be flown and why," Porter went on, "or finding someone from whom to borrow the money, who won't ask questions." He paused and smiled. "I have always wanted to borrow money from my government at a favorable rate."

"Give Chubby both ears and the tail," Lowell said.

"The trick is to give Jean-Philippe at least fifty-one percent of the stock immediately after we sign the contracts," Porter said.

"I owe you more than both ears and the tail," Jean-Philippe said.

"You don't owe me a goddamn thing," Porter Craig said. "You're family, Jean-Philippe."

"If someone will hand us the bottle," Lowell said, "Lieutenant Craig and myself will drink to that."

[THREE]
Over the River Plate
(Argentine–Uruguayan Border)
2245 2 February 1965

"Buenos Aires approach control," WOJG Enrico de la Santiago said into his microphone, "this is U.S. Army Eight-seven-seven, a Beechcraft Twin Bonanza, at 7,000 over the River Plate with Buenos Aires in sight. Request approach and landing at Ezeiza, please."

"U.S. Army Eight-seven-seven, contact Campo de Mayo approach control on 122.9."

"Buenos Aires, Army Eight-seven-seven, be advised that we are international. IFR from Pôrto Alegre, Brazil. We have been instructed to request Customs and Immigration services at Ezeiza."

"U.S. Army Eight-seven-seven, you have been diverted to Campo de Mayo. Contact Campo de Mayo approach control on 122.9."

"Understand 122.9," de la Santiago said. "Thank you."

He began to tune his radio.

"What the hell is that all about?" Jack Portet asked.

"More important, where *is* Campo de Mayo?" de la Santiago said.

"Johnny," Jack called, "we have been diverted to Campo de Mayo."

Oliver got out of his seat and knelt between the pilot's and copilot's seats as Jack searched for an approach chart to Campo de Mayo.

"There it is," Oliver said, pointing to a Jeppesen Aerial Chart.

"Right in the middle of a restricted zone, and clearly marked closed to all but ArgMil traffic," Jack added.

"Mayo approach control, U.S. Army Eight-seven-seven."

"*Ocho-siete-siete aqui, Campo de Mayo, ¿cual es su posición?*"

"*Dos mil metros sobre el Río de la Plata Creo que diviso Jorge Newbery.*"

"*Roger, Ocho-siete-siete. Lo tengo en el radar. Asuma curso 310 grados, y descienda a 1000 metros en este momento.*"

"Enrico, what's going on?"

"I told him where we were — that I was over the river at 6,000; that I thought I had Jorge Newbery, the city airport, in sight. He said he has us on radar and we are to descend to 3,000 feet on a course of 310 degrees."

The plane was in a gentle bank to the right. The compass needle was pointing almost to 310 degrees.

"Call him and tell him our chart shows a restricted zone," Oliver ordered.

"*Campo de Mayo, conteste . . . conteste . . .*" de la Santiago said into his microphone, "*Campo de Mayo, aqui U.S. Army Ocho-siete-siete. Mi mapa muestra que su campo está en una zona restringida. Éste es un avión del Ejército de los Estados Unidos.*"

"*Roger, Ocho-siete-siete. Éste es un aeropuerto*

restringido. Lo tengo a 2,000 metros en un curso de 310. Está aproximadamente a ocho kilometros de esta estación. Empiece su descenso ahora por una recta de aproximacion a la pista de aterrizaje 31. El altimetro es dos nueve nueve. Los vientos son insignificantes. Informe cuando tiene la pista de aterrizaje a la vista.”

"What was all that?" Oliver asked.

"Yes," de la Santiago reported, chuckling, "this is a restricted airfield. We have you on radar. You are cleared for a straight-in to Runway 31."

"What the hell is going on?" Oliver asked, chuckling.

"We're about to find out," Jack said. "I suspect those lights dead ahead are Runway 31."

"Gear down, flaps twenty," de la Santiago ordered.

Jack reached for the controls.

"Mayo, Ocho-siete-siete," de la Santiago said to his microphone. *"Tengo pista de aterrizaje treinta y uno a la vista.”*

"Gear down and locked," Jack reported. "You have twenty degrees of flaps. Johnny, go back and strap yourself in."

"Ocho-siete-siete, tiene permiso para aterrizar. Tome la primera calle de aproximacion conveniente a su izquierda. Dirijase a la base de operaciones, debajo de la torre de Control, donde se estacionará.”

"I really have to take a piss," Jack announced.

"Mayo, Ocho-siete-siete, en tierra a cinco minutos de la hora. Somos IFR Internacional de Puerto Allegre. ¿Puede cerrar nuestro plan de vuelo?”

"Ocho-siete-siete, su plan de vuelo ha sido cerrado. Bienvenidos a Campo de Mayo.”

"The tower says welcome to Campo de Mayo," de la Santiago reported.

"My mother was right," Oliver said. "I should have paid more attention to Spanish in high school."

Uniformed ground crewmen appeared with wands and directed de la Santiago in parking the airplane.

"Shut the sonofabitch down," Jack said. "I really need to take a leak."

"Here comes somebody. Here come a lot of people," de la Santiago said.

A large man in a blue sport coat and an open-collared yellow polo shirt walked across the tarmac toward the L-23. Four steps behind him came four men, two in what looked like Air Force uniforms, and two in what suggested they were Customs or Immigration officers.

"I believe you're senior, Captain," Jack said. "You deal with the natives."

Oliver got out of the airplane first and walked to the older of the Air Force officers and saluted.

"Good evening, sir," he said. "I am Captain John S. Oliver, U.S. Army."

The salutes were returned.

"Welcome to Campo de Mayo," one of the officers said in good English.

Warrant Officer Junior Grade Julio Zammoro was next off the plane.

He walked toward Oliver and the uniformed officers, obviously to provide his services as an interpreter. He raised his hand in a salute.

"Hola, Julio," the man in the sport coat said softly.

Zammoro turned to see who had spoken. Then he stopped walking, his hand still at his forehead.

"Willi," he said softly.

WOJG Enrico de la Santiago was now out of the plane, and Jack Portet and Otmanio followed a moment later.

Zammoro and the man in the sport coat walked to each other and embraced.

"Madre de Dios, me alegro de verlo, mi amigo," the man in the sport coat said. *"He oído distintos comentarios sobre usted. Uno decia que usted estaba muerto, el otro que usted estaba en la Isla de Pinos."*

"Ricky," Jack asked de la Santiago softly, "what's going on?"

"They must be friends," de la Santiago replied. "The Argentine said he was glad to see him, that he had heard both that Zammoro was dead and on the Isle of Pines." He paused and then added, "The Isle of Pines is Castro's worst prison."

"Estoy vivo y punto."

"¿Y Dolores?"

"Está en la Isla de Pinos."

"¡Mi Dios! ¿Y los niños?"

"Lo último que oí de ellos, es que están con Maria, la hermana de Dolores."

De la Santiago, his voice tight with emotion, translated the essence of the exchange: "He asked Zammoro about his wife; Zammoro said she's on the Isle of Pines and that their children are with his wife's sister."

The man in the sport coat gave Zammorro a final kiss on the cheek and let him go.

"You're the only captain," he said to Oliver in perfect English, "so you must be Captain Oliver. I am Lieutenant Colonel Rangio, and it is my privilege to welcome you to Argentina."

Oliver saluted.

"How do you do, sir?"

Rangio turned to the uniformed officers.

"Gracias. No se requerirán sus servicios. Estos señores están conmigo. Mande a alguien al Casino en media hora, para que se encargue de todo lo relacionado a los pasaportes."

"We're with him," de la Santiago translated softly. "We're going to the officers' club. He told the immigration officers to come there in half an hour."

The uniformed officers all saluted and marched away.

"I will take pleasure in meeting you all individually," Rangio said, "but I suggest we do that at the Casino. I'm sure you all would like to visit a men's room." He paused. "In fact, there is a men's room in the hangar, if that is a pressing problem."

"Sir," Jack said. "It is a pressing problem for me."

"Then, if you will follow me, Lieutenant?" Rangio said.

"Sir," Oliver said. "Our luggage?"

"I'll have someone bring it to the Casino," Lieutenant Colonel Rangio said.

"And sir," Oliver said, nodding toward Otmanio, "Sergeant First Class Otmanio is . . . not an officer."

"In a flight suit, who will notice?" Rangio replied with a shrug.

Twenty minutes later, they were all sitting around a very large, very low, round, glass-topped table in a room off the main dining room of the Campo de Mayo Casino, the officers' club.

White-jacketed waiters had laid an array of bottles — in case anyone preferred something other than champagne — and trays of cold cuts on the table, and then left, closing the door after them.

"When your manifest came into my hands," Rangio said, "and I saw Julio's name, I wasn't sure, of course, that he was my Julio, but I thought it possible, even likely. So I asked them to chill a little wine, in case there was occasion to celebrate."

Oliver thought: *If you saw the manifest, which was classified Confidential, Colonel, that means that you have access to Confidential messages addressed to our military attaché. Did you get the manifest from the attaché, or do you have someone in the embassy?*

Oliver smiled.

"Colonel, if Zam had said something about knowing you, I'm sure Colonel Felter would have advised you."

"Is that what they call you, Julio? 'Zam'?"

"Usually, Willi, they call me something more profane," Zammoro said.

"I thought perhaps that our friendship was something you didn't want known," Rangio said. "And I thought that it might prove awkward at Ezeiza if it suddenly came out. I knew that my friend Colonel Harris planned to meet you at Ezeiza, so I had you diverted here."

"I understand," Oliver said. "But what do we do about Colonel Harris? Our orders are to report to him."

"At this very moment, Colonel Harris and his very competent Sergeant Major Wilson, probably cursing the unpredictable Argentines, are en route from Ezeiza here to pick you up," Rangio said.

"Thank you, sir."

"And at this very moment, my good wife is sitting by the telephone to learn whether your Julio is our Julio," Rangio said. "So I have a favor to ask of you. If I swear to deliver him to the embassy transient quarters at eight tomorrow morning, may I take him home with me?"

"Absolutely," Oliver said. "And it doesn't have be 0800, either, Colonel. I plan to sleep most of tomorrow . . ."

Rangio took a card from his wallet and wrote a number on it.

"Call this, night or day, and I will have Julio where you want him within the hour."

"Thank you," Oliver said.

"And now, if you will excuse us? Colonel Harris knows where you all are."

Zammoro stood up and saluted.

"Thank you, Captain," he said.

"Don't be silly, Zam. Have a good time. See you tomorrow, or the day after."

Oliver waited until Rangio and Zammoro had left, then rapped his knuckles on the glass tabletop to get everyone's attention.

"Our orders, you will recall, are to tell Colonel Harris only what he has to know. And I don't think he has to know that Zammoro and Rangio are old friends. Any questions?"

Everyone shook their heads in understanding, and SFC Otmanio said, "Yes, sir."

"I wonder why Zammoro didn't say anything . . . back in the States?" Jack asked.

"I don't know," de la Santiago said. "But it could be because he was afraid they wouldn't send him down here knowing he and the SIDE guy are old pals."

"Yeah," Oliver agreed thoughtfully. "Anyway, Zam asked permission to spend the night with an old friend, name unknown, and I gave it to him. Okay?"

[FOUR]
Apartment 10-B
Malabia 2350 Palermo
(U.S. Embassy Transient Quarters)
Buenos Aires, Argentina
1130 3 February 1965

"Señor," the maid who came with the apartment said to Captain John S. Oliver, who was sharing a cup of coffee with Lieutenant Jacques Portet on a narrow balcony, "there is a gentleman from the U.S. Embassy to see you."

"Ask him to come out here, please," Oliver said.

Thirty seconds later, Mr. J. F. Stephens walked onto the balcony.

"Captain Oliver?" he asked, and when Oliver nodded, went on: "I'm J. F. Stephens, the embassy's administrative officer for housing and medical services."

"Sure you are," Oliver said, unable to restrain a smile. Colonel Lowell had told him to expect that the CIA station chief would make himself known, but not that he would be a CIA version of Felter, an absolutely unimpressive man in a mussed suit, who looked like anything but an intelligence agent.

"I really am," Stephens said. "Maybe you expected an American Michael Caine?"

Oliver and Jack Portet chuckled.

"How about a cup of coffee before you tell us what we can do for you?" Oliver said, offering his hand. "This is Lieutenant Jack Portet."

"I'd love some coffee," Stephens said, and gave his hand to Jack. "Welcome to Buenos Aires."

"Thank you," Jack said. He ordered coffee for all of them from the maid with sign language.

"No Spanish, huh?"

"Not a word."

"You really only need three," Stephens said. "*Baño, cerveza,* and *bife de chorizo*. Bathroom, beer, and New York strip steak."

Johnny and Jack chuckled dutifully.

"I really am, the admin officer for housing, I mean," Stephens said. "I came by to discuss housing with Warrant Officers de la Santiago and Zammoro and Sergeant Otmanio. You two can stay here, of course, until you go back to the States. Which will be when?"

"I wonder who wants to know," Oliver said. "The admin officer for housing or curious people in Langley?"

"Would you settle for both?"

The maid held out a tray with cups of coffee on it.

He said something in Spanish to her, and she pulled the tray back and went into the apartment.

"The only way I can drink the coffee here is to lace it heavily with cream," Stephens said. "Which in Argentina, fortunately, means real cream from a cow, rather than that 'dairy creamer' crap — mostly soybeans and chemicals — they give you in the States."

"I don't know when we'll be going back to the States," Oliver said. "Jack and I are newlyweds, so we'd like to leave yesterday. Our orders are to get Zammoro, de la Santiago, and Otmanio settled; to get a feel for the country and a feel for Señor Guevara. I want to see — I want us all to see — where he grew up; that sort of thing."

" 'Know thy enemy'?"

"I suppose," Oliver said.

The maid returned with the tray of coffee. In

each cup now floated a large chunk of cream.

"They call that café con crème," Stephens said as he reached for his cup. "Are the . . . what should I say, 'permanent party'? . . . around?"

"Otmanio went for a run," Oliver said. "He's a Green Beret. They do that sort of thing. De la Santiago went out to buy a newspaper — newspapers."

"I thought you were all Special Forces," Stephens said.

"There's the kind who runs and the kind that don't," Jack said. "Oliver and I are in Group Two."

"And Zammoro?"

"He's visiting a friend," Oliver said.

"Oh, really?"

"Yes, really," Oliver said.

"Are you going to tell me what that's all about?" Stephens asked.

"I beg your pardon?"

"There are two kinds of guys in my line of work," Stephens said. "I was sort of hoping that I had convinced Colonel Lowell and Father Lunsford that I was the kind who could be trusted."

"When they briefed us," Oliver said, "Father said you were better than most, and Colonel Lowell said he hoped we were all familiar with the adage 'beware of spooks bearing gifts.' "

"Okay, fair enough. Let me tell you what I know. After an emotional greeting at Campo de Mayo between your Mr. Zammoro and the guy who diverted your flight there, there was a sumptuous repast laid in a private room of the Campo de Mayo Casino."

"How do you know who diverted our flight?"

"I can count the people with the clout to do that on the fingers of one hand, leaving out the thumb. By a simple process of elimination — it wasn't the President, or General Pistarini, or the minister for aviation — I have a damned good idea who did it."

"Watch out for him, Jack," Oliver said. "He's clever."

"While Dick Harris and I — he's another good guy, by the way — were on our way from Ezeiza to Campo de Mayo, your Mr. Zammoro and his good herein-unnamed buddy left for parts unknown in said buddy's official car."

"How'd you find that out?" Jack asked.

"The waiters at the Casino talk too much," Stephens said.

"Just for the record, Jack, I made the decision to tell the housing officer here what that was all about," Oliver said. "And the answer is that I don't have the foggiest idea what that was all about, except that Zammoro and Colonel Rangio are apparently old and good friends."

"You didn't know beforehand?"

Oliver shook his head, no.

"De la Santiago thinks Zammoro was afraid they wouldn't send him down here if they knew he and Rangio were old pals."

"What did Zammoro do in the Cuban Army?" Stephens said. "Was he in the same line of work as Rangio?"

"I honestly don't know," Oliver said, and then had another thought: "How did you know he was in the Cuban Army?"

"I got a radio from some people in Virginia," Stephens said. "I know a lot about all of you, although, come to think it, you're supposed to be a bachelor." He paused and pointed to Jack. "The long arm of the draft caught you in the Congo," he said. "Where your father owns one airline, for which you flew, and is chief pilot of another. Right after you married some general's daughter, the Army recognized your all-around genius and made you an officer. . . ."

"Right before I married the general's daughter," Jack said, chuckling.

"De la Santiago was a captain in the Cuban Air Force, who worked for your father, then flew black B-26s in the Congo, and then joined the Army," Stephens said. "How'm I doing?"

"Otmanio?" Oliver asked.

"Otmanio, Jorge," Stephens said. "Puerto Rican. Joined the Army at seventeen. Jump School. Served with the Eighty-Second Airborne, 183rd Regimental Combat Team — my old regiment, by the way — made buck sergeant, applied for Special Forces, went to Vietnam as a demolitions man on an A Team, came back as an SFC with a Silver Star, two Purple Hearts . . . He's fluent in Spanish, of course."

"You guys are very good," Oliver said.

"I think they call that 'knowing your enemy,' " Stephens said. "Would it shock you to learn that there are people in an unnamed government agency — probably more than one agency, come to think of it — who gather at midnight in cemeteries to stick pins in a doll bearing a resemblance to one Colonel Sanford T. Felter?"

"No," Oliver said, chuckling.

"Presumably you have heard of 'guilt by association'?" Stephens said.

"No," Oliver said. "What's that?"

"It's contagious, and you got it," Stephens said. Oliver raised his hand above his shoulder, his thumb holding the pinkie down, the other fingers extended.

"Boy Scout's Honor," he said. "I didn't know that Zammoro knew Rangio, and — I don't *know*, of course — I don't think that Felter or Lowell knew either."

"The people in Virginia know only that he was a major in the Cuban Army," Stephens said. "Which, coupled with the fact that Castro has got his wife in that very nasty slam on the Isla de Pinos, makes me think he was in the same line of work as Rangio. Intelligence officers' records have a tendency to disappear."

"Yeah," Oliver agreed thoughtfully.

"If you tell Lowell, will he jerk him out of here?"

"I don't know."

"I would hate to see that happen," Stephens said. "That contact could be very valuable."

"Are you suggesting I don't tell Colonel Lowell?"

"I'm suggesting you have a decision to make about that that isn't covered in a field manual," Stephens said. "One you should not make like one of Pavlov's pooches."

"I was going to say 'Give me time to think about that,' " Oliver said.

"Good. I will interpret that as step one on your path toward concluding that this housing officer is trustworthy." He held up his hand in the Boy Scout salute. "I was an Eagle. What about you?"

"Me, too," Oliver said.

"And you, Lieutenant?" Stephens asked.

"I was never a Boy Scout," Jack said.

"That's a pity. Now I'll have to wonder if I can trust you," Stephens said. "Why don't we go get some lunch? I'll buy, mainly because I can put it down as a necessary on-duty expense."

"That's the Edificio Libertador," Stephens said, pointing out the window of his Chevrolet Impala at a wide, tall building. "Army Headquarters. Rangio has an office on the twelfth floor, right down the corridor from General Pistarini."

"Giving tours to tourists is in your job description, is it?" Oliver asked.

"My job description is a little vague," Stephens said. "Only tourists who agree with me get the tour."

"Agree with you about what?" Jack asked.

"That blowing the bearded bastard away would be really counterproductive," Stephens said. "You'd be surprised how few people feel that way. When vacationing in Virginia, I sometimes feel like that still, small, lonely, voice of reason."

"Uh," Oliver grunted.

"This is Avenida Libertador," Stephens said. "We're going to make a left here and drive around Plaza San Martín, past the Círculo Militar, which makes any officers' club I ever saw in the States look like a roadhouse."

Oliver and Portet were smiling.

"When Lowell and Lunsford were here, they stayed in one of the general officers' suites in the Círculo Militar, which, to someone in my line of work — I mean, as a housing officer — suggested that they knew someone important, like, for example, General Pistarini or Lieutenant Colonel Rangio. And sure enough, I got a skinny from my friends in Virginia a couple of days later, saying Lowell's father-in-law is Lieutenant General Count von Greiffenberg, head of German intelligence. Did you know that?"

"I did," Oliver said.

"I didn't," Jack said.

"A little bird told me the Argentines — which means Rangio at the orders of Pistarini — had a shoot-the-bearded-bastard-on-sight order out. The next thing I know is Colonel Lowell is playing polo with Pistarini —"

He paused and pointed out the window again, this time at an enormous turn-of-the-century French-style mansion.

"That's the Círculo Militar. It was built by the people who owned the Argentine version of *The New York Times*. Inspired by admiration for the Army, they gave it to them. I'd love to know what was behind that."

He continued around Plaza San Martín, slowed, and drove the Impala half onto the sidewalk in front of another turn-of-the-century building, his bumper against a sign that very obviously forbade parking.

"This is the Plaza Hotel," he said. "Inside is the oldest — and possibly the most expensive — restaurant in Argentina. I only get to eat here when I can put it on the expense account."

"They don't teach you to read in Virginia? Not even very graphic signs?" Oliver asked.

"You are with a duly accredited diplomat," Stephens said. "We get to park anyplace we want to. We're immune to Argentine law. You can probably guess how handy that is, on occasion."

"I'll bet," Jack said.

He led them into the restaurant, which was on the ground floor. The headwaiter greeted Stephens by name and bowed them to a table. A waiter immediately appeared.

"You guys want to trust me, or do you want to

gamble with your nonexistent Spanish?"

"We're in your hands," Jack said, chuckling.

Stephens ordered rapidly without looking at a menu. The waiter left.

"We're going to have to talk about diplomatic immunity," Stephens said. "But before we do, let me pick up where I left off before."

"Where was that?"

"Lowell playing polo with General Pistarini," Stephens said. "He's not bad, by the way. Not in Pistarini's league, but not bad. Anyway, when I talked to him afterward — the next day, they drank the night away at the Círculo Militar — Lowell told me that Pistarini had agreed to call off the contract on Guevara. I then concluded that Lowell was one of the good guys. There are bad guys in uniform, you may be surprised to learn. The defense attaché here is a real asshole."

"I've heard something to that effect," Oliver said, chuckling.

The waiter appeared with a bottle of wine and went through a formal routine of offering the cork for Stephens to examine and sniff, and then pouring a taste-size dollop of wine in his glass. Stephens nodded his approval, and the waiter poured the wine.

When the waiter had gone, Stephens went on.

"At that point, I decided to make myself useful to your noble enterprise, despite pointed hints from my friends in Virginia that I throw broken bottles and other impediments in your path. Am I getting through to you guys?"

"Yeah," Oliver said. "But you won't mind if I keep looking for the hook?"

"I would be disappointed if you didn't," Stephens said. "First, assuming Zammoro gets to stay, it would be handy as hell if you could get him a diplomatic passport. Right now, his status doesn't entitle him to one, and the Argentines don't like to approve them for anybody but colonels. . . ."

"What is his status?" Jack asked.

"Military staff of the embassy," Stephens said. "Dips get a white CD license plate. Mil Staff, which is just about everybody but the defense attaché, and the army and navy attachés, get blue plates. The Argentines leave them alone, but they don't have diplomatic immunity. There are exceptions. The cryptographic guys are Army warrant officers, but for obvious reasons, they have to have immunity. They call them 'communications officers' and get them diplomatic passports."

"So it wouldn't look suspicious if Zammoro got a diplomatic passport?" Oliver asked.

"The problem is usually the Argentines," Stephens said. "They don't want every Tom, Dick, and Harry parking on the sidewalk. But I suspect that Zammoro's old buddy could overcome any objections."

"What about de la Santiago?" Jack asked.

"He's a warrant officer; what would work for Zammoro would work for him. But again you'd need Rangio to grease the skids."

"And SFC Otmanio?"

"He's an enlisted man. That would really be pushing the envelope," Stephens said. "Which brings us to him. . . ."

"What's that got to do with anything?" Jack asked.

"It is an article of faith in diplomatic circles that enlisted men are children. Especially the unmarried ones. They require supervised living. They're not — the unmarried ones — even allowed to have cars, and they make them live together. Here they live with the Marine Guards. Only the Marine sergeant in charge, who is always married, gets his own apartment and can drive his own car."

"That's bullshit," Jack said.

"As a former Spec5" — an enlisted grade, equivalent to sergeant — "I of course agree, but I'm not the Secretary of State, who makes the rules. Is Otmanio married?"

"Yeah," Jack Portet and Johnny Oliver said at the same time.

"If his wife was here," Stephens said, "that would make things a lot better. He could have his own apartment, and drive a private car."

"Where are Zammoro and de la Santiago going to live?" Oliver asked.

"Embassy policy is that two bachelor officers share an apartment," Stephens replied. "The housing officer has the authority to grant waivers to that rule."

The waiter delivered two-inch-thick New York strip steaks, a lettuce and tomato and onion salad, and a huge mound of what looked like very thick potato chips.

"The steak is called *bife de chorizo,*" Stephens said. "The spuds are *papas a la provenzal.* Enjoy."

He signaled to the waiter to bring another bottle of wine.

"So what I have to do is see if Colonel Felter will send Otmanio's wife down here," Oliver said.

"What you have to do is decide whether you're going to tell Felter, or Lowell, which I suppose is really the same thing, that Zammoro and Rangio are old pals."

"Colonel Lowell said that if I was properly humble, you would let me use your radio link to your friends in Virginia," Oliver said.

"You want to call Felter?" Stephens asked, and when Oliver nodded, added: "And what are you going to tell him?"

"I'm going to think about that while I'm eating, and while we're on the way to wherever your radio link is."

[FIVE]
Office of the USIS Administrative Officer for
** Housing and Medical Services**
United States Embassy
Sarmiento 663
Palermo, Buenos Aires, Argentina
1505 3 February 1965

"White House Secure," a male voice said, the clarity surprising Johnny Oliver.

"Two-two-seven, please."

"Two-two-seven, Mr. Finton."

"John Oliver, Finton. Is the boss there?"

"Hold one."

"Felter."

"Oliver, sir."

"I know."

"Sir, I've been talking to Colonel Lowell's friend from Virginia."

"The CIA station chief? Stephens?"

The CIA station chief was sitting behind his desk, smiling. He had made it plain from the beginning that he intended to listen to the conversation. Oliver didn't like it, but it was Stephens's radio link to the White House secure switchboard, and there was nothing that could be done about it.

"Yes, sir."

"And?"

"It would make things easier for Otmanio if his wife was here. Otherwise, he's going to have to live with the Marine Guards, and can't have a private automobile."

There was a fifteen-second pause before Felter replied.

"No problem with that," Felter said. "As soon as I can get DA to cut orders, she'll be on a plane. What about Rangio? Any contact with him?"

"We were supposed to land at Ezeiza. We were diverted to the military field at Campo de Mayo. Rangio was there. It turns out he and Zammoro are old, and apparently close, friends."

"Shit," the CIA station chief said bitterly. Oliver wondered if Felter could hear him.

The pause this time was longer.

"That got by me somehow," Felter said. "Well, what do you want to do?"

Oliver didn't expect the question. He expected a decision, orders, not a request for his opinion.

"That association could be very valuable, sir," he said.

"That occurred to me. I asked what you want to do?"

"I would like to use his connection, sir."

"Why do you think he didn't tell us?"

"De la Santiago thinks he was afraid if you knew you wouldn't have sent him down here."

"De la Santiago's right. The question was, what do you think?"

"I agree with de la Santiago, sir."

"Then the question becomes, is he down there

as a team player or because it'll give him a clear shot at Guevara?"

"I'd vote for team player, sir."

Jesus, that was my mouth on full automatic! I didn't consider that response, I just made it.

There was another pause before Felter replied.

"Your call, Oliver," Felter said. "Anything else?"

"Diplomatic status for him and de la Santiago."

"The State Department tells me the Argentines won't do it."

"Zammoro's relationship with Rangio may change that, sir."

"You understand that if I insist that State ask for diplomatic status for them after they've said the Argentines won't give it, and they're proved right, they will make sure the President sees the egg on my face?"

"Yes, sir."

"You want to ask Rangio first?"

"I'll ask Zammoro to ask him. See what happens then."

"Let me know what happens then," Felter said. "Anything else?"

"No, sir."

"The sooner you're back here, the better, I guess you know," Felter said.

"Has something come up, sir?"

"You and Jack are the newlyweds," Felter said, chuckled, and hung up.

"White House Secure," a male voice said. "Are you clear?"

"Clear," Oliver said, and put the handset in its cradle.

"You had to tell him, huh?" Stephens asked.

"Army officers are like Boy Scouts," Oliver

said. "We're not supposed to lie, cheat, or steal."

"I think that's West Point cadets," Stephens said.

"Actually, it's Norwich," Jack said. "We had the honor code before Hudson High."

"Whatever," Stephens said. "If you really believe that, maybe you're in the wrong line of work. Lying, stealing, cheating, and worse, are part of this territory."

"What about 'all's fair in love and war'?" Jack asked.

"Maybe there's hope for you, at least, Lieutenant," Stephens said. "So what did the legendary Colonel Felter have to say?"

"You couldn't hear?"

"Call it confirmation of what I hope I heard," Stephens said.

"He's going to send Otmanio's wife down here," Oliver said. "And I was right, he didn't know Zammoro and Rangio are old buddies. He left the decision up to me."

"We lucked out," Stephens said. "I don't think you really understand how valuable that connection can be."

"He said he was honorable, not stupid," Jack said.

Stephens looked at Jack. One eyebrow went up, but he didn't respond.

"I suppose the next step is to talk to Zammoro," Oliver said. "Rangio gave me a number to call."

"Your next step is to make your manners to Colonel Harris," Stephens said.

"Okay," Oliver said. "Then Zammoro. I suppose you want to sit in on that, too?"

"Oh, no. By now Rangio has already warned Zammoro to stay away from me."

"Rangio knows who you are . . . what you do?"

"Oh, sure. I often wonder who we think we're fooling with these cover jobs."

[SIX]
Apartment 10-B
Malabia 2350 Palermo
(U.S. Embassy Transient Quarters)
Buenos Aires, Argentina
1715 3 February 1965

"That was quick," Johnny Oliver said to WOJG Zammoro when he walked into the apartment.

"Colonel Rangio promised to deliver me 'within an hour,' " Zammoro replied. "He is a man of his word."

"We're going to have to talk about your friend Colonel Rangio," Oliver said.

"Yes, sir," Zammoro said, as if he had expected this. He looked at Jack Portet. "With respect, sir, may we talk alone?"

"No, I want Lieutenant Portet in on this," Oliver said. "I told de la Santiago and Otmanio to go to the movies."

"Yes, sir," Zammoro said.

"Your credibility, Mr. Zammoro, and thus your usefulness to this mission, has been called into doubt," Oliver said. "The one way you might, repeat might, regain some credibility is, from this moment, give me the truth, all the truth, and nothing but the truth."

"Yes, sir."

"When and where did you meet Colonel Rangio?"

"In Argentina, sir, in 1952. I was sent to the Infantry School there. He was an instructor. And then I met him again in Cuba, in 1957."

"What was Rangio doing in Cuba?"

"He was ostensibly the commercial attaché of the Argentinean embassy."

"And actually?"

"He had been sent to Cuba by SIDE, sir."

"And you were, then?"

"An infantry officer, a major. I was in an infantry battalion."

"Not an intelligence officer?"

"General Batista used his intelligence service as a private police force," Zammoro said contemptuously. "No, I was not one of them, I was a soldier." General Fulgencio Batista was President of Cuba until the Castro-led revolution was successful.

"And how did you come to meet Colonel Rangio again?"

"He sought me out," Zammoro said. "He offered his help."

"What kind of help?"

"My regiment was then responsible for 'controlling' the insurrection in the Sierra Maestra mountains."

"You mean Castro?"

"Yes, sir."

"What was Rangio's interest in that?"

"Castro's medical officer — Ernesto Guevara de la Serna," Zammoro said.

"You knew he was an intelligence officer?"

"I knew he wasn't a 'commercial attaché.' When he told me he had just been promoted to lieutenant colonel — it wasn't hard to figure out."

"And what kind of help did he offer?"

"He let me know that if Guevara was killed, there would be no repercussions from the Argentine government. He had the idea that the reason our campaign against Castro was failing was because we were worried about trouble from the Argentines, and other South American governments."

"Was that true?"

"Captain, when senior officers are appointed to major commands because of their support of a corrupt regime, you don't get an efficient army."

"I suppose not. Is that what happened?"

"Yes. If Batista had let his good officers run the Army, he would probably still be President."

"What was the Argentine interest in Castro?"

"They knew Guevara was a Communist. This was, you will recall, when Castro was posing as a fighter against the corrupt regime of Batista. It was only after he took Havana that it came out he was a Communist. The Argentines had apparently told the United States what they knew, and the U.S. did nothing. It would have been in the Argentine interest for the Castro rebellion to fail, and for Guevara to die while it failed. There are Communists here, too, you know."

"Obviously, you didn't succeed in stopping Castro," Jack Portet said.

"We exchanged a gangster in an officer's uniform for a Communist," Zammoro said.

"And you felt you had to get out of the country," Oliver said.

"Just as soon as Castro was in Havana, he had Rangio declared persona non grata, but before he left he got word to me that I was on Señor Guevara's arrest and execute list. Guevara knew of my association with Colonel Rangio. And of course Fidel himself wasn't too happy with me. I took out a lot of his men."

"And your wife didn't get out," Jack said softly.

"She was arrested the day I arrived in Miami," Zammoro said. "She's in a cage — literally, a cage — on the Isla de Pinos, an island off the southern coast."

"Shit!" Jack said.

"Why didn't you tell somebody — General Hanrahan, Colonel Felter, Colonel Lowell, somebody — about this?" Oliver asked.

"I knew they would be — with ample justification — suspicious of anyone who had been an officer in Batista's army. I really wanted to get in Special Forces, and didn't want to put any obstacles in my way."

"Why did you want to get in Special Forces?" Jack asked.

"Right now, Lieutenant, who else in the world is interested in doing anything about stopping Communism in South America except Special Forces?"

"Why didn't you go to Argentina?" Jack asked. "You had the connection with Rangio."

"There are no foreigners in the Argentine Army," Zammoro said. "I couldn't have even enlisted as a private."

"The real question here, Zammoro," Oliver said. "Is whether you're a Special Forces officer who takes orders, or somebody in a Special Forces uniform who's going to take the first clear shot he gets at Guevara."

"Captain, you're a Norwich graduate, a professional officer. I'd hoped you would understand."

"Understand what?"

"I am a professional officer, too. Before I put on this uniform, I took a solemn oath before God to obey the officers appointed over me," Zammoro said. "If those orders are not to kill the Antichrist sonofabitch who has my wife in a cage on starvation rations, I will obey them, whether or not I like them."

Oliver looked into Zammoro's eyes for a long moment, then stood up.

"I need a drink," he said. "Anybody else?"

"A little scotch would go down nicely," Jack said.

"No, thank you, sir," Zammoro said.

Oliver went to the bar and returned with two glasses dark with whiskey. He handed one to Zammoro.

"Take it," he said. "Get your own booze, Jack," he added. "You're only a lieutenant, and a damned junior one at that."

Zammoro took the drink from Oliver but didn't taste it. Oliver waited for Jack to make a drink, then touched his glass to Zammoro's.

"Embassy policy is that two bachelor officers will share an apartment," he said. "The embassy housing officer, who is also the CIA station chief, says he can waive that rule. What do you think, Julio? You want to share an apartment with de la Santiago or not?"

"*Muchas gracias, mi capitán,*" Zammoro said, his voice thick with emotion. "*A sus órdenes, mi capitán.*"

Jack and Oliver looked at him curiously.

" '*Muchas gracias*' means 'thank you very much,' " Zammoro translated. " '*A sus órdenes, mi capitán*' means, 'I am at your orders, Captain.' "

"That's nice, Julio," Oliver said. "But I asked you a question."

Zammoro looked at the glass in his hand, then took a sip.

"If we were to have separate apartments against the policy, that might look odd," he said. "And I have no objections whatever to sharing an apartment with de la Santiago. On the other hand, it might be very useful if we had a second apartment. Could that be arranged?"

"I don't see why not," Oliver said.

[SEVEN]
1210 Avenida Tucaman
Buenos Aires, Argentina
1525 5 February 1965

Captain John S. Oliver, Lieutenant Jacques Portet, Warrant Officers Junior Grade Enrico de la Santiago and Julio Zammoro, and SFC Jorge Otmanio — all in civilian clothing — had been standing on the sidewalk before the ornate door of the turn-of-the-century apartment building about five minutes when a 1964 Chevrolet Impala with CD license plates and a CD sticker on its bumper drove up, slowed, inched halfway onto the sidewalk, and stopped.

Mr. J. F. Stephens got out and walked up to them.

"Kept you waiting long?" he asked, offering his hand to Oliver.

"We just got here," Oliver said.

"By the skin of our teeth," Jack said. "I thought Paris had the craziest drivers in the world."

"The Argentines try to excel in everything," Stephens said. He pointed down the street at a large building. "That's the Colón Opera House," he said. "When it was built, the architect's first order was to make it larger than the Paris Opera and the Vienna Opera."

"Really?" Jack asked, chuckling.

Stephens put out his hand to Otmanio.

"I'm Jack Stephens, the embassy housing officer," he said in Spanish.

"SFC Otmanio, señor."

"You don't have to call me 'sir,' Sergeant. I used to be a Spec Five," Stephens said, still in Spanish. "Welcome to Buenos Aires and the U.S. Embassy family. What do you think so far?"

"It's a beautiful city," Otmanio said.

"Pity you're married, Sergeant," Stephens said. "The women are spectacular, as you may have noticed."

"I've noticed," Otmanio said, smiling.

Stephens offered his hand to de la Santiago.

"Enrico de la Santiago," de la Santiago said.

"Portet tells me you used to fly together in Africa," Stephens said. "What kind of airplanes was that?"

"Most of the time, it was old Boeing C-46s," de la Santiago said.

"There are people here who don't speak Spanish," Jack Portet said.

"How unfortunate for you," Stephens said. "Bear with me, Jack."

He turned to Zammoro.

"You have to be Mr. Zammoro," he said, switching back to Spanish.

"I am."

"I understand you have friends here in Buenos Aires?"

"I do."

"How lucky for you. Have they been showing you around?"

"Yes."

"There's two apartments here. Fourth and sixth

floors. Would you prefer the fourth or the sixth?"

"It doesn't really matter," Zammoro said.

"Well, why don't we have a look at both and then you can decide."

"Whatever you wish," Zammoro said.

"Until Señora Otmanio gets here, we've been thinking of asking one of you to put the sergeant up. That would keep him from having to move in and out of the Marine Guards' house. Would that pose any problem for you, Señor Zammoro?"

"No," Zammoro said.

"You don't talk much, do you?" Stephens said, and then, without waiting for a reply, walked to the door and pushed a doorbell button.

An elderly Argentine in a suit opened the door to them.

Stephens introduced Zammoro, de la Santiago, and Otmanio as "embassy officers" who would be living in the two apartments, and told them that Señor Cavias was the porter, and the man to see if anything went wrong.

Then he led them to an open elevator, which appeared to have been added to the building before World War I, and finally switched to English.

"These are not reliable with more than three people aboard," he said. "And, since Rank Has Its Privileges, you and the Lieutenant and I will ride up to the sixth floor, where I shall send the elevator back down for these three. Okay?"

"Fine," Oliver said, a tone of impatience, or annoyance, in his voice.

When the elevator had risen far enough to be out of sight of Zammoro, Otmanio, and de la Santiago, Stephens reached in his pocket and handed Jack a sheet of paper.

"I am also a part-time mailman," Stephens said. "That came in just before I left the embassy to come here."

Oliver took it, read it, and handed it to Jack Portet.

SECRET

Central Intelligence Agency
Langley, Virginia

FROM: Assistant Director For Administration

DATE: 4 February 1965 2115 GMT

SUBJECT: Guevara, Ernesto (Memorandum # 44.)

TO: Mr. Sanford T. Felter
Counselor To The President
Room 637, The Executive Office Building
Washington, D.C.

By Courier

In compliance with Presidential Memorandum to The Director, Subject: "Ernesto 'Che' Guevara," dated 14 December 1964, the following information is furnished:

(1) (Reliability Scale Five) (From CIA, Havana Cuba) The Cuban Army is recruiting approximately five hundred (500) Negro soldiers from its ranks, telling them they will

---

be part of an "international contingent of freedom fighters."

(2) (Reliability Scale Two) (From CIA, Havana Cuba) It is rumored:

(a) The recruited troops are intended for use in Africa.

(b) They will be trained in secret camps somewhere in Cuba.

(3) Further information is being sought, and if developed, will be furnished to you.

Howard W. O'Connor
HOWARD W. O'CONNOR

SECRET

"I'll bet that ruined the whole day of the analyst who said it 'was highly unlikely' that the Cubans will take any military action on the African continent," Stephens said.

"Five hundred is a lot of soldiers for a covert operation," Oliver said.

"The minute things start going his way, he'll drop the covert and it'll become a liberation army," Stephens said.

"Michael Hoare didn't have anything like five hundred mercenaries —"

"Who?" Oliver interrupted.

"The South African Kasavubu hired to put down the Simba rebellion when his army couldn't do it," Jack said. "I don't think he had two hundred people, and very few of those could be called 'well-trained troops.' He recruited most of them in waterfront bars in Belgium and France."

"But they did take the Congo back, didn't they?" Stephens said. "Lesson to be learned: You guys better stop Guevara before he gets very far."

The elevator stopped with a lurch. Stephens slid the folding door open and waved them out. He punched a button on the control panel, then closed the door. The elevator began to descend.

Stephens led them across a tiled floor to a door and opened it.

The rooms were large and high-ceilinged, European. The obviously American furniture didn't seem appropriate, and Jack idly wondered why the embassy hadn't bought furniture locally.

They were still wandering around the apartment when de la Santiago and the others came in.

"The other apartment," Stephens said, now in English, "give or take, is identical to this one." He looked at Zammoro. "You're going to use one of them as a safe house, I take it?"

"Thank you for speaking English," Jack said.

"I was checking their Spanish," Stephens said.

"And?" Oliver asked.

"If they work on the accent, the different words, Zammoro and de la Santiago could *maybe* pass for Argentines, Chileans, or Uruguayans. Otmanio, no way. He's got a really strange accent."

"Spanish Harlem Spanish, mixed with Puerto Rican," Otmanio said.

"He's also going to attract attention because of his black skin," Stephens said. "There aren't many really black people in Argentina. My advice is keep your mouth shut."

Otmanio nodded.

"You're going back when?" Stephens asked.

"Tomorrow morning, we're going to fly to Córdoba. We should be back here by dark, and then Jack and I are on the 2315 Aerolineas flight to Miami," Oliver said.

"Córdoba, or Alta Gracia?" Stephens said.

"Alta Gracia," Oliver said.

"Whose idea is that?"

"Actually, it was a pointed suggestion from Colonel Felter," Oliver said.

"It's probably a good idea, but don't expect to see much," Stephens said. "I've taken that tour myself. You're going to have a guide, I hope?"

"Oh, sure."

"I presume the apartments meet your approval?" Stephens asked.

"They're very nice," Zammoro said.

"And convenient, too," Stephens said. "You can probably have lunch with your old buddy a lot."

"Excuse me?"

"Your old pal's office is at Leandro Alem, 26. That's just a couple of blocks from here."

"What's that?" Oliver said.

"Large office building," Stephens said. "Lots of people — in and out of uniform — standing around just inside the door and on the loading dock holding submachine guns. There's a rumor going around it's SIDE's secret headquarters."

Jack chuckled.

"I'll send a car to the transient quarters at

nine," Stephens said. "Give my regards to Miami."

He tossed a large stack of keys to Zammoro and walked out of the apartment.

XVI

[ONE]
Córdoba
Córdoba Province, Argentina
0955 6 February 1965

"Córdoba," Lieutenant Colonel Guillermo Rangio announced, "is the second largest city in Argentina, and the capital of Córdoba province. It is also the site of our aircraft factory, another expensive legacy of General Perón. Everybody knows and admits that it would be cheaper and more efficient to buy all our military aircraft from you Americans, or the British, than to try to make them ourselves, but if we did that, it would put a lot of people out of work here. And, another legacy of the general, the unions here are second in power only to the military, so the politicians throw our money away on our aircraft factory."

Everyone in the L-23 smiled.

He was sitting in the copilot's seat beside de la Santiago, wearing, like the others, a green coverall garment officially described as a "US Army Suit, Flight, Summer."

"There it is," he said, pointing out the window. "When we land, we will be directed to a hangar. With a little bit of luck, no journalist will see us land."

"Would that be a problem, Colonel?" Oliver asked.

"It would be all over the front page of *CLARIN* — which is our *New York Daily News* — tomorrow that Yankee spies were down here brazenly stealing Argentine technology while SIDE did nothing about it."

De la Santiago reached for the microphone and requested approach and landing instructions.

They were met at the end of the runway by a follow-me pickup truck, which led them to a hangar whose doors were wide open. De la Santiago shut off the engines and a dozen ground crewmen pushed the airplane into the hangar and turned it around. The hangar doors closed.

Jack Portet, who had ridden in the rearmost seat, opened the door and got out of the airplane. Two men in uniform approached.

"Good morning," Jack said.

Both replied in English.

"Good morning," one said.

"Welcome to Córdoba," the other said.

Otmanio got out next, followed by Oliver, then Rangio, Zammoro, and finally de la Santiago.

The two officers saluted Rangio, then embraced him.

Rangio put his arm around Zammoro.

"This is my dear friend Julio Zammoro," he said in English. "Formerly Major in the Cuban Army, and now an officer of the United States Army. My wife wept when she learned Castro has her friend, Señora Zammoro, on the Isla de Pinos."

Both officers saluted Zammoro, and then, shaking their heads in what could have been compassion or outrage, and was probably both, shook his hand.

Rangio motioned de la Santiago over to him.

"This is Enrico de la Santiago," he said, "formerly captain of the Cuban Air Force, now also a U.S. Army officer. Dr. Guevara personally murdered his grandfather with Enrico's grandmother and mother watching."

Both officers saluted de la Santiago, and again shook their heads as they shook his hand.

"And this is Sergeant First Class Otmanio," Rangio said. Otmanio saluted. "He is in the United States Special Forces, as are these gentlemen, Captain Oliver and Lieutenant Portet."

Salutes and handshakes were again exchanged.

"They are all here at the request of General Pistarini," Rangio went on. "To help us with a certain problem. Since you know we are going to Alta Gracia, I don't think I have to put a name on the problem, nor point out the importance of discretion vis-à-vis their presence here."

"No, sir," the two said, almost in unison.

"The ugly one, gentlemen," Rangio said, "is my deputy for this area, Major Ricardo Javez. And the other, really ugly one, Colonel Paolo Lamm, heads the Policía Federal in Córdoba Province. He is my wife's cousin."

Hands were shaken all around again.

"The cars are ready? And luncheon is arranged for?" Rangio asked.

"Yes, sir," the two said, again almost in unison.

"Well, then, gentlemen," Rangio said. "I suggest we get on with the tour."

He started taking off his flight suit, and the others followed. Under them, they were in civilian clothing. They tossed the flight suits into the L-23.

Three cars were waiting outside the hangar, a

1963 Buick and two 1962 Chevrolets. Rangio got behind the wheel of one of the Chevrolets and motioned Zammoro and Oliver to get in with him. Major Javez got behind the wheel of the second Chevrolet, and Jack, de la Santiago, and Otmanio got in with him. Colonel Lamm got in the Buick alone and, leading the little convoy, drove off.

There were signs all along the two-lane highway, posting a 110-km (about 70-mph) speed limit, and there were two gendarmerie posts along the thirty-mile road to Alta Gracia. The speed limits were ignored, and the little convoy sailed past the gendarmerie so fast the gendarmes barely had time to recognize the Policía Federal chief's Buick and salute.

They came to Alta Gracia, a town of about 30,000 people, and drove through its streets until they came to a residential area. The right turn signal on Colonel Lamm's Buick flashed. The two Chevrolets pulled to the curb and stopped. The Buick continued on.

Rangio got out of the his car and walked to the car behind him.

"The house directly across from here is where Dr. Guevara spent his childhood and early manhood," he said, indicating a small, well-cared-for house with a covered verandah behind a fence. "His parents still live in that house. From here, we will go to his parish elementary school, San Tomas Aquinas; and to his secondary school, San Pedro y San Paolo; and the football field where he tried to play football. He had asthma, which made it difficult for him, but he tried. He went from here to Buenos Aires, where he attended the university — which I have already shown you — and earned the degree of doctor of medicine."

A man came out of the house to the right of the Guevara de la Serna residence, and stood by the door and watched them.

Rangio got back in his car, gave them two minutes to study the house, and then drove off on the tour he had promised. They went into both schools, and into both churches. In the parish church of Saint Thomas Aquinas, Rangio led them down the aisle to the altar.

"Dr. Guevara was an altar boy here," he said. "What he has become very much distresses the priests and the good sisters, and they have no excuse for it."

There were high-school-aged boys playing soccer on the soccer field, and they watched the game in silence for several minutes before Rangio walked wordlessly back to his car and they drove off, back to Córdoba. Jack wondered what had happened to Colonel Lamm in the Buick, and decided that Lamm had felt his duties were over once he had shown them Guevara's home.

They drove up to the Hotel Crillon in Córdoba and went inside.

They were shown to a private dining room off the main dining room. Colonel Lamm was already there, and so was the man who had come onto the porch of the house next to Guevara's.

Rangio pointed to a table laden with wine bottles.

"I understand that Enrico will be flying," Rangio said, nodding at de la Santiago, "so he gets no wine. But for the rest of us . . . Unless someone would prefer whiskey?"

A waiter pulled a cork and poured a sample for Rangio's approval. He sipped it, nodded his approval, and the waiter began to fill glasses.

"The wine is from Córdoba Province," Rangio

said. "We like to think our Argentine wine is as good as any."

He waited until everyone had a glass, then raised his glass to the man who had come out on his porch to watch them.

"I would like to thank Señor Manuelo Frotzi for joining us," he said. "I happen to personally know that he is both a good Catholic and a patriot. He is in the difficult position of liking Ernesto Guevara de la Serna, who he watched grow up as the friend of his son Reynaldo, who is now a captain in the 1st Regiment of Grenadiers, stationed in Buenos Aires. I will arrange for Zammoro, de la Santiago, and Otmanio to meet with Capitán Frotzi in the next few days."

Señor Frotzi smiled uneasily at them.

"Unfortunately, Señor Frotzi doesn't speak English very fluently," Rangio went on, "but Colonel Lamm has explained to him who you are and what you are doing here, and thought he might be of some service to you."

Everybody shook Frotzi's hand.

Jack wondered if Frotzi really wanted to be helpful, or whether it was an invitation he couldn't refuse.

Over lunch, it quickly became apparent that Rangio's description of him was accurate. Frotzi was torn between his affection for Guevara, whom he had obviously looked upon as sort of another son, and at least embarrassment, and possibly shame, that "his" nice young man had turned into a communist revolutionary.

The picture Frotzi painted — his English was much better than Rangio had suggested; only an occasional translation was necessary — was that Che Guevara had had a perfectly normal childhood, marred only by the restrictions his asthma imposed on his athletics. There had been no indication, even, of leftist leanings, although his father and mother had supported the socialist-like programs of Juan Perón.

In the last serious talk he had had with him, Frotzi related, when Guevara was nearing the end of his medical education, he had candidly told him that he intended to stay in Buenos Aires, because doctors in the country had a hard time making a living, much less a lot of money.

The luncheon meeting lasted over two hours, and the array of wine bottles had just about been depleted when Rangio ended it.

"The norteamericano officers are flying home tonight; we're going to have to start back to Buenos Aires." He looked around the table. "Any last questions?"

No one replied.

"Sergeant Otmanio, you haven't said very much," Rangio said. "No questions?"

"Colonel," Otmanio said, just a little thickly. "I been sitting here trying to figure this clown out."

By the end of the sentence, it was obvious that Otmanio had done more than his fair share of depleting the wine supply.

"How is that, Sergeant?" Rangio said, not quite able to restrain a smile.

"I grew up in Spanish Harlem in New York, Colonel," Otmanio said. "Compared to what I had, Guevara has had it really knocked all of his life. He lives in a nice house, he goes to church, he doesn't do dope, he goes to medical school, and he wants to turn this country communist? From what I've seen, Colonel, all you Argentines want to do is eat, drink wine, and make babies. He knows what happens when the Communists take over. The first thing they do — I saw this all the time in Vietnam, and so did you, Captain Oliver — is blow away the nice people — like de la Santiago's grandfather, like Señor Frotzi, like his own father and mother, for Christ's sake! Where's he coming from? What the *fuck* is wrong with the sonofabitch?"

Oliver rolled his eyes. Otmanio saw this.

"Well, shit, Captain," Otmanio said. "He asked me."

Rangio chuckled.

" 'Eat, drink wine, and make babies'?" Rangio quoted. "An astute observation of the Argentine people, Sergeant." He paused, then went on seriously. "I have asked myself the same question — why? why? — many times, and never found an answer. If I had an answer, maybe it would be easier for people like you and me to stop him. And others like him. But then, Sergeant, what would people like you and me do for a living?"

Rangio stood up and looked at his watch.

"It's time we were going," he said.

[TWO]
Ezeiza International Airport
Buenos Aires, Argentina
2310 6 February 1965

Army Regulations provide that when junior officers such as Captain John S. Oliver and Lieutenant Jacques Portet are traveling on official business, they will be provided with the most economical passage. This translated to mean that Oliver was in Aerolineas Argentina's flight 7201's seat 39B, separated from the window on his left by one fellow passenger, and from the aisle on his right by another fellow passenger. Lieutenant Porter was similarly seated in 39E, on the other side of the aisle, one seat away from the window and one seat from the aisle.

It was going to be a long — nine-hours-plus in the air — and somewhat crowded flight to Miami.

A white-jacketed steward came down the aisle and stopped at row 39.

"Captain Oliver?"

"That's me."

"Will you come with me, please, Captain?"

"What's up?" Oliver asked.

The steward turned across the aisle and asked Lieutenant Portet if he would come with him.

Captain Oliver and Lieutenant Portet met in the aisle.

"What the hell is going on?" Portet asked. Oliver shrugged.

They followed the steward up the aisle to the door, where he turned and bowed them into the first-class compartment.

A man they had never seen before smiled.

"I am sure if Colonel Rangio were here, he would be mortified that there was some sort of mix-up," he said. "Your seat change should have been made before you boarded."

He pointed to two large, leather-upholstered first-class seats.

"That's for us?" Oliver asked.

"Colonel Rangio hopes that you have a pleasant flight, and will see you soon again," the man said. "And he thought that since you liked our Argentine wine, you might like to try some of our champagne."

He thrust a large paper bag at Oliver, who looked in and saw four foil-necked champagne bottles.

"He also hopes that you will be good enough to

take a bottle to Colonel Lowell and Major Lunsford," the man said.

"Certainly," Oliver said.

"And that you will be good enough to deliver this to Colonel Lowell," the man said.

He handed Oliver a white envelope. It was not sealed and was not addressed.

"Certainly," Oliver said. "I'd be happy to."

He put the envelope in his suit jacket pocket.

The man put out his hand.

"I, too, hope you have a very pleasant flight," he said, shook their hands, and walked to the aircraft door.

Johnny bowed Jack into the window seat, then sat down himself.

A stewardess appeared with two glasses of champagne.

"Champagne? Or would you rather wait until we're in the air?"

"Seize the opportunity, I always say," Jack said, taking a glass. "Thank you very much."

There was a whining noise.

"He's starting Inboard Two," Jack said. "Drink up."

"I wonder what's in the envelope?" Oliver said when they were still climbing to cruise altitude and the champagne had been replaced with a glass of Johnny Walker Black.

"It wasn't sealed," Jack said.

"I noticed," Oliver said. "On one hand, it would be reading somebody else's mail."

"And on the other," Jack said, "I'm sure you remember what Mr. Stephens said about lying, stealing, cheating, and worse, being part of this territory."

"You are a corrupting influence, Lieutenant," Oliver said, and took the envelope from his jacket pocket.

It contained two typewritten pages.

This is list of some of the personnel who will participate in the Cuban operation in the former Belgian Congo. I understand the American CIA rates the reliability of information of this nature on a scale of one to five, five being the most reliable. By that criteria, this information would be FIVE.

With the exception of Guevara, who is believed to be in or en route to Paris, all of the officers and most of the enlisted men are in one of the training camps secretly established in Pina del Rio Province, and identified as Pita 1, Pita 2, and Pita 3. Pita 2 and Pita 3 are still under construction.

In the parentheses following the officer's rank is the Swahili name these individuals will use in the Operation. One might logically deduce they have someone fluent in Swahili available to them.

(1) Guevara, Ernesto de la Serna
Major (Tatu)
No comment considered necessary

(2)
Dreke, Victor
Major (Moja)

Although he is not a professional officer, Dreke is a highly skilled guerrilla, who served with Castro and Guevara in the Sierra Maestra. He is a dedicated Communist, and a close and trusted friend of both Guevara and Castro.

Until this assignment, he has been Deputy Commandant of the Fight Against Bands of Counterrevolutionaries (Acronym from the Spanish, LCB). He is not adverse to executing persons believed to be counterrevolutionaries on the spot when and where detected.

Dreke is a very dangerous man, whose mission will probably be similar to that of a political commissar in the Soviet Army — that is, in addition to his military duties, he will do whatever is necessary to maintain communist zeal.

(3) Tamayo, José María Martínez
Ministry of the Interior officer (Mbili)
Martínez is a former military intelligence officer, whose function at the Interior Ministry has included supervision of the Secret Police.

(4) Gilbert, Raphael Zerquera, M.D.
Not Known (Kumi)
This would seem to indicate Ernesto Guevara de la Serna, M.D., plans to be too busy with other activities to serve as the operation's physician.

(5) Terry, Santiago
Captain (Ali)

Terry is not a professional soldier. He was "commissioned" as a reward for his service while with Castro in the Sierra Maestra mountains. He and Guevara and Dreke are the only officers who have any experience in waging guerrilla warfare.

(6) Pichardo, Norberto Pio
Lieutenant (Inne)
Pichardo is a recently commissioned officer who served in Infantry.

The following enlisted men are members of the cadre. Some of them served in the Sierra Maestra, but most are simply soldiers recruited from the Cuban Army because of their black skin. Few, if any, are believed to have guerrilla experience.

Sergeant Eduardo Torres Ferrer (Coqui),
Sergeant Julián Morejón Gilbert (Tiza)
Sergeant Victor Manuel Ballester (Telathini)
Sergeant Ramón Muñoz Caballero (Maganga)
Corporal Pablo Osvaldo Ortíz (Sita)
Corporal Pedro Ortíz (Saba)
Private Aldo García González (Tano)
Private Martín Chivás (Ishirini)
Private José Escudero (Arobaini)
Private Constantino Pérez Méndez (Hansini)
Private Angel Fernández Angulo (Sitaini)
Private Lucio Sánchez Rivero (Rabanini)
Private Noelio Revé Robles (Kigolo)

Oliver waited until Jack had read the second page.

"You think this is from that little bird we keep hearing about?"

"I wouldn't be surprised," Jack said. "And this little bird apparently still has some friends in Cuba."

[THREE]
International Arrival Terminal
Miami International Airport
Miami, Florida
0645 7 February 1965

A zealous officer of the U.S. Immigration and Naturalization Service, who Captain John S. Oliver had within three minutes of meeting decided was a chickenshit sonofabitch with the brains of a gnat, had delayed the return of Oliver and Lieutenant Jacques Portet into the land of their birth.

The INS officer, on inspecting their passports, had noticed they did not have an EXIT stamp indicating the time and date they had left the United States for a foreign nation. And here they were, returning from a foreign nation. Something, he concluded, was clearly amiss.

Captain Oliver had explained that he and Lieutenant Portet had left the United States on competent orders issued by the United States Department of the Army, which ordered them to proceed to Buenos Aires, Argentina, and such other places as duty required, and to travel by government and/or commercial air, rail, sea, and motor transport.

He produced copies of these orders and explained that he and Lieutenant Portet had departed the United States aboard a U.S. Army

641

aircraft, in which case having one's passport stamped was not required. He further explained that they had left the U.S. Army aircraft in Buenos Aires, Argentina, and were now returning, via commercial aircraft.

The INS officer's position was that their passports did not bear an EXIT stamp, and here they were trying to get them stamped RETURNED. Something was clearly amiss, and he could not admit them under such circumstances without consulting superior authority.

That superior authority functionary was normally on duty until 6 A.M., but he had left a little early (it was then 5:25 A.M.) and it would be necessary to wait for his replacement to come on duty at 6 A.M. The INS officer was deaf to Captain Oliver's plea that he and Lieutenant Portet were on an Eastern Airlines flight to Atlanta departing Miami at 0715, and if there was a delay, they were not going to be able to make it.

The INS superior authority functionary scheduled to go on duty at 6 A.M. had a little car trouble and did not make an appearance until 6:25 A.M.

When apprised of the situation, the INS superior authority functionary examined Captain Oliver's and Lieutenant Portet's orders and passports and quickly reached a decision.

"No problem," he said. "Welcome home."

Captain Oliver was perhaps a little distracted when he led Lieutenant Portet out of the Customs area into the terminal. He was intent on finding one of the "You Are Here" maps he knew were mounted on various pillars of the terminal concourse, so that he could determine where the hell he was, where the hell Eastern Airlines was, and maybe be lucky enough to get there in time to board the plane.

Finger on the "You Are Here" map, he paid absolutely no attention to the redheaded female who stepped up behind him — he did notice her perfume — until she spoke.

"Hey, there, soldier, looking for a good time?"

He turned to examine the redheaded female.

"I will be a sonofabitch," he said.

"I know," Liza Wood Oliver said, "but I married you anyway."

When, perhaps ninety seconds later, he removed his face from Liza's neck, he saw that Lieutenant Portet was similarly engaged with Mrs. Portet.

"Where's Allan?" he asked.

"With Jack's stepmother," Liza said. "I didn't want to wake him up this early."

"What's going on?"

"You're on ten days' leave, you and Jack," Liza said. "Colonel Lowell arranged it. And called Marjorie and suggested we might like to meet you —"

"I've got to call Lowell," Oliver blurted. "I've got something for him."

"And it won't wait?" Liza asked.

"Sometime today," Jack said.

"— and we're in Lowell's house in Ocean Reef," Liza said. "And driving that wonderful old Packard of his."

"What's that all about?"

"Halfway down here in Jack's Jaguar, Marjorie and I realized that we now had husbands to ferry around, and we really should have taken my car."

He laughed.

"I guess we're not used to being married women," Liza said. "I wonder why?"

[FOUR]
12 Surf Point Drive
The Ocean Reef Club
Key Largo, Florida
1005 7 February 1965

Oliver waited until Liza had closed the bathroom door and he heard the sound of the shower before reaching for the bedside telephone. Then he hung it up, went to his trousers and found his wallet and the number, and picked up the telephone again and dialed it.

"Strike Aviation Section, Sergeant McMullen, sir."

"Colonel Lowell, please, Captain Oliver calling."

"The Colonel's tied up, sir. Maybe I can be of help?"

"Thanks, but no thanks, Sergeant. Please tell him I'm on the line and holding."

"Yes, sir."

Lowell came on the line a moment later, but before he spoke to Oliver, Oliver could hear him speak to Sergeant McMullen: "I thought I told you, Mac, Oliver's on the anytime, anywhere list."

And then he spoke to Oliver.

"Sorry about that. I thought I told Mac you were on the good guy list, but the shake of his head and hurt look on his Irish face tells me I didn't. What's up, Johnny?"

Before Oliver could reply, Lowell added, "Christ, the brides did meet the plane, didn't they?"

"Yes, sir, driving your Packard. And we are now in your house. For which I am, we are, very grateful."

"I'm glad somebody's using both. How did things go down there?"

"I have a present for you from Colonel Rangio. Actually two presents. A bottle of Argentine champagne for you and Major Lunsford. And a letter, sort of, for you."

"What's the letter, sort of, say?" Lowell asked, then picked up on Oliver's hesitation. "Johnny, I hope you read it."

"Yes, sir. I thought maybe I should."

"So what's it say?"

"It's a list of people, name, rank, code name, who are going to Africa."

"Good God!"

"I think it's good stuff, sir. Things went very well with Rangio, because of Zammoro."

There was no reply for a long moment.

"I hate to interrupt your leave, Johnny, but I want the list, and I know Felter will. I was going to tell you to take it to Homestead Air Force Base — it's not far from where you are — and have them send it up here. But I really think I should talk to you both. Would it make things easier for you if I offered to buy lunch for the brides at the Homestead O Club at twelve-thirty or one?"

"We'll be there if you want us to, sir."

"I've got access to a T-37, but I don't like to fly into Ocean Reef in an Air Force airplane. And Geoff's got the Cessna at Bragg."

"I understand, sir. We'll be there at 1230."

The line went dead.

Johnny put the telephone back in its cradle and rolled onto his back.

" 'We'll' is who? And 'there' is where?" Liza asked.

She was standing in the bathroom door,

naked and dripping.

"The little red 'line in use' button on the bathroom extension lit up," she explained, "and suspicious wife that you better understand I am, I wondered who my husband was talking to."

" 'We'll' is all four of us. Colonel Lowell wants to buy us lunch at Homestead AF Base."

Liza looked as if she was going to say something. Johnny worried what it would be.

What she finally said was, "Well, for reasons I can't imagine, I seem to have worked up an appetite."

She turned and walked back into the bathroom.

After a moment, Johnny swung his legs out of bed and walked after her.

[FIVE]
Officers' Open Mess
Homestead AF Base, Florida
1220 7 February 1965

Lt. Col. Craig W. Lowell was waiting for them just inside the door.

Marjorie Portet went to him and kissed him.

"If you're here to tell us we don't get the ten days' leave, Uncle Craig," she said, "I'll kill you."

"You get the ten days — and probably more, if you ask for it," Lowell said.

"In that case, we're glad to see you," Marjorie said. "And thanks for letting us use your house."

"I just need a word with Johnny and Jack," Lowell said. He shook their hands. "Jack, have you had a chance to talk to your dad yet?"

"No, sir. He was leaving for Miami when we got to Ocean Reef. He said something about looking at airplanes."

"He's now the president of Intercontinental Air Ltd., and I'm surprised he didn't tell you."

"He's probably saving it for dinner," Jack said.

"More than likely," Lowell said. "You said you have a letter for me, Johnny?"

"A letter and a bottle of champagne," Oliver said.

Jack handed him a paper bag with the champagne, and Oliver handed him the envelope from Rangio.

"Let's go in and get a table," Lowell said.

"These young officers and their ladies are whooping it up on leave," Lowell said to the waiter, "and thus will require something intoxicating. I'm unfortunately on duty, and iced tea will have to do."

"Now that I know I'm not going to have another abbreviated honeymoon," Liza said. "I think I would like something . . ."

"Champagne?" Lowell asked.

"Why not?"

"They probably don't have any cold," Marjorie said.

"Do you?" Lowell asked the waiter.

"Yes, sir, of course," the waiter said.

"The Air Force lives much better than we poor soldiers," Lowell said. "I would have thought your father would have told you that. Bring them a bottle of something nice. After we have a sip, we'll order."

"Yes, sir."

Lowell took the two typewritten sheets from Rangio's envelope and read them.

"You showed this to Jack?" Lowell asked.

"Yes, sir."

"Very interesting, where Rangio tells us our friend is," Lowell said. "Especially since this is the last word from our friends in Virginia, who appear to be a day late again."

He handed Jack a sheet of paper.

SECRET

Central Intelligence Agency
Langley, Virginia

FROM: Assistant Director For Administration

DATE: 6 February 1965 1805 GMT

SUBJECT: Guevara, Ernesto (Memorandum # 51.)

TO: Mr. Sanford T. Felter
Counselor To The President
Room 637, The Executive Office Building
Washington, D.C.

By Courier

In compliance with Presidential Memorandum to The Director, Subject: "Ernesto 'Che' Guevara," dated 14 December 1964, the following information is furnished:

(Reliability Scale Five) (From CIA, Paris, France)

SUBJECT is in Paris, staying at the Cuban

Embassy. He is accompanied by (First Name Unknown) OSMANY; Emilio ARAGONÉS; (FNU) PAPITO; and (FNU) MANRESA.

SUBJECT visited the Louvre museum 1300–1630 Paris Time accompanied by an Antonio CARRIOOL, the Cuban Ambassador to Paris and an unknown official of the French Foreign Ministry.

Tonight, he and his entourage, plus CARRIOOL, are scheduled to attend a formal dinner at the ChiCom Embassy.

Howard W. O'Connor
HOWARD W. O'CONNOR

SECRET

Jack read it and handed it to Oliver, who read it and handed it back to Lowell.

Lowell folded it and put it into the Rangio envelope.

"I was going to carefully grill you about the Argentines," Lowell said. "To see if they were really on the team or just being charming. This makes that unnecessary, wouldn't you say?"

"I'm sure they're with us, sir," Oliver said.

"Sandy Felter will love this," Lowell said, tapping the envelope. "He'll send an FYI copy to the agency. You obviously made the right decision about Zammoro, Johnny. I think that will open a lot of doors."

"What decision about Zammoro?" Liza asked.

"I can't answer that," Lowell said. "And your husband can't with me sitting here. But I agree with Felter's observation that pillow talk is the one large hole in security that'll never get plugged."

"You're not going to tell us what *any* of this is all about, right?" Marjorie challenged.

"Right," Lowell confirmed.

"Do we at least get to ask what happens next?" Marjorie asked.

Lowell thought that over.

"Okay," he said. "After you leave, you report back to Bragg. Several weeks after that — maybe as much as a month after — Jack goes to the Congo —"

"For how long?" Marjorie asked.

"You better count on at least a month, and maybe a month or two longer," Lowell said. "Which, I think I should point out, is a considerably shorter period of time than a tour in Vietnam."

"And Johnny?" Liza asked.

"For the time being, Johnny stays at Bragg. Then he goes wherever he's needed, either to the Congo or South America. Unless something unexpected happens, neither will be gone from Bragg for very long."

"Isn't something unexpected happening inevitable?" Liza asked.

"Like you and Johnny getting married after all?" Lowell replied.

The waiter ended the conversation by delivering the champagne.

650

[SIX]
Room 637, The Executive Office Building
Washington, D.C.
1135 8 February 1965

"I didn't expect to see you," Colonel Sanford T. Felter said when Lieutenant Colonel Craig W. Lowell walked into his small office.

"I'm fine, sir," Lowell said. "Thank you very much for asking, sir. And might I inquire into the Colonel's all around well-being, sir?"

Felter did not reply.

"I'll settle for 'Hello, Craig,' " Lowell said.

"Hello, Craig. I didn't expect to see you," Felter said sarcastically, but there was a smile on his lips.

"What do we know new about our friend Ernesto?" Lowell asked.

"This just came in," Felter said as he opened a drawer in his desk, to come out with a sheet of paper.

SECRET

Central Intelligence Agency
Langley, Virginia

FROM: Assistant Director For Administration

DATE: 7 February 1965 1805 GMT

SUBJECT: Guevara, Ernesto (Memorandum # <u>52</u>.)

TO: Mr. Sanford T. Felter

> Counselor To The President
> Room 637, The Executive Office Building
> Washington, D.C.
>
> By Courier
>
> In compliance with Presidential Memorandum to The Director, Subject: "Ernesto 'Che' Guevara," dated 14 December 1964, the following information is furnished:
>
> (Reliability Scale Three) (From CIA Hong Kong)
>
> SUBJECT is reported to be in Peking for meeting(s) with Liu Chao Chi and other senior members of the Communist Party Secretariat.
>
> *Howard W. O'Connor*
> HOWARD W. O'CONNOR
>
> ## SECRET

"What's he doing in China?" Lowell asked when he had read it.

"Whatever it is, it's not good news," Felter said. "The least that will happen is that the Chinese will provide arms. That's not good news."

Lowell grunted his agreement, then smiled.

"Well, for a change, I am the bearer of good news," he said, and tossed Rangio's envelope on Felter's desk.

"What's this?" Felter asked as he took the two sheets of paper from the envelope. He raised his eyes to Lowell when he had read it.

"I got it from Johnny Oliver yesterday in Florida. He got it the night before in Buenos Aires from one of Rangio's men, who got on their Aerolineas plane to tell them they had a free upgrade to first class." He paused. "And earlier that day, the day they left Argentina, Rangio went with them to Córdoba, showed them where Señor Guevara lived, was an altar boy, where he played soccer, and introduced them not only to Guevara's next-door neighbor, but to the SIDE guy in Córdoba and the chief of the Policía Federal for Córdoba."

"Sounds too good to be true. 'Beware of the Argentines bearing gifts'?" Felter said.

"Both Oliver and Portet believe the affection between Rangio and Zammoro is genuine."

"As a result of which Rangio will happily arrange a clear shot at Guevara for Zammoro? Or vice versa?"

"According to Oliver, Zammoro takes being an officer seriously. . . ."

"Hang around him, maybe it'll be contagious," Felter said. "How did you get up here, anyway?"

"In a T-37," Lowell said. "I have developed a close relationship with my Air Force peers at Strike. They let me fly their airplanes."

"I don't want to know how you've developed that close relationship," Felter said, and chuckled, and then grew serious. "This Rangio/Zammoro thing really sounds a little too good to be true."

"Oliver said that when he 'counseled' Zammoro about not having told anybody about knowing

653

Rangio, Zammoro said something to the effect that he had taken an oath before God to obey the orders of those appointed over him, and he would obey those orders . . ."

He paused and took a slip of paper and read from it:

". . . 'even if those orders are not to kill the Anti-Christ sonofabitch who has my wife in a cage on starvation rations.' "

"You wrote it down?"

"Johnny Oliver did, he wanted to remember it exactly. And he gave it to me."

"And Oliver was taken in by this melodramatic announcement of loyalty and obedience to orders?"

"Yeah, Sandy, he was. And so was young Portet. And from the way they tell the story, and the way that Rangio came through with the names — which is more than the names, it's an admission he's got people close to the top in Havana — so am I."

"Well, it's moot," Felter said. He tapped Rangio's list of Cubans. "Between you and me, this will help my credibility with the President."

"Is that getting to be a problem?"

"There's one of me and — what's that sailor's prayer? 'My ship is so small and Your ocean so big'? — and so many CIA people with convincing mannerisms."

"You're pretty convincing yourself, Sandy," Lowell said, very seriously. "You have been right so many times when the Agency has been wrong."

"I feel like a tightrope walker working without a net," Felter said. "You only get to make one mistake under those conditions."

"I'll buy you lunch to cheer you up," Lowell said.

"No, but thanks anyway. I'm on my way to Camp David." He paused. "I'm glad to have this from Rangio."

"Anything special going on?"

Felter looked at him for a moment, then handed him a radio teletype message. Paper-clipped to it was a small sheet of crisp notepaper:

The Chief of Staff

I didn't know if you would get this in time for this afternoon's session.

OPERATIONAL IMMEDIATE
SECRET
1535 ZULU 7 FEBRUARY 1965
FROM: HQ US MILITARY ASSISTANCE
COMMAND VIETNAM
TO: DEPT OF THE ARMY WASH DC
IMMEDIATE PERSONAL ATTENTION C/S US
ARMY

CONFIRMATION OF RADIOTELECON THIS
HQ AND DUTY OFFICER SITUATION ROOM
HQ DEPT OF THE ARMY 1455 THIS DATE.

1. AT 1035 ZULU 7 FEBRUARY 1965
VIETCONG FORCES ATTACKED CAMP
HOLLOWAY, A FACILITY FOR US MILITARY

ADVISORS TO ARMY OF THE REPUBLIC OF SOUTH VIETNAM. CAMP HOLLOWAY IS SITED IN THE CENTRAL HIGHLANDS OF THE RVN, NEAR PLEIKU.

2.   INITIAL REPORTS INDICATE EIGHT (8) US MILADV PERSONNEL KILLED IN ACTION; ONE HUNDRED (100) US MILADV PERSONNEL WOUNDED IN ACTION; AND 10 (TEN) US AIRCRAFT DESTROYED.

3.   THE VC ATTACK ACHIEVED SURPRISE AND THE VC WERE ABLE TO WITHDRAW AFTER THE ATTACK WITH MINIMAL LOSSES.

4.   THE KIA, MIA, AND AIRCRAFT LOSSES, GIVEN IN (2) ABOVE, ARE CONFIRMED BUT PRELIMINARY, AND ADDITIONAL LOSSES OF KIA, MIA, AND A/C SHOULD BE ANTICIPATED.

5.   AN AFTER ACTION REPORT WILL BE FURNISHED ON COMPLETION.

GREGORY, MAJ GEN, USA
J-3 USMAC VIETNAM

SECRET

"That was delivered by one of the chief's aides," Felter said. "I've known him for a long time; he was one of my instructors at Beast Barracks at West Point, when I was a plebe."

Lowell's eyebrows rose, but he didn't say anything.

"I remember him with his nose against mine," Felter went on, "his spittle spraying my face. He told me I shouldn't expect to be around long — there was no room for wiseass New York Hebrews in his army. I don't think he's changed his opinion of me over the years; I don't think he's among my legion of admirers."

"Hell, Mouse, you won. He's the errand boy. And the chief is, otherwise he wouldn't have sent you that."

"I'd like to know if the chief sent me that because he thinks I'm a soldier, or because — obviously — the President wants me at the meeting he's called in response to this."

"You have the admiration of a lot of good soldiers, Mouse. Bellmon, Hanrahan, many others, and of course me," Lowell said. "What does this VC attack mean?"

"It means the commitment of more troops is now a certainty, rather than a possibility. The Marines are forming a reinforced regimental-size Expeditionary Force, the Ninth, for 'possible use' in Vietnam. Now they'll go for sure, and more troops — Marine and Army — will follow."

"Is this going to have any effect on us?"

"It already has. Finton got a call two days ago from the Air Force, saying that the C-130 that was supposed to pick up the black L-19 at Bragg won't, having been diverted to a mission with a higher priority, and that this unspecified higher-priority mission — obviously Vietnam — will also almost certainly delay indefinitely the airlift I asked for to take the Beaver, the H-13, et cetera et cetera to the Congo."

"I thought you had all the priority you needed?" Lowell countered.

Felter looked at him almost tolerantly, as if pained to realize that anyone he knew so well could be so dense.

" 'You know what we did last week?' " he mock-quoted. " 'While people are getting killed in Vietnam, while we have to replace the ten airplanes that got blown up in Pleiku, we flew to fucking *Africa* with a fucking L-19 and half a dozen grunts in the back.' "

He paused and went on.

"How long do you think that secret mission would stay secret?" he asked. "I may have to do it, but I really don't want to."

"Maybe that's not going to be as much of a problem as you think, Mouse," Lowell said. "Presuming you can come up with the money to charter a 707 from Intercontinental Air Ltd."

"I have absolutely no idea what you're talking about."

"Captain Jean-Philippe Portet is now president and chief executive officer of Intercontinental Air Ltd. That's the rest of the good news I flew all the way up here to tell you in person," Lowell said.

"He found the money to buy an airline with a 707?" Felter asked. A smile crossed his face.

"He didn't find it," Lowell said. "Our friends from Langley came to Florida, checkbook in hand, practically forcing it on him."

"This is a done deal?" Felter asked.

"It's a done deal," Lowell said. "And Cousin Porter done the deal, which means he really put the screws to the Agency. It may take them a while to figure it out, but Porter really screwed them. They provided the money, and they don't have any control whatever."

"And you really think this is a good thing?" Felter asked softly.

"You don't?"

"If you'd asked me, I would have told you under no circumstances to get Captain Portet involved with the Agency."

"Ah, come on, Mouse. They're always screwing us, and waiting for their next chance to do it again. Fuck them. For once we had the chance to screw them."

"They're not the enemy, goddamn it," Felter said. "There's a lot of good people over there."

"Name one."

"Stephens, for example. You told me he was helpful as hell in Buenos Aires. And Colby, for example."

"Who?"

"Bill Colby, the CIA station chief in Saigon."

"Oh, yeah. But, hell, he's one of us. He jumped into France in World War II with the OSS. He's not what you could call a standard Langley candy-ass chair warmer. Name somebody else."

"I don't want to debate this with you," Felter said. "But get this straight, Craig, get out of your 'Fuck you, CIA' frame of mind. That's not a suggestion, that's an order."

Lowell just looked at him.

"I gave you an order, Colonel," Felter said.

"Yes, sir."

"I'll have to go to the Director and try to pour oil on the troubled waters," Felter said. "He'll be at Camp David this afternoon."

"What do you want me to do about Intercontinental Air Ltd.?"

"If you took the wings off a Beaver, could you

get it in Portet's 707?"

Lowell considered the question.

"You'd probably have to take the landing gear off, too," he said. "Put it on some kind of skid, pallet, but yeah, I think so."

"Have Mr. Finton issue a purchase order," Felter said. "And for God's sake, don't take this as a license to steal from the government."

"Yes, sir."

"And make a real effort to think things through before you jump into something else, will you?"

"If I fucked up, Mouse," Lowell said. "I'm sorry."

"You should be," Felter said. "Whenever I hear the phrase 'loose cannon,' I see your face."

Felter looked at his watch, nodded at Lowell, and walked out of his office without another word.

[SEVEN]
Office of the Commanding General
John F. Kennedy Center for Special Warfare
Fort Bragg, North Carolina
1300 8 February 1965

"Major Lunsford requests a few minutes of your time, General," Captain Stefan Zabrewski boomed into Brigadier General Paul R. Hanrahan's office from the door.

Hanrahan, who was deep into paperwork, made a *"let him in"* sign with his fingers, but did not raise his eyes from the paperwork for perhaps sixty seconds. When he did, he saw Lunsford standing at rigid attention ten inches from his desk, his right hand holding a stiff-fingered salute.

Hanrahan returned it with a casual wave in the general direction of his forehead.

"The major is grateful the general is willing to give the major some of his valuable time without an appointment," Father said.

"I'm up to my ass in paper and in no mood for your sophomoric humor," Hanrahan said.

"May the major take that as permission to assume the position of Parade Rest, sir?"

"The major better have something pretty damned important on his so-called mind when he sits down," Hanrahan said.

"Thank you, sir," Father said, and slumped into the chair before Hanrahan's desk.

"Well?" Hanrahan asked impatiently.

"Sir, the major believes he will not be wasting the general's time. Sir, the major believes that an incipient rebellion, perhaps even a mutiny, is worthy of the general's time."

"Now you're really not funny, Father," Hanrahan said.

"What happened is that one of the cadre, a staff sergeant whose name I know but would prefer not to reveal, mistook a couple of the ASA guys for privates on a labor detail, and did the standard 'you and you come with me' routine, whereupon the senior of the ASA guys said, 'Go fuck yourself, I'm sick of you and your fucking kind,' or words to that effect."

"That's insubordination," Hanrahan said.

"Not if you're a Spec7," Father said, "and the guy you told to go fuck himself is a staff sergeant, E-6. I think that may be conduct unbecoming an NCO, but I don't really know. In defense of the sergeant, the ASA Spec7 was not wearing stripes."

"So what happened?" Hanrahan asked.

"The sergeant went looking for the Doubting Thomas, who he correctly believed was in the charge of the legs at Mackall to report the insubordination and the ASA guys went to Aunt Jemima, where he repeated that he and the other ASA guys were sick of being fucked with by every other Green Beanie with a room-temperature IQ, and they were right on the edge of unvolunteering for overseas duty of a classified and hazardous nature."

The Army Security Agency had provided Operation Earnest with twelve enlisted men, all of African heritage, all of whom were either skilled electronic technicians or high-speed radiotelegraph operators, and in many cases both.

"They're serious, or just pissed?" Hanrahan asked, now concerned.

"The Spec7 volunteered out of the White House Signal Agency, where he went to work every day in a suit, and had coffee served to him on duty from the presidential kitchen. That was the reason he didn't have stripes on his fatigues; he hasn't owned fatigues for years, and the Mackall supply room didn't have any Spec7 stripes to issue him when they issued the fatigues. There are just over a hundred Spec7's in the entire U.S. Army, I learned today. He's pissed and serious."

"Nobody told your guys who the ASA guys were?" Hanrahan asked.

"My guys know. The Mackall cadre does not. They didn't have the need-to-know."

"What's the root of the problem?"

"The ASA guys — and, Aunt Jemima tells me, the airplane guys as well, including Aunt Jemima and the other two pilots — do not at all like being regarded as a lesser specimen of soldier, for that matter of human being, by every — to quote Aunt

Jemima — 'high-level cretin whose claim to fame is having jumped out of a perfectly functioning aircraft while in flight.' "

Despite himself, Hanrahan had to smile.

"They sound like Craig Lowell," he said.

"That's part of this," Father said. "They know about Lowell, or think they do, and about Jack Portet. What's the real skinny on Lowell? Was his first jump really a HALO, as legend has it?"

"Yeah, it was," Hanrahan said, and then went on: "Special Forces, Special Operations, really got its start in Greece, with the U.S. Military Advisory Group, Greece. A lot of the people there — Felter and me, for openers — were parachutists, Rangers. Lowell was neither. But he was one hell of a special operations soldier there. A while back, they grandfathered everybody who had combat service in Greece into Special Forces. Felter and Lowell and me included. Lowell declined the honor, saying he didn't want anyone to think he was dumb enough to jump out of a perfectly functioning aircraft in flight."

Father chuckled.

"That sounds like him," he said.

"For a number of reasons, both Felter and I thought Lowell should be identified with Special Forces. It was 'suggested' to him that he apply for Special Forces, and he couldn't find the time. So one day a couple of years ago, he was here, and we suited him up in high-altitude gear so he could watch a HALO from a C-141 at 30,000 feet. He was standing on the open ramp, watching, when two HALO experts grabbed his arms and walked him over the edge. When he landed, I told him he was now a parachutist whether he liked it or not, and handed him jump wings and a Green Beret."

"He wears it now like he likes it," Father said.

"Afterward, he went to Benning and did a half a dozen other jumps, so he was entitled to wear the wings. I think he has a total of seven jumps, maybe eight."

"And these guys know about Portet," Father said.

"Leading up to what, Father?"

"They want jump wings and shiny jump boots, General," Lunsford said. "If it takes jumping out of a perfectly functioning aircraft while in flight, so be it."

"You're not serious?"

Lunsford nodded.

"Even Aunt Jemima and the other two pilots," he said.

"That's simply out of the question."

"That's what I told Aunt Jemima," Lunsford said, "to which he replied, 'Why? We've done everything here we have to. We're sitting around with our thumbs up our ass waiting for God only knows what to go to Africa.' Significant line: 'If Portet did it, why not us'?"

"Jesus H. Christ!"

"I didn't have an answer for him I could give with a straight face," Lunsford said.

"There's no way I could get spaces for them at Benning," Hanrahan said. "And even if I could, there's no time. Felter tells me by the time Portet and Oliver come off leave, there will be transportation. He's got some sort of civilian charter set up."

"I tried that," Lunsford said. "They've seen people jumping from Beavers and Hueys at Mackall, and they reasonably ask, 'Why not us?' "

"Because I don't have the authority to authorize

something like that, and you know it."

"We're back to Portet. If Portet did it, why can't we?"

"This is an absurd conversation, you realize that? These guys are soldiers, and soldiers can't go on strike."

"I don't think they would actually unvolunteer — they're soldiers, good soldiers, all of them — but unless you can think of something I can't to tell them, we're going to be taking to Africa twenty-five people we have just told we don't think are as good as us. That's going to shoot the old team spirit in the ass."

"Just for the sake of conversation — nothing more — if you were sitting in this chair, what would you do?"

"Exigencies of the service," Lunsford said.

"I can't get away with that here for twenty-odd people, and you know it."

"Are you humoring me, or do you really want to know what I would do?"

"I want to know, but that's not saying I'll do anything but snort."

"We have a little clandestine jump school here, let them make five jumps out of a Beaver and a Huey —"

"I don't have the authority to issue orders putting them on jump status," Hanrahan repeated. "And I don't want to pin wings on these guys only to have to tell them to take them off."

"All you have to do here is pin the wings on," Lunsford said. "Quietly, at Mackall."

"And the orders designating them Army parachutists?"

"I issue them in Africa," Lunsford said. "Classified Secret. 'The exigencies of the service having made it necessary for the following officers and men to participate in parachute operations in connection with a classified assignment, and having done so a minimum of five times, they are hereby designated Army parachutists.' You get a copy of the order, declassify so much of it as pertains to designation as Army parachutists, and direct that it be confirmed and made a matter of record."

"You'd need a microscope to see the line between what you're suggesting and knowingly and willingly issuing and/or uttering a false document."

"These guys want to be on the team," Lunsford said. "Why not prove to them we think of them that way? What about 'The Good of the Service'?"

"My God, Father!" Hanrahan said, and slumped back in his chair for a full sixty seconds.

"Do it," he said finally.

Lunsford rose to his feet and came to attention.

"Yes, sir. Does the major have the general's permission to withdraw?"

"The major has my permission to go fuck himself," Hanrahan replied. "If one of these guys so much as sprains an ankle, Father, I'll break both of your legs."

"Yes, sir. Thank you, sir."

Major Lunsford executed a perfect about-face movement and marched out of the office.

[ONE]

SECRET

Central Intelligence Agency
Langley, Virginia

FROM: Assistant Director For Administration

DATE: 13 February 1965 0810 GMT

SUBJECT: Guevara, Ernesto (Memorandum # 56.)

TO: Mr. Sanford T. Felter
Counselor To The President
Room 637, The Executive Office Building
Washington, D.C.

By Courier

In compliance with Presidential Memorandum to The Director, Subject: "Ernesto 'Che' Guevara," dated 14 December 1964, the following information is furnished:

(Reliability Scale Three) (From CIA,

Johannesburg, South Africa) SUBJECT believed to have arrived from unknown departure point, possibly Peking, in China aboard Air France Flight 811 0805 Zulu 12 February 1965. SUBJECT did not pass through South African passport facilities, and departed Johannesburg 1250 Zulu 12 February 1965 on UTA Flight 2332, probable destination Dar es Salaam, Tanzania.

(Reliability Scale Five) (From CIA Dar es Salaam, Tanzania) SUBJECT arrived Dar es Salaam 1645 Zulu 12 February aboard UTA Flight 2332 from Johannesburg, South Africa.

(Reliability Scale Three) (From CIA Dar es Salaam) SUBJECT is to meet with President Julius Kambarage Nyerere, despite official government denials that SUBJECT is in, or expected in, Tanzania.

Howard W. O'Connor
HOWARD W. O'CONNOR

SECRET

[TWO]
Camp Mackall, North Carolina
1205 19 February 1965

The Bell HU-1D "Huey" fluttered down to the crude Mackall airstrip as luncheon was being served to what was now — as of the day before yesterday — officially known as Special Forces Detachment 17.

When an army unit is activated, even down to company-sized units, there is almost always an activation ceremony. A band plays, and a senior officer presents the unit's colors to the sergeant major, and makes appropriate remarks. The new commander then makes appropriate remarks. The newly activated unit, in class A uniform then marches past a reviewing stand.

This did not happen with Detachment 17.

Master Sergeant William "Doubting" Thomas stood up in the mess at the evening meal and thumped on a stainless-steel water pitcher with a knife until he had everyone's attention.

"You will all be doubtless thrilled to know that as of yesterday, the Army has a new unit, Special Forces Detachment 17, and all you clowns are in it. Any questions?"

There was a chorus of voices, all asking essentially the same question, with variations of colorful profanity: "When the [expletive deleted] do we get out of this [expletive deleted] place?"

"The major says he hopes to have something about that tomorrow," Master Sergeant Thomas said, to be greeted by moans of disbelief.

The interim Table of Organization & Equipment under which Detachment 17 was formed called for six officers and thirty-five enlisted men. The officers were Major G. W. Lunsford, Commanding; Lieutenant Geoffrey Craig, Executive Officer; Captain Darrell J. Smythe, Aviation Officer; Captain J. Kenneth Williams, M.C., Surgeon; and three other Army aviators, one of whom was Lieutenant Jacques Portet, and the other two the first Morning Report stated were not yet joined.

Seniority would normally have dictated that Captain Smythe be the executive officer, but his only combat experience had been as an aviator. Geoff Craig was only a lieutenant, but Geoff had combat experience as a Green Beret and had been in the Congo during the Simba uprising. Experience, rather than regulations, counted.

Similarly, it was pointed out to Dr. Williams that he had zero experience in treating traumatic injury caused by gunfire — Dr. Williams was a parasitologist recruited from the Walter Reed Army Medical Center — and Sergeant First Class Amos T. Tyler, a Green Beret medic in Vietnam, had a hell of a lot of experience in that area. Dr. Williams was made to understand that, unless asked for his assistance by Sergeant Tyler, he would confine his services to keeping Detachment 17 as free as possible from tropical diseases and parasites.

The enlisted strength of Detachment 17 consisted of the original fourteen Green Berets, the twelve ASA communications technicians, and the nine aircraft mechanics and avionics technicians.

Major Lunsford did not — surprising nobody at all — show up first thing the next morning to inform the members of Detachment 17 when they could expect to leave the comforts of Camp Mackall.

But just as Detachment 17 was sitting down for the noon meal, when the Huey fluttered down onto the rather primitive landing strip near the tarpaper-covered frame shack that was the mess hall, the first passenger to get off was Major George Washington Lunsford. He was wearing camouflage fatigues.

"And there's General Hanrahan," someone said.

"And two other guys . . . officers," someone else said.

"What is that, beer?"

"That's what it is, and I'll be goddamned if that little guy carrying two cases isn't a full fucking bird colonel!"

A moment later, Major Lunsford, a case of beer under each arm, kicked the mess hall door open and bellowed, "At-ten-hut!"

Two seconds later, before anyone could fully rise from the plank benches, General Hanrahan, in fatigues and carrying one case of beer, marched in and ordered, "As you were."

He followed Major Lunsford to the serving line area of the mess, and when Lunsford had put his two cases of beer on the counter, set his beside it.

"Everybody here, Thomas?" General Hanrahan inquired.

"Everybody is presented or accounted for, sir," Master Sergeant Thomas replied.

"That's not what I asked, Thomas," General Hanrahan said.

"I sent Peters into Fayetteville, General," Major Lunsford offered. "He needed some stuff from Radio Shack."

Peters was Specialist Seven William D. Peters, the senior of the ASA communications experts.

"I said I wanted everybody here," Hanrahan said, a tone of annoyance in his voice. "Colonel Felter wanted to see him."

"I'm sorry, sir, I didn't know," Lunsford said.

Hanrahan let it ride; there wasn't much else he

could do. But he really wished that Spec7 Peters were here.

The other two officers — Colonel Sanford T. Felter and Lieutenant Colonel Craig W. Lowell, both in Class A uniforms, both cradling two cases of beer in their arms, went to the serving line and laid the beer on the floor.

General Hanrahan faced the officers and men of Special Forces Detachment 17.

"The officers with me today have been in this business since the beginning," he said. "We served together in Greece, and in other places. The taller is Lieutenant Colonel Craig W. Lowell. The other is Colonel Sanford T. Felter, General Staff Corps, Counselor to the President of the United States, and Action Officer, Operation Earnest."

Felter stepped onto one of the two-high stacks of beer cases. Even so, his head was lower than General Hanrahan's.

He put his hands on his hips and let his eyes slowly sweep the faces of Detachment 17, looking each man in the eye for a long moment.

He was formidable. His uniform was heavily laden with ribbons and qualification badges and patches. Topping the five rows of ribbons was one representing the Distinguished Service Cross, the nation's second-highest award for valor. Above that were the star and crest wings of a Master Parachutist, and above that the Combat Infantry Badge, with a star indicating the second award of the badge. There were clusters on his Silver Star, Bronze Star, and Purple Heart medals, indicating more than one award of each. He wore a Ranger tab on his sleeve, and his other breast pocket carried the insignia of the General Staff Corps and an array of parachutist's wings issued by half a dozen foreign governments.

By the time he had finished his visual sweep of the men of Detachment 17, the mess hall was absolutely quiet.

"By the power vested in me by God, the Commander-in-Chief, and General Hanrahan," Felter began sternly, "and largely because General Hanrahan tells me that you're all mentally retarded and deserve a little pity, I herewith declare a pardon for all of you, effective immediately."

It took a good fifteen seconds before the troops came to comprehension of what the little colonel with all those fucking medals and wings had just said. There were first a few nervous chuckles, and these grew to guffaws. They were now hanging on his every word.

"So far, you have been told you have volunteered for, and have been trained for, important and hazardous duty on the African continent," Felter went on. "Today, Colonel Lowell is going to tell you where you're going on the African continent and when and why. That information is highly classified, specifically, as Top Secret Earnest. That's not a joke. One loose mouth — one — can blow this whole operation out of the water. What you'll be doing is of great importance to our country, and is being carried out on the personal orders of President Johnson.

"As of midnight tomorrow night, you're all on a ten-day pre-embarkation leave. Anyone who can rise early tomorrow can leave then, but your leave will not start until midnight tomorrow night. So when you're home, resist the temptation to tell anyone what you're about to do. Anyone includes

673

your wife, or whoever else you're sharing your bed with. If you think you can get away with it, tell people you're going to be a military adviser to the South African Army. But don't even hint about where you're really going and why.

"President Johnson has asked me to convey to you his thanks for volunteering for this operation, and to wish you godspeed and good luck.

"As a young officer serving under then-Lieutenant Colonel Hanrahan in a war most people don't even know we had, I learned an important truth about Special Operations people. If you want them to pay attention during a briefing, make sure they have a beer in their hands. Your show, Colonel Lowell."

He stepped off the beer cases, ripped a case open, and signaled with his fingers for one of the sergeants to start passing out the beer.

When Lowell began the briefing, Felter looked around the room, pointed to Lunsford, Portet, and Thomas, and looked around for someone he couldn't find. Then he took a bottle of beer from a case and signaled for them to go to the rear of the mess hall. Hanrahan followed.

"Where's Bill Peters?" Felter asked.

"I sent him into Fayetteville," Lunsford said.

"I really wanted to see him," Felter said. "Why did you send him into town? I sent word I wanted everybody here."

Lunsford exhaled audibly.

"It is hard for someone named George Washington to tell a lie," Lunsford said. "The truth, Colonel, is that Peters is temporarily *hors de combat*, and we didn't want General Hanrahan to know."

"Why not?" Hanrahan challenged.

"Sir, the general will probably remember telling the major that he would break both of the major's legs if one of them so much as sprained his ankle."

"How bad is he?" Hanrahan asked, shaking his head.

"Nothing's broken," Lunsford said. "Tyler had his leg x-rayed. And it's not really sprained, but he took a hell of a whack on the horizontal stabilizer going out of the door of an L-20. Tyler thought it would be best if he put a cast on it."

"You're not telling me Peters was *jumping* from an L-20 when this happened?" Felter asked incredulously.

"Yes, sir," Lunsford said.

"Why was he jumping from an L-20, Father?" Felter asked softly.

"He didn't want to be a leg anymore, sir," Lunsford said. "None of them did."

"I knew there was something out of place," Felter said. He looked at the serving line end of the mess hall. "All those new Corcoran jump boots. Everybody's wearing jump boots, aren't they? Except Doctor Whatsisname."

"Sir, I brought Dr. Williams's jump boots with me on the Huey," Lunsford said. "He made his fifth, qualifying, jump last night."

"Everybody did this?" Felter asked incredulously.

"Yes, sir."

"When?"

"Well, sir, once they got the aircraft crated, and the communications up and running, there wasn't a hell of a lot for them to do —" Lunsford said.

"They *all* volunteered?" Felter said.

"To a man, sir," Lunsford said firmly.

Felter looked at Hanrahan.

"And DCSOPS gave you authority to conduct a jump school?"

"I'm afraid that's what some IG is going to ask me, Mouse," Hanrahan said.

"You can pin wings on them, I suppose," Felter said. "But how are you going to get it on their records so they can draw jump pay?"

"Major Lunsford has some very interesting ideas on how to do that, Colonel," Hanrahan said, looking at Lunsford.

"Well, if Major Lunsford's interesting ideas don't work, come to me. I think it was a good idea."

"Father sold me on the idea for team spirit," Hanrahan said.

"That, too, I suppose," Felter said thoughtfully, "but I was thinking of Mobutu and Colonel Supo," Felter said. "The brotherhood of those who jump out of airplanes." He smiled. "Can Peters travel?" he asked Lunsford.

"Tyler says he'll take the cast off in a week or ten days," Lunsford said.

"I mean right now?"

"Well, sir, he's on crutches," Lunsford said.

Felter took a sheet of paper from his inside pocket and handed it to Hanrahan, who read it, then passed it to Lunsford, who passed it to Portet.

SECRET

Central Intelligence Agency
Langley, Virginia

FROM: Assistant Director For Administration

DATE: 18 February 1965 1805 GMT

SUBJECT: Guevara, Ernesto (Memorandum # 58.)

TO: Mr. Sanford T. Felter
Counselor To The President
Room 637, The Executive Office Building
Washington, D.C.

By Courier

In compliance with Presidential Memorandum to The Director, Subject: "Ernesto 'Che' Guevara," dated 14 December 1964, the following information is furnished:

(Reliability Scale Five) (From CIA Dar es Salaam Tanzania) SUBJECT met with Demo KABILA, Tanzanian Foreign Minister and offered 30 (thirty) Cuban instructors and "appropriate arms" to "wage war against U.S. imperialism." KABILA accepted.

(Reliability Scale Five) (From CIA Dar es Salaam) In Dar es Salaam interview 16 February 1965 by Spanish language newspaper, Prensa Latina, SUBJECT was quoted as saying, "I am convinced that it is possible to create a common front of struggle against colonialism, imperialism and neocolonialism."

Howard W. O'Connor
HOWARD W. O'CONNOR

SECRET

"There seems to be no question that Guevara's going over there," Felter said. "The only question now is when, and in what strength. I'm afraid we're going to have to play the old Army game of hurry up and wait. I want to send Father, Portet, Thomas, and Johnny Oliver's friend. . . . What's his name?"

"Captain Darrell J. Smythe," Lunsford furnished. "Aunt Jemima."

Felter nodded. "Smythe," he said. "He jumped too?"

"Yes, sir," Lunsford said.

". . . over there as soon as possible. I don't want to give Mobutu a chance to change his mind, for one thing, and I want to get Thomas together with Colonel Supo."

He turned to Jack Portet.

"I spoke with your father on the way down here this morning," he said. "He apparently put the Intercontinental Air 707 through a 100-hour check, and found some things that have to be repaired. But he'll have the airplane ready by the time the team comes back from leave. On reflection, it made more sense to fly everybody and everything over there at once, rather than infiltrate the men a few at a time and rely on the Air Force to get the equipment to us when they can find the space. I'd rather save our priority until we need it."

"Yes, sir."

"So you charm Mobutu, decide where you want the 707, et cetera. You'll be the advance party, so to speak."

"Yes, sir," Jack said.

"Lowell told me he told you you would be here at least a month," Felter said. "Sorry, Jack, but it just can't be helped."

"I understand, sir," Jack said.

Felter looked as if he was going to say something else, something serious, but changed his mind.

"I want to tell you guys about Peters," he said, smiling. "He came over to my office from the White House and asked if he could speak to me personally. I said sure. He's always gone out of his way to take care of me."

"What was he doing in the White House?" Hanrahan asked.

"Making sure the President's communications don't break down," Felter said. "He had twenty guys working for him."

"So what's he doing here?" Hanrahan asked. "Why would he give that up for this?"

Felter smiled.

"He wants to be a *real* soldier," Felter said. "He said that when he came in the Army, he wanted to go Infantry, maybe even go to jump school. But he made the mistake of telling them he had a radio amateur's license. ASA is always looking for guys passing through reception centers who can read Morse *and* know about radios. So they put him in the Signal Corps and the ASA, and that's all he's done in the Army. Every time he applied for transfer, they told him he was essential. If he really raised hell, they promoted him. You know how few Spec7s there are in the Army? Probably less than a couple of hundred, and he's the youngest. Anyway, he told me he'd been reading my mail, knew what's going on with Operation Earnest, and knew that I levied the ASA for communications people. So he volunteered, and was told, again, he was essential. He said he knew I had the authority to levy him by name, and would I please do so, because I was his last chance of ever getting out of the ASA and 'back in the Army.' So I levied him by name, and the head of the ASA called me up and said I obviously didn't understand the situation, Peters was essential to the White House Signal Agency, and I just couldn't have him. I told him I had the priority, and wanted him. He said, 'Colonel, not as a threat, as a statement of fact, I'm going over your head with this one.' "

"Obviously," Hanrahan said, chuckling, "he wasn't familiar with your chain of command."

"I don't think he was," Felter said, smiling. "And I don't know if General Sawyer actually went to President Johnson, but the day before Peters came down here, he showed up at my office — it was the first time I'd ever seen him in a uniform — came to attention and saluted, and said he was reporting for duty. Then he started worrying that he wouldn't measure up to being around Green Berets. I assured him he didn't have to worry, all he had to do was make sure the communications worked, nobody expected him to eat snakes or jump out of airplanes."

"And we turn him into a parachutist," Jack said.

"I hope he got hurt after he got his fifth jump in," Felter said. "I suspect he *really* wants the wings and the shiny boots."

"On his fifth," Lunsford said. "He's got his five jumps."

"Don't let him do it again, Father," Felter said. "He's too valuable."

[THREE]
404 Avenue Leopold
Léopoldville, Republic of the Congo
1320 26 February 1965

The international operator informed Jack Portet that there was a problem with the circuits at the moment, his call to Fayetteville, North Carolina, could not be completed at this time, and suggested he try again later.

"*Merci beaucoup, mademoiselle,*" Jack said politely, hung up, and then angrily muttered, "Shit!"

Marjorie had taken the news that he was going to Africa now, rather than a month or so later, surprisingly calmly. It was nice to think that this was because she was, after all, an Army brat, and knew that Army wives have to get used to their husbands being sent off on short notice. But it was also possible that she was just putting on a bright face, and was pissed or hurt, or both.

But he had promised her that he would call the minute he got to Léopoldville, and he *had* called just as soon as they'd gotten to the house and he'd had a shower, so he had called her within an hour and a half of getting off the UTA flight from Brussels, which was close enough, and now the fucking circuits were having a problem.

He pulled open a shelf in his father's desk, found the number he was looking for on a typewritten list, and dialed it.

"*Le residence du Chef de l'Armée de la Republique,*" a male voice announced.

French, Jack thought. *They hate the Belgians and anybody else who speaks French, but they answer the phone in French.*

"This is Captain Jacques Portet of Air Simba," Jack said in Swahili. "I would be very honored if General Mobutu could find a moment to speak to me."

There was a long — at least two-minute — period of silence and then the operator came back on the line.

"Regrettably, the General cannot take your call at this time," he said in French,

"Would you be good enough to give General Mobutu a message for me?" Jack asked, again in Swahili.

"I will try," the operator said in French.

"Please inform General Mobutu that I am in Léopoldville, at my home, and would be honored if he could find the time to telephone me," Jack said in Swahili, then spelled his name and gave the number — three times, before the operator managed to get it right.

He put the telephone in its cradle and walked through the French doors to the verandah, then down to the swimming pool, where, as Spec7 Peters, his leg in a now-soiled cast that ran most of the way up his calf, watched from an umbrellaed table as Major Lunsford and Captain Smythe tried unsuccessfully to wrest a pink rubber swan from the massive arms of Master Sergeant Thomas.

"Get through?" Lunsford called to Jack.

"No."

"Hey, if Special Forces wanted you to have a wife, they would have issued you one," Lunsford said.

Jack gave him the finger.

"And Mobutu wasn't available," Jack added.

"Meaning?"

"He may call this afternoon. He may call tomorrow, or three days from now, or he may never call," Jack said. "Two variables affect the equation: One, they may not have passed my message on to him, and, two, presuming they did, he may not return the call for hours, or days, to make the point that he is important and I am not."

"You're going to have to try tomorrow if he doesn't call back today," Lunsford said.

Jack nodded, and sat down beside Peters.

"Anything I can get for you, Peters?"

"No, sir."

"Hungry?"

"I could eat a little something, yes, sir."

Jack looked up at the house, saw Nimbi, the houseboy, and mimed eating. Nimbi trotted to the table, and Jack spoke to him in Swahili. Nimbi nodded and trotted back to the house.

"Beer now," Jack said. "Steak and a salad in twenty minutes. Okay?"

"Sounds good."

When the beer was delivered, it drew Father, Doubting Thomas, and Aunt Jemima from the pool like a magnet.

Lunsford held up his bottle of beer.

"We're going to have to start paying you for the beer, accommodations, and chow," he said.

"Forget it," Jack said.

"No, it's one of the things we have to figure out," Lunsford said. "We're on separate rations, which means, apparently because the State Department has somebody who figures this out, we get standard separate rations pay, plus forty percent, because Léopoldville — all the Congo — is forty percent more expensive to live in than Washington, D.C. Same thing for the quarters allowance."

"Really?" Jack said, interested. He'd never thought of the subject before.

"Really," Lunsford said. "As of this moment, in addition to your other duties, you are Rations and Quarters Officer of Detachment 17. Once a month you will, as Rations and Quarters Officer, present a statement to me, stating that adequate quarters and messing facilities were not available. I will sign the first endorsement thereto, forwarding it to the military attaché for action, whereupon he will lay money on you, which you will then disperse to the troops."

"I have to do that?" Jack said.

"Yes, Lieutenant, you do," Lunsford said. "That's why we have junior lieutenants, to relieve their senior officers of dealing with petty administrative problems. Maybe, if you behave between now and then, I will assign the duty to one of the other pilots when they get here. But for now, you're it. Say 'yes, sir.' "

"Yes, sir," Jack said, chuckling, and then asked, "Even if we eat the rations they're going to ship us?"

"I don't want to eat them unless we have to," Lunsford said. "But once rations like that are issued, they're no longer accountable for. I thought they might be handy to pass out to our Congolese allies, but that would mean we'll have to find our own chow. What do you think?"

"Well, I don't mind eating lion," Jack said. "Or, for that matter, monkey or gorilla, but I don't know about the others."

There was silence.

"You got 'em," Lunsford said. "I thought Gimpy Peters's eyes were going to come out of his

684

head when you said 'monkey or gorilla.' "

"If we're in Stanleyville, there will be lots of first-class cooks looking for work," Jack said. "Vegetables and fish and eggs and pork won't be any problem, but we're going to have to figure out some way of getting in beef."

"That going to be expensive?"

"I don't think so. Ninety percent of the Belgians are gone from Stanleyville, and there was a food system that supplied them that no longer has customers. Everything but beef was available in Stanleyville, and still should be — or at least enough to feed the Detachment. They grow beef around Costermansville, and same story: Belgians gone, and the farmers looking for customers."

"The farmers weren't Belgians?" Peters asked.

"I don't know this for a fact, but I'd be pretty surprised if, after Mike Hoare's mercenaries ran the Simbas out, that the number-one boys on the farms didn't come out of the bush and go back to work, whether the boss was there or not. They make their living off the farms and ranches, too, and the number-one boys know as much about running the operation as the owners did."

"Interesting," Lunsford said.

"Don't take any heavy bets that I'm right," Jack said. "We'll only know for sure when we get there. In Costermansville, if that's where we wind up — Colonel Supo has his headquarters there — we can just take over a floor in the Hotel du Lac."

"Nice place," Lunsford said.

"You know it?" Jack asked, surprised.

"I met Pappy Hodges and Geoff Craig there when I was running around in the bush with the Simbas," Lunsford said. "And what's all this going to cost?"

"I think, not much. I know the people who run the hotel, so they won't try to gouge us, and I think they'll be glad for the business," Jack said. "So what happens if we don't need all the money Uncle is giving us?"

"Well, he ain't going to get it back," Thomas said. "That is, if the Rations and Quarters Officer is wise enough to delegate that responsibility to the senior NCO of this organization."

"Sergeants, as you should know, having been one, are the backbone of the Army," Lunsford said. "It would behoove you to pay attention to Sergeant Thomas. Say 'yes, sir.' "

"Yes, sir," Jack said.

"I was thinking of R and R," Lunsford said. "Christ only knows how long we'll be here. I'll set up a week's TDY to South Africa, every couple of months, on a roster. We will call them 'local purchases missions' and it won't be charged as leave. If there's excess money in the rations and quarters fund, we can pass it out to the troops."

"That's not legal," Captain Smythe protested.

Lunsford looked at him with his eyebrows raised.

"Since you have been a sort of half Green Beanie not quite long enough to get your sweatband greasy," Lunsford said, "I will overlook that stupid comment, Captain. But don't ever again offer a legal opinion of one of my decisions. Say 'yes, sir.' "

He was smiling, but Smythe — and everybody else — knew he was serious.

"Yes, sir," Captain Smythe said.

The steaks were served, and they were just about finished with them when there was movement on the verandah.

"Why do I think we're about to see General Mobutu?" Lunsford asked softly as two Congolese paratroopers moved quickly across the lawn to take up defensive positions, and two more stepped onto the patio.

"I didn't hear any sirens, did you?" Jack asked.

Lunsford shook his head.

"Maybe he knows he's important," Lunsford said.

Joseph Désiré Mobutu stepped onto the verandah, followed by Dr. Howard Dannelly. Mobutu was wearing camouflage fatigues and jump boots. Dannelly was in a tropical-weight gray suit.

"Jacques, mon vieux!" Mobutu called out, smiling and waving his hand as he came off the verandah and started across the lawn.

"Why do I think he wants something?" Lunsford asked softly as he got to his feet.

"Welcome, my general," Jack said in Swahili. "And you, Doctor."

Lunsford came to attention in his bathing trunks, and saluted. Mobutu returned it, then embraced Jack.

"I am here as a friend, not officially," Mobutu said in Swahili.

"Then hello, Joseph," Jack said. "Can I offer you a beer? Lunch?"

"Just a beer, thank you," Mobutu said, and sat down at the table, and motioned for Dannelly to take a chair.

Without orders, Nimbi came quickly across the lawn carrying a tray with more beer and a pitcher of orange juice.

Jack waited until Mobutu had taken a beer, and orange juice had been poured for Dannelly.

"General, may I present these three soldiers? This is Captain Smythe, who will be Colonel Supo's pilot; Master Sergeant Thomas, our sergeant major; and Specialist Peters, who will be in charge of communications."

Mobutu looked at each of them carefully.

Taking their cue from Lunsford, Smythe and Peters saluted.

"How do you do, sir?" Thomas said in English.

"Unfortunately, neither Captain Smythe nor Specialist Peters speaks either French or Swahili," Lunsford said in Swahili, "but we're going to try to teach them."

Mobutu smiled at Thomas, possibly because they looked as if they could be brothers, returned his salute, and offered him his hand.

"What's wrong with the little one's leg?" Mobutu asked. "And what is a specialist? Is he a soldier?"

"He is a fine soldier, my general," Thomas said in Swahili. "He hurt his leg during his last jump —"

"He's a parachutist?" Mobutu asked, doubtfully.

"Oh, yes, my general," Lunsford said. "And despite his injury, he insisted on coming here with us. He is perhaps the best special operations communications man in the Army. As a specialist of his grade, he is paid what a master sergeant is paid."

Mobutu beamed at Peters, reached for his hand, and pumped it enthusiastically. Peters, who hadn't understood a word of the exchange, smiled nervously.

"How is your wife, Captain Portet?" Dannelly asked in English.

"It's Lieutenant, Doctor," Jack corrected him, now speaking English. "And she is fine, and at this moment waiting for my call. There's trouble with the circuits."

"Mr. Finton tells me that her father is a fine Christian officer and gentleman," Dannelly said.

"And her mother is a fine Christian lady," Jack said.

"Well, then, I guess we can hope they will all be a good influence on you, can't we?"

"I'm sure they will be, Doctor," Jack said.

It was obvious from the look on his face that Captain Smythe was wondering what that exchange was all about.

"I said I was here personally, as a friend, Jacques," Mobutu said in Swahili. "We have to talk about Air Simba. Do you mind discussing a little problem in front of your friends?"

"Not at all," Jack said. "Major Lunsford is my friend as well as my commanding officer. I look on Sergeant Thomas as a friend as well as a master sergeant."

"But I'm sure you don't want to force the others to have to listen to a business conversation, do you?"

"With your permission, sir," Thomas said in Swahili to Lunsford, "I will take the others into the house."

"Granted," Lunsford said.

"Thank you," Mobutu said to Thomas.

Mobutu helped himself to another beer and waited until Smythe and Thomas, supporting Peters between them, made their way across the lawn to the verandah.

"There is a slight problem with the people who are going to finance the purchase of Air Simba,"

Mobutu began, now speaking French. "Somewhere they have gotten the idea that the company
is not in as good shape, financially, as your father
led me to believe it was, and I — my friends — told
the bankers it was."

"May I speak frankly, Joseph?" Jack asked in
French.

"We are friends," Mobutu said.

"My father has faith in the Congolese government," Jack said. "When he listed the assets of the
company, he treated the vouchers issued by the
government as cash. The bankers, possibly, being
bankers, do not share Dad's faith that as soon as
possible the government vouchers will be paid."

Mobutu did not reply.

"The second problem is that the bankers have
somehow formed the idea that your father has
more or less deserted Air Simba for greener pas-
tures, suggesting this is because he is fully aware
of the financial difficulties of Air Simba," Dr.
Dannelly said.

"They know he has resigned as chief pilot of Air
Congo, and is now living in the United States,"
Mobutu added.

"He told you about that, Joseph," Jack said.
"The U.S. government has asked for his services,
and he could hardly refuse. I thought you understood."

"*I* understand," Mobutu said. "It's the *bankers*
that don't understand."

"I'll help in any way I can, of course," Jack said,
"and so will Dad. But I don't know —"

"One of the solutions suggested," Dannelly
said, "is that your father return here for two or
three months, during which time General
Mobutu assures me the problem of the unpaid

vouchers can be taken care of. That would put the concerns of the bankers to rest."

Jack thought: *I wonder where that suggestion came from? You?*

"I don't see where that would be possible," Jack said.

"If he doesn't come back, the bankers will be convinced they are right about his having deserted what they think of as a sinking ship," Mobutu said. "And if that word got around, that Air Simba *is* a sinking ship . . ."

"What if Jack were to run Air Simba for a while?" Lunsford asked. "Would that help matters?"

"General Mobutu had considered that, frankly," Dannelly said. "But Jacques is in the Army. . . ."

"Perhaps something could be worked out," Lunsford said. "Unofficially, of course."

"You seem very willing to be of help," Dr. Dannelly said.

"Beware of Americans bearing gifts?" Lunsford said. "Would you be surprised if there were something in it for me?"

Mobutu chuckled.

"What would be in it for you?" he asked.

"If Jack were wearing an Air Simba uniform, and flying an Air Simba airplane, something he's done for years, the bankers would be reassured. . . ."

"And?" Mobutu asked.

"Air Simba flies all over the Congo, all over southern Africa, without questions being asked," Lunsford said. "That would help me do what I have been sent here to do."

"And now that the government, I understand, is

preparing to redeem the vouchers . . ." Mobutu said.

Meaning, of course, Jack thought, *that you will call the minister of finance in and "suggest" he redeem Air Simba's unpaid vouchers even if it means stripping the treasury of every last dollar instrument. Anything for a good cause, especially if that cause is "your associates" being able to borrow the money to buy Air Simba at forty, fifty cents on the dollar.*

"The bankers would be assured that Air Simba is solid financially," Jack said.

"Exactly," Mobutu said, almost triumphantly. Then a worried look crossed his face and he looked at Dr. Dannelly.

"I think," Dannelly said after a moment, "that everyone might profit if Captain — excuse me, *Lieutenant* — Portet became Captain Portet of Air Simba again for the next several months."

"And even afterward," Lunsford said. "If the Congolese Army were to charter Air Simba to support Colonel Supo."

"Yes," Mobutu said. "You could arrange this, Major Lunsford?"

"Consider it arranged, General," Lunsford said, and reached across the table with his hand extended. "Deal?"

Mobutu looked at Dannelly again, almost as if asking permission. Dannelly just visibly nodded his head, and Mobutu took Lunsford's hand.

Jack waited until Mobutu's paratroopers had followed Mobutu and Dannelly into the house before asking, "You think you can get away with me going back to Air Simba?"

"If I asked for permission, I would probably be told I'm out of my mind, so I just won't ask for

692

permission. Consider yourself placed on further TDY, Lieutenant, in a classified covert mission which will require your assumption of cover role. Hell, the CIA does it all the time, why not Detachment Seventeen?"

Jack shook his head.

Smythe, Thomas, and Peters appeared on the verandah and, moving at Peters's on-crutches pace, came back to the swimming pool.

"There has been a change in officer assignments," Lunsford said. "Captain Smythe, you are herewith appointed Rations and Quarters Officer of Detachment 17. Lieutenant Portet is relieved."

"What's going on?" Thomas asked.

"You tell them, Captain Portet, while I seek the gentlemen's rest facility," Lunsford said. "My back teeth, as they say, are floating."

He walked quickly across the lawn toward the house.

[FOUR]
The Oval Office
The White House
Washington, D.C.
1615 25 February 1965

The President of the United States was behind his desk, talking on the telephone, his voice cajoling, when a Secret Service agent opened the door. Colonel Sanford T. Felter was standing behind him.

It took a moment to catch the President's attention. Then Lyndon Johnson signaled with a pointed finger for Felter to enter, and for him to join the other two men in the room.

The other two men were the Secretary of State and the Director of the Central Intelligence

693

Agency. They both nodded somewhat coldly at Felter, but didn't speak. Felter sat down on one of the two couches on either side of a coffee table.

Then all three waited for the President to finish his telephone call.

He finally put the telephone in its cradle and walked to them, where he slumped into a wing-back chair.

"Well, Felter, what do you think?" Johnson asked.

"Think about what, sir?" Felter asked.

"For Christ's sake," Johnson flared, "give it to him!"

The Director of the Central Intelligence Agency handed Felter a radioteletype message. Felter began to read it.

"If you'd have given him that when I was on the phone," Johnson said rather nastily, "the three of us wouldn't be here staring at the goddamn table."

There was no response.

When he had finished reading the message, Felter looked at the President.

"Well, Felter?"

"It's surprising, sir," Felter said.

"Declarations of war are usually surprising, aren't they?" Johnson asked sarcastically, "and that's what that is, isn't it? A declaration of war?"

He snatched the message from Felter's hand and read from it.

" 'If one Vietnam is bad for the American imperialists, I say, give them three Vietnams,' " he read. "That's what the sonofabitch said, and he said it in front of the five hundred people at the . . . What the hell was it?"

"The Second Economic Seminar of Afro-Asian

694

Solidarity, Mr. President," the Secretary of State furnished.

"And you didn't think he was going to cause trouble in Africa," the President said, and turned to the Director of the CIA, "and you told me it was your 'best assessment' that he wasn't."

"I can only repeat, Mr. President," the Director said, "that I think that speech was hyperbole, nothing more."

"That's what I find surprising, sir," Felter said. "There should no longer be any question that Guevara's going to act in Africa, but that he would go public with an announcement like that is surprising. The Soviets have announced they and their allies have no interest whatever in starting revolutionary activity anywhere in Africa."

"So you would say you think it's an announcement of a change in Soviet policy?"

"I think we have to move on that presumption," the Secretary of State said.

"I asked Felter," the President said. "That's why I sent for him, to hear what he thinks."

"Yes, sir," the Secretary said.

"My gut reaction is that his mouth ran away with him," Felter said.

"I can't go along with that," the Secretary said.

"I'm still listening to Felter," the President said.

"He's been running around Africa, Mr. President," Felter said, "With the red carpet rolled out for him everywhere. I think it's entirely possible, and I don't mean to be flippant, that he's started to believe his own press releases."

"You want to explain that?" Johnson said.

"Mr. President, I've been thinking of who he really is . . . ," Felter said.

"The last I heard, he was the number-two man

in Cuba, a wholly owned subsidiary of the Kremlin, Incorporated," the Secretary of State said.

"The only difference between Ernesto Guevara and a thousand other would-be revolutionaries is that he has had a chance to act out his fantasies," Felter said.

"I would not call him a 'would-be' revolutionary," the Secretary said. "I would call someone who took over a country ninety miles off our coast and just about handed it to Moscow a successful revolutionary."

"Fidel Castro took over Cuba," Felter said. "Not Guevara."

"Guevara was, is, his number two," the Secretary argued.

"I would say Fidel's brother, Ramon, is his number two," Felter said.

"For Christ's sake, let Felter talk," Johnson snapped. "I already know what you two think!"

"Guevara is a physician," Felter said. "He was Castro's medic in the mountains. Obviously, they became very close friends, which very possibly is because they were the only two intellectuals there. People tend to forget that Fidel has a Ph.D. He's very bright, and so is Guevara, and it's natural they would be comfortable with each other. And Castro, I suggest, is not above wallowing in the admiration of another intellectual who thinks he walks on water. But being a close friend of El Supremo does not make somebody a skilled guerrilla."

"You're suggesting Guevara is incompetent?" the Director asked sarcastically.

"I hope to prove that soon in the Congo," Felter said. "That's why I want him kept alive, as a

failed, incompetent dreamer, rather than the mar-
tyred guerrilla genius who was brutally murdered
by fascist imperialists."

"So why has Castro been pushing his *doctor* as
the great guerrilla?" Johnson asked.

"Probably because it makes Cuba's — Russia's
— plans for South America, as well as Africa,
seem international. And there are Communists in
Argentina, and thinking that an Argentine,
Guevara, is a successful revolutionary is great for
their image, their morale."

Johnson grunted. "The basic question is why
did he give this declaration of war speech?"

"He probably believes everything he says, as he
probably believes he is a great guerrilla/revolu-
tionary," Felter said. "And the red-carpet treatment he's been given by everybody — including
the Chinese — has fed that misconception. I
would personally be surprised if Castro, much less
the Politburo, had any idea what he was going to
say about three Vietnams. They don't want to
alarm the rest of the world — they want to sneak
up on it and hit it from behind."

"You really think he's a loose cannon?" Johnson
asked.

"Yes, Mr. President," Felter said.

"How are things going in the Congo?"

"We're in the final stages of sending the team
over there, Mr. President."

"Using Intercontinental Air Cargo, Ltd.?" the
Secretary of State asked.

"As a matter of fact, yes," Felter said.

"Colonel Felter told me about that, Mr. Secretary," Johnson said, icily sarcastic. "And my
Director of the Central Intelligence Agency feels
that Intercontinental Air was a pretty good idea.

Isn't that so, Mr. Director?"

"Yes, Mr. President," the Director said. "We expect to be working closely with Felter in that area."

"And I'll tell you something else, Mr. Secretary," Johnson said. "General Whatsisname, the head of the Army Security Agency, came to see me to tell me that Felter wanted one of his sergeants, and if I went along with that, the entire White House communications system was going to collapse like a house of cards. So I told him to break out the signal flags" — Johnson mimed someone waving signal flags — "because I had told Felter he could have anything he needed to get this job done, and I meant it." He paused. "I think that's what they call a parable. A little story with a message. Did you get the message, Mr. Secretary?"

"Yes, Mr. President," the Secretary said.

"That will be all, gentlemen," the President said. "Thank you very much for coming."

He was back on the telephone before they left the Oval Office.

[FIVE]
Stanleyville Air Field
Stanleyville, Oriental Province
Republic of the Congo
0940 10 March 1965

The newly repaired communications equipment in the control tower came to life twenty minutes earlier than expected. The telephone message from the Kamina Air Base to Colonel Supo's headquarters in Costermansville had been very brief: "ETA 1000 Your Time 10 March Poppa."

"Stanleyville, Intercontinental Air Four-nine-three."

The voice, although clipped metallically, was obviously that of Captain Jean-Philippe Portet.

Captain Jacques Portet of Air Simba, who was wearing a white polo shirt, white shorts, and knee-high white socks, reached over the camouflage fatigue uniform shoulder of Captain Weewili of the Congolese paratroops (known to the U.S. Army as Spec7 William Peters) and took the microphone.

"Intercontinental Nine-three, Stanleyville," he said in English.

"Nine-three is at flight level ten, five minutes west of your station. Approach and landing, please."

"Nine-three, the winds are negligible. I haven't the foggiest idea what the barometer says, but it's a beautiful day here in Stanleyville. You are cleared as number one to Runway Two-six. There is no other traffic."

"Understand number one to two-six," Captain Portet said, as Major George Washington Lunsford, who was wearing the camouflage fatigue uniform of a lieutenant colonel of Congolese paratroops touched Jack's arm and pointed out the hole where the control tower window had once been. The 707 was in sight.

Jack nodded, handed Peters the microphone, and started down the stairs from the control tower. Lunsford followed him.

Colonel Jean-Baptiste Supo was standing just outside the terminal building with a small group of officers and soldiers of the Congolese Army.

Sergeant Major Tesio Chil and Sergeant Paul Joe, Supo's driver and bodyguard, were really in the Congolese Army, but Major Jemima and Captain Tomas were not.

There were — and had been, since first light — two companies of Congolese infantry on the field. All roads past the airfield had been closed and would remain so until further orders. In addition, three-fourths of the infantrymen formed a perimeter guard around the field. The remaining troops would be used to push the 707 from where it would be stopped on the taxiway to a recently emptied hangar.

Pushing the 707 was going to be necessary because the three aircraft tractors once stationed at the field had all been vandalized by the Simbas, and the jet exhaust from the 707 would (a) almost certainly set the dry uncut grass near the hangars on fire and (b) very possibly blow one or both of the tin-sided and tin-roofed hangars down if they tried to taxi the aircraft.

Captain Portet set the 707 down smoothly a moment later, taxied to the terminal, and shut it down. A dozen Congolese soldiers pushed the stairs to the rear door. The stairs were mounted on a Chevrolet pickup truck, the engine, glass, and tires of which had also been vandalized by the Simbas.

Master Sergeant Thomas/Major Tomas had managed to get the hydraulics of the stairs themselves working again, and removed the shot-up tires. It now rolled on its rims, but it rolled.

The cargo door of the 707 opened, and Lieutenant Geoff Craig appeared at the door, in uniform, carrying a cut-down Remington 1100 12-gauge shotgun in his hand. He glanced around, made a "follow me" gesture with his hands, and started down the stairs. Everyone had more of less expected that, but no one expected that the first person to follow him would be a Green Beret just barely meeting minimum-height regulations, carrying an Uzi submachine gun, and wearing colonel's eagles on his collar points.

"Jesus," Major Lunsford/Lieutenant Colonel Dahdi said. "Felter!"

Lunsford was waiting at the foot of the steps at attention, his hand raised in a crisp salute, when Felter came down there.

"Lieutenant Colonel Dahdi, sir," he barked. "Welcome to Stanleyville."

Felter returned the salute shaking his head.

"Let me guess, *Colonel*," he said. "Daddy as in Father, right?"

"It's spelled Dee Ay Aich Dee Eye, sir," Father said. "It was Colonel Supo's idea."

"And who's that? The Good Humor Man?" Felter asked on spotting Jack in his white clothing.

"That's Captain Portet of Air Simba, Sir," Father said. "That was General Mobutu's idea."

"And, just as soon as you found the time, you were going to tell me all about this, right?" Felter said.

"Sir, the commo and crypto equipment is on this airplane," Father said. "I was going to make all of this part of my very first report to the colonel, sir."

Felter looked at him a long moment, then smiled.

"Okay, that round goes to you, Father — excuse me, Dahdi," he said, then walked up to Colonel Supo and saluted.

"It's a pleasure to see you again, sir," he said in French. Then he spotted Doubting Thomas.

"Line them up, Sergeant," he said, gesturing at

701

the team coming down the ladder.

"That's *Major* Tomas, Colonel," Thomas said.
"All right, you guys. If anyone has a round in the
chamber, get rid of it. And then form on me."

When the team had cleared their weapons and
were lined up, Tomas called attention, did an
about-face, saluted, and barked, "Sir, the Detachment is formed."

Felter returned his salute, then saluted Supo
again.

"U.S. Army Special Forces Detachment 17. At
your orders, sir."

Supo returned the salute, then walked to the
double rank and shook the hand of each man.

He walked back toward Felter.

"Okay, the parade's over," Thomas barked,
hands on hips. "You know the drill. Get the aircraft unloaded."

"How long will you be with us, Colonel?" Supo
asked.

"I'm going back with the airplane," Felter said.
"But I wanted to bring them here to you, myself."

"How long will it take you to unload the aircraft?"

"In practice at Fort Bragg, they did it in
forty-four minutes, twenty seconds," Felter said.

"But you will have time for lunch?"

"Of course," Felter said. "Very kind of you,
sir."

Captain Portet of Intercontinental Air came
down the ladder and put his arm around the
shoulders of Captain Portet of Air Simba.

"Well, aren't you the fashion plate?" he asked.
"What's that all about?"

"I'll tell you over lunch," Jack said. "Every time
I called and got through, you weren't there, and I

thought you'd rather hear about my conversation with Mobutu straight, rather than relayed through Hanni or Marjorie."

"Okay. There'll be time. Marjorie has visions of you up to your ass in lions and cannibals in the bush," he said. "Shall I disillusion her?"

One hour and twenty-three minutes later, Intercontinental Air Ltd.'s Flight 1002 lifted off from Stanleyville, bound for Kamina, where it would take on fuel for the return flight to the United States.

It had left behind one partially disassembled DeHavilland L-20 Beaver; one partially disassembled Cessna L-19 Birddog; and other supplies, ranging from 10-in-1 rations and ammunition through aviation and ground radios and aircraft parts, so many of them that the airplane had been more than a little over the prescribed maximum gross takeoff weight when it left Pope Field, North Carolina.

It would return to Stanleyville, Colonel Felter informed Colonel Supo, just as soon as it could, within a week at the latest, bringing another partially disassembled L-19, a partially disassembled Bell H-13 helicopter (capable of use as either a medical evacuation aircraft or as an aerial gun platform with two .30-caliber machine guns, depending on what was fixed to the skids), additional supplies of all kinds, and, with a little bit of luck, two more aviators.

XVIII

[ONE]
Apartment B-14
Foster Garden Apartments
Fayetteville, North Carolina
1730 12 March 1965

When Mrs. Marjorie Bellmon Portet, who was wearing blue jeans and a sweater, answered her door, she found her father-in-law, Captain Jean-Phillipe Portet, and Colonel Sanford T. Felter standing there. Both were in full uniform, and neither looked very happy.

Her heart sank and her face went white.

"Jesus!" she said.

"If I can read your mind, honey," Felter said, "Jack is fine."

"Hello, Marjorie," Captain Portet said, and leaned forward and kissed her cheek.

"The other thing happens, as you damned well know," Marjorie said to Felter. She leaned down and kissed him on the cheek. "Come on in — you have just solved my booze problem."

"What booze problem is that?" Captain Portet asked.

"I had just — although I really wanted one — talked myself out of a double scotch because I know you shouldn't drink alone."

"Then we can all have a double scotch — I need one, too," Felter said. "And then we'll take you out for dinner."

She led him into the kitchen, where an unopened bottle of scotch sat on the bare kitchen table.

"What are you doing here?" she asked.

"Strange," Felter said, "I would have thought your first question would be 'How's my Jack?' "

"I have also been trying to force myself not to think about my Jack," Marjorie said. "Okay. How's my Jack?"

"When we left him, beer glass in hand, he was fine. He was all in white," Portet said. "Shirt, shorts, knee-high stockings, and shoes."

"What's that all about?" Marjorie asked, handing him a whiskey glass. "Jack, in white shorts?"

"And knee-high stockings," Felter said. "It's an involved story, but Jack is operating Air Simba, and that, apparently, is the uniform for that."

He touched her glass with his.

"I've had visions of him stalking around the steamy jungle while a lion, three lions . . . what do they call it? — a *pride* of lions — stalked him."

Portet chuckled.

"The only thing Jack's being stalked by is the number-one boy with a fresh supply of cold beer."

"We had lunch in the roof garden on top of the Immoquateur building," Felter added. "Broiled fish, steamed vegetables, white linen, crystal, china . . . very nice. But a little strange, really."

"How strange?" Marjorie asked.

"Stanleyville is a ghost town," Captain Portet answered for him. "You don't see much evidence — except for vandalized trucks and cars — that the Simbas were ever there, or for that matter very much evidence of the hell of a fight the Simbas put up when the Belgians jumped on it. A few bullet holes here and there, and lots of missing glass, but —"

"And there's virtually no whites, no Belgians," Felter interjected. "I don't know how many want to come back, but Jack said the government is discouraging those that do want to. Mobutu won't — can't — afford to station enough troops there to protect it."

"Jack's there," Marjorie said. "Who's protecting him?"

"Three Congolese paratroops," Felter said. "Colonel Supo — he's the Congolese officer running things — insists on that."

"If there's nobody there, why are they there?"

"They're going to use Stanleyville as sort of their air base," Felter said. "Supo has his headquarters in Costermansville, but the airfield for Costermansville is across the border in Rwanda, and keeping black airplanes there overnight, or for repair, would be awkward. They can land on a broad street —"

"Avenue Bernard," Captain Portet furnished. "In the daytime, and there are dirt strips out of town where they can stay overnight, but no place to maintain them."

"— once they get the planes up and flying," Felter went on. "Father Lunsford said they're — he and Jack and Doubting Thomas — probably going to move to Costermansville."

"I think that's probably because the Hotel du Lac in Costermansville is back in business," Portet said. "And Jack always liked staying there."

Felter chuckled.

"So, back to my first question, what are you doing here?"

"Having the airplane reloaded," Portet said.

"We couldn't carry everything in one haul."

"You're going back over there?"

"We're not," Portet said. "The plane is. None of the pilots that came with Intercontinental had ever been to Africa before, so I thought I should make the first trip a training flight. They're going to send a plane for Sandy, and you and I are on the 9:05 Southern flight out of here for Miami, via Atlanta, in the morning. Is there someplace I can rest my weary head?"

"Last question first," Marjorie said. "There's always room for you here, and I may even throw in breakfast, but I don't know about going to Miami with you."

"Hanni's orders," he said. "And thus have to be obeyed. We can talk about it over dinner."

"And if I can use your phone, honey," Felter said, "I will call my bride and tell her I'm back."

"Help yourself, Uncle Sandy," Marjorie said.

Damn it, I don't want to go to Miami.

Damn Jack. I'm worried sick, and he's having broiled fish in a roof garden, swilling beer, and running around in white shorts and knee-length socks.

Damn, I miss him!

At dinner in the main officers' club at Fort Bragg, and to which General and Mrs. Hanrahan and Captain and Mrs. Oliver were also invited — primarily, Marjorie decided, so that they could be brought up to date on conditions in the Congo, and be told what would be required of them — Mrs. Marjorie Portet had one additional drink of scotch whiskey, and two glasses of wine with the entrée, and a Grand Marnier with her coffee.

She also learned:

That Mrs. General Hanrahan had spoken only

that afternoon with Mrs. General Bellmon, who *really* wanted Marjorie to come home to wait for Jack.

That the Intercontinental Air 707 would, if things went well, and there was no reason they shouldn't, lift off from Pope the next afternoon at 1700. The crew was already out there, getting the aircraft ready.

That there was a *really* good program at Fort Bragg, personally run by Mrs. General-Commanding-the-XVIII-Airborne-Corps to keep the wives of young officers away on TDY busy and entertained.

That the Hotel du Lac in Costermansville, Republic of the Congo, was *really* nice, and that Jack would almost certainly be staying in the top-floor suite, which Air Simba kept permanently to house its crews.

That Mrs. Liza Wood Oliver was *really* looking forward to having Marjorie help her select furniture and drapes for the 2,700-square-foot three-bedroom Dutch Colonial that she and Captain Oliver had purchased at a price that was a real steal.

That it wasn't at all true that Central Africa was a steaming jungle. Costermansville, which was on the amazingly clear waters of Lake Albert — the Hotel du Lac's cocktail bar balcony was over the lake and you could see the fish in the water while you had your drinks — was a delightful place, 5,800 feet above sea level, and the climate always reminded Captain Portet of San Francisco: nice days and cool nights.

That, since the Intercontinental Air Cargo 707 wouldn't be carrying nearly as much weight as it had on the first flight, and given a decent jet stream, it was entirely possible that after taking on fuel in Casablanca, Morocco, it would be able to make Stanleyville with enough fuel remaining for the relatively short hop from there to Kamina, where it would refuel for the return flight to Miami.

That that would be a good thing, because there were all sorts of zealous Congolese bureaucrats who had to be dealt with at Kamina, and the authority at Stanleyville was now Lieutenant Colonel Dahdi, who wasn't about to ask questions about aircraft, weapons or anything else.

That, unfortunately, it looked as if Jack was going to have to stay in the Congo for at least ninety days, and maybe even a little longer. Maybe, if that happened, Marjorie could fly to Brussels, and Jack could fly up, and they could have at least a couple of days together.

"You do have your passport, don't you, honey?" Captain Portet inquired.

I'm drunk, Mrs. Marjorie Bellmon Portet decided. *I had that double scotch at the house, and another one here, and the wine, and then the Grand Marnier. What I'm thinking is the booze talking.*

[TWO]
Pope Air Force, North Carolina
1635 13 March 1965

"I'm sorry, ma'am," the Air Force air policeman said, "this is a restricted area. I can't let you through."

"I was told it was a restricted area," Marjorie said. "Captain Oliver expects me."

"Ma'am, I have my orders."

"Not all of them, apparently," Marjorie said.

"Please take me to Captain Oliver."

She was only a lieutenant's wife, but on the other hand, she had spent most of her life as a general's daughter. With that background, she spoke with a certain assurance.

"It's all right, Sergeant," Captain Oliver said to the air policeman. "I'll take care of Mrs. Portet." He waited until the sergeant had driven off.

"That's for Jack, huh?" he asked, nodding at her two suitcases. "We should have thought of that last night; it would have saved you the trip out here."

"Johnny, why don't you take off?" Marjorie said. "That way, you can truthfully say the last time you saw me I was talking to the crew, and you thought I was just going to give them suitcases for Jack."

"You're insane," he said, immediately taking her meaning.

"Last night, I thought I was drunk," she said. "But I'm stone sober now, and the question still is 'why the hell not?' "

"Oh, Jesus, Marjorie!"

Marjorie picked up her suitcases and started up the ladder to the cargo door of the 707.

She had just reached the top when a gray-haired man in a white shirt, the epaulets of which bore the four stripes of a captain, came out of the airplane.

"Can I help you, ma'am?"

"I'm Mrs. Portet," Marjorie said. "I'm going with you."

"Excuse me?"

"My father-in-law said he would try to phone before he caught the flight to Atlanta. Didn't he?"

"No, ma'am, he didn't."

"Well, no problem," Marjorie said. "I'm here."

She fished in her purse and came out with a set of car keys.

"Johnny," she called. "I almost forgot. Take care of Jack's car for me, will you, like a darling?"

He caught the keys.

Marjorie looked at the captain expectantly. After a moment, he understood she was waiting for him to pick up her bags.

He did so, and carried them into the airplane, and installed the new boss's daughter-in-law in a seat. Then he went back out onto the head of the movable stairs, intending to ask the Army captain what the hell was going on.

The Army captain was walking toward Base Operations, and when the captain called to him, apparently couldn't hear him.

"Oh, what the hell," the captain said, and signaled for the ground crewmen to move the stairs away from the fuselage.

Then, with a grunt, he hauled on the door until it began to move.

He walked through the cabin and stopped at Marjorie's chair.

"We'll be lifting off in a couple of minutes," he said. "Once we're in the air, there's a thermos of coffee on the bulkhead."

"Thank you very much," Marjorie said, giving him her most dazzling smile.

[THREE]
Quarters #9
Fort Bragg, North Carolina
1910 13 March 1965

"Good evening, sir," Captain John S. Oliver said to Brigadier General Paul R. Hanrahan, as Hanrahan got out of his car.

"Jesus, you scared hell out of me," Hanrahan said. "Why the hell are you lurking in the dark corners of my garage?"

"I thought it best if Mrs. Hanrahan didn't see me, General," Oliver said. "She would certainly have asked me what was on my mind."

"And what is on your mind that wouldn't wait until tomorrow morning? And that you didn't want my bride to ask about?"

"Sir, I think I have fucked up by the numbers," Oliver said.

"How?"

The door from the house to the garage opened. Patricia Hanrahan stepped into the garage.

"I thought I heard voices in here," she said. "Hello, Johnny. What's on your mind?"

"Captain Oliver was just about to tell me," Hanrahan said.

"Marjorie got on the Intercontinental Air 707," Oliver said.

"So what?" Hanrahan said. "It's her father-in-law's airplane, and I really suspect she has a good idea of what's going on."

"And then the airplane took off for Casablanca," Oliver finished.

"She can't do that," Patricia Hanrahan said.

"She did it, Mrs. Hanrahan," Oliver said. "And I'm the dummy responsible."

"Let's go in the house," Hanrahan said. "I need a drink, and I think Oliver could use one."

"What is she, crazy?" Patricia Hanrahan said.

"On reflection, Captain," General Hanrahan said several minutes later, "the situation is probably not as bad as it seems at first glance."

"Oh, Red," Patricia protested, "how could it be any worse? You're going to have to tell Barbara Bellmon. I won't." She paused and then warmed to the subject. "Why didn't you stop her, Johnny? Throw her over your shoulder if you had to?"

"You're right," Oliver said. "That's what I should have done."

"Or called the MPs," Patricia Hanrahan said.

"May I say something?" General Hanrahan asked, and when they both looked at him, he went on. "Legally, Marjorie did nothing wrong. She is twenty-one, and enjoys all the rights of any other citizen, which means if she wants to go to Africa, she can go to Africa."

"That's stupid, and you know it," Mrs. Hanrahan said.

"Possibly, but it's a fact," Hanrahan said.

"Bob Bellmon's going to go right through the roof, and so is Sandy Felter, and with every right," Patricia said.

"For the time being, we are not going to say anything to either Bob or Sandy," Hanrahan said. "Or anybody else."

"They'll find out," Patricia said. "You know they will."

"By the time they find out, I think she'll be back here," Hanrahan said. "And then it can be just a funny story to tell."

"What's funny?"

"Marjorie flew all the way to Africa to be with Jack, and then had to fly all the way back, because she didn't have a visa, and they wouldn't even let her out of the airport — just flew her straight home. Ha ha."

"I'm almost sure she doesn't have a visa for the Congo," Oliver said.

"The story I got was that it took Jean-Philippe Portet having to go to the Congolese ambassador personally and remind him he was a pal of General Mobutu to get visas for Felter and the others," Hanrahan said, and then had an unpleasant second thought: "Unless she's been planning this all along?"

"She said she got the idea last night at dinner," Oliver reported.

"And I know why," Patricia said. "The picture Sandy and Jean-Philippe painted for her of Jack all dressed in white and living in a hotel on a lake. No wonder she wanted to go. Men are such damned fools!"

"On that philosophical note, Captain Oliver, I think you can go home to your wife."

"Yes, sir," Oliver said. "Sir, their radio is scheduled to be on the Net no later than 2400 tonight. Should I send Father a heads-up?"

"No, you will not, repeat not, send Father a heads-up. If Father, or Jack, knew that Marjorie was coming, they would somehow arrange for the Congolese foreign minister to be waiting when the airplane landed with a visa and a bouquet of flowers."

"Yeah," Oliver agreed.

"They're not going to let her into the Congo without a visa," Hanrahan said. "She doesn't have

714

a visa, and I wouldn't be at all surprised if they turned her back at Casablanca, before she even gets to the Congo." He paused. "I'm glad you didn't throw her over your shoulder, Johnny. *That* would have been hard to explain to General Bellmon, and Jack would probably try to cast . . . punch you in the nose."

"Or both," Oliver said. "Good evening, Mrs. Hanrahan."

"Good night, Johnny," Patricia Hanrahan said.

"Tell Liza I detained you," Hanrahan said. "Everybody else on Fort Bragg thinks I'm a sonofabitch — why not Liza?"

[FOUR]
Stanleyville Air Field
Stanleyville, Oriental Province
Republic of the Congo
1230 14 March 1965

On the logical and universal military assumption that one never gets into much trouble giving priority to the desires of the senior commander, Major Lunsford/Lieutenant Colonel Dahdi had ordered that the L-20 Beaver — which would become Colonel Supo's personal aircraft — be reassembled first.

It had proved less difficult than planned for, for several reasons. When Jack had first flown into Stanleyville on one of the two remaining Air Simba Boeing C-46s, he had carried with him as much heavy maintenance equipment — jacks, cranes, that sort of thing — as weight would permit, as well as five Air Simba airframe and engine mechanics, hoping that the vandalism of Air Simba's third Boeing by the Simbas would

715

turn out to be repairable.

That hope hadn't turned out. There was no way really to tell how much damage had been done to it without giving it sort of a thousand-hour over-haul. They'd started on that. By the time the first Intercontinental flight landed, the bullet-shredded tires had been replaced and the C-46 rolled into one of the two hangars, where the work would be completed.

When the team's aircraft and engine mechanics — the soldiers recruited by Jack and Lunsford at Fort Rucker — saw the cranes Jack flew in to, if necessary, remove the engines from the C-46, it was immediately apparent to them that they could also be used to haul the L-20 fuselage off the skid on which it had been shipped while the landing gear was reinstalled, and when that had been accomplished, and the Beaver was sitting on its gear, to use the cranes to reinstall the Beaver's wings.

They had been prepared to "locally fabricate" makeshift wooden cranes from trees and had brought power saws and woodworking tools with them to do so. Practice at Camp Mackall had indi-cated this would take 1.5 or 2.0 days.

When the second Intercontinental Air flight called for approach and landing instructions at Stanleyville, the reassembly process of the Beaver was two days ahead of schedule. It was sitting on the tarmac with its engine running, and Captain Smythe/Major Jemima in the pilot's seat was about to take it off on its first test flight.

Captain Jacques Portet of Air Simba intended to serve as copilot.

"Well, it hasn't blown up so far," Aunt Jemima said. "Shall we see if it will fly?"

"Why not?" Jack replied, and, more from habit than necessity — only Captain Weewili/Spec7 Peters and one of his technicians were in the tower, installing newly arrived radios — put on earphones and reached for the microphone on the yoke.

"Oh, for Christ's sake," the earphones said in massive disgust. "Don't tell me the fucking radio is out in the fucking Beaver!"

"Station obscenely calling the Beaver, identify yourself," Jack said, sternly, into the microphone.

"Is that you, Captain Smythe?"

"This is Portet."

"I've been trying to raise you, sir. Intercontinental Air is ten minutes out."

"Well, I guess we better put off the test flight, then. I don't want to get run over by a 707."

Jack touched Aunt Jemima's arm, then made a cutting motion across his throat.

"The 707's ten minutes out."

"In that case, I guess I better find Sergeant Thomas and mobilize the stevedores," Aunt Jemima said as he began to shut the engine down. "Our noble leader is downtown playing tennis with Geoff Craig."

"War is hell, ain't it?" Jack said, and started to unfasten his harness.

[FIVE]
The Hotel du Lac
Costermansville, Kivu Province
Republic of the Congo
1745 16 March 1965

Howard Dannelly, M.D., was not in a good mood when he walked into the Hotel du Lac, and what he saw shortly afterward very nearly made him lose his temper, something he really hated to do.

It had been a long — and toward the end, very bumpy — flight in an Air Simba Boeing from Léopoldville. There had been a dozen Congolese young men in civilian clothing on the airplane. Dannelly knew they were soldiers, recent graduates of the parachutists school, intended as augmentation for Colonel Supo's inadequate forces, and in civilian clothing because they were going to have to pass through the airport in Kigali, just across the Rwandan border from Costermansville, and the Rwandan government didn't want soldiers passing through their airport.

They had apparently shed their military discipline with their uniforms, for not only had they brought two cases of beer onto the airplane, which they had promptly begun to consume, but, as Congolese country boys were prone to do with alcohol in their systems, began to say unkind and scatological things about the nearest white man. This was, of course, Dr. Dannelly, and the drunken paratroops of course had no idea who he was, or that he was fluent in Swahili.

Predictably, the first of them became nauseous when the bumpy weather began, and by the time the Boeing landed at the field at Kigali, most of them had become nauseous, some of them spectacularly so. His shoes and trousers had been splattered.

In the Kigali terminal building, there had been a particularly offensive — and apparently illiterate; he held Dannelly's documents upside down while he studied them intently — immigration officer who took great joy in showing that Rwanda was now independent, and black men could now annoy white men with impunity.

There was no bottled water in the Kigali terminal, and Dr. Dannelly knew better than to drink anything else.

Just as soon as he entered the Hotel du Lac, he went to the bar in search of at least two bottles of club soda.

And saw Jean-Philippe Portet's son sitting at a table in bathing trunks. There was a champagne cooler on the table. Young Portet was shamelessly staring at a young woman in a nearly lewd bathing suit, who was dancing alone to sensual music on the phonograph. The young woman — probably the daughter of one of the farmers who hadn't fled; she seemed too young to be married — seemed to revel in the attention.

Dr. Dannelly called to one of the boys for water, a little more loudly than he intended, and this caught young Portet's attention.

"Well, as I live and breathe," Young Portet called. "Dr. Dannelly! Come on over — there's someone I want you to meet."

Dannelly walked to the table.

"You may think you're clever, Mr. Portet," Dr. Dannelly said. "But your behavior is not only disgusting, but brings everything you say into question."

"Like my marriage vows, for example?"

"Yes, like your marriage vows."

"Judge not, Doctor, lest ye be judged," Young Portet said. "As it says in the Good Book." He raised his voice. "Sweetheart, come over here a minute, will you?"

The young woman walked to the table.

"Baby, this is one of the most important men in the Congo," Jack said. "Say hello to Dr. Howard Dannelly. Doctor, may I present my wife, Marjorie?"

"I'm very pleased to meet you, Mrs. Portet," Dr. Dannelly said after a perceptible pause. "And, I must say, I'm really surprised to see you here in Costermansville."

"Well, Doctor, you know. The Song of Solomon. 'Whither thou goest, I will go,' et cetera."

"Do you really read the Bible, Mrs. Portet?"

"Yes, I do," Marjorie said. "I think of myself as a Christian, and I'm even working on bringing the heathen I married into the fold."

"Well, I must say, Mrs. Portet, you have your work cut out for you."

"Call me Marjorie, please," she said. "And won't you join us? Can we offer you a glass of champagne?"

"Thank you no," Dannelly said. "I'm a member of the Church of Latter-Day Saints. We don't use stimulants."

"I've heard that," Marjorie said. "I've always wondered how you square that with what Christ said: 'Take a little wine for thy stomach's sake and thine other infirmities.' "

"I'd love to get into that at length with you, Marjorie," Dr. Dannelly said, "but right now I really would like some water."

Thirty minutes later, just before he excused himself to take a shower before dinner, Dr. Dannelly assured Mrs. Portet there would be no problem whatever with her visa. If she would entrust her passport to him, he would take it to Léopoldville the following day, have a friend — the Minister of Foreign Affairs — have someone stamp it, and then have it flown back to her in Costermansville on the next Air Simba flight.

[SIX]
Office of the Deputy Director
The Central Intelligence Agency
Langley, Virginia
0845 17 March 1965

The Director was sitting on one of the Deputy Director's matching couches and Howard W. O'Connor, the Assistant Director for Administration, didn't see him when he walked into the office.

"You wanted to see me, Paul?" O'Connor asked.

"I did," the Director said.

O'Connor turned.

"I didn't see you, sorry," he said. "Good morning, sir."

"Have you seen this?" the Director asked, and handed him a long, curling sheet of radioteletype paper.

TOP SECRET
1920 GREENWICH 16 MARCH 1965

FROM STATION CHIEF, BUENOS AIRES

TO DIRECTOR, CIA, LANGLEY
COPIES TO SOUTH AMERICAN DESK
    MR SANFORD T FELTER, COUNSELOR TO
    THE PRESIDENT
    THE EXECUTIVE OFFICE BUILDING
    WASHINGTON

1. THE UNDERSIGNED HAS BEEN
APPROACHED BY AN OFFICER RECENTLY
ASSIGNED TO THE OFFICE OF THE DEFENSE

ATTACHÉ HERE WHOM THE UNDERSIGNED HAS REASON TO BELIEVE IS IN A COVERT ASSIGNMENT IN CONNECTION WITH OPERATION EARNEST WHICH THE UNDERSIGNED HAS FURTHER REASON TO BELIEVE IS CONTROLLED BY MR. FELTER AT THE DIRECTION OF THE PRESIDENT.

2.   THE OFFICER HAS PROPOSED THAT HE WILL MAKE AVAILABLE INTELLIGENCE INFORMATION TO ME UNDER THE FOLLOWING CONDITIONS: HIS NAME WILL NOT BE USED OR FURNISHED TO THE AGENCY. ANY INFORMATION HE FURNISHES WILL BE TRANSMITTED OVER CIA FACILITIES WITH A COPY TO BE FURNISHED MR. FELTER BY OFFICER COURIER IMMEDIATELY UPON RECEIPT IN LANGLEY. THE INFOR-MATION WILL NOT BE PASSED, UNDER ANY CONDITIONS, TO ANYONE WITHOUT THE EXPRESS PRIOR PERMISSION OF MR. FELTER.

3.   THE UNDERSIGNED IS FULLY AWARE THAT ARRANGEMENTS SUCH AS DESCRIBED CONTRAVENE AGENCY POLICY, BUT FEELS AN EXCEPTION TO POLICY IS JUSTIFIED IN THIS CASE BECAUSE THE INTELLIGENCE OFFERED IS UNAVAILABLE FROM ANY OTHER SOURCE.

4.   IT IS RECOMMENDED THE INTELLI-GENCE FOLLOWING BE REGARDED AS THE EQUIVALENT OF CIA RELIABILITY SCALE FIVE.

ERNESTO GUEVARA ARRIVED AT JOSE MARTIN AIRFIELD, HAVANA, CUBA AT 1605 GREENWICH 14 MARCH 1965 ABOARD AIR FRANCE FLIGHT 6005 WHICH ORIGINATED IN ALGIERS, ALGERIA. GUEVERA'S ARRIVAL WAS NOT PREVIOUSLY ANNOUNCED TO THE PUBLIC, THE PRESS WAS EXCLUDED FROM THE DEBARKATION AREA, AND THERE WERE NO OFFICIAL WELCOMING CEREMONIES.

ALEIDA MARCH DE GUEVARA, HIS WIFE; HILDITA GUEVARA, HIS DAUGHTER FROM HIS PREVIOUS MARRIAGE; FIDEL CASTRO; CUBAN PRESIDENT OSVALDO DORTICÓS; CARLOS RAFAEL RODRÍGUEZ; EMILIO ARAGONÉS; ORLANDO BORREGO; AND THREE UNIDENTIFIED MINISTRY OF INDUSTRY FUNCTIONARIES WERE THE ONLY PEOPLE GIVEN ACCESS TO THE DEBARKA- TION AREA.

AFTER A SHORT MEETING OF THE ABOVE WITH GUEVARA, GUEVARA AND CASTRO (ONLY) LEFT THE AIRFIELD TOGETHER, AND WERE DRIVEN TO A MANSION AT CALLE BOLIVAR 117 WHICH IS SET ASIDE FOR CASTRO'S UNOFFICIAL AND PRIVATE USE. IT IS OF INTEREST TO NOTE THAT THE FEMALES WHO CUSTOMARILY RESIDE IN THE MANSION WERE REMOVED EARLY IN THE DAY AND HAVE NOT RETURNED.

THERE IS A CREDIBLE RUMOR CIRCU-

LATING THAT AS A RESULT OF THE "THREE VIETNAMS" SPEECH GUEVARA GAVE TO THE SECOND ECONOMIC SEMINAR OF AFRO-ASIAN SOLIDARITY GUEVARA IS IN DISFAVOR WITH CASTRO BECAUSE CASTRO WAS STRONGLY REBUKED BY THE SOVIET AMBASSADOR FOR THE SPEECH AND/OR CASTRO ALSO DISAPPROVES OF THE BELLIGERENT TONE OF THE SPEECH. THERE IS A FURTHER, LESS CREDIBLE, RUMOR THAT GUEVARA WILL, AT THE SUGGESTION/ REQUEST/DEMAND OF THE SOVIET AMBASSADOR, BE STRIPPED OF HIS POST AS MINISTER OF INDUSTRY SO THAT THE CUBAN GOVERNMENT CAN DENY THAT HE WAS SPEAKING/SPEAKS FOR THE CUBAN GOVERNMENT.

IT IS CONSIDERED UNLIKELY, HOWEVER, THAT ANY OF THE ABOVE WILL AFFECT THE CUBAN OPERATION IN AFRICA, ALTHOUGH GUEVARA'S ROLE IN THAT OPERATION MAY BE LIMITED.

5.   IN THE ABSENCE OF SPECIFIC INSTRUC- TIONS TO THE CONTRARY, THE UNDER- SIGNED INTENDS TO GO AHEAD WITH THE RELATIONSHIP DESCRIBED ABOVE.

J. P. STEPHENS
STATION CHIEF BUENOS AIRES

TOP SECRET

724

"I had not seen it, no, sir," O'Connor said when he had finished reading it.

"The only thing we had on this was a Reliability Three that Guevara was in Havana," the Director said.

"Yes, sir," O'Connor said, largely because he could think of no safe comment to make.

"I just told Paul that I wouldn't be at all surprised if Felter already has this information, and is sitting in the Executive Office Building waiting to see how long it takes for us to send it to him."

"How would he do that, sir?"

"The same way he found somebody who knows the address of the house where Castro gets his revolutionary ashes hauled," the Director said. "Clean that up, just the intel stuff, nothing about the deal Stephens has struck with Felter's man down there, and get it over to Felter by officer courier."

"Yes, sir."

"And you, Paul, you tell the South American desk that I am going to be very interested indeed — perhaps 'morbidly fascinated' would be a better choice of words — to see how much sooner Felter sends me stuff like this than our people do."

"My God, Castro shoots anybody and everybody he thinks *might* be turned," the Deputy Director protested.

"Well, I'd say he hasn't shot enough people, then, wouldn't you? Felter's source has got somebody in there, and at the top."

[SEVEN]
The Hotel du Lac
Costermansville, Kivu Province
Republic of the Congo
0950 19 March 1965

The seven-story Hotel du Lac was the tallest building in Costermansville.

After some rather convoluted business dealings, the sixth and seventh floors had been requisitioned, in the name of the Republic of the Congo, by Colonel Jean-Baptiste Supo, Military Commandant of Kivu Province, for use in military operations.

The requisition did not state that the military operation Colonel Supo had in mind was to provide space — and living accommodations — for Special Forces Detachment 17.

The King Leopold Suite of the Hotel du Lac — two bedrooms, an office, a sitting room, and a reception room, all of whose windows overlooked Lake Albert — had become Detachment 17's headquarters.

The smaller bedroom was now Major George Washington's Lunsford's office. The Detachment's executive officer, Lieutenant Geoffrey Craig, and the aviation officer, Major Darrell J. Smythe, shared what had once been some dignitary's private secretary's office, and the larger bedroom was now the commo center. Cables ran out of one of its windows up the side of the building to the antennae on the roof.

Lunsford, Smythe, Craig, Thomas, Peters, and Mr. Portet of Air Simba all had two-room suites on the seventh floor, which just about filled it up, and the enlisted men were housed on the sixth

726

floor, most of them with rooms of their own.

The management of the hotel was pleased with the arrangement, and not at all upset that some people might think the payment arrangements were questionable, perhaps even illegal. This was, after all, the Congo, and things were different in the Congo.

Colonel Supo had issued vouchers for the services provided, and it was even possible that at some time in the future they would be honored by the Congolese government. The management was going to provide an essentially identical bill to the commanding officer, SFDET-17 in the field, with the understanding that it would be paid in U.S. dollars immediately.

The SFDET-17 bill differed from the bill rendered to Colonel Supo's headquarters in that, in the SFDET-17 bill, the cost of beer, wine, and spirits served would be incorporated into the cost of the meals served, and the words "beer," "wine," and "spirits" would not appeared thereon.

There were already some radio antennae on the roof of the Hotel du Lac when Spec7 Peters/Captain Weewili went up the first time to see where he could install his antennae, and he was fascinated with what he found, much as when a car aficionado discovers a Model T Ford in daily use.

His antennae, including two dishes, were state of the art, so much so that he was a little uneasy when Lieutenant/Mr. Portet asked for an explanation of how everything worked. Just about all of the equipment he'd brought with him was classified, and you were supposed to have a need-to-know. He finally decided that, in these circumstances, Portet had the need-to-know anything and everything.

"Most of the aviation stuff is pretty standard," Peters explained. "But the commo is nonstandard, state of the art, and classified."

"How does it work?"

"We don't talk about it much," Peters explained, "but we're tied into the datalinks of the surveillance satellites. They have a reception capability — to turn the cameras on and off, you know, stuff like that — and we use that for our commo.

"First, we go through the usual encryption process, break it down into five character blocks. . . . You know how that works, I guess?"

Jack had nodded, although he really didn't have a clue how that worked.

"After we get the encrypted message on tape, then we condense it," Peters said.

"How does that work?"

"You put the encrypted tape on one machine, and a blank tape on a second machine. The first machine is running, say, 480 times as fast as the second machine. If, for example, you had 960 seconds of data, eight minutes' worth, it gets copied onto two seconds' worth of tape on the second machine. And most messages are a lot shorter than eight minutes, more like two, before condensation. When you condense a two-minute tape at 480 — and we can go as high as 960 and even 1920, but sometimes the tape won't take it that short — when you condense a two-minute tape at 480, you get a half-second uplink tape. You bury that in garbage — "

"What?"

"You send a long uplink tape . . . sometimes,

depending on how long the satellite will be over you, an hour, and hour and a half. They call it garbage because the five-character blocks which look like crypto aren't; they're meaningless, randomly selected. I brought about twenty hours' worth with me. So what you do is re-record say forty-five minutes of *that,* and you slip the half-second — sometimes shorter — crypto message in between a couple of characters in the garbage blocks. Still with me?"

"I don't know," Jack confessed.

"So we'll send that up to the satellite," Peters said. "The satellite records it, and then, when the satellite gets over Washington — actually, we have antennae farms at Vint Hill Farms Station in Virginia, and at Fort Meade, over in Maryland — the satellite downlinks it. Okay?"

"I'm beginning to be sorry I asked," Jack confessed.

"Then they run the tape fast through one of their machines, until they hit the trigger —"

"What trigger?"

"The crypto message has an impulse — like a 300-cycle tone, you know? The exact frequency is in a Signal Operations Instruction, so maybe one day it's 299 cps, and the next 1,202, and so on. Anyway, when the fast machine hits a trigger, it stops, backs up to the trigger, and then starts running at slow speed. That's fed to a crypto machine, and that's it. Out of the crypto machine comes the decrypted message."

Jack thought it over for a long moment.

"So what the bad guys have to do is play the whole tape — the garbage tape — looking for the trigger. . . ."

"Right."

"Which is hidden somewhere in a half-second encrypted message in tape maybe forty-five minutes long. . . ."

"Right."

"And if they get lucky, then all they have to do is break the encryption code?"

"Right. It's supposed to be foolproof, which probably means they're reading it in the Kremlin, or in Peking, before the courier can get it into Washington from Vint Hill Farms or Fort Meade."

"How often can you send, or receive, something?"

"We get a satellite about every four hours for half an hour, maybe forty-five minutes — it depends on the trajectory."

"Around the clock?"

"Sure."

"I find it hard to believe that the bad guys have somebody here listening for us to send a message to a satellite."

"Anything is possible," Peters said.

"But if there is, aren't we telling him here's a message the minute we start transmitting?"

"We transmit garbage twenty-four hours a day. Every five minutes, there's a two-second pause, long enough to shut off the garbage tape and turn on the crypto tape," Peters explained. "And then, when the crypto's finished, we wait for a two-second pause, and shut it down, and turn on the garbage again."

"I am awed," Jack said. "And I will be very surprised if it works."

Two hours later, when Geoff Craig handed him a printout from the cryptographic machine, there was proof that it worked:

```
SECRET

EARN0005 WASH DC 1405 ZULU 19 MARCH
1965
VIA WHITE HOUSE SIGNAL AGENCY

FROM: EARNEST SIX
TO: HELPER SIX

1-IMMEDIATELY ON RECEIPT ADVISE
LOCATION, CONDITION, VISA STATUS AND
ETA USA MRS. MARJORIE PORTET.

2-ETA LÉOPOLDVILLE LIEUTENANT JAMES C.
MOORE AND CWO3 FRANCIS CLAURE FROM
RUCKER VIA BRUSSELS ABOARD UTA 5621
1635 ZULU 22 MARCH.

FINTON FOR EARNEST SIX

SECRET
```

And three hours after that, at 3:15 P.M. local time, Colonel Sanford T. Felter (Earnest Six) also had proof that the burst transmission network to Costermansville was functioning well when he received the following from Major George Washington Lunsford (Helper Six).

```
SECRET
HELP0003 1605 ZULU 19 MARCH 1965
VIA WHITE HOUSE SIGNAL AGENCY
```

[EIGHT]
The Hotel du Lac
Costermansville, Kivu Province
Republic of the Congo
0950 23 March 1965

The reception room of the King Leopold Suite had been converted into the Detachment's conference room by moving the elegant furniture with which it had been furnished and replacing it with folding banquet tables and folding chairs from the hotel's basement storerooms.

Map boards had been locally fabricated from two-by-fours and sheets of plywood, and there was even a glossy mahogany speaker's lectern with a built-in public address system. It carried a beautifully carved insignia reading, "Rotary International, Costermansville, Belgian Congo."

With the exception of a few members of the Detachment — aircraft mechanics, a tower operator, and two Green Berets charged with their security — who were in Stanleyville, the entire Detachment had been assembled in the conference room. They were sitting around the banquet tables, which had been arranged in a U.

They were all now wearing the uniforms of Congolese paratroops, with the collar rank insignia of senior noncommissioned officers or junior officers. Lunsford had decided, Solomon-like, that E-7s would be captains, E-6s lieutenants, and everybody else who spoke Swahili senior sergeants. The seven E-5s who didn't speak Swahili were wearing sergeant's insignia.

Everyone was wearing U.S. Army parachutist's jump boots, rather than Congolese boots, as the result of another Solomon-like decision of Major Lunsford. The "old" Green Berets had put on Congolese boots when they had drawn their Congolese uniforms; many of the "new" Green Berets had not.

"What the hell, Geoff," Lunsford had announced when informed of the problem. "If it makes them feel good, why not?"

With the exception of their pistols — everyone had a Colt Model 1911A1 .45 ACP caliber semiautomatic pistol — their weapons were a mixture of Belgian and American. There were Fabrique National 7-mm automatic rifles from Colonel

733

Supo's ordnance stocks, and U.S. Army M-16 .223 rifles, including the short carbine version of that weapon, the Car-16.

Major Lunsford, Lieutenant Craig, and Sergeant Thomas were armed with cut-down Remington Model 1100 12-gauge shotguns. They had carried such weapons in Vietnam, having found they were both very effective close-range people killers, and easy to carry in aircraft. All three weapons and a case of 00-buckshot ammunition for them had been carried to Africa in a locked case, as Lunsford strongly suspected that if their weapons preference became known, everyone would want a shotgun, and he wanted most everybody to be armed with a rifle of one kind or another.

The weapons littered the banquet tables in the conference room, as everybody watched the door to see what the hell was up.

The door opened, and Lieutenant Craig walked in, stood to one side, and called, "Ah-ten-hut!"

Everyone in the room popped to attention.

Colonel Jean-Baptiste Supo, Military Commandant of Oriental, Equatorial, and Kivu Provinces, walked into the room, followed by two Congolese officers and finally Major Lunsford, who was wearing the uniform of a Congolese lieutenant colonel of paratroops.

Major Smythe walked up to Lunsford, saluted crisply, and announced, "Sir, the Detachment is formed."

Lunsford returned the salute, performed a crisp about-face movement, saluted Colonel Supo, and said, in Swahili, "Chief, the detachment is formed."

Supo returned the salute, then walked to the lectern.

"Be as you were," he said, in painful English. "I regret, I have not the English. Major Totse will do for me."

Major Alain George Totse stepped beside Supo.

"I am Major Totse," he said in heavily French-accented English, "I have the honor to be Colonel Supo's intelligence officer."

He stepped back and motioned for Colonel Supo to go to the lectern's microphone. Colonel Supo said something to him in Swahili, and Totse stepped forward to stand beside Supo.

Supo said something in English.

"Colonel Supo welcomes you to the Republic of the Congo and thanks you for offering to serve against a common enemy," Totse translated.

Colonel Supo said something else in Swahili.

"Colonel Supo," Major Totse translated with a smile, "says I am to take it from here."

Colonel Supo went to one of the empty chairs in the first row and motioned for Lunsford, Smythe, and Craig, who were still standing near the lectern, to join him.

Totse went to the map board, where there were two Belgian Army maps, one U.S. Army map, and one National Geographic Society map. He picked up a pointer, which had formerly been a billiards cue.

"My English is not so fine," he announced. "Be so good to interrupt when understand me you don't."

There were some muted chuckles.

Totse pointed to the U.S. Army map.

"This is where we are, Costermansville, in Kivu

Province," he said, "at the southern end of Lake Kivu. We are pretty much in the center of Africa. This is the source of the Nile River . . ."

He moved the pointer.

". . . just over the border in Rwanda."

He shifted the pointer to the west.

"This is Stanleyville, in Oriental Province, where you arrived in this country. When this trouble began, a revolutionary named Nicholas Olenga, who originally referred to himself — without ever having been an officer — as 'Major' Olenga, then 'Colonel' Olenga, and who now calls himself 'Lieutenant General' Olenga, began operations in Albertville, which is here on the shore of Lake Tanganyika."

He moved the pointer to show where he meant.

"The border between the Congo and Tanganyika runs down the middle of Lake Tanganyika.

"Now, in the beginning, Olenga's rebellion was spontaneity —"

"Spontaneous, Alain," Lunsford corrected him.

"Spontaneous, thank you, Father," Totse said. "Olenga is a Kitawala, which is a cult mixing primitive Christian faith — they expect the return of Christ any day — with native gods. They believe they have Dawa, which protects them from being shot.

"Inasmuch as Olenga's insurrection was unexpected, the Armée Nationale Congolese was not prepared for it. He took Albertville and marched on Stanleyville, and took that, and increased the size of his forces en route.

"Three things happened. It was necessary to request foreign assistance. A former British officer, Michael Hoare, who lives in South Africa, was recruited to form a mercenary force to resist Olenga and his Simbas. Hoare is a soldier, but he recruited his white mercenaries from the bars of the Belgian and French waterfronts. They are not soldiers. It is necessary for Hoare to shoot the insubordinate as a means of maintaining discipline.

"Olenga began to massacre Belgians and other whites in Stanleyville. The story that he cut their livers out and ate them is true. Major Lunsford was in Stanleyville and saw this.

"The Russians and the Chinese, who were apparently as surprised as we were at Olenga's success, began to try to supply him with arms and people to train his men.

"Aware of what that would mean, and to save the lives of the Belgians in Stanleyville, the Belgians provided parachutists, and you Americans airplanes, to jump into Stanleyville. The Belgians also supplied troops under Colonel Van de Waele. Those troops, and Major Hoare's mercenaries, succeeded in driving the Simbas from Albertville and Stanleyville. At the moment they are scattered, in small groups, all over this area, some in the bush around Albertville, some in the bush around Stanleyville, but with their greatest strength in the area of Luluabourg in Kasai Province."

He moved the pool pointer far to the east on the map to Luluabourg.

"For one reason or another, the ANC has been unable to completely eliminate the Simba in Kasai Province, which may explain why, as of yesterday, General Mobutu has added Kasai Province to Colonel Supo's responsibilities, and given him orders to eliminate the Simba and 'Lieutenant General' Olenga once and for all.

"I have no doubt this could be accomplished, and without the assistance of Major Hoare's mercenaries, were it not for the new threat of Guevara. If Guevara is coming to the Congo, we have to presume he is coming with Soviet support, which means with Soviet weapons and other supplies, and possibly with the assistance of the Chinese Communists as well.

"Now, so far Olenga's forces are not well-equipped or well-trained. Most of their weapons are those they captured from the ANC in the opening days of the trouble. If Guevara comes —"

"With respect, Alain," Lunsford interrupted. "*When* Guevara comes."

"I stand corrected," Totse said. "When Guevara comes, it will be necessary for him to get his men, and weapons, and supplies to the center of insurrectionist activity in Luluabourg. There is little doubt that both will arrive in the capital of Tanganyika, Dar es Salaam, which is here . . ."

He pointed to the far, eastern, coast of Tanganyika.

". . . on the Indian Ocean, by both ship and air. That's quite a distance. There's no way they could get them across the border where our countries join, which means they would have to be shipped across Lake Tanganyika, and then somehow transport them to Luluabourg.

"That raises the possibility of both men and matériel being shipped through the former French Congo, now known as Congo Brazzaville."

He moved the pointer again.

"You can see that Brazzaville is closer to Luluabourg than Luluabourg is to Lake Tanganyika.

"As Napoleon said, 'an army travels on its stomach', and that would seem to apply to a guerrilla force as well. The tactics devised by Colonel Supo to deal with this threat are as follows:

"First, now that Kasai Province is under his orders, he will use ANC Forces and Major Hoare's mercenary force, and the few aircraft that will now be available to him — several B-26 bombers, a few more T-28s, and a C-47 — to contain, and ultimately eliminate, the insurrectionists around Luluabourg.

"Colonel Supo believes that all that activity in Luluabourg area will discourage the Soviets — and the Cubans — from trying to increase their forces, or supply them, through Congo Brazzaville.

"That, of course, leaves them only the across-Lake-Tanganyika route. It is also possible that since they will soon learn the bulk of our strength is in the Luluabourg area, they may see it as an opportunity to strike in this area. It is communist doctrine, as we all know, to strike where the enemy is weakest, and when resistance is encountered, to bend like a weed in the wind.

"The terrain in this area is such that the insurrectionists can move a hundred meters off the road confident that we can't see them. And, until now, aerial reconnaissance has been unavailable to us. If we can find them, without them knowing they have been found, we can do them a good deal of harm. Furthermore, patrolling Lake Tanganyika by air will permit us to interdict much of what they try to ship across the lake."

He paused and smiled.

"Are you now getting the idea of why we're so glad to have you with us?"

"Major," Lunsford said. "With due respect to our aviators, overwhelming immodesty compels me to tell you that Special Forces is also pretty good at interdicting people — and their supplies — on the ground. In both friendly territory and the other kind."

"So you have been telling me, Father," Totse said.

"We're also pretty good at listening to other people's radio messages, Major," Spec7 Peters said.

"That of course would be very helpful," Totse said, and then went on. "I will be here as long as necessary to answer any and all questions, but before we get into that: Would you like to add anything, my colonel?"

Supo got up and walked to the lectern, looked around the room, and then said something in Swahili.

Totse translated. "The colonel says that when he was a young corporal, he was taught to conserve the things necessary to fight — that most of the time when they are gone, they are gone forever."

Supo spoke again, and again Totse translated:

"The colonel says that he thinks you are going to become very valuable tools to fight this war, and therefore he asks —"

Supo interrupted him in Swahili.

"The colonel *begs* you to conserve your airplanes, and yourselves, so that you will be valuable tools for a long time," Totse translated. "He says he cannot afford the loss of one airplane, or any one of you."

Lunsford stood up.

"With all respect, my colonel," he said. "When

we take care of this little job for you, and get on the plane to go home, I will bet you a case of beer that you will say, 'My God, am I glad to see them go!' "

"A soldier," Supo said in his painful English, "is never glad to say goodbye to another soldier."

He turned and marched out of the room.

[NINE]

SECRET

Central Intelligence Agency
Langley, Virginia

FROM: Assistant Director For Administration

DATE: 26 March 1965 1530 GMT

SUBJECT: Guevara, Ernesto (Memorandum # 63.)

TO: Mr. Sanford T. Felter
    Counselor To The President
    Room 637, The Executive Office Building
    Washington, D.C.

By Courier

In compliance with Presidential Memorandum to The Director, Subject: "Ernesto 'Che' Guevara," dated 14 December 1964, the following information from your sources in Buenos Aires, Argentina, is relayed as re-

---

ceived: (Reliability Scale: Not Applicable).

Begin Intelligence Relayed:

Ernesto Guevara de la Serna has secretly moved into a single family residential building controlled by the Fight Against Bands of Counterrevolutionaries (Acronym from the Spanish, LCB) at Calle Hernandez 134 in the La Corona section of Havana. Neither his wife nor daughter are with him.

He has shaved his beard and the top of his skull, apparently to give the appearance of a smooth shaven bald-headed man. He has also been fitted with prosthetic devices apparently intended to change the appearance of his lips.

It may be that he intends to use the name Ramón Benítez and travel on a Brazilian passport, but this has not been confirmed.

End Intelligence Relayed.

Howard W. O'Connor
HOWARD W. O'CONNOR

SECRET

XIX

S E C R E T

Central Intelligence Agency
Langley, Virginia

FROM: Assistant Director For Administration

DATE: 31 March 1965 1530 GMT

SUBJECT: Guevara, Ernesto (Memorandum # <u>66</u>.)

TO: Mr. Sanford T. Felter
Counselor To The President
Room 637, The Executive Office Building
Washington, D.C.

By Courier

In compliance with Presidential Memorandum to The Director, Subject: "Ernesto 'Che' Guevara," dated 14 December 1964, the following information from your sources in Buenos Aires, Argentina is relayed as received: (Reliability Scale: Not Applicable).

743

Begin Intelligence Relayed:

Victor Dreke was taken afternoon of 30 March 1965 to the house at Calle Hernandez 134 in the La Corona section of Havana by Alberto Chivina, an aide to Castro. Dreke, who will be Guevara's deputy, was introduced to Ramón Benítez, whom he either pretended not to recognize as Doctor Ernesto Guevara de la Serna, or actually did not recognize, which seems rather unlikely.

Dreke now has a Uruguayan passport in the name of Roberto Suárez Milían and Guevara one in the name of Ramón Benítez. Both are believed to be genuine Uruguayan passports furnished the Cubans blank. It is probable that other such passports have been made available by Uruguay, the Dominican Republic, and others.

When the masquerade was revealed, Dreke and Guevara finalized the roster of the personnel they intend to take with them to the former Belgian Congo.

The 113-man strong force was described by Guevara as a "column," and will consist of a General Staff, three platoons of infantry and one of artillery. So far as is known the column does not have small arms or artillery.

Guevara and Dreke and a small, unknown number of others will probably leave tomorrow on the regularly scheduled Aerolineas Cubana flight to Prague, Czechoslovakia, and probably move from Prague via Cairo, Egypt to Dar es Salaam, Tanzania aboard a scheduled Czechoslovak Air flight to Dar es Salaam, Tanzania, as soon as possible.

A roster of the revolutionary column will be furnished when available.

End Intelligence Relayed.

Howard W. O'Connor
HOWARD W. O'CONNOR

SECRET

MONTREAL, CANADA
PARIS, FRANCE
PRAGUE, CZECHOSLOVAKIA
VIENNA, AUSTRIA

SUBJECT: POSSIBLE MOVEMENT OF
ERNESTO "CHE" GUEVERA AND OTHERS

THE AGENCY IS IN POSSESSION OF
UNVERIFIABLE BUT PROBABLY RELIABLE
INTEL THAT ERNESTO "CHE" GUEVERA AND
VICTOR DREKE, AND PROBABLY A SMALL
GROUP OF UNIDENTIFIED OTHERS WILL
DEPART HAVANA CUBA 1 APRIL 1965
ABOARD AN AEROLINEAS CUBANA FLIGHT
TO PRAGUE, CZECHOSLOVAKIA, AND LATER
FLY TO DAR ES SALAAM VIA CAIRO ABOARD
A CZECHOSLOVAK AIR FLIGHT.

THE DIRECTOR PERSONALLY REPEAT
PERSONALLY IS VERY INTERESTED IN
CONFIRMATION OR DISPROVAL OF THIS
INTEL INCLUDING ADDITIONAL DETAILS
FOLLOWING: BOTH GUEVARA AND DREKE
MAY BE TRAVELING ON URUGUAYAN
PASSPORTS USING THE NAMES RAMÓN
BENÍTEZ AND ROBERTO SUÁREZ MILÍAN
RESPECTIVELY. GUEVERA MAY BE CLEAN
SHAVEN, WEARING GLASSES, HAVE THE TOP
OF HIS HEAD SHAVEN AND WEARING
PROTHESIS TO CHANGE THE SHAPE OF HIS
MOUTH.

THE FOLLOWING ACTION IS DIRECTED:

SURVEILLANCE OF CUBANA OR OTHER
AIRLINE FLIGHTS ORIGINATING IN HAVANA
CUBA AND TERMINATING AT OR PASSING
THROUGH LOCATIONS ABOVE, PLUS
GANDER, NEWFOUNDLAND, WILL BE
IMMEDIATELY ESTABLISHED AND
MAINTAINED UNTIL FURTHER NOTICE.

CONFIRMING OR DISPROVING REPORTS
PLUS ANY OTHER INTEL THAT CAN BE
GENERATED IN RE MOVEMENT OR
LOCATION OF GUEVARA AND/DREKE WILL
BE TRANSMITTED BY THE MOST
EXPEDITIOUS MEANS, INCLUDING
SATELLITE, TO CIA LANGLEY EYES ONLY
DIRECTOR CIA AND ASSISTANT
DIRECTOR/ADMIN.

FOR THE DIRECTOR
O'CONNOR ASST DIR/ADMIN

SECRET

[TWO]
Camp David
The Catoctin Mountains, Maryland
1430 1 April 1965

The President of the United States was not in a very
good mood.

For one thing, it was raining, and apparently
was going to rain all goddamn day, and he had

planned to shoot a little skeet, and he obviously couldn't shoot skeet in a pouring goddamn rain.

For another, the President didn't like what he was hearing about communist activity in the Dominican Republic from either the Director of the Central Intelligence Agency, the Chairman of the Joint Chiefs of Staff, the Chief of Naval Operations, or the Chief of Staff of the U.S. Army.

The Director had told him he considered it very likely that the government in Santo Domingo was very likely to be toppled by Communists, unless something was done almost immediately.

The Chairman had told him that he concurred with the Director's assessment of the situation, and recommended military intervention before that happened, as it would be much easier to keep the government there in power than it would be to restore it to power after a communist coup.

The Chief of Naval Operations had told him that he concurred with the Director's analysis, and the Chairman's belief that military invention was necessary, and recommended that a re-inforced regimental-size Marine landing force be formed and ordered to prepare for an invasion of the Dominican Republic.

The Chief had told him that he concurred with the Director and the Chairman's analysis and their recommendation of preventative establishment of an American military presence in the Dominican Republic, but had to respectfully disagree with his good friend the Chief of Naval Operations about how to do that.

For both military and political reasons, the Chief said, it would be better to use the 82nd Airborne Division. There was no way that the sailing of a Marine landing force could be kept from either the press or the Communists in the Dominican Republic. That might cause the Communists to act sooner than expected, and that would (a) topple the existing government, and (b) very likely cause the Marines, when they arrived, to have to execute a landing on hostile shores.

There was always, the Chief went on, a regiment of the 82nd at Bragg ready to enplane on no more than twenty-four hours' notice, and a second regiment would be available in another twenty-four hours.

The best way to send an American military presence into the Dominican Republic would be to jump an 82nd Regiment into Santo Domingo without warning, with of course the permission of the current government. Once the airport was secured, a second and a third regiment could be flown in. The Marines could thus land, without opposition, later.

The President of the United States did not like the mental pictures he was given of (a) some goddamn *Dominican* Fidel Castro giving the United States of America the finger; (b) parachutes filling the sky over Santo Domingo; or (c) Marines embarking from landing craft on the hostile shore of this goddamn banana republic.

"I want to think this over," the President announced. "And it's obvious we need some fresh thinking on the subject." He turned to his secretary. "Send for Felter."

The President's secretary did not tell Colonel Sanford T. Felter much more than that the President wished him to go immediately to the Pentagon helipad, where a U.S. Army Huey would be waiting for him.

He arrived at Camp David one hour and twenty-five minutes after receiving the President's secretary's call, and was immediately taken into the presence of the President, the Chairman, the CNO, and the Chief. He was wearing a somewhat mussed gray suit, and a cotton raincoat that obviously was not up to keeping him dry.

"Tell me about the Dominican Republic, Felter," the President greeted him.

"Sir, I don't know much about the Dominican Republic," Felter said. "That's not in my area of responsibility."

"Tell me what you do know," the President said.

The telephone rang.

The President's secretary answered it.

The President held up his hand to silence Felter while he waited to see if the call was for him.

"It's the White House Signal Agency," the President's secretary announced. "For Colonel Felter. They have the Léopoldville secure satellite link open for him."

"Tell them to reschedule —" Felter began.

"What's that, Felter?" the President asked.

"Sir, I had a message from Major Lunsford saying that he had to talk to me," Felter said. "So I asked the Signal Agency to —"

"Meaning he's in trouble in the Congo?" Johnson interrupted.

"I think meaning, Mr. President, that Major Lunsford has something he considers important to say to me. Maybe he needs a decision from me. But if there was trouble, sir — if someone has been injured, for example — I think that would have been in his message."

"Huh," the President snorted.

"I'll reschedule the link, sir," Felter said.

"No," the President said. He looked at his secretary. "We can put that on the speakerphone, right?"

"Yes, Mr. President."

The President looked at Felter.

"Do not, do not, tell him where you are, or who's also here. I don't want him worried about saying the wrong thing."

"Yes, sir."

The President pointed to a second telephone on a coffee table, and pointed at the couch beside it. "You sit there, Felter, and talk at the telephone; you don't have to pick it up, just push the speaker button."

"Yes, sir."

He sat down, still in his rain-soaked raincoat, and pushed the speaker button.

"Felter," he said.

"Sir, we have your secure satellite link to Léopoldville. You have eleven minutes, twenty seconds of sat time left."

"Thank you," Felter said. "Open it, please."

He pushed a button on the chronograph on his wrist.

"You there, boss?" Lunsford's voice said, having been sent into space and bounced back off a surveillance satellite, then relayed to two speakers mounted on the walls of the room in Camp David.

"How are you, Father? What's on your mind?"

"I need some more stuff, some more money, and your permission to kill the company man, and I need it yesterday."

The President looked at the director of the Central Intelligence Agency, which was frequently referred to informally as "the company."

"Tell me about the company man," Felter said.

"The sonofabitch thinks he's Eisenhower," Father said. "He sits on his fat ass in the embassy and draws arrows on maps."

"That's the problem?"

"The problem is, he's making assets available only to projects of which he approves. That means he's got jeeps and three-quarter-ton trucks in a fucking motor pool in Léopoldville, while we're — including Colonel Supo — riding around in requisitioned trucks, or walking. But, far fucking worse, the sonofabitch has the B-26s, the T-28s, and the C-47s in his fat little fingers and he told me flat out there is no way he's going to let us use them. And we need them, Colonel, if this thing is going to work."

"I'll see what I can do," Felter said, and looked at the director of the Central Intelligence Agency.

"If I had my druthers, I'd rather have permission to stick a spear up his ass and feed his corpse to the crocodiles," Father said.

"What else, Lunsford?"

"I need at least two more — four would be better — L-19s and two pilots for each."

"I'll speak with General Bellmon as soon as we're off, and get back to you."

"And twenty fixed-station transceivers, fifty backpack radios, and plenty of batteries for them."

"That can be arranged," Felter said. "What about the money?"

"Supo wants to buy information and dead Simbas with money, which in the bush means gold coins."

"How much are you talking about?" Felter asked.

752

The President picked up a telephone and spoke softly into it.

"Twenty-five thousand right now, and more later," Lunsford said.

"I think that can be arranged," Felter said.

"This link will shut down in fifteen seconds for a higher priority," the White House Signal Agency operator announced. "You are rescheduled for fifteen minutes at 2210 Zulu."

Felter looked at the President.

"The Signal Agency guy tells me that's when the next satellite will be available," the President said. "In about an hour and ten minutes. I think that should give Felter enough time to explain all of this to us."

"Mr. President," Felter said. "May I respectfully remind you, sir, that Major Lunsford, at your orders, was not aware that anyone but me was on this end?"

"He's one mean sonofabitch when crossed, isn't he?" the President said. "I'd really hate to have him threaten to stick a spear up my rear end." He paused. "Brief us on what's going on over there, Felter."

"Yes, sir."

"You going to need a map?"

"I'd like to have one, sir."

"Get him a map," the President ordered. "And while that's on the way, Felter, get out of that wet raincoat."

Two sailors, a chief petty officer and a seaman first class, quickly replaced the maps of the Dominican Republic and Santo Domingo on a very elegant polished-wood, tripod-mounted map board with a map of the Republic of the Congo and its environs, then lowered a sheet of acetate over it.

Felter saw that the map board was equipped with grease pencils in four colors and a pointer. As he picked up the pointer, he saw that it bore an engraved plaque: PROPERTY OF THE OFFICE OF THE CHIEF OF NAVAL OPERATIONS.

He guessed, correctly, that the CNO had planned to use the map to describe how the Marines would go into the Dominican Republic. And he guessed, again correctly, that the Chief of Naval Operations did not particularly like a lowly colonel in civilian clothing using his map board.

"The insurrectionist forces," Felter began, "known as the Simbas, are commanded by a self-appointed Lieutenant General Olenga. The Communists — not the Simbas themselves — refer to them as the Lumumbist Forces, after the late Patrice Lumumba, who, it is alleged, was assassinated in 1961 at the orders of Mobutu. So far as I know, Lumumba never laid eyes on Olenga.

"Following the Belgian jump on Stanleyville, and the roughly simultaneous military actions by the Belgians and the mercenaries of Major Michael Hoare, the Simbas were pretty well scattered all over these four provinces — Equatorial, Oriental, Kivu, and Kasai."

He used the pointer to indicate the locations of the several provinces.

"About the only effective Congolese officer dealing with the problem has been Colonel Jean-Baptiste Supo, like Mobutu a former sergeant major in the Belgian Force Publique. As of about ten days ago, Supo has been given responsibility for all the provinces, and our augmented

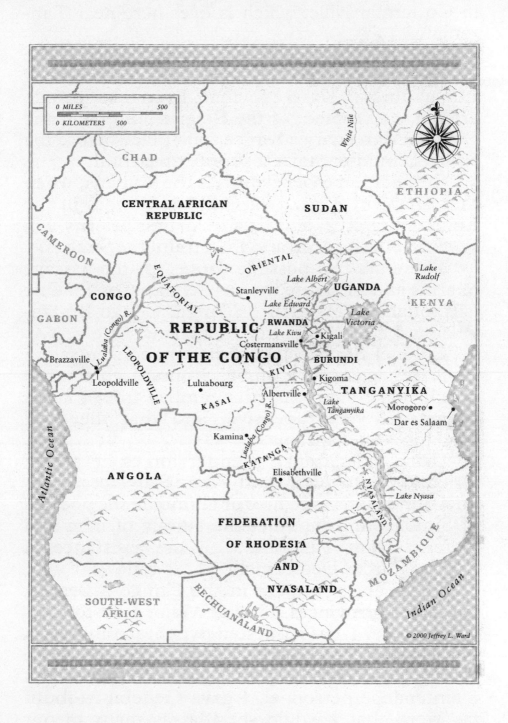

Special Forces team is attached to his headquarters in Costermansville, which is over here near Tanzania.

"Colonel Supo believes that the bulk of the on-the-run Simbas are in the vicinity of Luluabourg, in Kasai Province. Even these people are not well armed, as the Belgian jump and the Belgian/Mercenary advance took place before the Soviets could organize a supply operation.

"Colonel Supo believes that the Cubans, when they arrive in Africa, will join the Simbas in the Luluabourg area, and that their first priority will be to first better arm, and then train, the Simbas.

"There are two possible routes for the passage of arms and men into the ex–Belgian Congo. One is through the ex–French Congo, Congo Brazzaville, and the other is from Tanzania.

"Colonel Supo believes that by concentrating his forces against the Simbas around Luluabourg, it will make supplying the Simbas from Congo Brazzaville very expensive, and that they will therefore use Tanzania.

"Using what frankly slender forces he has in Oriental, Equatorial, and Kivu Provinces, Colonel Supo plans to reduce or eliminate the pockets of Simbas, and interdict the supply of men and matériel from Tanzania with the assistance of Special Forces Detachment 17, as follows:

"There are at present in the Congo a Beaver, two L-19s, and an H-13, and Major Lunsford, as you just heard, has requested two, preferably four, more L-19s. The aircraft are available, but we're having trouble finding enough black pilots and maintenance personnel. I gave General Mobutu my word that I would see that as many of our people as possible would be black."

"You're telling me, Colonel," the CNO said, "that you think you can patrol — and interdict men and matériel — in an area that huge with half a dozen spotter planes and what, forty men?"

"Yes, sir. Both Colonel Supo and Major Lunsford believe this can be done. With some help from the black B-26s and T-28s presently under the control of the company. We have no choice. President Kasavubu has publicly stated he will not have an American military presence in the Congo."

"I'd love to know how," CNO said.

"We are going to establish small outposts at dirt strip airfields at roughly fifty-mile intervals, from Basoko, west of Stanleyville, through Stanleyville, down to Costermansville, and then down Lake Tanganyika past Albertville to the Rhodesian border. There are apparently a large number of primitive airfields in the area, built by farmers and mercenaries, and not shown on aerial charts."

"How do you know this?" the Chief asked.

"One of the officers was formerly a pilot in the area, sir."

"A Congolese, you mean?"

"No, sir. An American officer. One of the two white Special Forces pilots. He was recently married to General Bellmon's daughter."

"I'll be damned," the Chief said.

"At each airstrip there will be a small detachment of Congolese soldiers, a supply of avgas and lubricants, and a radio able to maintain contact with our aircraft in the area, and with at least one other airstrip on each side. At every third or fourth airstrip, there will be a Swahili-speaking Special Forces soldier, and a platoon of Congolese soldiers.

757

"Until aerial reconnaissance was made available, Colonel Supo's forces have had great difficulty in locating the enemy, who can move two hundred yards off the roads and become invisible. Now they can be found, and kept under surveillance until ground forces can make contact."

"And you don't think the — what did you call them, Simbas? — are going to take out your outposts once they know what they're up to?"

"Colonel Supo believes that once they come to understand that as soon as an outpost learns of their presence, either accidentally, or by having friendly natives inform the outpost — and obviously Major Lunsford believes that twenty-five thousand dollars in gold is going to buy some friendship — or, especially, by attacking an outpost, that they will thereafter immediately become the hunted, that the outposts will be avoided at all costs."

"And how many of your outposts will have been overrun before they get that message?" the Chairman asked.

"That will probably depend, sir," Felter said evenly, "on how fast and how hard we can react when the first one, the first two, are attacked. I suspect that it is why Major Lunsford wants access to the T-28s and the B-26s. The only aerial gun platform he has available to him is the H-13, on which he can mount a couple of air-cooled Browning .30-caliber machine guns. He plans to bomb the Simbas with a technique developed in Vietnam. You pull the pin on a fragmentation grenade, and then place it in a quart Mason jar. The walls of the jar keep the firing mechanism from operating. The Mason jar is then dropped from an L-19. If the jar shatters, the grenade is activated."

"Jesus Christ!" the President of the United States said.

"And since the outposts are all on, or next to the few roads that pass through the bush in that area," Felter went on, "this will also deny the roads to the enemy as supply routes."

"You seem to be placing a hell of a lot of faith in the ability of this Major Lunsford," the Director said.

"It's well-placed," the President said. "Major Lunsford ran around in the jungles for four months passing himself off as a Simba. He's quite a character."

"There are certain things Supo's men cannot handle without assistance," Felter said. "They are short of transportation. The more jeeps and three-quarter-ton trucks they have available, the quicker they can respond to the detection of the enemy, and the easier they can keep the outposts resupplied. I wasn't aware that the agency had vehicular assets in the Congo. If I had been, I'd have asked for them. As it is now, I am flying in jeeps on our chartered 707.

"Tactically, if Supo can call on our — the agency's — black B-26s and T-28s when they encounter a large enemy force, or to interdict boats attempting to move men and matériel across Lake Tanganyika, it will make his job that much easier."

"I've heard about enough of this," the President said.

"Sir?" Felter asked.

"When you arrived, Colonel Felter," the President said, "we were discussing whether I should order sending the Marines or the Eighty-second Airborne Division into the Dominican Republic.

759

In either case, we are talking about thousands of men, hundreds of transport airplanes."

"Yes, sir?" Felter asked.

"I don't like the picture I'm getting of one of Lunsford's men all by himself in the middle of an African jungle, having to worry, if he's attacked, if anybody's going to come help him," the President went on. "So I'll tell you what's going to happen."

"Yes, sir?"

"When that satellite comes on again, Felter, you're going to get on the horn with Major Lunsford, you're going to give him my best regards, and you're going to tell him I said he's going to get everything he asked for. And then you, Paul, are going to tell your man over there that if I ever hear he didn't give Lunsford whatever he asked for, I will stick a spear up his ass myself."

[THREE]
The Office of the Ambassador
The Embassy of West Germany
Washington, D.C.
0900 2 April 1965

"Good morning, Erich," the ambassador said to the embassy's military attaché. "What have you got for me?"

They were both slight, trim, bald men of the same age who wore spectacles. They looked so much alike that when both were to attend a diplomatic reception, Colonel Erich Steitz, if at all appropriate, tried to wear his uniform, to preclude his being called "Your Excellency" and/or "Mr. Ambassador," and the ambassador being called "Colonel."

"A von Greiffenberg-gram, Your Excellency," Steitz said with a smile, and held out to him two sheets of paper.

"These things drive poor Dieter up the wall, you know," the ambassador said with a chuckle, making reference to Dieter von und zu Schaaf, the second secretary, who was in charge of administration, and liked to have two copies, preferably more, of everything.

"Yes, sir, I know," Steitz said. "But I would rather have Schaaf angry with me for not having copies of these than von Greiffenberg angry with me for giving him one."

"Me, too," the ambassador said, and took the two sheets of paper and read them.

CLASSIFICATION MOST SECRET
TRANSMISSION PRIORITY ONE
FROM MINISTRY OF SECURITY BONN
#65-4003
1300 BONN TIME 2 APRIL 1965

FOR ARMY ATTACHÉ
PERSONAL ATTENTION ONLY COLONEL
STEITZ
WEST GERMAN EMBASSY
WASHINGTON DC

ON RECEIPT ATTACHMENT 1 WILL BE
IMMEDIATELY DECRYPTED USING CODE
HEINRICH SIX AND DELIVERED BY YOU
PERSONALLY TO COLONEL SANFORD T.
FELTER, COUNSELOR TO THE PRESIDENT OF
THE UNITED STATES, EXECUTIVE OFFICE
BUILDING, WASHINGTON. YOU WILL SHOW

COLONEL FELTER THIS MESSAGE OF TRANSMITTAL, WHEREUPON HE WILL PROVIDE YOU WITH A CODE WORD INDICATING ITS RECEIPT WHICH YOU WILL THEN TRANSMIT TO ME. IT IS EXPRESSLY FORBIDDEN TO MAKE ANY COPIES OF EITHER MESSAGE OTHER THAN THE ONE COPY TO BE DELIVERED TO COLONEL FELTER.

VON GREIFFENBERG GENERALLEUTNANT DIRECTOR

ATTACHMENT 1 TO MINISTRY OF SECURITY #65-4003 (DECRYPTED)
COPY 1 OF 1 DUPLICATION FORBIDDEN

BONN 2 APRIL 1965

MY DEAR FRIEND SANDY:

THE URUGUAYAN CITIZENS SENOR RAMÓN BENÍTEZ AND SENOR ROBERTO SUÁREZ MILÍAN ARRIVED IN PRAGUE, TOGETHER WITH SIX OF THEIR COUNTRYMEN, WHOSE NAMES I REGRETFULLY CANNOT FURNISH AT THIS TIME, AT 2205 GREENWICH 1 APRIL 1965 ABOARD AEROLINEAS CUBANA FLIGHT 9880 FROM HAVANA, WHICH STOPPED AT GANDER, NEWFOUNDLAND EN ROUTE.

THEY WERE IMMEDIATELY TAKEN UNDER UNUSUAL CONDITIONS OF SECURITY TO A

HOUSE AT 407 ULBRECHTSTR, NOT FAR FROM THE AIRPORT, WHICH IS A SAFE HOUSE OPERATED BY STASI, AND HERETOFORE MADE AVAILABLE ONLY FOR EAST GERMAN AND SOVIET ACTIVITIES. I WOULD SUGGEST THIS TO BE CONFIRMATION OF SOVIET INVOLVEMENT IN THE OPERATION IN WHICH WE ARE INTERESTED.

BENÍTEZ AND MILÍAN HAVE RESERVATIONS ON CZECHOSLOVAK AIR FLIGHT 2332 PRAGUE/CAIRO/DAR ES SALAAM 2300 3 MARCH 1965.

I WILL ATTEMPT TO CONFIRM DEPARTURE, PASSAGE CAIRO AND ARRIVAL DAR ES SALAAM.

I AM SENDING THIS INFORMATION TO OUR FRIENDS IN BUENOS AIRES.

IT IS A PLEASURE FOR ME TO BE OF ASSISTANCE, AND HOPE YOU FIND THIS USEFUL. WITH THE WARMEST REGARDS TO YOU AND SHARON AND THE CHILDREN, AND OF COURSE CRAIG.

VON GREIFFENBERG

"I don't suppose you have any idea what this is all about?" the ambassador asked.

"This is apparently another of those cases

763

where the good Generalleutnant feels he can trust Oberst Felter with something we really don't have to know."

"I think one would naturally trust someone who plucked you from a Siberian labor camp more than most other people," the ambassador said. "What I don't really understand is why von Greiffenberg insists that I read these things."

"Von Greiffenberg, Mr. Ambassador, like the Lord, moves in mysterious ways."

The ambassador chuckled, and handed the sheets of paper back to Steitz.

"Thank you, Erich," the ambassador said. "When you see Felter, give him my best regards."

"I'll do that, sir."

[FOUR]
The Oval Office
The White House
Washington, D.C.
1045 2 April 1965

The President, the Director of the Central Intelligence Agency, the Chairman of the National Security Council, and the Chairman of the Joint Chiefs of Staff were discussing what the President twice in the last ten minutes had called "the goddamned Dominican Commies" when the door opened and the President's secretary stood waiting for the President's attention.

"What?" the President asked, somewhat abruptly.

"Mr. Finton has a memo for you, Mr. President."

Everyone in the room knew that Mr. Finton worked for Colonel Sanford T. Felter. The

Director of the CIA also knew that Finton was a bishop of the Church of Latter-Day Saints.

The President gestured for Finton to be admitted.

"Good morning," the President said, and held out his hand for the memorandum.

"Good morning, Mr. President," Finton said, and handed the President a White House interoffice memorandum.

The White House
WASHINGTON, D.C.

INTEROFFICE MEMORANDUM

CLASSIFICATION: Top Secret

DATE AND TIME: 1020 Washington Time 2 April 1965

FROM: Sanford T. Felter

TO: Eyes Only The President of the United States
Eyes Only The Director, CIA

By Hand

I have good reason to believe the following should be regarded as Reliability Scale Five.

Ernesto Guevara (traveling as Ramón Benítez) and Victor Dreke, his deputy, (travelling as Roberto Suárez Milían) both using

---

Uruguayan passports, arrived in Prague, together with six other Cubans, names not presently known, at 2205 Zulu 1 April 1965 aboard Aerolineas Cubana flight 9880 from Havana, via Gander, Newfoundland.

They were immediately taken under unusual conditions of security to a house at 407 Ulbrechtstr, not far from the airport. This is known to be a safe house operated by STASI, the East German State Security Service, and heretofore has been made available only for East German and Soviet activities. This would tend to confirm Soviet involvement in Guevara's operation.

Guevara and Dreke, traveling as Benítez and Milían, have reservations on Czechoslovak Air flight 2332 Prague/Cairo/Dar es Salaam 2300 3 March 1965.

Respectfully submitted,

Sanford T. Felter
Sanford T. Felter
Colonel, GSC, U.S. Army

As the President was reading it, Mr. Finton reached into his pocket and handed a carbon copy of the memorandum to the Director of the CIA.

"Thank you," the President said to Mr. Finton when he had finished reading the memorandum.

"And thank Colonel Felter."

"Yes, Mr. President," Mr. Finton said.

"You got anything for Felter?" the President asked when he saw that the Director of the CIA had finished reading his copy of the memorandum.

"No, sir," the director said.

"Thank you," the President said to Finton, dismissing him.

The President waited until the door closed.

"Well, do you still have doubts that Guevara is going to the Congo?" he asked.

"This would seem to suggest, if this can be relied on, Mr. President, that Guevara is going at least to Dar es Salaam," the Director said.

"Maybe you know something I don't," the President said. "Why do you think, since he's already been to Dar es Salaam as Che Guevara, that he's going back there with a phony name, on a phony passport, via Prague?"

"I just don't know, Mr. President," the Director said.

"Yeah," the President said. "That's what I thought."

[FIVE]

SECRET
URGENT

FROM : CIA LANGLEY 2 APRIL 1965 1310 GMT

TO: STATION CHIEFS:

ALGIERS, ALGERIA
BERLIN, GERMANY
CAIRO, EGYPT
DAR ES SALAAM, TANZANIA
MONTREAL, CANADA
PARIS, FRANCE
PRAGUE, CZECHOSLOVAKIA
VIENNA, AUSTRIA

SUBJECT: POSSIBLE MOVEMENT OF
ERNESTO "CHE" GUEVERA AND OTHERS
REFERENCE MY 03/5788 SUBJECT AS
ABOVE.

INASMUCH AS THERE HAS BEEN ZERO
RESPONSE TO REFERENCED MESSAGE, THE
DIRECTOR PERSONALLY SENDS THE
FOLLOWING FOR THE GENERAL
INFORMATION OF ALL CONCERNED:

GUEVERA AND DREKE AND OTHERS ARE IN
PRAGUE, SPECIFICALLY AT 407
ULBRECHTSTR.

THEREFORE, ATTEMPTED SURVEILLANCE AT
GANDER, BERLIN, ALGIERS AND VIENNA
MAY BE DISCONTINUED.

IT IS STRONGLY SUGGESTED THAT STATION
CHIEF PRAGUE OBTAIN PASSAGE ABOARD
CZECHOSLAVAK AIR FLIGHT 2332
DEPARTING PRAGUE 2300 3 MARCH 1965,
ON WHICH GUEVERA, DREKE, AND
POSSIBLY OTHERS WILL TRAVEL TO DAR ES

SALAAM ON URUGUAYAN PASSPORTS. STATION CHIEF CAIRO SIMILARLY SHOULD SURVEILLE CAIRO/DAR ES SALAAM LEG OF THIS FLIGHT.

IT IS STRONGLY RECOMMENDED THAT STATION CHIEF DAR ES SALAAM MEET THE AIRCRAFT AND, PRESUMING PRAGUE AND CAIRO PERSONNEL ARE ABOARD, WITH THEIR ASSISTANCE ATTEMPT TO KEEP GUEVERA, DREKE, AND POSSIBLY OTHERS UNDER SURVEILLANCE.

ALL CONCERNED ARE REMINDED IT IS THE FUNCTION OF THE AGENCY TO DEVELOP AND DELIVER INTELLIGENCE OF THIS NATURE, NOT RECEIVE IT FROM OTHERS.

CONFIRMING OR DISPROVING REPORTS PLUS ANY OTHER INTEL THAT CAN BE GENERATED IN RE MOVEMENT OR LOCATION OF GUEVARA AND/DREKE WILL BE TRANSMITTED BY THE MOST EXPEDITIOUS MEANS, INCLUDING SATELLITE, TO CIA LANGLEY EYES ONLY DIRECTOR CIA AND ASSISTANT DIRECTOR/ADMIN.

FOR THE DIRECTOR
O'CONNOR ASST DIR/ADMIN

SECRET

TOPSECRET

Central Intelligence Agency
Langley, Virginia

FROM: Assistant Director For Administration

DATE: 4 April 1965 1530 GMT

SUBJECT: Guevara, Ernesto (Memorandum # 69.)

TO: The President

Copy To: Mr. Sanford T. Felter
              Counselor To The President
              Room 637, The Executive Office
                Building
              Washington, D.C.

By Officer Courier

The Director believed The President would find the CIA generated intelligence reported herein of interest. In compliance with Presidential Memorandum to The Director, Subject: "Ernesto 'Che' Guevara," dated 14 December 1964, the following information is being furnished to Colonel Felter. (Reliability Scale Five).

Follows verbatim satellite transmitted message from James M. Foster, CIA Station Chief, Dar es Salaam, Tanzania:

TOP SECRET

1445 GREENWICH 4 APRIL 1965

FROM STATION CHIEF, DAR ES SALAAM
TO (EYES ONLY) DIRECTOR, CIA, LANGLEY
(EYES ONLY) DEPDIR ADMIN, CIA LANGLEY

   TWO INDIVIDUALS BEARING
URUGUAYAN PASSPORTS AND MEETING
DESCRIPTION OF GUEVERA/BENÍTEZ AND
DREKE/MILÍAN (YOUR 03/5788) ARRIVED
DAR ES SALAAM ABOARD CZECHOSLOVAK
AIR FLIGHT 2332 1550 4 APRIL 1965.
TOGETHER WITH SIX OTHERS THEY WERE
OFFLOADED UNDER CONDITIONS OF
UNUSUAL SECURITY AND TRUCKED TO A
FARM IN THE VICINITY OF MOROGORO,
APPROXIMATELY 75 MILES WEST OF DAR ES
SALAAM.

   THE SITE IS UNDER SURVEILLANCE.
INITIAL INFORMATION INDICATES THE NOW
DESERTED FARM, OWNED BY WHITES WHO
HAVE LEFT THE COUNTRY, WAS RENTED BY
AN EAST GERMAN FIRM BELIEVED TO BE
CONTROLLED BY STASI. PROVINCIAL
TANZANIAN POLICE HAVE ESTABLISHED
ROAD BLOCKS ON NATIONAL ROUTE A7.

   INASMUCH AS THIS STATION IS
PREPARED TO MAINTAIN AROUND THE
CLOCK SURVEILLANCE OF THE SITE,
ASSISTANCE OF PERSONNEL FROM OTHER
STATIONS IS NOT REQUIRED, AND IN THE

ABSENCE OF SPECIFIC INSTRUCTIONS TO THE CONTRARY, THEY WILL DEPART THE COUNTRY NLT 7 APRIL 1965.

JAMES M. FOSTER
STATION CHIEF DAR ES SALAAM

TOP SECRET

END CIA Dar es Salaam Message

Additional intelligence generated by CIA Dar es Salaam will be furnished immediately on receipt.

Howard W. O'Connor
HOWARD W. O'CONNOR

TOP SECRET

[SIX]
The Hotel du Lac
Costermansville, Kivu Province
Republic of the Congo
0900 5 April 1965

"I was worried sick about you," Mrs. Marjorie B. Portet greeted her husband when he, Major George W. Lunsford, Spec7 William Peters (in the uniforms of a Congolese lieutenant colonel and captain, respectively), and Lieutenant Geoffrey

Craig walked into the dining room of the hotel.

"The weather was lousy," Jack replied. "We had to spend the night."

"You could have sent word," Marjorie said.

"That's what we were doing, baby," Jack answered, a slight tone of impatience in his voice. "Setting up relay stations so we can send word when something like that happens."

"In other words, I'm being a bitch?"

"You said it, not me," Jack said.

"Children, children," Lunsford said. "If you keep that up, we will be forced to suspect the honeymoon is over."

"I forgive you," Jack said.

"Screw you," Marjorie said, but she kissed him.

A waiter appeared and took their breakfast order, and as a second waiter was pouring coffee, two Congolese paratroop officers, who had come to the Congo as Master Sergeant Thomas and Sergeant First Class DeGrew, appeared and sat down at the table.

"This came in last night, boss," Doubting Thomas said, and handed Lunsford a sheet of paper from the encryption machine.

Lunsford read it, then handed it to Geoff Craig, with a gesture meaning he wanted it passed around to the others. The way they were sitting, Jack got it last.

"Can I show this to my bride?" he asked.

"Who do you think ran the tape machines?" Marjorie asked. "I know what it says."

TOP SECRET
EARN0023 WASH DC 1740 ZULU 4 APRIL
1965
VIA WHITE HOUSE SIGNAL AGENCY

FROM: EARNEST SIX
TO: HELPER SIX

1-COMPLETELY RELIABLE SOURCE STATES
GUEVARA, DREKE, AND SIX OTHERS
ARRIVED IN DAR ES SALAAM 1530 ZULU 4
APRIL.

2-JAMES M. FOSTER, CIA STATION CHIEF
DAR ES SALAAM, APPARENTLY CONFIRMS
WITH REPORT CIA HAS GUEVARA, DREKE,
AND SIX OTHERS UNDER SURVEILLANCE ON
FARM IN VICINITY OF MOROGORO, 75
MILES WEST OF DAR ES SALAAM.

3-REFERENCE PREVIOUSLY FURNISHED
MANIFEST, SUPPLY FLIGHT FOUR WILL NOT
REPEAT NOT HAVE TWO JEEPS ABOARD
INASMUCH AS LÉOPOLDVILLE MOTORPOOL
NOW AVAILABLE. TWO L19 AIRCRAFT;
EQUIVALENT OF $25,000 IN GOLD SWISS
COINS; TWO ASA TECHNICIANS; AND ONE
L19/L20/H13 MECHANIC WILL BE ABOARD.
ETA WILL BE FURNISHED WHEN AVAILABLE.

FINTON FOR EARNEST SIX

SECRET

"I have the feeling," Father said, "that Mr. Foster disproves the general rule that most agency clowns cannot find their gluteus maximus with both hands."

"I'd like to talk to him," Sergeant Thomas said.

"My thinking exactly," Thomas said.

"I'd like to have an intercept team near that farm," Spec7 Peters said.

"Lieutenant Craig, with splendid enlisted men like these two, their thinking in complete synch with that of their beloved commander, how can we fail?"

"There are several possible problems," Geoff said. "Starting with the basic one that this CIA guy may tell you go to . . . up a rope. Sorry, Marjorie. Close on the heels of that one, how do we get to talk to him?"

"Captain Weewili and I have given the subject some thought," Thomas said. "And then we conferred at 0600 this very day with Major Alain George Totse himself."

Lunsford smiled, and made a gesture with both hands, meaning, "Well, let's have it."

[SEVEN]
Consular Section
Embassy of the United States of America
Dar es Salaam, Tanzania
1210 6 April 1965

"Good afternoon," Captain Jacques Portet of Air Simba said to the receptionist. "I'd like a word with the Consul General, please."

He was wearing a short-sleeved white shirt with the four-striped board of a captain in its epaulets, and crisply creased black trousers. Beside him stood a stocky African wearing a loose, somewhat soiled, white shirt and loose, somewhat soiled, white trousers, held up with a knotted cord, their frayed hems a good ten inches above his heavily callused bare feet. He wore both a necklace and a bracelet of wild pig teeth.

"Perhaps I can help you, sir. Mr. Foster is tied up at the moment," the receptionist replied. She was a striking, very tall, very black young woman who was made very uncomfortable by the shameless beaming approval being given her by the American's boy.

"I really would be very grateful if Mr. Foster could spare me just a moment of his time," Jack said. "And I really need to see him."

"I'll see what I can do," she said.

Mr. Foster appeared a moment later. He was a black man in his late twenties or early thirties, wearing a flamboyantly colored, diagonally striped shirt, yellow walking shorts, knee-length white stocks with a tassel at the top, and tasseled loafers.

"I'm afraid I can't give you much time," he said, glancing at his watch. "I've a luncheon appointment."

"I need just a moment of your time, privately," Jack said. "Could we step in there just a moment?"

The reception room had three small cubicles against one wall.

"Well, if you think it's important," Mr. Foster said.

He bowed Jack into the room ahead of him, followed him in, and was greatly surprised when the white American's boy followed him inside.

"Is uh . . . he . . . necessary for this?" Mr. Foster replied.

"I love those loafers," the boy said. "But where the hell did you get that shirt?"

"May I present Major George Washington Lunsford?" Jack said, smiling.

"Cutting to the chase," Father said. "I command Special Forces Detachment 17, in Costermansville, in the Congo. And you're the CIA station chief, and you've got Guevara and Dreke and some others under surveillance in a farm near Morogoro, about seventy-five miles from here."

"I have no idea what you're talking about, of course," Foster said.

"Right," Father said. "This is Lieutenant Jack Portet, one of my officers."

"How did you get in the country?"

"He got in by flying an Air Simba C-46 — that's his cover. And I got in by riding in the back. I guess you could say I'm passing for a native."

"Have you got some sort of identification?"

"Oh, come on," Lunsford said. "You have diplomatic immunity. I don't. And I don't want to get shot as a spy because the locals found an AGO card in my wallet. How long have you been a spook, anyway?"

"What can I do for you, Major?" Foster asked.

"First, can we find someplace larger than this phone booth, and secure? My lieutenant reeks of his wife's cologne, and it has a distressing erotic effect on me. And I don't want that splendidly stacked receptionist of yours taking notes."

"No problem there," Foster said. "She gets her paycheck from the same place I do. She's from Philadelphia."

He pushed open the door, waved them out.

"Close us for lunch, please," he said to the

receptionist, "and then come on in."

"Ah, would that we were meeting elsewhere," Father said when the woman came into Foster's office. "Bookbinder's, perhaps. The one on South Broad Street."

He smiled, expecting her shocked reaction.

She smiled.

"But we're not, are we?" she replied. "And the last time I was in Bookbinder's you had to wear shoes."

Father was only momentarily taken aback.

"Major George Washington Lunsford at your service, ma'am," he said, and made a sweeping bow.

"What's going on?" she asked of Foster.

"The rumor going around that there are Special Forces in the Congo? It's apparently true."

"If the Tanzanians catch you here, it would be awkward, as I suppose you know," she said.

"It would also probably be painful, so let's do what we can to keep that from happening, shall we?" Lunsford replied. "Are you going to tell me your name?"

"I don't think you have the need-to-know," she said.

"You're legal as far as the flight is concerned?" Foster asked.

"I'm here trying to buy aircraft engine parts," Jack said. "Major Lunsford is illegal."

"You're both illegal," she said. "You can probably get away with it. I'm not so sure about barefoot boy here."

"What is it you want?" Foster said.

"My mission is to frustrate Guevara's plans for the Congo," Lunsford said. When he saw something in her face, he added: "Yeah, we know he's here, and that you have him under surveillance on a farm near Morogoro."

"I'd love to know where you heard that," she said.

"The operative word is 'frustrate,' " Lunsford said. "We want him to return to Cuba alive and with his tail between his legs. That restriction does not apply to other Cubans, of whom, eventually, there will be about two hundred."

"I didn't hear that figure," she said.

"I can have nothing to do with that," Foster said, "with . . . uh . . . armed action against the Cubans, or anyone else."

"It will be a lot easier for us to interdict the movement of his people, and their supplies, if we have an eye on that farm," Lunsford said. "And it would be a lot easier for you to keep an eye on that farm if you had an intercept team listening to their communications."

"I asked for a team and was told no," Foster said. "That may change now, with him here."

"I'll loan you a team," Lunsford said.

"How would you get it into the country?" she asked.

"It's at the airport now, three ASA guys and two Special Forces. They're all black, and the Special Forces guys speak Swahili, one of them well. That one also speaks Spanish. All they'd need from you is transport to the area, and a supply of food."

"And you want us to relay the intercepts?" she asked.

"Oh, no, Katharine," Father said. "You don't mind if I call you Katharine, do you? You have that same, utterly charming Katharine Hepburn, between-clenched-teeth accent she had in *The Philadelphia Story*."

779

"Oh, aren't you clever!" she replied. "And, yes, I do mind you calling me Katharine. The question was, you want us to relay the intercepts? If so, it's out of the question. The ambassador wouldn't allow that."

"What I had in mind, Kate," Lunsford said, "was our guys uploading to a satellite, and then we'd forward them to you, for your information."

"You've got satellite authority?" Foster asked, surprised.

"And our own, as opposed to embassy, links," Lunsford said.

"I'd have to get clearance from my superiors," Foster said.

"This can't have anything to do with Langley," Father said. "I don't have authority to operate, black or otherwise, in Tanzania. If you ask Langley —"

"Well, I can't do it otherwise," Foster said.

"And I don't want anybody else to know, either, like that CIA jackass in Léopoldville."

"Then it's out of the question, I'm afraid," Foster said.

"Aw, hell," Lunsford said. "I was really hoping that you just might be in that small group of station chiefs — like Jack Stephens in Buenos Aires and Bill Colby in Saigon — who are more interested in getting the job done than in getting their tickets punched. I really should have known better."

"Didn't your Mommy ever tell you," she asked, "that you get more by being nice than by being an arrogant sonofabitch?"

"I don't have time to be nice," Lunsford said.

"Well, you can't put an intercept team in here," Foster said.

"I'm going to put an intercept team in here with or without your assistance," Lunsford said. "Get that straight."

"How are you going to stop him?" she asked. "And what are you going to do when he does, Jim? Turn them in? Tell Langley?"

"You sound as if you think this is a good idea," Foster replied.

She turned to Lunsford.

"If they are discovered, it will have to be understood, we never heard of them, or you."

"Naturally," Lunsford said. "And it will have to be understood that if I hear Langley's been told — and I would — or the Tanzanians, I will personally turn him into a soprano with a dull machete, and think of something equally interesting to do to you."

"My God, Cecilia!" Foster protested.

"Oh, what a pretty name!" Lunsford said. "Wouldn't you agree that's a pretty name for such a pretty girl, Lieutenant Portet?"

"Yes, sir," Jack said. "I certainly would, sir."

"So do we have a deal, Cecilia?" Father asked.

"That, of course, would be up to Mr. Foster," she said.

"Oh, Cecilia," Lunsford said. "Just when I was starting to really like you, you start playing silly games again."

"Meaning what?" she asked.

"Meaning you're really the station chief, and, frankly, my dear, you're not too good about keeping that the dark secret it's supposed to be."

"You really are a sonofabitch, aren't you?" she snapped, but there was a tone of admiration in her voice.

She walked to Foster's desk, picked up a

notepad, wrote something on it, and handed it to Lunsford.

"That's down by the waterfront," she said. "They'll be expecting your team anytime after three. With a little luck, we can move them. How much equipment do they have?"

"It will all fit inside a panel truck," Lunsford said.

"We can probably move them to Morogoro tonight," she said. "By then you should be almost back in the Congo."

"I guess dinner's out of the question, then, Cecilia?"

"For tonight, George, it is," she said. "But maybe sometime, when you're wearing shoes, we could talk about that again."

XX

ONE

Near Kigali, Rwanda
1845 6 April 1965

"Kigali, Air Simba Seven-two-seven understands I am number one to land on One-eight," Jack said into the microphone, then turned to Major Darrell Smythe, who was in the copilot's seat of the Boeing. "Put the gear down, please, Major, sir, and then go get in the back and try to look like an African."

Jack hadn't wanted to press one of the Air Simba pilots into making the flight to Dar es Salaam without knowing the purpose, and he couldn't tell them the purpose for a number of reasons, which left him with the choice of flying the C-46 alone — he had done so before, but it wasn't a smart thing to do — or taking one of the Army aviators along in the left seat. Smythe had the most twin-engine experience of all the Army aviators, and he had been drafted by Lunsford.

"Gear down and locked," Smythe reported a moment later, and then unstrapped himself and got out of the copilot's seat.

"Kigali," Jack reported, "Seven-two-seven turning on final."

Smythe stood in the narrow aisle between the pilot's and copilot's seats, and waited until Jack was lined up with Runway 18.

"In the interests of precision, Lieutenant, may I

783

remind you that I already look like an African, but now I will try to look like a *native* African."

"I stand corrected, Major, sir," Jack said as he reached for the throttle quadrant. "And may I say, sir, that you make a very credible native African in that costume. All the Tutu maidens are excited by the very sight of you."

"Fuck you, Lieutenant," Smythe said, and turned and walked into the fuselage.

Just as Smythe sat down beside Major George Washington Lunsford, there was a chirp of the tires and a just perceptible bump as Jack touched down.

Majors Smythe and Lunsford were dressed identically in loose white cotton jackets and trousers, except that Smythe wore crude sandals and dirty white socks, and Lunsford was barefooted. The sandals were necessary because Smythe's feet were soft and not callused, and he could not walk barefoot as Father could. The socks were necessary because an African with feet that were not heavily callused would attract attention.

The native costumes were necessary because the airport that served Costermansville was across the Rwandan border in Kigali. The Rwandan border was closed to Congolese military personnel, and to everyone else whose passport didn't have the proper visa.

Majors Lunsford and Smythe and the ASA intercept team and their Green Beret protectors — all wearing somewhat soiled white cotton shirts and trousers — had crossed the border into Rwanda in the bed of an Air Simba Ford pickup truck, sitting atop the crates of equipment the intercept crew was taking with them.

There also had been two cases of Simba beer in

the truck. One of them had been enough to get past happily smiling Rwandan border guards on the way in, and the other, Jack was reasonably confident, would get them past happily smiling border guards on their return.

The border guards were accustomed to Air Simba aircrews crossing the border to get to and from the Kigali airport, and many of them knew Jack by sight and reputation — he could always be counted on for a case of beer.

They hadn't even looked into the crates, which was fortunate, because the teams' weaponry, a supply of Composition C-4, and half a dozen thermite grenades had been packed on top of the communications equipment. The state-of-the-art, highly classified communications equipment could not be allowed to fall into the wrong hands, even if that meant torching it at the Rwanda border guard station, and to do that, the thermite grenades had to be right on top, rather than hidden someplace.

It had all gone off without a hitch on the way to Dar es Salaam, and there was less chance — the crates and the intercept crew were now in Tanzania — that anything would go wrong on the way back.

And nothing did.

And just across the bridge that spanned the river, and was actually the border, Jack stopped the Ford, and Aunt Jemima and Father got out of the truck bed and got in the seat with Jack.

Father was happily puffing on a fat, black cigar — his first since they'd left Costermansville — when Jack pulled the Ford up to the basement loading dock of the Hotel du Lac, on which First Lieutenant Geoffrey Craig, Spec7 William Peters, and Mrs. Jacques Portet were standing, obviously waiting for them.

"Something's wrong," Father announced. "Look at them."

They did not look happy.

Geoff Craig came down the landing dock steps as Father, Jack, and Aunt Jemima got out of the truck. Craig wordlessly handed a sheet of paper to Father, who read it, said, "Shit!" and handed it to Jack, who read it and handed it to Aunt Jemima.

SECRET
HELP0022 1730 ZULU 6 APRIL 1965
VIA WHITE HOUSE SIGNAL AGENCY

FROM: HELPER FIVE

TO: EARNEST SIX

REFERENCE MAP BAKER 08

1-AT 1425 ZULU 6 APRIL 1965, OUTPOST FOX RELAYED A RADIO REPORT FROM OUTPOST GEORGE STATING THAT UNUSUAL ACTIVITY IN THE BUSH HAD BEEN DETECTED AND CONGOLESE SOLDIERS ANTICIPATED AN ATTACK. WEATHER CONDITIONS AT THAT TIME PRECLUDED BOTH REINFORCEMENT OF OUTPOST GEORGE OR AN AERIAL RECONNAISSANCE THEREOF.

2-AT 1530 OUTPOST FOX RELAYED A RADIO REPORT FROM OUTPOST GEORGE STATING

THAT CONGOLESE SOLDIERS HAD DISAPPEARED LEAVING THEIR UNIFORMS BUT TAKING THEIR WEAPONS.

3-THERE HAS BEEN NO FURTHER COMMUNICATION WITH OUTPOST GEORGE.

4-AT 1615 THE WEATHER HAVING CLEARED SUFFICIENTLY TO MAKE AERIAL RECONNAISSANCE, AN L-19 FLYING OVER GEORGE REPORTED SIGHTING ONE APPARENTLY DISMEMBERED BODY; NO OTHER SIGN OF LIFE; AND EVIDENCE THAT GEORGE, INCLUDING GASOLINE SUPPLIES, HAS BEEN BURNED. UNDERSIGNED FORBADE THE L-19 TO LAND.

5-IN VIEW OF THE FOREGOING IT MUST BE PRESUMED THAT TECHNICAL SERGEANT CLARENCE D. WITHERS, RA23380767, SFDET17 IS MISSING IN ACTION AND MUST BE PRESUMED DEAD.

6-A CONGOLESE COMPANY STRENGTH TRUCK BORNE RECONNAISSANCE FORCE WILL DEPART OUTPOST EASY FOR OUTPOST GEORGE AT FIRST LIGHT AND AERIAL RECONNAISSANCE WILL RESUME AT FIRST LIGHT. FURTHER INFORMATION WILL BE FURNISHED AS AVAILABLE.

HELPER FIVE FOR HELPER SIX

SECRET

"What was Colonel Supo's reaction?" Father asked.

"He wants to see you four hours ago," Geoff Craig said.

"Let's go," Lunsford said, and walked quickly up the stairs of the loading dock.

[TWO]
Office of the Commanding General
The John F. Kennedy Center for Special
Warfare
Fort Bragg, North Carolina
1555 6 April 1965

"Administratively, Sandy," said General Paul R. Hanrahan, "how is this going to be handled?"

"Normal routine, I would suppose," Felter replied. "The Adjutant General sends the telegram —"

"The AG doesn't know yet, does he?"

"That just came in, Red," Felter said.

"Hold off on telling him, would you, please? At least until we know for sure."

"Don't get your hopes up, Red," Felter said. "I'll wait until I hear from you. You are talking about no later than tomorrow?"

"No later than tomorrow," Hanrahan said.

"Break it down," Felter said.

"White House Secure disconnecting," a male voice said.

"Ski!" Hanrahan called, raising his voice.

Captain Stefan Zabrewski, who had been standing just outside General Hanrahan's office from the moment the White House Signal Agency announced they had a secure call from Colonel Felter for General Hanrahan, stepped into the door.

"General?"

"One of the outposts was run over. It looks like SFC Withers has bought the farm."

"Shit!" Captain Zabrewski said, and then " 'Looks like', General?"

"He messaged that the Congolese with him had taken off. Then he went off the Net. An L-19 flew over, and saw a dismembered body."

"Goddamn!"

"Get me his address, the other personals," Hanrahan ordered. "Have the sergeant major put Padre Martin on ten minutes' notice in Class A's."

"Yes, sir."

"I will probably require an L-23 to send Wilson. I want us to do it, not some candy-ass AG notification team. And if it's anywhere this side of Nome, Alaska, I'll go myself."

"Yes, sir."

Captain Zabrewski returned in less than four minutes.

"Sir, RFD Laurinburg, North Carolina," he reported. "Next of kin, his parents."

"Thank God, he wasn't married with half a dozen kids," Hanrahan said, and then: "Sorry, I shouldn't have said that."

"I understand, sir," Zabrewski said, very softly.

"Where's Laurinburg?"

"About fifty miles, sir."

"Activate the chaplain," Hanrahan ordered. "Change that ten minutes' notice to I want him here in Class A's, when I get back from changing into mine. Same thing for Tony."

"Yes, sir."

"And make sure Tony has a road map. He's a good kid, but I've been lost with him before."

"Yes, sir. Sir, may I come along?"

"You don't have to, Ski. You understand that?"

"I knew Withers, sir."

"Okay," Hanrahan said.

[THREE]
Office of the Military Commandant of Kivu, Oriental, Equator, and Kasai Provinces
The Hotel du Lac
Costermansville, Kivu Province
Republic of the Congo
1910 6 April 1965

"Forgive our appearance, sir," Major George Washington Lunsford said as he entered the office of Colonel Jean-Baptiste Supo with Major Darrell J. Smythe and Lieutenants Geoffrey Craig and Jacques Portet. "We just got the word."

What could have been a smile flickered on the face of Colonel Supo as he returned Lunsford's salute.

"Totse, Tomas, and I have been at the map," Supo said, speaking French. "Deciding how best to deal with the situation."

Majors Alain George Totse and Doubting Thomas/Tomas were on their knees on the floor, on which a large map of Oriental and Kivu Provinces was laid out.

"The heavy question, boss," Doubting Thomas said, "is whether we can get the L-20 into George. It's one of the shorter strips."

"Why do we want to put an L-20 into George?" Lunsford asked as he dropped to his knees to look at the map.

"Because we can be there thirty minutes after first light," Tomas said. "And the reaction force — if there's no ambush — can't get there before nine-thirty, maybe later."

"Why the L-20?" Lunsford pursued.

"The sooner we get trackers on the site," Colonel Supo said, "the better. As Tomas has set it up, there would be six people in the L-20. The two trackers, myself, yourself, Tomas, and the pilot."

"You're going to the site, sir?"

"Yes," Supo said simply. "The question then is can we all go in the L-20, with two L-19s available for reconnaissance, or will it be necessary to make three trips in L-19s, which will then not be immediately available for reconnaissance?"

"I can put the Beaver in there," Jack Portet said. "Getting it out again with six people on it will be a little hairy."

"The trackers and Major Tomas will stay at George," Colonel Supo said. "Major Tomas leads me to believe he has some tracking experience himself."

"Yes, sir, he does," Lunsford agreed. "Sir, with respect, you don't think the Simbas will be at George, knowing we'll land there to see what happened?"

"They are neither sophisticated nor courageous," Supo said flatly. "As, apparently, neither were the soldiers I left with Captain Withers."

Lunsford didn't reply directly.

"What time's first light?"

"I figure we can get off the ground from the airstrip at five minutes to six," Doubting Tomas said. "I'd give my left nut for a D-model Huey for this."

"It will take us fifteen minutes to get to the airstrip," Lunsford said. "That means we'll have to leave the hotel no later than 0530. Order breakfast at 0500. Sound reveille accordingly."

Without really thinking about it, Jack and Doubting Thomas understood this to be an order; both said, "Yes, sir."

"I could bring the H13 out there," Geoff Craig said. "Once we're sure the landing zone isn't hot."

"Don't send it anywhere else," Lunsford ordered. "But don't start out there until you get the word." He paused and looked at Colonel Supo. "I am presuming, sir, that all of this meets with your approval?"

Supo nodded, indicating he approved.

"There is one other thing," he said. "The reaction force."

"Yes, sir?"

"I think it unlikely that there are Simbas in sufficient numbers in the area to give them the courage to attack the convoy," he said. "But the possibility exists. Would it be possible to provide some degree of aerial surveillance of the Force while it is en route to Site George?"

Lunsford nodded.

"Work it out, Aunt Jemima," he ordered, switching to English. "Either you take one of the L-19s, or Craig does."

"Sir," Major Smythe said, flustered. "I haven't understood a word of this conversation. You've all been speaking French."

"In that case, Geoff, you take it," Lunsford ordered in English. "You keep the H-13 hot to trot, Jemima, in case we need it."

"Yes, sir," Smythe said. "May I respectfully

remind you, Sir, that it is the aviation officer who normally makes flight assignments?"

"In other words, you want to fly the L-19?"

"Yes, sir, that would be my recommendation."

"Okay. Geoff, *you* keep the H-13 hot to trot."

[FOUR]
The Hotel du Lac
Costermansville, Kivu Province
Republic of the Congo
2125 6 April 1965

The mess of the military commandant of Kivu, Oriental, Equator, and Kasai Provinces was organized according to the customs of the Force Publique, which in turn was closely patterned after that of the Royal Belgian Army. Seating, in other words, was by rank. Seating was under the control of Colonel Supo's sergeant major, who shuffled people around until protocol was satisfied, and only then sent Colonel Supo's orderly to find the colonel and tell him his officers were assembled for dinner.

Colonel Supo sat in the middle of a long table, from the ends of which two other tables formed a U. Unless there was a distinguished guest, the seat to Colonel Supo's right was reserved for the next senior officer present. To Supo's left was the next junior officer. Seating by rank moved from right to left across the head table, and then down the tables forming the legs of the U.

Mrs. Marjorie Bellmon Portet was considered a distinguished guest, and sat at Colonel Supo's right. Her husband, in his role as acting general manager of Air Simba, was similarly considered a distinguished guest, but tonight, since he had elected to dress for dinner in the uniform of a first lieutenant of the U.S. Army, he found himself far down the right leg of the table. Lieutenant Colonel Dahdi found himself seated where Colonel Supo's Chef de Cabinet normally sat, to Colonel Supo's left. The Chef de Cabinet had personally assumed command of the relief column headed for Outpost George.

Next to him sat Major Tomas. He usually sat in that chair, in defiance of protocol, because Colonel Supo's sergeant major knew that Colonel Supo thought very highly of Major Tomas, and had informed his sergeant major that Major Tomas, like he himself, had once been a sergeant major, and there is of course an exception to every rule.

Tonight, Lieutenant Colonel Jemima sat next to Mrs. Portet, and next to Colonel Jemima sat Major Alain George Totse, Colonel Supo's intelligence officer.

Everyone in the dining room, except Mrs. Portet rose, without orders, when Colonel Supo entered his mess. Colonel Supo, who like everybody else was wearing paratrooper's camouflage fatigues, bowed to Mrs. Portet, kissed her hand, and sat down. Everyone else then sat down.

Waiters filled one of the two wineglasses before each plate with a Chardonnay from South Africa.

Major Totse (as the second senior, bona fide, Congolese officer present) rose, glass in hand, and everyone, this time including Mrs. Portet, also got to their feet.

"The President of the Republic of the Congo," he said.

Everyone took a sip of the Chardonnay.

"The President of the United States," Lieutenant Colonel Dahdi said, raising his glass.

Everyone took another sip of wine.

"Colonel Jean-Baptiste Supo," Major Totse offered.

Everyone but Colonel Jean-Baptiste Supo took a sip of wine.

"Our comrade, Sergeant Chef Clarence Withers. May he be in God's hands," Major Totse intoned.

Everyone took a sip of wine.

"To our comrades serving with Sergeant Withers," Lieutenant Colonel Dahdi offered. "May they be in the hands of God."

Everyone but the Americans sat down, without sipping their wine.

After an awkward moment, the Americans also sat down.

Half a dozen waiters began serving the first course, and pouring a very nice South African Merlot into the glasses of anyone who expressed an interest.

"Inasmuch as we are pressed for time," Major Totse said, "Colonel Supo hopes you will forgive him for intruding on our dinner with his appreciation of the situation."

The sergeant major ushered in two Congolese paratroopers pushing a map board. The map was of the eastern Congo, from a little north of Costermansville to a little south of Albertville on Lake Tanganyika.

"This is the location of Outpost George," Totse began, pointing to the map with a pointer. "It was constructed several years before independence on a cattle ranch owned by a Monsieur Delamm, to accommodate his Cessna Model 172 aircraft. The buildings of the now-deserted farm are approximately two point four kilometers west of the landing strip.

"Route Nationale Number Five, which is shown in red, runs in this area from Costermansville to below Albertville. It passes approximately point-five kilometers from Outpost George here, and is visible from Outpost George.

"To the west of Route Nationale Five, the terrain is gently rolling grassy hills, without much other vegetation. To the east of Route 5, however, there is heavy bush to the shore of Lake Tanganyika. That is a distance of approximately fifty miles. The road was built inland because — like the airfield at Outpost George — it could be easily bulldozed on the gently rolling hills. To go any farther east, it would have been necessary to remove the bush, which made no sense.

"Colonel Supo believes there are a number of Simbas in this area. The bush makes it a good place for them to hide from our patrols, and they can easily leave the bush, cross Route Five, and help themselves to the cattle from the ranches west of Route Five. Furthermore, since this area borders on Lake Tanganyika, it offers them a chance to retreat across Lake Tanganyika into Tanzania should the Army somehow locate them. Similarly, if the Soviets or Red Chinese make good on their promise to supply the Simbas, doing so across Lake Tanganyika would be the most convenient way.

"Colonel Supo believes that Outpost George was very likely attacked by a band of Simbas on a cattle-thieving mission. They had accidentally happened across it, and more because they thought a Congolese Army detachment would have equipment and supplies — and if nothing else, weapons — they could use, had overwhelmed it for that reason, rather than as an attack on an outpost per se."

Colonel Supo said something to Major Totse in Swahili, and Totse made the translation.

"Colonel Supo regrets that the price was the loss of the valiant Sergeant First Withers, but suggests it was not in vain. They will learn they cannot attack outposts without immediate retaliation."

Totse let that sink in a moment.

"The reaction force under Lieutenant Colonel Obesti will reach Outpost George at approximately 0900 tomorrow. They will have with them supplies of aviation fuels to replace those we must conclude were destroyed by the Simbas, and radios to replace those we presume were also lost. A larger detachment than was previously stationed at George, under the command of a captain, will replace the detachment that was at George.

"If it proves possible to land in the L-20 very early tomorrow — Colonel Supo believes it unlikely but possible that the Simbas may have rendered the runway unusable — it will have aboard two trackers, who will immediately begin to locate both the Simbas and the Congolese soldiers of the original Outpost George detachment. The trackers will carry with them radios to communicate both with Station George and the reaction force.

"If the runway has been rendered unusable — which Colonel Supo believes unlikely, as the Simbas probably did have the equipment to cause it serious damage — then it will be necessary to await the arrival at Station George of the reaction force, which will make the runway usable. If the L-20 can land, this will give the trackers a two-hour advantage.

"Lieutenant Colonel Dahdi and Major Tomas proposed to Colonel Supo that Major Dahdi and the two trackers be parachuted onto Outpost George as the first order of business tomorrow, but Colonel Supo decided against that proposal."

Colonel Supo said something in Swahili, and Major Totse translated:

"Colonel Supo is highly appreciative of the offer, but felt that there was a possibility that the Simbas might be on the site, or have it under observation, and he could no more afford to lose the two trackers than Colonel Dahdi could afford to lose Major Tomas."

When he had finished, Totse looked at Supo.

"Does that about cover it, sir?"

Supo replied in Swahili, and Totse translated:

"Colonel Supo would be pleased to hear from Colonel Dahdi and his officers any recommendations or suggestions."

"Anybody got anything to say?" Father Lunsford asked.

One by one, starting with the junior American officer present — Lieutenant Jacques Portet — the Americans shook their heads, no.

Supo spoke again.

"Colonel Supo again apologizes for interfering with our dinner, and suggests we now finish it," Totse translated.

The entrée was broiled fish, large firm white filets, served with asparagus and steamed potatoes.

[FIVE]
County Highway 17
Laurinburg, North Carolina
1725 6 April 1965

"What is this stuff?" General Hanrahan asked, gesturing out the window of the olive-drab Chevrolet sedan at tiny green buds sprouting through the earth in the fields on both sides of the dirt road.

"Tobacco?" Captain Zabrewski guessed from the front seat.

"Maybe soybeans," Chaplain (Lt. Col.) T. Wilson Martin suggested. "They grow a lot of soybeans in North Carolina."

"Not a bad-looking farm," Zabrewski said, and then the tone of his voice changed. "Check out the guy on the tractor at three o'clock."

All eyes moved to the left off the highway. At the far end of the field was a man riding a very large tractor.

They reached the house several minutes later. It was a rambling structure, mostly of concrete block construction but with additions of frame. It was neatly painted, and there was a neatly trimmed lawn running the length of the covered porch.

There were three barns, one of which looked as if it was about to fall down, the other two in much better shape.

Tony, General Hanrahan's driver, stopped the car on a concrete pad, large enough for half a dozen cars, in front of the house. Hanrahan was out of the car before Tony could open it for him.

Hanrahan walked briskly up the three steps to the porch and rang the bell. Chaplain Martin and Captain Zabrewski came after him as soon as they could. Sergeant Tony Calzazzo, the driver, looked indecisive for a moment, then leaned on the fender of the staff car.

There was no answer to the doorbell.

Without realizing that he was doing it, Hanrahan made a hand signal ordering flankers forward left and right. Captain Zabrewski immediately dropped off the porch and started to move around the house to the left. After a moment's hesitation, Chaplain Martin started to do the same.

"Heads up," Sergeant Calzazzo called softly.

Hanrahan turned and saw the tractor that had been in the far side of the field. It was now approaching the house.

Hanrahan walked off the porch onto the concrete pad and waited for the tractor driver to appear. Without really thinking about it, Chaplain Martin took up a position beside him, and Zabrewski and Calzazzo took up positions behind them. Calazzo came to the position of Parade Rest.

The tractor driver was a tall, lithe man in washed-nearly-white blue jeans and a light blue shirt. He had a straw cowboy hat on his head.

He stopped the tractor, looked at the four men, shut off the tractor, and crawled down from it.

"Mr. Withers?" Hanrahan asked.

The man nodded.

"My name is Hanrahan, Mr. Withers —"

"I know who you are, General," the man said. "There's a picture of you and Clarence on the mantel — when you handed him his flash when he came out of Camp Mackall."

The flash is the embroidered insignia of the fully qualified Special Forces soldier, worn on the Green Beret.

"Yes, sir," Hanrahan said. "Mr. Withers —"

"Why don't we go in the house?" Withers said. "I suspect I'm going to need a drink."

"Mr. Withers," Chaplain Martin said, "I'm Chaplain Martin. . . ."

"I was in the Army," Withers said. "I know a chaplain when I see one."

He walked up the stairs to his porch, then opened the unlocked door and held it, motioning them all to enter. When they had, he followed them inside.

"It's bad, isn't it?" he asked. "Let's have it."

"About as bad as it gets, Mr. Withers," Hanrahan said.

"I didn't think they'd send a general out here to tell me Clarence broke his leg, or got shot," Withers said.

He walked away from them, into the house, and returned almost immediately with a bottle of Wild Turkey bourbon and a stack of short squat glasses.

"You hold the glasses, Sergeant," he said to Tony Calzazzo, "and I'll pour."

"Yes, sir," Tony said.

Very soon everyone had a glass of whiskey.

"If you're a teetotaler, Chaplain," Withers said. "You don't have to drink that."

"I'm not a teetotaler," Chaplain Martin said simply.

"Clarence bought this out at Fort Bragg," Withers said, tapping the Wild Turkey. "My daddy taught me to drink good whiskey, and I taught Clarence, and he always brought me a couple of bottles when he came home. This is the last one. I was going to save it until he came home. Now I don't have to, right?"

"It looks that way, Mr. Withers," Hanrahan said.

He drained his whiskey glass.

"Goddamn, I'm going to miss him," Withers said. "He was a good boy, and his mama and I were so proud of him."

"You had every right to be," Hanrahan said. He raised his glass. "Gentlemen, I give you Sergeant First Class Clarence Withers."

He drained his glass, and the others followed suit.

"Did you know him, General? I mean, really know him, aside from giving him his flash?"

"Yes, I did," Hanrahan said.

"We were in Vietnam together, Mr. Withers," Captain Zabrewski said.

"No, sir, I did not," Chaplain Martin said.

"I saw him around," Sergeant Tony Calzazzo said. "But we wasn't buddies, or anything like that."

"So what happened to my boy, General? And when? And where? Hell, all he would say was that he was going someplace in Africa."

"Just before we came out, Mr. Withers, I had a telephone call telling me there had been word from Africa —"

"Where in Africa?" Withers interrupted.

"Mr. Withers, your son was on a classified assignment," Hanrahan said.

Goddamn it, I'm not going to tell this man — he doesn't have the need-to-know.

"He told me that," Withers said.

"What he was doing was advising the Congolese," Hanrahan said. "He was with a small detachment of Congolese soldiers, and they were apparently run over —"

"Apparently? Run over by who?"

"We lost radio contact with the detachment at 1530 Congo time — that would be ten-thirty this morning, here. There's a five-hour difference. They anticipated an attack, and there apparently was one."

"And no chance that he's a prisoner?"

"The Simbas rarely take prisoners, Mr. Withers," Hanrahan said. "I wouldn't want to give you false hope."

"The Simbas? That the bunch that was eating the white people in Stanleyville?"

"Yes," Hanrahan said.

"You think they ate Clarence?"

"I think that's very unlikely, Mr. Withers. We won't know until we can get people on the ground where this happened. That won't be until seven o'clock or so, tomorrow morning there. Two A.M. here."

"How'd you get your information so quick?"

"We sent them there with the best communication equipment we have," Hanrahan said.

"Satellite? You're bouncing your communication off a satellite?"

"Yes, sir. As a matter of fact, we are."

"I think we should have some more details by three or four o'clock tomorrow morning," Zabrewski said.

"Ain't that a bitch?" Mr. Withers said. "Until I read in the papers what happened over there in the Congo, saw it on the TV, I thought savages eating people was something out of a comic book. Now I'm going to learn, bounced off a satellite, whether or not savages ate my son."

"I don't think we'll learn that, Mr. Withers," Hanrahan said.

"General, I don't want to seem rude, but I'd rather you not be here when Clarence's mama gets home. Not knowing is worse than knowing, where she's concerned. I'll try to break this to her gently. If you could call, don't matter the hour, when you know something, I'd be grateful."

"Of course, sir," Hanrahan said. "The moment I get word, I'll call you."

"We going to get his body back?"

"I think we will."

"I don't want his mama to even suspect they ate him, or part of him," Mr. Withers said. "Sonofabitch. Excuse me, Chaplain."

Chaplain Martin waved his hand, indicating no apology was necessary.

[SIX]
The Hotel du Lac
Costermansville, Kivu Province
Republic of the Congo
0445 7 April 1965

Lieutenant Jacques Portet, using a rubber prophylactic, bloused the legs of his Suit, Flying, Tropical Climates, around the top of his parachutist's jump boots and then stood up and moved around to make sure that he had done so properly.

He looked up and saw his wife, who was in the bathroom in her underwear, looking thoughtfully at his reflected image in the medicine cabinet mirror.

"What are you thinking, baby?" he asked.

"You really want to know?"

He nodded.

"I came over here so I wouldn't have to sit in the apartment in Fayetteville, not knowing what you

804

were doing," she said. "Now I'm here, and I don't like knowing."

"I'll probably be back for supper, baby," he said.

"Sure, you will."

"Are you going to put some clothes on?" he asked. "Or are you going to breakfast like that?"

"Are you actually hungry?"

"If that's a suggestion, baby, I don't think we have time."

"No. I really want to know. Are you actually hungry?"

"Yeah, I am."

"I have no appetite at all for reasons I can't imagine," she said.

"You don't have to go down there for breakfast, baby."

"Yeah, I do," she said.

[SEVEN]
3 Degrees 60 Minutes 52 Seconds South Latitude
28 Degrees 9 Minutes 15 Seconds East Longitude
(Above Outpost George)
0705 7 April 1965

The DeHavilland L-20 Beaver came in over the crest of the enormous grass-covered gently sloping hill and flew over the Outpost George dirt strip at five hundred feet.

"There's a body down there," Major Tomas said, quite unnecessarily; everybody had expected to see a body — in the rear baggage compartment of the Beaver was a Container, Zippered, Impermeable, Human Remains, known as a "body bag"

— and everybody had seen one.

The Beaver was painted flat black, and bore no markings of any kind. Before Jean-Phillippe Portet had gone into business with the Gresham Investment Corporation and the Intercontinental Air Ltd. Boeing 707 had become available, Felter had thought it was going to be necessary to covertly insert the Beaver — and all the other aircraft — into the Congo from South Africa, and had ordered the paint job so that it could be "credibly denied" that the United States was supplying matériel of war to the Congo.

Although it had been decided by Colonel Supo — just about as soon as the Beaver had been reassembled in Stanleyville — to paint it in the camouflage pattern of the Congolese Air Force, and affix credible-looking but spurious Congolese registration numbers to it, it was still painted flat black. Aircraft paint, and paint-spraying equipment, was not available without raising questions. Both were scheduled to be on the next 707 supply flight, which was due possibly today, and more likely tomorrow.

No one saw — and everyone was looking hard — any bright little flashes that would mean someone was shooting at them. That meant one of two things: that no one was down there, or that there was someone down there smart enough to realize that it's much easier to shoot up an airplane on the ground than one flying five hundred feet in the air.

Jack flew across Route Nationale Number 5, and everyone tried to see something in the bush on the other side of the road.

"It's not Vietnam," Lieutenant Colonel Dahdi opined, "but it's close."

"Yeah," Major Tomas agreed. "But it's easier to track people if they have to hack their way through something like that. And even if there are paths down there, there's no way to hide footprints on them — they're bound to be wet."

Jack then dropped to two hundred feet and flew up and down Route 5 for about a mile in each direction.

One of the two trackers, both senior sergeants, got the attention of the other and pointed, with a grunt, to something he saw on the ground.

"With your permission, Colonel," Jack said, "I will make one more pass, lower, over the strip, and then land."

Supo, who was in the copilot's seat, nodded.

Everybody looked hard again, and no one saw anything on the dirt strip that suggested it wouldn't be usable. And everybody saw the body again. The head was separated from the torso, and so was one leg, from the knee down.

Jack put the Beaver into a steep turn, lined up with the runway, lowered the flaps, and retarded the throttle.

There was the sound of rounds being chambered in weapons, which was unnerving.

Jack touched down smoothly, but the runway was not smooth — crushed rock — and there was a loud roar from the undercarriage.

He kept his hand on the throttle until the point where he would no longer have runway or speed enough to take off again in a hurry, then rolled to the end of the strip and turned around.

He put his hand back on the throttle and picked up a little speed until he'd reached the "no-go" point, then retarded the throttle and taxied slowly to the far end of the strip. There he turned around again and taxied to the burned buildings about halfway down the field.

Everyone saw Sergeant First Class Clarence Withers's head resting about two feet from his torso. A horde of flies feasted on the pooled, now coagulated, blood in which it lay.

No one said anything.

Jack stopped the airplane.

Father Lunsford opened the door and jumped out, followed by Doubting Thomas. Both were armed with the short version of the M-16 rifle. They ran for twenty feet or so in opposite directions, dropped to their bellies, and waited to return any hostile fire.

The two trackers got out of the Beaver next. They were armed with FN 7-mm automatic rifles, which they carried cradled in their arms like bird hunters.

Last to get out, via the front doors of the Beaver, were Jack Portet and Colonel Supo. Jack was armed with an FN automatic rifle and a .45 ACP in a shoulder holster. He stopped the moment his feet touched the ground and loaded a round in the chamber. Colonel Supo had a Browning 9-mm automatic pistol in a web holster. He didn't take it from the holster.

After forty seconds — which seemed much longer — Father Lunsford stood up, and then Doubting Thomas. They walked to Withers's body.

Jack was surprised to see Thomas take an aerosol can of insect spray from the pocket on the calf of his paratrooper's camouflage trousers. He first sprayed the head of Withers's corpse, then the body. Jack felt nauseous.

I suppose that's not the first already-starting-

to-decompose body he's had to deal with.

Father walked to the rear door of the Beaver, climbed inside, and came out with the body bag.

Doubting Thomas was walking around the body, kicking at the grass with his boot. Then he started walking toward the burned buildings. He'd gone ten feet or so when he bent down and came up with a dog-tag chain. Then he looked farther, and finally found the two dog tags Withers had worn around his neck.

Father unfolded the body bag next to Withers's body and then pulled the zipper down. Thomas trotted up, reached for Withers's severed leg, and put it — not without effort; Withers had been a large, strong man — into the bag. Then, while he picked up the remaining leg of the torso, Father put his hands under Withers's armpits and they gently picked the rest of him up and lowered it into the body bag. Then Thomas went to Withers's head. He first closed the eyes, then gently pried the mouth open. He slid one of the dog tags into the mouth, picked up the head, and put it into the bag.

Then he closed the zipper.

"I deeply regret your sergeant's death," Colonel Supo said.

Lunsford met his eyes but said nothing.

Doubting Thomas went to the Beaver and took out backpack radios and other field gear.

The two trackers, Jack saw in surprise, were taking off their camouflage jackets and then their boots. They rolled the trouser legs halfway up their calves, and then they slipped into their web gear, and finally they put their arms through the straps of the backpack radios.

"The decision is of course yours, Major

Tomas," Colonel Supo. "You may go with Sergeant First Jette and track the Simbas, or with Sergeant First Nambibi and try to find the men who were here."

"I'll go with Jette," Thomas said without hesitation.

"Let's check this place out first," Lunsford said, and started to walk toward the burned-out buildings. Jack started after him, and then Colonel Supo, and finally Thomas.

The two trackers started to walk, barefoot, back and forth in an ever-expanding circle from Withers's body bag toward Route Nationale Number 5.

When they reached the burned-out, concrete-block buildings, there was the smell of burned wood, and burned gasoline, and of something sweeter.

Lunsford first peered through the door, then stepped into the building as far as he could. The charred roof timbers kept him from going far.

"Well, he got some of them," Lunsford said, and stepped out of the building.

Jack looked inside.

He saw the badly burned skull of one man, and then of another, and another, and finally of a fourth.

God, don't let me get sick!

He heard Lunsford ask, "Could these be your men, Colonel?"

"I think my men would have been out there, their heads cut off, with Sergeant Withers," Supo answered. "As a mark of contempt. These are probably the bodies of Simbas — it was easier to burn them than bury them."

"Your call, Colonel," Lunsford said. "What would you like to do now?"

Supo glanced at his watch.

"It's eight forty-eight," he said. "It will be nine, or later, when the reaction force gets here. I suggest there is nothing for us to do here, and therefore it would make sense to fly down Route Five until we meet the reaction force, tell them what we found here, and then return to Costermansville."

"Sir, we'll be returning Sergeant Withers's body to the States on the 707. Would it interfere with your schedule if we took Withers to Stanleyville before we went back to Costermansville?"

"Forgive me," Supo said. "I should have thought about that. Stanleyville, of course."

Rigor mortis had set in the body of SFC Withers. It was difficult to get his body bag into the Beaver, then strap it somewhat awkwardly into one of the seats, and by the time they had finished, everyone was sweat-soaked.

"Don't get your hopes up too high," Lunsford said to Thomas. "They've had a lot of time to hide. And don't do anything stupid."

"I'm going to get the bastards that did this to Clarence, boss," Doubting Thomas said matter-of-factly.

Then he saluted crisply and trotted off toward Sergeant First Jette, who was going to track the Simbas.

By the time the Beaver started, taxied to the end of the runway, and took off Thomas and Sergeant First Jette had already disappeared into the bush on the other side of Route Nationale Number 5.

[EIGHT]
2301 Kildar Street
Alexandria, Virginia
0425 7 April 1965

There was a telephone on the bedside table in the bedroom of Colonel and Mrs. Sanford T. Felter. And there was a second telephone inside the bedside table. It was in appearance identical to the telephone on top of the table, but it was not connected to the Alexandria exchange, but actually to the White House switchboard.

When it rang — actually buzzed, like an angry wasp — Felter was instantly awake and quickly took it from the cradle. There was no sense in waking Mrs. Felter.

"Felter," he said.

"Turn the light on, darling," Sharon Felter said. "You're probably going to have to write something down."

"Hold one for a secure call from Mr. Finton, Colonel," the male operator ordered. "Go ahead, Mr. Finton."

"Finton, sir," Finton said. "They just delivered a message from Helper."

"Read it," Felter ordered.

In Room 637 of the Executive Office Building, CWO(4) James L. Finton, who had been sleeping, fully dressed, on the too-small couch in the outer office, picked up the sheet of paper he had just received from the White House Signal Agency duty officer and read from it.

HELP0026 0925 ZULU 7 APRIL 1965
VIA WHITE HOUSE SIGNAL AGENCY

FROM: HELPER FIVE
TO: EARNEST SIX

FOLLOWING IS VOICE MESSAGE RECEIVED
FROM HELPER SIX PRESENTLY AIRBORNE
VIA WOOLWORTH TO THIS STATION.

1-REGRET CONFIRM DEATH OF SFC
CLARENCE WITHERS AS RESULT OF
INSURGENT ATTACK ON OUTPOST GEORGE.
REMAINS ARE BEING TRANSPORTED
WOOLWORTH. UNLESS ORDERED
SPECIFICALLY TO THE CONTRARY, INTEND
TO RETURN REMAINS TO FORT BRAGG ON
707. REMAINS ARE NOT REPEAT NOT
SUITABLE FOR VIEWING.

2-SFC WITHERS WHO WAS ALONE DURING
ATTACK DISPATCHED AT LEAST SIX
HOSTILES AND WOUNDED AT LEAST THAT
MANY BEFORE LOSING HIS LIFE. IT IS
INTENTION OF COLONEL J. B. SUPO, WHO
VISITED SITE WITH UNDERSIGNED TO
AWARD THE CONGOLESE MEDAL FOR
GALLANTRY IN THE GRADE OF CHEVALIER
POSTHUMOUSLY TO SFC WITHERS.
UNDERSIGNED, FULLY AWARE OF THE
CIRCUMSTANCES MAKING AN AMERICAN
AWARD AWKWARD NEVERTHELESS
RECOMMEND IN THE STRONGEST POSSIBLE

TERMS THE AWARD OF THE SILVER STAR
MEDAL TO SFC WITHERS.

3-SUPPORTED BY DET17 AERIAL
SURVEILLANCE AND AN ADVISOR ON THE
GROUND, AN ATTEMPT IS BEING MADE BY
CONGOLESE FORCES TO LOCATE THE
INSURGENTS RESPONSIBLE.

4-OUTPOST GEORGE WILL BE
RECONSTITUTED NO LATER THAN 1030
ZULU 7 APRIL 1965.

5-AN AFTER ACTION REPORT WILL BE
FURNISHED ON COMPLETION.

6-ADVISE SOONEST 707 ETA.

HELPER SIX

END VOICE MESSAGE

HELPER FIVE FOR HELPER SIX

SECRET

"I thought we sent him the ETA of the 707," Felter said.

"Sir, you authorized a twenty-four-hour hold to see if we could get some additional pilots."

"So I did," Felter said. "And we got them. But did they get off?"

"Yes, sir. And I sent the 707's ETA — before

1300 tomorrow — just now."

"I guess you better wake up General Hanrahan with this," Felter said. "He'll have to go to his office to take it, but that's what he said he wanted."

"Yes, sir."

"And do not, repeat do not, inform the AG yet."

"Yes, sir."

"And when you do that, you might as well go home, Finton."

"Mary Margaret's coming in at 0600, sir. I'll wait for her."

"If I'm not there when she gets there, tell her I'll be in early," Felter said.

"Yes, sir," CWO(4) Finton said. "Break it down, White House."

[NINE]
County Highway 17
Laurinburg, North Carolina
0530 7 April 1965

"Hello?"

"Mr. Withers?"

"Yeah."

"General Hanrahan, sir."

"I've been expecting your call."

"The news is very bad, Mr. Withers," Hanrahan said. "We have confirmation that Clarence has been killed."

"Yeah."

"I have some other information, Mr. Withers, that I really would not want to talk about over the telephone."

"You want to come here?"

"Yes, sir, if that would be all right."

"It'll take you what, an hour and a half to get here."

"Actually, sir, I'm calling from a motel — the Carolina — just outside Laurinburg on U.S. 401."

"Charley Taylor's place. It'll take you about ten minutes."

"We'll see you shortly, sir," General Hanrahan said.

Mr. Withers came down the steps from the verandah of his home when the olive-drab Chevrolet stopped on the concrete pad. He was wearing a windbreaker over a stiffly starched white shirt and gray slacks.

Hanrahan was out of the car before Tony could open the door for him. Chaplain (Lt. Col.) T. Wilson Martin and Captain Stefan Zabrewski clambered after him. A muscular Green Beret wearing the chevrons of a sergeant major got quickly out of the front seat.

"You must have got up pretty early to be here now," Mr. Withers said.

"We came by chopper, Mr. Withers —"

"Staff car and all?" Withers asked incredulously.

"Sergeant Calzazzo drove back over last night, Mr. Withers, with Sergeant Major Tinley . . ."

"Good morning, sir," Sergeant Major Tinley said.

"I know that face," Mr. Withers said. "You was with Clarence in Vietnam, right?"

"Yes, sir. We were in the same A Team. I'm sorry as hell about this, Mr. Withers."

"Yeah, we all are."

"Delmar," a female voice called from the verandah. "Ask the gentlemen to come inside."

"That's Clarence's mother," Delmar Withers said. "I was hoping you'd stay in bed."

"I want to know what happened," she said simply.

Withers waved his arm in a signal for them to go into the house.

"That's Tin Man, Clarissa," Withers said, pointing to Sergeant Major Tinley. "He was with Clarence in Vietnam. They was in the hospital together when they both got shot."

"Yes, I remember," Mrs. Withers said.

She led them through the house into the kitchen.

"Can I make breakfast?" she asked.

"No, ma'am," Hanrahan said. "Thank you just the same."

"Delmar told me to expect the worst news," she said. "Is that what you're here to tell us?"

"Yes, ma'am," Hanrahan said. "We have confirmation that Clarence was killed."

"The Lord giveth and the Lord taketh away," she murmured. "Praise God!"

"Amen," Chaplain (Lt. Col.) T. Wilson Martin said. "Mrs. Withers, I'm Chaplain Martin."

"How do you do?" she said, and gave him her hand. "What are you?"

"Excuse me?"

"We're Presbyterian," she said.

"I'm Presbyterian," Martin said.

"Most of the black people around here are Baptist," she said. "But the people who owned the place before the Civil War were Presbyterian, and we just stayed Presbyterian, afterward, Delmar's family and mine."

"Yes, ma'am," Chaplain Martin said.

"Ma'am," Sergeant Major Albert "Tin Man" Tinley said. "Maybe I'm out of line, but I knew him pretty well, and I know he would want his daddy to know he went out like a soldier."

"How do you mean?" Mr. Withers asked.

"He took six, maybe more, of the bastards with him, and wounded a lot more."

"That's quite enough, Sergeant Major," Chaplain Martin said sternly.

"It's all right, Chaplain," Mr. Withers said. "I can't find much wrong with calling the bastards who killed Clarence bastards."

"Not in front of the Reverend," Mrs. Withers said.

"When are you going to be able to bring him home?" Mr. Withers asked. "How long is that going to take?" When Hanrahan didn't immediately respond, Withers went on: "We are going to get him back, aren't we?"

"We have a supply plane en route to the Congo right now," Hanrahan said.

"That's where he was, in the Congo?" Mrs. Withers asked.

"Yes, ma'am," Hanrahan said. "The plane will reach the Congo tomorrow, and start back the next day, or the day after that. They'll bring Sergeant Withers with them. And they'll come directly to Pope Field at Fort Bragg."

"He bought a set of dress blues just before he went over there," Mr. Withers said. "They're here. I expect he'd like to get buried in them."

"I'm sure that can be arranged," Hanrahan said. "But . . . I don't know how to say this . . . the message we have said 'the remains are not suitable for viewing.'"

"What does that mean?" Mrs. Withers asked.

"It means he got shot up pretty bad when they killed him, right, General?" Mr. Withers said.

"Yes, sir."

"I think I'd like to remember him the way he was," Mrs. Withers said. "I don't think I'd like to see him. . . ."

"Goddamn," Mr. Withers said.

"There are two other things I have to tell you," Hanrahan said. "The first is that the Congolese government is decorating Sergeant Withers for his valor. Specifically, he's being awarded the Congolese Medal for Gallantry, in the grade of Chevalier."

"What about the U.S. Army?" Mr. Withers asked.

"He's been recommended for the Silver Star. But that often takes some time to work its way through the bureaucracy."

"And what's the other thing?" Mr. Withers asked.

"As I told you, as I think your son told you, he was on a classified assignment," Hanrahan said.

"I don't understand that," Mrs. Withers said.

"His being in the Congo, for some reason, was a secret," Mr. Withers said. "Right?"

"That's correct, sir," Hanrahan said.

"I don't understand," Mrs. Withers repeated.

"It doesn't really matter, Clarissa, when you think about it, does it?" Mr. Withers said.

"I guess not," she said.

"But you said, General?" Mr. Withers said.

"So far the Adjutant General's Department has not been officially notified of what happened," Hanrahan said. "They're in charge of handling all the details when something like this happens. But with your permission, sir, we'd like to bury Sergeant Withers. Send Special Forces soldiers to carry the casket, fire the volleys over the grave, that sort of thing."

"I'd like to carry Clarence's casket, ma'am," Sergeant Major Tinley said.

"What's the problem, then?" Mr. Withers asked.

"Well, I'm going to do everything I can to stop the normal procedure," Hanrahan said. "But sometimes . . . what's likely to happen, I'm afraid, is that the AG will send an official notification team from Third Army Headquarters."

"I get the picture," Mr. Withers said. "I was in the goddamned Army."

"Delmar, watch your language," Mrs. Withers said.

"With your permission, I'd like to leave Sergeant Major Tinley here to make sure that everything goes smoothly," General Hanrahan.

"Run the bastards off is what you mean," Mr. Withers said. "Well, he's the man to do it. Clarence said the Tin Man was the one meanest badass he'd ever met in his life."

"And I'd be happy to stay as long as you need me," Chaplain Martin said. "Actually, we've set up sort of a command post in the motel."

"Maybe, Reverend," Mrs. Withers said, "you could go see Reverend Pollman. First Presbyterian Church of Laurinburg. It's right on Maple Avenue — you can't miss it."

"I'd be happy to, ma'am," Martin said.

"I'd like to thank all of you for coming here like this, so early," Mr. Withers said. "And I expect we'll be seeing more of you in the week."

"Yes, sir. Is there anything I can do for you

before we go?"

"You're not going to go without me fixing you all breakfast," Mrs. Withers said. "And I won't take no for an answer."

"Yes, ma'am," Hanrahan said. "That would be very nice."

XXI

[ONE]
Stanleyville Air Field
Stanleyville, Oriental Province
Republic of the Congo
1250 8 April 1965

Captain James J. Dugan and First Lieutenant Paul
W. Matthews had been recruited — more than a
little hurriedly — respectively from the 1st Infantry
Division at Fort Riley, Kansas, and Headquarters,
3rd United States Army at Fort McPherson,
Georgia, for "a classified overseas flight status
assignment involving a substantial personal risk."
They had literally no idea where in the world they
were going until fifteen minutes after the Intercontinental Air Cargo Ltd. Boeing 707 had taken off
from Pope Air Force Base, North Carolina.

Then the captain had come into the cabin and
told them they were bound, via Casablanca,
Morocco, to Stanleyville, in the former Belgian
Congo. There, they would be met by a U.S. Army
officer, most probably Major G. W. Lunsford,
who would explain to them what they would be
expected to do.

It was fairly obvious to both that it would
involve flying L-19 aircraft, as two of that type aircraft, wings and landing gear removed, were on
skids in the fuselage of the 707, sharing space with
crates of radios, ammunition, and other military

822

supplies of one sort or another.

Plus three expensive suitcases and what looked like six months' supply of disposable diapers and other infant accoutrements.

Although both Captain Dugan and Lieutenant Matthews would have endured a fair amount of torture rather than admit this, they had both felt a flush of excitement during their recruitment, which had happened very much the same for both of them, although a day and more than a thousand miles apart.

There had been a message for them to call the Office of the Commanding General, which rarely happens to junior officers. When they had called, they were ordered to report to the airfield at a certain time.

There — in Dugan's case — the assistant division commander had been waiting for him, and in Matthews's case the Third Army's assistant chief of staff, G3.

A Major Hodges would be shortly arriving, they were told, to ask them to volunteer for a classified overseas mission. They were as free to reject the assignment, they were told, as they were to accept it. Major Hodges was acting on the verbal order of the chief of staff of the United States Army, who had personally telephoned the general to set this up. The matter was considered Top Secret.

Major Hodges arrived flying a Mohawk that had U.S. Army markings, but none of the to-be-expected markings indicating to which unit the aircraft was assigned. This was because Pappy Hodges had been at the Grumman Aircraft Plant at Bethpage, Long Island, picking up a new Mohawk when he got the call from Colonel Sanford T. Felter telling him that Finton had found two black aviators, one at McPherson and the other at Riley, and that Pappy was going to have to go to McPherson and Riley as soon as possible to see if the two met the requirements.

Requirement one would be their willingness to volunteer for a classified overseas assignment. Requirement two was professional qualifications. Since all Army fixed-wing aviators had learned to fly in the L-19, they obviously met that requirement, Felter said.

"Father needs black pilots right now," Felter had said. "We're not in a position to be choosy. The 707 leaves in four days, and if these two fellows can see lightning and hear thunder, I want them on it."

The four days they had spent after volunteering for a classified overseas flight duty assignment involving a substantial personal risk, and before boarding the 707 at Pope Air Force Base, had given both Captain Dugan and Lieutenant Matthews ample time to reflect on, and wonder whether, their impetuosity hadn't gotten their ass in a narrow crack.

That started before they arrived at Pope Air Force Base and were taken to a hangar guarded by Special Forces noncoms. Seeing that the hangar held an aircraft of an airline neither of them had ever heard of — Intercontinental Air Cargo, Ltd. — which was being flown by a captain who had a French accent and a Cuban who spoke very little English, did not restore their morale to any appreciable degree.

At the very last minute, after the 707 had been towed out of the hangar, three other passengers were escorted into the cabin by the captain with the French accent. One was an enormous black woman who had a sleeping blondheaded infant in her arms, and the third was a good-looking blonde, who had to be the infant's mother.

There was just time, before the engines were started, to ask a few discreet questions of the blonde. She said she was an Army wife about to join her husband, a first lieutenant.

"And where is that?"

"I don't think I'm supposed to say," she said.

She had a slight German accent.

Obviously, if the Army was permitting a lieutenant to have his wife and infant child accompany him, wherever they were going couldn't be all that rough.

They had no way of knowing, of course, that the Army was permitting Mrs. Geoffrey Craig to join her husband because there was very little they could do to stop her, and could only hope that the situation vis-à-vis lieutenants' wives of Special Forces Detachment 17 could be controlled somewhat better than it had been so far.

They had not, of course, been privy to the telephone conversation between Captain Jean-Phillipe Portet of Intercontinental Air Ltd., in Miami, and Colonel Sanford T. Felter, General Staff Corps, in Washington, D.C.

"Ursula Craig put an interesting question to me last night, Sandy," Jean-Philippe Portet had said.

"She wants to know," Felter asked immediately, "since Marjorie is over there, why she can't be? I was waiting for that."

"Close, but not quite. She asked me if I would take her and Mary Magdalene on the 707, or should she make other arrangements."

"Ursula Craig escaped from East Berlin by crashing through the Berlin Wall in a truck. She's not going to consider sneaking into the Congo without a visa much of a problem," Felter said. "Especially since Geoff — I'm sure — made sure she has access to lots of cash."

"If she wanted to go to Léopoldville —"

"I don't suppose we could get Hanni or Porter Craig — better yet, Helene Craig — to reason with her?" Felter interrupted.

"That failed," Jean-Phillipe said. "As I expected it would. Helene went berserk. Hanni finally managed to convince her that Ursula and the baby would be safe in Léopoldville."

"That's a thought," Felter said. "If we could get Marjorie out of Costermansville, to Léopoldville, that would be an improvement on what we have now," Felter said. "They could both stay at your place, right?"

"Of course. But how do we get them to do that?"

"What we *don't* do is order Marjorie to Léopoldville, or tell Ursula she can't go over there. That would guarantee both of them in Costermansville."

"So what do we do?"

"Ursula and Mary Magdalene know what happened in Stanleyville — they were there," Felter said. "I think they'd much rather be in Léopoldville. Maybe they can talk Marjorie into going there."

"So I should take them?"

"What choice do we have?"

As the 707 made its approach to Stanleyville, both Captain Dugan and Lieutenant Matthews noticed that both the blonde and the enormous black woman seemed disturbed, nervous; the black woman held the baby to her tightly, her lips pursed tightly, and the blonde woman seemed very tense.

Both officers suspected that the women were probably afraid of flying generally, and landing in some strange airport compounded that fear.

Once the 707 had stopped in front of the terminal, Captain Dugan and Lieutenant Matthews could see evidence of small-arms fire on the terminal building. And there were no Americans in sight, just Congolese paratroopers. Even more disconcerting, in the open door of a hangar just behind the terminal, a Congolese paratrooper was painting a somewhat crude coffin with what looked like flat black paint.

A movable stairs mounted on a badly shot-up pickup truck was pushed to the side of the 707 by a dozen or more Congolese paratroopers. The truck had no tires; it was rolling on its rims.

A stocky Congolese paratroop officer came quickly up the stairs.

"Lieutenant Colonel," Lieutenant Matthews, who made sort of a hobby of knowing the rank insignia of foreign armies, said softly to Captain Dugan. Dugan nodded.

The Congolese lieutenant colonel made his way past the L-19s and the crates and infant accoutrements toward the cockpit.

He saw them.

"The aircraft is now at the terminal," he said in heavily sarcastic English. "The captain has extinguished the 'Fasten Seat Belts' sign. What the hell are you two waiting for?"

Captain Dugan and Lieutenant Matthews unfastened their seat belts and stood up.

"Oh, Jesus Christ!" the Congolese lieutenant colonel said, in what sounded like Yankee English, to the blonde. "What are you two, gluttons for punishment?"

Then he said something in a language neither officer had ever heard before to the enormous black woman, who smiled at him and replied. It was the first time either officer had seen the woman smile.

"Good afternoon, Major Lunsford," the blonde said. "How nice to see you again."

Tears ran down her cheeks.

"Major Lunsford?" Captain Dugan wondered.

"Oh, Jesus, honey, don't do that," Lunsford said, and put his arms around her and the baby.

"I'm all right, Father," she said.

"Father"? Lieutenant Matthews wondered.

"Trust me, honey," Lunsford said. "Things are changed from the last time you were here."

He saw Captain Dugan and Lieutenant Matthews looking at them.

"What do I have to do, stick a boot up your ass to get you off the airplane?"

Captain Dugan and Lieutenant Matthews descended the ladder. A slight Congolese paratroop captain waited at the bottom.

Lieutenant Matthews saluted him, and a moment later Captain Dugan did so, too.

The Congolese returned the salute.

"You don't have to do that," Captain Weewili said, smiling. "I'm actually a Spec7."

[TWO]
5 Degrees 27 Minutes 08 Seconds South Latitude
29 Degrees 11 Minutes 19 Seconds East Longitude
(The Bush, Near Lake Tanganyika, Kivu Province, Congo)
1550 8 April 1965

It was not the almost impenetrable jungle that Hollywood Tarzan movies have taught us to envision when "African jungle" is mentioned. It was closer to "virgin forest." More trees — many of them ancient and enormous — than vines. A vast assortment of bushes — hence the term "the bush" — and a two- or three-inch-thick padding underfoot of rotting leaves and branches. It was warm — they were five degrees south of the Equator — but not oppressively so, and they were about five thousand feet above sea level, so while the humidity was high, it was not as oppressive as, say, the Florida panhandle, where Special Forces troops are trained in "jungle warfare."

Sergeant First Jette had not spoken more than a dozen words to Major Tomas since they had left Outpost George and crossed Route 5 and gone into the bush. When it had been necessary to communicate — not often: "Stop." "That way." "Listen." "Move." — he had done so with hand movements.

The Simbas were herding half a dozen head of cattle ahead of them, and the trail had not been at all hard to follow.

Jette had set the pace, a sort of a lope, and it had been all Doubting Thomas could do to keep up with him.

Jette put his left hand to his ear. "Listen."

Thomas heard the sound of mooing cattle, and he nodded.

Jette made signs indicating the direction, and that they should move. The path he chose was in the bush, parallel to the track, and his pace picked up.

By the time Jette held up his hand, "Stop" again, Doubting Thomas was breathing hard.

Thomas could now hear voices in addition to the mooing of the cattle, but he could not make out what was being said.

Jette began to move again, this time slowly and carefully, and then held up his hand again, "Stop," and pointed. He dropped to the ground and moved on his hands and knees through the bush, and finally signaled another "Stop."

The Simbas were no more than twenty yards away. There were nine of them, ambling along both sides of the cattle and to the rear of them. They were all armed, with an assortment of both rifles and machetes. A few had pistols, and one had a pair of binoculars hanging around his neck. Most of them had some piece of uniform clothing — Belgian officers' brimmed caps with the insignia missing; dress uniform tunics; camouflage fatigue jackets or trousers; Sam Browne belts — but not one of them was completely uniformed.

It would have been easy to take them all out, Doubting Thomas judged professionally, but that wouldn't make much sense. He looked at Jette for any sign that he wasn't going to obey the one order "Major Tomas" had given him: "Unless we're attacked, you will not shoot without my specific permission."

Jette was lying on his stomach, his arms folded

in front of him, resting his chin on his hands.

He knows what he's doing, Thomas thought approvingly. *There was no sense in going back into the bush. If the Simbas hadn't seen them yet, it was unlikely they would before, in their own good time, they ambled out of sight tending the cattle.*

As Thomas started to lie down near Jette, the rain started. It had been threatening to rain for an hour. It began with a few large drops, and then it came in a torrent. There was no way the Simbas would see them now. The rain would last no more than an hour or so.

Thomas touched Jette's leg and signaled that they were to move back into the bush. Jette nodded and said nothing, but there was a look in his eyes that told Thomas that Jette had no idea what he was up to.

Thomas walked 122 paces — he counted them — before he found what he was looking for: a natural clearing in the bush open to the sky.

He unbuckled and shrugged out of the backpack radio and then his web gear, then hung it all on a broken-off limb on a tree. Then he took his compass — he carried this hanging around his neck, next to his dog tags — and sighted it back to the trail the Simbas were using.

Sergeant First Jette squatted on the ground, holding his rifle between his knees, and watched him with unconcealed curiosity. He did not take off his pack.

"When do we kill the Simbas, Major, sir?" he asked.

"Not now, Sergeant First Jette," Thomas said. "First we must talk and think and see what weapons are available to us."

"Yes, Major, sir."

"Is there any question in your mind that you can track the Simbas to their base?" Thomas asked.

"It is not hard to track cattle, Major, sir."

"Do you think the Simba will stop for the night if they cannot reach their base by dark?"

"I think they will reach their base by dark."

"I was told it's fifty miles, eighty kilometers, from Route Five to the shore of Lake Tanganyika. We have come . . . what?"

It was obvious the question was difficult for Sergeant First Jette.

"Would you agree if I said we have come perhaps fifteen kilometers?"

"Yes, Major, sir."

Shit, he'd agree if I said we'd come two klicks, or two hundred.

"Why do you think the Simba base is so close to Route Five?"

"Far enough in the bush to make finding it hard, close enough to cross Route Five to steal cattle and easily drive them to the base."

That makes sense. I should have figured that out myself.

"I don't think this will work, but what the hell, I may get lucky," Thomas said, thinking out loud.

"Major, sir?"

Thomas went to his backpack radio, let the flexible antennae loose so that it popped erect, then turned the radio on and selected a frequency.

"George, George, Hunter One," he said to the microphone.

There was no answer, even after several tries.

He turned the radio off.

"Which means, Sergeant First Jette, that George's radios are not working; or that this radio is not working; or that this radio is working, but these fucking trees are in the way."

"Yes, Major, sir."

"And I really hate to climb trees," Thomas said, looked around the clearing, selected a large tall tree with sturdy limbs near one side of it, and, motioning Jette to follow him, walked to it, carrying the radio with him.

Jette boosted him onto a lower limb and Thomas climbed the tree. When he thought he was high enough, he dropped a nylon cord weighted with his pistol to the ground. Jette tied the cord to the backpack radio, the pistol to the radio, and Thomas hauled both into the tree.

"George, George, Hunter One," he called into the microphone.

There was no reply.

"George, George, Hunter One."

Shit.

"George, George, Hunter One."

This time there was a reply, an unexpected one.

"Hunter One, this is Birddog Three."

"Birddog Three, Hunter One, how do you read?"

"Five by five, Hunter."

"Can you raise George?"

"Negative. I am over George. No radios. The reaction force is there. Who is this?"

"Doubting Thomas."

"Geoff Craig. Where the hell are you?"

"About fifteen klicks, I think, in the Bush east of George."

"You think?"

"How are you fixed for fuel?"

"A little more than an hour. I'm about to sit down at George — they have fuel. I can see a truck loaded with jerry cans. What do you need?"

"What I'd like to do is pop a smoke grenade and see if you can find me."

"You need help?"

"What I'd like is for you to mark my location on a map, and send the reaction force here."

"You found the Simbas?"

"Yeah."

"Well, aren't you clever?"

"You going to try to find me or not?"

"I'm headed that way right now."

"It would be better if you didn't overshoot this location."

"Understood. Pop smoke in five minutes. You got any yellow?"

"Popping yellow in five minutes," Thomas said, turned the radio off, and started down the tree.

He took two yellow smoke grenades — all he had — and half a dozen others from his rucksack and gave them to Sergeant First Jette.

"You stand in the middle of the clearing, and when I yell down, pull this thing, and then toss it on the ground," he said. "It won't blow up."

"Yes, Major, sir," Sergeant First Jette said, dubiously.

"If I yell again, pull the pin on another yellow. Then any of the others."

"They will not blow up, Major, sir?"

"I give you my word of honor as a former Boy Scout," Thomas said, and motioned for Jette to give him another boost into the tree.

"Birddog, Hunter."

"Read you loud and clear, but I don't see no smoke."

"Popping smoke," Thomas replied. He looked down. "Pull the pin, Sergeant First Jette!" he called.

Sergeant First Jette pulled the pin, tossed the grenade onto the ground, and then ran as fast as he could to the shelter of a tree. After a moment, he cautiously peered around the tree as yellow smoke billowed from the grenade.

"I don't see no smoke," Birddog Three announced.

"Keep looking," Thomas said.

"Ah, there you are, you elusive clever devil!"

For the first time, Thomas could now hear the sound of the L-19's engine. But he couldn't see it, even when the sound told him Geoff Craig had flown directly over him.

"There's a trail about one hundred meters due south of the smoke. Can you see it?"

There was a pause before Birddog replied.

"You said a hundred meters *south?*"

"Affirmative."

"All I can see is treetops."

"Can you see the ground where I pulled the yellow?"

"I saw a little clearing when I flew over. I didn't see you."

"I'm in a tree. You got enough to mark your map?"

"Yeah."

"Well, maybe they can find the track we followed. The Simbas are herding a half-dozen cows."

"Tell me what you want done, Thomas."

"Go to George. See if you get them on the air. That would solve a lot of problems. Show them where we are, and have them start this way."

"You want all of them?"

"How many are there?"

"Looks like a company: three big trucks, two

835

pickups, and a jeep."

"I'd like to have about twenty shooters, maybe a .30-caliber Browning. No more than that."

"Can trucks use this track if they find it?"

"No, but the jeep might be able to make it. That would come in handy if somebody got dinged. Is it towing a trailer?"

"Yeah."

"Tell them to try to bring the jeep and the trailer."

"You want them now?"

"You might as well get them started now. But I don't want to start anything today. It's too close to dark. If we can get them assembled here, by the time they get here, I'll reconnoiter the Simba camp."

"I thought you said you found them."

"I did, but we stopped trailing just before I got on the horn. We don't think the camp is far from here. I'll have to check that out."

"Okay, Thomas. Watch your ass. If they get can't get their radios working, I'll come back."

"Thank you. Out."

"Birddog out."

Thomas took a small coil of nylon cord from his pocket and used it to lash the backpack radio more securely to the tree. Then he climbed down to the ground. He went to his rucksack and took from it a small, squarish pack, three inches thick and roughly a foot square.

Sergeant First Jette squatted on the ground, holding his rifle between his knees, and watched him with unconcealed curiosity.

Jette's eyes widened when Thomas unfolded the pack, turning it into a tent of sorts. There was a flat roof, held up by nylon lines tied to the trees Thomas had looked for and found. The walls were nylon netting reaching to the ground. The floor was separate, and held in place by tree branches Thomas cut and then sharpened and drove into the ground with the heel of his boot.

Thomas went back to his rucksack and took from it the aerosol can of insect spray he had used on Withers's corpse; a plastic bottle that had once contained shampoo; and another, smaller pouch. He went to the tent, raised the netting, sprayed it thoroughly, and then went inside, taking his rifle and pistol with him.

He was now out of the rain in an insect-free environment. Sergeant First Jette was squatting in pouring rain, slapping at an assortment of native insects upon which the rain had no apparent effect.

"If you will take your machete and cut us wood for a fire, Sergeant First Jette, I will share my tent with you."

"Major, sir, if I cut wood, it will not burn. It is wet."

"If you do not cut wood, you will stay there in the rain," Thomas said. "It's up to you."

"When do we kill the Simbas, Major, sir?"

"Not now, Sergeant First Jette," Thomas said. "In the morning. Now you cut wood and I clean my weapons and then eat. Or, if you do not cut wood, then you stay there in the rain and you do not eat."

Sergeant First Jette rose effortlessly to his feet from his squatting position, unhooked his machette from his web belt, and disappeared into the bush.

Thomas field-stripped his Car-16 weapon,

sprayed the mechanism with Three-In-One oil, reassembled it, chambered a round, and then laid it on the floor of his tent. Then he did the same thing with his .45 automatic, except that instead of laying it on the tent floor, he carried it with him while he went to the tree where he had hung his rucksack and web gear. He took another plastic-wrapped package from the rucksack and returned to his tent to wait for Sergeant First Jette to finish his wood collecting.

Jette came in about five minutes, his arms full of small limbs of trees.

"Shave some slivers from the bigger pieces," Thomas ordered. "Put them on the bottom, with some leaves from the ground, and then put the larger pieces over them, leaving enough room for air."

"With respect, Major, sir, I know how to lay a fire."

"But you do not know, you tell me, how to make a fire with wet green wood?"

"Wet, green wood, Major, sir, will not burn."

"Lay the fire, Sergeant First Jette, and then as we watch the fire burn, we will have our supper."

When Jette had laid the fire, making a nice conical shape of it, Thomas raised the netting and stepped out into the rain, carrying with him his machete and the plastic bottle that had once held shampoo.

He disappeared into the bush, returning in no more than two minutes with more tree branches, thick with leaves. He sharpened the ends and jammed them into the ground so that they shielded the fire Jette had laid from the rain.

Then he sprayed the fire bed with the contents

of the former shampoo bottle, took a Zippo lighter from his pocket, and ignited the liquid.

Sergeant First Jette's eyes widened in appreciation.

"When you have to build a fire in the rain, Sergeant Jette," Thomas said, "there's nothing like a little avgas. Write that down."

"I cannot write, Major, sir," Jette said.

Shit!

Thomas waited until the burning avgas had the leaves and chips burning well, and then added larger pieces of wood.

Without waiting to be told, Jette loped off into the bush and returned with another armful of wood.

"It seems to be burning nicely, Sergeant First Jette," Thomas said. "Put a few more pieces of wood on it, and then come in the tent."

Jette squatted before the fire and nurtured it until he was confident it would remain on fire, then went under the nylon netting.

Thomas handed him dinner: fried chicken and a cold baked potato from the kitchen of the Hotel du Lac.

"There is also two bottles of beer," Thomas said, "but you will have to get them from my rucksack. I forgot."

"I have beer," Jette said. "I did not know if the Major, sir, would approve."

"The major approves."

"You have been in the bush before, Major, Sir," Jette said.

"Not this bush, Sergeant. And not for as long as you. You are a master of the bush."

"What is your tribe?"

"I have no idea," Thomas said. "For all I know,

839

my family may have been from here. I look like you."

Jette nodded his acceptance of that.

"You talked to the airplane, Major, sir?"

"He told me the reaction force is at Outpost George. He will tell them to come here. I could not talk to them on the radio."

"When they get here, we kill the Simbas, Major, sir? When the rain stops? When it is dark?"

"It is best, Sergeant First Jette, to know all you can about the enemy and his position before you attack, and it is better to attack with twenty men than two."

Jette nodded his acceptance of that philosophy.

"Tonight, you and I will locate the Simbas precisely. And in the morning, with twenty men, and with a little luck, a machine gun, we will attack them."

Jette nodded again.

"The airplane will come back if I cannot talk to the reaction force on my radio, and he will tell us when they are coming."

Jette nodded again.

"Get the beer, Sergeant First Jette," Thomas said. "I always like a beer with my supper."

"Yes, Major, sir."

They had just finished their chicken and cold baked potato dinner when both heard the sound of the L-19's engine.

"Oh, shit," Doubting Thomas said aloud. "That means no reaction force radios."

He got to his feet and motioned for Jette to follow him.

It had stopped raining, but the ground and the tree were still rain-slick.

Here lies Master Sergeant William E. Thomas, who

busted his ass climbing a fucking tree.

"Birddog, Hunter, I'm back in the fucking tree. How read?"

"Five by five," Geoff Craig replied. "All their batteries are dead."

"Oh, shit!"

"Yeah. Well, they're on their way. Twenty shooters, no machine gun, and a jeep, no trailer."

"Okay."

"I'm going to Woolworth. There's batteries there. I'll be back at first light — first light here, I can take off from there in the dark — and I'll drop the batteries to the smoke clearing. When you hear my engine, pop yellow smoke."

"I have one only yellow. Can you get me more?"

"Sure."

"And four bottles of beer, and enough fried chicken for two."

"Done, and don't get yourself eaten by a hungry lion while I'm gone."

"Thanks, Lieutenant."

"Be careful, Bill. See you in the morning. Birddog out."

"Hunter out."

When he'd reached the ground again, Sergeant First Jette had a worried look on his face.

"What's bothering you?" Thomas asked.

"If we can hear the airplane, the Simbas can hear the airplane," Jette said.

"It's almost impossible to tell the direction of an airplane from the sound," Thomas said. "And he was flying close to the treetops, so they couldn't see him."

Jette considered that for a long moment, then nodded.

"If the Major, sir, wishes to sleep, I will stay awake," he said.

"We will take two-hour turns, Sergeant First Jette," Thomas said. "That way we both get some sleep."

Sergeant First Jette nodded.

[THREE]
Stanleyville Air Field
Stanleyville, Oriental Province
Republic of the Congo
1845 8 April 1965

"Woolworth, Woolworth, Birddog Three," Geoff said into his microphone.

"Where the hell are you?" the tower operator replied.

That was not the standard response of a tower operator, but the tower operator in this case was not a tower operator but rather Major George Washington Lunsford, and Major Lunsford had been troubled over the past six, even seven hours over several things.

For one thing, no one had been able to establish radio contact with Outpost George, and Major Lunsford had been unable to establish contact with Colonel Jean-Baptiste Supo to report the situation.

The last time Major Lunsford had seen Colonel Supo was when, after they had dropped off the corpse of SFC Withers, Colonel Supo and Lieutenant Jacques Portet had taken off in the Beaver for Costermansville. Inasmuch as neither Colonel Supo nor Lieutenant Portet was in Costermansville, the possibility existed that they and the L-20 were down somewhere between Woolworth

842

(Stanleyville) and Costermansville.

Further, although it was unlikely, the possibility that Outpost George had been overwhelmed again had to be considered. It was not possible to dispatch the reaction force to Outpost George, because the reaction force had already been dispatched to Outpost George, which opened the possibilities (a) that it had been ambushed after Major Lunsford had flown over it on Route 5 when it had been en route to Outpost George, or (b) that it had been overwhelmed after it reached Outpost George.

Under that circumstance, Major Lunsford had deemed it unwise to dispatch a reconnaissance team from either Outpost Fox or Outpost Item (the nearest outposts, on either side of George). Such reconnaissance teams would stand a high risk of ambush if, in fact, the reaction force had been overwhelmed before or after reaching Outpost George.

It would be wiser, Major Lunsford had decided, to wait until contact was established with Birddog Three (Lieutenant Craig), which, at Lunsford's order, was engaged at overflying all the outposts to determine (a) how long it actually (as opposed to theoretically) took to fly from one to the next and, (b) to test and judge the efficiency of the ground-to-air communications thereof.

Birddog Three's ETA at Woolworth had been 1630, opening the possibility that Birddog Three, now two hours and fifteen minutes overdue, was down somewhere, God only knew where.

If the reaction force had been overwhelmed, that would mean that it had been attacked by a superior force, which meant that everybody was now in a much larger ballgame, the ramifications of which Major Lunsford did not even wish to think about, but privately thought was going to be a three-star fucking mess.

In addition to which, of course, he had considered the possibility that he was going to have to be a notification team of one to tell Mrs. Jacques Portet that her husband was missing and to tell Mrs. Geoffrey Craig very much the same thing.

"I'm over the river, about ten minutes out. Will you light it up, please?"

"You sonofabitch!" Major Lunsford said, tossed the microphone to Spec7 Peters/Captain Weewili, and stormed down out of the control tower to see if he could find someone who could turn on the generator to power the runway lights without fucking that up, too.

"Birddog Three, Woolworth," Captain Weewili called. "Roger your request for runway lights. They should be on by the time you get here. The winds are negligible, and you are cleared for a straight-in approach to Two-seven. Report when you have the lights in sight."

"Roger, Woolworth."

"And have we got a surprise for you!"

"I heard," Lieutenant Craig replied.

Major George Washington Lunsford was waiting when Lieutenant Geoffrey Craig taxied the L-19 to the door of Hangar Two and shut it down.

"Where the fuck have you been, you sonofabitch?" he greeted him. "You've had everybody scared shitless."

Lieutenant Craig knew Major Lunsford well enough to know that if he really had his ass in a crack, Major Lunsford's greeting would have met the requirements of military courtesy and protocol in every minute detail. What he had here was a concerned friend.

"I tried to call," he said. "All I can do is talk into the microphone. I can't make the radio work."

"What's going on at Outpost George?"

"I just came from there. Aside from their shit-for-brains commo officer not having brought one — not-fucking-one — undead battery for their radios with them, they're in pretty good shape. Doubting Thomas has tracked the Simbas about fifteen klicks into the bush, and asked for twenty shooters and a jeep to be sent to him. They're on the way. I'm going to take off from here at oh dark hundred, to arrive over his position at first light and drop batteries to him."

Lunsford nodded but didn't respond.

"The Beaver's missing," he said.

"They should be in Léopoldville by now. They didn't get there?"

"Léopoldville?" Lunsford asked.

"The last I heard — Portet put out an 'anybody listening' — they were on their way to Léopoldville. He told me Supo decided he wanted to see Mobutu before he went to Costermansville."

"You talked to him?"

"Yeah. I asked him if he wanted the message relayed, and he said no. Supo would send word on a landline. They didn't get there?"

"I don't know," Lunsford said. "Since I didn't know they were going to Léopoldville, I didn't call Léopoldville to ask if they got there."

Lunsford shook his head, then marched purposefully toward the terminal building, which served as the command post for the Congolese soldiers guarding the field.

The guard outside was squatting on the ground, his rifle between his knees.

"The next time you don't get to your feet and salute me when you see me, I'm going to stick that rifle up your ass," Lunsford said in Swahili.

The guard quickly started to get to his feet as Lunsford walked past.

The officer in charge of the guard detachment was asleep in an office chair. Lunsford pushed it, hard, with his foot. The chair spun around as it moved across the floor.

"I hope I didn't disturb you, Lieutenant," Lunsford said politely.

The lieutenant got to his feet.

"I thought the colonel was gone for the day," he said.

"Have there been any messages for me?"

"I don't think so," the lieutenant said.

"Why don't we look?" Lunsford asked, and walked to a teletype machine, marked with the logotype of Sabena, the Belgian airline, but now connected to the Army network in Léopoldville. There was a large pile of teletype paper on the floor behind it.

Lunsford ripped it off the machine and started reading it.

"Here it is," he said finally, after he'd pulled about half of the coiled teletypewriter paper through his hands. "Sent from Léopoldville at two-fifteen this afternoon." He read from it in English: "Quote 'Immediately inform Lieutenant Colonel Dahdi that I am in Léopoldville and will come to Stanleyville tomorrow. Please meet me there and delay departure of supply aircraft until my arrival. Supo. Colonel Commandant.' End Quote." He looked at Craig. "I wonder what the hell that's all about?"

Craig shrugged.

The lieutenant was now standing at rigid attention.

"I should kick his ass around the block," Lunsford said, "but I don't think it would do any good."

He switched to Swahili. "Lieutenant, I don't think that Colonel Supo will be pleased that I had to find for myself a message at night that was supposed to be delivered to me at two-fifteen this afternoon. He will be here tomorrow."

The lieutenant winced.

"Well, for the good news," Geoff said. "I see the 707 made it in."

Lunsford looked at him.

"Lieutenant, have you ever heard that when you deliver a message that you feel will greatly surprise the individual to whom you are giving it, you should make him sit down first? So that he won't fall over and break his head, or his ass, or both?"

"Yes, sir, I've heard that. Should I sit down?"

"I think that would be a very good idea," Lunsford said. "Sit down, Lieutenant."

At first, Geoff had thought Lunsford was making a joke. When he saw that he was serious, he looked around and found a small chair, and sat down on it.

When he had, Lunsford told him that his wife, son, and Mary Magdalene were in the Immoquateur, probably having their dinner.

[FOUR]
Gregory & Gregory Funeral Home
730 North Main Street
Laurinburg, North Carolina
1350 8 April 1965

"I'm James L. Gregory," the somberly dressed, pale-skinned man said to Captain Stefan Zabrewski. "How may I be of service, sir?"

"There has been a death," Zabrewski said.

"May I offer my most sincere condolences?" Mr. Gregory said.

"And we're here to arrange for the funeral," Zabrewski said.

"And your relationship to the deceased?"

"I'm a friend," Zabrewski said. He nodded at Sergeant Major Tinley. "We're both friends."

"I see."

"SFC Withers's parents live here," Zabrewski said. "On a farm. Outside of town."

"SFC Withers?"

"The man who's dead," Zabrewski said.

"I see. Oh, I *see*. I take it you're speaking of Mr. and Mrs. Delmar Withers?"

"Yes, sir."

"They're fine people," Gregory said.

"Yes, sir."

"Normally, the family makes the arrangements. . . ."

"We're trying to spare them that," Zabrewski said.

"I understand."

"When did . . . What did you say, SFC?"

"Sergeant First Class, yes, sir."

"When did Sergeant Withers pass?"

"The day before yesterday."

"And you're just coming to us now?"

"Yes, sir."

"And where did he pass?"

"I'm afraid I can't tell you that, sir."

"Really? Why not?"

"I'm afraid that's classified information, sir."

"I see. And where are the remains?"

"I'm afraid I can't tell you that, either," Zabrewski said. "But Withers is on his way either to the States or to Pope Air Force Base right now, or shortly will be. He should get here the day after tomorrow, or the day after that."

"I presume the documentation is in order?" Gregory asked.

"Excuse me, sir?"

"I'm presuming Sergeant Withers passed outside the United States?"

"That's right."

"Well, as I'm sure you can understand, there are certain procedures that have to be followed. We'll need, of course, a certificate of death, as issued by the appropriate authorities. If death occurred in a foreign county, that will need verification by the Consul General — the *United States* Consul General — serving the country in which death occurred. Then there will have to be a copy of the autopsy, again verified by the Consul General, stating the cause of death, and that the remains are not infected with any of the contagious diseases. . . ."

"Captain Zabrewski, sir," Sergeant Major Tinley asked politely. "May I have a word with you, sir?"

Zabrewski was visibly surprised, but recovered quickly.

"Certainly, Sergeant," he said. "Will you

excuse us, please, Mr. Gregory, for a moment while we step into the corridor?"

"I'll just step outside for a few minutes," Gregory said, nodding at a door. "And when you're finished, you could just tap on the door."

"That's very kind of you, sir," Captain Zabrewski said. "Thank you very much."

When there was no tap on the door ten minutes later, Mr. Gregory cracked the door to see if he could be of some assistance.

Neither the captain nor the sergeant major was where he had left them, nor, when he looked, anywhere in the building.

Apparently, Mr. Gregory concluded, some sort of military emergency had come up.

[FIVE]
Office of the Corps Surgeon Headquarters
XVIII Airborne Corps
Fort Bragg, North Carolina
1445 8 April 1965

"Sir, General Hanrahan is here," SFC Stuart T. Cameron, the administrative NCO of the Office of the Corps Surgeon, announced.

Colonel Frederick A. Emmett, Medical Corps, rose to his feet.

"Please come in, General Hanrahan," he said.

Hanrahan, trailed by Zabrewski and Tinley, marched into his office.

"Thank you for waiting for me, Doctor," Hanrahan said.

Hanrahan did not believe it was necessary for medical officers to carry rank; he never addressed them by their rank; he called them all "Doctor," except those he personally admired and/or liked, whom he addressed as "Doc."

"My pleasure, General," Colonel/Doctor Emmett said.

"We have a little problem I hope you can help us with," Hanrahan said.

"Anything within my power, General."

"One of my men was killed the day before yesterday," Hanrahan began.

"I'm sorry."

"We all are. Good soldier."

"What happened to him?"

"That information is classified Top Secret/ Earnest," General Hanrahan said. "As of this moment, you have a Top Secret/Earnest clearance for those matters — only those matters — which in my judgment you have the need-to-know."

"Yes, sir."

"He was on an outpost in the former Belgian Congo, which was overrun by an insurrectionist group known as the Simbas."

"I didn't know we were in the Congo," Dr. Emmett said.

"His body was partially dismembered," Hanrahan said. "The head and part of one leg."

"Jesus!"

"His body is now, or shortly will be, en route by air to Pope."

"I see."

"My aide, Captain Zabrewski, and Sergeant Major Tinley," Hanrahan said, nodding at them, "have just come from a funeral home in SFC Withers's hometown, Laurinburg, which is about fifty miles from here. The funeral director told them they need all sorts of paperwork which we don't have, and have no way of getting."

"The AG isn't handling the return of the remains?"

"So far as I know, the AG hasn't been told of SFC Withers's death."

"Permission to speak, sir?" Sergeant Major Tinley asked.

"Granted," Hanrahan said.

"We were hoping it could be done here, Colonel," Tinley said. "The paperwork, I mean."

"I see," Colonel/Doctor Emmett said. "Captain, would you and the sergeant major step outside for a minute, please? I'd like a word with General Hanrahan."

"Yes, sir," they said, in unison, turned and walked out of the office.

When the door was closed, Colonel/Doctor Emmett looked at General Hanrahan and said, "Jesus Christ, Red, here we go again!"

"Doc, I can't help it."

"You know what it says in the *Manual for Court-Martial*? 'Any officer who willingly and knowingly issues, or causes to be issued, any document' —"

"— 'or statement he knows to be false,' " Hanrahan finished for him, " 'is subject to such punishment as a court-martial may direct.' The way I read that — *'or causes to be issued'* — I'm not asking you to do something I'm not doing myself."

"We've had this conversation before, haven't we? Too many times."

"And every time you've come through for me," Hanrahan said.

"Fuck you, Red. I'm thinking of the next of kin."

"Me, too, Doc. This is my fault. I should have known Zabrewski and the Tin Man would have gone to the funeral home without asking me first."

"That was the Tin Man? I've heard about him."

"Withers was on his A team in Vietnam."

"If they hadn't gone to the funeral director, I would have gotten another three-in-the-morning phone call, saying you're at Pope with a little problem, right?"

Hanrahan nodded. "Probably, certainly."

"I'm afraid that funeral director is going to smell a rat now."

"Zabrewski said he told him nothing except that the death took place outside the U.S."

"And if he makes a stink?"

"Then we're fucked."

"Same drill as last time? Understood?"

"Understood," Hanrahan said.

"If you can get the body off the airplane and off Pope without the Air Force knowing and into the hospital, I will do the autopsy. . . . Jesus, you said the head is severed?"

Hanrahan nodded.

"Well, that's the cause of death, then?"

"I'm hoping he was dead, shot, first," Hanrahan said.

". . . and sign the death certificate, and the no-communicable-diseases certificate. . . ."

"Which I thereupon stamp Top Secret, and give the funeral home a copy with the place of death et cetera, blacked out."

"Right. But not my signature, right?"

"I don't think they'd take it without your signature, and that seal, stamp, whatever, that makes little holes in the paper."

853

"What if the mortician wants the documents verified by a Consul General?"

"This happened before. I gave them a signed, stamped certificate saying that the Consular Verification has been accomplished but misplaced. I planned to do that again now."

"Now there's *willingly and knowingly issues,*" Colonel Emmett said.

Hanrahan shrugged.

"Between you and me, Red, what this fellow was doing, was it important? Is it worth all this?"

"Yeah, it was."

"Don't tell those two anymore than they have to know," Colonel Emmett said.

"They'll have to handle getting the body off the airplane. . . ."

"Anymore than . . . what's that you're always saying? . . . they have the need to know."

"Thanks, Doc," Hanrahan said.

[SIX]
Apartment 10-C, The Immoquateur
Stanleyville, Oriental Province
Republic of the Congo
1930 8 April 1965

First Lieutenant Geoffrey Craig put his arms around his wife and held her tightly against him. He was surprised at the depth of his emotion; he could not, literally, talk and he was aware that his chest was heaving.

Finally, he found his voice.

"You're out of your goddamned mind," he said.

"I love you too," Ursula said.

"Jesus Christ, Liebling, you know what

happened here!"

"I was in the hand of God then, and I am in the hand of God now. And with my husband."

Without taking his arms off her, he pulled his head back so that he could look at her face. That struck him dumb again.

After a moment he asked, "How the hell did you get on the airplane? What the hell was Portet thinking of?"

"I asked him if he would bring us, or whether I would have to get here myself. He knew I would come either way. Bringing me would be easier on Jiffy. And I could bring all the things I need for Jiffy on the plane."

"Jesus, Liebling, you can't stay here!" he said, and before she had a chance to respond, asked, "Does Felter know?"

Ursula nodded.

"He knew he couldn't stop me."

"I just don't understand your reasoning," Geoff said. There was a suggestion of anger in his voice.

"Marjorie is here," Ursula said.

"Marjorie's out of her goddamned mind too," he said.

"Marjorie is with her husband," Ursula said. "And now I'm with my husband, and Jiffy is with his Poppa."

"What the hell did my mother say?"

"She was a little hysterical," Ursula said matter-of-factly. "Then Hanni convinced her we would be safe in Léopoldville."

"And you're going to Léopoldville, just as soon as I can get you there!"

"You smell from under the arms," she said.

"What?"

"You need a shower."

"I spent all goddamn day in an airplane," he said. "Of course I need a shower."

"Well?"

"How's Jiffy?"

"Taking a nap. Mary Magdalene's with him."

"You brought her back, too?"

Ursula nodded.

"Maybe, by the time you have your shower, he'll be awake."

He looked at her.

"Just as soon as I can get you out of here, you're going to Léopoldville."

"You really smell," she said.

"So you keep telling me," he said.

She pointed toward the bathroom.

He shook his head, finally took his arms off her, and went into the bathroom and closed the door. He sat on the toilet and took off his boots, then stripped out of his flight suit and underwear and got under the shower.

Ursula looked at the closed bathroom door, then started taking off her clothing. When she judged he had had enough time to take off his clothing and get under the shower, she went to the bathroom, saw him vaguely behind the steamed glass door, smiled when she heard him talking to himself, then pulled open the glass door and got in the shower stall with him.

[SEVEN]
Apartment 10-C, The Immoquateur
Stanleyville, Oriental Province
Republic of the Congo
2055 8 April 1965

The word is surreal, Captain James J. Dugan decided as he looked around the living room of Apartment 10-C. *The last week has been* surreal, *from the moment I was told to call the Office of the Commanding General at Fort Riley. I know better than to think this is a dream from which I will wake up, but that's what it feels like, and the word for that is* surreal.

Captain Dugan was wearing the uniform of a major of Congolese paratroops, complete in every detail to the Browning 9-mm automatic pistol in a web holster. First Lieutenant Paul W. Matthews was wearing the uniform of a Congolese captain of paratroops.

As they had put on the uniforms, under the direction of a Congolese captain of paratroops named DeeGee, who confessed that he was really Sergeant First Class Andrew DeGrew of the 17th Special Forces Detachment, Lieutenant Matthews had made a little joke:

"Yesterday, I ain't never even *seen* a captain of Congolese paratroops, and today I are one."

When they had pressed Sergeant DeGrew for details of what was going on, DeGrew had politely told them that "The Major" would explain what was going on over dinner, which would be served at 2100 in Captain Portet's apartment.

Once satisfied with their appearance, DeeGee/DeGrew had left them alone in apartment 8-F with two bona fide Congolese paratroop sergeants, who would, DeGrew explained, serve as both their orderlies and their bodyguards. Using sign language, one of the sergeants had managed to communicate that there was beer, if the officers wished, and at 2050, the other had managed to communicate that it was time to go to dinner.

There were two paratroopers outside the door of Apartment 10-C, whom Dugan and Matthews judged to be bona fide because both bore facial scars obviously intended to enhance their beauty.

Captain DeeGee opened the door to them, a Car-16 slung from his shoulder, and indicated the direction of the living room.

A white man in a U.S. Army flight suit without any insignia of any kind was sitting on the floor playing patty-cake, patty-cake, with the blond infant who had been on the 707. The blonde was nowhere in sight.

There was a coffee table, on which had been arranged a selection of hors d'oeuvres, and a bare-footed African in a starched white jacket was standing behind a small bar. The Congolese lieutenant colonel now identified as Major Lunsford was at the bar with two other men: the captain of the 707, and the Congolese captain who had been at the foot of the aircraft steps and told them saluting wasn't necessary, he was a Spec7.

And I never saw a Spec7 before today, either, although I've heard of them, Captain Dugan thought.

A second barefoot black man in a starched white jacket came into the room through a swinging door, carrying a huge platter holding a small roast pig with an apple in its mouth. The enormous black woman from the 707 followed him, and showed him where she wanted it laid on a large dining table. Then she followed him back through the swinging doors.

"Welcome," the airline captain said. "Come on over and have a drink."

They walked to the bar.

"Good evening, sir," Captain Dugan said.

"Good evening, Captain," Lieutenant Matthews said.

"You're Major Lunsford, sir?" Captain Dugan asked, offering his hand.

"Welcome to the Congo, Captain," Lunsford said, shaking his hand, then offering his hand to Matthews with a nod.

"You've met Spec7 Peters, I understand?" Lunsford said.

"Yes, sir," they said in unison.

"The proud daddy on the floor is Lieutenant Geoff Craig, my exec."

Craig waved at them, then held the infant's arm so that the infant could wave too.

"Which one of you is better at dropping things from L-19 hardpoints?" Craig asked. "Specifically, into a clearing maybe twice the size of this room? A clearing in some really heavy bush?"

Dugan and Matthews looked at each other, but neither replied.

"Hey, you were asked a question," Lunsford said.

"Sir, I haven't flown an L-19 in some time," Matthews said truthfully.

"You came from where?" Father asked.

"Headquarters, Third Army, sir."

"Been flying the brass around in L-23s?"

"Yes, sir."

"Then you're the one from the Big Red One?" Lunsford asked Dugan.

"Yes, sir."

"And they have a lot of L-19s in the Big Red One, right?"

"Yes, sir. I've got some recent L-19 time."

"That means you don't get anything to drink, I'm afraid," Lunsford said.

"Sir?"

"At first light," Geoff said, "you and I are going to try to drop some batteries into a clearing in the bush. So we're shut off from the sauce tonight."

Mrs. Ursula Wagner Craig came into the room. She was wearing a simple, crisp-looking, yellow dress.

"And this, of course, is Miss — Mrs. — Stanleyville of 1965," Lunsford said. "Otherwise known as Mrs. Ursula Craig."

The enormous black woman came into the room, snatched the infant from the floor, and left with it.

"And that is the one meanest black lady I have ever met," Lunsford said. "The first time I met her, I came through that door" — he pointed — "doing my John Wayne act with a FN automatic rifle, and Mary Magdalene came through that one" — he pointed at the swinging door — "with murder in her eye, and a butcher knife in each hand. I have never been so scared in my life."

"She was protecting the baby," Ursula Craig said.

"Jacques said that when he got here," the airline captain said, "she scared him out of his wits, and she raised him."

"A word to the wise, therefore, gentlemen," Father said. "Don't cross Mary Magdalene. Understand?"

"No, sir," Captain Dugan said. "With respect, sir, I don't understand any of this. I don't know

860

what's going on, and I'm not sure I even know where we are."

"Okay," Lunsford said. "I'll try to make this quick so we can eat. You read in the papers about the Simbas, the people who occupied Stanleyville, and most of this part of the Congo, until the Belgians jumped on Stanleyville?"

"Yes, sir."

"Captain Portet's wife, Ursula, the baby, and Mary Magdalene were trapped here when the Simbas came. In this apartment. It belongs to Captain Portet. When the Belgians jumped, Jack Portet — he's Captain Portet's son, and a Special Forces officer — jumped with them, and of course headed right for the Immoquateur because his mother and Ursula and the baby were here, presuming the Simbas hadn't had their livers for lunch in the town square."

"Father, my God!" Ursula protested.

"They wanted to know what's going on here," Lunsford said, unabashed. "I'm telling them."

"Sir, with respect, and forgive me, Mrs. Craig," Captain Dugan said, "but you're not saying these people actually practiced cannibalism, are you?"

"Yes, I am," Lunsford said. "That's exactly what I'm saying."

"Sir, didn't I understand you to say you were here too?" Matthews asked.

Lunsford nodded.

"Then you jumped with the Belgians, too?"

"No. He was here when the Belgians got here," Geoff Craig said. "He was running around in the bush with the Simbas."

"We had Special Forces here then?" Matthews asked, genuinely surprised.

"And some people from the Army Security

Agency," Spec7 Peters said.

"And some people from the Army Security Agency," Lunsford agreed, smiling.

"We often work with Special Forces," Spec7 Peters explained with as much modesty as he could muster.

Craig and Lunsford exchanged glances but said nothing.

Geoff Craig had a flattering — from his perspective — thought: *If that skinny little bastard — especially since he's earned his jump wings — doesn't get himself blown away over here, there's no way he's going back to the White House Signal Agency.*

"Sir, what I don't understand is what Special Forces is doing here now," Matthews said. "Haven't the Simbas been . . . broken up? Don't the Congolese have the situation under control?"

"Well, if it wasn't for Che Guevara thinking that the way to bring the joys of Communism to the rest of the world is by encouraging the savages here to eat some more white people's livers, they would."

"*Ach, du lieber Gott, Vater,*" Ursula protested, so unhappy and disturbed that she reverted to her native German.

"You're not talking about the Cuban?" Captain Dugan asked incredulously. "The guy with the beard?"

Lunsford nodded.

"That's hard to believe," Dugan said.

"Truth is stranger than fiction," Lunsford said. "Write that down."

"My God, you're serious," Matthews said.

"Ernesto Guevara de la Serna, M.D. — who naively thinks we don't know — is at this very moment on a farm outside of Dar es Salaam,

Tanganyika, preparing to lead his quote 'forces of liberation' unquote across Lake Tanganyika into the Congo," Father said.

"He's a doctor?" Lieutenant Matthews asked incredulously.

"I'll be damned," Captain Dugan said.

"We have an ASA intercept team on him," Spec7 Peters said.

"So the question before you, Captain Dugan and Lieutenant Matthews, is do you want to stay here and help us stop the sonofabitch, at considerable risk to your skin, and no bands playing when you get home — if you get home — or do you want to get on the 707 when it goes back to the States tomorrow?"

"Sir, we volunteered for this assignment," Matthews said.

"You just think you did," Lunsford said. "You were recruited by Pappy Hodges, who could show the Virgin Mary how he'd marked his cards, then talk her into playing strip poker with him."

"Father, that's terrible!" Mrs. Craig said, but she was smiling.

"I don't want anyone here who doesn't want to be here," Father said. "And I think anyone who would want to be here is certifiable."

Matthews and Dugan looked at each other but said nothing.

"Just to make sure you know what you might be letting yourself in for," Lunsford said. "That coffin you saw us making at the field? We're sending a damned good soldier home in it with Captain Portet. He was on an outpost; the Congolese soldiers with him got scared and took off. He stayed and fought, and lost, and after he was dead, I hope, they cut off his head."

Captain James J. Dugan looked at Lieutenant Matthews, then at Lieutenant Craig.

He wet his lips.

"What time did you say we were taking off in the morning, Lieutenant?" he asked.

[EIGHT]

SECRET

Central Intelligence Agency
Langley, Virginia

FROM: Assistant Director For Administration

DATE: 8 April 1965 2330 GMT

SUBJECT: Guevara, Ernesto (Memorandum # 72.)

TO: Mr. Sanford T. Felter
Counselor To The President
Room 637, The Executive Office Building
Washington, D.C.

By Officer Courier

In compliance with Presidential Memorandum to The Director, Subject: "Ernesto 'Che' Guevara," dated 14 December 1964, the following information is being furnished:

From CIA Dar es Salaam, Tanganyika (Reliability Scale Five):

1-In the last 96 hours thirty Negro males of military age bearing Cuban passports have arrived in Dar es Salaam, all on tourist visas issued by the Tanganyikan Embassy in Mexico City, Mexico. No names are available at this time.

2-They arrived variously, in groups no larger than six, aboard various commercial flights from Cairo, Egypt (3); Prague, Czechoslovakia (3); and Paris, France (2).

3-Immediately on arrival all were transported by car or light truck to the farm in the vicinity of Morogoro, where Guevara and Dreke are known to be.

4-It is the opinion of the undersigned that most, if not all, of the group will leave the farm within the next seven days and attempt to enter the Congo, probably by crossing Lake Tanganyika from Kigoma in the Western Province.

Howard W. O'Connor
HOWARD W. O'CONNOR

SECRET

XXII

[ONE]
5 Degrees 27 Minutes 08 Seconds South
  Latitude
29 Degrees 11 Minutes 19 Seconds East
  Longitude
(The Bush, Near Lake Tanganyika, Kivu
  Province, Congo)
0440 9 April 1965

Doubting Thomas was surprised, and at first annoyed, that Lieutenant Colonel Henri Coizi, Colonel Supo's Chef de Cabinet, who had elected to personally command the reaction force, had also elected to personally command the reinforcement force of twenty shooters he had asked for.

Like most senior sergeants with something important to do, Master Sergeant Thomas believed the last thing needed to accomplish his mission was a goddamned lieutenant colonel to get in the way.

But at least the bastard's leading the column on foot, Thomas thought when first he saw Colonel Coizi, *not riding standing up in the jeep, like Patton.*

He had then stepped out of the bush.

Here lies Master Sergeant William Thomas, who was shot in the middle of the jungle at oh dark hundred by a trigger-happy African.

"Hold fire!" Lieutenant Colonel Coizi barked in a command voice that would have made him

866

perfectly at home on the parade grounds of Fort Bragg.

Thomas saluted crisply.

"Good morning, sir."

Coizi returned the salute as crisply.

"Major," he said.

"I expected the colonel a little earlier," Thomas said politely.

Like maybe at ten o'clock last night.

"We moved up from Outpost George last night, but I thought it best to wait just out of range until light," Coizi said. "I didn't want to get past your position, for obvious reasons. And I thought sending a scout to find you and Sergeant First Jette would be a good way to lose a scout. And, of course, I have no radios."

"Yes, sir," Thomas said.

"Where is Sergeant First Jette?"

"At our camp, sir. About a hundred meters into the bush."

"And the Simbas?"

"About two klicks — two kilometers — down the path, sir. Jette and I reconnoitered last night. There's about sixty of them, including some women."

"Well, why don't you and I go have a look? While we're gone, Jette can brief my men." He picked up on Thomas's hesitation. "Unless you would prefer to brief the troops while Jette and I go to see what we'll be facing?"

"Sir, what I would like to do, with your permission, is wait for the L-19 to drop batteries for your radios. I expect the aircraft at first light — right about now. And then, when we have your radios operating, you and I can have a look at the Simbas."

"Of course," Coizi said. "I should have thought of that. You'll have to forgive me. I am not used to being supported by aviation."

"Yes, sir."

"Where are the batteries going to be dropped?"

"In the clearing, sir," Thomas said, and pointed.

Coizi turned, called a name, and a Congolese officer walked quickly and silently up to him and saluted. He was young, very tall, and very black.

"Lieutenant Breque, do you know Major Tomas?"

"No, sir."

Tomas and Breque shook hands.

"Establish a perimeter guard," Coizi ordered. "We have what, four back radios?"

"And one in the Jeep, sir."

"My radioman can't carry them all," Coizi said. "Give me two strong men. I don't want Major Tomas carrying his own radio."

"Yes, sir."

"Send them to us," Coizi ordered, pointing toward the bush. "Batteries will be dropped to us from one of the little airplanes very shortly."

"Yes, sir."

"When they are, I will send Sergeant First Jette here to brief you and the men, and to test the radios. Major Tomas and I will then perform a reconnaissance."

"Yes, sir."

"You may go," Coizi said.

Lieutenant Breque saluted and returned to the column of shooters.

"I think he will do," Coizi said.

"Sir?"

"I promoted him yesterday — he was a sergeant

— to replace the lieutenant who was responsible for our having no batteries," Coizi said matter-of-factly. "I reduced him to the ranks. I probably should have had him shot."

"Well, the problem is solved," Thomas said.

"He's not the soldier Jette is," Coizi said. "I would have liked to have made Jette a sous-lieutenant, but Jette can't read or write."

"Yes, sir, I know."

Almost at the moment Tomas, Coizi, and the two soldiers carrying the radios stepped into the clearing, they could hear the sound of an L-19 engine.

Tomas hurriedly popped a yellow smoke grenade.

Three minutes later, just as Thomas reached his radio lashed to the tree trunk and turned it on, a black L-19 flashed over. It disappeared, and came back a minute later, this time much lower.

A few seconds after that, there was a crashing sound in the branches above Doubting Thomas, and as he snapped his head upward, a padded canvas bag crashed though limbs toward him, stopping — when the canopy of its parachute encountered the upper branches of the tree — no more than three feet from where he had propped himself in the tree.

By the time he had detached the bag from the shroud lines of the small parachute, and before he could start to lower it to the ground, the sound of the L-19's engine announced another pass, and this time, after it had flashed over again, the small cargo 'chute delivered its load to one side of the clearing, landing not far from where Lieutenant Colonel Coizi was standing.

"That had to be dumb luck," Thomas said aloud.

He finished lowering the battery bag to the ground, waited until Jette had untied the cord, hauled it up, and then unlashed his radio and started to lower it to the ground.

By the time he got to the ground himself, Coizi's radioman had already installed the batteries in one radio and Colonel Coizi was talking to the reaction force at Outpost George.

"That's very interesting," Coizi said to him when he was finished. "The other tracker, Sergeant First Nambibi, brought in two of the deserters at first light."

"What's going to happen to them?" Thomas asked.

"They'll be hung as soon as we get back to Outpost George," Coizi said, as if the question surprised him.

Thomas dropped to his knees by his backpack radio, switched it on, and picked up the microphone.

"Birddog, Hunter."

"Go, Hunter."

"We have both of them," he announced.

"You sound surprised," Geoff Craig's voice responded.

"George is on the air," Thomas asked. "Coizi's been talking to them."

"I heard," Craig responded. "We went there first. What happens now?"

"The bad guys are about two klicks due east. Coizi and I are going there now. Can you hang around? If they run, I'd like to know in what direction."

"I told you, Thomas, all I can see is treetops."

"You might get lucky," Thomas replied. "I'll stay on this frequency."

"Give me a call when you're ready," Craig replied.

"Thank you, Hunter Out," Thomas said.

He tried to pick up the radio and shrug into its harness, but one of the paratroops made it clear he was going to carry it for him.

Thomas gave in, although the idea of having the Congolese paratrooper carrying his radio made him nervous.

They took off on Withers when they thought they were in trouble. What are the chances I'm going to find myself alone out here, surrounded by cannibals, while the sergeant here lopes off into the bush carrying my radio?

He walked up to Lieutenant Colonel Coizi, who was standing with Sergeant First Jette.

"Anytime you're ready, Colonel," Thomas said. "With your permission, I'll take the point."

"And I will bring up the rear," Coizi said.

"Yes, sir."

"In the Force Publique, and now in the Armée Congolaise, I learned that when you order a commander to give you so many men, the men you get are the ones he thinks he can best spare," Coizi said. "Is it thus in the Special Forces?"

"I think it was probably that way in the Roman Legions, Colonel," Thomas said, smiling.

"Under those circumstances, I think it is wise that one of us bring up the rear, to make sure that if we start out with four people, we will have four people when we reach our objective. Do I make my point?"

"Yes, sir."

Coizi motioned one of the radio bearers to him

and relieved him of his automatic rifle. He examined it carefully, then charged the action and put the sling around his neck, which allowed him to carry the weapon with his hand near the trigger.

"You two follow Major Tomas," he said. "I will bring up the rear."

He gestured toward the bush.

"Whenever you are ready, Major Tomas," he said.

Thomas checked both his Colt Car-16 and his .45 pistol to make sure they were loaded and on SAFE, then started back through the bush to the trail.

There had been no indication the previous night that establishing a perimeter guard was in the Simba field manual, and when they were what Thomas guessed was half a klick from their encampment, he waited for Colonel Coizi to catch up with him and told him so. He finished up:

"Last night, there was one man sleeping by the side of the trail, around the next curve. That was all. We just went around him, and the encampment itself was maybe four hundred meters from where he was."

"I'll have a look," Coizi said. "There is really no reason for you to go. One man makes less noise than two."

He handed Thomas his FN automatic rifle.

"I think it's best that you keep this," he said.

"Yes, sir."

Coizi left the trail and entered the bush to the left. He was gone fifteen minutes, and came back through the bush so quietly that he startled Thomas.

"About half are still asleep," he said. "I think we

should move a little back down the trail, order my troops up, and wait for them, and then conduct our operation."

"Yes, sir," Thomas said. "Sir, may I ask what your plan is?"

"Of course," Coizi said. He squatted, and swept the leaves and twigs clear from a two-foot-square area, revealing moist earth. He took a twig and drew a rough map of the area.

"Here's the encampment, on both sides of the trail. I will send a half-dozen men to deploy the far side of it."

He drew an arc facing away from the lake.

"I was thinking you and Sergeant First Jette might wish to do this. The rest of the force will be here."

He drew another arc, longer and deeper.

"When the troops are in place, I will call for their surrender. That will not happen. I think their first reaction will be to retreat east, toward the lake. This force will (a) allow the women to pass; (b) shoot the men; and (c) ensure that the cattle do not remain in the Simbas' hands."

I don't think, Thomas thought, *that allowing the women to pass reflects some Congolese notion of chivalry toward the gentle sex.*

"If I am correct, and their first reaction is to flee eastward, when the first fire they receive is from the east, they will go in the other direction, most probably right down the path, where my force will take them under fire, which will probably send them back in an easterly direction, where, again, you will kill the men and allow the women to pass."

"Sir, why are you going to allow the women to pass? As opposed to taking them prisoner?"

"If we take them prisoner, we will have to feed them," Coizi said matter-of-factly. "And letting them 'escape' is the best way I know to spread the word quickly among other Simbas that when this group went on a cattle-stealing expedition, the Armée Congolaise found them, killed the men, and did not allow the cattle to fall into Simba hands."

Ten minutes later, with the permission of Major Tomas, Sergeant First Jette selected the half-dozen shooters they would take with them to the far side of the Simba encampment.

His instructions to them were simple:

"You will follow Major Tomas. I will bring up the rear. I will shoot any man who fires his weapon before either Major Tomas fires his or I fire mine. And I will shoot any man I even suspect is thinking of going into the bush."

Forty minutes after that, Thomas found a comfortable position behind a fallen tree and called Lieutenant Colonel Coizi to report they were in position.

"Very well," Coizi replied.

Two minutes later, there was the sound of one, or perhaps two, automatic rifles being fired, and then silence. There was no way of telling whether the weapons were in the hands of Coizi's men or the Simbas.

Two minutes after that, there was the sound of cattle moving, and shortly after that, two women appeared goading a milk cow down the path. More women and two other cows appeared shortly thereafter.

Thomas could see Jette, who had taken up a position much like his, prone behind a fallen tree thick enough and high enough to provide protection against rifle fire. When he looked now, Thomas saw that Jette was taking aim with his rifle, and he flicked the lever from SAFE to SINGLE SHOT and rested his left hand on the tree trunk as he waited for a suitable target to appear.

Two suitable targets appeared, male, armed Simbas, the second of them carrying a sword as well as an FN rifle.

Thomas decided he would take whichever one of the targets remained after Jette had taken the first shot. Since Jette would almost certainly take the first male, armed Simba, Thomas took a sight picture on the chest of the Simba with the sword.

When he heard the sound of a single shot from Jette's 7-mm rifle, Thomas squeezed the trigger of the Colt Car-16. The sword-bearing Simba dropped his rifle, looked at his chest in surprise, and then fell forward on his face.

When Thomas raised his head from the stock, he was surprised to see the first Simba running toward him as fast as he could run. He lowered his head, quickly got another sight picture, and fired. It was a hasty shot, and his aim was a little off. The bullet struck the Simba on the left shoulder, which caused him to turn to the left before falling down. Thomas hit him again before he was on the ground.

He was surprised that Jette had missed him; he had naturally presumed the Congolese noncom could take a man-sized target at no more than fifty, sixty yards.

Then he saw that the milk cow had fallen forward onto its front legs, and that its head was bloody. The women who had been goading it were nowhere in sight, although there was the sound of something crashing through the brush.

The second cow and its goaders were having trouble getting past the fallen cow. Jette's rifle fired again, and the second cow staggered and then fell on its side. Its goaders, both women, ran full tilt back up the path.

There was a third shot from Jette's rifle. Thomas couldn't see either man or beast, but it seemed safe to assume Jette had taken out the third cow.

Then, for several minutes, aside from a faint and diminishing rustling in the bush, there was silence.

Then there was a fusillade of fire, including what to Thomas' ears sounded like the ripping sound of a 9-mm Uzi machine pistol.

A minute or two after that, women — ten in all — came running down the trail, singly and in pairs.

Then there came the sphincter-tightening sound a rifle projectile makes when passing within feet of one's head. And then, immediately, two more such sounds.

"Shit," Thomas said, and slid backward to take advantage of the protection the tree trunk offered.

Here lies Master Sergeant William Thomas, killed by friendly African fire.

You can take a look, asshole. Nobody's shooting at you. That fire came from some idiot who wasn't paying attention when Colonel Coizi said, "Don't shoot down the path; we have people there."

He slid sideward behind the trunk until he reached the base of the tree, which had been uprooted when the tree had fallen. He very carefully got to his knees and peered around the root structure.

876

Here lies Master Sergeant William Thomas, who took a look when he should have had enough fucking sense to keep his fucking head down.

He could see nothing but the dead cows; the two Simbas he had taken down were hidden by the bush.

Neither could he see Sergeant First Jette or any of the other shooters. There was the sound of gunfire in the distance.

Then came the sound of something crashing through the bush, and he scanned the area quickly. The first life he saw was three cows, running as fast as they could.

Fuck it, those cows never did anything to me.

Then three more women, and behind them two, three, five, seven armed males.

He debated moving the lever from SINGLE SHOT to AUTO, decided to leave it on SINGLE SHOT, and moved back up the tree trunk so that he could steady his left hand on it.

He had just taken a bead on the chest of the first of the armed males when there was a deafening burst of fire from an FN rifle on AUTOMATIC. It was right over his head, and he turned and saw two of the shooters, standing erect, firing at the Simbas.

When he turned and looked for the Simbas again, they were nowhere in sight.

He issued an order.

"Get up here behind the log, and put those weapons on single shot," he ordered.

His voice sounded funny, and it took him a moment to remember — this was not the first time this had happened to him — that he had been deafened by the weapons firing so close to his head.

The two shooters obeyed his order, taking up positions behind the trunk of the fallen tree.

And then, for perhaps three minutes — which seemed much longer — absolutely nothing happened.

There was no sound of gunfire, no noises in the bush, and there was nothing, human or animal, to be seen.

And then Sergeant First Jette appeared, far to the right. He looked around, and Thomas sensed he was looking for him. Thomas raised his arm over the tree trunk and waved it until Jette saw it and waved back. Then Jette signaled that they should move down the trail in the direction of Colonel Coizi's men.

Thomas stood up and signaled for Jette to go first, he would bring up the rear.

The odds are that some nervous soul is going to take a shot first, and identify the target later, at anything coming down that trail. Let them shoot another African, not Mrs. Thomas's favorite son, Billy.

"All right, get going," he ordered the two shooters with him. "Form on Sergeant First Jette."

And you can relax, fellows. You can run off into the bush if you want to. Doubting Thomas has done all the killing he wants to for today.

Two minutes — a hundred yards — later, there was the sound of a single shot. As a reflex action, Thomas dropped to the ground.

He could see Jette standing up, pointing his rifle at the ground, and then firing. Jette moved twenty yards and fired again at the ground.

Christ, he's shooting the wounded!

Well, maybe they're already dead, but he's making sure.

It's a lucky thing I ordered him on point. I don't think I would have wanted to do that. I don't think I could have done that.

He got to his feet and started walking again.

There was the sound of single shots being fired from what sounded like several hundred yards away.

These are not nice people. They cut Clarence Withers's head off. And his leg. And I suppose there's a good chance that at least some of them were in Stanleyville, where they cut people's livers out and ate them.

But I still don't like the idea of shooting them to make sure they're dead.

The truth seems to be, Billy Thomas, that you're not nearly as tough as you like to think you are.

"I will leave Lieutenant Breque in charge here," Colonel Coizi said. "To dispose of the Simba bodies and collect their weapons. You and I and Sergeant First Jette will return to Outpost George in the jeep."

"Yes, sir," Thomas said.

"I would like to send a truck back for the dead cattle; it would be a waste to leave it here."

"Yes, sir."

The shooter who had been carrying Thomas's radio walked up to them.

Thomas switched it on.

"Birddog, you there?"

"I was beginning to think you were some lion's lunch," Geoff Craig's voice came back immediately. "What's going on down there?"

"We bushwhacked them."

"It's over?" Even clipped by the radio, the incredulity in Craig's voice was clear.

"Yeah, it's over. The good guys won. Colonel Coizi's taking me back to George in the jeep. Any chance you could pick me up there and get me out of here?"

"I've got one of the new pilots with me. I'll have to take him to Woolworth and then come back for you."

"Please," Thomas said.

"On my way," Geoff replied. "Birddog out."

"Hunter out," Thomas said, and turned off his radio.

[TWO]
Apartment 8-D, The Immoquateur
Stanleyville, Oriental Province
Republic of the Congo
1625 9 April 1965

Master Sergeant William Thomas, Special Forces Detachment 17, was sitting, in his underwear, on a chaise lounge on the balcony of the apartment. There was a bottle of Martel cognac on the floor beside him, but no glass. It was therefore apparent to Major George Washington Lunsford when he stepped onto the balcony that Doubting Thomas had been imbibing from the neck of the Martel bottle, and equally apparent that he had done so a great many times.

"Getting a head start on the cocktail hour, are you?" Lunsford asked.

He had more or less expected Thomas to hit the bottle. "Doubting Thomas" had earned the sobriquet in Vietnam, not as any kind of reference to Saint Thomas, who had doubted Jesus's resurrection until he had proof of it, but rather because he was given to sometimes nearly immobilizing pre- and post-operation introspection. *Why are we doing this? Why is Bill Thomas doing this? Why did we do this? Why did Bill Thomas do this?*

But the operative word is "nearly," Lunsford thought. *Thomas has never failed to perform, most often superbly, whatever he's been ordered to do. But before he did it, and after, he was often emotionally torn up.*

No one had ever mocked him — beyond the sobriquet — and Lunsford had often wondered whether this was because Thomas was a genuinely tough sonofabitch, whom anyone with sense would not intentionally cross, or because everyone seemed to understand, even respect, his doubts, even if they didn't share them themselves.

"I think I'll pass on the cocktail hour, thank you just the same, Major, sir," Thomas said, carefully pronouncing each syllable.

"Take a look at this, will you?" Lunsford said, handing him a sheet of typewriter paper. Thomas took it, and with a visible effort, focused his eyes on it. "I need to get it out on the next satellite."

SECRET
HELP0025 1600 ZULU 9 APRIL 1965
VIA WHITE HOUSE SIGNAL AGENCY

FROM: HELPER SIX
TO: EARNEST SIX

AFTER ACTION REPORT #2
REFERENCE MAP BAKER 08

1-REFERENCE MY HELP 0022 6 APRIL.

2-AT APPROXIMATELY 1600 ZULU 8 APRIL 1965 MSGT WILLIAM THOMAS WHILE ADVISING A CONGOLESE RECONNAISSANCE UNIT LOCATED THE SIMBA FORCE WHICH OVERRAN OUTPOST GEORGE. AT THE TIME OF DETECTION THE SIMBA FORCE CONSISTED OF APPROXIMATELY FORTY-FIVE (45) ARMED MALES AND FIFTEEN (15) ARMED FEMALES AND WAS APPROXIMATELY FIFTEEN (15) KILOMETERS DUE EAST OF OUTPOST GEORGE. THEY WERE HERDING SIX (6) HEAD OF CATTLE STOLEN FROM THE DESERTED CATTLE RANCH AT OUTPOST GEORGE.

3-AT APPROXIMATELY 0400 ZULU 9 APRIL 1965 A CONGOLESE REACTION FORCE OF APPROXIMATELY TWENTY (20) MEN COMMANDED BY LT COL HENRI COIZI AND ADVISED BY MSGT THOMAS MADE THEIR PRESENCE KNOWN TO THE SIMBA FORCE AND CALLED FOR THEIR SURRENDER. THE SIMBA FORCE RESPONDED WITH AUTOMATIC SMALL ARMS FIRE, AND THE REACTION FORCE ENGAGED. A FIREFIGHT LASTING APPROXIMATELY FIFTEEN (15) MINUTES ENSUED.

4-LOSSES TO THE REACTION FORCE: ZERO (0) KIA; ZERO (0) WIA

5-LOSSES TO THE SIMBA FORCE THIRTY

EIGHT (38) MALE KIA; ZERO (0) FEMALE KIA UNKNOWN WIA.

6-WEAPONS RECOVERED FROM SIMBA FORCE: 41 RIFLES OF VARIOUS MANUFACTURE, INCLUDING M-14 KNOWN TO BE IN POSSESSION OF SFC WITHERS AT OUTPOST GEORGE; 34 HANDGUNS OF VARIOUS MANUFACTURE, INCLUDING 1911A1 .45 PISTOL KNOWN TO BE IN POSSESSION OF SFC WITHERS AT OUTPOST GEORGE. IN ADDITION, FIVE HEAD OF CATTLE WERE RECOVERED.

HELPER SIX

SECRET

"That about cover it, Bill?" Father asked when Thomas looked up at him.

"Why not?"

"Is it accurate, or isn't it? Should I have it sent as is, or not?"

"You left out that Colonel Coizi hung the sergeant who ran off on Withers," Thomas said.

"We weren't involved in that," Father said, "or were we?"

"What they did was make a noose of commo wire —"

"We weren't involved, were we, Bill?"

"Coizi made me watch," Thomas said. "They made a loop of commo wire and hung that from a tree. Then they backed a truck up under it, put the poor bastard on the truck, put his head in the noose, and drove the truck away. It didn't break his neck, and it wasn't even doing a good job of strangling the poor bastard, so Coizi told Sergeant First Jette to pull down on him; that tightened the noose, and after a minute or so, he stopped jerking around."

He looked at Lunsford.

"While he was jerking around, everybody laughed. Funniest thing they'd seen in years."

"It's their business, Bill, not ours."

"There would have been some WIA, too, except they went around and shot the wounded."

"This is Africa, Bill."

"We're Africans, aren't we?" Thomas asked.

"I was born in Philadelphia," Father said.

"You know what I've been thinking, Father?"

Oh, Jesus. I hope he's not going to jump on the guilt wagon. I shouldn't have let them hang the guy. I should have stopped it.

"I'm getting a real hard-on for this Guevara bastard," Thomas said.

That was the last thing Lunsford expected to hear.

"How so?"

"He wants to use these fucking people. He doesn't give a shit about them."

"You're probably right."

"Probably, my ass. I'm abso-fucking-lutely on the money. He wants to be the big tamale in South America, and if that means a couple of thousand, a couple of tens of thousands of these poor fucking savages get blown away to get him there, that's fine with him."

Lunsford didn't reply.

"I shot two guys this morning," Thomas said. "Took the first one down with a chest shot; he didn't know what hit him. The second one I hit in the shoulder, and I had to shoot him twice. Okay. So maybe they did cut Withers's head and leg off. But Withers wouldn't have been here in the first place — none of us would — if that fucking Guevara wasn't trying to take over this country."

"I have to agree, Bill."

"So if it wasn't for Che fucking Guevara, Withers would be alive, right?"

Lunsford nodded.

"And so would those two savages I popped this morning, and all those poor fucking savages Coizi's shooters got, right?"

"Right."

"And now Che fucking Guevara is about to come across Lake Tanganyika in fucking person, right?"

"That's the intel, Bill."

"And if I pop the bastard — the only sonofabitch who really deserves to be popped — my ass is in a crack, right?"

"Very seriously in a crack, Bill," Lunsford said. "Don't even think about it."

"That's what I thought you would say," Thomas said.

He picked up the bottle of Martel and held it out to Lunsford.

"You want a little taste, Father?"

"Thank you," Lunsford said, and took a pull from the bottle's neck.

"I'm trusting you on this one, Father," Thomas said. "I really would like to pop Che fucking Guevara."

"Not popping him is going to cause him, and people like him, more trouble than popping him," Lunsford said.

"So I keep hearing."

"You going to be all right, Bill?"

"Yeah. I'll just have a couple more tastes and hang it up for the day."

"You're sure?"

"I'm already shit-faced. I don't want Craig's wife to see me this way."

"You're probably right."

"Tough broad, that one," Thomas said. "Coming here to be with her man. You have to admire that. I'd like to find one like that."

"Me, too," Lunsford said, and was genuinely shocked when an image of Cecilia The Real Dar es Salaam Station Chief flashed through his mind.

God, that's strange. I don't even know her last name. What triggered that? When Doubting Thomas called Geoff's wife a "tough broad"? And that isn't the first time I've thought of her, either.

What did she say? Maybe sometime, when you're wearing shoes, we could talk about dinner again.

"You know she got out of East Berlin by crashing through the wall in a truck?" Thomas asked admiringly. "Tough broad."

"I heard," Lunsford said. "You sure you're going to be all right, Bill? You want me to hang around?"

"With all respect, Major, sir, get the fuck out of here."

[THREE]
Room 637, The Executive Office Building
Washington, D.C.
0930 21 April 1965

Mary Margaret Dunne knocked politely at the door of Colonel Sanford T. Felter, and when he

886

motioned her to enter, handed him a sheet of paper. "Just delivered, Colonel," she said.
He took it and read it.

SECRET

Central Intelligence Agency
Langley, Virginia

FROM: Assistant Director For Administration

DATE: 21 April 1965 1345 GMT

SUBJECT: Guevara, Ernesto (Memorandum # 75.)

TO: Mr. Sanford T. Felter
Counselor To The President
Room 637, The Executive Office Building
Washington, D.C.

By Officer Courier

In compliance with Presidential Memorandum to The Director, Subject: "Ernesto 'Che' Guevara," dated 14 December 1964, the following information is being furnished:

From CIA Dar es Salaam, Tanganyika (Reliability Scale Five):

1-In response to an inquiry by US Ambassador, Tanganyikan Minister of Foreign

---

Affairs denied any knowledge of Cubans anywhere in Tanganyika.

2-Accompanied by a senior Tanganyikan police official, sixteen Cubans, including Guevara and Dreke, left the Morogoro farm on two trucks 2130 Greenwich 20 April 1965.

3-They are bound for Kigoma in the Western Province. They are in civilian clothing and armed with Belgian 7-mm automatic rifles and Israeli Uzi 9-mm machine pistols, but have no heavier arms, hand grenades, explosives, or other war matériel.

4-They will travel by a circuitous route, off major highways and possibly only at night. Estimated time of arrival in Kigoma before midnight 23 April 1965.

Howard W. O'Connor
HOWARD W. O'CONNOR

SECRET

"What I think we have here, Mary Margaret," Felter said, "is the exception to the rule. The CIA station chief in Dar es Salaam seems to have all his ducks in a row."

She chuckled.

"Extract the pertinent points and satellite it

to Lunsford."

"Right away. Would you like some coffee?"

"Is there any chocolate milk?"

"Coming right up."

[FOUR]
The Hotel du Lac
Costermansville, Kivu Province
Republic of the Congo
2215 22 April 1965

Specialist Five Charles K. Anderson, who was drawing extra proficiency pay for being both an Army Security Agency high-speed intercept operator and an ASA ultrahigh-frequency radio communications technician, and who was wearing the uniform of a lieutenant of Congolese paratroops, did not look much like the popular image of a paratroop officer, Congolese or any other kind.

He was five feet five inches tall, two months past his nineteenth birthday, and weighed 165 pounds. Among his peers he was known variously as "Tubby," "Fatso," and "Lumpy," and was privately thought of by Major George Washington Lunsford as "the fat kid from East Saint Louis."

Lunsford had been genuinely concerned — for the purposes of Operation Earnest, he really needed the fat kids' technical skills, and for the fat kid himself — when Anderson had shown up, displaying a wide array of white teeth for the irregular course in parachute jumping conducted at Camp Mackall.

Lunsford was absolutely convinced that Anderson could never have made it through the first week — much less the whole parachute course — at Fort Benning, but he had made it through the one at Camp Mackall.

And now he took great pride in being a paratrooper. He had confessed to Doubting Thomas that he could hardly wait to get back to East Saint Louis wearing his wings and Corcoran jump boots.

Anderson found Major Lunsford/Lieutenant Colonel Dahdi sitting at a table with Master Sergeant Thomas/Major Tomas, and the two white officer pilots and their wives on the hotel patio overlooking the lake. Lunsford and Thomas and the wives were drinking beer. The two pilots were drinking lemonade.

Anderson marched up to Lunsford, came to attention, saluted crisply, and announced:

"Just off the satellite, sir."

Lunsford — who was not particularly fond of saluting — returned the salute with parade-ground precision.

"Stand at ease," Lunsford ordered, and reached for the sheet of paper. He read it, then handed it to Geoff Craig.

OPERATIONAL IMMEDIATE
TOP SECRET

EARS 0007 2140 ZULU 22 APRIL 1965
VIA WHITE HOUSE SIGNAL AGENCY

FROM: EARS SIX
TO: HELPER SIX

1-FOLLOWING RECEIVED LANDLINE 2105
ZULU 22 APRIL 1965 QUOTED VERBATIM

"Anderson," Lunsford ordered. "Search out Colonel Supo, present my compliments, and ask the colonel if he would be good enough to join me."

Anderson popped back to attention, said "yes, sir," saluted, waited for Lunsford to return it, did what he thought was a perfect about-face movement, and marched off the patio.

"Thomas," Lunsford said. "You know what's faster than a corporal going to his first noncom's call?"

"I'll bet you're going to tell me," Thomas said.

"A brand-new paratrooper looking for somebody to show how tough he is," Lunsford said.

"That's not nice, Father," Marjorie Bellmon said. "He's a nice kid."

"I know," Lunsford said. "That's why I don't want him trying to stomp somebody; he'd lose. Have a word with him, Sergeant Thomas."

Thomas chuckled.

"He went to Coizi," Thomas said. "Asked him, the next time the Congolese jump, could he jump with them."

"No goddamn way! I don't want him breaking a leg, or worse. You have a word with him."

"I already did."

"Then have another one," Lunsford said. "You have the map in your pocket?"

Thomas dug for it.

"Can I see that?" Marjorie asked her husband, to whom Geoff Craig had passed the message.

"Ask the boss," Jack said.

"Why not?" Lunsford said.

Jack passed it to Marjorie, who read it and passed it to Ursula.

"What's this Barefoot Boy/Katharine Hepburn business?" Marjorie asked. "What's it all about?"

"It was love at first sight," Jack said. "You could hear the violins playing, and our beloved commander was drooling all over the consulate floor." He chuckled, and added, "All over his bare feet."

"Goddamn you!" Lunsford said, but more in surprise — *Gee, did I act that way?* — than in anger.

"Who is she?"

"Ostensibly, the CIA station chief's secretary in Dar es Salaam," Jack said.

"And actually?" Marjorie asked.

"The CIA station chief," Jack said.

"Well, so much for keeping that little secret," Father said. "I hate to stop this delightful chit-chat, but . . . I read that to mean Guevara and the others are taking boats at midnight from Kigoma. Am I right?"

"It looks to me as if she has somebody in

Kigoma," Jack said. "Maybe she even went there. It said 'landline.' "

"Thomas?"

"That's how I read it," Thomas replied.

"Geoff?"

"Yeah. That's how I would read it."

"We're all set up at the field and the outposts?"

"The bad news there is that there's sometimes morning fog," Jack said. "Which maybe Guevara knows about, and is counting on to keep him invisible."

" 'Take not counsel of your fears,' " Lunsford quoted. "General George S. Patton. The question was 'we're all set up at the field and the out-posts?' "

"Aunt Jemima is at Item," Craig said. "You want me to run this by you again, right?"

Lunsford nodded.

"Aunt Jemima is at Item," Craig repeated. "He'll fly up the middle from there. I'll fly down the middle from here. Jack will fly back and forth in a fifteen-mile pattern on the middle right out from Kigoma."

"Keep in mind that middle you keep talking about is the border of Tanganyika. We can't cross it."

Jack and Geoff nodded.

Colonel Jean-Baptiste Supo, trailed by Lieutenant Colonel Henri Coizi and Major Alain George Totse, came out of the hotel.

All the American men stood up. Supo and Totse kissed the hands of the women.

"Please be seated," Supo said.

Everyone sat down.

"We have some word, I gather?" Supo said.

"We have reliable information that they will

take boats from Kigoma at midnight, sir," Lunsford said. He did not show him the satellite message.

"The question then is where will they land?" Supo replied.

"If we can find them on the water, we can follow them," Lunsford said.

"There is sometimes morning fog in the area," Supo said.

Lunsford flashed a look at Jack.

"Let's have the map, please, Thomas," Lunsford said.

When the beer and lemonade glasses had been pushed aside, and the map laid in place, Major Totse stood over it.

"My colonel," he said. "This is what Colonel Dahdi and I propose for your approval. Now that we know when the boats will leave Kigoma, things are made somewhat more simple for us.

"Colonel Dahdi and I have made the following assumptions. The boats they will use will be small launches, for any number of reasons, starting with availability, and the probability that they are going to have to land on the shore. For planning purposes, we believe there will be two launches. Launches have a top speed, depending on water conditions, of fifteen knots.

"It is approximately thirty-five miles across Lake Tanganyika from Kigoma. So the absolute minimum travel time would be just a little over two hours. We further presume that they will wish to make the journey in darkness, which means, given sunrise at 0605 tomorrow, they can travel no further, under optimum conditions, than six hours at fifteen miles per hour, or ninety miles. They have to consider that for any number of reasons — primarily their detection — they may have to return to Tanganyika. That reduces their practical area of operation to a forty-five-mile arc from Kigoma.

"That arc would extend from Kalamba in the north to Kunanwa in the south. While there are no truck-capable roads in the bush between Kalamba and Kunanwa and National Route Five, there are paths, and both villages are closer to Route Five than any other village with paths in between.

"Colonel Dahdi and I have therefore concluded the launches will have either — or perhaps both — villages as their destination. I have therefore ordered reaction forces to move near both villages on Route Five. They will have orders not to engage, simply to observe.

"To ensure compliance with that order, we recommend that Colonel Coizi command the reaction force at Kunanwa and Major Tomas command — excuse me, *advise* — the reaction force at Kalamba. The Kalamba reaction force was used at Outpost George, and the men are aware of the confidence Colonel Coizi places in Major Tomas."

He paused.

"That's about it, sir," he said.

"The only question I have is the aircraft; they will be operating at night." He looked at Jack Portet. "You can land for refueling, et cetera, at night on those primitive strips?"

"We have radio communication with them, Colonel," Jack said. "When we call, they will send a radio signal, on which we can home, and when we are close, they will light the field."

"How?" Supo asked.

"There will be sand-filled tomato cans, soaked

in gasoline, marking the runways," Jack explained. "And, at one end or the other, depending on the wind, a truck will be parked with its headlights on. The pilot will land just past the truck."

"Is this a Special Forces technique, or something you learned when you were flying here?"

"A little of both, sir."

"And you think you will be able to see small launches on Lake Tanganyika at night?"

"I think so, sir. And we're going to take observers with us — give us two pair of eyes."

"And the Guevara party will not be aware they are under observation?"

"The aircraft are painted flat black, as you know, sir. They will be hard to spot at night."

"But the sound of the engines, certainly?"

"I doubt if they will be able to hear the engines over the noise of the engines in the launches, sir, and even if they could, it's very difficult to determine the position of an aircraft by sound."

Supo grunted.

"What I am thinking, gentlemen," Supo said, "is that if it were not for you, there is absolutely no way we could have detected the infiltration of this force into the Congo."

"Have we your permission to proceed, sir?" Lunsford asked.

Supo nodded.

"You will stay here, Colonel?" he asked.

"Yes, sir."

"Good hunting, gentlemen," Supo said.

"There is one thing, Jack," Lunsford said.

"Sir?"

"Have you picked your observer?"

"Everybody wants to go," Jack said. "I thought

I'd have them draw straws."

"Would you have any problems with Anderson?"

Jack considered it a moment.

"No," he said. "Why not?"

"I'll have him waiting in the lobby for you," Father said. "Will you excuse me, sir?"

"You'll be coming back?"

"I just want to tell Spec5 — Lieutenant Fatso — that he can go with Lieutenant Portet."

"Why are you smiling, Anderson?" Major Lunsford asked.

"Well, sir, I know most of the guys in the WHSA. The one we got from Ears and this one are really going to blow their minds, trying to figure out what's being said."

"What's being said is none of their business, Anderson," Lunsford said. "And nobody here's business, either. You read me?"

"Five by five, sir."

OPERATIONAL IMMEDIATE
TOP SECRET

EARS 0007 2205 ZULU 22 APRIL 1965
VIA WHITE HOUSE SIGNAL AGENCY

FROM: HELPER SIX
TO: EARS SIX

1-REFERENCE YOUR 0007

2-AS SOON AS FEASIBLE TRANSMIT FOL-
LOWING VERBATIM TO KATHARINE HEPBURN

START MANY THANKS I AM LOOKING
FORWARD TO OUR MIDNIGHT DINNER
WITHOUT DESI ARNAZ AND HIS FRIENDS
SOMETIME SOON BAREFOOT BOY

END

HELPER SIX

TOP SECRET

[FIVE]
**4 Degrees 47 Minutes 37 Seconds South
Latitude
29 Degrees 3 Minutes 09 Seconds East
Longitude
3,000 Feet Above Lake Tanganyika
0305 23 April 1965**

"Hey, Lieutenant!" Spec5 Anderson cried excit-
edly, "there's a couple of boats down there!"

"Can you be a little more specific, Fatso?" Jack
asked.

"Out the right side," Anderson replied. "A little
bit behind the wing."

"The way we say that, Fatso," Jack said as he
put the L-19 into a shallow turn to the left, "is
'possible sighting at 4:30.' Imagine a clock."

"Yes, sir," Spec5 Anderson said, chagrined.

"Specialist Anderson," Jack said a moment
later, "I think you have just won first prize in the
Find-The-Floating-Bastards Contest. The prizes
are both a cement bicycle and an all-expenses-

paid visit to the whorehouse of your choice in downtown Costermansville."

"You think that's them, Lieutenant?"

"Well, who else do you think would be headed across Lake Tanganyika at three-oh-five in the morning without running lights?"

"Jesus!" Anderson said.

"Get on the horn, Anderson, and call Helper Base. Say we have two unidentified launches just across the border on a straight-line course toward Kay One; estimate distance to Kay One fifty klicks."

"Yes, sir," Spec5 Anderson said.

[SIX]
**4 Degrees 50 Minutes 57 Seconds South
    Latitude
29 Degrees 17 Minutes 40 Seconds East
    Longitude
(4 Miles East of Kalamba, Kivu Province,
    Congo)
0525 23 April 1965**

"Hunter One, Birddog One."

"Go."

"They just turned north, toward shore, and are slowing down. I guess maybe seven, eight klicks West of Kay One. They are maybe a klick and a half from shore."

"Understand seven, eight klicks west, klick and a half from shore."

"You got it."

"Maybe you better haul ass; it's getting light. We don't want them to see you."

"I'll go up a little, and south. Let me know when you see them."

"They have some friends here."

"Interesting. Watch yourself."

"Birddog One, Hunter One."

"Go."

"I can't see them, but I can hear them. They're coming right at us."

"Okay. We're gone. Birddog one clear."

Master Sergeant William Thomas had taken with him two night-vision devices. One looked much like an outsize set of binoculars, and, since it was too heavy to hold to the eyes, came with a folding tripod. A cable ran from the "binoculars" to a large battery pack that sat on the ground.

The other was mounted on a U.S. Springfield Caliber .30-06 Rifle, Model 1903A4, and looked something like an oversight telescopic sight. It, too, had a power cable, which ran to a battery pack equipped with web straps, much like a rucksack.

The rifle-mounted device was not a binocular, nor as powerful as the other device, but there was really no way Thomas could have hauled it aloft in the tree he had chosen to surveil the shore of Lake Tanganyika.

And the rifle-mounted device had performed better than he thought it would.

He had picked up the launches when they were almost one thousand yards from the beach, and as they drew closer, he could make out first the forms of men aboard them, and ultimately, as they reached the beach, even facial characteristics.

One of the sixteen men who debarked from the second launch had an unlit cigar in his mouth. He was bald and clean-shaven.

Before he had completely waded ashore, a half-dozen men came out of the bush to greet him.

They embraced warmly.

The bald and clean-shaven man with the unlit cigar in his mouth, and one of the men who had come out of the bush, stood and watched the other men jump out of the launches into the shallow water, then begin to transport small packages and small arms from the launches to the shore.

The rifle-mounted light-intensifying sight had crosshairs. The rifle had been sighted at 150 yards.

Master Sergeant Thomas took a sight picture on the head of the bald, clean-shaven man with an unlit cigar in his mouth, and waited patiently, his finger on the trigger, until — as he knew he would — the bald, clean-shaven man with an unlit cigar in his mouth turned to look around, and he could center on the crosshairs on his nose.

He squeezed the trigger.

The firing pin extended into the empty chamber of the U.S. Springfield Caliber .30-06 Rifle, Model 1903A4. There was a metallic click.

"Got you, you Cuban cocksucker," Master Sergeant Thomas said with great satisfaction in his voice, then started to climb down from the tree.

[SEVEN]

SECRET
HELP0025 1050 ZULU 23 APRIL 1965
VIA WHITE HOUSE SIGNAL AGENCY

FROM: HELPER SIX
TO: EARNEST SIX

AFTER ACTION REPORT #9
REFERENCE MAP BAKER 08

1-AT APPROXIMATELY 0600 ZULU 23 APRIL 1965 SIXTEEN (16) ARMED MEN LANDED SURREPTITIOUSLY FROM TWO LAUNCHES APPROXIMATELY FIVE (5) KILOMETERS WEST OF KALAMBA, KIVU PROVINCE, CONGO.

2-THE LAUNCHES WERE PREVIOUSLY DETECTED BY SPEC5 CHARLES K. ANDERSON, AN OBSERVER ABOARD AN L19 PILOTED BY 1LT JACQUES PORTET CROSSING THE TANGANYIKA/CONGO BORDER. AFTER DISEMBARKING THE INFILTRATORS, THE LAUNCHES WERE OBSERVED ON A COURSE WHICH WOULD TAKE THEM TO KIGOMA, TANGAN-YIKA.

3-ONE OF THE INFILTRATORS WAS POSITIVELY IDENTIFIED AS MAJOR ERNESTO GUEVARA BY MSGT WILLIAM THOMAS, WHO ALSO BELIEVES MAJOR DREKE WAS IN THE PARTY. ALL BUT GUEVARA ARE NEGRO.

4-THE INFILTRATORS ARE APPARENTLY UNAWARE THAT THEY HAVE BEEN DETECTED. COLONEL JEAN-BAPTISTE SUPO BELIEVES THEIR DESTINATION WILL BE LULUABOURG IN KASAI PROVINCE, TO WHICH THEY WILL TRAVEL IN GROUPS OF

TWO OR THREE IN FARM VEHICLES. SUPO
HAS ISSUED ORDERS STATING THEY ARE TO
BE ALLOWED TO PASS THE CHECKPOINTS
HE HAS ESTABLISHED.

5-DETECTION OF THE INFILTRATORS WAS
MADE POSSIBLE BY EXTRAORDINARILY
ACCURATE AND TIMELY INTEL FURNISHED
BY STAFF OF CIA STATION CHIEF DAR ES
SALAAM.

HELPER SIX

SECRET

[EIGHT]
The Hotel du Lac
Costermansville, Kivu Province
Republic of the Congo
2105 23 April 1965

Master Sergeant William Thomas had just con-
fided in First Lieutenant Geoffrey Craig that he had
the crosshairs right on the bastard's nose when
Spec5 Kenneth Anderson walked into the bar with
a message.

"I suppose I can show you this, Lieutenant," he
said. "Before I show it to the major."

Craig read it, and said, "Congratulations,
Fatso, well-deserved."

He handed it to Master Sergeant Thomas,
who read it, snorted, and said, "The fucking

903

Green Hornet.[1] I will be damned."

```
SECRET
EARN0051 WASH DC 1910 ZULU 23 APRIL
1965
VIA WHITE HOUSE SIGNAL AGENCY

FROM: EARNEST SIX
TO: HELPER SIX

1-FOLLOWING FROM PRESIDENT OF THE
UNITED STATES QUOTE WELL DONE. KEEP
UP THE GOOD WORK END QUOTE.

2-BY VERBAL ORDER OF THE PRESIDENT OF
THE UNITED STATES, THE ARMY
COMMENDATION MEDAL IS AWARDED TO
1LT JACQUES PORTET, MSGT WILLIAM
THOMAS, AND SPEC5 KENNETH ANDERSON.
FURTHER, BY DIRECTION OF THE PRESIDENT
SPEC5 ANDERSON IS PROMOTED TO
SPECIALIST SIX.

3-EARNEST SIX HAS RELAYED YOUR
APPRECIATION OF EFFORTS OF STAFF OF
CIA DAR ES SALAAM TO DIRECTOR CIA.

FINTON FOR EARNEST SIX

SECRET
```

[1] The Army Commendation Medal, often referred to derisively as "The Green Hornet," is represented by a green ribbon with vertical white stripes. It is usually awarded for noncombat administrative excellence and ranks immediately above the Good Conduct Medal, which is awarded for three years' service without disciplinary infraction.

XXIII

Major Guevara (using the pseudonym Tatu) and the vanguard of Column One entered the Congo 23 April 1965, beginning the tremendous, heroic effort of revitalizing the Lumumbist forces to make them the nucleus of a new liberation army which would halt the enemy offensive and begin to recover the positions that had been lost. It was too late, for the Congolese people's rebellion was being wiped out by enormously superior enemy forces.

— "Cuban Involvement in Liberation Efforts in the Congo,"
Government Printing Office, Havana, Cuba, 1995

[ONE]

TOP SECRET
1820 GREENWICH 25 APRIL 1965
FROM STATION CHIEF, BUENOS AIRES

TO DIRECTOR, CIA, LANGLEY
COPIES TO SOUTH AMERICAN DESK
    MR SANFORD T. FELTER,
    COUNSELOR TO THE PRESIDENT

THE EXECUTIVE OFFICE BUILDING
WASHINGTON

THE FOLLOWING RECEIVED FROM US ARMY
OFFICER ASSIGNED US EMBASSY BELIEVED
TO BE CONTROLLED BY MR. FELTER. IT IS
RECOMMENDED THAT THE INTELLIGENCE
FOLLOWING BE REGARDED AS THE
EQUIVALENT OF CIA RELIABILITY SCALE FIVE.
IT IS TRANSMITTED IN ITS ENTIRETY AND
VERBATIM.

START

DEAR FRIENDS:

THANK YOU FOR THE INFORMATION
REGARDING THE TOURING CUBANS.

UNDER CAPTAIN SANTIAGO TERRY, WHO IS
BOTH A SKILLED GUERRILA AND A
DEDICATED COMMUNIST, APPROXIMATELY
ONE HUNDRED THIRTY (130) NEGRO
CUBAN SOLDIERS ARE EN ROUTE BY TRUCK
FROM CAMPS PITA 1 AND PITA 3 IN PINA
DEL RIO PROVINCE TO THE PORT OF
MATANZAS WHERE THEY WILL BOARD THE
CUBAN VESSEL "UVERA," A SMALL
FREIGHTER. THEY ARE CARRYING WITH
THEM A QUANTITY OF SMALL ARMS AND
OTHER WAR MATÉRIEL.

THE CAPTAIN OF THE "UVERA" HAS
OBTAINED FROM THE OBLIGING CAPTAIN

OF THE GREEK FLAGGED VESSEL "ACHILLES," NOW IN THE PORT OF SANTIAGO DE CUBA NAUTICAL CHARTS (INCLUDING TIDES) OF THE WEST COAST OF AFRICA, SPECIFICALLY OF THOSE LEADING TO THE PORT OF POINTE NOIRE IN THE FORMER FRENCH CONGO (CONGO BRAZZAVILLE). THE "UVERA" IS SCHEDULED TO SAIL AT 0400 CUBAN TIME 27 APRIL 1965.

UNDER THESE CIRCUMSTANCES IT SEEMS REASONABLE TO PRESUME THAT OUR MEDICAL FRIEND HAS DECIDED TO TEST THE EFFICACY OF REINFORCING HIS ARMY OF LIBERATION VIA CONGO BRAZZAVILLE.

AND SPEAKING OF OUR FRENCH AND GERMAN FRIENDS, YOU MIGHT WISH TO KEEP AN EYE, AS WE AND OUR MUTUAL GERMAN FRIEND ARE, ON THE FRENCH JOURNALIST REGIS DEBRAY, AND THE ARGENTINE/EAST GERMAN HAYDEE TAMARA BUNKE, WHO CALLS HERSELF TANIA. AN EXCHANGE HERE WOULD BE HELPFUL, TOO.

WITH OUR BEST REGARDS TO ALL OF YOU

END

J. P. STEPHENS
STATION CHIEF BUENOS AIRES

TOP SECRET

[TWO]
The Situation Room
The Pentagon
Washington, D.C.
05550 28 April 1965

Colonel Sanford T. Felter was in uniform. He was well aware that among the uniformed laborers in the Pentagon, the term "civilian" was almost always preceded by an — unspoken — profanity, "Goddamn."

His uniform wore the General Staff Identification Badge, and hanging around his neck on a dog-tag chain was a plastic identification badge, with a photograph of him in uniform. Its color and stripes identified him as an officer authorized access to the most secure areas of the Pentagon, including the offices of the Joint Chiefs of Staff — the offices of the Chairman, the Chiefs of Staff of the Army and Air Force, the Chief of Naval Operations, and the Commandant of the Marine Corps — and the Situation Room.

He sat, sipping at a mug of tea, in the rear of three rows of theaterlike seats against the wall. There were other colonels, and some one- and two-star generals and admirals, and a half-dozen ("Goddamn") civilian officials in the other seats. Felter was reasonably confident that if anyone noticed him at all, it would be presumed he was a gofer for one of the very senior Army general officers seated at the curving table between the seats and the wall of cathode-ray-tube displays.

The cathode-ray displays showed the location of American forces — a fleet of USAF C-130 transports with a regiment of the 82nd Airborne Division and a U.S. naval force of a hundred-odd ships — heading from the United States toward Santo Domingo, the capital of the Dominican Republic.

The Dominican Republic occupies the eastern two-thirds of an island 500 miles long and 150 miles wide, which sits 50 miles east of the U.S. naval base at Guantánamo Bay, Cuba, and about as far west of Puerto Rico. Haiti occupies the western third of the island.

The President of the United States had decided it was necessary to establish an American military presence in the Dominican Republic in order to preserve peace, protect lives, and keep its government from being overthrown by Communists.

The 82nd Airborne would jump on Santo Domingo at 0555 hours. It was believed the element of surprise would permit the paratroopers to land without serious opposition, seize the airfield, and prepare to receive reinforcements, which would be landed by — not parachuted from — a second and third wave of C-130s.

The transport aircraft would be protected both by USAF fighters from Homestead Air Force Base outside Miami, and by Navy fighters aboard aircraft carriers in the naval element. The naval element of the incursion force included a force of U.S. Marines who were prepared to invade a hostile shore, if this proved necessary, and to reinforce the Army.

Felter's attention was on one of the smaller displays, which showed the area from Havana, Cuba, to San Juan, Puerto Rico. It was data-relayed, some of it real-time, from satellites passing over, and from long-distance radar aboard Air Force radar planes and from radar aboard vessels of the naval element.

Every vessel on the sea appeared on the display, not unlike the displays used in air traffic control. Every vessel had a symbol, and most of them a code, that identified them.

Some did not, including one unidentified surface vessel apparently on a course from the north coast of Cuba that would place it in the path of the naval element. It was tentatively identified as a small merchant vessel of unknown ownership.

Felter watched with interest when this vessel was suddenly surrounded by a yellow circle. He was not surprised when, almost immediately, an adjacent display screen suddenly changed its display to another, closer-in, view of the unidentified surface vessel.

He sat his teacup on the floor under his seat and walked to the row of controllers. He quickly found the controller's display, which was a duplicate of the wall display of the close-up of the unidentified surface vessel. The controller was a Navy commander, who wore a headset, with a microphone before his lips.

The controller sensed Felter standing behind him.

"Colonel?" he asked.

"What have you got, Commander?"

The commander checked Felter's identification badge before answering.

"A medium-sized vessel, probably a merchantman, on a course that'll put it in the path of the naval element. But it may be a Russian intel vessel. I'm about to find out."

He pressed a lever that activated his microphone.

"Admiral," he said. "We have an unidentified

surface vessel on a course which will cross the naval element — possibly a Soviet intel trawler."

A vice admiral came to the controller, looked curiously at Felter, then at the display.

"Recommendation?" the vice admiral asked.

"Send a fighter from Navy Three to have a look," the commander said.

"I wish you wouldn't do that," Felter said.

"I beg your pardon, Colonel?" the vice admiral said, a little testily.

"Sir, I suspect that vessel is the Cuban vessel *Uvera*," Felter said. "I would rather they not know they've been surveilled. I recommend that we get a satellite identification."

"Thank you for you recommendation, Colonel," the vice admiral said sarcastically. "Commander, send a fighter from the naval element."

"Aye, aye, sir."

Felter walked to the row of desks where the very senior officers were seated.

"Admiral," he said to the Chairman of the Joint Chiefs of Staff.

"What can I do for you, Felter?"

"You're about to send a Navy aircraft to identify a ship off the coast of Cuba. I believe that ship to be the Cuban merchantman *Uvera*, not a Soviet intel trawler, and I don't want them to know they're being surveilled. I'd like it identified by satellite."

"You're going to tell me why, right, Colonel?"

"I believe she's carrying a force of about 120 Cubans to Congo Brazzaville, sir. I want them to think they're doing so secretly."

"Excuse me, Admiral," the Director of the CIA said. Felter had not seen him enter the room.

"Yeah, Dick?"

"I recommend you go with Felter's recommendation."

"Oh, Jesus H. Christ!" the Chairman of the Joint Chiefs said, then raised his voice. "Tennyson!"

The vice admiral scurried to the Chairman's position.

"If you've launched a plane to identify the ship Colonel Felter's talking about, abort the mission. Get the next satellite passing over to downlink a photo, and then run it through the computer. Give the results to me, the Director, and Colonel Felter."

"Aye, aye, sir."

"Thank you, sir," Felter said.

"We'll be in the movie seats, Admiral," the Director said to the vice admiral.

"Yes, sir," the vice admiral said.

"Thank you," Felter said to the Director when they were in the row of seats.

"Felter, we're on the same team. I like it a lot better when we're cooperating, not protecting our turf like a couple of mailmen fighting over delivery routes."

"I do, too," Felter confessed.

"When I saw you tilting your lance at that formidable Naval windmill, Don Quixote," the Director said, "I had one of my few inspirations."

Felter smiled.

"Which was?"

"What we have in Africa is a war between your people and my man in Léopoldville and a love affair between your people and my man in Dar es Salaam —"

"Maybe that's because your man in Dar es

Salaam isn't a man," Felter interrupted.

"You do hear things, Felter, don't you?" the Director said, smiling.

"Sometimes," Felter said, returning the smile.

"I would like to improve that situation," the Director said.

"I'm all for it. How?"

"What I thought, off the top of my head, is a conference in either Léopoldville or Dar es Salaam. I'll send someone senior — I'm thinking of Howard O'Connor — with orders to tell everybody to stop the bickering. If you were to send someone . . ."

"Léopoldville," Felter said. "I can't go myself. I can send Lieutenant Colonel Lowell. I will, if you also tell O'Connor he and Lowell will be there as equals."

"When?"

"How long will it take O'Connor to pack his bags?"

"You think I should propose to the Secretary of State that he send someone too?"

"I think that would unnecessarily complicate a good, simple idea."

Fifteen minutes later, the vice admiral walked up to Felter and the Director.

"Mr. Director, we ran a downlinked satellite photograph of the vessel in question through the naval computer. It has been identified, with a ninety-seven percent positivity, as the Cuban merchant vessel *Uvera*. I have details —"

"That won't be necessary, Admiral," the Director said. "All Colonel Felter and I wanted was to make sure, (a) that it was the *Uvera* and, (b) that they not be aware we know where

913

they are, and are going."

"Yes, sir."

"Admiral," Felter said, "would it be possible to send one of the flanking destroyers of the naval force close enough to the *Uvera* so that it would be seen? Taking no action, of course. I think if they saw a destroyer that did not inspect them, they might change course, in the belief they had escaped detection."

"Good idea, Felter," the Director said.

"I'll have the necessary orders issued, sir," the vice admiral said.

[THREE]

SECRET
EARN0059 WASH DC 1235 ZULU 4 MAY 1965
VIA WHITE HOUSE SIGNAL AGENCY

FROM: EARNEST SIX
TO: HELPER SIX

1-LTCOL CRAIG W. LOWELL REPRESENTING COL FELTER AND CWO (4) JAMES L. FINTON WILL DEPART WASHINGTON DC 1400 ZULU 6 MAY 1965 TWA FLIGHT 233 TO BRUSSELS AND DEPART BRUSSELS 0830 ZULU 7 MAY 1965 UFA 4545 TO LÉOPOLDVILLE. A SENIOR CIA OFFICER REPRESENTING DIRECTOR CIA AND AN ASSISTANT WILL TRAVEL TO LÉOPOLDVILLE APPROXIMATELY SAME DATES AND ROUTE BUT DIFFERENT AIRLINES NOT KNOWN TO UNDERSIGNED.

2-A CONFERENCE BETWEEN THE ABOVE, PLUS CIA STATION CHIEFS LÉOPOLDVILLE AND DAR ES SALAAM, PLUS ONE STAFF MEMBER OF EACH WILL BE SCHEDULED AS SOON AS POSSIBLE AFTER ALL PARTIES ARE IN LÉOPOLDVILLE. CIA STATION CHIEF LÉOPOLDVILLE WILL COORDINATE.

3-INASMUCH AS CONFERENCE SHOULD BE AS INCONSPICUOUS AS POSSIBLE LOWELL AND FINTON WILL TRAVEL IN CIVILIAN STATUS, AND EARNEST SIX SUGGESTS IF POSSIBLE CONFERENCE BE HELD IN HOME OF CAPTAIN PORTET.

4-YOU ARE DIRECTED TO MEET LOWELL AND FINTON ON ARRIVAL IN LÉOPOLDVILLE NOT IN US UNIFORM REPEAT NOT IN US UNIFORM AND ARRANGE FOR THEIR QUARTERS AND TRANSPORTATION. YOU AND SUCH US OFFICERS AS YOU MAY DESIGNATE WILL PARTICIPATE IN CONFERENCE NOT IN US UNIFORM.

FINTON FOR EARNEST SIX

SECRET

[FOUR]
404 Avenue Leopold
Léopoldville, Republic of the Congo
1930 8 May 1965

There were three Congolese paratroopers in front of the gate in the fence that surrounded the Portet property. One of them, a lieutenant, stepped in front of the black 1964 Chevrolet with a Corps Diplomatique license plate and identification badge and held his hand out to make it stop. The other two moved so, should it be necessary, they could quickly train their FN 7-mm automatic rifles on the car.

"What the hell is this?" D. Patrick O'Hara, who was the Deputy to the Assistant Director of the CIA for Sub-Saharan Africa, said to Mr. Howard W. O'Connor, the CIA's Assistant Director for Administration. Both were in somewhat mussed tropical-weight gray suits.

"We don't have diplomatic status," O'Connor said, and then added, "I would like to know what the hell is going on with all of this."

The embassy chauffeur stopped and rolled down his window.

"This is a U.S. Embassy car," the driver said.

The Congolese paratrooper lieutenant did not seem very impressed.

"Papers, please," he said in French.

"Can they do that to an embassy car?" D. Patrick O'Hara asked.

"Just give him your goddamn passport," Howard W. O'Connor said.

The Congolese lieutenant examined the passports and handed them back.

916

"Invitation, please?" he asked.

O'Connor fumbled in the pocket of his suit and handed it over.

Captain and Madame Jacques Emile Portet

Request The Honor of the Presence Of

HON. HOWARD O'CONNOR
AND GUEST

At cocktails and dinner to honor

Lieutenant General Joseph Désiré Mobutu
404 Avenue Leopold
Léopoldville, Republic of the Congo

At half past seven o'clock

1930 8 May 1965

The paratroop lieutenant examined the invitation, returned it, saluted, and motioned for the driver to proceed.

Three minutes later, an identical black Chevrolet, also bearing Corps Diplomatique insignia, rolled up. This one contained a black man and a black woman. The paratroop lieutenant held out his hand to stop the car, and the driver rolled down the window and protested that he was

917

driving a U.S. Embassy car carrying two American diplomats.

A major of Congolese paratroops in crisply starched camouflage fatigues stepped out from behind one of the gateposts.

"The lady is known to me, Lieutenant," he said in Swahili. "The man I never saw before. Check him carefully."

"Yes, my major," the lieutenant said, and did so.

Two minutes later — which seemed longer — it was apparent to the lieutenant that the man's papers were in order. He reported this to the major.

"Let them pass, then," the major said.

The car began to move.

As it passed the gatepost, the black lady ordered, rather imperatively, the driver to stop. The Chevrolet jerked to a stop. The lady rolled the window down.

"Well, look who got himself a pair of shoes," she said, and then, before he could reply, ordered the driver to drive on.

There were three houseboys in immaculate, stiffly starched jackets, black trousers, and no shoes, inside the door of the Portet home.

"Good evening, sir," Nimbi said, in French, to Howard W. O'Connor and his guest. "If you will be good enough to follow Ali, cocktails are being served by the pool."

Ali smiled at the two Americans and signaled to them that he would lead them to the pool.

O'Connor saw that a bar had been set up at the pool, that beyond the pool were two tennis courts, and beyond the tennis courts, the area was ringed

918

by Congolese paratroops, one every fifteen yards, keeping the fence under surveillance.

A strikingly beautiful young woman greeted them as they reached the pool.

"You must be Mr. O'Connor," she said.

"Yes, I am, and this is Mr. O'Hara."

"I'm Marjorie Portet," she said. "Welcome to my home . . . actually, my father- and mother-in-law's home. And welcome to the Congo, too, I suppose."

"Thank you very much," O'Connor said. "We're delighted to be here. Is there a Mr. Lowell here?"

"There's a *Colonel* Lowell here," Marjorie said. "Actually, tonight is his idea. He's over there with General Mobutu and Colonel Supo."

She inclined her head to indicate the bar.

O'Connor saw a tall, handsome white man in a white dinner jacket, the lapel of which sagged under the weight of an impressive array of miniature medals. There was an enormous medal of some sort hanging around his neck from a purple sash.

With him were two other white men in dinner jackets, and two Congolese officers, one in what in the U.S. Army would be called a Class A uniform, and the other in starched camouflage fatigues. The latter O'Connor recognized from his photos as Lieutenant General Joseph Désiré Mobutu, Minister for Defense and Chief of Staff of the Armée National Congolaise.

"Why don't you come with me?" Marjorie said. "Everybody's here but the people from Dar es Salaam, I think. I'll introduce you."

"Thank you very much," O'Connor said.

They started toward the group at the bar.

At the opposite end of the pool, there was another small group of people. Two white men in suits not unlike those of O'Connor and O'Hara, and two more in white dinner jackets were sitting at a table with a blond young woman. There was an infant on the table, being fed a banana by an enormous black woman.

The two men in the dark business suits got to their feet when they saw O'Connor and O'Hara, and intercepted them before they got to the bar.

"Good evening, sir," one of them said respectfully to O'Connor.

"Hello, Charley," O'Connor said to the CIA station chief, Léopoldville. He nodded at his deputy.

He desperately wanted to ask him what was going on, but with Madame Portet with them, that was obviously out of the question.

"We're about to meet General Mobutu," O'Connor said. "Have you met him?"

"Tonight," Charley said. "For the first time."

O'Connor resumed his walk toward Mobutu.

Craig Lowell smiled at O'Connor when he saw him coming.

A smile, O'Connor decided, *that is less an offer of friendship than one of amusement, and amusement at the expense of Howard W. O'Connor. I came here to do business, not attend a pool party.*

"And this, my general," Lowell said in French, and gesturing with his martini glass at O'Connor, "is the distinguished Howard W. O'Connor, Deputy Director of our Central Intelligence Agency."

"How do you do, General?" O'Connor said. "May I present my colleague, Mr. O'Hara?"

Mobutu shook their hands and said, "And these are my friends Dr. Dannelly and Colonel Jean-

Baptiste Supo," Mobutu said.

Everybody shook hands.

"And I think you know Mr. Finton, don't you?" Lowell asked.

"Good evening, sir," Finton said.

A houseboy appeared for their drink order.

O'Connor debated asking for something soft, but lost his resolve and ordered a gin and tonic. O'Hara followed his lead.

"I've been telling the general," Lowell said. "That you have taken the time from your very busy schedule to come here to coordinate our mutual efforts with regard to Señor Guevara and his friends."

"That's true," O'Connor said, and blurted, "And when are we going to have the time for that, Colonel?"

"I thought we'd do it over after dinner coffee," Lowell said. "I met with Colonel Supo and Major Lunsford this afternoon, and went over their plans. All we have to do is fit the CIA and its assets into the plan. That shouldn't take long."

O'Connor searched for words to reply.

"As I told the General," Lowell went on, "Colonel Felter meant it when he said this is a cooperative effort and we are going to have no secrets from Colonel Supo or General Mobutu. You don't have any problems with that, do you, Mr. O'Connor?"

Goddamn! O'Connor thought. *What the hell is wrong with the Director? He should have known Felter would sandbag him!*

"No, of course not," O'Connor said as sincerely as he could.

Lowell smiled at him, then looked over his shoulder.

"Well, everybody's here, I see," he said.

The secretary to the Consul General of the United States in Dar es Salaam and that luminary himself were being escorted across the lawn toward them.

"General," O'Connor said, "this is Mr. James Foster, the United States Consul General in Dar es Salaam, and his assistant, Miss Cecilia Taylor."

"How do you do?" Mobutu said, and there was another round of introductions, during which Lieutenant Colonel Dahdi — who had had to walk from the gate to the house — showed up.

"Actually, General," O'Connor announced, "Mr. Foster has duties beyond Consul General in Dar es Salaam."

"You are right, Major," General Mobutu said in Swahili, "she really is something to look at! An absolute beauty!"

"Well, since it's truth time," Lowell said, "why don't we confide in General Mobutu that Miss Taylor is actually the Dar es Salaam CIA station chief?"

"So Major Lunsford led me to believe," Mobutu said in French.

"Unfortunately, General," Cecilia Taylor said in perfect Swahili, "Major Lunsford talks too much."

Mobutu laughed out loud.

"You speak Swahili very well, mademoiselle," Mobutu said in French. "Are you familiar with the Swahili saying?" — he gave the saying in Swahili.

Dannelly and Supo laughed. Supo waved his finger — naughty boy — at Father Lunsford, who looked very uncomfortable.

"I've heard that, yes," Cecilia replied in French, and looked very uncomfortable.

"I don't speak Swahili," Lowell said.

"Or I," O'Connor said.

"What does it mean, Father?" Lowell asked.

"Not me," Father said.

"You may consider that an order to translate the General's comments, Major Lunsford," Lowell said.

For a moment, it looked as if Lunsford was going to refuse the order. Then he looked at Cecilia Taylor, who said, "Don't you dare!"

"Man who thinks he's in love can be counted upon to behave like orangutan in heat," he translated, "and show the world his red ass."

"If you gentlemen will excuse me," Cecilia said, "I think I will go powder my nose."

"Thanks a lot, General," Father said when she was out of sight.

"I wouldn't worry, my friend," Mobutu said. "She likes you. I could see it in her eyes. Women can sense warriors, and warriors attract women."

[FIVE]

Immediately after the dessert plates had been cleared from the table, as houseboys served both coffee and cognac, two Congolese paratroopers carried first a tripod, and then a map board, into the dining room.

I'll be a sonofabitch! He's actually going to do it! Howard W. O'Connor thought.

Lieutenant Colonel Craig W. Lowell stood up, cradling a cognac glass in his hand, rolling the cognac around in the glass.

"This is where, in times past," Lowell said, looking at O'Connor, "the ladies retired, while the gentlemen sipped at their cognac and puffed on their cigars. But times have changed, and I would like to begin this session by offering my thanks, and that of Colonel Felter, to Marjorie and Ursula. Major Lunsford has told me how much they have contributed to Operation Earnest. Thank you, ladies."

I'll be a sonofabitch! O'Connor thought again.

Colonel Supo clapped his hands, and in a moment, General Mobutu joined in.

This has gone too goddamn far!

"Colonel," O'Connor said. "I feel that I have to raise the question of security."

"This place is secure, Howard," Lowell said. "With General Mobutu here, it's probably the most secure place in the Congo."

I didn't tell this sonofabitch he could call me by my Christian name!

"I was referring to the ladies' security clearances," O'Connor said.

"Oh. Well, Howard, the ladies have Top Secret/Earnest clearances."

"But they're not government employees, Colonel, they're dependents."

"Major Lunsford, who granted the clearances, knew that, Howard," Lowell said. "Anything else?"

O'Connor shook his head, no, but then asked, "Lunsford has the authority to grant clearances?"

"Three of us do," Lowell said. "Colonel Felter, Major Lunsford, and myself. It's all in order, Howard."

"Mon general," Lowell asked in French. "Would you like to say anything before we begin?"

Mobutu shook his head, no.

"Mon colonel?"

Supo shook his head, no.

"I understand you would like to have Major Lunsford take this over?"

"I have not the good English," Supo explained.

"Major Lunsford?" Lowell said, motioning Lunsford to his feet and then helping him pull the sheet of oilcloth that covered the map over the top of the map board. Lunsford then stepped in front of the map. He held part of a billiards cue in his hand, to use as a pointer.

"Guevara and the other Cubans," he said in French, "who entered the Congo on 23 April reached Luluabourg . . . here" — he pointed out Luluabourg with the cue — "in the early-morning hours of 7 May, yesterday. A second group of approximately 130 Cubans, under Captain Santiago Terry, debarked from the Cuban vessel *Uvera* in Pointe Noire, Congo Brazzaville, at 0600 6 May. Nineteen of them, under Captain Terry, were immediately trucked to the Congo River, near Matadi" — he used the pointer again — "and entered the Congo here, where they were met by Laurent Mitoudidi, who calls himself 'general' and is *chef de cabinet* of the revolutionary staff military council. . . ."

"May I ask, Major," O'Hara asked in not very good French, "the source of your intelligence?"

"Colonel Supo," Lunsford replied.

"We are not completely without intelligence sources," Mobutu said, sarcastically, in French.

"We believe they will reach Luluabourg either today or early tomorrow," Lunsford went on. "Orders have been issued to the roadblocks to let them pass."

"May I ask why?" O'Connor asked.

"*One,*" Lunsford said, "nineteen Cubans aren't going to make a perceptible change in the insurgent forces; *two,* this way, we'll have all the Cubans in one place; and *three,* they will not be aware that we have them under surveillance. And, maybe, *four:* there were 130 men and a quantity of arms on the *Uvera.* Inasmuch as they think their route into the Congo is secure, they will probably use the same route to move both men and matériel in a truck convoy, bypassing the roadblocks when possible, and overrunning the roadblocks they can't bypass. We're working on a plan to have the convoy disappear."

"Disappear?" O'Connor asked.

"We will surveil their progress from the entry point at the Congo River to Luluabourg. They don't have many options so far as a route goes — it's either National Route Five, Sixteen, or Twenty — and at the appropriate point, we will simply make the supply convoy disappear. The Cubans will be moved somewhere — probably Stanleyville — where they can be secretly court-martialed —"

"Court-martialed?" O'Connor interrupted. "*Secretly* court-martialed?"

"International law permits the court-martial of armed foreign nationals detected in a country during an armed insurrection, with the intent of supporting the insurrection," Lunsford said as if delivering a classroom lecture. "The details of the court-martial — court-martials — do not have to be made public until the insurrection has been suppressed, and law and order restored, when they are required to be furnished to the International Court of Justice in The Hague."

"In other words, you intend to shoot the Cubans?" O'Connor said.

"It's my understanding, Howard," Lowell said,

"that with the exception of Guevara, whom the Congolese government, like our own, does not wish to make into a martyr, the Congolese government intends to court-martial any foreign national who comes to the Congo armed, and intending to join or assist the insurgents. What punishment will be meted out is, of course, something the Congolese will determine."

In other words, yes, you're going to shoot the Cubans.

"That's one of the places where you, or at least your airplanes, come in, Howard," Lowell went on. "Colonel Supo may have to move a company-size force in a hurry, and he'll need your C-47s to do that. This plan presumes he'll have access to three C-47s for twenty-four hours when he calls for them. Is there going to be a problem with that?"

O'Connor turned to the CIA station chief, Léopoldville.

"Charley?"

"The C-47s have more on their plate than they can handle, sir," Charley said, "supporting Hoare's mercenary force in their suppression of the insurgents in the Luluabourg area."

"I'm sure that Major Hoare would be delighted to give up his air transport for a twenty-four-hour period if that meant the interdiction of a convoy of men and matériel intended to reinforce the insurgents he's dealing with," Lowell said. "I know I would."

"Make the aircraft available to Major Lunsford," O'Connor ordered.

"We won't know where to hit the convoy until Colonel Supo makes that decision," Lunsford said.

927

You mean, O'Connor thought, *until you make that decision.*

". . . which means," Lunsford went on, "that we won't know which of the airfields we'll use until just before we use them. What we would like to do is send Portet to Kamina. He knows just about every field in the area; he's landed at just about every field in the area."

The translation of that is you want your guy at Kamina to make sure Charley's aviation people "cooperate fully" with your request for Charley's C-47s.

"Any problem with that, Howard?" Lowell asked.

"I can't think of any," O'Connor said. "Charley?"

"I was wondering, frankly, why you can't use Portet's — Air Simba's — C-46s for this."

"They're being used, openly, under contract to the Congolese Army, to supply Colonel Supo's forces," Lunsford said. "And, of course, they're supporting, covertly, our covert operations. Once we have the convoy in our hands, they can be used to take the prisoners to Stanleyville, and to distribute the war matériel wherever Colonel Supo wants it, but they can't be used to transport a company of paratroopers; we need the C-47s for that."

"Hoare won't like it," Charley said.

"It doesn't matter what Major Hoare likes or dislikes," General Mobutu said. "He is in the employ of the Congolese Army; he will take orders from the Congolese Army."

"I presume that question is settled?" Lowell asked after a moment, then, when O'Connor nodded, added: "Go on, please, Major Lunsford."

"Colonel Supo has some agents with the insurgents in the Luluabourg area," Lunsford said. "The problem with them is getting their intel out in time for it to be of any use. The way Colonel Supo plans to deal with that is — with our assistance — to establish two outposts in the area around Luluabourg, one of the low land and the other on the plateau, which is five thousand feet above.

"We have reason to believe — Colonel Supo's agents have told us — that Mitoudidi plans to retake Albertville, in Katanga Province, here" — he pointed to Albertville, which was at the midpoint of the shore of Lake Tanganyika — "because (a) it will give him a port for resupply from Tanganyika; (b) restore the credibility the insurgents lost when Major Hoare's men ran him out of it; and (c) because he believes the Cubans will give him the necessary muscle to do so."

"And you think he can take it back from Hoare?" O'Connor asked. "And what about the Congolese Army?"

"Colonel Supo," Lowell said, "who, as I think you know, was recently given responsibility for Katanga Province, believes that he can keep Albertville from being taken again, with the forces he is in the process of moving there. If the Cubans participate in the attack — and Colonel Supo believes Mitoudidi will not attack *without* the Cubans — and that attack is a spectacular failure, Colonel Supo believes this will destroy the credibility of the Cubans with the insurgents, and the credibility of 'General' Mitoudidi with the Congolese people. The advantages of that, obviously, would be enormous.

"Going off at a sort of tangent," Lowell went

on, "Colonel Supo wants the Congolese Army — not Major Hoare's mercenaries — to win quote 'The Second Battle of Albertville' unquote, which would make it clear that the Congolese Army has things under control without any outside assistance, and again, the advantages of that would obviously be enormous."

And if you and your Green Berets aren't "outside assistance," what the hell are you? O'Connor thought, and then he had a second thought: *No. I'm wrong. The whole world knows about Michael Hoare and his mercenaries, and nobody knows about these Special Forces people. If they can help Mobutu and Supo to really hand Mitoudidi a licking, this arrogant sonofabitch is right, "the advantages of that, obviously, would be enormous."*

"So the problem is reduced, essentially," Lowell said, "to make sure that Mitoudidi does lose the Second Battle of Albertville, and the way to do that, Colonel Supo believes, I believe, and Major Lunsford believes, is (a) to keep up the interdiction of military matériel, and Cubans, both across Lake Tanganyika and coming across the Congo River from Congo Brazzaville, and (b) to have accurate and timely intel vis-à-vis Mitoudidi's intentions, and that brings us back to Major Lunsford's outposts in the Luluabourg area."

"How are you going to get that intelligence?" Cecilia Taylor asked. It was the first time she had spoken.

"Colonel Supo's agents have the intel, Miss Taylor," Father Lunsford said. "The problem is getting it out before it's yesterday's news."

"How are you going to solve *that* problem, Major Lunsford?" she asked.

"We're making up sort of A Teams, mixed Congolese and American," Lunsford said, and paused. "You know what I'm talking about?"

"I know what an A Team is," she said.

"The teams will consist of two American Special Forces people who speak Swahili," Lunsford went on, "and have experience in Vietnam in running around in the bad guy's backyard without getting caught. There will be at least one, maybe two, ASA radio people. There will be six Congolese paratroopers, and two of those six will be what the Congolese call trackers. The trackers will establish contact with Colonel Supo's agents, bring their intel to the outpost, where it will be relayed to L-19s flying overhead on a regular schedule."

"These ASA people," O'Hara said. "They're technicians. Can they survive in the bush?"

"We ran them through a jackleg course at Fort Bragg," Lunsford said. "They'll be all right. And they all want to go."

"And what if a team is detected?" O'Hara pursued.

"The worst possible scenario?" Lunsford asked rhetorically. "That's when we'll need some more air support. We don't have, and can't get, because that would blow the covert nature of this operation, any extraction choppers — Hueys — so if a team is discovered, we'll first send in the T-28s and the B-26s to suppress fire while we jump reinforcements in from C-47s. If we can do that, jump in a platoon of Colonel Supo's shooters with some heavier weaponry — machine guns, mortars, et cetera — and maintain the air cover over the position, Colonel Supo and I figure we can get a reaction team to the site on the ground before things go down the tube."

"And that brings us . . ." Lowell said, looking at the Léopoldville CIA station chief, ". . . Charley, is it?"

"My name is Willard, Colonel," the CIA station chief said reprovingly. "Charles M. Willard."

"I thought I heard Howard call you 'Charley,' " Lowell said. "Sorry."

"It's Charles, Colonel, Charles M. Willard."

"Well, now that that's been straightened out, *Charles,*" Lowell said, "as I was saying, *Charles,* that brings us to the vehicles in your motor pool. Which is, as I understand it, at Kamina?"

"I have some vehicular assets at Kamina, but none that can be diverted from supporting Major Hoare and his forces."

"Tell me something, Howard," Lowell said. "I was under the impression that you and I were sent here by our bosses to make sure that my people and your people, who have had little disagreements in the past, kissed, made up, and were made to understand we're on the same team. Was I wrong?"

"That's essentially correct, of course," O'Connor said.

"Don't you think it's about time you passed that on to Charles, here?"

"I'm not sure I know what you mean, Colonel," O'Connor said.

"Yes, you do. And I've had about all I intend to take of Mr. Willard."

"Is that so?" O'Connor flared.

"Yes, it is. I'm right on the edge of suggesting to Colonel Supo that he requisition all of the vehicles in the Kamina motor pool."

And you would do just that, wouldn't you, you sonofabitch?

"What I think, Colonel," O'Connor said, "is that Mr. Willard was simply trying to make you aware that Major Hoare's operations would be severely curtailed if you took the vehicular assets at Kamina —"

"I didn't tell him how many vehicles I need," Lowell snapped. "So how could he make that judgment?" He paused. "I'm right on the edge of calling this conference off and telling my boss that what he and your boss thought was a pretty good idea failed in the execution."

"How many vehicles are you going to need, Colonel?" Cecilia turned and asked.

"Six two-and-a-half-ton six-by-six trucks, with trailers; a fuel truck; a wrecker; two jeeps; and two three-quarter-ton trucks, with trailers," Geoff Craig said. "Colonel Supo will provide the drivers from the reaction force."

"That doesn't sound unreasonable to me," Cecilia Taylor said. "Why can't you do that, Charley?"

"Welcome to the team, Miss Taylor," Lowell said.

Charles Willard gave her a dirty look and then looked to Howard W. O'Connor for support and got none.

"That can probably be arranged," Willard said finally.

"Probably?" Lowell asked softly.

"I think we can probably save a lot of time here if I put it this way, Charley," O'Connor said. "Very simply, you are to make sure that Major Lunsford's people get whatever they ask for as your first priority. Do you understand?"

"Welcome to the team, Howard," Lowell said.

"Inasmuch as it has been made clear that I no

longer enjoy the confidence of the Agency," Willard said, as if he had rehearsed the phrase, "I officially request relief and transfer to other duties at the earliest possible time."

"Oh, Charley, don't be an ass," Cecilia said.

"Come on, Charley," O'Hara said placatingly.

"Sir," Willard said, looking at O'Connor, "I officially request relief and transfer to other duties at the earliest possible time."

O'Connor looked around the room. Both Mobutu and Supo were fascinated with the exchange. Lowell's and Lunsford's looks were contemptuous. Miss Cecilia Taylor looked unhappy, as did Mrs. Geoffrey Craig and Madame Jacques Portet. Lieutenants Portet and Craig were making a valiant effort to keep straight faces.

"We can talk about this in the morning," O'Connor said. "But I think that's all we'll need from you tonight, Charley."

Willard stood up and walked out of the room.

"I regret, sir, this unfortunate —" O'Connor said, to Mobutu.

The general waved his hand. *These things happen.*

"Colonel Lowell, is there anything else I can do to show you, and General Mobutu and Colonel Supo, that we are, in fact, on the same team?"

"There is one thing," Lowell said. "Miss Taylor."

"What about Miss Taylor?" O'Connor asked.

"To replace Willard," Lowell said. "I think everybody in this room would be happy if she were the CIA station chief here."

Jesus Christ, that came from left field!

But why not?

She's smart, she gets along with Lunsford . . .

"Sir, I was forced to replace Willard with Cecilia Taylor. I'm afraid the job was a little too much for him. And she has a close working relationship with Felter's man, Major Lunsford. I happen to know Felter's man, Lowell, thinks it's a good idea."

"Cecilia?" O'Connor asked.

"That possibility never entered my mind," she said.

"You told me yourself that Jim Foster was as much on top of things in Dar es Salaam as you are," O'Connor said.

She raised both hands, palm upward, in a gesture of surrender.

"I'll have to have the concurrence of Mr. O'Hara, of course, and of the Director," O'Connor said.

"I think we have a new station chief," O'Hara said. "The Director will understand why this had to happen."

[SIX]

TOP SECRET
1420 GREENWICH 10 MAY 1965

FROM STATION CHIEF, BUENOS AIRES

TO DIRECTOR, CIA, LANGLEY
COPIES TO SOUTH AMERICAN DESK
     MR SANFORD TO FELTER,
     COUNSELOR TO THE PRESIDENT
     THE EXECUTIVE OFFICE BUILDING
     WASHINGTON

THE FOLLOWING RECEIVED FROM US ARMY

OFFICER ASSIGNED US EMBASSY BELIEVED TO BE CONTROLLED BY MR. FELTER. IT IS RECOMMENDED THE INTELLIGENCE FOLLOWING BE REGARDED AS THE EQUIVALENT OF CIA RELIABILITY SCALE FIVE. IT IS TRANSMITTED IN ITS ENTIRETY AND VERBATIM.

START

DEAR FRIENDS:

IT WAS LEARNED TODAY THAT SEÑORA CELIA DE LA SERNA DE GUEVARA, DR. ERNESTO GUEVARA'S MOTHER, HAS BEEN ADMITTED TO THE STAPLER CLINIC, AVENIDA CORONEL DIAS, PALERMO, BUENOS AIRES. SEÑORA GUEVARA IS SUFFERING FROM CANCER. SHE IS 59 YEARS OLD.

ERNESTO LYNCH GUEVARA, DR. GUEVARA'S FATHER, HAS MADE HIMSELF RESPONSIBLE FOR HIS EX-WIFE'S HOSPITAL BILLS, WHICH SHOULD BE VERY LARGE, AS SHE IS INSTALLED IN A LARGE PRIVATE ROOM IN PROBABLY THE BEST FACILITY FOR CASES OF THIS NATURE IN ARGENTINA.

SEÑORA DE GUEVARA'S PROGNOSIS IS THAT SHE IS CLOSE TO DEATH, POSSIBLY WITHIN DAYS. IT IS KNOWN THAT HER FORMER HUSBAND YESTERDAY VISITED THE SOVIET EMBASSY HERE, HAVING HEARD

```
THE SOVIETS HAVE DEVELOPED A CURE
FOR CANCER.

BEST REGARDS

END

J. P. STEPHENS
STATION CHIEF BUENOS AIRES

TOP SECRET
```

[SEVEN]
Kamina Air Base
Katanga Province, The Congo
1615 13 May 1965

Major John D. Anderson, an assistant military attaché, and the senior pilot of the U.S. Embassy in Léopoldville, turned on final to Runway 27, called for gear down and twenty-degree flaps, and looked over his shoulder at his sole passenger.

She was the last goddamned person in the world anyone would think was the head spook for the CIA in the Congo, but that was the fact. Her predecessor, Charley Willard, who Anderson had always thought was a pretty good guy, if a little self-important, had apparently fucked up big-time somehow and gotten his ass shipped back to the U.S. of A. on twenty-four hours' notice. The next day, Miss Cecilia Taylor had walked into his office and introduced herself as Charley's replacement. She was ostensibly a cultural affairs officer.

But she was the head spook, the CIA station chief, and she knew what authority came with that. This morning, she had walked into his office and, politely, sure, but in a this-is-an-order tone of voice, told him she wanted to be at Kamina at 1630, and what time did she have to meet him at the airport so that he could fly her there in the L-23?

She would be at Kamina for two or three days, she said, and would get word to him when he was to fly back and get her.

He told her two o'clock, and she was there at two o'clock, and she smiled at him, and his copilot, and said "Hello," but not one other word.

"You're strapped in all right, ma'am?" Major Anderson asked.

"Yes, I am, and if we're going to work together, could you call me Cecilia?"

"I'd be happy to," he said. "My first name is John."

"I'll shake your hand, John," she said with a smile, "when you don't need it to steer the airplane."

"Is someone going to meet you here, ma' . . . Cecilia, or should I radio for a car?"

"Someone's going to meet me," she said. "But thank you."

A follow-me jeep led the L-23 to the tarmac in front of one of the hangars, and as he turned it around, he glanced into the hangar and saw an L-19, painted flat black all over, with no markings of any kind, on which three Congolese were working. They were wearing what looked like GI mechanic's overalls.

A Congolese lieutenant colonel drove down the

tarmac in a jeep, and Major Anderson did a double take.

I know that sonofabitch. He's the Green Beanie that was in the Air Simba hangar when the other Green Beanie, the aviator, told me they would fly my airplane to Stanleyville by themselves, thank you just the same.

"Cecilia," Major Anderson said helpfully, "the last time I saw that Congolese light colonel in the jeep there, he was wearing a U.S. Army Special Forces major's uniform."

"John," Miss Taylor said, "I'm sure you're mistaken."

"No, really."

"Major, you are mistaken," Miss Taylor said, with that voice-of-command tone again in her voice, "I know you are mistaken."

"Yes, ma'am," Major Anderson said.

The Congolese lieutenant colonel walked up to the wing root of the L-23, saluted Miss Taylor, and spoke to her in Swahili. She replied in Swahili, and he helped her off the wing root and into the jeep, then returned to the L-23, where he opened the luggage door with what looked like experience and took out her luggage, put it in the jeep, got behind the wheel, and drove off.

Major Anderson told the copilot to watch while the tanks were topped off, and he would check the weather.

"The pilot recognized you, Colonel," Cecilia said.

"There was a minor flap when we first got here," Father said. "Felter told him he wanted the L-23 — Jack Portet flew it — and that idiot thought we needed him to fly the airplane. It was like we were stealing his little rubber duckie."

"You often refer to peers as idiots, do you?"

"Only when they are," Father said.

"Where are we going?"

"First to your quarters, then I thought we would tour your motor pool. The guy now in charge of the motor pool is one of my guys. SFC Doc Jensen. Great big guy from Chicago, speaks pretty good Swahili. After that, I thought I would show you your air force. The pilot in charge is a Cuban. Good guy, knows what he's doing, has the motivation, and knows and likes Jack Portet from the time Jack was teaching them how to fly the -26s at Hurlburt. The problem was the idiot you replaced."

"Tell me something, Lunsford," she said. "How much did you have to do with your colonel asking O'Connor to transfer me here?"

He turned and looked at her.

"When Colonel Lowell made that suggestion, I was in the 'is that my brain or my heart thinking' part of the thought process. He spoke before I could make up my mind."

"Let's clear the air," Cecilia said. "We have a professional relationship, and that's all it's going to be."

"You got it," Lunsford said.

Lunsford pulled the jeep up before the verandah of a large, single-story, tin-roofed house with an immaculately trimmed lawn and shrubbery.

"This is the VIP guest house. Colonel Supo told me to tell you he hopes you'll be comfortable here."

"You like Supo, don't you?"

"He confirms my theory that a lot of sergeant majors should be colonels, and vice versa," Lunsford said. "He's smart, and a good soldier."

Two barefooted houseboys trotted down to the jeep and took Cecilia's luggage, not quite being able to conceal their surprise that a black-woman-not-following-her-colonel-husband was to occupy the VIP guest house.

There was a living room, with flowers on all the tables, and a dining room, set for dinner for one, and with a bottle of champagne in a cooler.

"That your idea or Colonel Supo's?" Cecilia asked.

"The champagne is my idea," he said. "A little thank-you for not caving in to your boss when Willard was showing his a— ignorance."

"His ass, you mean," she said. "My, you do talk dirty, don't you, Major?"

"I try not to around you," he said. "You got something you want to do here, powder your nose or something? The houseboys will take care of your luggage. I got SFC Jensen and Jose Whatsisname waiting for you, and it's going to be dark soon."

"Yes, thank you, I would like to powder my nose," she said.

"Have you worked for Major Lunsford long, Sergeant?" she asked of the massive Green Beret from Chicago in the Congolese captain's uniform. "Before you came to the Congo, I mean?"

It was a routine question, intended to put him at ease.

"Oh, yes, ma'am," he said. "I was Father's medic on half a dozen excursions into Cambodia."

"I wasn't aware we had troops in Cambodia," she said.

"Not *troops*," he corrected her. "Special Forces A Teams," and then he caught her meaning. "You told me she was the new head spook," he challenged Lunsford.

"As indeed she is," Lunsford said. "I told Jensen, Miss Taylor, that you had all the appropriate security clearances."

"I made a couple of excursions with Lieutenant Craig, too," Jensen said. "When he was an enlisted swine."

Cecilia realized she couldn't think of a response to that, so she changed the subject.

"You're a medic?" she asked. Hearing that this enormous man who looked as if he could pull arms off at the shoulders was a medic had genuinely surprised her.

"I can do anything but open the cranial cavity," Jensen said matter-of-factly. "When I get my twenty in, I'm going to be a male nurse."

"We talked about that," Lunsford said. "You're going to medical school and be a doctor, Doc."

"Father thinks I'm a lot smarter than I am, ma'am," SFC Jensen said.

Conclusion to be drawn, Cecilia thought: *Major Lunsford has earned the respect and admiration of his subordinates, and Major Lunsford pays genuine attention to the concerns of his subordinates, not just lip service. There is more to him than he shows the world.*

It became obvious in the next fifteen minutes that, in addition to being able to perform any medical procedure with the exception of opening the cranial cavity, SFC Doc Jensen was a soldier-type soldier.

There were Congolese soldiers standing in front of the vehicles Charley Willard has been unwilling to part with. They came to attention when they saw Jensen coming.

She examined the vehicles casually.

"They seem to be in good shape, Doc," she said.

"You should have seen them when I got here," he said. "They were really in shi— bad shape. Hoare's ass— mercenaries either didn't know to maintain a vehicle, or didn't care."

Jose Whatsisname, whose name turned out to be Elias Sanchez, was, so to speak, at the other end of the social spectrum. He — like many of the other B-26 and T-28 pilots — had been an officer in the pre-Castro Cuban Air Force.

He was now wearing the uniform of a Congolese lieutenant colonel. He was, Cecilia decided, of mixed blood. Like herself, he had long hair, and he was almost as dark as she was. Not as dark as Lunsford or Doc Jensen, but dark.

And it was obvious that he was torn between relief at being out from under Charley Willard's orders and deep Latin macho concern at now being under the orders of a woman. The being-under-her-orders part bothered him, not the woman. He lost no time as he showed her his flight line, before turning on a warm smile and hoping that she would be free to join him for dinner at the officers' mess.

"Well, I'm sorry, but Colonel Dahdi and I already have plans," she said.

"Good try, Jose," Father said.

Their final stop was the hangar in which Major

Anderson had seen the flat-black L-19 and what he mistakenly thought were Congolese working on it. There she met Major Darrell J. Smythe and the three suddenly-recruited-from-Fort-Rucker aircraft mechanics. Smythe, Lunsford told her, was going to provide what they called "radio cover" for the outposts to be established at Luluabourg, flying over them on a staggered schedule to receive the intelligence gathered by Colonel Supo's agents and passed to the trackers, and finally radioed to the L-19 by the ASA people with the mixed A Teams on the ground.

His interest in seeing the L-19 was perfectly maintained was understandable, Cecilia thought. If the engine failed and the L-19 went down in the trackless bush, that would be the end of Major Smythe.

Smythe's respect for Lunsford was obvious.

Barefoot Boy is obviously a special type of man.

Watch it, Cecilia. The last thing you want to do, for a long list of reasons, is get emotionally involved with Major George Washington "Father" Lunsford.

"I'll come by here at about eight and pick you up," Father said to Cecilia as they sat in the jeep outside the VIP house. "You just tell the house-boys what you want for breakfast, and when."

"That would be fine," she said.

"Unless you'd like to have breakfast with us — Aunt Jemima, Jose, and Doc — in the mess," he said.

"That sounds even better," she said.

"Then I'll pick you up about quarter past seven?"

"Fine."

"Is that where you planned to have dinner? The

mess?" she asked.

He took her meaning.

"Good question," he said. "I can't go there, can I? Jose Whatsisname will know we didn't really have plans. No problem. I'll find something."

"Would there be enough food in the house for both of us?"

"Sure."

"Then we'll have dinner here."

"You sure you want to do that?"

"We have an understanding, don't we? Our relationship will be professional, period?"

"That's bullshit and you know it," Father said.

"My, we do talk dirty, don't we, Major?"

"I'm not very good at this game," Lunsford said. "I don't understand women, and never have. I can usually tell when men are lying to me, but I'm not good at that with women, and especially not with you."

"What have I said that makes you wonder if I'm lying?"

"I just told you," he said. "With that professional relationship, period, bullshit."

"It would be an enormous mistake for both of us to get involved," she said.

"We're not talking about enormous mistakes," Father said. "We're talking about do you want to, or not."

"Want to what or not?"

"Shit, there you go again. You know goddamn well what I'm talking about."

She met his eyes but said nothing.

"I suppose the bottom line is that I'm pretty stupid," he said. "I just can't understand how you can drive me crazy, and the only reaction I get from you is that I'm a soldier who talks dirty."

"I drive you crazy?"

"When Jose Whatsisname came on to you, I wanted to slit his throat," Father said.

That "slit his throat," Cecilia decided, *is not a figure of speech.*

"I can only repeat that it would be an enormous mistake for us to become involved," Cecilia said.

"How the hell would we know that until we do?" Father asked. "Do you always go by the goddamned book? Don't you ever take a chance? For Christ's sake, for all you know we could be the greatest goddamned thing since sliced bread!"

She looked at him without speaking, got out of the jeep, and turned to look at him again.

He was sitting, both hands on the steering wheel, looking straight ahead.

She turned and walked onto the verandah, and there thought of something to say.

"George, come on in the house," she called.

"What?"

"I said, 'George, come on in the house,'" she said. "I am not going to call you 'Father.'"

By the time he got in the house, she was in the corridor, looking into the dining room. She did not turn when she heard him walk up behind her.

"What now?" she asked.

"Well, we could open that bottle of champagne — it's probably still cold — and sit in there or in the living room and make small talk, or we could take that bottle into the bedroom."

She turned around and snapped, furiously, "Did you really think you were going to walk in here and jump in my bed? Just like that?"

"I didn't know," he said. "It was worth asking. And when you think about it, what's wrong with it? I don't think you play by other people's rules any more than I do. And, Jesus Christ, I've never wanted anything more in my life."

I should slap his face and tell him to get the hell out of here.

She looked into his eyes.

"If that was over the line," he said, "and looking at your eyes, I guess it is, it's because I don't know where the goddamn line is."

She reached up and touched his cheek. He stiffened but made no other move.

"Give me five minutes," Cecilia heard herself saying. "I need a shower. And then bring the champagne."

"I need a shower too," he said.

"You're not actually suggesting we take one together?" she asked incredulously.

"Why not?"

My God, I'm out of my mind!

In for a penny, in for a pound.

She took her hand from his cheek, found his hand at his side, and took it, and led him down the corridor to her bedroom.

XXIV

[ONE]

SECRET
HELP0039 2220 ZULU 14 MAY 1965
VIA WHITE HOUSE SIGNAL AGENCY

FROM: HELPER SIX
TO: EARNEST SIX

SITUATION REPORT #37
REFERENCE MAP BAKER 11

1-EARS ONE RELAYED INTEL FROM SUPO'S
SOURCES AT LULUABOURG POSITIVELY
LOCATING GUEVERA, DREKE AND BULK OF
CUBANS AT NEW CAMP SET UP ON
LULUABOURG PLATEAU APPROXIMATELY
FIVE (5) KILOMETERS FROM KIMBARA.
COORDINATES 65545/23009. HEREAFTER
LULUPLAT.

2-SAME SOURCE REPORTS GUEVERA ILL,
PROBABLY SUFFERING FROM TROPICAL
FEVER OF SOME KIND, WHICH MAY EXPLAIN
CUBAN MOVEMENT TO LULUPLAT, WHICH
IS 5,000 FEET ABOVE MAIN SEA LEVEL,
COOLER, LESS HUMID, AND LESS INSECT
INFESTED.

[TWO]

TOP SECRET
1920 GREENWICH 16 MAY 1965

FROM STATION CHIEF, BUENOS AIRES

TO DIRECTOR, CIA, LANGLEY
COPIES TO SOUTH AMERICAN DESK
        MR SANFORD T FELTER,
        COUNSELOR TO THE PRESIDENT
        THE EXECUTIVE OFFICE BUILDING
        WASHINGTON

THE FOLLOWING RECEIVED FROM US ARMY
OFFICER ASSIGNED US EMBASSY BELIEVED
TO BE CONTROLLED BY MR. FELTER. IT IS
RECOMMENDED THE INTELLIGENCE
FOLLOWING BE REGARDED AS THE
EQUIVALENT OF CIA RELIABILITY SCALE FIVE.
IT IS TRANSMITTED IN ITS ENTIRETY AND
VERBATIM.

START

DEAR FRIENDS:

IT WAS LEARNED TODAY THAT AS A RESULT

949

OF HAVING LEARNED THAT SEÑORA CELIA DE LA SERNA DE GUEVARA'S SON IS DR. ERNESTO GUEVARA, THE AUTHORITIES OF THE STAPLER CLINIC INFORMED HER FAMILY THEY NO LONGER WISHED TO PROVIDE MEDICAL SERVICE TO HER, AND SHE HAS BEEN TRANSFERRED TEMPORARILY TO THE ENGLISH HOSPITAL BUENOS AIRES WHILE OTHER HOSPITAL ACCOMMODATIONS CAN BE FOUND. HER PROGNOSIS REMAINS GRAVE WITH DEATH POSSIBLY IN LESS THAN A WEEK.

BEFORE GOD AND ON MY HONOR AS AN OFFICER, I SWEAR TO YOU THAT NO ONE YOU MET IN ARGENTINA OR KNOWN TO ME WAS RESPONSIBLE FOR THIS DESPICABLE ACTION ON THE PART OF THE STAPLER CLINIC. AN INITIAL INVESTIGATION SUGGESTS THAT CERTAIN SENIOR PERSONNEL CONNECTED WITH THE STAPLER CLINIC ARE REFUGEES FROM EAST GERMANY, AND THEIR HATRED FOR ALL THINGS COMMUNIST MUST HAVE OVERWHELMED THEIR SENSES OF COMMON DECENCY.

WITH REFERENCE TO THE ARGENTINE/EAST GERMAN HAYDÉE TAMARA BUNKE, "TANIA": WE WERE INFORMED BY OUR MUTUAL GERMAN FRIEND THAT SHE HAD BEEN LOCATED IN EAST BERLIN, AND WAS TRACED TO HAVANA. WE HAVE LEARNED THAT SHE WAS LAST WEEK SENT, USING A

URUGUAYAN PASSPORT IN HER OWN NAME, TO LA PAZ, BOLIVIA, TO SERVE AS A DEEP COVER AGENT IN PLACE FOR ACTIVATION WHEN DR. GUEVARA BEGINS TO LIBERATE SOUTH AMERICA. THIS STRONGLY SUGGESTS TO ME THAT HE PLANS TO BEGIN IN BOLIVIA. IF THIS INFORMATION BECOMES KNOWN TO BOLIVIAN AUTHORITIES, IT IS BELIEVED TANIA WILL BE IMMEDIATELY TERMINATED, AND THEREFORE THE BOLIVIAN GOVERNMENT HAS NOT REPEAT HAS NOT BEEN GIVEN THIS INTELLIGENCE.

BEST REGARDS

END

J. P. STEPHENS
STATION CHIEF BUENOS AIRES

TOP SECRET

[THREE]
9 Degrees 59 Minutes 28 Seconds South
    Latitude
20 Degrees 33 Minutes 39 Seconds East
    Longitude
(Route Nationale No. 39, The Bush, Near
    Saurino, Katanga Province, Congo)
1310 16 May 1965

Smythe's flat-black L-19 was at 3,500 feet above, and perhaps a quarter mile behind, a Ford and Peu-

951

geot truck convoy moving through the bush. So far as Smythe had been able to see, there was no other traffic on the road for five miles or so in either direction.

He had been following the four-truck convoy for about an hour, ever since it had passed through Saurino. He hadn't had to stay on its trail like a bloodhound. There was only one road capable of taking the trucks within seventy miles; all he had to do — had done — was make wide circles, which every ten minutes brought the convoy in sight again.

He had flown over the road at a very low altitude the day before with a surprisingly pleasant and cheerful — even, for once, happy — Father Lunsford in the backseat, looking for a place to set up the ambush. Lunsford had apparently done this sort of thing before, because when he saw the hill, with a curving road running along its side, he had pointed it out and told Smythe to land as close as possible so they could reconnoiter on the ground.

Smythe had landed the L-19 on the highway itself, after determining there was no traffic on it that would reach the landing site within the twenty minutes Father said he would need to have a look.

Then he had flown Father back to Kamina, where Lunsford immediately reported to that absolutely stunning lady from the CIA, and then, in two flights, had flown Master Sergeant Thomas and a Congolese sergeant first named Jette to the site.

They would remain overnight, preferring that to a sixty-plus-mile trip in a jeep or three-quarter-ton truck from Kamina.

Doubting Thomas told him it was his military creed: "Never stand if you can lie down; never run if you can walk; and whenever possible, go by air."

Like he was about many things Doubting Thomas said, in what appeared to be absolute sincerity, Smythe was really not entirely sure how serious he was.

Trucks under SFC Jensen had set out from Kamina at first light, carrying a platoon-plus of Congolese paratroopers. They were now in the bush a half-mile on either side of where Thomas and Jette were in position.

"You should be able to see them any moment now, Jesse James," Captain Darrell J. Smythe said into his microphone. "They're about halfway up the hill, about to make the turn."

"I have a visual, Aunt Jemima, thank you very much. I think you can have the cavalry sound the charge," Thomas said into his microphone.

He laid the microphone on the ground beside him and picked up a black pistol that looked something like the legendary Luger 9-mm Parabellum. It was, in fact, a Ruger Mark II .22 Long Rifle Caliber semiautomatic pistol, to which had been added what the Army called a "suppressor" — the term "silencer" was either not wholly accurate, or politically incorrect. There was an eight-inch cylinder attached to the forward end of the barrel.

When fired, the sound was a soft *thut*.

Sergeant First Jette had required a practical demonstration of the weapon — Thomas had set up quart cans of tomato juice beside one of the Kamina runways — before he was willing to accept that, although it went *thut* instead of *bang* when fired, it was still a real pistol.

Once convinced, Jette was enthralled with the weapon, and Thomas realized he was going to have to fabricate yet another wholly dishonest official document, this one stating that One Each Pistol, Ruger, .22 LR, SN 14-48070 had been lost while conducting operations against a hostile force. It was either that or fight Jette to the death to get it back.

Thomas also had a little trouble convincing Jette that his concept of shooting tires out on a truck — firing a clip of 7-mm rifle ammunition at them — would not be as efficacious in this situation as what he intended to do.

"We don't want these guys to hear gunfire, Jette," he had explained. "That would make everybody in all four trucks nervous, and they would come out of the trucks with their weapons ready to shoot anything they saw. This way, they won't even hear the *thut thut* as we shoot little holes in the front tires. The tires will not blow out, but they will quickly go flat, and they will get out to see what happened, leaving their weapons in the truck. And then the cavalry will roll up, from behind and in front of them, with machine guns over their cabs, and their beds full of shooters with their weapons trained, and if these people have the brains to find their ass with both hands, they will just put their hands up. Get the picture?"

"You have done this before, Major, sir?"

"I have done this before."

Thomas stood up and signaled that the trucks were about to be upon them. He couldn't see Jette, but he knew that Jette could see him.

Then he went back into the bush, no more than two meters from the road, behind a large tree, and

954

took up a position where he could rest his elbows while holding the Ruger with both hands.

The sound of the first truck grew louder, and then he could hear the sound rocks made when they shot out from under tires as the trucks entered the bush.

Here lies Master Sergeant William Thomas, who took a rock between the eyes on a deserted road in the Congo bush.

And then he sensed the truck next to him before he actually saw it.

When he saw the tire, he squeezed the trigger.

Thut, thut, thut, thut.

The second truck appeared. He didn't fire at it. The second and fourth trucks were Jette's.

The third truck appeared.

Thut, thut, thut, thut, and, what the hell, *thut, thut.*

The Ruger's magazine held ten cartridges.

The fourth truck passed him.

When it was out of sight around the bend, Thomas stood up and signaled Jette to have a look through the bush.

Then he picked up his microphone.

"Do I get the purple stuffed gorilla?" he asked.

"The first truck has pulled to the side," Major Smythe reported.

"Where's the cavalry?"

"About a quarter mile in each direction," Smythe reported.

Not quite a minute later, a military truck roared past him, a Congolese paratrooper standing in the front seat manning a 7.62 machine gun in a ring mount, its bed jammed with paratroopers holding FN 7-mm rifles.

And then the second.

He didn't see SFC Doc Jensen, which meant he was with the trucks coming in the other direction,

"The cavalry is at the scene," Smythe reported. "Lots of hands in the air. Good show, Thomas!"

"Right you are, Percival," Thomas said. "You want to come down and pick me up?"

"You don't want to go to the scene of your victory?"

"No," Thomas said. "I don't."

And I don't want to think what's going to happen to those poor bastards once they get their fair, by-the-goddamned-book court-martial.

Well, shit, they knew what they were letting themselves in for. Why the fuck didn't they stay in fucking Cuba?

He slipped his arms into the backpack radio and came out of the bush and started walking down the hill to where Smythe would land the L-19.

He found the microphone.

"Custer, Custer, Jesse James," he called.

"Go, Jesse," Jensen replied immediately.

"Start walking down the hill. Aunt Jemima will fly you out of here."

"I'd rather stay with my trucks."

"The way this works, Doc, is that I tell you what to do, and you do it. I'll wait for you. Jesse James clear."

Thomas walked slowly down the road, looking over his shoulder from time to time until he saw Doc Jensen coming down the road after him.

Then he stopped and waited for him to catch up.

"What's going on, Thomas?"

"Father wants us out of here, that's what's happening," Thomas said. "Did you hear that 'good show' bullshit from Aunt Jemima?"

"I think he wants to be an English officer and gentleman," Doc said. "But I sort of like him."

"Yeah, me, too."

He pointed toward the sky, where Aunt Jemima's flat-black L-19 was making its approach to National Route 39.

[FOUR]

SECRET
HELP0041 2220 ZULU 16 MAY 1965
VIA WHITE HOUSE SIGNAL AGENCY

FROM: HELPER SIX
TO: EARNEST SIX

AFTER-ACTION REPORT #5
REFERENCE MAP BAKER 11

1-AT APPROXIMATELY 1200 ZULU 16 MAY 1965 CAPT DARRELL J. SMYTHE FLYING RECONNAISSANCE IN AN L-19 NEAR SURINO, KATANGA PROVINCE, CONGO OBSERVED A FOUR TRUCK CONVOY ON ROUTE NATIONAL 39 SUSPECTED OF TRANSPORTING CUBAN FORCES INTENDED TO REINFORCE CONGOLESE INSURGENTS IN THE LULUABOURG AREA.

2-THIS INTEL WAS FURNISHED TO A CONGOLESE REACTION FORCE AT KAMINA, ADVISED BY SFC ALFRED JENSEN, AND TO A RECONNAISSANCE PATROL IN THE AREA ADVISED BY MSGT WILLIAM THOMAS.

3-AT APPROXIMATELY 1330 ZULU 16 MAY 1965 THE CONVOY WAS HALTED BY THE CONGOLESE REACTION FORCE APPROXIMATELY 35 MILES EAST OF SURINO. MSGT THOMAS AND SFC JENSEN WERE LATER SEPARATELY INFORMED BY CONGOLESE OFFICERS THAT EIGHTY-TWO (82) ARMED INDIVIDUALS BELIEVED TO BE CUBAN NATIONALS WERE TAKEN INTO CUSTODY, TOGETHER WITH A LARGE QUANTITY OF SMALL ARMS AND OTHER MILITARY MATÉRIEL.

4-THERE WAS COMPLETE SURPRISE AND THE ALLEGED CUBANS WERE TAKEN INTO CUSTODY WITHOUT THE EXCHANGE OF GUNFIRE. CONGOLESE AUTHORITIES BELIEVE THAT THE STOPPING OF THE CONVOY WAS CONDUCTED WITHOUT GIVING THE ALLEGED CUBANS TIME TO INFORM INSURGENT FORCES IN THE LULUABOURG AREA THAT THEY WERE BEING STOPPED. ALTHOUGH NEITHER WAS PRESENT AT THE ACTUAL STOPPING OF THE TRUCKS AND SUBSEQUENT ARREST OF THE ALLEGED CUBAN NATIONALS MSGT THOMAS AND SFC JENSEN CONCUR.

5-CONGOLESE AUTHORITIES HAVE INFORMED THE UNDERSIGNED THAT IF INVESTIGATION REVEALS THE ALLEGED CUBANS ARE IN FACT ARMED FOREIGN NATIONALS IN THE CONGO WITH THE INTENT OF OVERTHROWING THE

GOVERNMENT BY FORCE, THEY WILL BE DEALT WITH UNDER INTERNATIONAL AND CONGOLESE MILITARY LAW, WITH APPROPRIATE REPORTS TO BE MADE TO THE INTERNATIONAL COURT OF JUSTICE AT THE TERMINATION OF THE CURRENT STATE OF NATIONAL EMERGENCY.

HELPER SIX

SECRET

[FIVE]
404 Avenue Leopold
Léopoldville, Republic of the Congo
1205 20 May 1965

Nimbi, the houseboy, led Miss Cecilia Taylor to what he referred to as "Les Madames," who were sitting in their bathing suits at one of the umbrellaed tables by the swimming pool.

Mary Magdalene, the enormous black woman Cecilia had seen before, was sitting at the shallow end of the pool, her feet in the water, her flowered dress hiked nearly to her waist, playing with the Craigs' baby.

Madame Ursula Craig and Madame Marjorie Portet smiled at her — and then at each other — when they saw her.

"Good morning, Cecilia," Ursula said. "You look like you could use a glass of orange juice."

"I could, thank you very much," Cecilia said.

"We all need orange juice, Nimbi," Marjorie

959

ordered. "And Miss Taylor will be staying for lunch."

"That's very kind of you, and I accept. But the reason I'm here is because Major Lunsford asked me to meet him."

"He'll be here soon," Marjorie said. "He's at the airport with my Jack, deciding which of the redundant-shipments goes where," Marjorie said.

"Excuse me?"

"The Air Force, to everyone's surprise, finally delivered a planeload of redundants early this morning," Marjorie said.

"Redundants?"

"The way I understand it, the Air Force insisted they could support Operation Earnest. Felter didn't believe them, of course, but gave them the shopping list, meanwhile making sure my father-in-law actually delivered what we needed with the Intercontinental Air Cargo 707. . . ."

She paused and, smiling naughtily, asked, "I thought they called Father last night about it? Didn't he tell you?"

"Major Lunsford was at my apartment, on some business, when he had a call," Cecilia said. "I suppose that's what it was."

"When the plane landed, the pilot wouldn't turn the stuff over to anyone but Father, Cecilia," Marjorie said. "So when the attaché called here, I gave him your number."

"I feel like I'm explaining to my mother why I was out all night," Cecilia said.

"Apropos of nothing whatever," Marjorie said, "I think I can say without fear of contradiction that Special Forces Detachment 17 is very happy to see their beloved commander happy, and grateful to whoever, or whatever, is making him happy."

"My God, you mean everyone knows?" Cecilia asked.

"All of us know," Marjorie said, "and not one of us would say a word outside the clan."

"How did you know George was at my apartment?" Cecilia asked.

"I'm the unofficial adjutant, I guess," Marjorie said. "I'm the one people come to find Father, so he tells me where he's going to be. So I knew where to find him when the attaché called."

"At half past three in the morning," Cecilia said.

"Oh, was it that late? I never looked at the clock," Marjorie said.

"The hell you didn't," Cecilia said, and added: "I never thought I would behave like this — was *capable* of behaving like this."

"None of us did," Marjorie said. "I think they call it 'lust,' as in 'unbridled lust.' It sneaks up from behind, and quite literally sets you on your behind."

"Marjorie!" Ursula said reprovingly, but with a smile.

"Actually," Marjorie said. "Just before you came, Ursula and I decided we were going to have a word with you, just between us girls, but first things first."

She took a sheet of paper from her purse and handed it to Cecilia.

"This is what Father wanted you to see," she said.

```
SECRET
EARN0087 WASH DC 1035 ZULU 20 MAY
1965
VIA WHITE HOUSE SIGNAL AGENCY

FROM: EARNEST SIX
TO: HELPER SIX

FOLLOWING RECEIVED FROM ZAMMORO IN
BUENOS AIRES

SEÑORA CELIA DE LA SERNA DE GUEVARA
DIED OF LUNG CANCER AT 1230 BUENOS
AIRES TIME 19 MAY 1965.

FINTON FOR EARNEST SIX

SECRET
```

Cecilia handed it back.

"I suppose you saw the other one," she said, "where they threw the poor woman out of the hospital?"

Both Ursula and Marjorie nodded.

"I can't understand that," Cecilia said.

"I'm not saying it's right," Ursula said. "But I can understand it."

"Ursula used to live in East Germany," Marjorie said. "But, quickly changing the subject, how are your quarters here in Léopoldville?"

"They're what you'd expect for the secretary to the Cultural Affairs Officer," Cecilia said. "A fifth-floor walk-up overlooking the Stanley Basin."

"We're all living here, and there's still three unused bedrooms," Ursula said.

"You're not suggesting I move in here?"

"We're suggesting you'd attract less attention often spending the night with your American girl-friends here . . ."

"Than with my American boyfriend at my flat?"

"Actually, I was thinking your Congolese light colonel boyfriend," Marjorie said.

"God, I forgot about that. . . ."

"Then you cave in to our irrefutable logic and will?"

"I suppose I should feel like a shameless slut, but I don't," Cecilia said.

"If it's with the right guy," Marjorie said, "I have learned that feeling like a slut is not necessarily all that bad."

[SIX]
404 Avenue Leopold
Léopoldville, Republic of the Congo
1735 21 May 1965

Father Lunsford, Marjorie Portet, and Ursula Craig were sitting at one of the umbrellaed tables by the pool, watching Mary Magdalene splashing around the shallow end of the pool chasing Jeffy. Father and Ursula were drinking beer, Marjorie what looked like a gin and tonic.

"Where's Jack?" Cecilia Taylor asked as she slipped into the chair beside Lunsford, managing to run her fingers across his shoulders as she did so.

"He took a C-46 load of redundants to Kamina," Father said. "He'll be back tomorrow, probably, or the day after."

"Oh, he's left already?" Cecilia asked.

Taking supplies to Kamina wasn't the only reason Jack was going there, and Cecilia knew it. But Ursula and Marjorie were at the table, and they didn't have the need-to-know, and Cecilia knew that too.

Colonel Supo had told him he had been thinking. And what he had been thinking was that if they didn't interdict any of the launches crossing Lake Tanganyika from Kigoma, that might be suspicious. If, Colonel Supo said he had been thinking, one of the T-28s to which he now had access could interdict the odd launch, giving the impression that it had been discovered by accident — an air patrol had just found it by luck — that would, he was thinking, convince the insurgents that there were certain risks in sending launches across the lake.

That would make them more cautious, thus reducing the frequency and number of launches they would attempt to send across Lake Tanganyika. And, of course, if they sank the odd launch now and then, that would consign X many pounds of supplies to the bottom of the lake, and force the insurgents not only to get more supplies but also to buy another launch and find a crew capable and willing to sail it across the lake, where the enemy, it was known, sometimes got lucky and came across a launch and sank it with all hands.

That's what he had been thinking, Colonel Supo said, and what did his good friend Lieutenant Colonel Dahdi think of his thinking?

Colonel Dahdi said he was in complete agreement with Colonel Supo, but that he would have to discuss it with Miss Taylor.

Miss Taylor, when Lunsford had discussed it with her over lunch, had thought it was a good idea, with certain caveats. She had rather liked Major Lunsford's notion that it was better to make the insurgents' replacements simply disappear than to engage a replacement launch under conditions in which there might be survivors who could guess that there were agents in Kigoma transmitting intel vis-à-vis the departure of launches from that port.

"And we have to be very careful, George, to make sure we don't sink some innocent smuggler. Your ASA people in Kigoma can get a message to Kamina or the T-28s how fast?"

"They can talk to the B-26s in the air, but not the T-28s."

"So why don't we send Jack Portet in a B-26 — not to fly it, I want the Cubans to fly it — to make sure they get the right launch, and make it disappear?"

"Great minds think alike," Father had said to Cecilia, "about love and war."

He did not think it necessary to tell her that he was going to tell Jack to make absolutely sure that when the trigger on the B-26's control yoke was depressed, firing the six .50-caliber Browning machine guns in the nose, he wanted that trigger depressed by someone who really knew what he was doing, and that Jack would almost certainly decide he was the man for the job.

"He wanted to get to Kamina before dark," Father said. "So, how was your day at the office, dear? To tell you the truth, I've never really understood what a 'cultural affair' is. Making love to classical music?"

He waited for appreciative laughter. He didn't get so much as a chuckle.

"They're all a little retarded, Cecilia," Marjorie said. "It takes some getting used to."

"The courier from the embassy in Brazzaville brought me something," Cecilia said. "A total of nine Cubans, including one positively identified as Captain Roberto Agramonte, have arrived, two and three at a time, on various airlines, but mostly Air France, in Brazzaville. Agramonte went right to the Foreign Ministry. Our source there said he told the Foreign Ministry people he was there to, quote, 'coordinate the reception of Column Two,' unquote, whatever that means."

"It probably means no more than another fifty men," Father said. "Guevara's got delusions that he's Napoleon. He's divided the . . . what — thirty, forty — people he's got on the plateau into the troops and the general staff. We'd call it a platoon."

"I thought you weren't supposed to underestimate the enemy," Cecilia said.

"What's to underestimate? All he's done so far is sneak into the country — *think* he's snuck into the country — set himself up in a shack city on a plateau in the middle of nowhere, and get sick. And he's supposed to be a doctor."

"I wonder if he knows about his mother?" Cecilia asked.

"The intercept teams haven't picked up anything," Father said. "I suppose news like that would have to go from the Cuban Embassy in Buenos Aires to Havana, to Dar es Salaam, and then they'd have to relay it to Luluabourg."

[SEVEN]
Kamina Air Base
Katanga Province, The Congo
1100 23 May 1965

Father Lunsford found Jack Portet, who was wearing a flight suit, eating breakfast — ham and eggs, a croissant, orange juice and coffee — in the officers' mess.

"Is that breakfast or lunch?" Lunsford asked, slipping into a chair beside him and reaching for the coffeepot.

"I was up most of the night in a B-26," Jack said. "And, apparently aware that I was getting some well-deserved rest, the maintenance officer ordered T-18 engine run-ups outside my window, starting at nine. I finally gave up trying to get some sleep. What are you doing here?"

Lunsford did not respond to the question; instead, he asked lightly:

"And did you do something useful, while you were up most of the night?"

"Are you going to send an after-action report?" Jack asked seriously.

"No. The B-26s are an Agency operation. And since we don't fly their airplanes — we don't fly their airplanes, do we, Jack?"

Portet met his eyes and snorted.

"No, sir, I don't think you could find anyone who would say that I was flying the B-26 last night, when it blew a launch into many small pieces."

"And since we don't fly their airplanes," Lunsford went on, "there's really no reason for us to send an after-action report, is there?"

"I guess not," Jack said.

967

"But, hypothetically speaking, if an after-action report was being sent, what do you think it would say?"

Jack thought about that a moment, then replied:

"Acting on information everyone on the B-26 really hopes was reliable, a forty-odd-foot launch was detected in the Congolese waters of Lake Tanganyika — maybe a mile over the border. Said vessel was on a course for Kalamba. Said vessel did not display running lights. Persons aboard said vessel, on seeing a B-26 aircraft coming at them with gear and flaps down at about two hundred feet, fired upon said B-26 with what appeared to be small-caliber automatic weapons, whereupon said B-26 blew said launch into small pieces with a ten-second burst of .50-caliber machine-gun fire from the six Brownings in the nose of said B-26."

"Hypothetically speaking, what would you say the chances were the boat was able to report their predicament before it went down?"

"Zero," Jack said.

"Chances of survivors?"

"Zero."

"Not even hanging on to pieces of the boat?"

"From the fireball, I'd say it was carrying a couple hundred gallons of gasoline as cargo. Plus some high explosives. Nobody swam away from that one."

"Now that they know how to do it, can the Cubans do this on their own from here on in?"

Portet thought that over before replying.

"You have two problems with *our* Cubans," he began. "The first is that they'll happily blow any boat out of the water that they even suspect has their communist countrymen aboard, and, two, they are wondering, aloud, why they can't just blow Guevara and everybody else on the Luluabourg plateau away."

"I'll have Cecilia speak to them," Lunsford said.

"What makes you think they'll listen?"

"Because she'll make it clear that anybody who disobeys orders will get shipped back to the States," Lunsford said. "They wouldn't like that. Here at least they can do something against Guevara."

[EIGHT]

TOP SECRET
HELP0039 2115 ZULU 23 MAY 1965
VIA WHITE HOUSE SIGNAL AGENCY

FROM: HELPER SIX
TO: EARNEST SIX

SITUATION REPORT #43

1-FOLLOWING, IN WHICH MATA HARI CONCURS, SHOULD BE FURNISHED TO CIA.

2-AT 0915 ZULU 23 MAY 1965 ASA SOURCES INTERCEPTED A RADIO MESSAGE TRANSMITTED FROM KIGOMA, TANGANYIKA AND SIGNED BY COLONEL LAURENT MITOUDIDI, AS CHIEF OF STAFF OF THE REVOLUTIONARY STAFF MILITARY COUNCIL, ADDRESSED TO "TATU" (GUEVARA) IN LULUPLAT. IT USED A CODE NORMALLY

USED ONLY BY CUBAN EMBASSY IN DAR ES SALAAM, AND IS THEREFORE CONSIDERED LEGITIMATE. IT ORDERED GUEVARA TO "PREPARE TO ATTACK AND LIBERATE ALBERTVILLE AND HOLD IT AGAINST ALL MERCENARY AND REACTIONARY FORCES." NO SPECIFICS WERE GIVEN.

3-WE HAVE DRAWN THE FOLLOWING CONCLUSIONS:

A.   GUEVARA HAS, PROBABLY BECAUSE HE HAS NO OTHER CHOICE, PLACED HIMSELF AND CUBANS UNDER ORDERS OF MITOUDIDI. MITOUDIDI IS HAVING HEARTS AND MINDS PROBLEMS WITH CIVILIAN POPULATION IN ORIENTAL, KATANGA, AND KASAI PROVINCES BECAUSE OF BOTH HIS INABILITY TO OUST HOARE'S MERCENARIES AND/OR SUPO'S FORCES FROM ALBERTVILLE, STANLEYVILLE, OR ANYWHERE ELSE, AND BECAUSE OF THE UNDISCIPLINED BEHAVIOR OF HIS TROOPS. THERE HAVE BEEN MANY CONFIRMED REPORTS OF ATROCITIES AGAINST CONGOLESE CIVILIANS IN THE AREAS INFESTED BY SIMBAS, RANGING FROM THEFT OF FOOD AND LIVESTOCK, FORCIBLE RECRUITMENT OF MEN INTO SIMBAS, TO RAPE AND MURDER.

B.   MITOUDIDI IS SPENDING MORE AND MORE TIME IN KIGOMA AND LESS TIME ANYWHERE IN THE CONGO. THERE IS

REASON TO BELIEVE THAT HE BOTH LIKES THE BROTHELS AND OTHER ATTRACTIONS OF KIGOMA AND IS ALSO AFRAID OF BEING CAPTURED BY HOARE'S OR SUPO'S FORCES IN THE CONGO. INASMUCH AS COLONEL SUPO NOW HAS COMMAND OF ALL CONGOLESE FORCES IN THESE PROVINCES, THIS SITUATION WILL CERTAINLY BECOME WORSE FOR HIM.

C.   COLONEL SUPO BELIEVES, AND MATA HARI AND UNDERSIGNED CONCUR, THAT SHOULD IT BE POSSIBLE FOR GUEVERAN FORCES, WITH SOME SIMBA ASSISTANCE, TO RECAPTURE ALBERTVILLE, MITOUDIDI COULD CLAIM A MAJOR SIMBA VICTORY, AND HIS HEARTS AND MINDS PROBLEMS WOULD BE DIMINISHED. SHOULD AN ATTACK ON ALBERTVILLE FAIL, HE COULD PLACE THE BLAME ON GUEVARA AND HIS FORCES. THEREFORE, HE WILL PRESSURE GUEVARA TO MAKE THE ATTACK AT THE EARLIEST POSSIBLE TIME.

D.   ALTHOUGH, SINCE HE HAS ENCOUNTERED GREAT DIFFICULTY IN AUGMENTING THE SMALL FORCE HE HAS WITH HIM AT LULUPLAT, GUEVARA MAY BE RELUCTANT TO MAKE THE ATTACK, HE WILL PROBABLY BE FORCED TO DO SO IN ORDER TO SOLVE HIS OWN HEARTS AND MINDS PROBLEMS WITH MITOUDIDI. IN THIS CONNECTION, IT MUST BE REMEMBERED THAT GUEVARA THINKS OF HIMSELF AS THE

LEADER OF THE AFRICAN LIBERATION MOVEMENT. IF AN ATTACK ON ALBERTVILLE SUCCEEDED, HE COULD AND ALMOST CERTAINLY WOULD CLAIM THE CREDIT FOR BEING THE GENERAL.

E. BASED ON HIS ASSESSMENT OF THE STRENGTH AND ABILITY OF THE MITOUDIDI FORCES, AND PRESUMING THAT CURRENT INTERDICTION EFFORTS OF CUBAN REINFORCEMENTS FROM BOTH TANGANYIKA AND CONGO BRAZZAVILLE WILL CONTINUE TO BE SUCCESSFUL, SUPO BELIEVES THAT WITH THE AUGMENTATION OF, OR REPLACEMENT OF, HOARE'S MERCENARY FORCES IN THE ALBERTVILLE AREA BY CONGOLESE ARMY FORCES, ADEQUATELY SUPPLIED, CURRENTLY TAKING PLACE, IT WILL NOT BE POSSIBLE FOR GUEVARAN FORCES TO RETAKE ALBERTVILLE. MATA HARI AND UNDERSIGNED CONCUR.

F. MATA HARI AND UNDERSIGNED CONCUR THAT IT MUST BE KEPT IN MIND THAT NEITHER MITOUDIDI OR GUEVARA ARE TRAINED OFFICERS, AND THAT BOTH ARE DESPERATE AND EGOTISTICAL AND MAY TAKE ACTION AT ANY TIME THAT OTHERS WOULD REGARD AS ILL ADVISED.

HELPER SIX

TOP SECRET

NINE

TOP SECRET
2015 GREENWICH 8 JUNE 1965

FROM STATION CHIEF, LÉOPOLDVILLE,
CONGO
00025

TO DIRECTOR, CIA, LANGLEY
COPIES TO SOUTH AMERICAN DESK
          MR SANFORD T FELTER,
          COUNSELOR TO THE PRESIDENT
          THE EXECUTIVE OFFICE BUILDING
          WASHINGTON

1. AT 0635 8 JUNE 1965 A MESSAGE
FROM "TATU" (GUEVERA) IN LULUPLAT TO
CUBAN EMBASSY DAR ES SALAAM WAS
INTERCEPTED BY HELPER PERSONNEL,
DECRYPTED FROM CUBAN CODE SUGAR
FOUR, AND FURNISHED BY HELPER SIX TO
THE UNDERSIGNED.

2. GUEVARA REPORTS PROBABLE DEATH
BY DROWNING IN LAKE TANGANYIKA OF
COLONEL LAURENT MITOUDIDI, CHIEF OF
STAFF OF REVOLUTIONARY STAFF MILITARY
COUNCIL WHILE MOVING BY LAUNCH
FROM KIMBAMBA TO NEW LOCATION OF
HQ FOR GENERAL STAFF.

3. AIRCRAFT OPERATING IN SUPPORT OF
COLONEL SUPO REPORT INTERDICTION

AND SINKING OF LAUNCH KNOWN TO BE CLANDESTINELY TRANSPORTING MATÉRIEL AND PERSONNEL FOR GUEVERAN OPERATION IN THIS AREA AND AT THIS TIME.

4.   IT IS PROBABLE THAT COLONEL LAURENT MUDANDI WILL REPLACE MITOUDIDI. MUDANDI, NOW IN DAR ES SALAAM, IS A CHINESE-TRAINED RWANDAN TUTSI AND MAY DEMONSTRATE MORE INITIATIVE THAN MITOUDIDI HAS.

C. R. TAYLOR
STATION CHIEF LÉOPOLDVILLE

TOP SECRET

[TEN]

TOP SECRET
2015 GREENWICH 14 JUNE 1965
00031

FROM STATION CHIEF, LÉOPOLDVILLE

TO DIRECTOR, CIA, LANGLEY
COPIES TO SOUTH AMERICAN DESK
        MR SANFORD T FELTER,
        COUNSELOR TO THE PRESIDENT
        THE EXECUTIVE OFFICE BUILDING
        WASHINGTON

5. REFERENCE MY 00025 8 JUNE 1965

6. INTEL FROM COLONEL SUPO'S AGENTS IN LULUPLAT RELAYED BY HELPER SIX PERSONNEL

A-CONFIRMS PRESENCE OF COLONEL LAURENT MUDANDI IN LULUPLAT REPLACING MITOUDIDI AND EXERCISING CONTROL OVER GUEVERAN FORCES. B-REPORTS MUDANDI HAS CANCELLED ATTEMPT TO RETAKE ALBERTVILLE AND INSTEAD HAS ORDERED ATTACK "BY END OF MONTH" ON HYDROELECTRIC PLANT AT BENDERA.

7. BENDERA IS CURRENTLY GARRISONED BY APPROXIMATELY THREE HUNDRED (300) CONGOLESE TROOPS, NOT PARACHUTISTS, AND APPROXIMATELY EIGHTY (80) MERCENARIES UNDER MAJOR MICHAEL HOARE PRIMARILY CHARGED WITH SECURITY OF HYDRO-ELECTRIC PLANT AND DAM.

8. COLONEL SUPO WILL SECRETLY IF POSSIBLE REINFORCE BENDERA WITH APPROXIMATELY FIFTY (50) PARATROOPS WHO WILL BE ADVISED BY HELPER PERSONNEL AND SUPPORTED BY HUNTER RECONNAISSANCE AIRCRAFT.

C. R. TAYLOR
  STATION CHIEF BUENOS AIRES

TOP SECRET

[ELEVEN]
Bendera, Katanga Province, Congo
0540 29 June 1965

Master Sergeant William "Doubting" Thomas was having very disturbing doubts of the wisdom of his having taught Sergeant First Jette the fine points of rifle marksmanship as they applied to a U.S. Springfield Caliber 30.06 Rifle, Model 1903-A4 equipped with a Bausch & Lomb 4- to 8-power telescopic sight.

On the one hand, Jette had been an apt pupil. He was a natural shot. They came along every once in a while. Thomas had known a few. Although he had never in the last decade failed to qualify as High Expert with every weapon in the special forces arsenal, Thomas knew he was not a natural shot; he had to work at it. Jette, on the other hand, had apparently been endowed at birth with a degree of hand–eye coordination that had permitted him to do at least as well — after firing no more than 200 rounds through the first '03-A4 he had ever seen — as his teacher.

While Jette could not put a 168-grain bullet into the eye of a gnat at 100 yards, as the phrase goes, he *could* regularly hit the neck of a Simba beer bottle bobbing in Lake Albert at 250 yards — invisible to the naked eye at that distance. This told Thomas that Jette's brain was able to compute the time it took the bottle neck to swing from one side to the other and the time-in-flight of his bullet, and send the appropriate message to his muscles.

There was no problem vis-à-vis Sergeant First Jette's marksmanship, but rather with his military/political sophistication. Jette was having a good

976

deal of trouble understanding why he was absolutely forbidden to shoot any of the Simbas and their Rwandan and Cuban allies who were about to attack Bendera without having first obtained the permission of Major, Sir, Tomas in every instance.

The concept of permitting an enemy to escape when one had the ability to shoot him in the forehead was just about out of Sergeant First Jette's ability to comprehend, although Thomas had tried to explain the situation to him many times.

Sergeant First Jette had also had trouble with the concept of protecting one's hearing by the insertion of earplugs, and was going along with that strange idea solely because of his respect for Major, Sir, Tomas, whom he respected both as a soldier and as someone who knew how to move silently and invisibly through the bush almost as well as he himself did. Perhaps even a little better.

"Now what I think will happen, my friend," Major, Sir had explained, pointing at a map, "is that our friends will come out of the bush here, into this open area. Their primary objective will be to take the power-generating plant, here. It's about half a klick — five hundred meters — from the edge of the bush."

Jette nodded.

"We know they don't have artillery," Thomas had gone on, "although they may have mortars, and they know that the power station is guarded by Major Hoare's mercenaries. They also probably know that there will be no more than fifteen mercenaries on duty, and that the rest of the mercenaries will be in Bendera, and that it will take from ten to fifteen minutes for them to come to the power station from Bendera, once the attack starts.

"So what they will probably try to do is sneak up to the power station, overwhelm the mercenaries, and set themselves up to repel the mercenary counterattack fifteen minutes later. Then, when everybody — mercenaries and Congolese soldiers — has rushed to the power station, they will attack Bendera with the bulk of their forces. You understand me, Sergeant First Jette, my friend?"

Jette nodded.

"What they *don't* know is that we expect them; the attack will not be a surprise. And they don't know that we have twenty-five paratroopers with a machine gun here, on this side of the field, and another twenty-five with another machine gun here, on the other side of the field.

"And they don't know about you and me, my friend. We will be here, on the roof of the power station building. What you and I are going to do is take down their officers. Now, we don't want to do this until they have come — probably crawled — most of the way across the field. The paratroops will not open fire until the Americans with them tell them to, and the Americans will not do that until we fire. You understand?"

Jette nodded again.

"The idea is that if the Simbas and the Rwandans are most of the way across the field before we fire at them, the paratroops will be able to kill more of them before they retreat back into the bush than they would if we shot a couple of them the minute we saw them. We are going to have to be patient. Understand?"

Jette nodded.

"I have my orders from Colonel Dahdi that this man is not to be shot," Thomas said, showing him — for the tenth time — a half-dozen photographs of Ernesto Guevara de la Serna, M.D. "Colonel Dahdi will be very angry with me, and Colonel Supo will be very angry with you if we kill this man."

"Why is that, Major, sir?" Jette asked for the tenth time.

"Because those are our orders, Sergeant First Jette," Thomas replied, "and we as soldiers obey our orders even if we do not understand them."

"Yes, Major, sir," Jette said. "But what if he is killed by the paras?"

"Then you and I will still be in trouble," Thomas said. "Life is not fair, my friend."

"No, it is not, Major, sir," Sergeant First Jette agreed solemnly.

"You and I will be side by side on the roof," Thomas said. "I will tell you which of them to shoot. You are not to shoot anyone unless I tell you, you understand?"

Jette nodded.

"Let's go," Thomas had said, getting out of the jeep and then reaching in the back for the cased sniper's rifles, a rucksack, and a backpack radio.

The mercenary sergeant in charge of the power station guard detail was standing in the dark by the door of the power station. He was a short, stocky Frenchman with a pockmarked face.

Thomas had met him the night before, in Bendera, when finalizing the plans for the defense of the city and the hydroelectric plant with the mercenary commander, Major Michael Hoare.

Hoare knew that Thomas and the two Americans who had come with Supo's elite paratroopers were Americans and Green Berets, but that information was not shared with any of his officers or men. If Hoare suspected he was dealing with a

979

master sergeant, a sergeant first class, and a staff sergeant, rather than a major and two captains, he gave no sign.

He was actually very charming — Thomas had liked him at first sight — and completely agreed with the plan for the defense of the city and hydroelectric plant Supo and Father Lunsford had drawn up, but not before he had studied it carefully and asked what Thomas thought were intelligent questions about it.

There was little doubt in anyone's mind that the Simbas had spies all over the area, and that the Simbas knew many — perhaps most — of the details of Hoare's defense plans. The spies would immediately report anything out of the ordinary to the Simbas. It was therefore necessary to keep from both Hoare's mercenaries and the regular Congolese troops that there was a ninety-percent certainty that the power station would be attacked at first light, and Bendera itself, once the power station had been attacked and reinforcements had been sent to defend it.

The Congolese paratroopers had moved into the area in trucks with their tarpaulins in place, and there was no reason to think that anyone knew they were in the bush, and would move into their positions in the predawn darkness.

But the mercenary sergeant who would be in charge of the guard detail at the power station from 0600 had to be told that "a Congolese officer and his sergeant" would go into the roof of the building before dawn, and Hoare had sent for him, and told him.

The mercenary sergeant had made it clear that he did not like the idea of having a Congolese officer and a sergeant first on "his" roof, especially when Major Hoare told him it was none of his business what they would be doing, and, further, that he was to do whatever Major Tomas told him to do.

Hoare had picked up on the concern in Tomas's eyes, and when the mercenary sergeant had been dismissed, asked him if something was bothering him.

"I'm wondering, Major, if I have to tell that guy what to do, if he'll do it."

"He will do it," Hoare said. "I've ordered him to do it."

Tomas had still looked doubtful.

"We instill a high degree of obedience in our enlisted men by a swift system of punishment," Hoare explained conversationally. "The first instance of disobedience is punished on the spot by shooting them in the fleshy part of the leg. The second instance, we shoot them in the forehead. Sergeant Taller has already been shot in the leg. By me."

Jesus H. Christ! He means it!

"I suppose that would work," Thomas had said.

"Good morning, Sergeant," Thomas said, in French, to the mercenary sergeant. "I didn't see you standing there. And I guess you didn't see me; otherwise you would have saluted."

With obvious reluctance, the mercenary sergeant saluted, and Thomas returned it.

"It will not be necessary for you to tell your men that we are here," Thomas said. "Just show me how to get to the roof, and keep everyone off it until I tell you otherwise."

The mercenary sergeant nodded.

"What have you got in those long cases, Major? Rifles?" he asked.

"I could have sworn I heard Major Hoare tell you that what we're doing is of no concern of yours," Thomas said coldly.

The mercenary sergeant turned and wordlessly entered the building, waving his hand for Thomas and Jette to follow him.

The flat roof of the redbrick building turned out to be ideally suited for Thomas's purposes. There was a small wall, three feet high, more than high enough to conceal a prone body. Every ten feet or so along the wall — presumably to allow rain to drain off — the wall was level with the flat floor of the roof.

Thomas took two pillows marked "Hotel Du Lac" from the rucksack, tossed one to Jette, and then, bending it double, laid his in one of the depressions in the wall. Then he slid his Springfield from its case and laid the forearm on the pillow.

When he looked for Jette, he saw that Jette had finished doing the same thing. Thomas reached into the rucksack again, found the two pair of 8×57 Ernst Leitz, Wetzlar binoculars and handed one to Jette. Finally, he took out two bandoliers of .30-06 ammunition in five-round stripper clips and tossed one of them to Jette.

Then he dragged the backpack radio to his left side, checked the frequency, and turned it on.

"One, two, Hunter," he said to the microphone.

"One, go Hunter."

"Two, go Hunter."

"One more time, try not to shoot any white men," Thomas said.

"My mother warned me there would be days like this," a voice Thomas thought was probably

One — Sergeant First Class Omar Kelly — replied.

There was immediate confirmation of that.

"Hunter, Two." (Staff Sergeant Leander Knowles). "Say again daylight."

"Oh-five-fifty-five. It's getting to be that time. Four minutes."

"I hope they're late," One said. "I really like to lay a machine gun before I shoot it."

"That's enough radio chatter," Thomas said.

He propped himself up on his elbows and studied the vague visible end of the bush. He could see nothing.

Five minutes later, he could.

He picked up the microphone.

"Got what looks like a point man thirty meters from the right," he said.

"One, got 'em."

"Two, I got him."

Thomas set the binoculars down and put the rifle to his shoulder. He glanced at Jette and saw he had already done so.

When he put his eye to the telescopic sight, he could not see the man he had seen before.

Shit, don't tell me they know how to make like a snake!

He picked up activity at the edge of the bush. Four men stepped into the clearing, then dropped out of sight in the grass.

Thomas moved the scope ten yards into the field and saw movement, then a leg, or an arm.

"Ten meters ahead of the ones who just came in," he called to Jette.

"I see him," Jette said.

"Don't shoot him. Use him to show you where the others are."

Another man appeared at the edge of the bush and put binoculars to his eyes. Thomas examined him carefully through the scope.

He was black, but probably — because of the binoculars; the neatness of his uniform, and the fact he was wearing boots — a Cuban.

Thomas had already made up his mind to take down only Cubans. They had come here to cause trouble; if they didn't know what they were letting themselves in for, they should have. Simbas and Rwandans were going to have to be taken down, but let the Congolese do that.

"The man with the binoculars is mine, Jette," Thomas said softly.

"Yes, Major, sir."

Thomas found the point man again, and tracked him for a minute or so.

Then he tracked the others. After about five minutes, he was able to judge that about fifty men were making their way across the field, and, in his professional judgment, doing so pretty professionally. None of them — and the light was right for him to get a good look through the Bausch & Lomb sight — looked at all like Dr. Ernesto Guevara. For that matter, he hadn't seen anyone who didn't look as if he was black.

"Hunter, One, about fifty, I'd guess," the radio announced. "And it looks as if that's all of them."

"I'm going to let them get a little closer," Thomas replied. He looked through the scope again, and called to Jette. "The sixth man behind the point man is mine, too, Jette."

"Yes, Major, sir."

Thomas reached into one of the pockets of the cotton bandolier and took out the two five-round clipper clips it held, then took another two clips out. He pulled the bolt of the '03-A4 back, charged the magazine, and then slid the bolt handle forward and down. Then he reached for and took off the safety.

He flexed his shoulders, squirmed around on his belly, and did the other little things a marksman of his caliber and experience does to prepare to fire.

Then, close, there was a burst of automatic rifle fire and a siren began to growl.

Goddamn it, one of those mercenaries was wider awake than I thought he would be! Or maybe that mercenary sergeant wasn't as dumb as he looks, suspected something was coming off, and told the others to really keep their eyes open.

He swept the field through the scope, wondering if, once they had been fired on, and heard the squealing siren, if they would just retreat back into the bushes.

And all this fucking work will be for nothing!

But the attacking force was attacking, not retreating. And on their feet, rushing across the field toward the power station.

And there were half a dozen people waving their arms at the others, encouraging them to move forward.

Like that stupid fucking statue at the Infantry School. "Follow me, men! This way to where you get your ass blown away."

"Jette, shoot anybody wearing boots!" he called.

He found the man with the binoculars again, took in a breath, let half of it out, put the intersection of the crosshairs on the man's chest, six inches below his chin, and squeezed one off.

A half second later, he heard Jette's '03-A4 firing.

Goddamn loud! Oh, shit, after all the speeches I made to Jette, I forgot to put my goddamned earplugs in my ears!

Here lies Master Sergeant William Thomas, who was run over by a Mack truck he didn't hear coming because he was as deaf as a fucking post because he was too fucking dumb to use his earplugs!

By the time he had worked the action and found another target, he could hear the sound of the machine guns, and as he tightened his finger on the trigger again — but before he could squeeze one off — his target dropped his rifle, slid to his knees, and then fell forward on his face.

It took him almost five seconds to find another target, and he had to take that one down by laying the crosshairs on his back, twelve inches from the base of his skull.

XXV

"Mr. President," the Secret Service agent announced, "the Secretary of State is here."

"Send him in," the President said impatiently. "You know I sent for him."

"And Colonel Felter, sir."

"Him, too, for Christ's sake!" the President said.

The Secretary of State entered the Oval Office, followed by Colonel Sanford T. Felter. He looked around and saw the Director of the Central Agency was also in the room.

"Good morning, Mr. President," the Secretary said.

The President grunted.

"Good morning, sir," Colonel Felter said.

The President grunted again, and waved both men onto the couch across from the coffee table. He was sitting by the table in one of two identical armchairs. The Director was in the other.

The President slid a sheet of radio-teletype paper across the glass-topped coffee table to the Secretary.

"Now let those lying bastards try to tell us they

987

aren't helping the bastards in the Congo, and 'have no knowledge' of any Cubans in either the Congo or Tanganyika," the President said.

The Secretary picked up the message and read it.

TOP SECRET
2015 GREENWICH 30 JUNE 1965
00066

FROM STATION CHIEF, LÉOPOLDVILLE

TO DIRECTOR, CIA, LANGLEY
COPIES TO SOUTH AMERICAN DESK
        MR SANFORD T FELTER,
        COUNSELOR TO THE PRESIDENT
        THE EXECTUVIE OFFICE BUILDING
        WASHINGTON

1.   REFERENCE MY 00031 8 JUNE 1965

2.   DURING THE PERIOD 25–28 JUNE HUNTER AERIAL RECONNAISSANCE SURVEILLED WHAT WAS BELIEVED TO BE AN INSURRECTIONIST FORCE NUMBERING APPROXIMATELY THREE HUNDRED (300) MOVING COVERTLY FROM LULUABOURG TOWARD BENDERA IN KATANGA PROVINCE INTENDING TO ATTACK BOTH THE CITY OF BENDERA AND THE HYDROELECTRIC PLANT FOUR (4) KILOMETERS FROM BENDERA. AT 1600 GREENWICH 28 JUNE 1965 THE FORCE WAS LOCATED TWO (2) KILOMETERS FROM THE HYDROELECTRIC STATION.

3.   HAVING BEEN ADVISED BY MAJOR G. W.

LUNSFORD THAT SUCH AN ATTACK WAS HIGHLY LIKELY COLONEL JEAN-BAPTISTE SUPO SECRETLY REINFORCED THE MERCENARY AND CONGOLESE GARRISON WITH APPROXIMATELY FIFTY CONGOLESE PARATROOPERS ADVISED BY MSGT WILLIAM THOMAS, SFC OMAR KELLY AND SSGT LEANDER KNOWLES OF SEPCIAL FORCES DETACHMENT 17.

4.   MAJOR LUNSFORD AND COLONEL SUPO WERE IN AGREEMENT THAT THE ATTACK WOULD PROBABLY BE IN TWO PHASES, AN ASSAULT ON THE HYDROELECTRIC PLANT OUTSIDE BENDERA, TO BE FOLLOWED, ONCE THE PLANT WAS IN INSURGENT HANDS, BY AN ATTACK ON THE CITY, AND SUPO ORDERED THAT THE AMERICAN-ADVISED FORCE OF CONGOLESE PARATROOPS BE DEPLOYED AT THE POWER-GENERATING STATION.

5.   THE INSURGENT ATTACK BEGAN AT APPROXIMATELY 0600 GREENWICH 29 JUNE, WHEN APPROXIMATELY FIFTY (50) INSURGENTS ATTACKED THE HYDROELECTRIC PLANT. BY 0615 THE ATTACK HAD BEEN REPELLED, WITH A LOSS TO THE INSURGENTS OF NINETEEN (19) KIA AND FOURTEEN (14) WIA, ALL OF THE LATTER BEING TAKEN PRISONER. THERE WERE NO FRIENDLY KIA OR WIA. THE REMAINDER OF THE INSURGENT FORCE ATTACKING THE POWER PLANT RETREATED INTO THE BUSH.

6.   AT 0630 A FORCE OF ONE HUNDRED (100) CONGOLESE AND FORTY (40) MERCENARIES BEGAN TO PURSUE FROM BENDERA THE BULK OF THE INSURGENT FORCE WHO ALSO RETREATED INTO THE BUSH.

7.   A SEARCH OF THE KIA ESTABLISHED FROM IDENTITY DOCUMENTS THAT FOUR (4) WERE CUBAN, AND AN ADDITIONAL THREE (3) WERE PROBABLY CUBAN. A DIARY RECOVERED FROM THE BODY OF SERGEANT EDUARDO TORRES FERRER TRACED IN DETAIL HIS MOVEMENT AND THAT OF CAPTAIN VICTOR DREKE AND OTHERS FROM PITA CAMP #1 IN CUBA TO THE CONGO VIA PRAGUE, CZECHOSLOVAKIA AND DAR ES SALAAM, TANGANYIKA. THE IDENTITY DOCUMENTS OF ALL CONFIRMED CUBANS AND PHOTOGRAPHS OF THEIR CORPSES ARE IN THE HANDS OF MAJOR LUNSFORD PENDING INSTRUCTIONS.

8.   INTERCEPTED RADIO MESSAGE FROM CAPTAIN VICTOR DREKE IN BUSH NEAR BENDERA TO GUEVERA AT LULUPLAT REPORTED FAILURE OF ATTACK, AND SAID THAT ONCE FIRING STARTED, MANY RWANDANS HAD FLED ABANDONING THEIR WEAPONS, AND MANY CONGOLESE INSURGENTS HAD REFUSED TO FIGHT AT ALL.

9.   INTERCEPTED RADIO-TELETYPE

MESSAGE FROM GUEVARA IN LULUPLAT TO CUBAN EMBASSY DAR ES SALAAM RELAYED REPORT OF FAILED ATTACK AND STATED GUEVARA'S POSITION THAT IF COLONEL LAURANCE MUNDANDI HAD NOT DENIED HIM PERMISSION TO PARTICIPATE IN THE ATTACK "EVEN AS POLITICAL COMMISSAR" THE ATTACK WOULD HAVE BEEN SUCCESSFUL AS HE "COULD HAVE INSPIRED REVOLUTIONARY FERVOR IN THE ATTACKERS." COMPLETE TRANSCRIPTS OF THE EIGHT (8) MESSAGES WILL BE FURNISHED AS AVAILABLE.

10. COLONEL SUPO BELIEVES (LUNSFORD CONCURS) THAT COMPLETE ANNIHILATION OF RETREATING INSURGENT FORCE WOULD BE LESS PRODUCTIVE THAN PERMITTING FORTY TO FIFTY (40 TO 50) PERCENT OF FORCE TO RETURN TO LULUPLAT, AS THIS WILL INSURE NEWS OF DEFEAT WILL QUICKLY SPREAD THROUGHOUT BOTH INSURGENT COMMUNITY AND NATIVE POPULATION AND IS PROCEEDING ACCORDINGLY.

C. R. TAYLOR
STATION CHIEF LÉOPOLDVILLE

TOP SECRET

"You've seen that, right, Felter?" the President asked.
"Yes, sir."

"What would you have me do, Mr. President?" the Secretary asked.

"If we told your man Taylor right now to get those identity documents, the diary, and the pictures of the dead Cubans here, how long would that take?" Then he saw the smile on the Director's face. "Did I say something funny?"

"Mr. President, my 'man' in the Congo is actually a woman," the Director said.

"Really? I'll be damned! And how does she get along with Major Lunsford?"

"Sir, there is every indication that Major Lunsford and Miss Taylor are working very well together," Felter said.

"How long?" the President said.

"Well, sir, material of that sort has to be handled carefully," the Secretary said. "If there is a State Department courier in Léopoldville, or the area, it would be approximately twenty-four hours from the time he received the material until he could deliver it here."

"And if there's not a State Department courier handy?" the President asked. There was a tone of impatience in his voice.

"Then add, sir, the time it would take to get a courier to Léopoldville, from wherever we locate one, to that twenty-four hours."

"That's bullshit!" the President snapped. "Christ, how many officers do we have in Léopoldville right now? What's wrong with, say, one of the military officers, the military attaché, bringing it here?"

"That could be done, I'm sure, Mr. President," the Secretary said.

"Then do it. And no more than twenty-four hours after we have a look at those documents, to make sure we're not being sucker-punched, I want you — you, personally — doing a Joe McCarthy at the United Nations."

"Excuse me, sir?"

The President stood up, waving imaginary papers over his head in his hand.

"I have in my hand here proof that the Cubans are in the Congo," he said, "stirring up trouble, attacking the legal government of the Congo, and that — despite the repeated denials of the government of Tanganyika — they are doing so with the approval and support of the government of Tanganyika."

He looked at everybody triumphantly, then added: "The difference between you and Senator McCarthy, of course, will be that *we do have the goddamn proof*. Major Lunsford got it for us."

The President sat down.

"I'd like to think about that a moment, Mr. President," the Secretary said uneasily.

The President looked at Felter.

"For Christ's sake, Felter, don't tell me that you, of all goddamned people, agree with him?"

"Sir, it's not my position to offer —"

"You don't think it's a good idea to take this diary, the ID cards, all of it to the UN? Yes or no, goddamnit! Your position, Colonel, is whatever I tell you it is."

"No, sir. I don't, not at this time. I think we should get this material to the States as quickly as we can, but I don't think we should rush to the UN with it."

"You going to tell me why not?"

"Well, for one thing, even with the proof, they could — probably would — continue to deny it, sir. And if what we're after is to get the Tanganyikan — and Congo Brazzaville — governments to stop permitting the Cubans to use their ports to move men and matériel, I think the way to do that is without a confrontation. They're both liable to get their backs up — that would earn them, they might think, the admiration of other African nations for standing up to us — and they know we already disapprove, so they have nothing to lose. Right now, our interdiction efforts are apparently successful, and the insurgents' 'liberation' campaign is getting nowhere. And they know that, too. It very well might occur to them that since there is no apparent good — from their perspective — resulting from their cooperation with the Cubans, it would be in their interest to shut off the routes, which would (a) allow them to claim they're doing everything to claim to help the cause of peace, and (b) remove the threat that we are capable of going before the UN and proving to the world that they were lying."

The President looked at him, dubiously thoughtful.

"Mr. President, I rather agree with Colonel Felter," the Secretary said.

"Now, *that* really makes me suspicious," Johnson said.

They all waited for him to go on.

"How long would it take to get our ambassador to Tanganyika here?" he asked.

"Twenty-four, thirty-six hours, sir," the Secretary said.

"Why don't we get him here and see what he has to say?" Johnson said.

"Mr. President, if I may make a suggestion?" the Director said.

"Why not?"

"Miss Taylor, until very recently, was my station chief in Dar es Salaam. She probably has a very good idea of current Tanganyikan thinking?"

"You're not suggesting, I hope, that your station chief is more tuned in than my ambassador?" the Secretary said.

"I was thinking, simply, that she has the knowledge, and that she could bring the diaries, photographs, et cetera, with her," the Director said.

"Mr. President," Felter said. "At about this time, our supply plane is approaching Stanleyville. It will return to the States as soon as it's serviced."

"And could bring this lady? Is that what you're saying?"

"Yes, sir."

"Send her a satellite message to her to be on that plane," the President ordered. "With the ID cards, the diaries, and the photographs."

"Yes, sir," the Director said.

"And tell her to bring Major Lunsford with her," the President said. "I want his assessment of the situation."

[TWO]
Old Original Bookbinder's Restaurant
South Broad Street
Philadelphia, Pennsylvania
1745 5 July 1965

Of those invited, H. Wilson Lunsford, M.D., and Mrs. Lunsford arrived first. They were accompanied by Charlene Lunsford Miller, Ph.D., Stanley Grottstein Professor of Sociology at Swarthmore College, who had not been invited and whom Father Lunsford really wished hadn't invited herself.

He rose as his father walked to the table in the upstairs private room, shook his hand, hugged him, and then embraced his mother, a slight, trim, light-skinned, gray-haired woman.

"What's going on, George?" his father asked.

Miss Cecilia Taylor looked a bit uncomfortable under the frankly curious gaze of Dr. and Mrs. Lunsford and the even more fascinated gaze of the woman who had to be the sister George had described as being politically located somewhere to the left of Vladimir Ilich Lenin.

"There's someone I wanted you to meet," Father said.

"Aren't you going to say 'hello' to your sister, George?" Mrs. Lunsford asked.

"Hi, Charley," Father said. "What's new at Joe Stalin U?"

"Behave, George, for God's sake!" Cecilia ordered in Swahili.

Dr. Miller did not reply, but she looked at Cecilia with even greater curiosity.

"Mother, Dad," Father said. "This is Cecilia Taylor."

"I'm very happy to meet you, Miss Taylor," Dr. Lunsford said sincerely.

"And so am I," Mrs. Lunsford said. "I'm Esther Lunsford."

"How do you do?" Dr. Miller said.

"In here, Daddy!" Cecilia said, as a couple walked past the open door of the private dining room.

"Where the hell is the champagne?" Major Lunsford inquired as L. Charles Taylor, a very tall, light-skinned man who looked like the successful attorney he was, came into the room followed by his wife, also tall, and a waiter carrying a champagne cooler in each arm.

"Hey, Wilson," Mr. Taylor said. "How are you?"

Mrs. Taylor kissed Mrs. Lunsford on the cheek, and then Dr. Miller.

"Why am I not surprised?" Major Lunsford asked in Swahili.

"Ssssh," Miss Taylor said, in what could have been just about any language.

"What's going on here?" Mr. Taylor asked.

"I don't get kissed?" Miss Taylor asked.

"Oh, baby, I'm sorry," Mr. Taylor said, and bent over and kissed her.

"What are you doing here?" Mr. Taylor asked.

"Whatever it is, Charley," Dr. Lunsford said, sounding very happy, "it involves your daughter and my son and champagne."

"Jesus Christ!" Mr. Taylor said, taking a good look at Major Lunsford, who was in a light blue seersucker suit.

"Daddy, this is George," Cecilia said.

"I knew you in short pants, George," Mr. Taylor said, offering him his hand. "The last I heard, you had gone in the Army. What are you doing now? A doctor like your dad?"

"I'm still in the Army, sir," Major Lunsford said.

"Are you really?" Mr. Taylor said. He sounded surprised.

"We would both like to apologize for this," Cecilia said. "But it was either do it this way, or go back to the Congo without seeing you all, and together, and telling you."

"Telling us what, darling?" Mrs. Taylor asked, sounding a bit uneasy.

"Go back to the Congo?" Dr. Miller asked.

"We're on the six-o'clock Pan American flight to Durban in the morning," Cecilia said. "From New York."

"Tell us what, darling?" Mrs. Taylor repeated.

Cecilia extended her left hand, on which was a diamond engagement ring. She had had it on her finger for just over five hours.

"Oh, my God!" Mrs. Taylor said.

"I'll be damned!" Mr. Taylor said.

"Well, well," Dr. Lunsford said, beaming.

"What are you doing in the Congo?" Dr. Miller asked.

"I'm with the embassy there," Cecilia said.

"Are you really?" Dr. Lunsford asked. "And that's where you two met?"

"Right," Major Lunsford said.

"So what are you doing here? And why do you have to go back right away?"

"There was a conference in Washington," Cecilia said, having decided, with her fiancé on the train from Washington, that it probably would not be a good idea to tell their parents that they had spent two days at Camp David, where, among other things, they had had dinner with the President of the United States and Mrs. Johnson. "Just a quick trip. We have to go back to work."

"Why don't we open the champagne?" Major Lunsford suggested.

"Good idea," Dr. Lunsford said.

The waiter began to open one of the bottles of champagne.

"You're stationed in the Congo?" Mr. Taylor asked of Major Lunsford. "I didn't know we had troops in the Congo."

"I'm an adviser to the Congolese Army," Major Lunsford said.

"He's a Green Beret," Dr. Miller said. It sounded like an accusation.

"Are you really?" Mr. Taylor asked.

"It's supposed to be a secret, but the word is out," Dr. Miller said. "We're training the fascist army of Kasavubu to wipe out the liberation movement."

"Put a lid on it, Charley," Major Lunsford said.

"It's a disgrace, our being there," Dr. Miller continued.

"Well, somebody had to show them how to bayonet babies, Charley," Major Lunsford said.

"George!" Mrs. Lunsford said warningly.

"George, shut up," Cecilia said in Swahili.

"What language is that?" Dr. Lunsford asked.

"Swahili," Major Lunsford and Miss Taylor said in unison.

"And what is it, if you don't mind my asking, Cecilia, that you do in the Congo?" Dr. Miller asked.

"I'm attached to the Office of Cultural Affairs," Cecilia said.

"And what does that entail?" Mrs. Lunsford asked.

"Well, a number of things," Cecilia said. "We arrange for American symphony orchestras to visit the Congo, for example."

"And right now," Major Lunsford said, "Cecilia is pushing hard to get a troupe of Tutsi folksingers over here."

Mrs. Lunsford wondered why that earned George a dirty look from Cecilia. It sounded like an innocent remark.

Everyone was now holding a champagne glass.

"This isn't quite what I had in mind for Cecilia's engagement party," Mr. Taylor said, "but may I suggest we toast the engaged couple?"

"Here, here," Dr. Lunsford said.

Everyone took a sip of champagne.

"Did you propose in Swahili, George?" Dr. Lunsford asked. "And how did you two meet, incidentally? At the embassy?"

"I think I proposed in English," Major Lunsford said.

"We met at the embassy," Cecilia said.

"So you know what he's doing over there? And you approve?" Dr. Miller challenged.

"We don't talk much about our work," Cecilia said quickly.

"And when do you plan to be married? And where?" Mr. Taylor asked.

"We thought we would wait until we come home," Cecilia said.

"Oh, good!" Mrs. Taylor said.

"And when will that be, when you come home?"

"We talked about that in Washington," Cecilia said. "It shouldn't be long now. Maybe eight months, maybe six, maybe even less."

The President of the United States: *How long will it take before Guevara throws in the towel, Lunsford? Off the top of your head?*

Major G. W. Lunsford: *Sir, presuming we can continue to successfully interdict his replacement stream, and that Colonel Supo's plans to gradually take control of the area now under insurgent control are successful, a matter of months.*

The President of the United States: *How many months, Lunsford?*

Major G. W. Lunsford: *Eight at the outside, Mr. President. Possibly no more than four or five.*

The President of the United States: *Is there*

anything I can get you to speed that up any?

Major G. W. Lunsford: *I don't believe so, Mr. President.*

The President of the United States: *You don't want anything at all?*

Major G. W. Lunsford: *Sir, I'd like to get one of my men promoted.*

The President of the United States: *Oh?*

Major G. W. Lunsford: *Master Sergeant Thomas, sir. He's really doing more than a master sergeant should.*

The President of the United States: *See to it, Felter.*

Colonel Sanford T. Felter: *Yes, sir.*

"Anytime you're ready, sir," the waiter said to Major Lunsford.

"Now," Major Lunsford said.

"We're having first steamed clams and then lobster," Cecilia said. "I hope that's all right. George and I talked about having clams and lobster here in Bookbinder's when we first met in the Congo."

"That sounds fine," Mr. Taylor said.

"Great! There's no such thing as too much lobster," Dr. Lunsford said.

"I can't eat any crustacean," Dr. Miller said.

"No problem, Charley," Major Lunsford said. "I'll eat yours, and you can have a hamburger or something."

[THREE]

TOP SECRET
1905 GREENWICH 14 JULY 1965
00074

FROM STATION CHIEF, LÉOPOLDVILLE

TO DIRECTOR, CIA, LANGLEY
COPIES TO SOUTH AMERICAN DESK
          MR SANFORD T FELTER,
          COUNSELOR TO THE PRESIDENT
          THE EXECUTIVE OFFICE BUILDING
          WASHINGTON

1.   INTERCEPTED MESSAGE FROM
GUEVARA IN LULUPLAT TO CUBAN
EMBASSY IN DAR ES SALAAM REPORTS
THAT OVER GUEVARA'S OBJECTIONS THREE
(3) RWANDAN TROOPS INCLUDING MAJOR
(FIRST NAME UNKNOWN) MITCHELL SENIOR
RAWANDAN PRESENT AT BENDERA WERE
EXECUTED FOR COWARDICE AT BENDERA.

2.   INTEL FROM SUPO'S AGENTS RELAYED
VIA HELPER INDICATES THAT THERE HAVE
BEEN APPROXIMATELY FORTY (40) TUTSI
AND RWANDAN DESERTIONS FROM
LULUPLAT.

C. R. TAYLOR
STATION CHIEF LÉOPOLDVILLE

TOP SECRET

[FOUR]

TOP SECRET
1020 GREENWICH 7 AUGUST 1965

FROM STATION CHIEF, BUENOS AIRES

TO DIRECTOR, CIA, LANGLEY
COPIES TO SOUTH AMERICAN DESK
       MR SANFORD T FELTER,
       COUNSELOR TO THE PRESIDENT
       THE EXECUTIVE OFFICE BUILDING
       WASHINGTON

THE FOLLOWING RECEIVED FROM US ARMY OFFICER ASSIGNED US EMBASSY BELIEVED TO BE CONTROLLED BY MR. FELTER. IT IS RECOMMENDED THE INTELLIGENCE FOLLOWING BE REGARDED AS THE EQUIVALENT OF CIA RELIABILITY SCALE FIVE. IT IS TRANSMITTED IN ITS ENTIRETY AND VERBATIM.

START

DEAR FRIENDS:

AT 0630 6 AUGUST 1965, THE RUSSIAN FLAGGED VESSEL "FELIX ZDHERSINSKI" UNDER CHARTER TO THE CUBAN GOVERNMENT SAILED FROM MARIEL, CUBA FOR POINTE NEGRO, CONGO BRAZZAVILLE, WITH 200 CUBAN SOLDIERS FROM PITA CAMP 2 ON BOARD.

BEST REGARDS

[FIVE]

TOP SECRET
1905 GREENWICH 18 AUGUST 1965
00101

FROM STATION CHIEF, LÉOPOLDVILLE

TO DIRECTOR, CIA, LANGLEY
COPIES TO SOUTH AMERICAN DESK
MR SANFORD T FELTER, COUNSELOR TO
THE PRESIDENT
THE EXECUTIVE OFFICE BUILDING
WASHINGTON

1.   INTERCEPTED MESSAGE FROM
GUEVARA IN LULUPLAT TO CUBAN
EMBASSY IN DAR ES SALAAM REPORTS
THAT CUBAN LED INSURGENT FORCES AT
APPROXIMATELY 1000 GREENWICH 17
AUGUST 1965 SUCCESSFULLY AMBUSHED A
CONGOLESE ARMY CONVOY ON ROUTE
NATIONALE 16 APPROXIMATELY 25
KILOMETERS FROM ALBERTVILLE.

2.   REPORT STATES THAT CONVOY CONSISTED OF A LIGHT TANK, AN ARMORED TRUCK AND A JEEP WITH TRAILER; THAT SEVEN (7) PERSONNEL IN CONVOY WERE KILLED, AND ALL VEHICLES SET ON FIRE; AND THAT OTHER CONVOY PERSONNEL ESCAPED INTO BUSH.

3.   REPORT STATES THAT ALL KIA WERE WHITE MERCENAIRES AND ALL WERE BELIEVED TO BE U.S. CITIZENS.

4.   INFORMATION FROM COLONEL SUPO REPORTS THAT MAJOR HOARE'S MERCENARY FORCE REPORTS AN OVERDUE CONVOY IN THAT AREA CONSISITNG OF A FRENCH PANHARD ARMORED CAR (NOT A TANK); A STAKE BODY TRUCK WITH METAL REINFORCEMENT; AND A JEEP WITH A TRAILER. HOARE STATES NO REPEAT NO U.S. CITIZENS IN HIS MERCENARY FORCE.

5.   MAJOR LUNSFORD REPORTS THAT ALL REPEAT ALL OF SPECIAL FORCES DETACHMENT 17 PERSONNEL ARE ACCOUNTED FOR AND THAT NONE REPEAT NONE OF HIS MEN WERE ANYWHERE NEAR THE SITE OF THIS INCIDENT.

6.   A CONGOLESE REACTION FORCE IS EN ROUTE TO THE SITE OF THE REPORTED INCIDENT.

C. R. TAYLOR
STATION CHIEF LÉOPOLDVILLE

TOP SECRET

SIX

SECRET
HELP0073 2220 ZULU 27 AUGUST 1965
VIA WHITE HOUSE SIGNAL AGENCY

FROM: HELPER SIX
TO: EARNEST SIX

AFTER ACTION REPORT #14
REFERENCE MAP BAKER 11

1-REFERENCE MY AFTER-ACTION REPORT #5

2-HAVING BEEN ADVISED BY MATA HARI THAT APPROXIMATELY TWO HUNDRED (200) CUBANS WHO HAD DEBARKED FROM RUSSIAN VESSEL "FELIX ZDHERSINSKI" IN POINTE NOIRE, CONGO BRAZZAVILLE 21 AUGUST 1965 HAD SURREPTITIOUSLY CROSSED CONGO RIVER INTO THE CONGO IN GROUPS OF APPROXIMATELY TWENTY (20) DURING THE PERIOD 22–24 AUGUST, AERIAL SURVEILLANCE OF ROUTE 39 WAS BEGUN AS OF 0001 ZULU 24 AUGUST.

3-AT APPROXIMATELY 0900 ZULU 25 AUGUST 1965 1LT GEOFFREY CRAIG FLYING RECONNAISSANCE IN AN L19 NEAR SURINO, KATANGA PROVINCE, CONGO OBSERVED A FOUR TRUCK CONVOY ON ROUTE NATIONAL 39 SUSPECTED TO BE THE CUBANS EN ROUTE TO JOIN GUEVARA IN LULUPLAT.

4-THIS INTEL WAS FURNISHED TO THE CONGOLESE REACTION FORCE AT KAMINA, ADVISED BY MSGT WILLIAM THOMAS, AND AT APPROXIMATELY 1210 ZULU 25 AUGUST 1965 THE CONVOY WAS INTERDICTED APPROXIMATELY 35 MILES EAST OF SURINO, IN THE SAME LOCATION AS THE INTERDICTION REPORTED IN AFTER ACTION REPORT #5.

5-ONE HUNDRED NINETY-SEVEN (197) CUBANS AND A SUBSTANTIAL QUANTITY OF SMALL ARMS AND OTHER MATÉRIEL WERE SEIZED BY THE REACTION FORCE. THE CUBANS WERE TAKEN BY SURPRISE AND IT IS HIGHLY UNLIKELY THAT THEY WERE ABLE TO COMMUNICATE THAT THEY HAD BEEN STOPPED TO EITHER LULUPLAT OR CONGO BRAZZAVILLE.

6-CONGOLESE AUTHORITIES HAVE INFORMED THE UNDERSIGNED THAT IF INVESTIGATION REVEALS THE ALLEGED CUBANS ARE IN FACT ARMED FOREIGN NATIONALS IN THE CONGO WITH THE INTENT OF OVERTHROWING THE GOVERNMENT BY FORCE, THEY WILL BE DEALT WITH UNDER INTERNATIONAL AND CONGOLESE MILITARY LAW, WITH APPROPRIATE REPORTS TO BE MADE TO THE INTERNATIONAL COURT OF JUSTICE AT THE TERMINATION OF THE CURRENT STATE OF NATIONAL EMERGENCY.

CRAIG FOR HELPER SIX

SECRET

[SEVEN]

TOP SECRET
1035 GREENWICH 2 SEPTEMBER 1965

FROM STATION CHIEF, BUENOS AIRES

TO DIRECTOR, CIA, LANGLEY
COPIES TO SOUTH AMERICAN DESK
        MR SANFORD T FELTER,
        COUNSELOR TO THE PRESIDENT
        THE EXECUTIVE OFFICE BUILDING
        WASHINGTON

THE FOLLOWING RECEIVED FROM US ARMY OFFICER ASSIGNED US EMBASSY BELIEVED TO BE CONTROLLED BY MR. FELTER. IT IS RECOMMENDED THE INTELLIGENCE FOLLOWING BE REGARDED AS THE EQUIVALENT OF CIA RELIABILITY SCALE FIVE. IT IS TRANSMITTED IN ITS ENTIRETY AND VERBATIM.

START

DEAR FRIENDS:

A DELEGATION FROM THE SUPREME COUNCIL OF THE REVOLUTION OF THE CONGO, HEADED BY PRESIDENT GASTON SOUMIALOT, ARRIVED IN HAVANA 1600 HAVANA TIME 1 SEPTEMBER AND AT 1900 MET WITH RAUL CASTRO AND OTHER SENIOR OFFICIALS (NOT FIDEL).

IN A SOMEWHAT HEATED CONFRONTATION SOUMIALOT ACCUSED CUBANS OF NOT MAKING GOOD ON THEIR PROMISE TO SEND "SEVERAL HUNDRED, AS MANY AS FIVE HUNDRED" TRAINED SOLDIERS TO HELP WITH THE REVOLUTION. RAUL CASTRO REPLIED THAT THEY HAD SENT ALMOST 400 SOLDIERS SO FAR, AND HAD RECEIVED WORD THAT A COLUMN OF 200 CUBAN SOLDIERS HAD LANDED IN PUNTA NEGRE CONGO BRAZZAVILLE 21 AUGUST AND THAT THE CUBANS COULD NOT BE HELD RESPONSIBLE FOR WHAT HAPPENED TO THEM THEREAFTER; GETTING THEM TO THE WAR ZONE WAS RESPONSIBILITY OF CONGOLESE.

RAUL CASTRO ASKED FOR AN EXPLANATION OF FAILURE OF ATTACK ON (UNIDENTIFIED) HYDROELECTRIC PLANT, STATING HE HAD BEEN INFORMED BY CAPTAIN DREKE THAT SUBSTANTIAL NUMBERS OF REVOLUTIONARIES HAD REFUSED TO FIGHT. SOUMIALOT STATED THAT DREKE WAS A LIAR, WHEREUPON CASTRO TERMINATED CONFERENCE.

BEST REGARDS

END

J. P. STEPHENS
STATION CHIEF BUENOS AIRES

TOP SECRET

[EIGHT]

SECRET
HELP0099 2220 ZULU 18 SEPTEMBER 1965
VIA WHITE HOUSE SIGNAL AGENCY

FROM: HELPER SIX
TO: EARNEST SIX

INTELL REPORT #19

1 ON 1 SEPTEMBER 1965 THE
GOVERNMENT OF THE CONGO PUBLISHED
A NOTICE TO MARINERS THAT ANY VESSEL
ENTERING CONGOLESE WATERS OF LAKE
TANGANYIKA WITHOUT PRIOR NOTICE WILL
BE PRESUMED TO HAVE HOSTILE INTENT
AND WILL BE DEALT WITH ACCORDINGLY.
UNCONFIRMED REPORTS INDICATE SEVEN
(7) LAUNCHES HAVE BEEN DEEMED TO
HAVE HAD HOSTILE INTENTION AND WERE
SUNK BY CONGOLESE COAST GUARD
VESSELS AND/OR AIRCRAFT.

2 ON 14 SEPTEMBER MATA HARI ADVISED
UNDERSIGNED THAT THREE HIGH-RANKING
CUBAN OFFICIALS, (FIRST NAME UNKNOWN)
PADILLA; (FNU) COLMAN; AND DIONOSIO
OLIVA HAD ARRIVED IN DAR ES SALAAM VIA
AIR FRANCE FROM CAIRO AND WERE TAKEN
TO THE FARM AT MOROGORO.

3 ON 15 SEPTEMBER ASA INTERCEPTED
AND DECRYPTED RADIOTELETYPE MESSAGE
FROM MOROGORO TO "TATU" (GUEVARA)

SIGNED OLIVA STATING HE AND COLMAN AND PADILLA WERE LEAVING FOR KIGOMA IN MORNING AND LOOKED FORWARD TO SEEING HIM IN VERY NEAR FUTURE.

4 ON 17 SEPTEMBER ASA INTERCEPTED AND DECRYPTED MESSAGE SIGNED BY OLIVA, SENT BY LANDLINE FROM KIGOMA TO MOROGORO AND RELAYED TO TATU AS RADIOTELETYPE. PERTINENT EXTRACT "HAVE BEEN ADVISED BY LOCAL OFFICIALS THAT TRANSITING LAKE TANGANYIKA IS HIGHLY DANGEROUS BECAUSE OF FASCIST AERIAL SURVEILLANCE. CAN YOU COME TO KIGOMA?"

5 ON 17 SEPTEMBER ASA INTERCEPTED AND DECRYPTED MESSAGE FROM LULUPLAT TO CUBAN EMBASSY DAR ES SALAAM SIGNED TATU. PERTINENT EXTRACT "ADVISE OLIVA (1) TATU CANNOT COME TO KIGOMA (2) THERE IS ALWAYS AN ELEMENT OF RISK IN A WAR OF LIBERATION."

CRAIG FOR HELPER SIX

SECRET

[NINE]

TOP SECRET
1035 GREENWICH 4 OCTOBER 1965

FROM STATION CHIEF, BUENOS AIRES

TO DIRECTOR, CIA, LANGLEY
COPIES TO SOUTH AMERICAN DESK
        MR SANFORD T FELTER,
        COUNSELOR TO THE PRESIDENT
        THE EXECUTIVE OFFICE BUILDING
        WASHINGTON

THE FOLLOWING RECEIVED FROM US ARMY OFFICER ASSIGNED US EMBASSY BELIEVED TO BE CONTROLLED BY MR. FELTER. IT IS TRANSMITTED IN ITS ENTIRETY AND VERBATIM.

START

DEAR FRIENDS:

BY NOW I'M SURE YOU ARE AWARE THAT DR. FIDEL CASTRO HAS READ TO THE CUBAN PEOPLE DR. ERNESTO GUEVARA'S LETTER TO HIM, ANNOUNCING HIS RESIGNATION, IN THE FOLLOWING WORDS: "I FORMALLY RESIGN MY POSITIONS IN THE LEADERSHIP OF THE PARTY, MY POST AS MINISTER, MY RANK OF COMMANDER, AND MY CUBAN CITIZENSHIP. NOTHING LEGAL BINDS ME TO CUBA."

WE HAVE BEEN WONDERING HERE IF THIS, ESPECIALLY THE LAST SENTENCE, SUGGESTS THERE IS CONCERN THAT DR. GUEVARA'S ACTIVITIES IN THE CONGO WILL FAIL,

POSSIBLY SOON, AND THAT DR. CASTRO WANTS TO DISTANCE HIMSELF AND CUBA FROM DR. GUEVERA, AND HAVE WONDERED IF YOU ALSO HAVE BEEN THINKING ALONG THESE LINES.

ON THE OTHER HAND, IT MAY SUGGEST THAT DR. GUEVERA WISHES TO DISASSOCIATE HIMSELF FROM A CUBAN FAILURE IN AFRICA AND RETURN TO THIS CONTINENT AS AN ARGENTINE WHO WAS SUCCESSFUL IN AIDING DR. CASTRO, AND NOW WISHES TO LIBERATE THE REST OF SOUTH AMERICA.

BEST REGARDS

END

J. P. STEPHENS
STATION CHIEF BUENOS AIRES

TOP SECRET

[TEN]

SECRET
HELP0111 2005 ZULU 10 OCTOBER 1965
VIA WHITE HOUSE SIGNAL AGENCY

FROM: HELPER SIX
TO: EARNEST SIX

INTELL REPORT #22

1. AT 0900 ZULU 10 OCTOBER 1965 ASA INTERCEPTED AND DECRYPTED THE FOLLOWING RADIO MESSAGE FROM "SIKI" (CAPTAIN OSCAR FERNANDEZ MELI) BELIEVED TO BE IN VICINITY OF FIZI, KATANGA PROVINCE TO "MOJA" (CAPTAIN VICTOR DREKE) IN LULUPLAT:

BEGIN

FOR MOJA: THE SOLDIERS ARE ADVANCING ON FIZI AND THERE'S NOTHING TO STOP OR EVEN DELAY THEM. WE ARE MOVING FROM FIZI TO LUBONDJA. I WILL TRY TO DESTROY THE BRIDGES. TELL TATU MY TRIP WAS A FAILURE. SIKI.

END

2. COLONEL SUPO HAS ADVISED THE UNDERSIGNED THAT A RECONNAISSANCE TEAM OF FIVE (5) CONGOLESE PARATROOPS (ADVISED BY SSGT LEANDER KNOWLES) MOUNTED IN TWO JEEPS ARMED WITH .30 CALIBER BROWNING MACHINE GUNS ENTERED THE VILLAGE OF FIZI AT APPROXIMATELY 1115 ZULU 10 OCTOBER 1965, AGAINST NEGLIGIBLE RESISTANCE, AND THAT AS OF 1210 ZULU THE VILLAGE IS NOW IN THE HANDS OF CONVENTIONAL CONGOLESE TROOPS.

3. AT 1205 ZULU THE RECON FORCE BEING

ADVISED BY SSGT KNOWLES CAME UPON A GROUP OF INSURGENTS ATTEMPTING TO PLACE DEMOLITIONS CHARGES ON THE BRIDGE ACROSS THE LUVIDJO RIVER. THE INSURGENTS FLED ON SEEING THE RECON SQUAD APPROACHING.

PORTET FOR HELPER SIX

SECRET

[ELEVEN]

SECRET
HELP0114 1905 ZULU 12 OCTOBER 1965
VIA WHITE HOUSE SIGNAL AGENCY

FROM: HELPER SIX
TO: EARNEST SIX

INTELL REPORT #24

1.   FOLLOWING RECEIVED FROM SSGT LEANDER KNOWLES 1605 ZULU 12 OCTOBER 1965. KNOWLES IS ADVISING RECONNAISSANCE TEAM OF CONGOLESE PARATROOPS IN VICINITY OF LUBONJA, KATANGA PROVINCE.

BEGIN

FOR HUNTER SIX: PATROL ENTERED LUBONJA UNOPPOSED 1530 ZULU.

AWAITING SUPO'S TROOPS TO OCCUPY. INSURGENTS AND CUBAN ALLIES ABANDONED SUBSTANTIAL QUANTITIES OF WEAPONS, INCLUDING MORTARS, AND ONE HIGHLY INTOXICATED CUBAN CORPORAL, AS THEY WITHDREW. KNOWLES, SSGT.

END

CRAIG FOR HELPER SIX

SECRET

[TWELVE]

SECRET
HELP0117 1905 ZULU 14 OCTOBER 1965
VIA WHITE HOUSE SIGNAL AGENCY

FROM: HELPER SIX
TO: EARNEST SIX

INTELL REPORT #27

1. PERTINENT EXTRACT OF ASA DECRYPT OF RADIOTELETYPE MESSAGE FROM "TATU" (GUEVARA) IN LULUPLAT 1505 ZULU 14 OCTOBER 1965 TO CUBAN EMBASSY DAR ES SALAAM FOLLOWS:

BEGIN

CONCERNING FALL OF LUBONJA: OUR MEN'S ATTITUDE WAS WORSE THAN BAD. THEY LEFT WEAPONS THAT WERE UNDER THEIR RESPONSIBILITY, SUCH AS MORTARS, IN THE HANDS OF CONGOLESE AND THEY WERE LOST. THEY DIDN'T SHOW ANY FIGHTING SPIRIT. LIKE THE CONGOLESE, THEY THOUGHT ONLY ABOUT SAVING THEIR OWN SKINS, AND THE RETREAT WAS SO DISORGANIZED THAT WE LOST ONE MAN AND STILL DON'T KNOW HOW, BECAUSE HIS COMRADES DIDN'T KNOW IF HE GOT LOST, WAS WOUNDED OR WAS KILLED BY THE ENEMY. I HAVE DISARMED ALL THE CONGOLESE WHO SHOWED UP HERE. TATU.

END

HELPER SIX

SECRET

[THIRTEEN]

TOP SECRET
HELP0119 0855 ZULU 16 OCTOBER 1965
VIA WHITE HOUSE SIGNAL AGENCY

FROM: HELPER SIX
TO: EARNEST SIX

INTELL REPORT #30

1.   THE UNDERSIGNED HAS BEEN ADVISED
BY COLONEL SUPO THAT HE HAS ORDERED
"OPERATION SEVEN" TO BE EXECUTED AS
OF 0001 ZULU 16 OCTOBER 1965.

2.   THIS WILL BE A THREE-PRONGED
ATTACK INTENDED TO DRIVE THE
INSURGENTS TOWARD AN ENCIRCLEMENT
ON THE SHORE OF LAKE TANGANYIKA.
RECONNAISSANCE ELEMENTS OF THE
FORCE, SUPPORTED BY SF DETACHMENT 17
AERIAL RECONNAISSANCE, ARE CONGOLESE
PARATROOPS ADVISED BY OFFICERS AND
NCOS OF SF DETACHTMENT 17.

3.   THE MAIN ATTACK FORCE CONSISTS OF
CONGOLESE PARATROOPS AND
MERCENARY TROOPS UNDER MAJOR
MICHAEL HOARE. ONCE TERRITORY FALLS
UNDER THEIR CONTROL, THE MAIN ATTACK
FORCE WILL BE REPLACED BY
CONVENTIONAL CONGOLESE TROOPS.

END

HELPER SIX

TOP SECRET

FOURTEEN

TOP SECRET
HELP0124 0855 ZULU 24 OCTOBER 1965
VIA WHITE HOUSE SIGNAL AGENCY

FROM: HELPER SIX
TO: EARNEST SIX

INTELL REPORT #34

1. FOLLOWING RECEIVED FROM HELPER SIX
IN THE LULUPLAT AREA.

BEGIN

1.   AT 0535 ZULU 24 OCTOBER 1965 A
RECON FORCE OF CONGOLESE
PARATROOPS ADVISED BY MAJ G. W.
LUNSFORD AND WOJG WILLIAM THOMAS
ENTERED THE AREA IN LULUPLAT KNOWN
TO BE THE HEADQUARTERS OF "TATU."

2.   THE INSURGENT FORCES BECAME
AWARE OF THE APPROACH OF THE RECON
FORCE WHEN IT WAS NECESSARY FOR THE
RECON FORCE TO FIRE APPROXIMATELY
TWO HUNDRED FIFTY (250) ROUNDS OF
SMALL-ARMS FIRE AND TWELVE (12) HAND
GRENADES AT WHAT WAS BELIEVED TO BE
TWO (2) INSURGENT PICKETS ON
PERIMETER GUARD. NO DEAD PICKETS
WERE FOUND.

3.   WHEN THE RECON FORCE ACTUALLY
ENTERED THE HEADQUARTERS AREA, THE

INSURGENTS HAD FLED INTO THE BUSH, AFTER SETTING "TATU'S" QUARTERS ON FIRE, AND ATTEMPTING OTHER DEMOLITION ACTIVITIES.

4.   THE INSURGENTS LEFT BEHIND SUBSTANTIAL STOCKS OF WEAPONS AND AMMUNITION, FOOD STORES, RADIOTELETYPE EQUIPMENT, SOME DOCUMENTS POSSIBLY OF INTEL VALUE, AND TWO SPIDER MONKEYS KNOWN TO HAVE BEEN THE PROPERTY OF "TATU." SAID SIMIANS HAVE BEEN PLACED INTO THE CUSTODY OF WOJG THOMAS, WHO, FOR PURPOSES OF IDENTIFICATION, HAS NAMED THEM "FIDEL" AND "ERNESTO."

5.   "TATU" AND OTHER FORMER OCCUPANTS OF THE HEADQUARTERS AREA ARE APPARENTLY HEADED FOR LAKE TANGANYIKA. THEY ARE UNDER OUR AERIAL SURVEILLANCE, AND THIS RECON TEAM WILL PURSUE AT A DISCREET DISTANCE.

END

CRAIG FOR HELPER SIX

TOP SECRET

[FIFTEEN]

TOP SECRET
EARNEST 0081 0910 ZULU 2 NOVEMBER
1965
VIA WHITE HOUSE SIGNAL AGENCY

FROM: EARNEST SIX
TO: HELPER SIX

1   SECRETARY OF STATE HAS BEEN
ADVISED BY US AMBASSADOR, DAR ES
SALAAM, THAT CUBAN AMBASSADOR TO
TANGANYIKA WAS INFORMED 1600 ZULU 1
NOVEMBER 1965 BY TANGANYIKA FOREIGN
MINISTER THAT TANGANYIKA HAS "DECIDED
TO END THE NATURE OF THIS ASSISTANCE
TO THE CONGOLESE NATIONAL LIBERATION
MOVEMENT."

2   US AMBASSADOR WAS INFORMALLY
TOLD THIS MEANS TANGANYIKA WILL NO
LONGER PERMIT TRANSSHIPMENT OF
PERSONNEL OR MATERIEL ACROSS ITS
TERRITORY, BUT THAT AS A
"HUMANITARIAN" POLICY IT WILL GRANT
"TEMPORARY" REFUGE TO ANYONE FLEEING
THE CONGO WHO MAY HAVE BEEN
INVOLVED IN "LIBERATION" ACTIVITIES.

FINTON FOR EARNEST SIX

TOP SECRET

[SIXTEEN]

TOP SECRET
HELP0191 1205 ZULU 4 NOVEMBER 1965
VIA WHITE HOUSE SIGNAL AGENCY

FROM: HELPER SIX
TO: EARNEST SIX

1.   FOLLOWING IS AN EXERPT OF
DECRYPTED RADIOTELETYPE MESSAGE
FROM OSCAR FERNÁNDEZ PADILLA, HEAD
OF THE CUBAN INTELLIGENCE STATION IN
DAR ES SALAAM, TO "TATU" (GUEVARA)
(LOCATION UNKNOWN AT THIS TIME) 0900
ZULU 4 NOVEMBER 1965.

BEGIN

I AM SENDING YOU, VIA COURIER, A LETTER
FROM FIDEL. ITS KEY POINTS ARE:

1.   WE MUST DO EVERYTHING EXCEPT THAT
WHICH IS FOOLHARDY.

2.   IF TATU BELIEVES THAT OUR PRESENCE
HAS BECOME EITHER UNJUSTIFIABLE OR
POINTLESS, WE HAVE TO CONSIDER
WITHDRAWING.

3.   IF TATU THINKS WE SHOULD REMAIN
WE WILL TRY TO SEND AS MANY MEN AND
AS MUCH MATÉRIEL AS HE CONSIDERS
NECESSARY.

4. WE ARE WORRIED THAT YOU MAY WRONGLY FEAR THAT YOUR DECISION MIGHT BE CONSIDERED DEFEATIST OR PESSIMISTIC.

5. IF TATU DECIDES TO LEAVE THE CONGO, HE CAN RETURN HERE OR GO SOMEWHERE ELSE WHILE WAITING FOR A NEW INTERNATIONALIST MISSION.

6. WE WILL SUPPORT WHATEVER DECISION TATU MAKES.

7. AVOID ANNIHILATION.

END

FATHER AND I FOUND PARA 5. INTERESTING

CRAIG FOR HELPER SIX

SECRET

[SEVENTEEN]
The Hotel du Lac
Costermansville, Kivu Province
Republic of the Congo
2045 20 November 1965

Captain Weewili/Spec7 Peters found Lieutenant Colonel Dahdi/Major Lunsford sitting on the patio overlooking the lake drinking coffee with Captain Darrell J. Smythe, and Lieutenants

Geoffrey Craig and Jack Portet.

"What have you got, Peters?" Lunsford asked, both hope and impatience in his voice.

War is hell, and the worst part of the hell is the goddamned waiting.

Two days before, Guevara had radioed — a voice message in the clear; his cryptographic equipment apparently no longer available to him — to Kigoma, saying that he was withdrawing, and to prepare the launches for the evacuation.

There had been no reply to the message, but since it had been heard by three different American radio intercept teams — one of them now operating outside Kigoma — it seemed reasonable to presume that it had been received by the Cubans in Kigoma.

Unless, of course, the Tanganyikan government had gone further than ending "the nature of its assistance to the Congolese National Liberation Movement" and had shut down the Cuban radio station in Kigoma, or even arrested the Cubans.

That had posed an entirely new problem. If Guevara couldn't get across Lake Tanganyika, that would, obviously, leave him in the Congo. And there was nothing he could do in the Congo but surrender, or do something stupid, like charging some of Supo's troops, inviting them to shoot him.

The mission, of course, was to chase the bastard out of the Congo with his tail between his legs, not disappear, and certainly not to get himself on the front pages of the world's newspapers —

GUEVERA, FAMED FREEDOM FIGHTER, PERISHES IN HEROIC FIGHT TO THE DEATH IN CONGO

About 1600 that afternoon, the ASA intercept operators had intercepted another message — in Morse code, not encrypted — from Guevara, to someone named Changa, who was apparently in charge of the launches in Kigoma. Guevara said that he had two hundred men to evacuate and to send the launches.

This time, there had been a reply. "Changa" reported that he had been "detained" by Tanganyikan authorities, but had been released, and would attempt to cross the lake "tonight."

There had been no further messages, and none from Thomas or any of the others who were following the retreating Cubans and Simbas.

"Mr. Thomas called — voice message in the clear — sir, relayed from Outpost Mike — that's all he can talk to," Peters said. "He wants to know if you can come talk to him."

"He wants me to come there?" Lunsford asked incredulously.

"Yes, sir," Peters said. "He gave the coordinates."

Peters laid a map on the table and pointed.

"He said he walked the road; you can land on it."

"For Christ's sake, it's dark," Lunsford muttered.

Jack Portet got out of his chair and bent over the map. Thomas was pointing to a road near the shore of Lake Tanganyika, about ten kilometers south of Kibamba.

"I know that road," he said. "I can get in there — presuming he can light the runway with gasoline — in an L-19."

Lunsford looked at him dubiously.

"I can even get in there in the Beaver," Portet

1025

added. "It's mostly clear in that area, nothing on either side of the road, no power lines, et cetera."

"Doubting Thomas wouldn't want me there unless he has a problem," Lunsford thought aloud. "You really can get in there?"

Portet nodded.

"If you're going in the Beaver," Spec7 Peters said, "there'd probably be room for a radio. We could talk to the guys in Kigoma with it, without a relay."

"A radio you'd have to operate, right?" Lunsford challenged. "You have some kind of a death wish, Peters?"

"Or, for that matter, sir," Peters argued, "to Kamina, in case you wanted to call in T-28s or B-26s."

Lunsford gave him a look of mystification.

"As well, of course, to Colonel Supo," Peters said. "The radios Mr. Thomas has with him won't do that."

"If Portet can get in there in a Beaver, Aunt Jemima," Lunsford asked, "presumably you could get in there in an L-19?"

"I was about to suggest, sir," Captain Smythe said, "that Lieutenant Portet go in first in an L-19, possibly taking Peters — or maybe Peters's radio — with him, and once we know we can make a landing, I bring you and whoever else in the Beaver."

"I'll go with Portet and the radio in the Beaver," Lunsford said. "You bring Peters in an L-19." He turned to Craig. "You hold the fort, Geoff."

"Yes, sir."

"How long will it take to get there?" Lunsford asked of Jack Portet.

"Thirty-five, forty minutes," Jack replied.

"About an hour, counting time to get from here to the farm strip."

"Message Mr. Thomas to prepare the strip and to shoot a flare," Lunsford ordered. "ETA one hour, we'll call him from the area."

Major Lunsford looked out the copilot's window and saw the Beaver's wing strut and right wheel, and absolutely nothing else. He pushed himself up in the seat and got a better look out the windscreen, and saw absolutely nothing but the whirling propeller.

"I know exactly where I am," Major Lunsford said to Lieutenant Portet. "This is Africa. Somewhere to the left is Lake Tanganyika. But I wonder about you. How the hell are you going to find this road?"

Portet smiled at him, then reached for the microphone on the control yoke.

"Hunter One, Teeny-weeny Airlines One," he called.

"Go, Teeny-weeny," Thomas voice came back immediately.

"Hold your mike open for sixty seconds, please," Portet said.

"Acknowledged," Thomas replied.

Jack touched Lunsford's shoulder and pointed to the Radio Direction Finder indicator.

"He's over there somewhere," he said, and banked the Beaver to the left until the needle was where he wanted it.

"Hunter One, pop the flare when you hear me," Portet called, and reached over his shoulder from the trim control, putting the Beaver into a shallow descent.

"Acknowledge," Thomas replied.

"How are you going to keep from flying into the ground?" Lunsford asked, genuinely curious.

"I know the altitude of the lake from the charts," Portet said. "I will just make sure I'm fifteen hundred feet above the lake." He pointed to the altimeter.

Three minutes later, to their right, a bright yellow light appeared in the sky, and then slowly began to descend.

"I have your flare," Jack said to the microphone as he turned the Beaver toward the flare. Then he turned to Lunsford. "The trick here is to tell him when to light the gasoline," Jack said. "The sooner I see it the better, but I don't want the lights to go out just when I turn on final."

He pressed the microphone button again.

"Can you give me the winds, please?" he asked.

"From the south," Thomas replied. "Not much."

"You copy, Aunt Jemima?" Jack asked.

"Yeah, and I have the flare, too."

"When you have the field in sight," Jack ordered, "do three-minute three-sixties at the north end. Do not try to follow me in. We'll replenish the lights."

"Got it," Aunt Jemima

The flare disappeared.

"Shit," Jack said. "Thomas, I've lost the flare. Pop another one."

There was no acknowledgment, but thirty seconds later another bright light appeared in the sky, close enough so they could see the parachute under which it floated.

"Got it, light it up," Portet ordered.

There was a sixty-second wait, and then an orange light appeared on the ground and quickly turned into a line of fire. A moment later, another light appeared, and the second line chased after the first.

"You may begin praying now, Major," Portet said as he turned on final. He turned on the landing light, but Lunsford could see only the two parallel lines of burning gasoline.

Thirty seconds later, there was a rumble as the landing gear touched down on Katanga Provincial Route 23.

Jack stopped the airplane, turned it around, and taxied down the "runway" toward the headlights of a jeep. By the time he reached it, the gasoline "runway lights" were flickering out.

The jeep — now visible in the landing light — was parked to the side of the road. Portet taxied past it fifty yards farther down the road, turned around again, and shut down.

By the time they climbed down from the Beaver, Thomas was waiting for them.

He saluted Lunsford as a reflex action, and Lunsford returned it.

"I thought you'd come in an L-19," Thomas said.

"Aunt Jemima's up there in an L-19," Jack said. "Can we light the runway again?"

Thomas shouted orders in Swahili, and two jeeps — both with pedestal-mounted air-cooled .30-caliber Browning machine guns — that neither Lunsford or Portet had seen, suddenly started their engines and turned on their headlights, and started moving slowly along the runway. Congolese paratroopers kneeling in the rear seat poured gasoline from five-gallon jerry cans.

"Why the Beaver?" Thomas asked.

"Weewili suggested we could use a better radio to talk to Kamina or Colonel Supo," Lunsford said. "Weewili's in the L-19 with Aunt Jemima."

"That's good news," Thomas said. "Boss, you're going to have to talk to Supo."

"About what?"

"The situation is this," Thomas said. "Guevara and maybe thirty Cubans and a mixture of maybe two hundred, maybe more, Simbas and Tutsis are on the lakeshore about eight klicks from here. Kelly and Jette — you know Jette?"

Lunsford nodded.

"SFC Kelly, Jette, and another tracker are in a tree keeping an eye on them. The bad guys are all fucked up. Chaos time. They know the boats are coming for them tonight, and they suspect there's not going to be room for everybody.

"When I was up there a while ago, with SFC Kelly — he understands Spanish — he told me he heard Guevara trying to talk himself into staying — doing a George Armstrong Custer at the Little Big Horn — but that Dreke finally talked him out of it."

"Good," Lunsford said.

"The problem is the Congolese — our Congolese — and the mercenaries. They're about twenty klicks from the beach. They smell blood. The Congolese I understand — the Simbas have been killing their people, raping their women, and they want revenge for that, plus they have this warrior idea that when you have the chance, you kill your enemy. I don't know what's with the mercenaries, but they want to wipe everybody out too. I had a nasty session with a mercenary 'captain' — who just about told me to go fuck myself when I said the plan was to let everybody get in the boats."

1030

"Shit," Lunsford said.

"Major," Thomas said, very seriously, "Colonel Supo told me I had his permission to take down any mercenary who refused my orders."

"Hoare told me that was his version of Company Punishment," Lunsford interrupted.

"Now, I'll do it, if you tell me to —"

"No. Once Aunt Jemima gets on the ground with Peters, we can get on the radio with Supo. He can deal with his troops and the mercenaries."

"They should be about through pouring gas . . . ," Jack said.

"Get on the horn with Aunt Jemima and tell him," Lunsford ordered.

Jack crawled back into the Beaver and turned on the master buss.

Lunsford turned to Thomas.

"Bill, you did the right thing, telling me to come here."

"I want to go back to the shore, okay?"

"If you think that's where you should be," Lunsford said.

"That's where I belong, Father," Thomas said.

"Mr. Thomas," Major Lunsford said formally, "your orders are to take whatever action you deem necessary to ensure that Guevara is allowed to get on a launch."

"Yes, sir," Thomas said. "And Captain Dreke? Is he on the protected-species list too?"

Lunsford took a moment to reply.

"Let them go, Mr. Thomas," he said. "All of them. And that applies to Kelly and the two trackers."

"Yes, sir."

[EIGHTEEN]
**5 Degrees 27 Minutes 19 Seconds South
  Latitude
29 Degrees 17 Minutes 24 Seconds East
  Longitude
(The Bush, Near Lake Tanganyika, Kivu
  Province, Congo)
0240 21 November 1965**

Warrant Officer (Junior Grade) William E. Thomas aligned the crosshairs of the light-intensifying sight mounted on his U.S. Springfield Rifle, Caliber .30-06 Model 1903A4, on the forehead of Ernesto Guevara de la Serna, M.D., who was standing in ankle-deep water on the shore of Lake Tanganyika, holding the line of a forty-foot pale blue launch.

"Bang, you're dead, Ernesto," he said softly, then moved his sight to the yellow forty-foot launch run aground next to the blue one. He wandered around the people in the boat until he came to the face he was looking for. It was on a man standing in the stern of the launch, next to the coxswain. He aligned the sight on this man's forehead.

"Bang," Thomas said. "And you, too, Captain Victor Dreke, sir."

Ten minutes later, when even the amazing capabilities of the light-intensifying sight failed to give him anything more than a vague picture of two boats heading out into Lake Tanganyika, Thomas lashed the rifle to the tree and turned to the backpack radio lashed to the tree. He turned it on and put a set of earphones on his head.

"Helper Six, Hunter One," he said, softly, into the microphone.

"Go, Bill," Lunsford's voice replied immediately.

"The people we are interested in departed the Congo aboard two launches at zero two four five hours," Thomas reported. "They're hungry and dirty, and I actually felt a little sorry for them."

"What are you going to do now?"

Here lies Warrant Officer Junior Grade William E. Thomas, who was shot to death in the Congolese jungle by an illiterate Congolese soldier who mistook him for a Cuban.

"I thought I'd wait here until daylight, to see what happens."

"You and Kelly?"

"Right."

"Okay. Give us a call if anything turns up. And when you'll be at the landing strip. I'll send Portet back in the Beaver for you and Kelly."

"Thank you. Will do. Hunter One, clear."

XXVI

[ONE]

From *The Philadelphia Inquirer*, January 15, 1966:

MISS CECILIA TAYLOR BRIDE

Miss Cecilia Taylor was united in holy matrimony to Major George W. Lunsford by the Reverend Dr. Charles Chedister at the First Methodist Church of Bala Cynwyd during an afternoon service today.

Miss Taylor, a graduate of Temple University, is the daughter of Mr. and Mrs. L. Charles Taylor of Bala Cynwyd. Major Lunsford, a graduate of the University of Pennsylvania, is the son of Dr. and Mrs. H. Wilson Lunsford of Swarthmore.

The bride was given in marriage by her father. Miss Taylor's matron of honor was Mrs. Marjorie Bellmon Portet. Lieutenant Geoffrey Craig served as Major Lunsford's best man.

Following a reception at the Union League of Philadelphia, the couple departed on a wedding trip to Miami, Florida. They will reside in Buenos Aires, Argentina, where Major Lunsford has been assigned as an assistant

---

military attaché of the U.S. Embassy, and Mrs. Lunsford will assume duties as Deputy Chief of the Cultural Affairs Section of the embassy.

From the Newark (N.J.) *Star-Ledger*, January 17, 1966:

OUR BOYS IN THE SERVICE

Army Specialist Seven William D. Peters, son of Mr. and Mrs. Howard Peters of 365 Weequahic Avenue, Newark, has been promoted to Warrant Officer (Junior Grade).

A 1961 graduate of Weequahic High School, Warrant Officer Peters entered the Army in June 1961. He is a qualified parachutist and a communications specialist.

He has recently been assigned to the U.S. Embassy in Buenos Aires, Argentina, where he will work in the communications section.

From *The Washington Post*, January 20, 1966:

ARMY WILL TRAIN ARGENTINES

By Charles E. Whaley

The Pentagon confirmed today that the Argentine government has asked for, and the

U.S. Army will provide, a small group of U.S. soldiers, most likely to be selected from Special Forces units (Green Berets), to train Argentine troops in U.S. parachuting, mountain rescue, cold weather survival, radio communication and other special military techniques.

The group, which will "almost certainly not exceed twenty officers and men," will depart for Argentina probably within thirty days.

[TWO]

SECRET

Central Intelligence Agency
Langley, Virginia

FROM: Assistant Director For Administration

DATE: 2 February 1966 0405 GMT

SUBJECT: Guevara, Ernesto (Memorandum # 87.)

TO: Mr. Sanford T. Felter
Counselor To The President
Room 637, The Executive Office Building
Washington, D.C.

By Courier

In compliance with Presidential Memorandum to The Director, Subject: "Ernesto 'Che' Guevara," dated 14 December 1964, the following information, provided by the FBI, is furnished:

From CIA Prague, Czechoslovakia (Reliability Scale Five).

SUBJECT arrived Prague 1650 GMT 1 February 1966 aboard Aeroflot Flight 9003 from Dar es Salaam, Tanganyika via Cairo. SUBJECT is using Cuban Diplomatic passports in name of Ramón Benítez. SUBJECT was met by Cuban ambassador and Czech officials and was taken by car to residence of Cuban ambassador.

Howard W. O'Connor
HOWARD W. O'CONNOR

S E C R E T

[THREE]

TOP SECRET
1520 GREENWICH 26 MAY 1966

FROM STATION CHIEF, BUENOS AIRES

TO DIRECTOR, CIA, LANGLEY
COPIES TO SOUTH AMERICAN DESK
          MR SANFORD T. FELTER,
          COUNSELOR TO THE PRESIDENT
          THE EXECUTIVE OFFICE BUILDING
          WASHINGTON

A RIOT FOLLOWED A BEFORE-DAWN POLICE ATTEMPT TO BREAKUP A DISORDERLY STUDENT MEETING AT THE SCHOOL OF ECONOMIC SCIENCES ON AVENIDA CÓRDOBA IN DOWNTOWN BUENOS AIRES TODAY.

RIOTING STUDENTS, SOME CARRYING PLACARDS WITH PHOTOGRAPHS OF ERNESTO "CHE" GUEVARA, AND OTHERS RED FLAGS, PROTESTING A SHORTAGE OF UNIVERSITY FUNDS, OVERTURNED AND BURNED A CAR, SMASHED SHOP WINDOWS AND STREET LAMPS AND THREW COBBLESTONES AT POLICE FOR MORE THAN TWO HOURS.

IN A PRIVATE LUNCHEON CONVERSATION TODAY AT THE CIRCULO MILITAR WITH MAJOR G. W. LUNSFORD, LIEUTENANT GENERAL PASCUAL PISTARINI, COMMANDER IN CHIEF OF THE ARGENTINE ARMY, SAID "THE COMMUNIST SITUATION IS GETTING OUT OF CONTROL AND SOMETHING MUST BE DONE."

C. B. TAYLOR
STATION CHIEF BUENOS AIRES

TOP SECRET

[FOUR]

SECRET
1710 GREENWICH 31 MAY 1966

FROM STATION CHIEF, BUENOS AIRES

TO DIRECTOR, CIA, LANGLEY
COPIES TO SOUTH AMERICAN DESK
      MR SANFORD T. FELTER,
      COUNSELOR TO THE PRESIDENT
      THE EXECUTIVE OFFICE BUILDING
      WASHINGTON

FOLLOWING ARE WHAT ARE CONSIDERED
SIGNIFICANT EXTRACTS FROM THE SPEECH
GIVEN YESTERDAY BY LIEUTENANT GENERAL
PASCUAL PISTARINI, COMMANDER-IN-CHIEF
OF THE ARGENTINE ARMY AT CEREMONIES
MARKING THE 156TH ANNIVERSARY OF THE
FOUNDING OF THE ARGENTINE ARMY: "THE
ARMY IS AN INSEPARABLE PART OF THE
NATIONAL COMMUNITY, LEGALLY INVESTED
WITH THE RESPONSIBILITY OF ASSURING
THE DOMESTIC PEACE, AND IT MUST
FULFILL ALL OF ITS OBLIGATIONS. THE ARMY
DOES NOT ONLY REPRESENT A
PHILOSOPHY, BUT IS ALSO RESPONSIBLE
FOR THE AUTHORITY WITHOUT WHICH
THERE CAN BE NO FREEDOM."

C. B. TAYLOR
STATION CHIEF BUENOS AIRES

SECRET

FIVE

SECRET
1305 GREENWICH 29 JUNE 1966

FROM STATION CHIEF, BUENOS AIRES

TO DIRECTOR, CIA, LANGLEY
COPIES TO SOUTH AMERICAN DESK
        MR SANFORD T. FELTER,
        COUNSELOR TO THE PRESIDENT
        THE EXECUTIVE OFFICE BUILDING
        WASHINGTON

1.   AT APPROXIMATELY 0100 GMT (2100 BUENOS AIRES TIME) 28 JUNE 1966 TROOPS SEIZED RADIO STATIONS AND COMMUNICATION CENTERS IN BUENOS AIRES, AND THE PUBLIC WAS INFORMED THAT LIEUTENANT GENERAL PASCUAL PISTARINI, COMMANDER IN CHIEF OF THE ARGENTINE ARMY HAD "WITHDRAWN THE ARMY'S RECOGNITION OF THE MINISTER FOR WAR."

2.   AT 0440 GMT PRESIDENT ARTURO ILLIA, SPEAKING FROM THE CASA ROSADA, WHICH WAS GUARDED BY TROOPS OF THE SAN MARTIN REGIMENT OF GRENADIERS, ANNOUNCED THAT PISTARINI HAD BEEN DISMISSED AND HE WAS ASSUMING THE DUTIES OF COMMANDER-IN-CHIEF OF THE ARMY.

3.   AT 1105 GMT AIR SECRETARY BRIGA-

DIER MARIO ROMANELLI ANNOUNCED THAT A JUNTA CONSISTING OF PISTARINI, ADMIRAL BENINO VARELA (CHIEF OF NAVAL OPERATIONS), AND BRIGADIER ADOLFO T. ALVAREZ (COMMANDER IN CHIEF, AIR FORCE) WERE EXERCISING "NATIONAL AUTHORITY" PENDING THE SWEARING IN OF LIEUTENANT GENERAL JUAN CARLOS ONGANIA AT NOON TODAY. ONGANIA WAS FORMERLY CINC OF THE ARMY.

4.   DEPOSED PRESIDENT ILLIA IS BELIEVED TO BE UNDER HOUSE ARREST. IT IS BELIEVED THE COUP WAS ENTIRELY BLOODLESS.

C. B. TAYLOR
STATION CHIEF BUENOS AIRES

SECRET

[SIX]

SECRET
2205 GREENWICH 7 JULY 1966

FROM STATION CHIEF, BUENOS AIRES

TO DIRECTOR, CIA, LANGLEY
COPIES TO SOUTH AMERICAN DESK
        MR SANFORD T. FELTER,
        COUNSELOR TO THE PRESIDENT

THE EXECUTIVE OFFICE BUILDING
WASHINGTON

1.   ON 4 JULY AT THE INDEPENDENCE DAY PARTY AT THE AMERICAN CLUB OF BUENOS AIRES, LIEUTENANT GEOFFREY CRAIG WAS APPROACHED BY LIEUTENANT COLONEL RICARDO FOSTERWOOD, AIDE-DE-CAMP TO LIEUTENANT GENERAL PISTARINI, AND INFORMED THAT PISTARINI HAD ARRANGED FOR A MEMBERSHIP FOR HIM IN THE SAN JORGE POLO CLUB AND THAT HE HOPED HE WOULD ACCEPT.

2.   ON 6 JULY FOSTERWOOD TELEPHONED CRAIG AND INVITED HIM TO PLAY IN "AN INFORMAL POLO MATCH" AT THE SAN JORGE CLUB AT 1300 LOCAL TIME 7 JULY 1966. ON ARRIVAL AT THE CLUB, CRAIG LEARNED THAT HE WOULD BE PLAYING WITH PRESIDENT ONGANIA, GENERAL PISTARINI, AND LIEUTENANT COLONEL GUILLERMO RANGIO, THE DEPUTY DIRECTOR OF S.I.D.E.

3.   FOLLOWING THE POLO MATCH, PISTARINI TOLD CRAIG THAT HE SHOULD TELL HIS UNCLE (OBVIOUSLY REFERRING TO LIEUTENANT COLONEL CRAIG W. LOWELL) THAT THE NEW ARGENTINE GOVERNMENT WOULD CONTINUE TO HONOR ALL ASPECTS OF THE ARRANGEMENT HE HAD STRUCK WITH LOWELL WITH REGARD TO GUEVARA.

4.   FOLLOWING THE CRAIG/PISTARINI CONVERSATION, RANGIO GAVE CRAIG AN ENVELOPE WHICH CONTAINED THE MATERIAL QUOTED BELOW, AND "SUGGESTED" THAT CRAIG MAKE A HABIT OF TAKING A COCKTAIL EVERY MONDAY, WEDNESDAY, AND FRIDAY AT 1700 LOCAL TIME AT THE JOCKEY CLUB. CRAIG INFERS THIS IS BECAUSE THIS WOULD PROVIDE RANGIO AN OPPORTUNITY TO MEET WITH HIM IN WHAT WOULD APPEAR TO BE A SOCIAL CIRCUMSTANCE.

BEGIN RAGIO INTEL

DEAR FRIENDS

I'M SURE YOUR ACQUAINTANCES IN THE CIA WILL BE INTERESTED TO LEARN THAT OUR FRIEND THE DOCTOR IS NOW "SECRETLY" RESIDING IN A LOVELY VILLA IN THE VINALES AREA OF PINAR DEL RIO PROVINCE, CUBA, WIDELY BELIEVED TO HAVE BEEN THE PROPERTY OF A CIA AGENT.

IT IS NOW THE HEADQUARTERS OF A "SECRET" TRAINING CAMP BEING USED TO TRAIN A DOZEN CUBAN OFFICERS FOR SERVICE IN BOLIVIA.

THEY ARE:

DARIEL ALARCN RAMIREZ. ("BENINO"; 28; SERVED WITH OUR FRIEND IN THE SIERRA AND IN AFRICA.)

ELISIO REYES ("ROLANDO"; 26; SIERRA AND FORMERLY HEAD OF CUBAN NATIONAL POLICE INTELLIGENCE.)

ANTONIO PANTOJA ("OLO"; 33; SIERRA)

LEONARDO TAMAYO ("TAMAYITA"; 37; SINCE 1957, GUEVARA'S BODYGUARD)

RENE TAMOYO ("ARTURO"; 31; BROTHER OF LEONARDO; CLANDESTINE OPERATIONS FOR STATE SECURITY)

GUSTAVO DE HOED ("ALEJANDRO"; 29; SIERRA AND FORMERLY VICE MINISTER OF INDUSTRY)

MIGUEL HERNANDEZ OSORIO ("MANUEL"; 35; SIERRA)

ALBERTO FERNANDEZ MONTES DE OCA ("PACHO"; 31; WITH GUEVARA IN PRAGUE AFTER GUEVARA LEFT THE CONGO; SERVES AS HIS COURIER TO BOLIVIA)

OCTAVIO DE LA PEDRAJA ("MOROGORO"; 31; A PHYSICIAN; SIERRA AND CONGO)

ISRAEL REYES ZAYAS ("BRAULIO"; 33; SIERRA AND CONGO)

JUAN VITALIO ACUNA ("JOAQUIN"; 41; SIERRA; IS A COMANDANTE)

ANTONIO SANCHEZ DIAZ ("MARCOS"; 35;

SIERRA; ALSO A COMANDANTE)

JESUS SUAREZ GAYOL ("RUBIO"; 33; SIERRA; VICE MINISTER FOR SUGAR)

IT WOULD APPEAR, TO JUDGE FROM THE BACKGROUNDS OF THESE PEOPLE, THAT, PROBABLY SMARTING FROM THE HUMILIATION IN THE CONGO, AND DETERMINED TO BE SUCCESSFUL IN BOLIVIA, GUEVARA HAS RECRUITED THE BEST GUERRILLA FIGHTERS AVAILABLE IN CUBA. WE THINK IT SIGNIFICANT THAT TWO OF THEM ARE COMANDANTES, A VERY SENIOR RANK IN THE NEW CUBA.

EXACTLY WHEN THEY WILL GO TO BOLIVIA IS UNKNOWN AT THIS TIME, BUT IT SHOULD BE IN THE NEAR FUTURE.

BEST REGARDS

END RADIO INTEL

C. B. TAYLOR
STATION CHIEF BUENOS AIRES

SECRET

[SEVEN]

TOP SECRET
ARG 0019 2300 ZULU 30 AUGUST 1966
VIA WHITE HOUSE SIGNAL AGENCY

FROM: POLO SIX
TO: EARNEST SIX

AFTER-ACTION REPORT #1

REFERENCE US ARMY MAP SERVICE MAP
4774 BOLIVIA

1-DURING THE PERIOD 27 THROUGH 30
AUGUST, THE UNDERSIGNED TRAVELED TO
LA PAZ, BOLIVIA BY US ARMY L23 AIRCRAFT,
PILOTED BY 1LT GEOFFREY CRAIG AND
WOJG ENRICO DE LA SANTIAGO. OTHER
MEMBERS OF THE PARTY INCLUDED
LIEUTENANT COLONEL GUILLERMO RANGIO
OF THE ARGENTINE ARMY, WOJG JULIO
ZAMMORO AND MISS CECILIA TAYLOR.
UNDER THE CIRCUMSTANCES, IT WAS
CONSIDERED NECESSARY TO MAKE THE
IDENTITY OF THE CIA STATION CHIEF
BUENOS AIRES KNOWN TO LTCOL RANGIO.

2-CONFERENCES WERE HELD IN A SAFE
HOUSE CONTROLLED BY CIA STATION
CHIEF LA PAZ WITH A DELEGATION OF
BOLIVIAN ARMY OFFICERS HEADED BY
LTCOL ENRICO CUPULL, WHOM BOTH CIA
STATION CHIEF LA PAZ AND LTCOL RANGIO
CONSIDER "RELIABLE," AND WITH WHOM
WOJG ZAMMORO IS PERSONALLY
ACQUAINTED. CIA OFFICERS, RANGIO, AND
UNDERSIGNED STRONGLY EMPHASIZED
THE POSITION OF THE US GOVERNMENT
THAT GUEVARA MUST BE FRUSTRATED IN

HIS EFFORTS TO TAKE OVER BOLIVIA, BUT
KEPT ALIVE. CUPULL STATED THAT HE
PERSONALLY DISAGREED WITH THAT
POLICY, AND FURTHERMORE, THAT IT
WOULD BE DIFFICULT TO KEEP GUEVARA,
OR ANY CUBANS, ALIVE "AFTER THEY START
GUERRILLA ACTIVITIES." CIA STATION
CHIEFS LA PAZ AND BUENOS AIRES
INTENDED TO SEPARATELY STRONGLY
RECOMMEND DIPLOMATIC EFFORTS AT
HIGHEST LEVEL TO ENSURE COOPERATION
OF BOLIVIAN GOVERNMENT IN THIS
REGARD.

3-THERE WAS, WITH EXCEPTION OF
KEEPING GUEVARA ALIVE, A MEETING OF
MINDS ON MEANS TO FRUSTRATE GUEVARA
IN BOLIVIA. CUPULL WENT SO FAR AS TO
STATE IT MIGHT BE A "GOOD IDEA" TO
HAVE ZAMMORO REMAIN IN BOLIVIA, OR
GO THERE SOON, WHERE HE COULD
"EASILY ASSUME COVERT IDENTITY OF
BOLIVIAN ARMY OFFICER." CIA OFFICERS
FEEL THIS WOULD BE A GOOD IDEA, BUT
UNDERSIGNED DOES NOT FEEL HE HAS
AUTHORITY TO MAKE THIS DECISION, AND
WILL WAIT FOR GUIDANCE.

4-INTEL HAS SHARED BETWEEN RANGIO,
UNDERSIGNED, CIA OFFICERS AND CUPULL,
INCLUDING LIST OF PERSONNEL CUBANS
ARE TRAINING FOR BOLIVIAN SERVICE.
BOLIVIANS INFORMED US THEY ARE AWARE
THAT GERMAN/ARGENTINE HAYDEE

TAMARA BUNKE, "TANIA" WHO IS LIVING IN LA PAZ AS LAURA GUTIERREZ BAUER, IS A DEEP COVER CUBAN AGENT WHO IS UNDER SURVEILLANCE. THEY ALSO HAVE REGIS DEBRAY, A FRENCH JOURNALIST, UNDER SURVEILLANCE, AND REPORTED THAT HE HAD BEEN MEETING WITH MOISES GUEVARA (NO RELATION), A COMMUNIST MINERS' LEADER KNOWN TO BE PREPARING TO CONDUCT REVOLUTIONARY ACTIVITIES AGAINST THE BOLIVIAN GOVERNMENT. NO ACTION AGAINST EITHER IS PLANNED BY BOLIVIAN GOVERNMENT AT THIS TIME.

5-FINALLY, CUPULL STATED THAT A 1500-HECTARE (3700-ACRE) FARM (ACTUALLY WILDERNESS) IN THE SOUTHEAST OF BOLIVIA WAS PURCHASED, OSTENSIBLY FOR USE AS A PIG FARM, IN THE LAST FEW DAYS BY KNOWN BOLIVIAN COMMUNISTS, AND THAT THE PROPERTY WAS IDEALLY SUITED AS A BASE FOR GUEVARA'S OPERATIONS. AFTER ASSURANCES FROM CUPULL THAT DOING SO WOULD NOT CAUSE ALARM, WE OVERFLEW AND PHOTOGRAPHED THE FARM ON OUR RETURN TO ARGENTINA.

6-THE RIVER ÑANCAHAZÚ (WHICH IS DRY DURING THE SUMMER) RUNS THROUGH THE PROPERTY, ON WHICH ARE LOCATED A FEW PRIMITIVE FARM BUILDINGS AND LITTLE ELSE. IT IS AT THE EDGE OF A TROPICAL DESERT EXTENDING EASTWARD

TO THE PARAGUAYAN BORDER. IT IS 150 MILES SOUTH OF VERA CRUZ, TO WHICH A DIRT ROAD LEADS. IT IS 150 MILES FROM THE ARGENTINE BORDER, AND 12 MILES FROM THE NEAREST TOWN, LAGUNILLAS. THE TERRAIN IS HILLY AND THERE ARE FEW ROADS CAPABLE OF TAKING ANYTHING BUT A JEEP. IT (AND THE AREA AROUND IT) IS IDEALLY SUITED FOR GUERRILLA EVASIVE OPERATIONS, BECAUSE OF THE TERRAIN, THE HEAVY FORESTS, AND THE LACK OF ROADS.

7-IN VIEW OF THE FOREGOING, IT IS RECOMMENDED THAT THE UNDERSIGNED BE GRANTED PERMISSION TO OFFER TO UNOFFICIALLY TRAIN BOLIVIAN FORCES IN GUERRILLA DETECTION TECHNIQUES UTILIZING SPECIAL FORCES PERSONNEL PRESENTLY IN ARGENTINA. RANGIO BELIEVES CUPULL WOULD ACCEPT SUCH AN OFFER, ESPECIALLY IF IT WERE TO BE UNDER THE CONTROL OF ZAMMORO.

G. W. LUNSFORD, MAJ INF

TOP SECRET

TOP SECRET
EARNEST 0134 1405 ZULU 31 AUGUST 1966
VIA WHITE HOUSE SIGNAL AGENCY

FROM: EARNEST SIX
TO: POLO SIX

1-REFERENCE YOUR AFTER-ACTION REPORT # 1

2-IN RE ZAMMORO MOVING COVERTLY TO BOLIVIA. YOUR CALL. DIRECTOR CIA CONCURS.

3-IN RE UNOFFICIAL TRAINING PROGRAM AS OUTLINED. PRESUMING CONCURRENCE OF RANGIO, APPROVED. DIRECTOR CIA CONCURS. ZAMMORO TO COMMAND. WOJG WILLIAM THOMAS BEING ASSIGNED OFFICE OF MILATTACHE US EMBASSY LAPAZ TO ASSIST.

FELTER, COLONEL, GSC
COUNSELOR TO THE PRESIDENT

TOP SECRET

[EIGHT]

CONFIDENTIAL
ARG 0019 2125 ZULU 3 OCTOBER 1966
VIA WHITE HOUSE SIGNAL AGENCY

FROM: POLO SIX
TO: EARNEST SIX

SITUATION REPORT #16

1-THE FOLLOWING ARTICLES FROM THE BUENOS AIRES HERALD ARE FORWARDED FOR GENERAL BACKGROUND INFORMATION. YOUR ATTENTION IS INVITED TO SUBPARAGRAPH TWO OF 4- BELOW.

2-EXTRACT FROM HERALD OF WEDNESDAY 14 SEPTEMBER 1966

TOYNBEE ARRIVES TOMORROW.

ARNOLD J. TOYNBEE, THE BRITISH HISTORIAN AND ADVOCATE OF INTERNATIONAL PEACE, WILL ARRIVE FROM URUGUAY TOMORROW, AND REMAIN ABOUT ONE MONTH IN ARGENTINA. HE WILL LECTURE AT THE UNIVERSITIES OF BUENOS AIRES; LA PLATA; CUYO; TUCUMAN AND AT THE WAR COLLEGE.

3-EXTRACT FROM HERALD OF TUESDAY 27 SEPTEMBER 1966

PRINCE PHILIP ON PRIVATE VISIT

THE ON-AND-OFF VISIT OF PRINCE PHILIP, HUSBAND OF QUEEN ELIZABETH II OF BRITAIN, FINALLY CAME TRUE YESTERDAY. PRINCE PHILIP ARRIVED IN BUENOS AIRES FOR A 23-DAY VISIT DESPITE THE QUESTIONS ASKED IN PARLIAMENT ABOUT HOW HE WAS GOING TO MANAGE ON THE

50 POUND STERLING TRAVEL ALLOWANCE GRANTED TO ALL BRITISH TOURISTS.

HE IS HERE OFFICIALLY AS THE PRESIDENT OF THE INTERNATIONAL EQUESTRIAN FEDERATION AND WILL PRESIDE AT THE OPENING OF THE HORSE SHOW AND JUMPING CHAMPIONSHIP ON SEPTEMBER 30.

A FRONT-PAGE EDITORIAL IN THE EVENING NEWSPAPER "CRONICA," DESCRIBING HIM AS AN "UNDEROCCUPIED PLAYBOY," ASSURED THE PRINCE HE WAS NOT WELCOME IN ARGENTINA.

4-EXTRACT FROM HERALD OF SUNDAY 2 OCTOBER 1966

PHILIP TAKES A TUMBLE

PRINCE PHILIP, HUSBAND OF QUEEN ELIZABETH II OF ENGLAND, RECOVERING FROM A FALL FROM HIS HORSE, TEAMED WITH PRESIDENT ONGANIA FOR A 5-4 POLO VICTORY YESTERDAY. THE WIN WAS A PLEASANT CHANGE FOR PRINCE PHILIP, WHOSE VISIT HERE HAS BEEN MARRED BY DAILY ANTI-BRITISH DEMONSTRATIONS.

PRESIDENT ONGANIA AND PRINCE PHILIP TEAMED WITH TWO CRACK PLAYERS, JUAN CAVANAGH AND GEOFFREY CRAIG, FOR A HARD-PLAYED GAME AT THE MILITARY SAN

JORGE CLUB. WHILE GALLOPING BEHIND THE BALL, PRINCE PHILIP ATTEMPTED A QUICK SWERVE AND FELL FROM HIS HORSE. HE IMMEDIATELY REMOUNTED AND CONTINUED THE MATCH.

AT THE END OF THE POLO MATCH, A LUNCHEON WAS SERVED AT THE SAM JORGE CLUB IN HONOR OF THE VISITING PRINCE. PRESIDENT ONGANIA AND MEMBERS OF BOTH TEAMS WERE PRESENT, AS WERE 60 GUESTS.

G. W. LUNSFORD, MAJ INF

CONFIDENTIAL

[NINE]

TOP SECRET
ARG 0019 2205 ZULU 25 OCTOBER 1966
VIA WHITE HOUSE SIGNAL AGENCY

FROM: POLO SIX
TO: EARNEST SIX

SITUATION REPORT #23

1-LTCOL RANGIO HAS PASSED THE FOLLOWING INTEL FROM HIS SOURCES TO THE UNDERSIGNED:

A.   GUEVARA, WHO HAS SHAVED OR PLUCKED THE HAIR FROM THE ROOF OF HIS SKULL, HAS DYED THE REMAINING HAIR GRAY AND IS WEARING BOTH SPECTACLES AND A PROSTHETIC DEVICE TO ALTER THE SHAPE OF HIS MOUTH, AND AN UNKNOWN NUMBER OF OTHERS DEPARTED HAVANA UNDER CONDITIONS OF GREAT SECRECY ABOARD MEXICANA FLIGHT 6363 FOR MEXICO CITY 1630 ZULU 24 OCTOBER 1966, PRESUMABLY FOR BOLIVIA.

B.   MRS DOLORES DIAZ DE ZAMMORO HAS BEEN REPORTED BY THE CUBAN INTERIOR MINISTRY TO HAVE DIED "OF COMPLICATIONS OF INFLUENZA" AT THE ISLA DE PINOS "DETENTION FACILITY" AND TO HAVE BEEN IMMEDIATELY BURIED THERE "BECAUSE OF THE DANGER OF CONTAGION."

2-RANGIO, WOJG WILLIAM PETERS, SFC EDWARD YOUNG, AND UNDERSIGNED WILL DEPART VIA L23 (CRAIG, SANTIAGO FLYING) FOR LAPAZ 2300 LOCAL TIME FOR FOLLOWING PURPOSES:

A-EXCHANGE OF INTEL RE APPEARANCE OF GUEVARA AND PROBABLE ARRIVAL IN BOLIVIA.

B-POSSIBLE ESTABLISHMENT OF COVERT ASA INTERCEPT STATION(S) WITHIN BOLIVIA.

[TEN]
La Paz International Airport
La Paz, Bolivia
1530 3 November 1966

"That has to be him," Lieutenant Colonel Guillermo Rangio said, pointing through the one-way glass in the wall overlooking the Immigration Desk toward a middle-aged man wearing a snap brim fedora.

He spoke in English, out of courtesy to Major George Washington Lunsford and Warrant Officer (j.g.) William E. Thomas, whose Spanish was not very fluent.

All three were in uniform, Rangio because he was performing an official visit to the security division of the Bolivian Army, and Lunsford because he'd decided that he and Thomas would really attract less attention as army officers than as black men in business suits.

"You sure, Colonel?" Thomas asked, seeking confirmation, not a challenge.

1055

"That man meets the description I have," Rangio replied, just a little coldly. "You have seen Dr. Guevara before, Mr. Thomas?"

"The last time I saw the sonofabitch, sir," Thomas said. "He was getting into a boat on the shore of Lake Tanganyika."

He made a cross of his index fingers and held it over his forehead. Rangio understood the gesture to mean Thomas had had Guevara in the cross-hairs of his sight, and chuckled.

"And he didn't look like that, Mr. Thomas?" Rangio asked.

"Not much," Thomas said.

"That's him, Thomas," Julio Zammoro said. He was wearing the uniform of a Bolivian major of infantry.

"Well, then, I'm impressed as hell," Thomas said. "As they say, he could have fooled me."

"I don't really understand the disguise," Rangio said thoughtfully. "Castro has something like thirty-five hundred men in his Anti-Counter-revolutionary police. They obviously suspect — know — we have agents, who know what's happening and when. Who does he think he's fooling, even with hair plucked out?"

"I noticed that word in the heads-up," Thomas said. "He really 'plucked' his hair out? It's not just shaved?"

"Plucked," Rangio confirmed. "I understand it was rather painful."

"Ego, Julio," Lunsford said. "He's right on the edge of being an egomaniac. He's the only one in disguise, because the others are anonymous, and he, on the other hand, is famous."

"I don't think I've ever seen a photograph of him without his beard," Lieutenant Colonel

Enrico Cupull of the Bolivian Army said.

"I have," Rangio said. "He's a rather good-looking young man."

"Who only you, Willy, of this group would recognize on the street — or passing through immigration," Lunsford said. "Making my point. He sees himself as a world-famous guerrilla; he therefore needs to be disguised."

"I would," Zammoro said, "recognize him, I mean, with a beard or without, in a suit, in fatigues —"

"Well, he's through," Cupull said. "Give me a moment to make sure he's left the terminal, and then we'll go have our lunch at the club."

Cupull left the room with the one-way mirror overlooking the line of Immigration stations, and returned several minutes later to report that the bald-headed man they'd seen was carrying a Uruguayan passport issued to Adolfo Mena González, who told the Immigration officer that he was on a fact-finding mission for the Organization of American States, and had the documents to prove it.

"I'd love to know if they're real, or not," Cupull said. "And if real, who issued them."

"They are probably genuine," Zammoro said. "And the passport, too. In my experience, bureaucrats tend to do favors for both sides, in the logical presumption that one side or the other will win, and they can then claim to have been on their side all along."

"I'm sure you're right, Julio," Cupull said, and then smiled. "And now let us go for our lunch. As the beef in Argentina, as everyone knows, is next to inedible, I have arranged for what I think is known in the U.S. as a barbecue."

As they were having their coffee in the officers' club, an officer reported to Cupull, who listened carefully, thanked him, and then offered the report to the others.

"Dr. Guevara is at this moment," he related, "conversing with your fellow Argentine, Willy — Señora Laura Gutierrez de Bauer, formerly known as Haydee Tamara Bunke, and sometimes as 'Tania' — in suite 316 of the Hotel Copacabana on Prado Boulevard. The Bolivian Communists with him are pretending they do not know he is Guevara, although last night, when arranging tomorrow's transport, they used the phrase 'to transport Che Guevara to the farm in Ñancahazú' several times."

"I'm sorry about your wife, Zammoro," Doubting Thomas said to Zammoro as they used the urinal.

"Thank you," Zammoro said.

"Was I right not to pop the sonofabitch in the Congo?"

"You had no choice, Bill," Zammoro said. "You are a soldier — you had your orders."

"Sometimes I forget my orders," Thomas said. "Zam, I had my crosshairs on his forehead, and it's been a long time since I missed at that range."

"You are a soldier," Zammoro repeated. "You had your orders. You did the right thing, Bill."

[ELEVEN]

TOP SECRET
ARG 0065 2010 ZULU 1 DECEMBER 1966
VIA WHITE HOUSE SIGNAL AGENCY

FROM: POLO SIX
TO: EARNEST SIX

SITUATION REPORT #33

REFERENCE US ARMY MAP SERVICE MAP
4774 BOLIVIA

1-LTCOL CUPULL HAS PASSED THROUGH
MAJOR ZAMMORO THE FOLLOWING INTEL
FROM HIS SOURCES TO THE UNDERSIGNED:

SEÑOR CIRO ALGARANAZ, A LAW-ABIDING
BOLIVIAN PIG FARMER, HAS REPORTED TO
BOLIVIAN AUTHORITIES HIS SUSPICIONS
THAT THE NEW OWNERS OF A PIG FARM ON
THE RIVER ÑANCAHAZÚ ADJACENT TO HIS
ARE IN FACT ENGAGED IN THE DRUG
TRADE, BASING HIS SUSPICIONS IN PART
ON "THE FUNNY WAY" THEY SPEAK
SPANISH.

ON BEING COMMENDED BY MAJOR
ZAMMORO FOR HIS SERVICE TO THE STATE,
AND REMINDED THAT SUSPICIONS ARE NOT
PROOF, ALGARANAZ WAS HAPPY TO GO
ALONG WITH ZAMMORO'S SUGGESTION
THAT A SOLDIER BE ASSIGNED TO WORK IN
CIVILIAN CLOTHES ON HIS FARM IN ORDER
THAT HE MAY KEEP AN EYE ON THE
SUSPECTED DRUG TRAFFICKERS. THE ONLY
ROAD TO THE "DRUG TRAFFICKERS"
PROPERTY RUNS PAST SEÑOR ALGARANAZ'S
HOUSE.

[TWELVE]

TOP SECRET
ARG 0019 2300 ZULU 2 FEBRUARY 1967
VIA WHITE HOUSE SIGNAL AGENCY

FROM: POLO SIX
TO: EARNEST SIX

AFTER-ACTION REPORT #4
REFERENCE US ARMY MAP SERVICE MAP
4774 BOLIVIA

1- AFTER HAVING BEEN ADVISED THAT
INTERCEPTS OF ENCRYPTED
RADIOTELETYPE MESSAGES FROM
ÑANCAHAZÚ TO HAVANA (WHOSE CALL
SIGN FOR THIS PURPOSE IS "MANILA")
REVEALED THAT GUEVARA "AS A NEAR
FINAL STEP IN THE TRAINING PROCESS"
INTENDED TO LEAD HIS MEN ON A
TWO-WEEK TRAINING MARCH LTCOL
CUPULL APPROVED A SURVEILLANCE OF
THE MARCH BY BOLIVIAN TROOPS.

2-WOJG WILLIAM THOMAS IN HIS COVERT
ROLE AS SUBOFICIAL MAYOR (SGT MAJOR)
TO MAJOR ZAMMORO OF LTCOL CUPULL'S

STAFF JOINED THE PATROL WHICH
DEPARTED FROM THE BOLIVIAN GARRISON
TOWN OF CAMIRI 1 FEBRUARY 1967.

G. W. LUNSFORD, MAJ INF

TOP SECRET

[THIRTEEN]

TOP SECRET
ARG 0019 2300 ZULU 16 FEBRUARY 1967
VIA WHITE HOUSE SIGNAL AGENCY

FROM: POLO SIX
TO: EARNEST SIX

AFTER ACTION REPORT #7

REFERENCE US ARMY MAP SERVICE MAP
4774 BOLIVIA

1-THE UNDERSIGNED AND MAJOR
ZAMMORO MET WITH WOJG WILLIAM E.
THOMAS AT COORDINATES 2909/4512 AT
1600 ZULU 15 FEBRUARY WITH THE
INTENTION OF RECEIVING THOMAS'S
REPORT OF GUEVARA TRAINING MARCH
AND RELIEVING HIM OF HIS ADVISER ROLE
TO RECONNAISSANCE PATROL.

2-THOMAS DESCRIBED THE CONDUCT OF

THE GUEVARA PATROL AS "A CHINESE FIRE DRILL," STATING THAT THEY HAD INADEQUATE AND IMPROPER EQUIPMENT, INADEQUATE OR NO MAPS, POOR MARCH DISCIPLINE, HAD EXHAUSTED THEIR RATIONS, AND, IN THE ABSENCE OF AN ABILITY TO HUNT MORE ADEQUATE GAME, WERE FORCED TO EAT PALM HEARTS, MONKEYS, HAWKS AND PARROTS. HE REPORTED FURTHER THAT TWO BOLIVIAN COMMUNISTS HAD PERISHED ATTEMPTING TO CROSS THE ÑANCAHAZÚ RIVER, WHICH IS SWOLLEN BY RAIN AT THIS TIME OF THE YEAR.

3-STATING THAT HE BELIEVED IT WAS ENTIRELY POSSIBLE THAT GUEVARA MIGHT PERISH ON THE MARCH, AND THAT, IN ANY EVENT, IT "WOULD BE INSANE FOR THEM TO KEEP IT UP MORE THAN A FEW DAYS MORE," THOMAS REQUESTED PERMISSION TO REMAIN WITH THE RECONNAISSANCE PATROL, AND WAS GIVEN PERMISSION TO DO SO.

G. W. LUNSFORD, MAJ INF

TOP SECRET

[FOURTEEN]

TOP SECRET
ARG 0019 2300 ZULU 25 FEBRUARY 1967
VIA WHITE HOUSE SIGNAL AGENCY

FROM: POLO SIX
TO: EARNEST SIX

AFTER-ACTION REPORT #18

REFERENCE US ARMY MAP SERVICE MAP
4774 BOLIVIA

1-MAJOR PAOLO DESAZ, COMMANDING
OFFICER OF BOLIVIAN TROOPS IN CAMIRI,
WHO HAS NOT BEEN MADE AWARE OF
LTCOL CUPULL OR MAJOR ZAMMORO'S
ANTI-GUEVARA ACTIVITIES, AND NOT GIVEN
ANY INTEL, NEVERTHELESS BECAME
SUSPICIOUS OF ACTIVITIES AT ÑANCAHAZÚ
AND BEGAN PATROL ACTIVITIES IN AREA,
INCLUDING AERIAL RECONNAISSANCE BY
BOLIVIAN L-19 AIRCRAFT.

2-ON 22 FEBRUARY TWO BOLIVIAN
COMMUNISTS TOOK ADVANTAGE OF
ABSENCE OF "RAMON" (GUEVARA) AND
OTHERS FROM ÑANCAHAZÚ FARM AND
ATTEMPTED TO DESERT. THEY WERE
CAPTURED BY DESAZ TROOPS AND DURING
INTERROGATION REVEALED EVERYTHING
THEY KNEW, WHICH DID NOT INCLUDE
THAT "RAMON," COMMANDER OF CUBANS,
IS GUEVARA.

3-CUPULL IS DELAYING TRANSMISSION OF DESAZ'S REPORT TO LA PAZ, BUT CANNOT DO SO FOR LONG.

4-WOJG THOMAS REPORTS BY RADIO THAT GUEVARA-LED TRAINING MARCH IS STILL "STUMBLING AROUND" IN WILDERNESS, OUT OF FOOD, POSSIBLY LOST, AND A MINIMUM OF FOURTEEN DAYS' MARCH FROM ÑANCAHAZÚ FARM.

5-CUPULL'S OBSERVER ON ALGARANAZ FARM PHOTOGRAPHED PASSENGERS OF PICKUP TRUCK EN ROUTE TO ÑANCAHAZÚ FARM. THE TRUCK IS REGISTERED TO LAURA GUTIERREZ BAUER IN LA PAZ, AND SHE AND FRENCH JOURNALIST REGIS DEBRAY HAVE BEEN POSITIVELY IDENTIFIED BY PHOTOS AS PASSENGERS IN PICKUP TRUCK.

G. W. LUNSFORD, MAJ INF

TOP SECRET

[FIFTEEN]

TOP SECRET
ARG 0044 2300 ZULU 20 MARCH 1967
VIA WHITE HOUSE SIGNAL AGENCY

FROM: POLO SIX
TO: EARNEST SIX

AFTER-ACTION REPORT #35

REFERENCE US ARMY MAP SERVICE MAP
4774 BOLIVIA

1-WOJG WILLIAM THOMAS REPORTED 19
MARCH 1967 THAT GUEVARA-LED TRAINING
MARCH, "HAVING FINALLY FOUND ITS WAY
HOME," WAS ONE DAY'S MARCH FROM
ÑANCAHAZÚ FARM. GUEVARA STILL ALIVE
BUT SICK.

2-AT 1135 ZULU 20 MARCH 1967
RENDEVOUS WAS EFFECTED WITH
RECONNAISSANCE PATROL. THOMAS, WHO
LOST APPROXIMATELY TWENTY-FIVE
POUNDS DURING PATROL, WAS FLOWN TO
BUENOS AIRES IN L-23 BY 1LT CRAIG AND
WOJG DE LA SANTIAGO. FOLLOWING
DISCREET PHYSICAL EXAMINATION IN
ARGENTINE CENTRAL MILITARY HOSPITAL
BUENOS AIRES ARRANGED BY LT COL
RANGIO, THOMAS WILL BEGIN SEVEN-DAY
RECUPERATIVE LEAVE, NOT CHARGEABLE AS
ORDINARY LEAVE.

G. W. LUNSFORD, MAJ INF

TOP SECRET

[SIXTEEN]

TOP SECRET
ARG 0044 2025 ZULU 23 MARCH 1967
VIA WHITE HOUSE SIGNAL AGENCY

FROM: POLO SIX
TO: EARNEST SIX

SITUATION REPORT #42

REFERENCE US ARMY MAP SERVICE MAP
4774 BOLIVIA

1-AT APPROXIMATELY 1615 ZULU 23
MARCH 1967, A PATROL OF CAMIRI-BASED
BOLIVIAN SOLDIERS WAS AMBUSHED
APPROXIMATELY 15 KILOMETERS FROM
ÑANCAHAZÚ FARM. ONE (1) KIA; THREE (3)
WIA; TWO (2) MISSING.

2-UNDER CIRCUMSTANCES LTCOL CUPULL
MUST NOW FULLY REPORT ON HIS AND
MAJOR ZAMMORO'S ACTIVITIES IN AREA.

3-CUPULL'S OBSERVER ON ALGARANAZ
FARM REPORTED "TANIA" AND REGIS
DEBRAY PASSING AS THEY LEFT
ÑANCAHAZÚ FARM.

4-CUPULL BELIEVES AMBUSH WILL RESULT
IN FAR GREATER BOLIVIAN ARMY REACTION
AGAINST CUBANS, OVER WHICH HE WILL
HAVE LESS CONTROL.

[SEVENTEEN]

TOP SECRET
1820 GREENWICH 27 MARCH 1967

FROM STATION CHIEF, LA PAZ, BOLIVIA

TO DIRECTOR, CIA, LANGLEY
COPIES TO STATION CHIEF, BUENOS AIRES
      ARGENTINA
      MR SANFORD T. FELTER,
      COUNSELOR TO THE PRESIDENT,
      THE EXECUTIVE OFFICE BUILDING
      WASHINGTON

1-GENERAL RENÉ BARRIENTOS BECAME
PRESIDENT OF BOLIVIA AS OF 2815
GREENWICH 27 MARCH 1967.

2-THE UNDERSIGNED CONSIDERS IT
GERMANE TO REPEAT THE EXTRACT OF THE
PRIVATE CONVERSATION BETWEEN
BARRIENTOS AND THE UNDERSIGNED OF
24 MARCH 1967, FOLLOWING THE AMBUSH
BY CUBANS OF BOLIVIAN ARMY UNIT,
PREVIOUSLY FURNISHED.

BEGIN QUOTE

KEEP HIM ALIVE? WHAT WE SHOULD DO IS BEHEAD THE COMMUNIST (OBSCENITY) AND STICK HIS HEAD ON A POLE ON THE BOULEVARD PRADO.

END QUOTE

3-THE UNDERSIGNED AGAIN RECOMMENDS IN THE STRONGEST POSSIBLE TERMS THAT DIPLOMATIC REPRESENTATIONS AT THE HIGHEST LEVEL BE MADE VIS-À-VIS U.S. GOVERNMENT POLICY RELATIVE TO ERNESTO GUEVARA.

DONALD J. MACNAMARA

STATION CHIEF BUENOS AIRES

TOP SECRET

[EIGHTEEN]

TOP SECRET
EARN0225 WASH DC 1405 ZULU 29 MARCH 1967
VIA WHITE HOUSE SIGNAL AGENCY

FROM: EARNEST SIX
TO: POLO SIX
    STATION CHIEF BUENOS AIRES

1-PRESIDENT BARRIENTOS WILL SHORTLY NAME LIEUTENANT COLONEL ANDRÉS SELICH, DEPUTY COMMANDER OF THE PANDO REGIMENT OF MILITARY ENGINEERS STATIONED AT VILLEGRANDE, TO OVERALL COMMAND ANTI-GUEVARAN ACTIVITIES IN BOLIVIA.

2-PRESIDENT BARRIENTOS HAS REQUESTED, AND US GOVERNMENT WILL FURNISH ASAP, A SPECIAL FORCES UNIT TO TRAIN A BATTALION OF BOLIVIAN RANGERS. CAPT JOHN S. OLIVER, WHO HAS BEEN KEPT ABREAST OF ALL DEVELOPMENTS, WILL COMMAND.

3-SELICH, OF YUGOSLAVIAN BACKGROUND, IS WELL KNOWN TO OUR FRIEND IN GERMANY. HE HAS AGREED WITH OUR GERMAN FRIEND THAT GUEVARA SHOULD BE KEPT ALIVE, AND WILL DO WHATEVER HE CAN IN THIS REGARD. SELICH HAS BEEN INFORMED OF ACTIVITIES OF CUPULL (OF WHICH HE WAS AWARE) AND ZAMORRO/THOMAS (OF WHICH HE WAS NOT) AND BELIEVES INFORMING BARRIENTOS AND OTHERS OF CUPULL/ZAMMORO/THOMAS ACTIVITIES WOULD BE COUNTERPRODUCTIVE.

4-SELICH WILL INITIATE CONTACT WITH LUNSFORD, BUT NOT, REPEAT NOT, WITH CIA STATION CHIEF LA PAZ. LUNSFORD IS AUTHORIZED RELAY BETWEEN CIA AND SELICH AND TO PROVIDE SELICH WITH

WHATEVER ASSETS HE CONTROLS, TO INCLUDE USE OF THE L-23 TO TAKE GUEVARA, IF CAPTURED, TO ARGENTINA FOR FURTHER SHIPMENT.

5-YOU ARE DIRECTED TO MAKE THIS ORDER KNOWN TO LIEUTENANT COLONEL CUPULL AND LIEUTENANT COLONEL RANGIO.

6-DIRECTOR CIA CONCURS.

SANFORD T. FELTER, COLONEL, GSC

COUNSELOR TO THE PRESIDENT OF THE UNITED STATES

TOP SECRET

[NINETEEN]

TOP SECRET
1650 GREENWICH 21 APRIL 1967

FROM STATION CHIEF, LA PAZ, BOLIVIA

TO DIRECTOR, CIA, LANGLEY
COPIES TO STATION CHIEF, BUENOS AIRES
        ARGENTINA
        MR SANFORD T. FELTER,
        COUNSELOR TO THE PRESIDENT,
        THE EXECUTIVE OFFICE BUILDING

WASHINGTON

1-FRENCH JOURNALIST REGIS DEBRAY WAS ARRESTED BY BOLIVIAN ARMY NEAR MUYUPAMPA EARLY LAST NIGHT.

2-DEBRAY WAS IN COMPANY OF KNOWN BOLIVIAN COMMUNIST BUSTOS WHO WAS ON WANTED LIST. THEY WERE APPARENTLY TRYING TO LEAVE GUEVARAN FORCES FOR LA PAZ. DEBRAY WAS IN POSSESSION OF COUNTERFEIT IDENTIFICATION AND OTHER INCRIMINATING MATERIAL AND WILL PROBABLY BE COURT-MARTIALED.

DONALD J. MACNAMARA
STATION CHIEF BUENOS AIRES

TOP SECRET

[TWENTY]

TOP SECRET
ARG 0061 1935 ZULU 1 SEPTEMBER 1967
VIA WHITE HOUSE SIGNAL AGENCY

FROM: POLO SIX
TO: EARNEST SIX

SITUATION REPORT #56

REFERENCE US ARMY MAP SERVICE MAP
4774 BOLIVIA

1-MAJOR ZAMMORO, WHO WAS PRESENT AS OBSERVER, REPORTS THAT AT APPROXIMATELY 2200 ZULU 31 AUGUST 1967 A UNIT OF BOLIVIAN EIGHTH ARMY (CAPTAIN MARIO VARGAS SALINAS) UNDER CONTROL OF LTCOL SELICH AMBUSHED A PARTY OF GUEVARAN CUBANS AT THE CONFLUENCE OF RIO GRANDE AND MASICURI RIVERS.

2-FRIENDLY LOSSES NONE. GUEVARAN FORCE LOSSES SEVEN (7) KIA; FIVE (5) WIA; SIX (6) PRISONERS.

3-ZAMMORO POSITIVELY IDENTIFIED CORPSES OF COMANDANTE JUAN VITALIO ACUNA, "JOAQUIN"; AND GUSTAVO DE HOED, "ALEJANDRO," FORMERLY CUBAN VICE MINISTER OF INDUSTRY.

4-PRISONERS STATED THAT "TANIA" HAD BEEN WITH GROUP AND AFTER A SEARCH HER CORPSE WAS FOUND SEVERAL MILES DOWNSTREAM.

5-ON BEING ADVISED OF ACTION, PRESIDENT BARRIENTOS PERSONALLY RADIOED SALINAS STATING (A) HE HAD BEEN PROMOTED TO MAJOR AND (B) THAT "TANIA" WAS TO BE PLACED IN A COFFIN AND GIVEN A CHRISTIAN BURIAL. WHEN SALINAS ADVISED THAT "TANIA" WAS KNOWN TO BE AN ATHEIST, PRESIDENT BARRIENTOS REPLIED "SO MUCH THE BETTER."

G. W. LUNSFORD, MAJ INF

TOP SECRET

[TWENTY-ONE]

TOP SECRET
ARG 0074 1935 ZULU 7 OCTOBER 1967
VIA WHITE HOUSE SIGNAL AGENCY

FROM: POLO SIX
TO: EARNEST SIX

SITUATION REPORT #64

REFERENCE US ARMY MAP SERVICE MAP
4774 BOLIVIA

1-LTCOL SELICH ADVISES TROOPS UNDER
HIS CONTROL BELIEVE THEY HAVE
GUEVARA AND REMNANTS OF "BOLIVIAN
LIBERATION ARMY" NUMBERING LESS THAN
TWENTY-FIVE (25) MORE OR LESS
SURROUNDED IN CANYON NEAR LA
HIGUERA ON RIO GRANDE.

2-IT IS BELIEVED TROOPS ARE BOLIVIAN
RANGERS TRAINED BY CAPT OLIVER AND HE
MAY BE PRESENT AS OBSERVER. MAJOR
ZAMORRO EN ROUTE TO RELIEVE HIM IF
THIS IS THE CASE.

G. W. LUNSFORD, MAJ INF

TOP SECRET

TOP SECRET
ARG 0075 1705 ZULU 8 OCTOBER 1967
VIA WHITE HOUSE SIGNAL AGENCY

FROM: POLO SIX
TO: EARNEST SIX

SITUATION REPORT #65

REFERENCE US ARMY MAP SERVICE MAP
4774 BOLIVIA

1-ZAMMORO, WHO RELIEVED OLIVER AS
OBSERVER, REPORTS THAT AT 1310 LOCAL
TIME 8 OCTOBER 1967, BOLIVIAN ARMY
ATTACKED GUEVARAN FORCES NEAR LA
HIGUERA. A FIREFIGHT ENSUED.

2-AT APPROXIMATELY 1405 LOCAL TIME,
SERGEANT BERNARDINO HUANCA
ACCEPTED THE SURRENDER OF ERNESTO
GUEVARA, WHO RAISED HIS HANDS AND
STATED, "DON'T SHOOT. I AM CHE
GUEVARA. I AM WORTH MORE TO YOU
ALIVE THAN DEAD." ZAMORRO CONFIRMS
IDENTITY OF PRISONER, WHO WAS
WOUNDED IN LEFT LEG. HE WAS ARMED
WITH A US CARBINE M2, WHICH HAD BEEN
STRUCK BY A BULLET AND RENDERED
USELESS, AND WITH A US M1911A1
.45-CALIBER PISTOL FOR WHICH HE HAD
NO MAGAZINE.

3-LT COLONEL SELICH HAS PERSONALLY
RADIOED OFFICER NOW IN CHARGE OF
GUEVARA THAT HE IS TO BE GIVEN
MEDICAL TREATMENT AND NOT HARMED IN
ANY WAY. SELICH NOW EN ROUTE SITE BY
HELICOPTER. L-23 ON TEN-MINUTE ALERT
TO TRANSPORT GUEVARA TO ARGENTINA.
LTCOL RANGIO AND I WILL ACCOMPANY.

G. W. LUNSFORD, MAJ INF

TOP SECRET

[TWENTY-THREE]

TOP SECRET
ARG 0075 1105 ZULU 9 OCTOBER 1967
VIA WHITE HOUSE SIGNAL AGENCY

FROM: POLO SIX
TO: EARNEST SIX

SITUATION REPORT #66

REFERENCE US ARMY MAP SERVICE MAP
4774 BOLIVIA

1-ZAMMORO REPORTS LTCOL SELICH
PERSONALLY TRANSFERRED GUEVARA TO
THE SCHOOL HOUSE AT LA HIGUERA LATE
YESTERDAY AFTERNOON, WHERE GUEVARA

IS BEING GUARDED AGAINST BOTH AN ATTEMPT, CONSIDERED UNLIKELY, TO RESCUE HIM, AND OTHER DANGERS.

2-ZAMMORO AND SELICH BELIEVE THAT UNLESS HE IS DISSUADED BY HIGHEST ECHELONS OF US GOVERNMENT, BARRIENTOS WILL ORDER EXECUTION OF GUEVARA WITHIN HOURS.

3-ZAMORRO STATES SUFFICIENT SPECIAL FORCES STRENGTH IN AREA WOULD PERMIT TRANSPORT OF GUEVARA FROM IMMEDIATE AREA AND INTO ARGENTINA DESPITE WISHES OF BOLIVIAN GOVERNMENT. UNDERSIGNED CONCURS. L-23 ON TEN-MINUTE CALL. REQUEST GUIDANCE.

G. W. LUNSFORD, MAJ INF

TOP SECRET

[TWENTY-FOUR]

TOP SECRET
EARN0250WASH DC 1420 ZULU 29 MARCH 1967
VIA WHITE HOUSE SIGNAL AGENCY

FROM: EARNEST SIX
TO: POLO SIX

```
STATION CHIEF BUENOS AIRES

1-REPRESENTATIONS AT THE HIGHEST
POSSIBLE LEVEL REPEAT AT THE HIGHEST
POSSIBLE LEVEL WITHIN THE HOUR HAVE
FAILED TO CONVINCE PRESIDENT
BARRIENTOS OF WISDOM OF US POSITION
VIS-À-VIS GUEVARA.

2-BY DIRECTION OF THE PRESIDENT, NO US
OFFICIAL REPEAT NO US OFFICIAL WILL
TAKE ANY REPEAT ANY ACTION TO
CONTRAVENE THE WISHES OF PRESIDENT
BARRIENTOS IN THIS MATTER.

3-DIRECTOR CIA IS AWARE OF THIS
DECISION AND DIRECTS COMPLIANCE.

SANFORD T. FELTER, COLONEL, GSC
COUNSELOR TO THE PRESIDENT OF THE
UNITED STATES

TOP SECRET
```

[TWENTY-FIVE]
The Laundry Room
Nuestro Señor de Malta Hospital
Vallegrande, Bolivia
1205 10 October 1967

A Bolivian sergeant, recently graduated from the
Bolivian Ranger School, and wearing his new uniform, which included a green beret, not looking

entirely confident about what he was doing, raised his brand-new U.S. Carbine Caliber .30 M1 and challenged the two men at the door of the laundry room. They, too, were wearing green berets, and fatigue uniforms, and almost certainly were U.S. Army Special Forces officers and instructors. He just hadn't met these two.

"Off-limits!" the sergeant announced firmly.

The one thing he had heard again and again during his training from the U.S. Green Berets was that orders were orders and had to be obeyed, even if you didn't like them, and even if following them was going to get you in trouble, which he suspected was going to be the case here.

Major Zamorro, who was sitting on a chair tilted back against the mud wall of the laundry room, looked away from the body on the table and at the door.

"It's all right, Sergeant," Major Zammoro said. "Let them pass."

"*Si, señor,*" the sergeant said with obvious relief.

The two U.S. Army Special Forces officers moved through the door.

"Oh, shit!" Warrant Officer Junior Grade William E. Thomas said when he saw what was there. The bearded, longhaired, bare-chested, barefooted body of Ernesto Guevara de la Serna, M.D., was lying on a crude stretcher laid atop a stone laundry basin.

Guevara's eyes were open and his fists were clenched. There were several entrance wounds, including one in the thorax, from which most of the blood had been wiped.

Major George Washington Lunsford turned to the man in the chair. "Who actually did it?"

Major Julio Zammoro met Lunsford's eyes for a very long moment. Then he pushed himself erect and wordlessly walked out of the laundry room. Lunsford watched him go. Then, after a final look at the body, Lunsford and Thomas followed him.

Afterword

The remains of Ernesto "Che" Guevara were buried secretly not far from where he met his death.

In 1999, skeletal remains of a corpse buried without a coffin were determined by DNA evaluation to be those of Guevara, and were returned to Cuba.

In the first days of the millennium, speaking at the dedication of an enormous memorial to Guevara in Havana, Fidel Castro described Guevara as "Christlike."